DECOLONIZING THE HINDU MIND

Born in a Flemish Catholic family in Leuven, Belgium, in 1959, Dr Koenraad Elst graduated in Philosophy, Chinese Studies and Indo-Iranian Studies from the Catholic University of Leuven. He became interested in communal disputes in India during a stay at the Benares Hindu University, and wrote his first book on the budding Ayodhya conflict. While establishing himself as a columnist for a number of Belgian and Indian papers, he frequently returned to India to study the various aspects of its ethno-religio-political configuration and to interview the country's religious leaders and thinkers. *Decolonizing the Hindu Mind* is based on his doctoral thesis, submitted at Leuven in 1998. He has written copiously on multiculturalism, language policy issues, ancient Chinese history and philosophy as well as on subjects such as comparative religion and the Aryan invasion debate.

Decolonizing the Hindu Mind

Ideological Development of Hindu Revivalism

KOENRAAD ELST

RUPA

Published by
Rupa Publications India Pvt. Ltd 2005
7/16, Ansari Road, Daryaganj
New Delhi 110002

Sales centres:
Prayagraj Bengaluru Chennai
Hyderabad Jaipur Kathmandu
Kolkata Mumbai

P-ISBN: 979-81-291-0746-5
E-ISBN: 978-81-291-4076-0

Seventh impression 2023

10 9 8 7

Typeset by Pradeep Kumar Goel, New Delhi

Printed in India

Dedicated to the memory of my father,

Dr. jur. René Elst (1924-92)

"Hij was rechtvaardigheid"

Contents

Acknowledgements

My thanks are due to all those who made the completion of this text possible, starting with the elements, the ancestors, and so on down to mainly the following people. My wife Christel more than shared the hardships intrinsic to a writing job of this magnitude, and her effort in making it possible was inevitably greater than that of all others, perhaps including me. Access to primary sources, human and textual, was given to me by some of the people whose work is also the object of this research, most notably K.R. Malkani, Sita Ram Goel and Devendra Swarup. Practical and material help was given me by Kashi Nath Singh, Veer Bhadra Mishra, Pradeep Goel, Sujit Dhar, Manju Jhaver, Shrikant Talageri, Tushar Ravuri and Gopi Maliwal; and by Manohar Shinde, Arvind Ghosh, Krishna Bhatnagar, Satinder Trehan, Shrichand Chawla, Anand Bemra, Rama Shastry, Jaidev Rao, Raj Dave, Yamini Liu, Graydon Chiappetta, and Raman Srinivasan. For academic insights on the subject-matter, I should thank the late Professor Kedar Nath Mishra (Benares Hindu University), Professor Edmund Weber (J.W. Goethe University, Frankfurt), Professor Gopal Krishna (Wolfson College, Oxford), and my supervisor, Professor Gilbert Pollet. The list, let it be repeated, is not exhaustive.

This book is based on the main part of my doctoral dissertation, accepted by Katholieke Universiteit Leuven in 1998. For reasons of space, several peripheral chapters have been left out here and will be published separately. Conversely, some argumentative sections which I had left out of my dissertation at the suggestion of my supervisor have been reincluded, and the general tone and conclusions have been made more forthright than was affordable in a dissertation. It follows that the responsibility for controversial statements in this study does not lie with my Alma Mater, the examiners or my supervisor, but is entirely my own.

Leuven, Belgium **KE**
20 January 2001

Note on language and transcription

The present study is a text written in English, but in an age when different standards of English legitimately co-exist, this needs some specification. As to spelling, when in doubt I have followed the *Concise Oxford English Dictionary, 1986* and its occasionally surprising norms ("labour organization"), except in quotations. It is possible that I have failed to doubt on occasions when I should have, in which case deviations from the Oxford standard may occur. In quotations, Indian English is often retained, which includes many uncommon cases of using or not using the article, peculiarities in the use of capitals and word order, and borrowed native vocabulary. I have considered it unnecessarily pedantic to add "corrective" parentheses to such expressions unless they really disturb fluent comprehension.

Indian words are spelled as in Indian English texts, without any cumbersome diacritical marks, except in italicized "quotation words". Names are given in the form used by the person concerned, e.g. one may write *Mukherji* and another *Mookerjee*. Don't look for the diacritics in non-italicized words, which are to be considered Indian-English words, and even in italicized book titles they may be absent if that is how the authors chose to spell them. Words derived from Arabic are given in their Persian-Urdu pronunciation, as is common in India, e.g. *Hadîs* or *Zimmî* rather than *Hadîth* or *Dhimmî*. For words in Indian languages given in transcription, I have had to settle for a compromise, partly due to the typographical limitations of my antiquated word-processor, partly in order to stay close to the ordinary Indian-English spelling which will be used alongside the occasional transcription: following the system adopted in many Indian scholarly publications, [sh] and [ch] will be used as in regular English spelling. Allowance should also be made for v/w alternation in Sanskrit/Hindi words, both letters representing the English [w]. The choice between the Sanskrit form with *-a*, the Hindi form without *-a* (*Râma/Râm*) and the Dravidian form with *-an/am* (*satya/sathyam*, *Shrinivâs/Shrinivâsan*) depends purely on the context.

Glossary

abhinava: young
âdâb arz: Muslim greetings, hello
adhiniyam: act (of legislation), law
adhyâtmik: spiritual
âdivâsî: "aboriginal", Christian term for the tribals
âdmî: "scion of Adam", man
advaita: "non-two-ness", monism
agnihotra: Vedic fire-ceremony
agrahâra: land granted to Brahmin community, Brahmin village
ahl: people
ahl-e-kitâb: "people of the Book", the Abrahamic religions
AICC: All-India Congress Committee
AIR: All-India Radio
akhand: unbroken, united, continuous
akhârâ: arena, martial monastery
AMU: Aligarh Muslim University
âlim (pl. *ulemâ*): Islamic scholar
Allâh (from *al-Ilâh*, "the god"): Arab deity, God
X amar rahe: "may X remain immortal", long live X
amîr: commander, rich man
amîr-al-mominîn: commander of the faithful, caliph
anushîlan: devotedness
archanâ: worship
ârya: noble, gentleman; Hindu
âshram: stage of life; hermitage
ASI: Archaeological Survey of India
avarna: casteless
avatâr: incarnation of a deity
âyat: sign, verse of the *Qur'ân*
âyatollah: "sign of God", high-rank Shiite clergy
âzâd Kashmîr: "Free Kashmir", i.e. Pak-Occupied Kashmir
âzâd Hind fauz: Free India Army, INA—Indian National Army
âzâdî: "freedom"
azân: public call to Islamic prayer
Bajrang Dal: "team of Hanumân", VHP youth wing
bandh: strike
bania: trader

baudhik: RSS ideological session
bhajan: Hindu devotional song
BHU: Benares Hindu University
[X-Y] bhâî-bhâî: "[X and Y are] brothers"
bhakta: devotee
bhakti: devotion, popular devotional theism
Bhangî: sweeper, a Scheduled Caste
Bhârat: "(chakravarti) Bharata's land", India
BIMS: *Bhâratîya Mazdoor Sangh* (Indian Labour Union)
BJP: *Bhâratîya Janatâ* Party, Indian People's Party
BJS: *Bhâratîya Jana Sangh*, Indian People's Association
BMAC: Babri Masjid Action Committee
BMMCC: Babri Masjid Movement Co-ordination Committee
bodhi: awakening, enlightenment
Brahman: the Absolute, pure consciousness
brâhmana/brahmin: Vedic religious specialist
brahmavâda: "doctrine of the Absolute"
BSP: *Bahujan Samâj* Party, Dalit "Party of the Masses"
buddha: the Awakened one
burqa: veil covering Muslim woman's face
CBI: Central Bureau of Investigation
chakra: wheel
chakravarti: "wheel-turner", all-India monarch
Chamâr: "leather-worker", a Scheduled Caste
Chandâla: funeral worker, a Scheduled Caste
charkha: spinning-wheel
Congress-I: Indira Congress
CPI: Communist Party of India
CPI(M), CPM: Communist Party of India (Marxist)
CWC: Congress Working Committee
d.: *deciduit* (Latin), "he died (in year X)"
dakait/dacoit: armed robber
Dalit: "broken", oppressed, downtrodden, untouchable
Dâr-al-ulûm: "place of learning", Islamic academy
dashanâmî: prestigious monastic order founded by Shankara
DAV: Dayanand Anglo-Vedic, an *Arya Samâj* college
Dhamma (Pali, from Sanskrit *dharma*): Buddhism
dhanush: a measure equal to four cubits
dharma: duty, world order, religion
Dharm Sansad: roughly "religious parliament", *sâdhu*s' assembly
dharna: sit-down strike
dhoti: cloth covering hips and legs
dîn: religion, Islam
DMK: *Dravida Munnetra Kazhagam*, Tamil Progressive Federation
dûrdarshan: television, Indian state broadcast
DRI: Deendayal Research Institute

ekâtmatâ: "animated by a single self", integrated
fanâ: ego-extinction, God-absorption, goal of Sufi mysticism
Fâraizî: nineteenth-century Islamist movement in Bengal
fatwa (pl. *fatâwa*): authoritative opinion by a *mufti*
FISI: Friends of India Society International
garbha grha: "womb-house", sanctum sanctorum of temple
GATT: General Agreement on Tariffs and Trade
ghar-wâpasî: "home-coming", reconversion to Hinduism
ghât: bathing-place
gherao: lock-in strike
gûndâ: street-fighter, petty criminal
Granth: book, Sikh scripture
guna: quality, characteristic
gurû: "heavy one", teacher
gurudwara: "teacher's door", Sikh temple
gurukul: traditional Hindu school
hadîs, hadîth (pl. *ahâdîs*): an act or saying of the Prophet
hajj: pilgrimage to Mecca
Hari: Vishnu
Harijan: "God's people", (former) Untouchables
hidâya: guidance
HMS: *Hindû Mahâsabhâ*, Hindu Great-Assembly
homa: a popular Vedic ritual
HS: *Hindû Sabhâ*, Hindu Assembly
huzûr: Sir
îdgâh: place of assembly for Muslim prayers
imâm: prayer-leader in mosque
INA: Indian National Army (1943-45, under S.C. Bose)
inqilâb: revolution
ISI: Inter-Services Intelligence, Pakistani secret service
ISS: Islamic Sevak Sangh, "Islamic Servers' Association"
IUML: Indian Union Muslim League
jagîr: landed property, fief
jagîrdâr: (esp. absentee) landlord
janjû: *yajnopavît*, sacred thread as sign of Vedic initiation
JD: *Janatâ Dal*, People's Group
janmabhûmi: birthplace
janmasthân: birthplace
jâti: endogamous group, caste
jât-pat: caste principle, casteism
jî-huzûrî: "yes, Sir"-ism, toadyism
jihâd: "effort", Islamic struggle against unbelievers
jizya: tax levied on unbelievers
JNU: Jawaharlal Nehru University
JP movement: mass agitation (early 1970s) led by Jayaprakash Narayan
kâfir: unbeliever (in Islam)

karma: work, mechanical cause-effect relation (esp. across incarnations)
kar sevâ: manual participation in temple-building
karunâ: compassion
keshdhârî: "keeping one's hair", a *Khâlsâ* Sikh
khalîfa, caliph: "replacer (of the Prophet)", emperor of Islam
Khâlsâ: purity, (Sikh) Order of the Pure Ones
khânqâh: sufi hospice
khilâfat: caliphate, Islamic empire
Khuda: "self-created", God
Khuda hâfiz: "God be your protector", goodbye
khudî: selfhood, self-actualization
kîrtan: devotional chant
kror, crore: ten million
kshatriya: ruler or warrior by class
kufr: unbelief (in Islam)
kula: extended family
kulapati: head of family; rector of *gurukul*
kurtâ: loose shirt
lâkh: one hundred thousand
Lingâyat: member of the reformist Vîrashaiva ("stalwart Shivaite") sect
Lok Sabhâ: People's Assembly (national lower chamber)
madrasa: Muslim school
mahant: managing temple-priest
Mahâr: a Scheduled Caste in Maharasthra
maidân: open square
mandal: circle, symmetrical pattern; group
mandir: temple
masjid: mosque
math, mutt: abbey, monastery
mathâdi: porter
maulâna: title of Islamic scholar
mâyâ: magical creating power, illusoriness of creation
mâyâvâd: doctrine that the world is an illusion
mazhab: sect, religion, Sunni legal tradition
melâ: festival, fair
millat: religious community
mitra: friend
MLA: Member of Legislative Assembly
Mo'min: believer
Mapilla, Moplah: "son-in-law", Malayali Muslim
muazzin: man who gives âzân
mufti: Islamic jurisconsult
mukti: liberation; desireless state of mind
X murdâbâd: death to X, down with X
mûrti: idol
mushrik: practitioner of *shirk*, "associator", polytheist

Nadwat-al-Ulemâ: "meeting-place of Islamic scholars"
nawâb: honorofic plural of *naib*, "deputy", prince
nirguna: without characteristics, formless
nirvâna: desireless state, ego-extinction
NRI: Non-Resident Indian, expatriate Indian
pâdeshâh: king, Moghul emperor
pâdeshâhî: rulership, sovereignty
padyâtra: foot-march
pâk: pure
pakkâ: impeccable
panchâyat: "council of five", caste or village council
panth: "path", sect, school of thought
paramparâ: teacher-pupil chain, tradition
pardâh: "curtain", veiling and seclusion of women
paraia, pariah: an untouchable caste in Tamil Nadu; untouchable
peshwa: prime (minister), viz. of Shivaji's dynasty
pîr: a sufi, a Muslim mystic
POK: Pak-Occupied Kashmir
pradesh: province, state of the Union of India
PUCL: People's Union for Civil Liberties
pûjâ: devotional ritual, worship
purusha: "scion of Puru", man
qaum: nation, community
qâzî, qâdî: Islamic judge
Rahîm: "the Merciful", Allah
râjpût: "king's son", a warrior caste
râjya, râj: kingdom, regime
Râjya Sabhâ: State Assembly (national upper chamber)
Râm Râjya: "Rama's kingdom", ideal polity
Ramzân, Ramadân: Islamic month of fasting
râshtra: state
râshtrapati: president
rath: chariot
rathyâtra: chariot procession
Refah Partisi: Prosperity Party, Islamist party in Turkey
r.: *regnabat* (Latin), "he ruled (from year X to year Y)"
RRP: *Râm Râjya Parishad*, a traditionalist party
RSS: *Râshtrîya Svayamsevak Sangh*, National Volunteer Corps
sâdhana: a way or discipline of spiritual practice
sâdhu: Hindu monk, ascetic
sahajdhârî: non-*Khâls*â Sikh
salâm: "peace", greetings
salâm alaykum: "peace be with you"
samâj: society
samiti: committee
sampradâya: sect, tradition

sanâtana: eternal
Sanâtana Dharma: Hinduism
sangh: community, association
sannyâs: (vow of) renunciation
samskâra: ritual, psychic impression
samskrti, sanskriti: culture
sarai: "mansion", inn on caravan route
sarna (Munda): sacred grove, tribal religion
satî, suttee: "good woman", widow's self-immolation
Sayyid, Syed: title of Prophet's descendent
senâ: army, militia
shâkhâ: branch, RSS unit
shakti: power, goddess
shankarâchârya: head of one of the five *Dashanâmî* centres
Sharîf: noble, title of Prophet's descendant
sharî'a, shariat: "path", Islamic law
shâstra: Hindu religious book, esp. containing rules
shîla: rule, precept
shilâ: stone
shilânyâs: laying the first stone of a building
shirk: "association (of stars, ancestors etc. with God)", polytheism
shuddhi: purification, conversion ritual
shûdra: member of labouring class
sindûr: vermillion stripe in parting of Hindu wife's hair
sipâhî, sepoy: soldier
So-'ham: "Him am I", statement of monistic oneness
SP: *Samâjwâdî* Party, Socialist Party
SP: *Swatantra* Party, the liberal "Independence Party"
stûpâ: monument covering a Buddhist relic
sâûbâ: province
sûfî: "wool-clad", Muslim mystic
sûrâ: chapter of the Quran
sûrya-namaskâr: salute to the sun, ritual or exercise at sunrise
swadeshî: "of one's own country", native produce, self-reliance
swarâjya: self-rule, independence
talâq: Muslim unilateral divorce, repudiation
tapas: austerity
tawhîd: unity (of God), Islamic monotheism
tilak: Hindu mark on forehead
tîrth: ford, place of pilgrimage
tîrthankara: "ford-maker", ancient Jain sage
tushtikaran: appeasement
umma: the community of Islamic believers
UP: Uttar Pradesh, formerly United Provinces (of Agra and Oudh)
(Durgâ) vâhinî: "brigade (of the tiger-goddess)"
vaishya: member of the trading class

vanavâsî: forest-dweller, tribal
varna: "colour", one of the four ranks in society
Veda: "knowledge", ancient corpus of hymns
Vedânta: "end of Veda", Vedic philosophy
VHP: Vishva Hindû Parishad, "World Hindu Council"
Vidhân Sabhâ: Legislative Assembly, provincial parliament
vihâra: Buddhist monastery
Wahhabî: follower of Arab reformer Abdul Wahhab
wahî: inspiration, Quranic trance
WTO: World Trade Organization
yajna: sacrificial ritual
yajnopavît: sacred thread as token of Vedic initiation
zamîndâr: landlord
zimmî, dhimmî: non-Muslim as subject of Muslim state
X zindâbâd: long live X

Introduction

ABOUT THIS PROJECT

A history of ideas

My intention in writing this contribution to the study of Hindu revivalism, as a wider trend in Indian politics and public opinion expressing itself through diverse organizations and individual authors, is to provide an overview of the ideas animating this movement, with particular attention to its view of the religions and ideologies which have been in a hegemonic position in the last centuries, and with which Hindu revivalism has a relationship of unilateral or mutual hostility; and to its internal differences of opinion.

Hindu nationalism, or *Hindutva*, as given expression by the Hindû Mahâsabhâ (HMS, "Hindu Great-Assembly") and the family or *parivâr* of organizations around the Râshtrîya Svayamsevak Sangh (RSS, "National Volunteer Association"), including the Bhâratîya Janatâ Party (BJP, "Indian People's Party"), is the numerically most important tendency within the broader movement which goes by the name of Hindu revivalism. There is already a considerable literature about these organizations, including good biographies, studies of the sociological background of the movement's personnel and other factual aspects.[1] As we shall see, some academic studies and numerous journalistic reports carry a heavy and usually unabashed ideological bias, or innocently borrow that bias from their partisan though well-reputed Indian sources; but that need not prevent us from consulting them as useful repositories of material data about membership figures, caste background, election

[1]Three classics, generally objective and full of factual information, are Craig Baxter: *The Jana Sangh*, 1966; Walter Andersen and Shridhar Damle: *The Brotherhood in Saffron*, 1987; and Bruce Graham: *Hindu Nationalism and Indian Politics*, 1990. Less well-known but recommended is Gérard Heuzé: *Où Va l'Inde Moderne?* (French: "Whither modern India?"), 1993.

results, and the like.[2] However, a lot remains to be added, in particular about the ideological dimension, which remains relatively neglected in objective studies and grossly misrepresented in the more crusading type of studies.

For that matter, the most interesting formulations of Hindu revivalist thought have been provided by individuals outside the said organizations. Most of them have not even been noticed by established India-watchers, and I have presented a first survey of their work here.

Scope

The period which interests us primarily is the period of Hindu revivalism's breakthrough to political prominence, *c.* 1988-1998, when mass campaigns and electoral victories brought Hindu revivalist leaders on the front pages worldwide. The presence of the BJP in Parliament is an eloquent indicator of this stormy evolution: from two *Lok Sabhâ* seats in 1984 to 161 in 1996 and 179 in 1998, enough to form a Government and win a confidence vote with the help of its allies. Even the mere fact of having a few allies in 1996 and a great many in 1998 constituted a clean break with its earlier untouchability.

But our focus is not on the performance of political parties, though their party doctrines and manifestoes will be studied. It is mainly in the realm of ideas that the decade under consideration has witnessed a revolutionary breakthrough, mostly thanks to the efforts of Ram Swarup, Sita Ram Goel, and Arun Shourie. My position is that in their work, we see Hindu thought come into its own after centuries of either being of a provincial and unconvincing quality, or being in the shadow of the ideologies occupying the seat of political hegemony, chiefly Islam and a string of European imports, now united under the umbrella of "secularism".

To put this recent ideological rapid in perspective, I have chosen to selectively extend the horizon of this investigation back to the pioneers of

---

[2]A less than neutral attitude is in evidence in David Ludden, ed.: *Making India Hindu*, and in Christophe Jaffrelot: *The Hindu Nationalists in India*. More extreme cases (scholarship as crusade) are Arthur Bonner, ed.: *Democracy in India, a Hollow Shell*; and Lise McKean: *Divine Entreprise*. Among Indian publications, crusading books on this subject far outnumber dispassionate studies. Fairly sober examples of the former include Bipan Chandra: *Communalism in Modern India*, and Gyanendra Pandey: *The Construction of Communalism*. Crude examples include Tapan Basu et al.: *Khaki Shorts and Saffron Flags*. A more dispassionate study is Malik Singh: *Hindu Nationalists in India*.

Hindu revivalism in the late nineteenth century: Swami Dayananda Saraswati, Bankimchandra Chatterjee and Swami Vivekananda, and more recent stalwarts of Hindu revivalism like Swami Shraddhananda, Sri Aurobindo, Swatantryaveer Savarkar and Guru Golwalkar. Our treatment of them need not be comprehensive, since they already form the objects of a considerable literature, so we can concentrate on those aspects in their work most directly relevant to the contemporary ideological debate.

The broadness of our subject-matter implies that we have had to limit our investigation in other ways. Contentswise, no analysis of Hindu economic thought will be hazarded, first because I do not feel qualified, and secondly because it is very fluid now, with books on India's economic prospects (like those on China a decade earlier) being outdated by the time they get published. Even within the Hindu movement, it is unclear where the ongoing debate on economy vs. ecology and on *Swadeshi* ("native produce", a cherished nationalist motto) vs. globalization (in which India has so far been a great winner, at least economically) is headed.[3]

Likewise, we shall not deal with Hindu techniques of self-organization, nor with the existing strategies of mass mobilization, a popular topic in academic writing about Hindu revivalism.[4] Also, the caste background of the movement, another much-discussed aspect, will interest us only in passing, partly also because I object to the now-common reduction of everything Hindu to a caste calculus.[5] In a panel discussion about the 1996 *Lok Sabhâ* election results, at the 1996 South Asia Conference in Madison, Wisconsin, an official of the Indian Embassy rose to remark, quite rightly, that every speaker thus far had explained voter behaviour exclusively in terms of caste, as if Indian voters cannot have other levels of group identification, other types of collective interests, or convictions rather than interests. Of course, Hindu revivalist positions regarding the caste system will be considered, but this aspect of the matter will be kept in proportion.

The main focus will be on the actual programmatic and ideological statements of Hindu revivalist thinkers and organizations, on their position

[3]As if to illustrate the non-monolithic Hindu Nationalist position on economic policy, the RSS has recently been criticizing the BJP Government for, in the words of *Organiser*'s Rajesh Agarkar (26.4.1998), putting "Swadeshi on backburner".

[4]E.g. Tanika Sarkar and Urvashi Butalia, eds.: *Women and the Hindu Right*, or Praful Bidwai *et al.*: *Religion, Religiosity and Communalism*.

[5]See e.g. the caste distribution of BJS-BJP representatives in Madhya Pradesh, in C. Jaffrelot: *The Hindu Nationalists*, p.559.

vis-à-vis rival religions, and on their critique of the really existing secularist system. Though we may follow ongoing debates till after the time of the BJP's accession to power (March 1998), a description and evaluation of the BJP's performance in government will remain outside the scope of this study.

Sources

This study is not a secret history or a biography based on a perusal of private or otherwise nearly-inaccessible documents. On the contrary, it concentrates on the milestones, the major ideological statements of Hindu revivalism. It provides an overview, which means that we have to cover a fairly large number of authors from different persuasions and organizational obediences. Rather than scratch for unsuspected elements in remote corners of our subject-matter, which limitations of space would not permit anyway, I shall deal with the texts which form the ideological backbone of Hindu revivalism.

I have also made only a sparing use of the numerous interviews and informal talks I have had with insiders. After I had written my preliminary study on the Ayodhya controversy, well-liked in Hindu circles because its conclusion went in favour of their (well-established but then temporarily controversial) thesis that the Babri mosque had been built in forcible replacement of a Hindu temple, I was suddenly welcome to attend meetings and have interviews with practically all the Hindu revivalist leaders and thinkers.[6] Unlike some of my colleagues, I did not have to tell lies about myself to get past the distrust against Western India-watchers which the uniformly negative coverage of the Hindu movement has aroused there. Yet, I prefer to base my conclusions in this study on publicly accessible documents, not on uncontrollable statements made in private.

One invaluable advantage of this bit of "participant observation" has been the opportunity to verify (assuming a minimum of knowledge of human character on my part) whether Hindu revivalists, especially those

---

[6]To the extent that the Hindu revivalist publishing-house Voice of India offered to publish my thesis on the Ayodhya dispute: *Ram Janmabhoomi vs. Babri Masjid* (1990). Later, the relationship soured a bit as a result of my criticism of RSS-BJP policies, see e.g. BJP Executive member Kanchan Gupta: "Reply to Koenraad Elst", *Observer of Business and Politics*, 14/15.1.1997, a reply to my columns on BJP policies *ibidem*, 6/7.12.1996.

in powerful organizations, mean what they say. It is quite common among professional Hindutva-watchers to use only documentary information, often produced by the movement's declared enemies, without ever having met a single human representative of the movement itself. Consequently, it is equally common to publicize allegations about Hindu revivalist spokesmen which no one with inside knowledge could possibly sustain, e.g. to call the mild-mannered and soft-spoken BJP leader Lal Krishna Advani a "demagogue"[7] or the BJP's "fearsome rabble-rousing president"[8], qualifications which are hard to match with the fact that Advani is criticized precisely for his soft line.[9]

It is also very common in hostile writings about Hindu revivalists to admit grudgingly that their statements are unobjectionable in themselves, then to allege that it is all merely a code for an entirely different message.[10] I shall have occasion to discuss specific examples, but as a general rule, my findings are not such as to justify this unscholarly tendency to impute motives and to tell people what their "real" as opposed to their stated opinions are. I choose to be naïve and to discuss what my study objects have actually said and written, rather than their "real" intentions as revealed to God all-knowing.

---

[7]Thus, Brian Barron in the BBC *Assignment* documentary on the BJP in May 1991. Advani's alleged "demagoguery" was also the reason for hanging his picture in the rogues' gallery of the Simon Wiesenthal Center's Tolerance Museum (Los Angeles) for a few months in 1999, in the company of Saddam Hussein and Idi Amin.

[8]John Zubrzycki: "India's powerbrokers scuttle to fend off fundamentalists", *Sunday Times*, 12.5.1996.

[9]It is often alleged that Advani "whipped up his followers during the siege of the Ayodhya mosque [on 6 December] 1992", as in Freddy De Pauw: "Een goede man in een slechte partij" (Dutch: "A good man in a bad party", said about A.B. Vajpayee, supposedly "a liberal in a fundamentalist party"), *De Standaard*, 20.3.1998. According to eye-witnesses, the crowd pushed him aside when it attacked the mosque, and he got tears in his eyes; the next day, when he was to make a statement, he was depressed and Arun Shourie narrowly saved him from making a weak and apologetic statement. In a *BJP Today* editorial (16.11.1997), Advani noted that V.S. Naipaul and Nirad C. Chaudhuri justified the demolition, but he himself still "regretted the manner in which this happened".

[10]E.g. the para "Sangh doublespeak", in Y. Ghimire and L. Rattanani: "Harvesting the Shame", *India Today*, 15.2.1993; Mani Shankar Aiyar: "BJP-speak: Language in the age of Hindutva", *Sunday*, 7.2.1993; or the caption "Nationalist Hindu party seduces India with moderate façade", in Catherine Vuylsteke: "Het 'monster' aan de macht" (Dutch: "The 'monster' in power"), *De Morgen*, 6.2.1998.

Language

Language is a highly political issue in India.[11] Among the topics which we will have to leave aside in this study is the communal dimension of the Hindi-Urdu controversy, the movement for linguistic provinces and other instances of language politics. However, we cannot forego noticing that Hindu activists often refer to "the English-speaking elite" as their main enemy.

It is undeniable that the ruling elite has thrown its full weight behind attempts to preserve the privileged position of English and to prevent the linguistic decolonization of India, most decisively by sabotaging the implementation of the constitutional provision that Hindi replace English as the Indian Union's official language by 1965.[12] Most of them stand to lose in their individual careers if deprived of this simple advantage of language proficiency by the demotion of English. Incidentally, most India-watchers are far from neutral in this matter (as in the religio-political controversy): unlike former BBC correspondent Mark Tully, who is convinced that the predominance of English in India is harmful to intellectual life and to democracy, many academic India-watchers only laugh at the "nativist" position.[13]

Yet, it must be kept in mind that in the present context, "English-speaking" represents more a Westward cultural orientation than mere mastery of the language, which by itself says little about whether one is pro or contra Hindu revivalism. Indeed, an important constituency of Hindu revivalism consists of English-educated businessmen, engineers and professionals, many of them having relatives settled in the West (if not Non-Resident Indians themselves), people who want India to make progress and who believe that progress must be based on solid cultural

[11]About the political struggles over the official languages, see S. Dwivedi: *Hindi on Trial*.

[12]Art. 343: "(1) The official language of the Union shall be Hindi in Devnagari script. ... (2) ... for a period of fifteen years from the commencement of the Constitution, the English language shall continue to be used for all the official purposes of the Union".

[13]Mark Tully said as much in his lecture at the Asian Studies Department of Katholieke Universiteit Leuven, November 1997. I got an impression of the views of the Indologist establishment during a panel discussion about education through the mother tongue at the 1996 South Asia Conference in Madison, where the cream of American Indology lambasted and ridiculed the "nativist" position while a lone Indian educationist researcher, who had been a primary school teacher herself, testified about the pupils' stunted intellectual growth resulting from education through a foreign language.

rootedness. Hindu revivalism is by no means confined to provincial and uneducated circles. From Sri Aurobindo down to Arun Shourie, many of its spokesmen have been just as familiar with the West and as fluent in English as their opponents. But to them, English is just a language, while for the "English-speaking elite", it is a fortress.

Even those who have had little exposure to Western influence usually take the trouble of mastering English so as to be more effective in communicating their ideas. No matter how much most Hindu revivalists may regret it, English is still the language of political and intellectual life in India, and they adapt to this reality.[14] Most important ideological statements of this movement are available in English, so that ignorance of Hindi (or Marathi etc.) is no excuse for the substandard coverage which it has been receiving at the hands of most journalistic India hands. On the other hand, I readily accept that in the present case, knowledge of Bengali, Marathi and perhaps other vernaculars would have given me access to more sources; but then this is not the last study of Hindu revivalism, I trust. For the present purpose of making the first-ever in-depth study of contemporary Hindu revivalist doctrine, the consultation of English and Hindi material has yielded more than enough information.

Methodology: back to basics

As to method, I will not try to win a prize for originality. On the contrary, I insist on going back to basics. The way to find out about the thought animating a social, cultural and political movement is simply to listen and read what its acknowledged spokesmen have to say. If this seems obvious, a survey of the primary sources, basis of the prevalent discourse on Hindu revivalist ideology is a painful eye-opener, as we shall see. I am not approaching this material with a particular theory or sociological model in mind, not in the sense that I imagine myself being free of preconceptions and intellectual conditioning, but in the sense that I want to avoid doing injustice to the subject-matter by subjecting it to Procrustean schemes. The need of the hour is to get acquainted with what Hindu revivalists are really saying.

---

[14]I have had to conduct only a handful of interviews in Hindi, e.g. with Bajrang Dal leader Vinay Katiyar (Ayodhya, 3.11.1990). Likewise, consulting some Hindi literature has been helpful, but I cannot say that it has substantially altered the picture which one gets through English-medium sources, e.g. that *Panchjanya* reveals RSS positions not disclosed in *Organiser*.

I also intend to restore objectivity. This is an urgent necessity in view of two challenges. The more subtle challenge to the principle of objectivity is the "postmodern" form of Marxism (quite powerful in American universities) which denies the very notion of objective knowledge, which assumes that knowledge is conditioned by one's social belonging, and which insists that "all research in the social sciences has a political agenda".[15] This means in practice that once you have identified an author as a representative of the wrong interest group, his arguments are *ipso facto* wrong or vitiated. In a large part of the academic publications, this position is implicit in their way of foregoing any serious evaluation of arguments formulated by Hindu revivalists, as if the identification of the propounder of the argument as a "Hindu fundamentalist" were sufficient to put it beyond the pale of rational discourse. Thus, the Hindu litany of grievances against the inequalities imposed on Hinduism by the Indian state (which makes up a very large part of this literature) is commonly only mentioned as an object of ridicule, never of proper investigation.

The second problem is that many India-watchers who have ordinary notions of objectivity (i.e. who ignore the stratospheric questioning of this very concept by postmodernists), have none the less published books and papers on the present topic which suffer serious lapses from the normal scholarly standards. The exacting standards of objectivity are obviously a permanent challenge to scholars in any field, but this field, or at least its present-day state of the art, presents some peculiar problems. In some cases, the bias may be in the mind of the India-watcher, but the overriding problem is that even scholars and journalists who do try to be objective are handicapped in this endeavour by their reliance on Indian sources which have considerable standing but are none the less far from objective. There is, apparently, an assumption of cultural solidarity between Western India-watchers and their Indian colleagues: the former consider the latter as "our men in India", as representatives of enlightened modernity who stand above the ongoing conflicts between the native barbarians. The assumption is not even shaken by the conspicuous fact that many Indian academics use very partisan language when addressing the issue of Hindu revivalism.

---

[15]Thus spoke Biju Mathew in the discussion after I read my paper on "Linguistics and the Aryan Invasion Theory" at the Annual South Asia Conference, Madison 1996. This is a postmodern variation on the old Marxist attacks on "bourgeois objectivity".

However, we shall show in the next section that the very basics of this research are highly problematic: numerous presumably non-partisan sources are tainted by a partisan involvement which outsiders tend to ignore or misunderstand, and even the terminology which conditions the whole discourse on India's religious conflict is often unclear and sometimes the object of deliberate manipulation. My intention in this study is to avoid these traps and clear away the cobwebs at the only entrance to a real understanding of Hindu revivalism, viz. to let the primary sources speak.

Some problematic terminology

What follows is a brief glossary of the typical terminology encountered in the primary and secondary literature on Hindu revivalism. A number of these terms represent false trails, theories or rhetoric which contribute nothing to our understanding of Hindu revivalism, sometimes in spite of their tremendous popularity as explanation models in circles with little knowledge of the primary material. Others are very ordinary terms whose meaning suddenly becomes problematic when used in this context.

Hindu revivalism

The subject-matter on which we will focus is most aptly termed Hindu revivalism, a broad trend in nineteenth-and twentieth-century India which seeks to *revive* Hinduism after a benumbing near-millennium of political, ideological and psychological subjection to Islamic and Western hegemony. In practice, Hindu revivalism is a many-pronged attempt to ensure the survival of Hinduism by integrating the gains of modernity in Hindu civilization (in that sense, it is of course not a revival of anything ancient in unchanged form), as well as by intellectually and politically fighting off the perceived threats posed by Islam, Christianity and a string of secular ideologies, of which Marxism is the most articulate.

In some respects, the movement embraces contributions of modernity which are so radical that it would be more apt to speak of "reconstruction" rather than of "revival" of Hinduism. Most notably, the anti-casteist stand of the movement constitutes a sharp break with what Hinduism stood for in preceding centuries. The Maratha/Peshwa reconquest of much of India from Muslim rule in the eighteenth century is a favourite point of reference of the movement, but Peshwa regimes were typically casteist to an unprecedented and caricatural extent (e.g. prohibiting untouchables from entering towns in late afternoon, as their lengthening shadows would fall on other people, thus "polluting" them). But under British rule, and exposed to subversion by Christian and Islamic missionaries, casteism proved to be a luxury which Hindu society could no longer afford, so an anti-casteist line was adopted, embracing the gradual dissolution of what had long been its defining structure.

The Hindu revivalist movement perceives itself as the cultural chapter of India's decolonization. This means that it tries to free the Indians from the colonial condition at the mental and cultural level, to complete the process of political and economic decolonization. The need for "reviving" Hinduism springs from the fact that the said hostile ideologies (mostly Islam) have managed to eliminate Hinduism physically in certain geographical parts and social segments of India, and also (mostly the Western ideologies) to neutralize the Hindu spirit among many nominal Hindus. Even among committed Hindus, there is not always much life in Hinduism, except in the elementary sense that the rituals are still performed. Ignorance and inertia are rampant, and these too are enemies which Hindu revivalism seeks to defeat. In fact, ignorance sometimes informs distorting versions of Hindu tradition propagated by Hindu revivalist ideologues themselves.

One of the effects of centuries of immersion in a colonial psychology is an inferiority complex and an attitude of self-reproach. As prominent lawyer Nani Palkhivala once remarked: "India is like a donkey carrying a sack of gold. The donkey does not know what it is carrying but it is content to go along with its load on its back."[16] One intellectual project is to rediscover the ancient and not-so-ancient treasures of material culture and ingenuity which colonialism has obscured or destroyed. This effort is shared with other Indian intellectuals, e.g. with Claude Alvares who shows how "attempts were made to destroy non-Western technologies", and until recently if not today, "even the idea that other cultures may have had thriving technologies was calculatingly destroyed".[17] The basic sense of loss at the hands of colonialism has its parallels in other cultures, e.g. in Muslim protestations that the "awesome, sophisticated and wide-ranging publication industry" which grew in the Muslim world seven centuries

---

[16]Quoted by Anand Shankar Pandya: *Relevance of Hinduism in Modern Age*, p.12.

[17]Claude Alvares: *Decolonizing History: Technology and Culture in India, China and the West, 1492 to the Present* (1979). See also Alvares' review of Dharampal: *Indian Science and Technology in the Eighteenth Century*, in *Illustrated Weekly*, 15.8.1986.

before its European counterpart, "was systematically killed off by the colonial powers, along with the Muslim systems of education and medicine".[18]

Sometimes this debate is about very practical policy matters, e.g. the Green Revolution, supposedly an agricultural success story of the Western approach transplanted to the Third World, is criticized as a disaster-bound disruption of better-adapted native agricultural techniques.[19] Ecology is one favourite sphere where Hindu apologists of every school feel vindicated by recent developments: the "Western" approach to nature leads to global suicide, while the "Hindu" approach has always been one of "sustainable development".[20] However, once it gets technical, Hindu revivalists have until recently merely followed suit, adding more fervour than substance to the argument developed by more secular compatriots.

In spite of occasional bouts of chauvinistic bluster, Hindus are not very aware of the treasures of their civilization; most RSS people, who chant a kind of litany of the names of great Hindus at their gatherings, would not be able to say with any precision what was so unique about the contribution of a Pânini or an Aryabhatta. By contrast, all modern-educated Hindus are acutely aware of the "evils of Hindu society" which hostile authors and a hostile syllabus have highlighted no end. Therefore, a few scholars have also endeavoured to pull Hindu attention away from, as it were, the mote in the Hindu eye and towards the beam in the eye of the critics, e.g. by studying the "evils of Muslim society", in reaction against the apologetic justification of Islamic hegemony with claims of the superiority of the Islam's social philosophy.[21] So far, this attempt to take the debate on to the enemy half of the field remains a marginal endeavour.

---

[18]Ziauddin Sardar and Merryl Wyn Davies: *Distorted Imagination*, pp.96-7. This book on the Rushdie affair contains a chapter, "Enter, the Brown Sahib", which provides a fairly precise Muslim parallel to Hindu polemic against the anglicized alienated elite.

[19]See e.g. Dr. Vandana Shiva's reply to Green Revolution defender Norman E. Borlaug in *The Ecologist*, Sep. 1997, p.211-12.

[20]The trend is in evidence both among Indians and Western Orient-lovers, e.g. Ranchor Prime: *Hinduism and Ecology*; or Maneka Gandhi (Sanjay Gandhi's widow, and a Minister in the Governments led by V.P. Singh 1989-90, Chandra Shekhar 1990-91 and A.B. Vajpayee 1998-): *Heads and Tails*, on vegetarianism; or M. Vannucci: *Ecological Readings in the Veda*; and *passim* in the works of Ram Swarup, David Frawley *et al.*

[21]For such justification, see e.g. M.N. Roy: *Role of Islam in History* (1939), and Mohammed Habib: introduction to the 1952 Aligarh edition of Elliott & Dowson: *History of India as Told by Its Own Historians*, vol.2. For a Hindu probe into the problems of Muslim society, see Arun Shourie: *The World of Fatwas* (1995).

It is none the less symptomatic for an increased self-confidence, and possibly one element in the beginning of a new cycle of Hindu expansion.

Traditionalism

A contentswise limitation on this study is that we will not consider Hindu traditionalism, the anti-modern tendency most visibly represented by the late Swami Karpatri and the the former and the present Jagatguru Shankaracharya of Puri. They too have tried to "revive" Hinduism, but in a purely reactionary sense. The difference is most conspicuous in the attitude towards the caste system: the revivalist tendency seeks to unite Hindus across caste lines, while the traditionalists would insist on preserving untenable and burdensome institutions like Untouchability, thus effectively excluding themselves from competitive modern politics. The option to simply go back to the pre-colonial period as if nothing had happened is, of course, not really open.

On the other hand, it is remarkable that even these traditionalists have not been able to keep modernization out altogether, e.g. the *Sanâtana Dharma Sabhâ* ("Eternal Religion Council"), founded in 1895 to counter the emergent Hindu reformism, made it its business to propagate Vedic religion by making its literature easily available, without verifying whether every buyer was a properly initiated twice-born Hindu.[22] The decision of the regional traditionalist organizations to set up an all-India platform, the *Bhârata Dharma Mahâmandala* ("Indian religious federation", Mathura 1902), prefigured the creation of the reformist *Vishva Hindû Parishad* ("World Hindu Council", 1964) and of the *Dharma Sansad* ("Religious Parliament"). Another typical modern-Hindu element creeping into traditionalist discourse, but otherwise typical of the reformist discourse of a Swami Vivekananda, was the insistence that Hinduism is not just for Hindus, that it is the universal religion.

In spite of common causes like the anti-cow-slaughter movement, the traditionalists have more often distanced themselves from the Hindu revivalist movement, which they consider blatantly heterodox. Secularists do not mind taking the most conservative Hindu institutions, which object to the Hindu revivalist anti-caste drive, as allies against reform-Hindu

[22]As remarked with some sarcasm by J.N. Farquhar: *Religious Movements*, p.321-22. *Sanâtana Dharma Sabhâ*: "Eternal Religion Council".

activism. For example, Dipak Malik relates with explicit satisfaction how monastic institutions in Varanasi, along with the business community, refused to join the Ayodhya movement.[23] Likewise, many Hindu priests in Ayodhya have long refused to join the RSS's Ayodhya campaign, not because they reject the Hindu claim to the disputed site, but because their quarrel with the RSS over traditional social structures is so fundamental.

For over two decades after independence, they have had, apart from a sizable presence inside the Congress, their own political party, the *Râm Râjya Parishad*, which was entirely dependent on the personal leadership of Swami Karpatri and faded out after his death. Though a legitimate topic for further study, this traditionalist current will only receive peripheral attention here.

Hindu fundamentalism

It should already be clear from the above that the movement under consideration cannot be called "Hindu fundamentalism". The reason is not that, as Hindu revivalists commonly argue, "a Hindu cannot be a fundamentalist because this concept belongs in the Biblical-Quranic tradition". The role of "scripture" is indeed not exactly the same in Hinduism as in the "religions of the Book", among other reasons because there is a plurality of Hindu scriptures. But for all practical purposes, the same opposition to reform with reference to some ancient scriptural dictum is in evidence in Hindu traditionalist circles as you find among Jewish, Christian or Muslim fundamentalists.

The point is rather that that segment of Hindu opinion which we are considering in the present study, does not belong to this scripturalist tendency, even though it may embellish its manifestoes with an occasional (and often creatively reinterpreted) Vedic quotation. Most certainly, it is "not fundamentalist in the sense of being scripturalist".[24] Fundamentalist movements first of all oppose the lukewarm and compromising tendencies within their own religion; such is not the case at all in Hindu revivalism, which focuses on confronting non-Hindu doctrines or social forces and uniting all Hindus.

For this reason, I must object to the general title of Chicago

[23]Dipak Malik: "Three Riots in Varanasi", *South Asia Bulletin*, 1994, p.56.

[24]Niels C. Nielsen: *Fundamentalism*, p.107.

University's prestigious *Fundamentalism Project*, edited by Martin Marty and Scott Appleby, though I have used some of its studies with profit.[25] Thus, Buddhism has a militant face in Myanmar and Sri Lanka against non-Buddhists, but this has nothing whatsoever to do with the defining "fundamentalist" concern of scripturalism vs. modernism. Admittedly, it is hard enough to find an accurate term covering all the forms of contemporary religious ferment and militancy with which the project tries to deal; I would have tried it with something like "self-reassertion of religions". That term would invite the objection that it excludes the purely instrumental assertion of religious values by non-religious interest groups, literally the use of religion for political or economic ends, which I consider a real but overrated and separate phenomenon. We should not blur our understanding of the genuine reassertion of religion as an autonomous concern by reducing religion to more mundane factors.

The only component of the current under consideration which could be called "fundamentalist", i.e. seeking to revive Scripture as normative for today's society and attacking those co-religionists who have allegedly deviated from Scriptural purity, is the *Arya Samâj*, founded in 1875 and now long past its prime but still standing out as a *progressive* movement. In the case of Hinduism, it so happens that many of the traditional inequalities, injustices and unwholesome customs of Hindu society are not attested in Vedic scripture, and even less so in the Arya Samaj's own understanding of it. This made it possible to present a programme of social equality as a return to the Vedas.

An illustration of the difference between progressive fundamentalism and reactionary traditionalism was provided by the following incident. Swami Nishchalananda, the 145th Jagatguru Shankaracharya of Puri made headlines by interrupting a ceremony in Calcutta's Sharadeshwari Ashram, a women's religious community, to protest against the chanting of the Vedas by a woman (spring 1994) when in fact, some of the Vedic hymns were written and doubtlessly also chanted by women.[26] The incident shows the difference between traditionalism, which freezes a religion at the stage which one remembers from childhood (when women

---

[25]For the present topic especially Ainslie T. Embree: "The function of the RSS: to define the Hindu nation", in M.E. Marty and R.S. Appleby: *The Fundamentalism Project*, vol.4, *Accounting for Fundamentalisms*, p.617-52.

[26]See e.g. Brigitte Ars: "Vrouwen lezen de Veda's" (Dutch: "Women read the Vedas"), *India Nu* (Utrecht), July 1994.

were not allowed to chant the Vedas), and fundamentalism, which goes back to the roots and may have a progressive thrust. In the *Arya Samâj*, girls get the complete Vedic initiation, as apparently they used to in the Vedic age itself.[27]

Otherwise, "fundamentalism" in the true sense of the word is not in evidence in the Hindu revivalist movement. Of course, a certain allowance should be made for journalistic vagueness in the use of such terms, which need not indicate malicious intent. Still, the term "fundamentalism", originated in anti-modernist tendencies in Christianity, does not help in a proper understanding of what India-watchers assume to be the "corresponding" Hindu phenomenon.

Hindu communalism

One of the most frequently-used terms in India-watching is "communalism", a term unknown to most Westerners. Its roots lie in the British colonial policy of taking "communities" as the relevant units in recruitment or in the allotment of seats in representative assemblies. Originally, the term had no pejorative connotation, but Indian nationalists in the freedom movement objected to these "communal" policies which allegedly aimed at keeping the Indian population divided. Indeed, the biggest worry of the freedom movement was the "communalist" collaboration of the Muslim League with the colonial administration: in exchange for "communal" electorates and recruitment quota, the party claiming to represent the Indian Muslims agreed to stay aloof from the anti-British agitation.

Today, "communalism" is one of those labels allotted exclusively to people who reject it; it is a term of abuse. Even people who advocate communal recruitment quota (a demand recently revived by an array of Muslim organizations) are now self-described "secularists" and signatories to every new "National Manifesto (People's Rally, All-India Front etc.) Against Communalism". Just two examples from the most extreme corners of Islamic militantism, which support the demand for communal quota in recruitment: the All-India Milli Council passed a resolution on 1.9.1996 "strongly opposing the communal and fascist

[27]In the Dutch Hindu community, not only the reformist *Arya Samâj* but also the *Sanâtanis* (traditionalists) are now training girls as *panditâs* and priests, as shown on OHM (*Organisatie Hindoe Media*, the Dutch Hindu TV programme), 2.5.1998.

forces";[28] and S. Ausaf Vasfi of the *Jamaat-i-Islami* (whose Pakistani wing has campaigned for decades, and with success, for the desecularization of the state) attacks "communalism" in the name of "secularism".[29] I cannot recall a single issue of the Islamist papers *Radiance* and *Muslim India* which failed to brandish "secularism" and denounce "communalism".

This distortion of an otherwise well-defined and useful term started in the 1920s, when Congress leaders took to using it for (i.e. against) Hindu organizations, even though the latter *opposed* communal electorates and recruitment quota which the Congress had endorsed. Even when Congress became a party to the Partition of India on a communal basis (Pakistan for Muslims, India for non-Muslims), which these Hindu organizations kept on opposing, Congress kept on denouncing the latter as "Hindu communalist". All the same, during his speech in court (1948), Nathuram Godse, Hindu Mahasabha member and the murderer of the Mahatma, unselfconsciously attacked Gandhi's compromise with (Muslim) "communalism" and repeatedly pledged his allegiance to a united India which should be democratic and "non-communal". "Anti-communal" arguments were standard HMS parlance before Nehru popularized the terms "secularism" and "Hindu communalism".

To justify this shift in meaning, a symmetry was assumed between minority organizations which favoured the communal principle and Hindu organizations which opposed it, in the sense that both defended the perceived interests of their own community. The definition of the term was changed. The effective meaning of *communalism* in post-Partition India is explicitated by the Marxist historian Bipan Chandra as "the belief that because a group of people follow a particular religion they have, as a result, common social, political and economic interests".[30] Or: "It is the belief that in India Hindus, Muslims, Christians and Sikhs form different and distinct communities which are independently and separately

---

[28]Reported in *Muslim India*, Feb. 1997, p.87. *Milli* = "of the Muslim *millat*", i.e. "religious community conceived as a nation". In the Ottoman Empire, any tolerated religious community (Greek Orthodox, Maronite etc.) was called a *millet*; in India, the term refers specifically to the Muslim community and is often interchangeable with *ummah*, "the worldwide Muslim community".

[29]S. Ausaf Vasfi in *Radiance*, 18.8.1996, reproduced in *Muslim India*, March 1997, p.102.

[30]B. Chandra: *Communalism in Modern India*, p.1.

structured or consolidated; that all the followers of a religion share not only a community of religious interests but also common secular interests, that is, common economic, political, social and cultural interests", etc.[31] This definition is generally accepted and used, e.g. by Saral Jhingran: "By 'communalism' is meant the assertion that the secular interests of a group of persons are coextensive with its religious identity."[32]

This definition is, unfortunately, quite wrong. It does not satisfy the defining criterion of a definition, viz. that its semantic domain be coterminous with the phenomenon it seeks to define. When Bipan Chandra and Saral Jhingran talk about "communalism", they certainly include issues like the agitation against cow-slaughter, the Hindu and Muslim agitations concerning the temple or mosque in Ayodhya, and the *Satanic Verses* affair. In each of these examples, purely religious concerns are at stake: the leaders of these agitations are not telling their followers that they have "common economic, political, social and cultural interests", but that the birthplace of Rama or the fair name of the Prophet is being violated. These controversies are not covered by Bipan Chandra's definition of "communalism".

The kernel of truth in his definition is that some "communalists" seek to promote the interests of their religion and religious community by extending the community's identity and solidarity into secular spheres. But that was already outlined in the old British definition, viz. communalism is the principle that communities defined by religious identity are treated as units of political organization. Today, the usage has become so imprecise that any conjunction of the phenomena "religion" and "conflict" is called "communalism".

The fact that nowadays the label "communalist" is systematically applied to people who never describe themselves as such, and most of whom go out of their way to deny that they are "communalists", should caution scholars to handle it with utmost care. It may be legitimate to sit down and collect evidence for the thesis that "the Hindu nationalists are communalists", but it is not legitimate, at least not from the viewpoint of scholarly or journalistic deontology, to routinely replace their chosen self-description with the externally imposed label "communalist".

---

[31]B. Chandra: *Communalism in Modern India*, p.1.

[32]Saral Jhingran: "Religion and communalism", in P. Bidwai *et al.*, eds.: *Religion, Religiosity and Communalism*, p.78.

The normal practice is to label a movement with the name it gives itself, e.g. even though most ruling parties in Europe at the time of writing pursue free-market economic policies, we still call them "socialist" (strictly meaning that they pursue the nationalization of the means of production, which they do not) simply because that is what they call themselves. A Trotskyite or Maoist agitator may call them "lackeys of global capitalism" (and in the 1930s even as "social-fascists"), yet no newsreader or political analyst will think of identifying a Socialist prime minister in those terms.

Imposition of an exonym, especially a pejorative one like "communalist", must be considered a statement of involvement in an anti-Hindu-revivalist or so-called "anti-communal" crusade; or of ignorant reliance on such sources not recognized as partisan. People are welcome to their crusades, and they may even produce some real scholarship in the service of their crusades, but it is best to remain aware of the nature of their work, and not to assume that it is objective simply because it is adorned with academic references. In this study, based on primary sources, the term *communalism* will be used only sparingly, viz. only where I believe I can justify it in terms of its proper definition.

Two more remarks to keep the topic of "communalism" in perspective. It deserves to be noted that one of the trend-setting attacks on "Hindu communalism" was undoubtedly the "Report of the Enquiry Commission Appointed by the Council of the All-India Muslim League to Inquire into Some Muslim Grievances in Congress Provinces", better known as the *Pirpur Report* (1938), which lists Muslim grievances in Congress-ruled provinces.[33] These include: being blamed by Congress ministers for starting riots, being insulted by the singing of the "idolatrous" anthem *Vande Mâtaram*, "Hail Mother(land)", the non-recognition of Urdu as all-Indian link language, Gandhi's talk against cow-slaughter, and this: "The Indian National Congress' concept of nationalism is based on the establishment of a national state of the majority community in which other nationalities and communities have only secondary rights. The Muslims think that no tyranny can be [as] great as the tyranny of the majority."[34]

---

[33]The Pirpur Report is reproduced in K.K. Aziz: *Muslims under Congress Rule 1937-39. A Documentary Record*, vol.1, p.307-86.

[34]In K.K. Aziz: *Muslims under Congress Rule 1937-1939*, vol.1, p.311.

Exactly this allegation of majority tyranny ("majoritarianism") later became the standard argument against the BJP, and like the Congress in 1938, the BJP exhausts itself in denials, but to no avail. Though the Muslim League was the very incarnation of communalism (foisting communal electorates, communal weightage in representation and communal job quota on India), its attacks on Congress, Mahatma Gandhi and even Jawaharlal Nehru were remarkably similar to the post-Independence "secularist" critique of "Hindu communalism".

Secondly, now that "communalism" has become a term of abuse, it may be noted that communalism as historically applied had certain achievements to its credit. Some religions naturally have a lot of implications on society, in the form of rules of behaviour, dietary prescriptions and taboos, a calendar, family law, conception of authority and most of all a sense of community, of "us" as distinct from "them". Therefore, the Ottoman Empire embarked on a communalist policy and divided (or rather, formally acknowledged the existing division of) the population in *millet*s, "religious communities": the Maronites, the Armenians, the Greek-Orthodox, the Jews etc. In spite of the institutionalized inequality between Muslims and non-Muslims, this system provided for a secure political status and a large internal autonomy to each of the non-Muslim communities. Balkans specialist Professor Mon Detrez has called this "the best thing which ever happened to the Balkans"[35], because unlike under Christian rule, this allowed minorities to survive and to preserve their identity: a "multicultural society". From a secularist angle, one might object that this identification of Ottoman subjects by their religion vastly increased the hold of religion on the people; but pragmatically speaking, in an age when religiosity was an omnipresent and acknowledged value, this was a relatively benign system.

The same system is still applied in the Islamic Republic of Iran, so that the Armenian, Jewish and Zoroastrian minorities are recognized as separate units with their own representatives in Parliament and with a certain (communal, non-territorial) autonomy; and likewise in Pakistan. One has to admit that without this system, there would probably not be any representatives of the minorities in these Parliaments.

That this system is the "lesser evil" in predominantly Muslim societies has been illustrated in Turkey, where equality before the law regardless of

---

[35]Interview about the crisis in ex-Yugoslavia, BRTN (Flemish) radio, 1995.

religion was enacted under Western pressure after France and Britain saved the Ottoman Empire in the Crimea War. Violence against the minorities increased, e.g. the anti-Armenian pogroms in the 1890s (not to mention the Armenian genocide of 1915), and the secular Turkish Republic saw the pogroms expelling the Greeks from Istambul in the 1950s and the gradual expulsion of the Assyrian and Chaldaeic Christians from the South-east in the subsequent decades. In 1900, after centuries of Islamic rule and the *millet* system, Christians still formed a third of the population of Turkey; by 2000, after a century of semi-secular (Young-Turk) and militantly secular rule, their presence had been reduced to less than 1 per cent. But of course, it doesn't follow that the communal system which proved its use in the Ottoman empire must be emulated in a modern republic like independent India.

Hindu nationalism

A term which is accepted as a self-description by most Hindu revivalists is "Hindu nationalist". After the Ayodhya-related excitement with its media exaggerations died down, the more responsible Western media have decided to settle for this term when discussing the RSS and BJP. Some did so even earlier: "The BJP is often described as a Hindu fundamentalist party. More correctly, it espouses Hindu nationalism, a concept which it claims encompasses Muslims and people of other religions."[36]

It should, however, be realized that nationalism is only one possible articulation of Hindu revivalism. From Swami Vivekananda to Ram Swarup, a number of Hindu thinkers have sought to formulate Hindu concerns in terms of universal civilizational values. In the case of the famous Bengali poet Rabindranath Tagore (who belonged to the oldest Hindu revivalist organization, the *Brahmo Samâj*), this universalism even led to a distinctly anti-nationalist position.[37] Hindu Nationalism was developed by V.D. Savarkar and M.S. Golwalkar in the 1920s and 30s as an instrument to promote the interests of Hindu society and culture in the context of the freedom movement. It is not certain nor universally conceded that this was the right instrument, and it may well become less important in the future. Today, however, it is numerically and politically by far the dominant variety of Hindu revivalism.

[36] "The party that might have won", *The Economist*, 22.6.1991.

[37] See Ashis Nandy: *The Illegitimacy of Nationalism. Rabindranath Tagore and the Politics of Self.*

Hindu nationalism, or India's form of "cultural nationalism", is a self-description used in the post-Independence period by the main political embodiments of Hindu revivalism, the *Hindû Mahâsabhâ* (HMS, 1915-), the *Bhâratîya Jana Sangh* (BJS, 1951-77) and the *Bhâratîya Janatâ* Party (BJP, 1980-). It should be kept in mind that in India, "nationalism" doesn't have the negative connotations which it has in Western intellectual circles. On the contrary, the term is hallowed by its association with the freedom movement. It is also of little use trying to catch this nationalism in one of the proliferating "models" of nationalism. For the people concerned, it simply means "love of one's country", and in all other respects its meaning can vary: it is not a bourgeois or petit-bourgeois movement (as Marxists would have it) except in some instances, it does not generally seek to establish cultural homogeneity except that sometimes it may, it is an agent of modernization except in some respects, etc.[38] I assume a future expert on nationalism will be able to apply all the right labels, but he will need to know the facts first; I have concentrated on the facts themselves, and use "nationalist" in the most general and intuitive sense, largely because that is how the term is used by the people concerned when they apply it to themselves.

Hindutva

Another term which Hindu nationalists themselves often use, and which is now effectively a synonym of "Hindu nationalism", is *Hindutva*. This neologism, somewhat clumsy in that it combines a Persian root (*Hindû*, equivalent to Sanskrit *Sindhû*) with a Sanskrit suffix, was coined in 1923 by Vinayak Damodar Savarkar and literally means "Hindu-ness", the criterion being: "He who considers India as both his Fatherland and Holyland". It is distinct from "Hinduism", in that it designates the "Hindu nation" rather than "Hindu religion". The "Hindu nation" is conceived as including Indians belonging to semi-Hindu religions like Sikhism and Buddhism (whose sacred sites associated with the founders lie in India), but whether it also includes Indian Muslims and Christians is a point of disagreement within the movement. For Savarkar, at least, they cannot be Hindus as long as the origins and sacred sites of their religions lie in West Asia. The organized Hindu nationalist movement is often caustically referred to as "the Hindutva brigade".

---

[38]For theories of nationalism, I have consulted H. Kohn: *Nationalism, Its Meaning and History*, and J. Hutchinson and A.D. Smith: *Nationalism*, among others.

The Hindu Right

In Leftist writings, it is not uncommon to see Hindu revivalism, particularly its political section, described as "the Hindu Right". Though there is nothing pejorative in the term "right" in itself (on the contrary, for ages this was the "right" side, while the left side was associated with abnormality and evil, see for example, the semantic development of the Latin word for "left", *sinister*), ever since the French Revolution it has become associated with the reactionary defenders of social injustice, the moribund forces of the past. In practice, the very word "Rightist" carries an inherent Leftist bias. The parties journalistically described as "Rightist" (British Tories, German Christian-Democrats, American Republicans, etc.) very rarely call themselves that; only "extreme-rightist" parties do that. Most parties to which the metonymic term "Rightist" is applied, identify themselves by means of descriptive terms like "conservative".

We shall have the occasion to look into the programmes of Hindu revivalist parties and notice a number of points which are more Leftist than Rightist. The term *Hindu Right* only applies if an extreme-Leftist viewpoint is assumed (as is effectively the case for numerous Indian *Hindutva* critics): only from that angle is Hindu nationalism consistently found to one's Right. To the extent that Hindu revivalism rejects the Marxist reduction of history to economic factors, a refusal which Marxism construes as a camouflage for support to the status-quo in economic power equations, Hindu revivalism is of course non-Marxist and, if you want, non-Left.

But the decisive objection against the term *Hindu Right* is that the people concerned will not accept it. In fact, the BJS explicitly described itself as "centrist", e.g.: "As a centrist party, the Jana Sangh has been subjected to attacks both from the extreme right as well as the extreme left."[39] One workable measure of objectivity and neutrality in newsreading and scholarship is whether people and groups are classified with terms in which they recognize themselves. When we apply this simple yardstick of objectivity to the available literature on Hindu revivalism, we find most of it wanting.

---

[39]A.B. Vajpayee: foreword, in BJS: *Party Documents 1951-1972*, p.v. Vajpayee, whom I would classify as Left-leaning, has been called a member of a "Hindu extreme-Right party", and "the chief of the extreme Right" by Myriam Tricoci: "Quel visage pour Vajpayee?" (French: "Which face for Vajpayee?"), *Le Vif/L'Express*, 20.3.1998.

Islam

In the often heated debates on Islam which accompany the increasing presence and visibility of Islam in the West, some people make a bid for the intellectual high ground by overruling any claims pro or contra Islam with the announcement that "Islam does not exist". Usually, the proof given is a reference to the diversity within the Muslim world: Uighurs are different from Mauretanians, Ismailites aren't Sunnis, etc. This reasoning is obviously invalid, for it denies the existence of most classes in nature and society, none of which consists of identical members. Or does the fact that Arabian thoroughbreds, Shetland ponies and Flemish draught-horses exist side by side, prove that "the horse species does not exist"? By the same reasoning, Christianity, Hinduism etc. would also "not exist".

But the fact is that these categories do exist, even if catching each of them in a single definition is sometimes hard to do. In the case of Islam, the matter is fairly simple: "Islam is the belief in the existence and unity of the Creator-God and in the status of Mohammed as His final Prophet".[40] This has many smaller implications, for the second part of the definition implies acceptance of the Quran as God's own word, hence acceptance of the unchangeable validity of all its contents, and obedience to its commandments. The farther we go from the core beliefs, the more differences in interpretation and hence in implementation may appear, but about these core beliefs, there is unanimity: they define Islam. I am aware that this "essentialist" approach is out of fashion, but here I consider it entirely apt. It satisfies an important criterion for terminology: it will certainly not be rejected by the people concerned, for to orthodox Muslims it is obvious that Islam has belief in Allah and Mohammed as its defining essence. In Indian history, at any rate, Muslims rarely had difficulty in deciding who was a Muslim and who was not.[41]

---

[40]This is the content of the Islamic creed (*shahada*, "testimony"), which is recited upon conversion to Islam.

[41]In Pakistan, by contrast, problems have arisen concerning the borderline case of the Ahmadiyas, who call themselves Muslims but whom the Pakistani state declared non-Muslims in 1974. In 1954, the Munir Report had inconclusively tried to decide the question on the basis of an agreed definition (for excerpts, see Baljit Rai: *Muslim Fundamentalism*, p.41-4): under the general definition, the Ahmadiyas certainly qualify, but the *Ulamâ* decided that "belief in the prophethood of Mohammed" must be understood as "belief that Mohammed is the final prophet". This excludes the Ahmadiyas, because they believe in a prophet who came *after* Mohammed, viz. their own sect's founder, Mirza Ghulam Ahmad (1838-1908); see Mirza Bashiruddin Ahmad: *Invitation to Ahmadiyyat*, 1926.

Discourse on the history and culture of the Islamic world would greatly profit from a popularization of Daniel Pipes' distinction between "Islamic" and "Islamicate".[42] The latter term refers to all the cultural elements which the Muslim world has acquired and which have come to be identified with Islam. Thus, mosques are generally recognizable by their typical architecture, which cartoonists can easily evoke with a few strokes of the pen to make sure that the reader recognizes the environment of the depicted scene as Islamicate; yet, there is nothing strictly "Islamic" (Quran- and Sunna-based) about this architecture, which was largely borrowed from the conquered peoples of Byzantine West Asia.

Arts and sciences of the Muslim world belong to the "Islamicate" category, except in so far as it is strictly based on the doctrinal core of Islam. Thus, the non-figurative (geometrical or calligraphic) character of the designs adorning mosque walls is the direct consequence of the Islamic prohibition on depictions of human or animal beings, and may therefore be considered a feature of "Islamic" culture. By contrast, the Moghul school of painting is part of "Islamicate" culture but is, strictly speaking, an offence against "Islamic" doctrine, for which reason the orthodox emperor Aurangzeb closed it down. To describe Moghul painting (a Hindu contribution to Islamicate culture) as a "contribution of Islam to India's composite culture", as secularist discourse has it, indicates a muddled understanding of Islamic religion and Islamicate culture.

In this study, I will settle for the more common adjective "Muslim" when referring to the whole of "Islamicate" culture, and reserve "Islamic" for references to the doctrine of Islam *stricto sensu*. "Islamist" will serve as a neutral and general term for all forms of assertive or militant or purist Islam, avoiding controversial terms like "fundamentalist".

At this point, people often blur the issue by bringing up the many impurities in the religious practice of people classified as Islamic believers. They will say, for example, that many Indian Muslims are not pure monotheists nor faithful followers of Mohammed because they make pilgrimages to the tombs of saints, a form of "idolatry" which is forbidden in the strict reading of Islam. However, Islam does not change nor cease to exist simply because people practise it in an impure manner and mix it with non-Islamic attitudes and customs in their own lives. Quite rightly, Muslim purists will say in such cases that "these practices are un-Islamic",

[42]Developed in D. Pipes: *In the Path of God. Islam and Political Power.*

but continue to recognize the people involved as Muslims, because formally they stand by the two basic beliefs of Islam, monotheism and Mohammed's prophethood.

The beliefs and behaviour of Muslims consist of "Islam plus other things", including influences of their pre-Muslim ancestral culture, of the modern world, and of general human nature. Therefore, the cultural achievements of Muslims are not necessarily a merit of Islam, and the misbehaviour of some Muslims is not necessarily symptomatic of what Islam has inculcated in them. The distinction between "Muslims" and "Islam" is extremely important in the present discussion. Many Hindus say that Islam is a great religion, but Muslims are a problem. Others take the opposite view: the Hindu-Muslim conflict is due not to some collective character defect in the Muslims, but to the intrinsically conflicting doctrine of Islam, which pious and otherwise good-natured Muslims feel duty-bound to stand by. The second view leads to an ideological critique of Islam, while the first leads to cruder anti-Muslim attitudes and sometimes to physical confrontation.

Macaulayism

Islam has occupied a position of hegemony in most of India for more than five centuries (*c.* 1206 to *c.* 1717-1857) and proved strong enough to force a Partition on India in 1947. Till today, the conflict with Islam is treated as the most newsworthy aspect of Hindu revivalism. Christianity never occupied a similar position, for British rule was essentially secular. Marxism came a lot closer to political hegemony, being the dominant paradigm in Indian academe from the 1950s onwards and strongly influencing Indian politics under Jawaharlal Nehru and Indira Gandhi.

But Indian Marxism as such has been only a passing phase in a much larger trend known as *Macaulayism*, named after the British administrator Thomas Babington Macaulay, who in 1835 initiated an education policy designed to create a class of people Indian in skin colour but British in every other respect.[43] "Macaulayites" are those Indians who have interiorized the colonial ideology of the "White Man's Burden" (as Rudyard Kipling called it in a famous poem): the Europeans had to come and liberate the natives, "half devil and half child", from their native

[43]The full text of Macaulay's *Minute on Education* is reproduced as appendix 4 in A.H. Khan: *The Rediscovery of India*.

culture, which consisted only of ignorance, superstition and the concomitant social evils; and after this liberation from themselves, these Indians became a kind of honorary Whites.

Macaulay's policy was implemented and became a resounding success. The pre-Macaulayan vernacular system of education was destroyed, even though British surveys had found it more effective and more democratic than the then-existing education system in Britain.[44] The rivalling educationist party, the so-called Orientalists, had proposed a Sanskrit-based system of education, in which Indian graduates would not have been as estranged from their mother civilization as they became through English education, and in which they could have selectively adopted the useful elements of Western modernity, more or less the way Japan modernized itself.[45] But thanks to Macaulay, modernization became the preserve of a class which was foreign to India not because it happened to be foreign, but because it was groomed in a foreign cultural atmosphere and ultimately chose to be foreign.

As Ashis Nandy, a Christian critic of old and new forms of colonialism, has observed: "Schooling is the chosen instrument of alienation. The brightest children are snatched away from familiar surroundings to be introduced in schools based on the Western model. When they leave, they speak the language of the coloniser and can no longer communicate with their own people."[46]

A Hindu revivalist diagnosis is given by Ram Swarup: "Above all, there appeared a class of Hindu-hating Hindus who knew all the bad things about Hinduism. Earlier invaders ruled through the sword. The British ruled through *Indology*. The British took over our education and taught us to look at ourselves through their eyes. They created a class Indian in blood and colour, but anti-Hindu in its intellectual and emotional

---

[44]About the findings of these British surveys, see Dharampal: *The Beautiful Tree: Indigenous Indian Education in the 18th Century*; and J. Dibona: *One Teacher, One School: The Adam Reports on Indigenous Education in 19th-Century India*. In his review article ("The 'Beautiful Tree' that the British destroyed", *Organiser*, 28.10.1984), Ram Swarup quotes Brigadier-General Alexander Walker, *c.* 1795: "No people probably appreciate more justly the importance of instruction than the Hindus".

[45]About the victory of the Anglicists over the Orientalists and the native traditions of education, see Sri Kumar Acharya: *The Changing Pattern of Education in Early Nineteenth Century Bengal*.

[46]Ashis Nandy: "Propagating an Indian Model", *Sunday Mail*, 14.1.1990, p.35.

orientation. This is the biggest problem rising India faces—the problem of self-alienated Hindus."[47]

It is this class of Hindu-born "Macaulayites" which has inherited the mantle of the colonial ruling class. Its most conspicuous representative was the first Prime Minister of free India, Jawaharlal Nehru, then sometimes nicknamed "India's last Viceroy", and recently evaluated as "the English gentleman who came to ruin India".[48] Reviewer Joseph Shattan starts out with describing Jawaharlal's father Motilal Nehru as "in Macaulay's famous phrase, 'Indian in blood and color, but English in taste, in opinions, in morals and in intellect'. ... There being no vacancies at Eton, in 1905 he packed 15-year-old Jawaharlal off to Harrow, determined that the boy grow up a proper English gentleman. He succeeded beyond his wildest dreams, and years later, at Cambridge, Jawaharlal wrote his father asking permission to transfer to Oxford: 'Cambridge is becoming too full of Indians.' Those disliked countrymen, much to their ruin, would one day be led by Jawaharlal".[49]

A Hindu commentator observes about Nehru: "One has to read his writings and speeches, and evaluate his policies from a Hindu point of view, to realize that so far as Hindus and Hinduism are concerned, he was a combined embodiment of all the imperialist ideologies—Islam, Christianity, White Man's Burden, and Communism—that have flooded this country in the wake of foreign invasions or interventions. And by the time he assumed command, he represented a sizable and powerful class of self-alienated Hindus which had started taking shape during Muslim rule, and had multiplied fast under the British dispensation."[50]

This class of mostly Hindu-born Macaulayites has shaped the institutions of post-1947 India including its de facto state ideology, secularism. After its most prominent representative, applied Macaulayism is often called "Nehruvian secularism".

---

[47]Ram Swarup: "Hindu Renaissance", *Organiser*, 10.12.1995.

[48]Title of a review of Stanley Wolpert's book *Nehru: a Tryst with Destiny* by Joseph Shattan, *American Spectator*, Feb. 1997. David Aikman, reviewing Vishal Mangalwadi's book *India: the Grand Experiment* (*American Spectator*, Oct. 1997), agrees with Mangalwadi that "Nehru's grandiose state socialism was robbing the Indian countryside to finance Soviet-style industrial five-year plans".

[49]Joseph Shattan: review of Stanley Wolpert's book *Nehru: a Tryst with Destiny*, in *American Spectator*, Feb. 1997.

[50]S.R. Goel: *Hindu and Hinduism, Manipulation of Meanings*, p.19.

Secularism

In Europe, its continent of origin, secularism is not an ideology in its own right, it is only a practical arrangement between Church and State, viz. their separation. Secularism (French: *la laïcité*, "lay-ness") means that the State shall not in any way promote any religion, whether by propagating it through official channels, by discriminating in favour of its votaries, or by imposing its commandments through the rule of law. In a broader sense, secularism as a cultural tendency means that religion is "kept in its place" if not discarded altogether, in order to let people decide their destinies on the basis of purely human and this-worldly considerations.

In India, the Constitution of 1950 affirms the secular character of the Republic implicitly, but the explicit affirmation that India is a "secular" state was only added to the Constitution in 1976. This addition took place under the ominous configuration of Indira Gandhi's Emergency dictatorship (1975-77), without a proper parliamentary debate. The 42nd Amendment changed the self-definition in the Preamble, "sovereign democratic Republic", to: "sovereign socialist secular democratic republic". In India, like in Western secular states (France, the USA), the Constitution does not give any place to religious institutions in the structure and functioning of the polity, though it guarantees freedom of religion.

Surprisingly, this non-involvement of religion and specifically of Hinduism in the Indian polity is not much of a concern to Hindu revivalists.[51] The reason may simply be that they have more pressing concerns, while some lip-service to Hinduism in the Constitution would not make much difference to the flourishing of Hinduism in civil society anyway. The anger of Hindu revivalists is directed not against "secularism" in its proper meaning but against what it calls "pseudo-secularism", the alleged practice of favouritism toward the non-Hindus under the cover of "secularism". It is only as an armchair pastime that secularism itself may be questioned once in a while.

According to N.S. Rajaram, the very mention of "secularism" as a political principle is a lingering manifestation of the colonial condition, a

[51]An exception is Swami Muktananda Saraswati: *Vartamân Indian Samvidhân* (Hindi: "The contemporary Indian Constitution", the word *Indian* serves to emphasize its English rather than *Bhâratîya* origin), a traditionalist critique of the non-*Shâstrik* Constitution.

faithful copying of a cultural property of the former colonizers.[52] In this view, you could call it the Indian counterpart of colonial-age Senegalese or Congolese children in history class reciting: *"Nos ancêtres, les Gaulois"*.[53] For, this version of secularism, which mistrusts religion and is ever-vigilant to keep the slightest taint of religion out of public life, builds on the European and not on the Indian experience of relations between state and religion. In Europe, these were such that the exclusion of religion from politics was hailed as a solution; but Rajaram sees no reason for transplanting this "solution" to India, where the corresponding problem did not exist, where for example no pope ever forced a Galilei to recant. This transplantation allegedly ignores the radically different experience of Hindu history.

In this view, European secularists wanted man to be emancipated from the mind control exerted by authoritarian religious establishments in the name of dogmatic and irrational belief systems, a situation which did not obtain in India at all. To be sure, religion in the sense of belief in supernatural interventions was and is certainly widespread in India. Moreover, a religious conception of political authority also prevailed, with kings being enthroned with Brahminical rituals.[54] However, Hindu states always supported religious pluralism, and Hindu tradition never stifled debate, never stood in the way of science and in its early stage even incorporated and encouraged it.

In the Vedic age, India was very religious, but it was also ahead of the rest in mathematics and astronomy.[55] Thus, the geometry of the *Shulba Sûtra*s, geometrical appendices to the manuals of ritual (*Shrauta Sûtra*s), include the oldest known formulation of the theorem named after

---

[52]This alleged uselessness of European secularism for India is one of the main theses of N.S. Rajaram: *Secularism, the New Mask of Fundamentalism*, the other being the positive harmfulness of its incorporation in the strategy of Islamism and other anti-Hindu forces.

[53]"Our ancestors, the Gauls", the typical first lesson in old French and Belgian history books; its transplantation to the African colonial setting without adaptation to local realities is a classic example of the alienating effect of the colonial condition.

[54]About the religious foundation of political authority in ancient India, see A.K. Coomaraswamy: *Spiritual Authority and Temporal Power in the Indian Theory of Government* (1942).

[55]See e.g. M.D. Pandit: *Mathematics as Known to the Vedic Samhitas*, detailing such novelties as the first decimal system and the oldest names of "astronomical" numbers such as quadrillions and quintillions (p.20). Arabs still call the decimal number system *rakmû'l-Hindî*, from *Hind*, "India".

Pythagoras, developed in the context of Vedic altar-building.[56] Modern Hindus are fond of recalling this scientific element in their tradition, e.g. by quoting Carl Sagan: "Hindu cosmology gives a time-scale for the earth and the universe which is consonant with that of modern scientific cosmology", as opposed to the limited Biblical-Quranic cosmology, which was protected against more far-sighted alternatives by a vigilant religious orthodoxy.[57] Like in other ancient civilizations, in Hindu India priests and scientists were often the same persons; the conflict between religion and reason is not the primitive condition but a contingent historical development in post-classical Europe, parallelled to an extent by the stagnation of Muslim culture from the twelfth century onwards.[58]

Hindu India has also had no history of book-burning, of executing heretics or confining dissidents to lunatic asylums.[59] The Buddha could preach his heterodox doctrine till his old age without ever being persecuted. As Dutch indologist Sjoerd de Vries writes: "In Indian society, an amazing tolerance vis-à-vis people of unusual opinions has existed for ages. ... Only very few instances are known where conflicts have erupted for the sake of religion. Not until the advent of Islam did India get acquainted with religious persecution."[60]

Because of this Hindu tradition of free enquiry in both the worldly and the spiritual spheres, Hindu revivalists declare that India has no need of European secularism. Freethinkers and philosophical minorities did not need to feel threatened by the religious colouring of public life, so the need to remove religion from the public sphere did not arise. Materially, Hindu pluralism differed little from the modern European spirit of free enquiry which promoted secular institutions, so there is no questioning of the

---

[56]See e.g. N.S. Rajaram and D. Frawley: *Vedic Aryans and the Origins of Civilization*, Ch.4, with reference to the work of A. Seidenberg: "The ritual origin of geometry", *Archive for History of Exact Sciences*, vol.1, p.488-527; and "The origin of mathematics", *ibid.* vol.18, pp.301-42.

[57]Carl Sagan interviewed in *New India Digest*, March 1997.

[58]See also S.N. Balasubrahmanyam: "Science in India. Reintegrating a forgotten heritage", *Times of India*, 10.2.1996.

[59]This is, of course, no reason to overlook irrational elements in Hindu social practice as it really existed until recently, e.g. the belief that widows were magically responsible for their husbands' deaths and should therefore be treated as death-carriers and hence as a kind of untouchables. Hindus were free to denounce such beliefs, but this didn't stop these beliefs from being operative by force of established custom.

[60]Sjoerd de Vries: *Hindoeïsme voor beginners*, p.79.

desirability of propagating this attitude, but explicitating its native pedigree would only do justice to Hindu civilization.

There is an avalanche of literature about the problem of secularism in India.[61] I will not add too many pages to it, for I don't want this study to get side-tracked into a discussion of secularism as such, nor of what secularists say about Hindu revivalism. The point is that the movement under consideration was never intended to be a movement for or against secularism, and only produced some (diverse) viewpoints on secularism when being harangued about it by its opponents. N.S. Rajaram rejects the antagonism of secular vs. non-secular as "a false problem", pleading that the real issue is "pluralism—an environment in which different views and practices can co-exist. And this means that we must confront its arch-enemy: exclusivism which tolerates nothing that conflicts with the dogma of a chosen elite."[62] Implied is that Hindu religion, along with a certain secular freethinking modernity, is on the right side of "pluralism", while its enemies, Islamic and Christian religion, along with secular ideologies like Nazism and Marxism, are cases of "exclusivism".

If there is so much misunderstanding and so little real knowledge about Hindu revivalism today, it is largely because of the prejudicial application of Procrustean schemes like "secularism" and "communalism" which simply don't fit the subject. Nevertheless, in deference to the prevalent conceptualization of India's "communal" conflict, due attention will be paid to the views of secularism which the Hindu revivalist movement developed along the way, and to its own allegedly anti-secular project of a "Hindu state".

PSEUDO-SECULARISM

Ever since Jawaharlal Nehru gave it currency, the term "secularism" has been very popular in India: most parties and politicians call themselves "secular". Even Muslim activists whose counterparts in Turkey or Egypt denounce secularism as a demonic betrayal of Islam, call themselves "secularists". Check the editorials of Syed Shahabuddin's monthly *Muslim India*, or the Jamaat-i-Islami weekly *Radiance*: they brandish

---

[61]Most are from a Marxist or at least a militantly secularist angle, e.g. V.K. Sinha, ed.: *Secularism in India*; Iqbal Narain: *Secularism in India*; Radhey Mohan, ed.: *Secularism in India*. One which inclines towards the Hindu viewpoint is M.M. Sankhdher: *Secularism in India, Dilemmas and Challenges*.

[62]N.S. Rajaram: *Secularism, the New Mask of Fundamentalism*, pp.4-6.

"secularism" in every issue. Only the most extreme and least adroit Islamic organizations speak out against secularism, e.g. the self-styled *Milli Parliament* based in Aligarh has affirmed that "secularism is anti-Islamic and *harâm*".[63]

This general enthusiasm for "secularism" in itself should indicate that the meaning of the term has undergone a drastic change in India, and that it is irresponsible to use the term as if it had its established Western meaning (which most India-watchers do). Just as the English word *deception* has a radically different meaning from its French look-alike *déception* (= disappointment), the British-English word *secularism* radically differs in meaning from its Indian-English look-alike *secularism.* A professional interpreter who translates *déception* as *deception* is incompetent, and an India-watcher who translates the Indian-English term *secularism* into standard English as *secularism*, has a similar problem.[64]

If this judgment seems too harsh, consider the performance of Indian secularism during the *Satanic Verses* affair. Salman Rushdie's novel *The Satanic Verses* was first presented to the Indian public in September 1988 by *Sunday*'s Shrabani Basu (interview) and *India Today*'s Madhu Jain (review plus excerpts). Rushdie had sneeringly told Basu, who asked if he apprehended riots: "It is a funny view of the world that a book can cause riots." Five months later, amid a spate of Rushdie-related riots in Britain, Pakistan and India, on that fateful Valentine Day of 1989, Ayatollah Khomeini pronounced his death sentence against Rushdie. Five years after that, *Sunday* editor Vir Sanghvi retrospectively commented that it is a funny world indeed, and wondered: "Do we realise how that hastily-ordered ban has changed India forever? ... When the Government promptly submitted to this illiterate hysteria, it convinced

---

[63]See *Qaumi Awaz*, 17.11.1994, reproduced in V.P. Bhatia's column in *Organiser*, 18.12.1994; and Varsha Bhosle: "Dangerously silly Milli", *Sunday Observer*, 11.2.1996. *Harâm*: forbidden. Other *Millî* (i.e. of the Muslim nation) resolutions include a call for separate electorates (MPs elected by joint electorates are denounced as "lackeys of the Hindus") and the creation of autonomous states in Muslim-majority areas.

[64]A quotation which some would find apt here is Arthur Bonner (*Democracy in India*, p.81): "Applying European terms to societies with different histories should be done with caution lest they imply equivalency where there is none." However, in spite of its different history, the term *secularism* in its original meaning could in principle be applied to India, and implemented as a policy, just as *democracy* or *republic* can; the problem is not history but a deliberate decision to distort the meaning of the term *secularism*.

[Hindus] that secularism had become a code phrase for Muslim appeasement."[65]

Syed Shahabuddin, opposition MP, read about *The Satanic Verses* in the two magazines mentioned, and without delay, he petitioned Prime Minister Rajiv Gandhi to ban the book. Shahabuddin had also been planning a potentially violent Muslim march on Ayodhya, and the pragmatic Rajiv Gandhi considered this novel by a distant British writer an excellent bargaining chip to keep Shahabuddin humoured. If it could dissuade Shahabuddin from endangering the lives of numerous Indians, the Prime Minister considered it opportune (not to say: his duty to the nation) to ban the book. Rushdie may not have expected the ban in India, yet: "Rushdie cannot even have the solace of claiming that he was not forewarned about his impending fate. The Indian advisor of Viking/ Penguin, Khushwant Singh, had made it clear to him, after reading the manuscript of the controversial novel, that its publication would definitely outrage the Muslims and could even spark off bloodshed. Singh's well-meaning advice was ignored."[66]

One would have expected Indian secularists to support Rushdie. This was indeed the case with some of them, e.g. those around N. Ram's Communist fortnightly *Frontline*, which printed Rushdie's open letter to Rajiv Gandhi in protest against the ban.[67] Former Attorney-General Soli Sorabjee called the ban "yet another surrender to the forces of fundamentalism and intolerance".[68] An *Indian Express* editorial attacked this attempt at "thought control", but its editor, Arun Shourie, was routinely rubbished as a "Hindu communalist".[69] Among political parties, the champions of secularism remained silent; the BJP was "the only party to condemn the ban".[70]

[65]Vir Sanghvi: "Liberal first, secular second", *Sunday*, 27.2.1994.

[66]Parwez Hafeez: "Rushdie is no hero", *Hindustan Times*, 12.2.1995. Remark that Khushwant Singh successfully opposed demands for a ban on his own novel *Delhi* (1989), deemed offensive to Indian Muslims with its enumeration of atrocities committed by Muslim conquerors of India, though not directly to Mohammed and the basics of Islam.

[67]Salman Rushdie: "'They have got things backwards'", *Frontline*, 29.10.1988.

[68]Quoted in *India Today*, 31.10.1988.

[69]Arun Shourie's view on this and related controversies are presented in A. Shourie: *Religion in Politics* (second, expanded edition 1989), *Indian Controversies* (1993) and *A Secular Agenda* (1993).

[70]David Devadas in *India Today*, 31.10.1988.

By contrast, numerous leading Indian secularists supported the ban on *The Satanic Verses*, e.g. newspaper editors Khushwant Singh, Girilal Jain, M.J. Akbar, Vir Sanghvi and Dileep Padgaonkar.[71] The Press Council condemned the pre-publication of some excerpts as "an aberration from the path of ethical rectitude".[72] Commentator Pranav Khullar, while extolling Nehru for ignoring a colonial ban on seditious literature before 1947, described how the washerman, the vegetable vendor and others whom he asked had never heard of Rushdie, then concluded by defending the ban with the remarkable argument: "Nobody cared a hoot for Rushdie. In a free country people have the right not to read him."[73]

In a panel discussion about communalism, secularist S. Guhan replied to a question about the Rushdie affair with an attempt at even-handedness: "You say that you have been denied the opportunity to read the book, just because the Muslims said that it contains heretical reflections on the Prophet. You say that this is not fair. I on the other hand would defend the banning of that book for this simple reason: ... whether you like it or not, the 80 million Muslims of India have a certain feeling for their Prophet."[74] After protests from the audience that there are numerous anti-Hindu books freely available in India, so that this ban amounts to a case of double standards, Guhan came up with a way to restore equality: "By all means let people protest against the books that condemn Hinduism. ... If you find a book that hurts the Hindu sensibilities, make a demand for banning it!"[75] This was his concept of secularism at its most even-handed: ban all

---

[71]In 1988, the late Girilal Jain was still a secularist, though about to convert to Hindu nationalism in the enthusiasm of the Ayodhya movement. Throughout, he remained a spokesman for *Realpolitik*, and like his friend Rajiv Gandhi he didn't think Rushdie worth the loss of lives and property; therefore, even after becoming a Hindu Nationalist, he never regretted his support for the ban.

[72]*Indian Express*, 13.11.1990. By contrast, the Nepali weekly *Janjyoti*, when asked by Nepal's communications minister to discontinue the serialization of *The Satanic Verses* because it hurt the sentiments of the fast-growing Muslim minority, refused (*The Times*, 30.10.1990).

[73]Pranav Kullar in the *Patriot*, 12.12.1990.

[74]S. Guhan: "Dark Forebodings", in Jitendra Bajaj, ed.: *Ayodhya and the Future India*, p.87. The number of Indian Muslims already exceeded 100 million.

[75]S. Guhan: "Dark Forebodings", in Jitendra Bajaj, ed.: *Ayodhya and the Future India*, p.87.

criticism of religions.[76] In this case, Indian secularism proves to be not just different from, but the very opposite of secularism as it is understood in the West.

Muslim secularists generally took the same position. Asghar Ali Engineer declared that research books should not be banned, but: "It's a different matter if any religion or holy book is attacked. Then the book can be banned. You can say I have no belief in religion or God. That is fine. But using abusive language, like Salman Rushdie did, is an attack. It hurts people's sentiments."[77] Dina Vakil claimed, with reference to Rushdie-related riots: "Events that have taken place since the ban have vindicated the government's stand."[78] Saifuddin Soz, MP for the Kashmiri Muslim party National Conference, "congratulated the government for having banned the novel", though he preferred a "total ban" on the production, circulation and import of the book. Soz said that Rushdie's book was "decidedly detrimental to India's unity and the way of life of the Indians, which is secularism".[79]

One prominent Muslim who did protest against the ban, albeit only in 1992, was Mushir-ul-Hasan, pro-Vice-Chancellor of Jamia Millia Islamia, the Muslim university of Delhi. He told an interviewer: "I think the ban should be lifted. I think every person has a right to be heard and to be read."[80] Overnight, he became the target of a campaign by students and professors of Jamia Millia. Though he buckled, apologizing and saying he never meant to demand the lifting of the ban, he had to stay away from his own university. The day he showed up again, he was severely beaten up and had to be hospitalized. Student leader Nasser Jamal explained the

---

[76]Token banning of anti-Hindu publications to create a semblance of even-handedness and neutralize criticism of bans on anti-Islamic books has been practised by the governments of both India and Bangladesh, e.g. according to *Hinduism Today*, 1993/7, the latter banned a Bengali book titled *Shrishtir upor Drishti* ("Vision of Creation") which "gives imaginary and distorted information about Gods, Goddesses and the origin of Hinduism", apparently to counterbalance the ban on Taslima Nasrin's novel *Lajja*.

[77]A.A. Engineer interviewed by Sharmila Joshi, *Times of India*, 16.4.1995.

[78]Dina Vakil: "The 'Satanic' reverses", *Times of India*, 10.1.1991.

[79]Quoted in Times of India, 18.11.1988.

[80]Quoted in Arun Shourie's discussion of the affair: "The point we always evade", *Observer of Business and Politics*, 18.5.1992; included in his book *Indian Controversies*, p.363-70.

agitation: "This university is secular. We will not tolerate statements against any religion."[81] Here is a "secularism" which would shut Voltaire's mouth, i.e. physically shut it.

In retrospect, *Sunday* editor Vir Sanghvi questions the wisdom of this type of secularism: "In 1988, secular liberals found their secularism in conflict with their liberalism. The liberal view would have been to fight the ban: but *the secular thing to do was to ban something that could offend Muslims*. ... We should have preferred our liberalism over what we saw as secularism. ... In my view, 'likely to cause offence to religious fanatics' is not a good enough reason for censorship."[82] Here, Sanghvi sees secularism as potentially opposed to liberalism, whereas in the Western understanding, "liberalism" (both in its Anglo-Saxon and its Continental sense) implies "secularism", or at the very least the freedom to discuss and question religion. Sanghvi also explicates the operative meaning of "secularism", viz. "to ban something that could offend Muslims". Though he apparently changed his mind on the rights and wrongs of banning *The Satanic Verses*, he still cannot get himself to openly disown this rather peculiar definition of "secularism".

It should be clear by now that the self-described "secularism" of the Indian elite is a special case meriting closer inspection. Secularism in India is certainly not a neutral position, as Western India-watchers tend to assume. In fact, it is one of the warring parties in India's religious conflict. This is a rather consequential insight, for it means that reliance on the presumed neutral Indian sources describing themselves as "secularist" (a reliance which pervades the entire non-Indian literature on the present topic) is actually a reliance on the version of one of the warring parties, which is the very last thing to do in scholarship. Maybe we shouldn't put it this extreme, but we shall none the less see a list of serious instances below.

In this study, I will continue to describe as "secularists" all those who call themselves that; after all, in most cases it is their "secularization", away from Hindu religion, which has brought them to their current (including pro-Muslim) positions. By contrast, in their unease about the semantic manipulation of "secularism", Hindu revivalists question the very use of this term. Seeing that the policies actually carried out by the secularists are not in conformity with the dictionary meaning of

[81] Quoted by Parsha Venkateshwar Rao jr.: "Discordant notes", *Indian Express*, 10.5.1992.
[82] Vir Sanghvi: "Liberal first, secular second", *Sunday*, 27.2.1994; emphasis added.

"secularism", they allege that India is controlled by "pseudo-secularists". Some of them sum it up in one simplistic sentence: "Secularism means being anti-Hindu".[83] They profess not to reject the principle of secularism, meaning "genuine secularism" or "positive secularism", and accuse the establishment and the other parties of "pseudo-secularism", meaning "discrimination against Hindus justified in the name of secularism".

The classic example given is the Shah Bano case of 1985: repudiated by her husband, the Muslim woman Shah Bano went to court to force him to pay alimony, which Islamic law forbids; the Supreme Court upheld her claim on the basis of equality before the law (Hindu women would have the right to alimony in her case), but under Muslim pressure, Rajiv Gandhi's Congress Government voted a law overruling the verdict and reaffirming the Islamic rules on divorce, at least for Muslims.[84] This way, the distortion of Indian secularism by favouritism towards the Muslims ("Muslim appeasement"), or at least towards the Muslim leaders who act as "contractors" of the "Muslim vote-bank", became an arguable proposition.

Gandhian secularism

To complicate matters further, there is yet another typically Indian understanding of the term "secularism": the Gandhian doctrine of "equal respect for all religions", *sarva-dharma-samabhâva*. Thus, if a Hindu Minister attends an Islamic festival, this religious act is considered "secular", meaning something like "transcending religious identity". In practice, the term *secular* can also mean "tolerant" or "religiously pluralistic".

It is in this and only in this sense that you can call Indonesia a "secular" state: its Constitution requires every citizen to worship "one God", but the citizens are free to identify this God as Allah, as Ganesha or Jesus Christ or the Buddha. The underlying idea is that religion, not just the majority religion (Islam) but any mature religion, is a factor of responsible behaviour and a force of social cohesion; therefore, the state should be religiously neutral ("secular") not by opposing or discouraging religion, but by harnessing the social force of all religions towards positive

---

[83] See e.g. A.S. Pandya: *Hypocrisy of Secularism*.

[84] A collection of predominantly Muslim views of the affair is A.A. Engineer, ed.: *The Shah Bano Controversy*; a collection of mostly Hindu nationalist views is the Jagarana Prakashan's unsigned anthology, *The Shah Bano Controversy: Nation Speaks Out*.

national goals. This was also Gandhiji's vision for India: a state which treats all religions equally, but which values and encourages religion instead of opposing and discouraging it. If we follow the dictionary meaning of "secularism", Mahatma Gandhi was by no means a secularist, for he opposed the separation of religion and politics both in principle and in practice; but in India, it is not uncommon to present him as a model secularist.

Hindus typically claim that Hinduism is by nature "secular", in this sense at least: "Indian secularism, in the sense of equal reverence for all religions, was not born on January 26, 1950. ... It predates the Constitution, the freedom movement, ... It is part of the spiritual conviction of this country as expressed in the Vedas and the Upanishads."[85] The soft-line BJP leader Atal Behari Vajpayee claims that "the Indian concept of secularism is more positive", because unlike the Western variety, it "is not against any religion".[86] Clearly, what Vajpayee refers to as "secularism" could more properly be called "religious pluralism".

In contrast with Gandhiji's "equal respect for all religions", the mentality in the dominant class could best be described as "unequal disrespect for all religions". Hindus alienated from Hinduism have a typical psychology of self-hatred, of trying to exorcize their Hindu identity by striking anti-Hindu postures and joining hands with all anti-Hindu forces. They strike committed Hindus as being pro-Muslim or pro-Christian, but many of them feel contempt for these non-Hindu religionists as well, particularly when the latter question secularism (the original concept) from their own angles.[87] This class was the successor of the British administration, but whereas the latter also felt some patronizing sympathy for its colourful subjects and their cultural expressions, the Nehruvian ruling class did not.

---

[85]S. Gurumurthy: *Secularism, the Great Debate*, p.4.

[86]A.B. Vajpayee: *Secularism, the Indian Concept*, p.15.

[87]The most articulate Indian critique of secularism as such is voiced neither by Hindus (who, when asked, swear by "genuine secularism") nor by Muslims (whose ideal of a restored Caliphate is less appealing to modern people and therefore rarely highlighted before "secular" audiences), but by Christians, e.g. by Ashis Nandy or Mark Tully, or by convert Vishal Mangalwadi (*Missionary Conspiracy: Letters to a Post-modern Hindu*, 1996), who gives new life to old Christian arguments against secular modernity as exemplified by "the disastrous French Revolution" (p.203).

Marxism

Sometimes vocal participants in the present debate will be qualified as "Marxist". That is not a term of abuse but simply a descriptive term for the stated political commitment of numerous participants in the "communalism" debate, for even card-carrying Communists are still highly present in India's media and academic sector.[88] Thus, in a mainstream newspaper, a columnist describes Chairman Mao as follows: "a great revolutionary, an able strategist, a poet and a philosopher, he was above all a soldier-saint who led his country to salvation."[89] Communist Party (Marxist) president Harkishen Singh Surjeet regularly poses with portraits of Lenin and Stalin, which are still part of the standard equipment of CPM offices.[90]

It can be useful to know about the political commitment of sources on which India-watchers base their own views of the Hindu revivalist movement. Thus, the editor of a leading British intellectual weekly was rightly cautioned not to present "the *Economic and Political Weekly* and *Frontline* [the two most-cited Indian sources on "communalism"] as voices of genuine radical dissent. Both are of Stalinist-Maoist pedigree and should the country's Communist Parties achieve exclusive power at the national level, neither journal is likely to promote the right of dissent it enjoys in India today".[91]

In allotting political labels to persons, I intend to be more circumspect than the Marxists themselves are (they systematically label all Hindu revivalists as "RSS men" if not "Hindu fascists"). Of course, I don't pretend to know every author's personal involvement, and allowance should be made for changes in people's commitment; for example, after the implosion of the Soviet Union, quite a few scholars at Jawaharlal Nehru University, the Mecca of Indian Marxism, left the CPI for the

---

[88]When speaking at MIT (April 1993), I was interrupted by a Muslim in the audience who objected to my description of R.S. Sharma as a "Marxist", which he considered a term of abuse.

[89]G.S. Gandhi: "Revered revolutionary", *Pioneer*, 26.12.1995.

[90]See e.g. Ishan Joshi: "HKS Surjeet", *Outlook*, 5.1.1998, with Surjeet posing before a picture of Lenin.

[91]Premen Addy: "Unfair to Gandhi", *London Review of Books*, 31.7.1997. To illustrate the slanted standards of these papers, Addy points out that *Frontline* columnist and CPM leader E.M.S. Namboodiripad (who died just when the BJP came to power in March 1998) "described Gandhi as a Hindu fundamentalist".

Congress Party.[92] So, the safest criterion is simply to go by the presence or absence of a conspicuous Marxist viewpoint or conceptual framework in an author's writings, then to label that particular argument, rather than the author himself, as "Marxist". In a number of cases, however, the Marxist label is certified by Marxist sources. Thus, Romila Thapar and R.S. Sharma are quoted at some length as representatives of Indian Marxist thought in *A Dictionary of Marxist Thought*.[93] Irfan Habib has titled a recent collection of his papers *Essays in Indian History. Towards a Marxist Perspective.*

To Marx, Hinduism "was the ideology of an oppressive and outworn society, and he shared the distaste of most Europeans for its more lurid features. ... he was as sceptical as his Hindu followers were to be of any notion of a Hindu 'golden age' of the past."[94] Marx upheld the colonial view that India was not a country properly speaking, merely a stretch of land with a meek conglomerate of peoples passively waiting for the next conqueror. For him, the question was not whether it was right to colonize India, merely whether colonization by Britain was preferable (and in his view, it was) to colonization by the Turks or the Czar.[95]

Marx's Indian followers have remained true to his view. They reject the very concept of India as a national unit and only accept India's unity and integrity to the extent that they consider it strategically useful (e.g. in 1970-75 when they sincerely believed that they were about to come to power in Delhi). In an interview in *Le Monde*, Romila Thapar cheerfully predicted that India won't be able to stay together.[96] CPM Politburo

---

[92]There have also been more radical conversions, e.g. Hindu-leaning columnist Swapan Dasgupta is a convert from Trotskyism, as noted in an exchange on the *Letters* page of the *London Review of Books*, 20.6 and 4.7.1996. As we shall see, most of the leading Hindu revivalist thinkers of the past decades have a Marxist past. But at present we are concerned with a lighter type of conversion, from hard Left to soft Left (a common phenomenon in Europe in the 1970s), motivated more by a "ride with the tide" attitude.

[93]Tom Bottomore, ed.: *A Dictionary of Marxist Thought*, entry Hinduism, pp.203-06.

[94]Tom Bottomore: *Dictionary of Marxist Thought*, p.203, paraphrasing Karl Marx: *The First Indian War of Independence* (a collection of his articles on the 1857 Mutiny in the *New York Daily Tribune*, published in Moscow 1959), p.156. See also Marx: *Notes on Indian History*.

[95]In an unabashed defence of colonialism, M.A.G. van Meerhaeghe ("De schadelijke 'ontwikkelingshulp'", i.e. "the harm done by aid to developing countries", *De Standaard*, 5.3.1991) invokes the authority of Karl Marx: "Even Marx admitted that British rule in India was beneficial to that country."

[96]Interview in *Le Monde*, spring 1993, reproduced in *India*, Brussels, June 1993.

member Sitaram Yechury calls India a "multinational country" with "many nationalities".[97] CPM leaders Jyoti Basu and Ashok Mitra have declared that if the BJP were to come to power, West Bengal would secede from India, and that "India was never the solution" anyway.[98]

In every conflict, they have stood on the anti-Hindu and usually also on the anti-Indian side: betraying Quit India activists to the British in 1942, supporting the Pakistan scheme in 1945-47, supporting the separatist *Razâkâr* militia in Hyderabad state in 1948, siding with China in 1961-62, supporting the Muslim claim in the Ayodhya controversy. As a Western Marxist observer admits: "Uncompromising opposition to Gandhi and his cherished Hindu convictions meant that communists were cut off in a considerable measure from the mainstream of the patriotic struggle."[99] While in other Third World countries, Marxists have supported cultural anti-colonialism and encouraged national pride, Indian Marxists are generally opposed to anti-colonial developments in the cultural sphere.

Though Marxism in India is by no means out yet, it has definitely lost much of its vigour during the 1990s, partly as a result of international developments, partly due to the feedback from reality in states ruled by the Communist Party (Marxist). A disappointed Bengali Leftist comments on CPM rule in West Bengal: "The Marxist rule of the last two decades has been an unmitigated disaster for West Bengal. ... Marxism has ensured that West Bengal will become an industrial desert. By blocking investment, both indigenous and foreign, the red trade unions have ensured that the number of unemployed remains high, providing endless supplies of 'revolutionary cadres' from the ranks of the lumpen proletariat."[100]

After the Soviet implosion, many an Indian Marxist or Left-talking opportunist has switched to free-market liberalism but remained as

---

[97]S.R. Yechury: "Election verdict: the meaning of the mandate", *New India Digest*, Sep. 1996. Remark that a glossy magazine invites a Stalinist hard-liner to contribute the analysis on the election results (much of it a predictable attack on the BJP), but never a BJP man: the latter are only allowed into the debate as objects, not as participants.

[98]The latter quote of Ashok Mitra's is used as title: "India was nooit de oplossing", by Bas Heijne, *NRC Handelsblad*, 20.3.1993. When in 1998 the BJP did come to power, the Communists failed to carry out this threat, apparently because the CPM gerontocracy had lost its youthful fervour.

[99]Tom Bottomore: *Dictionary of Marxist Thought*, p.205.

[100]Amulya Ganguli: "From red to saffron?", *Hindustan Times*, 13.4.1998.

determined a Macaulayite and secularist, at least in the first stage. Indeed, the intense polarization for and against Hindutva in the early 1990s is partly due to a regrouping of Leftist forces on the cultural front after they found that their fortunes on the socio-economic front were down: "Deprived of the old legitimacy which the non-existent but effectively advertised success of the Soviet Union and China conferred on them, leftist intellectuals must now hang on desperately to Nehru. Secularism ... and not socialism has to be their battle cry."[101] The effect on international opinion is that "the 'secularist' and 'anti-Hindu-communalist' platform assures them the support of not only the Muslims at home and abroad but, interestingly enough, of a lot of people in the West."[102]

At the academic level, at least, this is very much the situation: Indian Marxists are welcomed in American seminars as privileged commentators on "Hindu communalism". It is ironic as well as disturbing that a movement which still swears by Lenin (whose October 1917 coup d'état deposed the first democratic Russian Parliament) and Stalin, is hailed in Western universities as the guardian of a civil polity against the encroaching barbarism of Hindu revivalism.

Yet, Indian Marxists sometimes become the allies of the Hindu nationalists. Thus, when non-Marxist secularists compromised with Islamist forces on the Shah Bano and Salman Rushdie issues, hard Marxists stood firm in their rejection of religious politics, so that along with the Hindu nationalists, they opposed the Government's concessions to the Islamists. Or for a different example, though Marxist intellectuals are very much part of the "English-speaking elite", working-class party cadres in West Bengal have promoted Bengali medium education instead of English.[103] On the economic front too, Marxists and Hindutva activists have made common cause in recent years, especially in agitations against the multinationals and the GATT/WTO treaty. This trend is paralleled by Marxist-nationalist ad hoc alliances against globalization in Russia, Europe and the USA.

---

[101]G. Jain: "Confusion, uncertainty await us in coming months", *Sunday Mail*, 19/26.11.1989. The parallel with the contemporaneous shift from socio-economic to cultural issues (multiculturalism, homosexual rights etc.) among Western Leftists is obvious.

[102]G. Jain: "Confusion, uncertainty await us in coming months", *Sunday Mail*, 19/26.11.1989.

[103]Ashis Chakrabarti: "Politics of language", *Indian Express*, 23.4.1998. A CPM spokesman is quoted: "English education is elitist and gives an unfair advantage to a small percentage of the people against an overwhelming majority."

The "Other"

One of the most fashionable ways to misunderstand the Indian religious situation is in terms of "the Other". This popular term carries two distinct meanings, one based on the writings of the French-Jewish philosopher Emmanuel Lévinas, the other on Edward Said's much-discussed book *Orientalism* (1978).

To start with the latter, it is often alleged that Hindu revivalism has borrowed an "Orientalist construct" of a mythical Hinduism which never existed but was imagined by eighteenth-and nineteenth-century Europeans as the contrastive "Other" of European civilization. Third-world cultures in the process of decolonization and seeking to assert some kind of identity are tempted by "a small yet taunting little voice that ... says: You could be Somebody's Other".[104] Thus, it is said with some justification that the Western construction of "the Orient" as "spiritual", in contradistinction to the "materialist West", has been interiorized by Hindu revivalists from at least Swami Vivekananda onwards.

A typical example of this type of "deconstruction" of the "Orientalist" factor in Hindu self-perception is this observation by Peter van der Veer about the trend towards religious tolerance in the eighteenth century in Europe, when it was colonizing India: "A growing emphasis on religious tolerance as a positive value is thus related to the marginalization of religious institutions in Europe. ... This discourse is then brought to bear on the Muslim and Hindu populations incorporated in the modern world-system. Muslims, the old rivals of the Christian West, are labelled 'fanatic' and 'bigoted', while Hindus are seen in a more positive light as 'tolerant'. At the same time, this labelling explains why Muslims have ruled Hindu India and why Hindus have to be 'protected' by the British. In short, what I want to argue here is that the attribution of 'tolerance' to Hinduism is a specific orientalist history of ideas. As such, it has also come to dominate Hindu discourse on Hinduism".[105]

---

[104]Rustom Bharucha: "Somebody's Other. Disorientations in the Cultural Politics of Our Times", *Economic and Political Weekly*, 15.1.1994.

[105]P. Van der Veer: *Religious Nationalism*, p.67. I am not aware of British invocations of a need to "protect" the Hindus in justification of the colonization of India, though of course they must have felt good, *after the fact*, about the Bengali Hindu enthusiasm for their defeat of their Muslim ruler Siraj-ud-Daula at Plassey in 1757. By contrast, the nineteenth-century colonization of Africa which was frequently justified in advance (often by progressive opinion) as a way of liberating the blacks from the Arab slave-traders.

It should be clear, however, that this Orientalist construction could not have come about without a certain basis in reality. Though "tolerance" is a very recent addition to the Hindu religious vocabulary, the historical reality of Hindu society is that foreign and dissident religions were effectively *tolerated*, as proven by the history of the Jews or the Parsis in India. Likewise, there is much truth in Voltaire's enthusiastic Orientalist assumption that unlike Judaism, Christianity and Islam, the Indian and Chinese "religions" were not based on prophetic "revelations" but on a purely human contemplation of reality. Or for a similar example pertaining to Islam: the Orientalist association of Islam with sensuality was partly the result of internal European concerns in the Victorian Age, but it was none the less correct in so far as Islam does have a more positive appreciation of sex than Christianity.

Also, the implicit allegation that an identity based on "Otherness" vis-à-vis the dominant colonial worldview is illusory need not be taken as a condemnation pure and simple. When looked at from the viewpoint of the colonized native struggling to regain his self-respect, this critique of the purely derivative or illusory character of an orientalism-based identity can be understood as encouraging a more serious and more historical rediscovery of the native culture as it really was, without the intrusive reference to the colonizer's model.[106]

The nastier application of "Otherness" discourse is the one affirming a "rejection of the Other" (as diagnosed in Lévinas' reflections on the Holocaust)[107] as an explanatory characterization of Hindu hostility against Islam. Many scholars assume that Hindu revivalism is just another typical case of the contemporary worldwide trend of "identitarian" politics: part of a strategy to artificially construct a common Hindu national identity

---

[106]Various viewpoints on the Orientalism-related instance of Otherness have been developed, see e.g. Ashis Nandy: *The Intimate Enemy. Loss and Recovery of Self under Colonialism*, or Vinay Lal: "Beyond alterity", *Economic and Political Weekly*, 4.2.1995.

[107]See E. Lévinas: *Totalité et Infini*, and for recent introductions, see e.g. Arno Münster: *La Différence comme Non-Indifférence. Ethique et Altérité chez Emmanuel Lévinas*, and John Llewelyn: *Emmanuel Lévinas. The Genealogy of Ethics.* It is insufficiently realized that Lévinas' now-ubiquitous discourse on "alterity" and "the face of the Other" is borrowed in large measure from the German-Jewish mystic philosopher Martin Buber.

through polarization with a hostile outsider or Other[108] But that is a case of forcing the unwilling facts into a preconceived pet theory.

That Hindu society does not reject "Otherness" has amply been proven throughout history. First of all, there was plenty of "Otherness" inside Hindu society: whatever the evils of the caste system, it did accommodate the continued diversity of cultural identities. As Hindutva spokesmen never tire of reminding us, the Jews and the Zoroastrians have been welcome to their "Otherness" ever since they were allowed to settle in India.[109] Christianity is a more complicated matter, which will perfectly illustrate the various aspects of the issue at hand. The Christianity of the Syrian refugees who settled in Kerala in the fourth century was distinguished from Hinduism by its ritual and doctrinal "Otherness", and suffered no hostility in consequence. By contrast, missionary Christianity brought by the colonizers is strongly disliked by Hindu activists, not because of its "Otherness", but because of its declared objective to eliminate Hinduism through conversion, i.e. because of its *rejection of Hinduism's "Otherness"*.[110]

This then is also the reason for Hindu hostility to Islam as enunciated in numerous Hindu revivalist texts. Islam's difference or "Otherness" has nothing to do with it, as the Hindu record of hospitality to the Moplahs ("sons-in-law", Arab traders who married Hindu girls in Kerala) shows. But Hindus perceive Islam as anti-pluralistic and intolerant of what is from

---

[108]Predictably, it is the French India-watchers Gérard Heuzé (*Où Va l'Inde Moderne?*) and Christophe Jaffrelot (*Les Nationalistes Hindous*) who give a central place to these concepts, but some Indian secularists have by now adopted this terminology as well, e.g. Shohini Ghosh ("The misguided morality squads", *The Hindu*, 19.2.1995) makes her point against moralistic opposition to "Western" indecency by reformulating the rejected "xenophobic" position as follows: "This intrusive and alien 'other' constantly vitiates the purity of 'Indian culture' by introducing elements that are supposedly 'un-Indian'."

[109]BJP critic Kuldip Nayar ("Will India stay secular?", *Hindustan Times*, 23.12.1992) testifies: "Jewish leaders have told me that India is the only country in the world where the Jews never faced religious persecution."

[110]See e.g. V. Neckebrouck: *De Stomme Duivelen. Het Anti-Missionair Syndroom in de Westerse Kerk* (Dutch: "The mute demons. The anti-missionary syndrome in the Western Church"), a critique of the assumption of many European Christians that the mission is a thing of the past.

the Islamic viewpoint the "Otherness" of Hinduism.[111] For this reason, they use the same somewhat inflated references to the Holocaust when speaking of their experiences with Islam, notably the Partition massacres of 1947 and the Bengali genocide of 1971. It is undeniable that there exists a widespread hostility to Islam among Hindus, and that this hostility is articulated if not cultivated by a number of Hindu revivalist authors; but it is sloppy thinking to construe this hostility in the fashionable terminology of "Otherness".

Siege psychology

It is said that Hindu revivalists display a "siege mentality", an allegedly irrational fear of being encircled by enemies. The phenomenon is not uncommon, e.g. the Muslim League used to attract Muslim support with the cry of "Islam in danger". Likewise, secularist demonstrations against Hindutva are often announced with slogans about "secularism in danger". And yes, Hindus have a similar catch-phrase: "Hinduism under siege". BJP leader Atal Behari Vajpayee has lamented that the Hindus felt beleaguered to the point that India now has a majority with a "minority complex".[112]

The "pseudo-secularism" outlined above is perceived as a symptom of a larger strategic configuration of forces. The strange alliance between secularists and Islamists, sometimes extended to include other groups with genuine or artificial grievances against the Hindus, is considered as a "siege" of Hindu society organized or facilitated by the Nehruvian state, rallying to its cause all those whom Islamic and Western colonialism have managed to set apart from Hindu society: "...the Muslim and British invasions of India, though defeated and dispersed, have yet managed to crystallize certain residues—psychological and intellectual—which a battered Hindu society is finding very difficult to digest. These residues are now in active alliance with powerful international forces, and are being aided and abetted on a scale which an impoverished Hindu society cannot match. And lastly, though at loggerheads amongst themselves, these

---

[111]In his book *La Pureté Dangereuse* (French, approximately "The Dangerous Concern for Purity"), a classic of Otherness discourse, Bernard-Henri Lévy highlights precisely the Islamic intolerance of Otherness, with reference to the Taslima Nasreen affair and the terror campaign by the Algerian *Groupe Islamique Armé*. Note that *Pâkistân* and *Khâlistân*, two explicitly anti-Hindu state projects, both mean "Land of the Pure", i.e. purified from Hindu elements.

[112]Quoted by Swapan Dasgupta: "Defying common sense", *Indian Express*, 1.6.1996.

residues have forged a united front which is holding Hindu society under siege."[113]

Rather than lazily dismiss this perception as "paranoia", we should give this viewpoint a hearing, just as most scholars in this field have given a hearing (and often unqualified support) to secularist warnings of "secularism in danger". It may be pointed out, however, that some Hindu revivalists have criticized the whole idea of a united front of all anti-Hindu forces as a fantasy: a scare fantasy on the Hindu side and a pipe-dream on the opposite side.[114]

Swapan Dasgupta rarely misses an occasion to draw attention to new developments which pinprick this fantasy, e.g. when in 1996, "Vajpayee demolished the myth of the BJP lacking support of the Dalits, the Scheduled Tribes and the Sikhs".[115] Important sections of the three groups mentioned have joined the BJP, always denounced as a party of Brahmins and Banias. They also have a long history of hostility towards the Muslims, yet anti-Hindu ideologues within them as well as Islamic strategists and secularists have tried to involve them in a broad "anti-BSO" front (BSO or "Brahminical Social Order" being a hostile and reductionist term for Hinduism, devised precisely to attract lower-caste Hindus to the non-Hindu side).[116] But social realities prove stronger: "For example, in Kanpur—fast replacing Meerut, Moradabad and Mau as the centre of Muslim assertiveness—the pitched sectarian battles are fought between Muslims and Dalits. The city is sharply polarised along communal lines, with the Dalits constituting the Hindu storm-troopers and voting BJP. ... The so-called solidarity of the disadvantaged is a creation of radical intellectuals."[117]

---

[113]S.R. Goel: *Hindu Society under Siege*, pp.5-6.

[114]The Muslim-Sikh-Christian-Dalit-Backward front against the "Brahminical social order" is a frequent theme in the editorials of Syed Shahabuddin's monthly *Muslim India*, as in those of V.T. Rajshekar's fortnightly *Dalit Voice*.

[115]Swapan Dasgupta: "Defying common sense", *Indian Express*, 1.6.1996.

[116]The term BSO was launched by V.T. Rajshekar, editor of the Bangalore fortnightly *Dalit Voice*, and is currently being given academic respectability, e.g. by Suranjit Kumar Saha: "The Brahminic Social Order and Tribal Society", in Arthur Bonner, ed.: *Democracy in India, a Hollow Shell*, pp.65-80.

[117]Swapan Dasgupta: "Traditional antagonisms", *Indian Express*, 14.7.1994. This finding will not convince the said radical intellectuals, for it could be explained as the result of manipulation by the wily Brahmin-Bania combine behind the BJP, which has propagated a "false consciousness" among the Dalits, contrary to their "objective class interests".

As for the international support to anti-Hindu agitations in India, there is undeniably a flow of money from the Arab peninsula to Islamic organizations, and from the West to the Christian missions (as well as from the overseas Hindus to Hindu organizations), but there are other facts too. Thus, Kashmiri separatism is not actively supported by Muslim countries except for Pakistan. The Christian separatists of the National Socialist Council of Nagaland claim to represent an independent country, yet it cannot boast of even the faintest semblance of Western recognition. The powerful Christian press will occasionally support Muslim causes like the Ayodhya mosque, but the fate of the Christians in Pakistan inevitably limits the scope for Muslim-Christian friendship.[118]

And so on: the *idea* of a united anti-Hindu front with international backing is very real, and to that extent the Hindu perception of being "under siege" has a basis in fact, but in social and political practice, this anti-Hindu front has no more than a fragmentary and intermittent existence. Even its most important component, the alliance between Islamist forces and the secularists (as in the Rushdie affair), is under permanent strain because it is so counternatural.

Westernization

The Hindu revivalist movement, of which the BJP is one (imperfect) emanation, perceives itself as essentially an anti-colonial movement, eager to complete the job of political decolonization with its missing component: cultural decolonization. This much it does have in common with Islamists in Egypt, Algeria and other countries, for example in 1992, French Muslim convert Abdullah Herbert explained the Islamist wave in Algeria as a matter of "completing political and economic decolonization with cultural decolonïzation".[119] The English-speaking elite, by contrast, and its mediatic and academic segments in particular, are the cultural heirs of the colonial system and consequently the enemies of Hindu Revivalism. This includes those Marxists who have always been up in arms against real or perceived forms of neo-colonialism in the political and economic

---

[118]Christian-Muslim tension, very strong in the North-East, is one of those blind spots in India studies. For a recent example elsewhere in India: in Hyderabad, "a group of Muslim youths attacked a missionary school and church for alleged blasphemy of Islam and prophet Mohammed in a moral science textbook" (*Pioneer*, 28.8.1997).

[119]Prof. A. Herbert speaking at the 6th Conference of European Muslims in Genk (Belgium), April 1992, see my report of the conference, K. Elst: *De Islamitische Zuil*, p.30.

sphere: "Those members of the Third World elite who never lose an opportunity to lash out against the West have been the worst affected by the colonisation of the mind. They speak in the language of the opponents and subscribe to their values."[120]

The pressure to Westernize is the most conspicuous form of this colonial mentality: "Colonialism has a long way to go before it is vanquished! Our nations are ostensibly independent, but our minds still remain enslaved. Because a second more pernicious wave of colonisation has begun, working insidiously on the minds of the colonised. It tries, with the connivance of our own elite, to persuade us that there is only one way to progress, the Western way. ... the so-called policies of development and modernisation as they have been formulated by Third World leaders are serving no other purpose but to destroy our culture without even ensuring material prosperity in return."[121]

One aspect of this "psychological colonization" is the demonization of native civilization: "The Indian press, like most of its Third World counterparts, puts a premium on all that is modern and condemns as degenerate all that is traditional. ... In order to put the stamp of legitimacy on modernisation, we have to believe that the traditional civilisation was inhuman."[122] Instilling guilt about the "evils of Hindu society" is indeed a favourite weapon of the secularist elite. On the other hand, some native, as also some Western customs *deserve* to be demonized; and in Hindu revivalism, we do see a repudiation of certain traditional Hindu customs deemed harmful to contemporary Hindu interests. Conversely, certain Western contributions are objectively superior to their Hindu counterparts, and are eagerly incorporated in Hindu revivalist discourse, which contains pleas for "modernization without Westernization" (the cultural counterpart of the economic policy line of "liberalization without globalization").

---

[120]Ashis Nandy: "Propagating an Indian Model", *Sunday Mail*, 14.1.1990, p.35. From his writings on Gandhi (e.g. *At the Edge of Psychology*, pp.70-98), it appears that Nandy criticizes the Hindu nationalists on the same ground: Hindus are interiorizing colonial ideals of "virility" and military strength as opposed to native "feminine" ideals of "sensitivity". In fact, martial ideals were just as much part of Hindu as of Western culture; the image of Hindus as passive and meek is (with apologies for the voguish term:) an *Orientalist construct*.

[121]Ashis Nandy: "Propagating an Indian Model", *Sunday Mail*, 14.1.1990, p.34.

[122]Ashis Nandy: "Propagating an Indian Model", *Sunday Mail*, 14.1.1990, p.36.

Instances of selective Westernization can certainly be discerned in the programmes of Hindu revivalists. They like to point out that Hindu civilization was at one time a pioneer in scientific thought and enquiry, and that after falling behind in the last centuries, it is only true to its original character if it interiorizes the fruits of progress achieved by other nations. It would be trivial to cite the benefits of modern technology here. More importantly, in the polemic against Christianity and Islam, some Hindu revivalists have discovered that there is hardly a better weapon than the findings of modern scholarship.[123] Conversely, those Hindu revivalists who spurn the opportunity to make use of the findings of modern scholarship, notably the RSS movement, usually cut a poor figure when it comes to arguing their case.

This openness to modern scholarship is a major difference with the Islamist movement. Though the latter is also often led by people with modern education or who have studied in the West (for example, Turkey's Islamist leader Necmettin Erbakan is an engineer, just like Vishva Hindu Parishad leader Ashok Singhal),[124] and though the Islamists may adopt Western media and technology, Islamism firmly keeps out the spirit of critical enquiry. Educated Hindus are confident that a confrontation with rational thought will cost Hinduism only some deadwood, some superstitious accretions, but that the core of Hinduism is capable of surviving the exposure to the light of reason. As Shrikant Talageri writes: "Hindus should adopt as open an attitude to *pantha-chikitsâ* ["diagnosis of sects"] of Hinduism as to that of Islam and Christianity: there is nothing to fear, since Hinduism in its essence will shine out white and pure in comparison with Islam and Christianity in *their* essence. It will only be cleansed of impurities which stand in its *own* way."[125]

---

[123]Thus, Sita Ram Goel's book *Jesus Christ, an Artifice for Aggression* (an unnecessarily aggressive title which doesn't really cover the contents) contains an overview of rationalist and skeptical Bible scholarship from the West. In his speech before the Catholic Bishops' Conference of India (published as *Missionaries in India*), Arun Shourie challenges the bishops to inform their followers about the findings of modern research on the origins of Christianity. Goel also republished the biographies of Prophet Mohammed by British authors William Muir and D.S. Margoliouth and Daniel Pipes' book *The Rushdie Affair*.

[124]Likewise, RSS leader Rajendra Singh and former BJP president Murli Manohar Joshi are professors of Physics. The sciences became perhaps the most important recruiting-ground for new BJP cadres in the 1990s; even in the Marxist-dominated Jawaharlal Nehru University, the RSS student organization won the elections for the Student Union in 1996 and again in 2000.

[125]Shrikant Talageri in S.R. Goel, ed.: *Time for Stock-Taking*, p.229.

A new powerful ally of the Westernized elite has recently appeared on the scene, a new avenue of penetration into Hindu society: the influence of globalization and Western pop culture spreading through the new media, now present in the remotest village. Its foreseeable effect will be an increase in cultural self-forgetfulness at the mass level. This way, the globalized market could replace Nehruvian state control of education and culture as the leveller of Hinduism.[126] On the other hand, the estrangement from the cultural roots may stimulate a more conscious (if more selective) return to those roots or at least to a modernized Hindu identity reconnecting with them. This outcome is suggested by past experience: to a large extent, the pioneers of Hindu Revivalism have been Westernized urban intellectuals, living in the kind of cultural half-way condition which the modern media are now spreading to the villages.

Majoritarianism

Hindu nationalists are often accused of "majoritarianism", an allegation which they themselves kind of invite by protesting against "minorityism". The latter term means that the minorities are given privileges or a veto right against democratic majority decisions; usually, it is used in cases of concessions of Muslim demands, or what is called "Muslim appeasement".[127] Thus, the Hindu Nationalists surmise that a majority of Indian citizens favour a ban on cow-slaughter, yet Nehru and his successors opposed it because they didn't want to go against minority feelings. So, they often allege that Congress and Janata Governments have systematically practised "minorityism".

[126]When new TV channels were thoroughly changing India's media landscape (*c.* 1994), secularists including columnist Tavleen Singh in *Indian Express* argued that if a bit of television can be a threat to India's much-touted 5000-year-old culture, then perhaps this culture isn't all that great and worth preserving. This presupposes the fallacious assumption that the most precious things are also the most robust, as if the brain were more robust than the bones. A precious heritage may not be able to compete under the rules of the downward-levelling free market.

[127]"Appeasement" was originally the term used by the HMS to describe Mahatma Gandhi's policy of repeated unilateral concessions to the Muslim League in the hope of dissuading it from pursuing its Pakistan project. The implied reference to Neville Chamberlain's policy of "appeasement" vis-à-vis Adolf Hitler is deliberate: at the time, the Muslim League openly compared its own position (that Muslims were part of the Muslim commonwealth and not of India, and that they should politically accede to the former and separate from the latter) with that of the Sudeten Germans who were "liberated" from Czechoslovakia by Hitler's intervention.

Conversely, "majoritarianism" is the position that a majority has the right to determine the face of a country, whether in symbolic respects or in actual legislation. It is in effect a pejorative term for "democracy", especially democracy in its unalloyed "one man one vote" form, in which a majority can take decisions without bothering about the religious background of the decision's supporters or opponents. On issues which pit a large community against a small community, this tends to allow the larger community to vote its own wishes into law. Thus, until recently England prohibited all work on Sundays, which was a Christian commandment turned into law, and atheists or Jews who did not specially care for the Sunday just had to abide by that law. It is an intrinsic feature of democracy that it is majoritarian. In South Africa, the anti-Apartheid campaigners used to describe their democratic "one man one vote" demand as "majority rule". And effectively, it is now impossible to elect a South-African president who is hated by the Black majority, but it is perfectly possible and democratic to elect a President who is unacceptable to the White, Coloured or Indian minorities, if he is the choice of the majority; just as it is possible in any democratic country with a Leftist majority to impose a Leftist president on the Rightist minority.

If we put it this crudely, some people may object that it is "undemocratic"[128] for a majority to ride roughshod over the minorities, e.g. journalist M.J. Akbar claims that: "The true test of a democracy is the justice that the minority gets in the system."[129] Well, no. When Socrates as a one-man minority was eliminated by Athenian democracy, that was certainly narrow-minded, intolerant and other deplorable things besides; but it was not undemocratic. Athens passed the true test of a democracy by implementing the will of the majority, viz. to eliminate Socrates (the choice between exile and death was generously left to the philosopher himself). Of course, the present writer is in favour of Socrates' right to free speech and of a system in which minorities "get justice"; but you cannot

---

[128]The term *democracy* itself could have figured in our list of oft-manipulated terms; witness the *German Democratic Republic* or Pol Pot's *Democratic Kampuchea*. Nowadays its distortion is less blatant but still common, especially in the usage of the term to describe the *contents* of a policy or programme (viz. if it is anti-nationalistic, anti-religious, pro-consumerist, pro-multiculturalist and pro-American) rather than its procedure of decision, which alone can be properly characterized as "democratic" or "undemocratic".

[129]M.J. Akbar in *Illustrated Weekly of India*, 22.12.1990.

deduce those desirable things from the single concept of *democracy*. You cannot invest "democracy" with all possible virtues. So, "tyranny by the majority" is and remains an inherent danger of democracy. And this would bring us to an old debate: in order not to lapse into barbarism, democracy needs the basis of a strong ethical culture in the population. Generally speaking, democracy has certain cultural prerequisites which fall outside the institutional democracy concept itself.

One curb on unalloyed "majoritarian" democracy could consist in veto powers conceded to smaller units (though this means that a minority can impose its will on the majority, which obviously detracts from the "democratic" character of the system). This is what David Ludden refers to in his criticism of BJP "majoritarianism": "As a majoritarian movement, Hindu nationalism defines the Indian nation as a whole and seeks to displace and remove alternative, pluralistic definitions."[130] A "pluralistic" definition seems to imply a recognition of subnationalities or other units below the level of the nation.

However, it is important to understand that this critique of "majoritarianism" intrinsically presupposes a *communalist* perspective: the nation is not one, is not a single unit which can take political decisions, but it is a composite of communities, one of which may be the majority, but each of which has its own sovereignty. The citizen does not participate in the decision-making process as just a citizen, but as a citizen qualified by his membership of a subnationality. Moreover, in the present debate, it is minorities defined by religion which are accepted as legitimate contenders for the status of a "minority" entitled to "get justice".

In secular countries, there may be subnationalities defined by region or language (and that only for very limited purposes), but it is unconstitutional and in fact unthinkable that a proposal of law in France, the US or any other secular country were to be subjected to the approval or disapproval of groups defined by religious identity. Thus, no matter how sinful the Catholic community may consider the legalization of abortion, there is no question of a modern Government giving representatives of the Catholic community a veto right against a democratically enacted law permitting abortion, nor even the right to have a separate minority law applying to Catholics alone. In those countries, a citizen is simply a

[130]David Ludden: *Making India Hindu*, p.14.

citizen, and his adherence to a majority or minority religion is strictly ignored. In France, it is even illegal to inquire about someone's religion in public life, e.g. in job interviews. That is real secularism.

That very policy, accepted as a matter of course in Western secular democracies, is precisely what Ludden describes as the "majoritarian" programme of the Hindu nationalists: to treat "the Indian nation as a whole", in particular, to have a Common Civil Code which applies to all citizens regardless of religion, replacing the present "pluralistic" Civil Code which differs according to religion. By contrast, the "alternative, pluralistic definitions" envisaged by Ludden introduce the notion of separate communities as relatively sovereign building-blocks of the nation. But that is *exactly* what the British in India used to call the "communal" principle.

This example of a controversial term may serve to illustrate how easily outside observers get entangled in the intricacies of India's "communal" problem; how they lose their neutrality by taking sides already in the stage when terms are defined; and how they may even end up on the side which they imagine they are criticising, i.e. "communalism". I therefore consider it better to avoid neologistic exonyms like "majoritarianism", which simply have nothing to do with the ideological self-definition of the movement under consideration.

PROBLEMS IN THE PERCEPTION OF HINDU REVIVALISM

Impact of the opinion climate

This study was not written in a vacuum. An entire opinion climate has been palpably present, which is bound to influence the reader (not excluding the academic specialist) in a certain direction. I am in no position to dislodge an established opinion climate, but I do want to caution the reader that certain commonly-held opinions about India and Hindu revivalism are no more than just that—opinions. Views on a large phenomenon like Hindu revivalism naturally stretch across the whole opinion spectrum, but those which dominate the international media and the channels likely to have influenced my readership, are almost uniformly hostile, sometimes ferociously hostile. About Hindu revivalism, we may say what an earlier researcher has said about the Druze community, viz. that they "were judged almost entirely in the light of sources written by their adversaries; hence many misconceptions about them persist to this day."[131]

This complaint is also heard from the people directly concerned, the Hindu revivalists themselves (though the predominant tendency in the RSS and among independent Hindu revivalist authors has for long been to ignore media and academic opinion). Of course, I am aware that most contenders in political struggles complain of unfair treatment by the media (if only to assume the underdog role), and that many of them also find individual outsiders to support them in this complaint.

Thus, it is a standard Muslim complaint that Islam is always highlighted in connection with barbarity and terrorism, and some non-Muslim authors have been willing to second that complaint, for example, Edward Said, a Palestinian Christian. Sometimes, this complaint is entirely justified (and liable to comparison with the Hindu situation), for example where Said shows how extremely partisan, unfair and distorted the American coverage of the Iranian revolution and subsequent hostage crisis (1979-80) was, how blatantly unbalanced its choice of "expert" commentators, how it "place[d] everything the Iranians said and did out of moral bounds".[132] Likewise, scholars James Piscatori and Dale F. Eickelman complain that "violence is never far from popular assumptions of Muslim politics".[133]

On the other hand, against this common complaint, the German journalist Klemens Ludwig argues that "in spite of all rhetoric about a Muslim *Feindbild* [enemy-image, bogey], Islam is supported by a strong lobby, not only in political and business circles but also in circles which consider themselves as enlightened and multicultural", specifically media opinion leaders who have become Islam's first line of defence against criticism.[134]

There is a logic to this. In cultural circles, progressives use Muslim immigrants as allies against their national-conservative enemies. As for business circles and the politicians catering to their interests: important

[131]Ismail K. Poonawala, reviewing Nejla M. Abu-Izzeddin: *The Druzes*, in *Journal of African and Oriental Studies*, 1996, p.601.

[132]E. Said: *Covering Islam*, a study of bias in the media coverage of Islam, p.90.

[133]Foreword to Bruce Lawrence: *Shattering the Myth: Islam beyond Violence*, p.xiii.

[134]Klemens Ludwig, quoted in Hilde Keteleer: "'Met de Koran in de hand worden vrouwen onderdrukt'" (Dutch: "Quran in hand, they oppress women"), *Markant* (Antwerp), 14.7.1994.

Muslim countries are wealthy but not very dynamic in building a competitive industry, which makes them an ideal market for Western industry (exactly the opposite counts for India, an ambitious high-tech competitor with as yet only limited purchasing power). To stay on good terms with the Muslim countries and to compensate for the latter's anger at Western support to Israel, Western powers, most of all the USA, promote Muslim-friendly policies, for example the all-out American support to Turkey, to Bosnia and indeed to Pakistan in its quarrels with India. This inevitably conditions the coverage in a large section of the media, which in the case of India reporting is anything but anti-Muslim.

So, complaints about unfair treatment should not be accepted uncritically. In the present case, should we be wary of being taken in by a predictable but unwarranted and at any rate self-serving complaint of unfair treatment, this time voiced by Hindu revivalists? Are we, like Edward Said, somehow missing the counter-evidence that the movement under consideration, far from being the underdog, actually disposes of "a strong lobby"? Or is there really something to their complaint? I propose we do our own fact-finding, with an emphasis on the international coverage of the Hindu revivalist phenomenon.

For starters, consider the following case. When the BJP lost the elections for the Legislative Assembly of Uttar Pradesh in 1993, some papers claimed that a Scheduled Caste politician belonging to the winning Backward Caste alliance (SP-BSP) had been murdered by a vengeful "upper-caste BJP".[135] In reality, the murder victim, Kala Bachcha, was a BJP candidate.[136] Such misreporting with inversion of guilt could hardly have been cooked up at editorial offices outside India; either it was done quite deliberately by interested parties in Delhi, then gullibly copied by foreign press correspondents; or, more likely, the original information was insufficiently explicit about the political identity of the victim, so that this gap was filled during the editing process on the purely deductive assumption that "BJP = Hindu = oppression of lower by upper castes", ergo "an ex-Untouchable must have belonged to the anti-BJP camp"; or perhaps "BJP = fundamentalist = terrorist, ergo BJP commits murders". At any rate, the net result was en exchange of aggressor and victim, arguably the most hurtful form of misinformation.

---

[135]E.g. *De Standaard*, 12.8.1994.

[136]Kala Bachcha ("black kid"), nickname of Munna Sonkar, belonging to the Sonkar (or Khatik, pigherd/butcher) Scheduled Caste, had distinguished himself as a mob leader in earlier communal riots, according to Paul Brass: *Theft of an Idol*, p.228.

For a more important example, affecting the entire Western press for years on end, consider the coverage of the Kashmir conflict. The cause of the conflict is routinely misrepresented in the false claim that "in 1990, militant Muslims took to arms after Jagmohan, the authoritarian Indian governor of the state, had reacted excessively to a peaceful demonstration".[137] In fact, the armed insurrection had started in autumn 1989 with the accession of the presumedly pro-Muslim government of V.P. Singh and his Kashmiri Muslim Home Minister Mufti Mohammed Sayeed, months after the end of Jagmohan's first term in office, and Jagmohan had been sent in again in January 1990 (by Home Minister Sayeed, who was to praise Jagmohan's accomplishments in Parliament on 25 April 1990) to remedy the situation.

With the publicity given to the phenomenon of "ethnic cleansing" in ex-Yugoslavia, one could have expected a sympathy wave in favour of the Kashmiri Hindus, who were collectively hounded out of the Kashmir Valley in 1989-90. Nothing of the sort ever materialized, if only because most foreign media simply refrained from reporting this event.[138] When at all forced to admit the fact, some commentators added insult to injury by claiming that the exodus of the Hindu population was part of a strategy which *triggered* (instead of being caused by) the Islamic insurrection, a strategy masterminded by Jagmohan (as alleged by Congress MP and columnist Mani Shankar Aiyar)[139] or by the BJP. Though the BJP was practically non-existent in the Kashmiri Pandit community (whose

---

[137]Tim McGirk in *The Independent*, reproduced in *De Morgen* (Brussels), 26.8.1995: "Een trektocht te ver" ("A trek too far"). McGirk also under-reports the number of Hindu refugees as 90,000 instead of over 200,000; but at least, he acknowledges their existence, till today a rare event in the Anglo-Saxon media.

[138]E.g. Edward Desmond: "Himalayan Ulster", *New York Review*, 4.3.1993, a lengthy review of a number of books on Kashmir, manages to keep this Hindu-cleansing out of view, even though at least one of the books under review (viz. Jagmohan: *My Frozen Turbulence in Kashmir*) deals with the refugee crisis in some detail. Desmond knowingly and deliberately suppressed this information.

[139]M.S. Aiyar: "Kashmir is not Bangladesh", *Sunday*, 17.10.1993. In his reply, "Setting the record straight" (*Sunday*, 7.11.1993), Jagmohan counters: "Aiyar wants the public to believe that the Kashmiri Pandits are so unintelligent that they left their comfortable homes and beautiful Valley at the instance of a pied piper called Jagmohan, and not by the militants' strategy of 'killing one and frightening one thousand'. He ignores the hard fact that eminent Kashmiri Pandits had been butchered before I took over". During his two terms as governor (ending months before, and starting months after the start of the insurrection), Jagmohan was not a BJP man. He accepted a BJP ticket in the 1996 elections and won a Lok Sabha seat from Delhi.

political sympathies were predominantly Leftist), a Flemish India-watcher claimed in 1995: "The BJP, which controls the whole of India, has also infiltrated Kashmir and convinced the Hindus there to leave, so that the Army could move in."[140]

Most of the attention was given to the plight of the insurrectionists in their confrontation with the security forces, who were sometimes even blamed for acts of the former, e.g. the exploding of the *Chrar-e-Sharif* mosque in 1995.[141] The BBC's dramatizing coverage of clashes between separatists and security forces has been criticized by Indians (not just Hindu revivalists) as a "misrepresentation" which "won't wash", "cleverly mixed" and "extreme", but to no avail.[142] At any rate, the opinion climate in key sections of the media was not favourable to publicity for the plight of the Kashmiri Hindus. Till the time of this writing, most references to the Kashmir conflict in the international media fail to mention the Hindu refugee problem.

This deliberate and systematic distortion of information on the Kashmir crisis is more than just a deontological problem: it is a matter of life and death. If proper information had created public opinion against the Pak-backed terrorists in Kashmir, Western governments might well have withheld weapons deliveries to Pakistan and exerted serious pressure to end the proxy war which Pakistan has been waging against India in Kashmir and on other fronts. Instead, reporters have objectively supported the prolonging of the Kashmir crisis with its ever-rising death toll.

A case study in the winds of change

While the first half of the 1990s saw a peak in the anti-Hindu bias in international India-watching, the second half saw a a partial return to

---

[140]Marc Colpaert in *Radio Trottoir* (BRTN Radio 1, Brussels), 5.8.1995. To describe the (alleged, actually non-existent) presence of this Indian political party in Kashmir as "infiltration" betrays the assumption that Kashmir is foreign territory to India.

[141]The siege of the Chrar-e-Sharif mosque, ending in the (probably pre-arranged) escape of the occupants and the destruction of the building, became a classic proof of "Muslim appeasement" in Hindutva rhetoric when the Government provided the occupants with *biryani*, a meat dish, in sharp contrast with the unyielding suppression of the Hindu agitation in Ayodhya in autumn 1990. As L.K. Advani commented: "Bullets for the *kar sevaks*, biryani for the Kashmiri militants".

[142]Shubhra Gupta: "All is calm", *Sunday*, 7.11.1993, who also develops a parallel critique of Doordarshan's rosy picture of the Kashmir situation. Hindu NRIs have shown me bunches of copies of their mostly unpublished "letters to the editor" of a variety of media in which they allege gross misreporting on the Kashmir problem.

common sense. An example of this evolution, from vaguely critical to downright hysterical and then back to a more factual coverage is provided by the Catholic missionary monthly *Wereldwijd* (Antwerp). The paper usually conveys fairly sympathizing viewpoints about exotic cultures; about Hinduism, this was also the case up to 1985.[143] To be sure, Hinduism was described as "the religion of unredeemed man", and Christianity was advertised as the solution, but I see nothing wrong in value judgments and evaluative comparisons, not even when one's own religion happens to come out on top. Until 1985, Hindu revivalism in its contemporary form was not even noticed, and at first it was only mentioned in passing, as "a fundamentalist movement like the RSS".[144]

In 1986, the Hindu revivalists are called "fundamentalists", modern Hinduism is described by interviewee Prof. Romila Thapar as "a denial of pluralism", partly based on "myths" (meaning stories about atrocities by the Muslim invaders of yore). At the time, the BJP had two seats in the *Lok Sabhâ*, but the reporter consistently pretends that the Government does the bidding of the "fundamentalists". There is also a section about "Catholic ashrams", featuring saffron-clad missionary Bede Griffiths, without a hint that Hindus consider him a swindler.[145] So far, so good.

The main source in this report, however, is V.T. Rajshekar, editor of the Bangalore-based fortnightly *Dalit Voice*. No information is given about the credentials of this man, but it is good to know that after being sacked as *Indian Express* reporter for collusion with Khalistani terrorists, he became India's foremost spokesman of anti-Brahminism. He frequently alleges that Brahmins pull all the strings in India, a position adopted lock, stock and barrel by the *Wereldwijd* reporter: "The orthodox Brahmins control the RSS while the 'progressive' Brahmins lead the 'national' parties including the Communist parties. The intention is that Brahmins always rule, no matter who wins the struggle."[146]

---

[143]E.g. Toon van Bijnen: "Bangalore", *Wereldwijd*, July 1979, and: "Hindoeïsme vandaag", May 1980.

[144]Marc Colpaert: "India", *Wereldwijd*, Dec. 1985.

[145]About the Catholic Ashram movement, see Catherine Cornille: *The Guru in Indian Catholicism*, for a sympathizing account, and S.R. Goel: *Catholic Ashrams, Sannyasins or Swindlers?*, for a hostile account.

[146]Marc Colpaert: "Hindoeïsme", *Wereldwijd*, March 1986. This view of the omnipresent Brahmin conspiracy controlling the Communist Party along with the Congress and the BJP, is worked out in detail in V.T. Rajshekar: *Dialogue of the Bhoodevatas. Sacred Brahmins vs. Socialist Brahmins. Bhûdevatâ*: "god on earth", a traditional epithet of the Brahmins.

Actually, the orthodox Brahmins denounce the reformist RSS as heterodox, but let that pass. More remarkable is the similarity with Hitler's rhetoric of how world Jewry was behind both capitalism and Bolshevism, all the more so because Rajshekar does combine anti-Brahminism with anti-Semitism. Indeed, catering to a largely Muslim readership, he regularly publishes anti-Jewish items and alleges a secret collusion between Israel and the "Jews of India", meaning the Brahmins.[147] All the while attacking the Hindus as "Nazis" (and many other terms of abuse besides), he also writes: "Muslims approved the persecution of Jews by Hitler who believed that as long as Jews existed in the world there would be no peace in the world. This is coming true as the Jews are controlling the Pentagon and CIA, not to speak of Lebanon and West Asia."[148]

Let us assume that the reporter, who has quoted from *Dalit Voice*, had overlooked such passages and was unaware of Rajshekar's agenda. But what he did quote was still somewhat worrying, e.g. that "a Hindu cannot be human", and that the *only* solution for Hindus is to convert out of Hinduism. About the RSS, even ordinary social work on the Christian missionary model is described in hateful terms, for example, it "*besieges* the aboriginal tribes and *infiltrates* among the untouchables", exactly the language which the RSS uses to characterize the work of the Christian missions. The reporter is candid about his own assent to Rajshekar's explicitly quoted views: "Thus argues V.T. Rajshekar. The facts appear to put him in the right."[149]

In 1991, at the height of the Ayodhya controversy, *Wereldwijd* calls the RSS a "militia" consisting of "Nazis" who "want to perpetuate the

---

[147]E.g. In his booklet *Brahminism* (1983), Rajshekar describes Brahminism as the mother of both Nazism and Zionism, inscribing both words in the swastika on the cover. He accuses the Mossad of having killed Rajiv Gandhi during the 1991 elections in order to create a sympathy wave to bring a Congress Brahmin (Narasimha Rao) to power (1.11.1992), exposes Theosophy as a joint venture of Tamil Brahmins and White Freemasons, another Zionist front (16.1.1993), etc.

[148]*Dalit Voice*, 1.11.1992. *Dalit Voice* advertises The Protocols of the Elders of Zion ("get a copy from the Iranian embassy", 1.12.1991), and accuses the Zionists of having brought both Lenin and Hitler to power (16.1.1993), and of having planted Monica Lewinsky in the White House in order to make Bill Clinton toe the line (1.9.1998). When French scholar Léon Poliakov protested against the misuse of his book *Le Mythe Aryen*, Rajshekar defended his term "Jews of India" with more allegations of Jewish-Brahmin collusion (1.7.1992). Rajshekar is invalidated as a quotable source more by his crankiness than by his political incorrectness.

[149]Marc Colpaert: "Hindoeïsme", *Wereldwijd*, March 1986.

monopoly and the power of the Brahmins".[150] This time, the sources quoted include *Dalit Voice*, interviewee Dr. J. Kananaikil, who leads the (Christian) Indian Social Institute in Delhi, and Rajni Kothari, who had applauded the newly enacted reservations for Other Backward Castes (which pit them against the upper castes) as having "the capacity to finish off the supremacy of Vedic Hinduism", and who is quoted as asserting that caste struggle is inevitable and necessary.

A picture captioned "Muslims on the steps of the Babri Masjid in Ayodhya" shows a functioning mosque in some other place, thus giving the impression that the Ayodhya controversy was about a functioning mosque which Hindu militants wanted to snatch from the local Muslim community, when in fact it was mosque architecture functioning as a Hindu temple since 1949. (After the violence in Ayodhya in late October and early November 1990, many newspapers including *De Standaard* and the *New York Times* published such wrongly chosen or wrongly captioned pictures. It got even worse in the more popular press, for example, a Dutch glossy magazine showed Khalistani terrorists wielding machine guns with the caption: "Fundamentalist Hindus near the demolished Babri Masjid").[151]

In 1995, the "fundamentalist RSS" is accused of the "deification of political leaders", with reference to the political ascendancy of film stars in Andhra Pradesh and Tamil Nadu: "Since then, Tamil Nadu politics is in the hands of fascist film stars."[152] In fact, the RSS (referent of the "fascist" smear) hardly had a presence in Tamil Nadu, but presumably Jayalalitha Jayaram, ex-filmstar and then Chief Minister, had proven "fascist" enough by encouraging Vedic education (now also for Scheduled Castes) and earmarking funds for the upkeep of temples. We also get to read the old canard that "RSS militants murdered Mahatma Gandhi". In fact, none of the conspirators belonged to the RSS, which was officially cleared of all suspicions; the actual murderer, Nathuram Godse, had left the RSS a decade earlier precisely because he wanted a more militant political involvement, as he confirmed during his speech in court.[153]

And then, after election victories, the Hindu nationalists came to power, for 13 days in May 1996, and somewhat more durably in March

---

[150]Jan Landman: "Hindoeïsme", *Wereldwijd*, Feb. 1991.

[151]*Avenue* (Amsterdam) 1995/1, photograph by Raphael Gaillarde/Gamma/ABC Press.

[152]Marc Colpaert: "Kinderen van een mindere god" (Dutch: "Children of a lesser god"), *Wereldwijd*, Feb. 1995.

[153]See N. Godse: *Why I Assassinated Mahatma Gandhi*, para 29 and para 114.

1998. Nazis and fundamentalists, Hitler and Khomeini rolled into one, they were set to change India into one vast concentration camp; that at least is what you could legitimately expect on the basis of the earlier reports. Yet, in 1998, after the BJP victory, the title of the on-the-spot report becomes: "When the Gods wake up", and one of the captions reads: "Today, Hindu consciousness is waking up in the people themselves."[154] We get anti-colonial talk from Vishvanath Lawande, a veteran of the Goa liberation movement (which achieved decolonization in 1964) and from philosopher Claude Alvares, who accuses all parties (BJP included) of following the same Western development model. But Alvares acknowledges the rise of the BJP as a logical symptom of a welcome general revival of religion and abandonment of religion-free secularist attitudes among the intellectuals, and he admits that the BJP programme of economic self-reliance ("one of the few Gandhian legacies to survive") is proven right by the crisis of the East-Asian economies.

Feminist Urvashi Butalia delicately calls the rise of the BJP "a delicate affair". Why, are women's groups suffering attacks from BJP reactionaries? Not quite: "The party addresses the same issues and speaks the same language as the—originally mostly Leftist—women's groups: violence against women, dowry, lack of education etc." All right, she claims that she goes to the root of the problems while the BJP remains superficial, "bringing a quick solution to a village or region with some money"; but still, this is not the reactionary oppressive BJP we used to read about.[155]

Muslim Marxist poet Ali Sardar Jafri is quoted as attacking not the BJP but one of the BJP's own scapegoats, globalization, as a "new colonialism". Finally, Sikh woman poet Gagan Gill gets to answer the question whether she is "afraid of the Hindu party BJP": "I think that all demons have to come out of their dens, so that you can exorcize them. And moreover, the people have had to miss Hindu tradition for so long, so you have to give them the chance to relate to their heritage. The BJP movement has rediscovered the Hindu tradition. They have won votes with it. And if they want to put Hinduism back in the syllabi, so what? That should have been done long ago."

---

[154]Jan Landman: "Als de goden ontwaken", *Wereldwijd*, May 1998.

[155]Three years earlier, in 1995, Urvashi Butalia co-edited the book *Women and the Hindu Right*, an implacable critique of the RSS and BJP.

It is still a sign of a strongly partisan attitude that for more than a decade, all the interviewees asked to enlighten the readership about Hindu Revivalism were outsiders, many of them openly hostile to the movement; never did the reporters consider it necessary to approach insiders for a first-hand explanation. In a paper which always extols the value of interreligious dialogue, that neglect is something of a statement in itself. However, to let outsiders say the things which were just quoted from the May 1998 issue is an even more convincing clearance than any *pro domo* statement by an acknowledged spokesman of the movement could have been.

The same trend is in evidence in another Flemish monthly, the secular, government-sponsored *De Wereld Morgen*. Its coverage of Hindu revivalism had always been rather fragmentary and mostly hostile. When its editors asked me for an article about the Ayodhya affair, I gave them the facts based on primary sources, but they prefaced my article (which they did publish) with an editorial article of the same length, based on sources like *Frontline*, which said all the opposite things, a unique move in the paper's history.[156]

But then, in 1997, they published an interview with Jaya Jaitley, a spokeswoman of the socialist *Samatâ* ("equality") Party, which had concluded an electoral alliance with the BJP in 1996 (and again in 1998, so that the nominally Christian party leader George Fernandes became Defence Minister in Vajpayee's cabinet). She was asked how such a pact with the devil was possible, and she replied that "the BJP is not that fundamentalist at all. In the five states where the BJP is in Government, there are no problems between Hindus and Muslims. Corruption there has decreased strongly. Our chairman George Fernandes is a Christian. He co-operates with the BJP without problems. By isolating the BJP, you will only make it more extremist. Finally, the BJP too is against the globalization as we know it today. We can also influence it somewhat on that point. That is not unimportant when you know that the BJP gets 30 per cent of the vote."[157] So, here was a trustworthy socialist witnessing to the emerging perception that the BJP was not such a monster after all.

---

[156]K. Elst: "Wie heeft er schrik van het hindoe-fundamentalisme" (Dutch: "Who's afraid of Hindu fundamentalism?"), and Chris Verschooten: "Een test voor de demokratie?" ("A test for democracy?"), *De Wereld Morgen*, Dec. 1990.

[157]Interview with Jaya Jaitley, *De Wereld Morgen*, March 1997.

If this change in attitude is found in an Indian paper (as it is in many of them), it might be dismissed as just a matter of opportunism. But these Flemish monthlies have little to gain or lose by taking this side or that in an Indian dispute. So, the evolution in their treatment of Hindu Revivalism reflects a real change in opinion. It also shows something else: when these papers published attacks on the RSS and BJP which now seem wildly exaggerated, they did so in good faith, because that just happened to be the information fed to them by Indian sources which they considered reliable. Once they were given a different version, they didn't mind publishing that one also, but until then, the hate-BJP version was practically the only one which had come through their information channels for years on end.

In the years 1989-94, a massive and implacable hatred of Hindu revivalism in the English-Indian press totally coloured the information flow, and it will take some time before the effect of this opinion wave on the non-specialist media dies down. In the general media, a diversification has taken place since, with some papers still taking a virulently anti-BJP line, after the example of Indian Communist papers like *Frontline*, and others following the opinion shift in the mainstream segment of the English-language Indian media. The actual position taken by the foreign media largely depends on their sources, which are now more diverse in their opinions than the uniform hostility of the early 1990s. Certain media opted for a cool-headed coverage years ago (e.g. the London *Economist*), while others have continued to be fiercely hostile (e.g. the *New York Times*).

Whether the more neutral line is followed or the old hostility is revived on occasion often depends on random factors like the personal idiosyncrasies of the junior correspondent to whom the India reporting is entrusted, but may also result from political choices, e.g. the projection of political struggles at home (which may also include a Muslim factor or an antagonism between minority and majority) on to the political configuration in India, or, in the case of the powerful Anglo-American media, their governments' alliance with Pakistan. At any rate, for the period under consideration, we have to reckon with distorted reporting and hostile analysis, both in the media and in specialized publications. If anything, the latter are more firm in their commitment to combat rather than study the Hindu revivalist movement, as we shall see in some of the following sections of this chapter.

The Anglo-secularist bottleneck

The international media coverage of Indian politics is based on an information flow which passes through a uniquely narrow bottleneck: a handful of Indian English-language papers, which are faithfully copied by press correspondents in Delhi. Editors in Paris or New York have India very low on their list of priorities, and they don't scrutinize the sources used by the India desk in filling the limited space allotted to it. Further, because India is a democracy, no one has an attitude of suspicion vis-à-vis Indian sources, the way most people had a healthy skepticism vis-à-vis the Soviet media. Therefore, a handful of people in the leading media can get away with pushing their own reading of Indian reality. For the period under consideration, my finding is that their version, the only one which reached the international public, was not that of neutral observers, but embodied the views and prejudices of one very specific class.

Unlike in China, where the ruling class during much of the past century has waged an unrelenting and high-powered struggle against native culture and religion, the impact of the Nehruvian secularist elite in India has always been limited. Its sway has never really extended beyond the strictly public sphere: the dominant media, academe, and politics. There, the smallest deviation from the Nehruvian line could be punished forthwith. A typical example is the case of G.G. Swell, presidential candidate for the opposition in 1992. He belonged to a minority (Christian) and to a Scheduled Tribe while his Congress opponent, Shankar Dayal Sharma, was a Brahmin; an outsider would think that this should have made him the natural candidate of the secularists and the Left. However, when the BJP promised to support his candidature, he returned the compliment by declaring that the BJP is not a "communal" party. At once, a group of vocal secularists including Syed Shahabuddin and Rajmohan Gandhi (grandson of the Mahatma) announced that they withdrew their support to G.G. Swell. Congress and the Communists supported Sharma *en bloc*. Swell's caste, religion or political programme had not changed, but his saying something nice about the BJP was enough to get him ostracized.

By contrast, in the administration, the army and the private sector, this quasi-McCarthyist taboo on any expression of Hindu identity or sympathy for Hindu Revivalism was never that strong, and in some quarters, it simply remained non-existent. However, the secularist hard core did man those sectors which control the information flow, and therefore the picture of Hindu nationalism among international India-watchers differed sharply from the opinions which common Indians had formed about it on the basis of their real-life experiences with it.

At the end of the period under consideration, even the core areas of secularist control started opening up somewhat to the winds of change. This became evident at the time of the 1996 elections and increased in proportion with the cracks appearing in the anti-BJP coalition led by Deve Gowda and then by Inder Kumar Gujral, when a surprisingly large number of media people and second-rank Congress politicians abandoned their tough anti-BJP talk, apparently for no better reason than that the BJP seemed set to take over after the next elections (which took place sooner than expected, in February 1998).

In some cases, this may be due to a genuine change of heart following the generally uncontroversial governance provided by the BJP in the states it had ruled in the preceding years, which suggested that the BJP was not such a monster after all. This impression was shared by the masses: "Then, there is a growing realization among the electorate, including a section of the minorities, that BJP's portrayal is somewhat exaggerated".[158] Others thought that the BJP had been a monster in the past (thus justifying their past anti-BJP crusades), but that the party had changed, that it "is endeavouring to recast Indian nationalism in another mould by going away from a narrow and retrograde definition of what constitutes the basis of the national community towards another, more open and flexible definition".[159] This was also the position taken by Mohiuddin Shah, a spokesman of the Kashmiri Muslim party National Conference, who said that the BJP "*was* a communal party. Now, it has softened its stand and may take up the national agenda".[160]

The professional India-watchers in the West have so far been slow to pick up this trend. When the BJP came to power very briefly in May 1996, a lonely James Clad reassured the Western readers that "the BJP will

[158]Yogesh Vajpeyi: "Confronting Contradictions", *Indian Express*, 22.1.1998.

[159]Dileep Padgaonkar: "India's defining moment: can BJP transcend itself?", *Times of India*, 29.12.1997.

[160]"NC, including Soz, to abstain from trust vote", *Indian Express*, 28.3.1998; emphasis added.

continue in India's secular path".[161] Otherwise, Atal Behari Vajpayee's accessions as Prime Minister in 1996 and 1998 were greeted with a strange silence. Here were the people who had been described in terms of Hitler and Khomeini, now they actually came to power in the world's largest democracy, a fledgling nuclear power, a giant of the next century, and nobody came forward to explain to the public just what this BJP stood for. After the 1998 elections, the Western media paid much more attention to Sonia Gandhi and her accession to the Congress presidency than to the BJP, as if not Vajpayee but the Italian widow had come at the helm of the nation. Perhaps they were embarrassed that their earlier alarmist writing about the BJP suddenly seemed so unrelated to the real world.

THE MARXIST FACTOR

So far, no one seems yet to have questioned the reliability of the privileged Indian sources of information which led to the extremely partisan reporting in the past decade. It is in a different context that Rajni Kothari, political scientist and a socialist himself, briefly described the relevant background development, viz. how under Indira Gandhi's regime (1966-77, 1980-84), the Left "did make a major effort at influencing not just the polity but also a number of scientific and educational institutions, a variety of government and semi-government committees, inner councils of the party and Parliament, a considerable cross-section of the mass media as well as important journals which they came to control. After all, in the Stalinist view of things the intellectual-scientific domain is extremely important. ... Meanwhile, the country also drifted more and more into the Soviet dragnet which had its local networks of individuals, research institutions and funding agencies which gradually forced many intellectuals and bureaucrats to fall in line."[162] Though now waning, this politicized background of the dominant Indian discourse on Hindu revivalism is extremely important to keep in mind when evaluating Indian claims about Hindu revivalism.

Kothari mentions Delhi University, Aligarh Muslim University (AMU) and of course Jawaharlal Nehru University (JNU) by name, but the

---

[161]James Clad: "The world ought to be able to live with Bharatiya Janata", *International Herald Tribune*, 22.5.1996.

[162]Rajni Kothari: "Dangers to democracy. The challenges from within", *Times of India*, 22.9.1995.

Indian Council of Historical Research would also deserve mention, as well as the key positions acquired by combative Marxists in the University Grants Commission, the Indian History Congress, the Indian Council of Social Science Research and other institutions; and this move to capture the intellectual sector obviously also extended to the media. The job of mapping out this Marxist bid for control of the intellectual, media and educational space, which has a history stretching from Nehru to Inder Kumar Gujral (who, as Prime Minister in 1996-97, nominated prominent Marxists including Romila Thapar in the selection committee of Doordarshan programmes),[163] remains to be done. For now, it will suffice to remind the readership that a lot of the information and analysis presently available about the Hindu revivalist movement is the fruit of deliberately politicized research programmes.

What this means in practice is not that books by JNU professors should henceforth be ignored, simply that they have to be handled with care and with constant alertness to their political background. Such vigilance is actually a standard requirement of any proper scholarship, and the only unusual thing here is that in the past decade so many scholars have neglected this rule when dealing with secondary accounts of Hindu revivalism.

The symmetry fallacy

Very often, misreporting or misinterpretation of data in the media is wholly unintentional. Correspondents distort the information not because they feel compelled to do so by their political convictions, but as a result of intellectual failings. One relatively innocent factor is a general tendency to mental laziness, which leads to a blind application of schemes from better-

---

[163]Until 1997, the overseers of programme selection were accountable to Parliament, but Gujral's committee was accountable only to the Executive, which was of course in sympathy with its own nominees. In an interview (*India Today*, 8.12.1997), the chairman of the freshly constituted *Prasâr Bhâratî* (= Broadcasting) Board, S.S. Gill, announced that he wanted to take action against the phenomenon of wildly popular religious TV serials, "this damn thing" as he called it. He would tolerate no dissent or interference: "We've been selected. Now it's our discretion and our judgement that has to prevail. Every serial on the air right now is going to be reviewed. If it doesn't come up to our standards it will be thrown out without ceremony." The statement was criticized by Shiv Charan Singh: "Should BBC or CNN show scriptural serials?", *Organiser*, 18.1.1998. Nothing came of Gill's plans, for a few weeks later, the Gujral Government fell, and the BJP-led Government restored parliamentary control.

known parts of the world to the Indian situation. A typical case is the assumption of *symmetry*, attributing the same motives and policies to both parties in the Indo-Pak or Hindu-Muslim conflict.

The most common mistaken presumption of symmetry is that between "Muslim Pakistan" and "Hindu India". Thus, a French commentator writes about the Partition: "But henceforth, there were two countries of the pure ones, purely Muslim Pakistan and, in spite of Nehru's profound secularism, Hindu India. Purely Hindu."[164] A Flemish commentator likewise sees British India partitioned into "a greater Hindu India and a smaller Muslim Pakistan who both saw their minorities as undesired intruders and opted for an archaic kind of purity".[165] In fact, India is by no means a Hindu state; it was not based on the refusal to co-exist with others, as Pakistan was; and it is not squeezing out its minorities, as Pakistan is. The best refutation is provided by the highly anti-symmetrical migration stream: the constant trickle of Hindu refugees from Pakistan and Bangladesh is not matched by a similar trickle of Muslim refugees from India, but by a vast movement of Muslim migrants from Bangladesh illegally settling in India.

For a less dramatic illustration of the symmetry fallacy, consider the fate of Salman Rushdie's 1995 novel *The Moor's Last Sigh*, a book attacking Bal Thackeray, leader of the Maharashtrian Hindu party Shiv Sena, and arguably also lampooning Hinduism as such.[166] Because of the symmetry fallacy, Indian and Western media predicted that Bal Thackeray would pronounce some kind of a fatwa against Rushdie, after the Ayatollah's example in the *Satanic Verses* case. Tim McGirk's article was mis-titled: "Rushdie satire infuriates Hindu extremists", for he could only

---

[164]Vladimir Razine: "La pureté, une sale maladie" (French: "Purity, a dirty disease"), *L'Evénement du Jeudi*, 12.1.1989.

[165]Paul Pelckmans: "Geen zondebokken voor de Moor", *Streven*, June 1996, p.527.

[166]The character *Raman Fielding* represents Bal Thackeray, the common denominator being that both last names were names of British novelists. *Thackeray* is an uncommon transcription of *Thakre*, so chosen because Bal's father was an admirer of nineteenth-century novelist William Makepeace Thackeray (who, incidentally, was greatly influenced by eighteenth-century novelist Henry Fielding). The very title *The Moor's Last Sigh* suggests a parallel between the situation in Mumbai and "the Moor's last sigh", meaning the final expulsion of the last Moorish ruler from Granada, Spain, in 1492, an event also known as "the tears of Boabdil" (when he was told by his mother to "cry like a woman for what you failed to defend like a man"). In other words, it obliquely imputes to the Shiv Sena the intention to expel the Muslims from India, after the Spanish example.

report that "there's no threat so far" according to the book's distributor, and that the Shiv Sena leadership had not seen the book yet; the rest was prediction and speculation.[167] And the predicted event never materialized: no bookshops were attacked, no copies of the book were burnt, no statement was made. Finally, journalists went and begged Thackeray for some comment. He replied laconically that he would have his secretary read the book and then maybe say something, maybe not.[168]

As for the BJP, its leader Atal Behari Vajpayee called the idea of banning the book "wrong", for the simple reason that "if you don't like a book, you are at liberty not to read it".[169] The most humourless comment was made by the Hindu Students' Forum of Britain, who called Rushdie "intellectually bankrupt" and concluded with a request to the British Government to let Rushdie arrange his own security rather than have it at taxpayers' expense.[170] And BJP economist Jay Dubashi poured out his contempt over Rushdie: "I do not know why Rushdie has to write such trash year after year. ... For the likes of Rushdie, India is not a country but a background for his books which rubbish India and the Indians. ... Those who cannot rise above the level of gutters are doomed to live in them."[171] But no call for a ban, even there. A mild customs ban was finally imposed by the Congress Government, reportedly because a dog in Rushdie's book was called *Jawaharlal*, but possibly also because it would not take chances with the Shiv Sena, considering the press "reports" about its "impending" retaliation.[172]

But the symmetry fallacy proved so strong that even after the fact, at

[167]Tim McGirk in *The Independent*, London, 29.8.1995. About the *Last Sigh* non-affair, see K. Elst: "Kroniek van een aangekondigde boekverbranding—die er niet kwam" (Dutch: "Chronicle of a book-burning foretold—which didn't take place"), *India* bimonthly (Brussels), March 1996, or K. Elst: foreword/postscript to Daniel Pipes: *The Rushdie Affair*, Indian reprint.

[168]An article reporting this was wrongly titled: "Thackeray seeks to stifle Rushdie's *Last Sigh*", *Indian Express*, 2.9.1995.

[169]Speaking to Swapan Dasgupta, as reported in S. Dasgupta: "Lessons in Tolerance", *Indian Express*, 17.9.1995.

[170]Quoted in S. Dasgupta: "Lessons in Tolerance", *Indian Express*, 17.9.1995.

[171]Jay Dubashi: "Mother India—Part II", *Organiser*, 15.10.1995.

[172]In December 1995, a group of intellectuals staged a demonstration to protest against the ban on *The Moor's Last Sigh*, which they failed to do in the case of an earlier ban on a Rushdie book. This was yet another case of asymmetry, as reader V.L. Dev pointed out in a letter (*Outlook*, 14.2.1996): "The intellectuals who ... read passages from *The Moor's Last Sigh* should now read some passages from *The Satanic Verses*. Indeed, they should protest against the 'mother of all bans'".

least one journalist maintained that Thackeray had followed in Khomeini's footsteps, and that Rushdie's book "was also prohibited by these [Hindu] fundamentalists, and they too threatened to murder him".[173] Other journalists have not written this explicitly, but by never correcting their initial predictions, they too have propagated the impression that Hindu nationalists are Khomeini-like book-burners.

Even when we dig up one case of actual Hindu book-banning, we find the symmetry thesis refuted. In one incident, the Shiv Sena did confiscate from the Mumbai news agents all copies of an issue of *India Today* in which Khushwant Singh had called the seventeenth-century freedom fighter Shivaji a "bastard", and it announced it would not let Khushwant Singh's books be sold. When Rushdie apologized and even reconverted to Islam, the Ayatollahs refused to show mercy, but when Khushwant Singh apologized to the fans of his "bastard", the affair was immediately closed, and bookstalls next to the Shiv Sena headquarters still sell *Khushwant Singh's Joke Book*.

Impact of the symmetry fallacy

In journalism, the symmetry fallacy leads to a systematic projection of bits of established "knowledge" about the already ill-understood phenomenon of militant Islam on to the total unknown of militant Hinduism. Thus, it is routinely alleged that the goal of Hindutva is a Hindu "theocratic state", a concept neatly defined in Islam but unknown in Hinduism. It is my considered opinion that the major part of media "background information" on Hindu revivalism consists in the purely deductive application of the symmetry fallacy, projecting half-digested ideas about Islam on to Hinduism.

The Sikhs, whose religion supposedly takes a midway position between Islam and Hinduism, also fall into place once the symmetry between Hindus and Muslims is assumed: during the Partition massacres, Hindus and Muslims killed each other "and the Sikhs, in between the two, were hit from both sides".[174] In reality, during the Partition massacres, the Sikhs functioned as arch-Hindus, favoured targets of Muslim fury in West Panjab and the most assiduous Muslim-slayers in East Panjab, with no Hindu-Sikh clashes in sight.

---

[173]Sus van Elzen: "India en Pakistan: het land was te groot", *Knack*, 13.8.1997. Like its title, "The country was too big", the article seeks to justify the Partition.

[174]Sus van Elzen: "India en Pakistan: het land was te groot", *Knack*, 13.8.1997.

A rather consequential effect of the symmetry fallacy is that the organized Hindu movement, like so many West-Asian Islamist groups, has been labelled "terrorist". Activists of the largest Hindu organization, the RSS, sometimes have visa problems because the security services of some countries have booked the RSS as "terrorist". Some scholars have also put it in writing that the RSS is "terrorist".[175] But they ought to get down to specifics: who are the secularist or Muslim leaders assassinated by the RSS? Where are the airplanes they hijacked or blew up? Whom did they kidnap for ransom or political concessions? These things have all been done by Sikh and Muslim separatists whom the Indian press refuses to label as "terrorists" (the approved term is "militants"), but it doesn't follow that Hindus must have behaved likewise.

Even in the most fundamental data concerning the Hindu-Muslim conflict, this symmetry fallacy plays a distortive role, for "Hindu identity" and "Muslim identity" are two very different concepts. To be a Hindu, it is not necessary to adhere to a specific belief, whereas belief is the defining condition of Muslim identity. More importantly, the Indian Muslim community was (except for a minority of descendants of invaders) carved out of the pre-existing Hindu society; the reverse does not apply. This has implications for a favourite type of anecdote in secularist writings, viz. instances of Hindu-Muslim syncretism, which are usually assumed to be instances of the two sister communities coming to meet each other half-way, and are therefore promoted among the religion-prone illiterate masses as, so to speak, "the poor man's secularism". In fact, the apparent symmetry is very superficial.

Thus, in an influential Congress plea for Hindu-Muslim unity which invokes the treasure of Hindu-Muslim syncretism, it is said: "The Hindus especially, already accustomed by their priests to all sorts of minor gods and goddesses, ... readily adopted into their pantheon and scheme of worship takiyas, maqbaras, dargahs and masjids. ... Millions of Musalmans to this day offer milk and eatables on the altar of Shitala, the goddess of small-pox, in villages, and many other Hindu shrines are worshipped by them."[176]

---

[175]E.g. S. Wolpert: *Tilak and Gokhale*, p.94.

[176]*Report of the Congress Committee of Enquiry into the Cawnpore Riots* (1931), reproduced in N.G. Barrier: *Roots of Communal Politics*, p.128. *Takîya*: Sufi hermitage; *maqbara*: grave, mausoleum; *dargâh*: a Sufi's "court" turned into a memorial after his death; *masjid*: mosque.

The Hindus worshipping at Sufi shrines have *adopted* such Muslim sites *into* their pantheon of venerable objects, and no Hindu priest is haranguing them about it because Hinduism has no doctrine excluding particular objects from veneration, and also because in many such cases, the Muslim buildings enumerated are known or believed to have replaced demolished Hindu temples, the underlying original object of veneration. By contrast, the Muslims worshipping donkey-borne goddess *Shîtalâ* have simply *failed to outgrow* this Hindu practice, which was an integral part of the religious life of that one ancestor who agreed to convert to Islam, a practice which remained in the family out of habit even though the convert abjured it upon conversion by pronouncing the Islamic creed ("There is no god but Allah"). Sacrificing on the altar of a Hindu goddess is blatantly in conflict with the Islamic doctrine of monotheism, which is why Islamic *Tablîgh* workers are actively trying to weed it out.[177]

If you want to understand Hindu revivalism, equating it with the "corresponding" phenomenon in Christianity or Islam is not going to help, on the contrary. Neither should we rely on the application of universal theories, which could only be universal if they are based on an exhaustive empirical study of *all* the phenomena covered, i.e. of the "fundamentalisms" of *all* religions, including the Hindu one. So, before or instead of assuming a common denominator for Hindu and other revivalisms, let us make a factual study of this one movement, regardless of its eventual symmetries and differences with other movements elsewhere.

Ignoring the Hindu voice

One of the original points about the present study is that I will actually quote Hindu revivalist sources when trying to get an idea of the Hindu revivalist position. In writing about India, it is all too common to starkly ignore the Hindu voice. Among Western authors, this disdain for Hindus is very robust, so far unaffected by all the anti-Eurocentric soul-searching of recent years.[178] In the Asian Studies departments in Western universities,

---

[177]*Tablîgh*: "propaganda", viz. to islamize nominal Muslims, to make them replace lingering non-Islamic customs with a purely Islamic lifestyle. See for example, Maulana Wahiduddin Khan: *Tabligh Movement*.

[178]For some examples (other than those given here) of the disdain with which Hindus are treated without being given a proper hearing, see K. Elst: *Update on the Aryan Invasion Debate*, pp.52-5.

there is a remarkable contrast between the political sympathy of the staff in the Chinese and Islamic sections for their study domains and the sharp hostility for Hinduism (and for India to the extent that it is the current political embodiment of Hindu civilization) among the India experts.[179] The only Hinduism which they like is museum Hinduism; any Hinduism that displays a will to survive is treated with the same horror that would be aroused if a mummy were to show signs of life.

Consider for example, the contempt for Hindu authors, among Westerners and some anglicized Indians, in the case of the topic "criticism of Mahatma Gandhi". A great majority of the Indian population and of Gandhi's fellow Congressmen were Hindus. One would therefore expect some of his critics also to have been Hindus. And effectively: Sri Aurobindo was ever sarcastic about Gandhi, Swami Shraddhananda was in mutual conflict with him in 1922-26, Veer Savarkar attacked his policies in his capacity of HMS president (1937-43), and Gandhi's murderer Nathuram Godse, undisputably his most hard-hitting critic, formulated a detailed critique during his defence speech in court.[180] Yet, not one of these Hindu revivalist critics of Gandhi is even mentioned in B.R. Nanda's much-acclaimed book purportedly dealing with Gandhi's critics, *Gandhi and His Critics*.

The Hindu voice is ignored in all kinds of debate. It is often absent in general presentations of comparative religion, very common in our multiculturalist days, where the Jewish view of a given topic is presented by a Jew, the Islamic one by a Muslim, etc.,—and the Hindu one by an Indologist, mostly a Western Christian or agnostic.[181] It is even muzzled to a large extent when the discussion specifically concerns the Hindu revivalist movement itself. Thus, an article by Antony Copley about the Hindutva inroads into the notion of secularism quotes profusely from writings by declared critics of Hindutva like Mushirul Hasan, Praful Bidwai and Sarvepalli Gopal, but of its 64 footnotes, not one is a direct

[179]Thus, a spokesman of Leiden university's institute for Islamic studies (ISIM) projects as the institute's social goal, "to debunk the myth of the Islamic threat", according to the cover-story by Marion van 't Verlaat: "De mythe van het islamitisch gevaar ontkrachten", in *Mare, Leids Universitair Weekblad*, 13.1.2000. Ever heard of an Indian studies institute which went public with a programme of "refuting the myth of the Hindu revivalist threat"?

[180]Published as N. Godse: *Why I Assassinated Mahatma Gandhi*.

[181]E.g. the *Journal of Dharma*, 1997/4, is devoted to the topic of law in the different religions, all represented by their own spokesmen except for the section on Hinduism, which is contributed by a Christian.

reference to a Hindutva source.[182] Only four references claim to reproduce the words of Hindutva spokesmen, and they have been taken from secondary, non-Hindutva sources: two from newspaper reports (and we know how journalistic accounts are often less than accurate), and two from Bruce Graham's standard work *Hindu Nationalism*.

Rajeev Bhargava's book discussing various criticisms of Indian secularism (though occasioned by an argument launched by a Christian)[183] naturally deals mostly with the perceived Hindu "threat to secularism". Yet, its eight-page bibliography contains *not a single* Hindu revivalist source.[184] The chapter on Hinduism in Niels Nielsen's survey *Fundamentalism, Mythos and World Religions* quotes all manner of outside sources, from Hegel to the *New York Times*, but only two of its 24 references are from a Hindu revivalist spokesman, both pretty old hat (by M.S. Golwalkar, d. 1973), and both borrowed through secondary sources.[185] It is possible to be an acclaimed expert on "Hindu fundamentalism" without having touched a single publication by a spokesman of that movement.

David Ludden has edited a book, published in India as *Making India Hindu* and in the USA as *Contesting the Nation* (1996), which contains twelve expert contributions on Hindu "communalism". The works included in the combined bibliography may have been consulted by all twelve or by just one of the contributors, but those missing have certainly been overlooked or ignored by all twelve experts. While containing ten titles by Asghar Ali Engineer, a declared campaigner against Hindutva, it contains just one by otherwise prolific and very influential Hindu writers like Balraj Madhok, H.V. Seshadri and Arun Shourie, and one BJP publication—but not a single BJP resolution or speech by its presidents, no HMS or RSS resolution or manifesto, and no book or article by seminal authors like Ram Swarup and Sita Ram Goel. Its basis in primary sources is extremely slender, and most quotations are from earlier academic Hindutva-watchers and from Indian sources openly hostile to the movement which they purport to study.

In the South Asia section of his book on "religious nationalism", Mark

---

182Antony Copley: "Secularism Reconsidered: from Gandhi to Ayodhya", *Contemporary South Asia*, 1993, 2 (1), pp.47-65.

183Ashis Nandy: "An anti-secularist manifesto", *Seminar*, October 1985, and other publications of his.

184Rajeev Bhargava, ed.: *Secularism and Its Critics*.

185Niels Nielsen: *Fundamentalism, Mythos and World Religions*, p.111, n.13 and n.15.

Juergensmeyer presents Sikh separatism and Lankan Buddhist nationalism through a number of contemporary spokesmen, some of whom were personally interviewed by the author; by contrast, Hindu nationalism with its immensely more numerous personnel and publications, is presented through just two primary quotations, and antiquated ones at that (by V.D. Savarkar, from 1923 and 1939), plus secondary material by neutral and hostile outsiders.[186]

The Ayodhya evidence debate (about whether there had really been a temple at the site of the controversial Babri Masjid before the latter was built) provides an example of wide complicity in muzzling the Hindu voice.[187] To my knowledge, not one Western scholar has covered the debate on the basis of primary material, all of them merely relaying the anti-temple account of partisan Indian authors. Thus, Brian K. Smith bases his account of the evidence debate wholly on an article from the Communist fortnightly *Frontline*, giving the game away by relaying some of the consensual canards circulating among secularist polemicists, for example that ASI director-general B.B. Lal had "found absolutely no evidence of any pre-existing temple at the site" (in fact, Lal had found the bases of a pillared building which either may or may not have been a Hindu temple, and later came out in support of the more recent and more decisive archaeological findings which Smith's source prematurely, and till today unprovenly, dismisses as fraudulent).[188]

To get an idea of the treatment of the subject by partisan Indian sources, consider this instance. Asghar Ali Engineer writes on the cover of his *Babri Masjid Ram Janmabhoomi Controversy* (1990): "Future generations will have a right to know what the controversy was about", but then takes care to include only a few token statements for the Hindu side which are either on peripheral aspects of the debate or belong to the clumsier variety of Hindutva polemic.

---

[186]M. Juergensmeyer: *The New Cold War?*, Ch.4.

[187]I am not discussing the Ayodhya controversy in this book, for I have briefly done so elsewhere, see K. Elst: "The Ayodhya Debate", in G. Pollet: *Indian Epic Values*, pp.21-42; a comprehensive analysis of the no-temple argumentation is forthcoming. For some recent additional information, see N.S. Rajaram: *Profiles in Deception. Ayodhya and the Dead Sea Scrolls*.

[188]Brian K. Smith: "Re-envisioning Hinduism and evaluating the Hindutva movement", *Religion* (Academic Press, London), 1996/2, p.124, based on Sukumar Muralidharan: "Scientific fraud: the 'kar seva' archaeology", *Frontline*, 15.1.1993.

He repeats the same exercise in his sequel *Politics of Confrontation* (1992): a few token pro-Hindu articles are included, hand-picked for harmlessness (whether by incompetence or by focusing on a peripheral aspect of the controversy), but not those on the central question of the historical evidence, least of all the official presentation of evidence by the Vishva Hindu Parishad prepared during the government-sponsored scholars' debate in December-January 1990-91.[189] Juxtaposing the temple-and-demolition evidence with the counter-argumentation would have drawn attention to the fact that the latter consisted only in attempts to sow doubts concerning some of the pro-temple testimonies; not in any positive indications for a no-temple and no-demolition scenario (as if the anti-temple party had been asked to sit in judgement upon evidence submitted to it by pro-temple supplicants, when in fact both parties were in the arena as equal contenders, both expected to prove their own position).[190] The net outcome of the debate was that the pro-temple team of scholars had defeated the no-temple party fair and square, which the latter implicitly conceded by staying away after an embarrassingly uneven session (24 January 1991); but don't expect to find this information in Engineer's publications.

Incidentally, this concealment job by Engineer and by the entire secularist academic establishment amounts to an unwitting admission of the outcome of the Ayodhya polemic: if a schoolboy comes home on Proclamation Day and remains conspicuously evasive about his exam results, you don't have to actually see his report to know what those results are like. This may be an understandable ploy in the case of a losing contestant, but not in that of scholars pretending to be neutral reporters on a contest. To comment on such manipulation, we might take inspiration

---

[189]VHP: *The Great Evidence* (1991); also published by Voice of India as *History vs. Casuistry*.

[190]The only formal attempt to take the pro-temple evidence apart was R.S. Sharma *et al.*: *Historians' Report to the Nation* (1991). The authors represented the Babri Masjid Action Committee during the government-sponsored scholars' debate in 1990-91; their booklet contains no evidence, it is merely a comment on a selection of the arguments presented by the Hindu side. Much is also being made by secularists of Richard Eaton: *Essays on Islam and Indian History* (2000) but this merely tries to explain the acknowledged fact of temple destructions in general as the result of non-religious factors. Even if the argument had not been wholly unconvincing, it would still have no effect on the evidence regarding the specific case of Ayodhya.

from Engineer's own words on the same cover: "It is not only violence which has to be condemned but also distortion of history and intellectual dishonesty."

Similarly, Gyanendra Pandey, in an article titled "The New Hindu History", claims to discuss the version of history spread by "the Ayodhya movement", but actually keeps its official statements on history along with the supportive expert opinions (by academics of his own rank)[191] out of view.[192] Instead, he concentrates on a few Hindi pamphlets by Hindu traditionalists with no training in history whatsoever, who rely on local traditions, which of course are hardly "new".[193] In another article, Pandey repeats the same exercise: strictly leaving out any mention of genuine historians, he attacks "Hindu historiography" in the shape of the same Hindi pamphlets and also one "Hindu historian", who turns out to be non-historian and journalist Girilal Jain (whose quoted statement, which Pandey ridicules, happens to be correct).[194] To write one piece after another about "Hindu historiography" without quoting or even mentioning a single Hindu historian: Pandey can get away with it because in Indian academe, this is the done thing.

Most consequentially, the Penguin book *Anatomy of a Confrontation* edited by S. Gopal, for most foreign India-watchers the *only* Ayodhya book within reach, carefully keeps Hindu contributions to the debate out of the picture. Thus, friend and foe have repeated again and again that the Vishva Hindu Parishad had a list of 3,000 mosques standing on the sites of

---

[191]E.g. Harsh Narain: *The Ayodhya Temple-Mosque Dispute*, and R. Nath: *The Baburi Masjid of Ayodhya*.

[192]G. Pandey: "The New Hindu History", in J. McGuire, P. Reeves & H. Brasted: *Politics of Violence*, pp.143-58; an earlier version was published as "Modes of History Writing. New Hindu History of Ayodhya", in *Economic and Political Weekly*, 18.6.1994.

[193]This is not to say that their claim that dozens of battles have been waged in defence of Ayodhya during centuries past, ridiculed by Pandey (in J. McGuire et al.: *Politics of Violence*, p.147), is altogether spurious. These folk traditions may have a core of truth in them. Compared with Europe and China, India kept on using far more perishable writing materials until the nineteenth century, and oral traditions are sometimes the only source of information for a period which has left only little documentary evidence.

[194]G. Pandey: *Hindus and Others*, pp.9-10. Girilal Jain is quoted as claiming that the disputed site had been known as *Janmasthân* since well before the British period. This is well-attested by a number of eighteenth-century sources (not to speak of the twelfth-century inscription claimed to have been found at the site in December 1992), see Harsh Narain: *The Ayodhya Temple-Mosque Dispute*.

(and often built with materials from) demolished temples.[195] One would expect such a key document in such an earth-shaking controversy to be discussed threadbare by historians, but I invite the reader to go through the scholarly literature on the Ayodhya affair and locate even a single discussion of this list. In the vast majority of articles and books on the subject, it does not even figure in the bibliography.

Blacking out Hindutva self-expression is a matter of deliberate policy: "After the Babri structure came down, Shri N. Ram thundered at a conference in Delhi that the print media owed it to the nation as much as to itself to black out fully statements and activities of the Hindutva brigade."[196] But it is one thing to do so for a Marxist editor in his own newspaper, and quite another for scholars to do so in academic publications purporting to study Hindutva ideology.

Numerous written attempts to explain what lies behind the Hindu upsurge in 1989-92 have cast their searchlight everywhere except at the explicit self-explanation of the movement itself. Hindu activists are treated like animals in a zoo: to know more about them, you can read the signboard in front of their cages, written by real human beings, but don't expect those dumb creatures to speak for themselves. The abnormality of this treatment of Hindu revivalist thought in academic publications may be grasped more clearly if we compare it with the treatment given to Islamist activists. Muslim communalists themselves are invited to do the quoting, and to act as competent interpreters of not only their own but also their opponents' viewpoints. Let us mention some well-known examples.

Asghar Ali Engineer is one of the most frequently quoted authorities on "Hindu communalism". But what is his own involvement? He is director of the *Institute of Islamic Studies* and calls his own position quite openly "an Islamic point of view".[197] He is welcome to his point of view,

---

[195]The list of temple-mosques is included in A. Shourie, S.R. Goel et al.: *Hindu Temples, What Happened to Them*, vol.1. The number given there is actually "around 2,000" (cover text), a numerical detail which allows you to separate those who have read the book from those who merely put it in their bibliographies on the basis of secondary sources which have also neglected to read it, e.g. Brian K. Smith: "Re-envisioning Hinduism", *Religion*, 1996/2, p.124, mentions "a list of 3000 sites"...

[196]Hemant Hemmady: "Intolerance of the champions of freedom of speech", *Organiser*, 9.2.1997.

[197]E.g. in A.A. Engineer: "Problems of Communal Harmony: an Islamic Point of View", *Mainstream*, 18.1.1986. Chairman Mao never called himself anything except a Communist, yet Western journalists were adamant in claiming that he was not a real Communist, just an "agrarian reformer"; likewise, an avowedly "Islamic" viewpoint is relayed as "secular", aptly indicating the shift in meaning of the latter term.

but the record shows that a Hindu counterpart of his would never be quoted or interviewed as an expert, merely questioned as a suspect, as an object of investigation rather than a subject of discourse. When accomplished Hindu intellectuals find reasons to support this or that Hindu revivalist cause, they are not listened to or invited to give their expert clarification. Only their name is cited, not as a competent reference, but as illustration for the assertion that "the middle-class is getting contaminated with the communal virus".

But Mr. Engineer, at least, is something of a reformer, a progressive within the limits imposed by Islam. By contrast, Syed Shahabuddin is one of India's most outstanding, even proverbial, fanatics. He took a leadership role in all the recent campaigns of Islamist mobilisation, including the Shah Bano case, the Babri Masjid movement and the demand for communal job reservations.[198] He personally unleashed the *Satanic Verses* affair. Yet, it is claimed that Shahabuddin is "widely recognized to have strong secular leanings".[199] A fine scholar like Gérard Heuzé calls him a "liberal".[200] Perhaps he was misled by the fact that Shahabuddin, unlike most *Ulemâ*, speaks English and even manages some voguish jargon like "post-modernism" (appropriated as a trump card against modernity with its inherent questioning of pre-modern belief systems like Islam). But if Shahabuddin is a liberal, how should we imagine Heuzé's idea of an extremist?

Likewise, a contribution by Syed Shahabuddin is included in a leading Leftist weekly and another one in a respected political science monthly in India.[201] A leading American Islam-watcher, John Esposito, has edited a

[198]Shahabuddin's demand is actually for "universal reservation" (with, after the BJP's plan of giving reservations to women, "an inbuilt quota for women within each quota"), as stated in his editorial: "Reservation in legislatures for women—at best a political gimmick and at worst an elitist manoeuvre", *Muslim India*, Oct. 1996, pp.434-36. Universal reservation means the generalization of the communal principle, and approaches the corporate system of representation favoured by Benito Mussolini.

[199]Z. Sardar and M.W. Davies: *Distorted Imagination* (on the Rushdie affair), p.186.

[200]G. Heuzé: *Où va l'Inde moderne?*, p.8.

[201]Syed Shahabuddin: "Should Muslim Indians remain silent?", *Mainstream*, 17.2.1996; and in *Politics India*, November 1997. Remark the expression "Muslim Indians", which the editor of *Muslim India* uses in preference to "Indian Muslims". For the RSS, this is a constant source of irritation ("anti-national!"), because it puts "Muslim" first. However, Shahabuddin's expression describes the people concerned as essentially "Indians", who are additionally qualified as "Muslim"; if anything, it is the more common expression "Indian Muslims" which in that framework of thought would have to be questioned as "anti-national".

strictly academic book titled *Islam in Asia. Religion, Politics and Society.* The part on Indian Muslims and their struggle with the Hindu majority is written by an American together with, yes, Syed Shahabuddin.[202] Let me clarify that I am not pleading for an embargo against contributions by Shahabuddin or anyone else; I am only drawing attention to the contrast between the treatment which he receives and the exclusion which has struck leading Hindu intellectuals like Arun Shourie during the period under consideration.[203]

Likewise, when the BBC wanted to do a documentary serial on Islam, it commissioned Akbar S. Ahmed, known for positions which are, at the very least, polemical.[204] A secularist reviewer notices "Ahmed's fall from scholarly neutrality", for example: "He hates Muslims with non-Muslim wives, who drink whisky and whose children have Hindu names. ... And he is all praise for Imam Bukhari and Syed Shahabuddin", India's proverbial Muslim communalists.[205] Again, Akbar Ahmed is entirely welcome to his opinions, but the point is: it is simply unthinkable that the BBC would entrust its programmes on Hinduism to Ahmed's Hindu counterparts.

A perverse selectiveness

When Hindu revivalist sources are quoted at all, preference is given to sources or statements which put the movement in a bad light. The most frequently quoted Hindu nationalist publication in the secondary literature is RSS leader Guru Golwalkar's *We, Our Nationhood Defined*, a rambling

---

[202]Syed Shahabuddin and Theodore Paul Wright, Jr.: "India: Muslim Minority Politics and Society", in John Esposito, ed.: *Islam in Asia*, pp.152-76. A recent and valuable contribution by T.P. Wright is: "The BJP/Shiv Sena Coalition and the Muslim Minority in Maharashtra: the Interface of Foreign and Domestic Conflict", *Journal of South-Asian and Middle-Eastern Studies*, winter 1998, pp.41-50.

[203]It is only in 1997 that, under a changing political configuration, a symptomatic change took place: the respected publishing-house HarperCollins (Delhi) offered to republish Shourie's latest five books as a glossy set as well as in paperback. As a consequence, these dissident books became widely available, even in railway station bookstalls throughout India.

[204]The serial was based on Akbar S. Ahmed's book *Discovering Islam* (1988), and both versions practise apologetics, sometimes to a comical extent, e.g. in the documentary, he proved Islam's spirit of synthesis by showing that in the Aya Sophia in Istanbul (which he mistranslates as "city of Islam", p.87, actually from Greek *eis tèn polin*, "to the city"), Christian mural paintings had not been removed, "merely" painted over. On the TV serial was based yet another book by Ahmed: *Living Islam* (1993).

[205]Parsa Venkateshwar Rao jr.: "The apology of clichés" (a review of Akbar Ahmed: *Living Islam*), *Indian Express*, 27.6.1993.

pamphlet written in 1938, a juvenile mistake which Golwalkar himself withdrew from circulation in 1948, and which the vast majority of living Hindu nationalists has never read. Hindutva-watchers just can't get enough of it: the majority of Golwalkar quotations in scholarly literature is taken from that pamphlet, though he was not the RSS supremo at the time (while his numerous later statements made when he was, are given much less attention) and though he himself later repudiated it.

Practically every paper on Hindutva quotes this line of Golwalkar's: "From this standpoint, sanctioned by the experience of shrewd old nations, the foreign races in Hindusthan must either adopt the Hindu culture and language, must learn to respect and hold in reverence Hindu religion, must entertain no idea but those of the glorification of the Hindu race and culture, i.e. of the Hindu nation, and must lose their separate existence to merge in the Hindu race; or may stay in the country, wholly subordinated to the Hindu Nation, claiming nothing, deserving no privileges, far less any preferential treatment—not even citizen's rights."[206] This is the most-quoted Hindutva statement by far.[207]

Thus, Niels Nielsen's chapter on Hindu fundamentalism offers only two actual Hindutva quotations, and one of these is the inevitable Golwalkar line. In Nielsen's case, the quotation is made even worse by leaving out the crucial term "or":[208] Golwalkar gives the minorities two options, either glorifying Hinduism *or* staying on as a kind of *zimmî*s, second-class residents without citizen's rights; but in Nielsen's rendering, they lose even that choice and will *in every case* fail to get citizen's rights.[209]

With or without such manipulations, it is this type of pre-independence statement, long forgotten by the Hindutva activists themselves, which are all over the place in the otherwise limited quotation part of purportedly scholarly papers on Hindutva. By contrast, in their

---

[206]M.S. Golwalkar: *We*, pp.47-8/pp.55-6. Where two page numbers are given for the same quotation from this book, the first refers to the original 1939 edition, the second to the 1947 reprint of the second edition.

[207]E.g. N. Ram: "The fascist basis of Hindutva", *Observer of Business and Politics*, 19.1.1993; Sitaram Yechury: *Pseudo-Hinduism Exposed*, CPI(M), Delhi 1993, p.2-3, and "What is this Hindu Rashtra?", *Frontline*, 12.3.1993, or p.14 of its republication as a separate booklet: *What Is this Hindu Rashtra?*, Frontline, Madras 1993.

[208]Niels Nielsen: *Fundamentalism, Mythos and World Religions*, p.111, n.13 and n.15.

[209]*Zimmî*: non-Muslim tolerated and protected by an Islamic state in exchange for payment of toleration tax and compliance to a list of disabilities, e.g. not criticising Islam, not bearing arms, etc.

official training programme, all activists of the RSS, BJP and related organizations, i.e. millions of people, today, are taught Deendayal Upadhyaya's philosophy of "Integral Humanism", formulated in his 1965 booklet *Integral Humanism*, and now the official party ideology of the BJP. Yet, discussion of Integral Humanism in the whole scholarly literature on Hindutva does not exceed a few pages. And even these few pages don't really amount to a "discussion", merely a mention, for example, the eleven lines which Bruce Graham devotes to Integral Humanism are about its place in Deendayal Upadhyaya's career, not its contents.[210]

Sometimes the Hindu voice is relayed, but only its basest register. When you want the Marxist viewpoint on a social conflict, you interview a party leader or quote from a study by some Marxist academic, rather than the trade-union militant on strike using foul language against the big fat capitalists. When you want the Muslim viewpoint on the Hindu-Muslim conflict, you get interviews with or invited contributions by articulate Muslim intellectuals like Rafiq Zakaria or Asghar Ali Engineer. By contrast, in writings about Hindu revivalism, the spotlights are as much as possible on the rumour mills (and of course, false rumours about girls being raped by members of the other community do play an evil role in the genesis of riots, on both sides) and on the irresponsible speeches by firebrand orators like Sadhvi Ritambhara.

Psychiatrist and secularist Sudhir Kakar devotes a paper to a famous or notorious speech by Sadhvi Ritambhara, given in Hyderabad in April 1991 and heard all over India on audio-cassette.[211] This young nun counted as the proverbial spokeswoman of militant Hinduism. In 1996, she stood trial in Delhi under Article 153 (A) of the Indian Penal Code (which punishes speech insulting other religions or communities) for a speech she gave in Delhi in late 1990, reportedly for the words: "We should be ready to do or die for the establishment of a Hindu state."[212] Finally, the court "acquitted [her] of the charge of making inflammatory speeches and

[210]Bruce Graham: *Hindu Nationalism and Indian Politics*, p.86.

[211]Sudhir Kakar: "The construction of a new Hindu identity", in K. Basu & S. Subrahmanyam: *Unravelling the Nation*, pp.204-35. His discussion of Sadhvi Ritambhara's famous speech makes up the section titled "The virtuous virago", pp.216-30. Off stage, Sadhvi Ritambhara makes a serene and friendly impression (as a renunciate should), as when I met her at the Vishva Hindu Parishad national conference venue in Mumbai, December 1995.

[212]"Judgement on Ritambhara reserved till Tuesday", *Patriot*, 10.2.1996. See also "Order reserved in Ritambhara's case", *Times of India*, 10.2.1996. The expression "do or die" was popularized by Mahatma Gandhi when he started the Quit India agitation in 1942.

whipping up communal sentiments, passing strictures on the Central Government for instituting a politically motivated case against her."[213] It was neither the first nor the last time that Hindu nationalists were saved by the courts.

Meanwhile, Sadhvi Ritambhara is a favourite quotable source. In the London *Times*, the allegation that the VHP is a "sinister influence" which "threaten[s] India's 120 million Muslims with ethnic cleansing", is proven with a speech by Sadhvi Ritambhara: "Playing on Hindu reverence for sacred cows, she shocked her simple rural audiences with tales of Muslims slaughtering the animals merely to please the palates of Arab sheiks."[214] The only commentators cited in the full-page article are Romila Thapar and Asghar Ali Engineer, both declared crusaders against Hindutva, but no Hindutva spokesmen of their level of sophistication were contacted. Incidentally, it is an easily verifiable fact that Indian Muslims do slaughter cows (along with sheep and goats) to commemorate Abraham's sacrifice, and it is also well-established that India exports beef to the Arabian peninsula, though the slaughterers are not exclusively Muslim.

Sudhir Kakar treats us to some interesting quotations, for example: "And as for unity with our Muslim brothers, we say: 'Brother, we are willing to eat sevian (sweet noodles) at your house to celebrate Eid but you do not want to play with colours with us on Holi. We hear your calls to prayer along with our temple bells, but you object to our bells. How can unity ever come about? The Hindu faces this way, the Muslim the other. The Hindu writes from left to right, the Muslim from right to left. The Hindu prays to the rising sun, the Muslim faces the setting sun when praying. ... The Hindu keeps a moustache, the Muslim shaves the upper lip. Whatever the Hindu does, it is the Muslim's religion to do its opposite. ... If you want to do everything contrary to the Hindu, then the Hindu eats with his mouth: you should do the opposite in this matter too."[215]

Very colourful indeed, though in naked violence potential it is certainly matched by the calls to *jihad* frequently heard from Islamist rostrums. But more importantly, it remains questionable whether the

---

[213]"Ritambhara let off, strictures on Centre", *Indian Express*, 15.2.1996. The verdict is reproduced in full in S.R. Goel: *Freedom of Expression*, pp.39-46.

[214]John Zubrzycki: "India's powerbrokers scuttle to fend off fundamentalists", *Sunday Times*, 12.5.1996.

[215]Sudhir Kakar: "The construction of a new Hindu identity", in K. Basu and S. Subrahmanyam: *Unravelling the Nation*, p.230.

Sadhvi's idiosyncrasies justify the exclusion of more competent representatives of the movement from Kakar's consideration. It is a highly significant detail that the speech does not figure in Sudhir Kakar's bibliography: he had to make do with the audio-tape, for the speech has never been printed. The main business of the RSS publishing-house Suruchi Prakashan is to publish the speeches of the Sangh Parivar spokesmen, yet it did not consider Sadhvi Ritambhara worthy of this honour. Even so, in spite of the Sadhvi's junior position in the Sangh Parivar, it is her speech, and not the published speeches of the acknowledged and representative leaders, which Kakar singles out to illustrate "the construction of a new Hindu identity".

As Sudhir Kakar certainly knows, leading Hindu revivalist authors oppose the shrill twist which such people give to their cause, e.g. Swapan Dasgupta writes: "To hold today's Muslims responsible for the sins of past Muslim emperors is about as obscene as holding the German youth guilty of the depredations of Hitler. Sadhvi Ritambhara may rave and rant about the need to fix the progenies of Babar once and for all, but this is a view exclusive to the minuscule lunatic fringe."[216] Meanwhile, outside observers can only guess what the Sadhvi's Muslim counterparts are saying from their pulpits, for a Rafiq Zakaria is never placed in the position of having to distance himself from their rhetoric, which is never highlighted at the expense of his own more diplomatic formulations of the Muslim viewpoint.[217] Readers who have no direct access to the Indian press, will also remain uninformed about what Swapan Dasgupta and other capable spokesmen have to say, for their arguments are kept out of sight in the literature on Hindu revivalism.

To Hindus, I would say that they have no cause for complaint, as it is in their own power to stop giving food to this unbalanced reporting by terminating the shrill propaganda which their own activists *à la* Ritambhara make. But to observers, I could only point out that their reporting is indeed unbalanced.

---

[216]Swapan Dasgupta, quoted with approval by Rafiq Zakaria: "The Indian Muslims: Are They Really Pampered?", *Illustrated Weekly of India*, 2.1.1993.

[217]When asked questions about Sadhvi Ritambhara, L.K. Advani said (quoted in *Muslim India*, Dec. 1996, p.554): "It is not fair! It is like asking Deve Gowda about Taslimuddin." Mohammed Taslimuddin, MP after defeating Shahabuddin for the Kishanganj seat in 1996, could indeed serve as a Muslim counterpart to Sadhvi Ritambhara; but he was made a Minister in Deve Gowda's Government, while she was never made a Minister in any BJP Government.

Off on a tangent

Imagine the following irritating experience. You are having breakfast, with the radio news programme in the background. The newsreader introduces an item which interests you: some new development has taken place, and he begins his story about it with an introductory sentence mentioning the topic. You start to listen attentively, but then, some family member has also heard what the story is about, and starts giving his opinion about it. You want to hear the new facts of the matter and postpone discussion till afterwards, but your relative cannot wait, and replaces the flow of hard information with a much less interesting flow of comment, which at any rate could have waited until after all the information was in.

That, more or less, is how contemporary Hindu revivalism is studied. Instead of hearing out the whole story, many observers are satisfied with just the first fragment of hard information and from that point onwards, they replace the facts with extrapolations and opinions. It is not that they ignore the facts about Hindu revivalists altogether; but they take just enough primary material to establish their credibility, then go off on a tangent and develop theories which are only dimly related to reality.

Given the limited and strangely selective use of primary source material, it is no surprise that in the secondary literature on Hindu revivalism, you come across claims and allegations which are not just wrong, but are even the diametrical opposite of reality. Among numerous inconsequential errors, I may cite the claim that "the BJP's smashing electoral success in 1991 was due partly to the tragic assassination of the Congress party's main candidate, Rajiv Gandhi".[218] On the contrary: the BJP's electoral breakthrough was curtailed by the assassination, which created a sympathy wave and a much better result for Congress in the states which went to the polls after the assassination than in those which had gone before that.

Quite often, these "errors" are not inconsequential, but pertain to the fundamental nature of the Hindu revivalist phenomenon. Thus, it is alleged in *Time* magazine that in 1947, RSS members "accused Mohandas Gandhi of favoring Muslims through his policy of egalitarianism".[219] This

---

[218]Mark Juergensmeyer: *The New Cold War? Religious Nationalism Confronts the Secular State*, p.88.

[219]Sudip Mazumdar: "A taste of power", *Time*, 27.5.1996.

clever amalgamation of Gandhiji's pro-Muslim policies with his apparently egalitarian anti-untouchability policies obscures the twin facts that the Hindutva movement was against the former and in favour of the latter. What Hindutva critics held against Gandhi's Muslim policy was precisely that it did *not* treat Hindu and Muslim citizens as equals, but conceded ever more privileges to the Muslims (for example, his last-ditch proposal to Jinnah to accept Muslim/non-Muslim parity in parliament, making one Muslim equal to three non-Muslims). But since egalitarianism is deemed a good thing, the fiercely anti-Hindutva weekly judged it more opportune to twist things a bit.

When something good has to be reported for which the BJP could take credit, the political responsibility for the reported development is generally omitted. Thus, in 1998 it was reported that air pollution in Delhi had substantially decreased, the role of the Delhi government was acknowledged, but very rare were the foreign media which also added that the government in the preceding term had been formed by the BJP. When the BJP state government of Uttar Pradesh acted against corruption, dismissing corrupt civil servants, this was reported as the kind of policy which India badly needed, but the name of the ruling party was not given.[220]

For an example at the level of political science, it is alleged in a much-quoted Marxist publication on the RSS: "The *frequent* representations of Hindutva as a spontaneous mass movement in search of Hindu identity naturalizes and suppresses a whole history of meticulously organized efforts towards a Hindu Rashtra."[221] Actually, no one is deliberately "suppressing" the "whole history of meticulous efforts", least of all the RSS itself, which prides itself on its "efforts".

To my knowledge, no important commentator has ever denied or completely overlooked the decisive role of the organizational preparation by the RSS. For, not only do Indian academics impute total responsibility for the Hindu "communalization" ("awakening") to the RSS, de facto denying the role of local "spontaneous" initiative in constructive work as

---

[220]Thus for example in *De Standaard*, 28.10.1998.

[221]Tapan Basu *et al.*: *Khaki Shorts, Saffron Flags*, p.1; emphasis added. In the same vein about religious riots: "A common fallacy is that these passions are 'natural' and that the violent struggle is an explosion of pent-up feelings", according to Peter van der Veer: *Religious Nationalism*, p.7.

well as in riots. Even the RSS itself never depicted Hindu mass demonstrations as "spontaneous"; quite to the contrary, it always emphasizes the crucial role of its own long-term organizational work.[222]

By the way, Marxists who know the history of the labour struggle are in no position to deny genuineness to a movement just because it has been meticulously organized by activists. In the Marxist view, agitators have to make their target audience conscious of its objective collective interests; and that is precisely how the Hindutva activists see their own activities. Truly spontaneous mass movements seldom come to anything; demanding that Hindu (or any) mass agitation be spontaneous and nothing but spontaneous is a demand for suicidal ineffectiveness and guaranteed failure.

For another example: "At the heart of Hindutva lies the myth of a continuous thousand-year-old struggle of Hindus against Muslims as the structuring principle of Indian history. Both communities are assumed to have been homogeneous blocs—of Hindu patriots, heroically resisting invariably tyrannical, 'foreign' Muslim rulers."[223] This is not backed up by any quotation from an RSS source. It could not be, for the position described is definitely not the RSS position. The perception of medieval history as a continuous Hindu-Muslim struggle is indeed widespread:[224] this much is the correct starting-point from which sloppy extrapolations are made. But the RSS view of history is not one of "homogeneous blocs", on the contrary: in the RSS view, Hindu society was defeated by Muslim invaders because it was *not* sufficiently homogeneous, which is why the RSS makes it its business to organize the Hindus into a more homogeneous society.

In RSS pamphletteering, there is frequent reference to Hindu traitors, particularly Jayachandra, the king of Kanauj who allegedly made common

[222]Though RSS workers individually are extremely modest, the RSS collectively is full of self-congratulatory bluster, witness its publications, e.g. the brochure *RSS, Spearheading National Renaissance*, or H.V. Seshadri, ed.: *Dr Hedgewar, the Epoch-Maker*.

[223]Tapan Basu *et al*: *Khaki Shorts*, p.2.

[224]And even this is not as absolute as commonly assumed. During the Ayodhya campaign, the main BJP-VHP line of argument against Babar's mosque as a "monument of foreign domination" was the "secular" position that "Hindu and Muslim Indians" had jointly fought "the foreign invader Babar". Its basis in reality was the fact that India-based Muslim Pathans (the Lodi and the Suri dynasties) also fought Babar and his successors and even took the innovative step of employing a Hindu general, Himu. But it hardly follows that these Pathans fought for "India", let alone for the Hindu cause.

cause with invader Mohammed Ghori against Prithviraj Chauhan of Delhi. Thus, Golwalkar describes Jayachandra as "the person most responsible for the defeat of Prithviraj", and Moghul vassal Raja Mansingh as "the person who hounded Rana Pratap from forest to forest". After mentioning a few similar cases, he concludes: "There was a veritable race of such traitors".[225] The RSS is painfully aware of the non-bloc nature of historical Hindu resistance to Islam.

A final example may be chosen from among the numerous references to the single most important element in enemy-images of Hinduism, viz. the caste system.[226] Christophe Jaffrelot, France's most-quoted Hindutva-watcher, claims: "The BJP is hostile to the policy of quota in favour of the low castes."[227] In fact, this much is true, that individual Hindu revivalist authors could be cited as opposing reservations.[228] But this should certainly not be extrapolated to the BJP. In a privately circulated collection of 69 critical articles about Prime Minister V.P. Singh's decision to extend the quota system (already well-established for Scheduled Castes and Tribes since 1950) to the Other Backward Castes, we do not find a single BJP author, but we do encounter well-known secularists like Mani Shankar Aiyar, A.S. Abraham, Dileep Padgaonkar, M.N. Buch, Bipan Chandra *et al.*[229]

When starting out as a Hindu party, the BJS made things difficult for itself by combining an affirmation of Hindu identity (which in a simple conservative attitude might have included a defence of the existing caste system) with a reform programme for Hindu society. In the 1950s this was already pointed out by foreign observers: "What weakens the Hindu parties in their political efforts is their failure to have a clear-cut political programme for returning to the old order".[230] At no point has the BJP opposed a decision to extend quota to this or that caste, if only because it

---

[225]M.S. Golwalkar, *A Bunch of Thoughts*, p.144.

[226]During his lecture in Leuven University, November 1997, Mark Tully related how people sometimes tell him: "I think Hinduism is a disgusting religion because of the caste system." And it is by no means only laymen whose view of Hinduism can be summed up in this one sentence.

[227]C. Jaffrelot, interviewed by François Schlosser: "Les intouchables entrent dans le jeu", *Le Nouvel Observateur*, 16.5.1996.

[228]Individual Hindu Revivalist opponents to caste-based job reservations include Arun Shourie (editorials in *Indian Express*, 22/23/24/25.8.1990) and Meenakshi Jain (columns in *Indian Express*, 18.9, 5.10 and 17.10.1990).

[229]Hari Prasad Lohia, ed.: *Political Vandalism*, 2 vols.

[230]Richard L. Park and Irene Tinker, eds.: *Leadership and Political Institutions in India* (1959), p.21.

doesn't want to antagonize the large Backward Caste constituency. In its recent election manifestoes, it has consistently upheld the principle of positive discrimination in favour of Backward sections, e.g.: "Continue with the current reservations policy for the Other Backward Classes till they are socially and educationally integrated with the rest of society."[231] So, Jaffrelot's statement is simply untrue, though it is the received wisdom confirmed by most foreign experts.

When we try to guess why an expert would go public with such flatly untrue statements, it might perhaps (like the symmetry fallacy) be another case of a purely deductive claim, i.e. "Arun Shourie opposes quota; Shourie supported the BJP on Ayodhya; *ergo* the BJP opposes quota"; or more generally "Hinduism = Brahminism, ergo militant Hinduism = struggle against anything which threatens Brahmin supremacy". Even celebrated experts on Hindutva are not above such sloppy thinking, let alone the general media.

The meaning of words

The politicized character of Hindutva-watching leads to unabashed manipulations of the semantics of established terminology. Authors simply announce that they will apply to Hindu phenomena terms which do not properly apply, but which are preferred simply for their stigmatizing force. This is not to be taken lightly, for any meaningful communication, and *a fortiori* scholarly discourse, is based on agreed meanings of terms. The very first rule of logic is: *a* = *a*, "a term retains the same meaning throughout the discourse". Violation of this rule is the most elementary violation of scholarly method, betraying either a very fundamental incompetence, or else something even more worrying.

Thus, in her published (and widely acclaimed) Ph.D. thesis about the political and commercial forays of Hindu gurus, Lise McKean starts out by innovatively conceptualizing "spirituality" as "a complex of ideas and practices that uses referents to ultimate values to legitimate the authority and self-interested actions of specific political groups".[232] Considered closely, this redefinition of an established term is of a breathtaking brutality. You cannot just walk in and allot new meanings to words, especially when you are going to discuss statements by and interviews

---

[231]BJP: *Election Manifesto 1998*, p.35.

[232]Lise McKean: *Divine Enterprise. Gurus and the Hindu Nationalist Movement*, p.xv-xvi.

with people who routinely use that same word in its established meaning. Nobody, but strictly *nobody* who refers to his own pursuits as "spirituality", will ever conceptualize it in the sense outlined by Lise McKean. Even that subset among professionals of spirituality which does dabble in politics, and among them even those who merely use "spirituality" as a smokescreen to "legitimate self-interested actions of political groups", can only use that smokescreen precisely because everyone agrees on the profoundly non-political, inward-oriented meaning of the term "spirituality".

For another example, Christophe Jaffrelot endeavours to add the label "racist" to all the hostile labels which Hindu nationalism is already carrying.[233] Likewise, Salman Rushdie describes anti-Muslim actions of the "Ravana gang", apparently the Shiv Sena, as "racial hatred".[234] It is well-known that many Hindu authors (Bipin Chandra Pal, Veer Savarkar, Guru Golwalkar) have used the word "race" when speaking about the Hindus; Sri Aurobindo even spoke of the "Aryan race".[235] But in pre-War English, the word *race* often simply meant "people, ethnic group", not "race" in the biological sense. The fact is that racism does not play any role at all in Hindu thinking about Hindu–Muslim relations or about the ideal Hindu state.

But then, on what does Jaffrelot base his allegation? Already in the formulation of his *demonstrandum*, he shifts from "racism" to "hierarchical integration" of the Muslims, as if hierarchy were intrinsically based on race. And the key proof of this "hierarchical" programme is—what else?—the worn-out line from Golwalkar's admittedly muddled booklet *We, Our Nationhood Defined*, inviting the Muslims to "adopt the Hindu culture" or else to "*remain* in the country"

---

[233]C. Jaffrelot: "The ideas of the Hindu race in the writings of Hindu nationalist ideologues in the 1920s and 1930s: A concept between two cultures", in P. Robb: *The Concept of Race in South Asia*, pp.327-54.

[234]Salman Rushdie: *Midnight's Children* (London 1982), p.72, quoted with approval by Jim Masselos: "The Bombay riots of January 1993: the politics of urban conflagration", *South Asia*, vol.17, 1994, p.79.

[235]In December 1914, Sri Aurobindo, when discussing theories about the "Aryan and Dravidian races" (*India's Rebirth*, p.104), adds in a footnote: "I prefer not to use the term *race*, for race is a thing much more obscure and difficult to determine than is usually imagined. In dealing with it the trenchant distinctions current in the popular mind are wholly out of place." Yet, after this he used the term many more times, in keeping with English usage.

(no ethnic cleansing here) in a position "*subordinated* to the Hindu nation", "deserving no privileges, far less any preferential treatment—not even citizen's rights".[236]

Golwalkar's statement was disowned by its author, who withdrew the booklet from circulation in 1948. It was never repeated later and was in fact contradicted numerous times in more recent Sangh Parivar writings, for example, all BJP election manifestoes since 1980 have affirmed the principle of legal equality regardless of religion. Can France's star BJP expert feign to ignore this? Golwalkar's statement is reprehensible in that it imposes on Muslims a position of second-class citizens, on the model of the *Zimmî* position of non-Muslims in Islamic states, but that does not constitute *racism*, not even a little bit of it, any more than the inequality between Muslims and non-Muslims in Islamic states constitutes racism.[237]

In Golwalkar's booklet *We* itself, many statements off-hand refute Golwalkar's alleged "racism", first of all by proving that he consistently gives the word *race* the meaning of "nation" or even "society", of which outsiders can become members, quite in contrast with a biological race. Golwalkar repeats *ad nauseam* his assimilationist (or in French terms, *Jacobin*) position, viz. that the Muslims should assimilate themselves into Hindu society, for instance: "Culturally, linguistically, they must become one with the National race; they must adopt the past and entertain the aspirations for the future of the National race; in short, they must be 'Naturalised' in the country by being assimilated in the Nation wholly."[238] This is the diametrical opposite of Hitler's plans with the Jewish "race", which was largely assimilated into German society and which he first of all forced to dissimilate again.

The point is also made, in the most straightforward terms, by the seed ideologue of Hindu nationalism, Veer Savarkar: "After all there is throughout this world so far as man is concerned but a single race — the

---

[236]Golwalkar: *We*, pp.55-6, quoted by Jaffrelot in Robb: *Concept of Race*, p.345; emphases mine.

[237]It is a different matter that the inferiority of the non-Muslim, applied to the black animists, was soon expanded into the concept of the inferiority of the blacks as a racial group, so that Islamic black slavery (an 800-year-old system when the Portuguese and other Europeans became partners in it) was historically the cradle of modern racism, as documented by Bernard Lewis: *Race and Slavery in the Middle East*. In principle at least, a white Christian or a brown Hindu would be legally inferior to any Muslim, whether white, brown or black.

[238]Golwalkar: *We*, p.54, quoted by Jaffrelot, in Robb, ed.: *Concept of Race*, p.344.

human race, kept alive by one common blood, the human blood. All other talk is at best provisional, a makeshift and only relatively true. Nature is constantly trying to overthrow the artificial barriers you raise between race and race. To try to prevent the commingling of blood is to build on sand. Sexual attraction has proved more powerful than all the commands of all the prophets put together. Even as it is, not even the aborigines of the Andamans are without some sprinkling of the so-called Aryan blood in their veins and *vice-versa*. Truly speaking all that one can claim is that one has the blood of all mankind in one's veins. The fundamental unity of man from pole to pole is true, all else only relatively so."[239]

These explicit anti-racist positions are all the more remarkable when you consider that until *c*. 1940, even biological racism was fully respectable in British India, most notably in the British preference for the imaginary "martial races" (Gurkhas, Sikhs) as opposed to the "effeminate races" (Bengalis), and in their colour prejudice against the native "Aryan brown".[240] Moreover, all Hindu revivalist ideologues were entirely clear about the well-known fact that Indian Muslims were mostly descendents of Hindus converted to Islam, so that the Hindu-Muslim conflict was one between sections of a single Indian race.

In spite of this thorough refutation of his position by explicit and authoritative statements (which he has, in fairness, acknowledged), Jaffrelot refuses to admit that the absence of biological discrimination definitively absolves the Hindu ideologues from the suspicion of "racism". Instead, he attributes to them "more a racism of domination than a racism of extermination ...: the Other is not excluded but he can only be integrated at a subordinate rank."[241] Borrowing from Gyanendra Pandey, he calls this "upper-caste racism".[242]

---

[239]Savarkar: *Hindutva*, p.90, also quoted (minus sentences 2 to 5) by Jaffrelot, in Robb: *Concept of Race*, p.340.

[240]See e.g. Lionel Caplan: "Martial Gurkhas: The Persistence of a British military discourse on 'race'", in P. Robb: *The Concept of Race in South Asia*, pp.260-81. The term "Aryan brown", with "Aryan" meaning "Hindu", is from a poem by Rudyard Kipling: "Now it is not good for the Christian's health to hustle the Aryan brown..." Colour prejudice against the Hindus was already widespread in the Muslim period, when *Hindu* was a common Persian synonym for "black" (often pejorative), approximately the skin-colour of what Amir Khusrau called "the crow-faced Hindus".

[241]Jaffrelot, in Robb: *Concept of Race*, p.354.

[242]G. Pandey: *Hindus and Others*, p.252, quoted by Jaffrelot in P. Robb, ed.: *Concept of Race*, p.347.

The distinction between a "racism of domination" and a "racism of extermination" is meaningful: while white settlers in Patagonia or Tasmania effectively endeavoured to "exterminate" the natives, the white cotton-planters in Alabama or South Carolina merely wanted to "dominate" the blacks, to "integrate them at a subordinate rank", not to kill or exterminate their dearly-paid human investment. But the point is: both varieties can only be put on the common denominator of "racism" because both presuppose a race theory, a theory which divides mankind in biological categories and then draws political conclusions from that division. Such is not the case at all with the Hindutva ideologues, who never tire of repeating that the Indian Muslims are flesh of their flesh, estranged only by the imposition of a foreign religion.

Why then do Pandey and Jaffrelot insist on describing as "racist" the Hindutva scheme of integrating the Muslims in the projected Hindu state, which has nothing to do with race at all? Given Jaffrelot's honest listing of anti-racist statements by Golwalkar and Savarkar, we would like to think of a more honourable explanation, but we cannot help wondering: could Pandey and Jaffrelot have been so eager to stigmatize Hindu nationalism that they thought it worth their while to distort the meaning of the central term in their plea?

That much, at any rate, is admitted openly by an Indo-Australian researcher who has likewise expanded the meaning of the incriminating term "racism" for political purposes: "I hope that this Indian debate will have some relevance for my Australian audience"[243], viz. for the struggle against anti-Asian racism there; never mind that race is not by any stretch of the imagination the issue between Hindus and Muslims. He concedes that he is distorting the word's meaning but is unapologetic about it: "There are, of course, particularly 'Indian' twists to this story, and it is also true that 'racism', properly speaking, has social-Darwinist connotations and should not be conflated with 'ethnicity'. Yet, for me, the popular word 'racism' has the advantage of not making India look 'peculiar'."[244]

So, instead of studying the Indian situation, he projects his Australian concerns on to it, never mind that this will certainly distort the picture of

---

[243]Dipesh Chakrabarty, of Melbourne University: "Modernity and ethnicity in India" (*South Asia*, vol.XVII, 1994, special issue, pp.143-55), p.144.

[244]Dipesh Chakrabarty: "Modernity and ethnicity in India", *South Asia* 1994, pp.144-45. Whether the Hindutva position vis-à-vis the Muslims really shares traits with Australian racist attitudes vis-à-vis Asian immigrants, such as exclusion and segregation, is another question.

his purported study object. This state of affairs is pretty grim: scholars openly proclaim their partisan position and their disrespect for the most elementary deontology of scholarship. And they need not fear any adverse consequences in their careers, on the contrary.

Unabashed bias

The fundamental mistake of Western India-watchers is to assume that secularism means some kind of neutrality, of being "above" the warring parties in the inter-religious conflict, so that self-described secularists must be unbiased. That is not the case at all. Most Indian secularist journalists and academics on whom Western India-watchers rely for their information have never pretended to be neutral. They usually start out quite openly by describing "Hindu communalism" as one of India's major *problems*. This may be right or wrong, but it is most definitely a partisan stand, for many others in India consider Hindu Revivalism as a *solution*.

The practice of quoting partisan Indian sources as uncontroversial authorities is widespread, for example, the French Leftist monthly *Le Monde Diplomatique* reproduces an article by one Teesta Setalvad, introduced as the editor of the Mumbai monthly *Communalism Combat*, i.e. someone who has made a profession of her partisan position vis-à-vis Hindu revivalism ("communalism").[245] The record indicates that her pro-Hindu counterparts would never get a tribune in the same monthly.[246] She only quotes authors who are militantly hostile to Hindu revivalism, e.g. Praful Bidwai, a Marxist scholar at the Nehru Memorial Library, whose assessment of Hindu revivalism is: "utterly despicable, base and crass".[247]

But strangely, while Indian secularist scholars don't make the faintest attempt to keep up appearances of neutrality, most of their Western contacts, rather than hearing a professional alarm bell ring to put them on alert against biased information, simply follow suit. Indeed, to an extent, Western observers follow the lead of their Indian sources, and openly declare their partisan interest in the topic of "Hindu communalism". Thus,

[245]T. Setalvad: "Les nationalistes hindous, menace pour la démocratie", *Le Monde Diplomatique*, July 1997.

[246]In April 1991, *Le Monde Diplomatique* also filled two pages with invective against the organized Hindu movement. One of the contributions, by Vijay Singh, "Mourir pour un temple" ("To die for a temple"), was largely an (unacknowledged) excerpt from *Understanding the Muslim Mind* by Rajmohan Gandhi, another signatory of every anti-Hindutva manifesto.

[247]P. Bidwai's column in *Illustrated Weekly of India*, 22.12.1990.

an Australian professor starts out by calling the BJP "undoubtedly 'a political problem'" and ends with lamenting "the evils of Hindutvism".[248]

It could just as well be argued that the Congress Party has been independent India's number one problem, for example, its sycophantic culture of dynastic rule and flattery of bosses has stifled initiative and dissent, its way of trying to be all things unto all men has pre-empted clear political choices, it has no internal democracy and has once imposed the Emergency on India. Come to think of it, these flaws of Congress explain the persistent anti-Congressism of some Communist and regional parties which in 1996-98 even kept them from joining hands with Congress in a solid anti-BJP front.[249]

Lise McKean's book *Divine Entreprise. Gurus and the Hindu Nationalist Movement* provides a good testimony to the prevalent opinion among academic India-watchers. In his laudatory review, Jeffrey J. Kripal correctly calls her conceptual framework "decidedly Marxist".[250] Her work (which has the one great merit of showing the continuity between spiritual and political Hinduism, a fact ignored by most Western followers of Hindu gurus) was accepted as a Ph.D. thesis, published by a prestigious publishing-house (University of Chicago Press), and acclaimed by reviewers in most professional journals. This means that at least a dozen experts have carefully read it, and approved of it. Yet, the book displays an unabashed bias. The only critical review of it known to me, by Daniel Gomez-Ibanez, points out its "serious flaws of scholarship" and its "obvious bias, verging on hostility", as well as its gross allegations ("the sect's coercive and punitive powers"; "greed, guile and violence that secure their status as spiritual leaders") which are not based on even a single specific fact presented at any place in her book.[251]

Neither flaws nor bias could prejudice her jury or her publishers' reading committee against her, not even to ask her to soften her language or check a few details. This, I think, constitutes an authoritative testimony to the prevalent opinion climate in a sector where objectivity ought to be the norm. Not that I object to her explicitness in choosing sides; again, it is

[248]Don Miller: "Mosque, temple and crypt"; *South Asia*, special issue 1994, pp.129-42.

[249]E.g. the Leftist call for "a clear-cut polarisation of forces in the Indian polity ... without the Congress inhabiting the middle ground and *fudging issues* in what has become its patented style", by Sukumar Muralidharan: "Politics after Ayodhya", *Frontline*, 12.12.1997; emphasis mine.

[250]J.J. Kripal in *International Journal of Hindu Studies*, 1997, p.208.

[251]Daniel Gomez-Ibanez: "Book Review", *News Report* (spring 1997) of Wisconsin University's Center for South Asia; quotes on p.19, p.23.

perfectly possible to produce real scholarship in the service of a crusade, and it is perhaps better that bias is explicitated than that a false pretence of neutrality is kept up. However, having read a great deal on Hindu revivalism in the last few years, I have never come across a study with the opposite bias which has received the same red-carpet welcome in the small world of India-watchers.

The price of tolerance

A typical feature of the power equation in the opinion climate of the past decade is that for Hindutva observers, Hindus are (or were) damned if they do, damned if they don't. Thus, if they demolish the Babri Masjid, it proves that they too are intolerant, and that anything they may say about the Muslims actually applies to themselves; but if they are tolerant, they are accused of trying to swallow the minorities by "assimilative communalism" (like a "boa constrictor")[252] and "repressive tolerance".[253] If they were to reject democracy, this would obviously be denounced as "fascist", but because they abide by democracy, this itself is given a pejorative twist as "majoritarianism". For millennia, Hindu India had been the proverbially rich country, and for long, the wily money-making "Hindu *bania*" (merchant) had been a favourite enemy-image projected by the Indian Muslims and Leftists, and given new flesh more recently by the economic successes of the overseas Hindus; yet, when Nehru imposed stagnation on India's economy with his Soviet-style five-year plans, the secularists called the disappointing economic results of this non-Hindu policy "the Hindu rate of growth".[254]

Consider, for a more serious example, this allegation by a Christian missionary: "India's constitution witnesses to the fact that Hinduism's famed liberalism is sometimes remarkably intolerant of the beliefs of others: Parsis, Christians and Jews have their own marriage and inheritance provisions, but Buddhists, Jains and Sikhs are all treated as

[252]The "boa constrictor" allegation is borrowed from *Dalit Voice* by Marc Colpaert: "Hindoeîsme", *Wereldwijd*, March 1986, and is most popular in pleas for the separate identity of Sikhism which is "threatened" by Hindu accommodativeness.

[253]The latter term was applied to Hinduism, acknowledging its tolerance but turning it into something sinister, by Arun Shourie (*Hinduism: Essence and Consequence*, 1979), then still strongly under the influence of Marxism.

[254]The story of how the term was thought up by the Nehruvian, Raj Krishna, and launched into the public arena by the *Times of India* in an editorial at the time of his death, is told by Raj Krishna's friend S.R. Goel in a letter, "Nehruvian rate of growth", *Indian Express*, 5.5.1994.

Hindu groups."[255] A separate law system for Sikhs, Jains or Buddhists has never existed in history. It takes a fervent anti-Hindu animus to detect "remarkable intolerance" in the recognition of this fact by India's Constitution, a text which is not the handiwork of "Hinduism" anyway. And it takes a remarkable forgetfulness about realities in the rest of the world to describe as "remarkable intolerance" what most Constitutions of democratic countries consider evident and necessary, viz. that the same laws should apply to all citizens regardless of religion.

Some authors even manage to turn the bright record of BJP state governments in containing communal violence against the BJP. In Uttar Pradesh, four Chief Ministers performed as follows: under V.P. Singh (non-BJP), the monthly average of casualties (dead and wounded) in communal violence was 29, the monthly average number of Muslims killed was 8; for N.D. Tiwari (non-BJP), the figures were 28 and 3; for Mulayam Singh Yadav (non-BJP), they were 98 and 17; and for Kalyan Singh (BJP), they were 5 and 1.[256] Sikh secularist Tavleen Singh writes: "Let us also remember that it is the Congress Party, not the BJP, which has presided benignly over some of the worst Hindu-Muslim riots in Indian history: Meerut, Maliana, Bhagalpur, Bombay."[257] The BJP itself proudly reports: "Above all, we have proved in the States where the BJP is in power that we can maintain communal peace and harmony; we can ensure security of life and property; and we can protect the honour and dignity of the minority communities."[258] Now, if a BJP source cites this fact, this is not interpreted as reassuring, but as a *threat*: "What they say: 'Muslims are safe in BJP-ruled states'. What they mean: 'Vote for the BJP or face communal riots.'"[259]

---

[255]Rev. Martin Forward: "Gods, Guides & Gurus", *Areopagus*, Trinity 1993, p.39. The article is also a good example of how Western observers swallow a certain propaganda, e.g. the Muslim League classic that Muslims in India are "a beleaguered and threatened minority". (p.41)

[256]B.P. Singhal (former Additional Home Secretary): "Definition of secularism", *Indian Express*, 24.8.1992. The minority death rate in communal violence in Uttar Pradesh was even lower under the several BJP governments after 1992.

[257]Tavleen Singh: "Pot calls the kettle black", *Indian Express*, 19.5.1996.

[258]BJP: *Election Manifesto 1998*, p.36.

[259]"Sangh doublespeak", in Y. Ghimire and L. Rattanani: "Harvesting the Shame", *India Today*, 15.2.1993. In an alternative strategy, some journalists replace the fact with its opposite, the counterfactual claim that "violence between Hindus and Muslims increases in states where the BJP is in power"; thus Catherine Vuylsteke: "Het 'monster' aan de macht" (Dutch: "The 'monster' in power"), *De Morgen*, 6.2.1998, basing herself on more recent columns in *India Today*.

In a sense, Hindus, and likewise India, make it all the worse for themselves by simply being so tolerant. When it comes to tolerating difference, there is hardly a place like India, as a well-known Indian Muslim testifies: "I come from an Indian Muslim family, but I experience India as a very pleasant country, whereas in Pakistan I feel ill at ease. You would think it should be the reverse. But in spite of its many defects, India is a rich and open society, while Pakistan is culturally an impoverished and closed society."[260]

Another testimony by an Indian Muslim confirms this: "My family of orientation migrated from India to erstwhile East Pakistan, although I did not experience any discrimination personally from the 'majority' Hindu community in India".[261] A third one argues that Muslims are better off in India than in Pakistan: "Two pictures, one in the Arab News and the other in the Gulf News, arrested my attention. One showed Indian Muslims offering prayers near the historic Taj Mahal in Agra in peace. The other showed people praying in a Karachi mosque with paramilitary forces guarding the worshippers."[262] And a fourth one confirms: "In Saudi Arabia, there is peace but no freedom. In Pakistan, there is freedom but there is no peace. In India, Muslims enjoy both peace and freedom."[263]

In the long run, this openness is certainly the right policy, but in the short run, the results of tolerance can be perverse. India is hospitable even to its critics, and the latter eagerly accept the invitation. All those NGO activists working in Indian tribal areas can openly support separatism and still stay in India or return there after vacation.[264] Foreigners who like to do some "drain inspection"[265] can do it at leisure in India, focusing on Hindu

---

[260]Salman Rushdie speaking to interviewer Thomas Harder, *Groene Amsterdammer*, 13.9.1995.

[261]Habibul Haque Khondker: "An open letter to Taslima Nasreen", *Economic and Political Weekly*, 13.8.1994.

[262]Saaed Naqvi, quoted by Sahil Brelvi: "Muslims in India", *Organiser*, 24.8.1997.

[263]Maulana Wahiduddin Khan, quoted by Parsha Venkateshwar Rao jr.: "The thinking theologist", *Indian Express*, 7.1.1996.

[264]Of all NGO activists dealing with Indian tribals or minorities susceptible to separatism, I have never heard or seen one defend the Indian viewpoint. Organizations like *India-Werkgroep Vlaanderen* and *India-Werkgroep Nederland*, not to speak of the India cells of the World Council of Churches, generally support every possible source of subversion and separatism in India. Thus, Wilco Brinkman, writing of Manipur ("Manipur, een mini-staat", *India Nu*, bimonthly of the India-Werkgroep Nederland, Utrecht, Jan. 1997), speaks of an "Indian invasion", of "Indian colonial oppression" and about rice being "exported from Manipur to India", implying that India is a foreign country.

[265]Term introduced by Mahatma Gandhi in his comment on the book *Mother India* by Katherine Mayo, a catalogue of all the bad things she could find in India.

society: it is fun to be in India, and there is no need to fear reprisals. It takes courage, and the willingness to forgo future visas, to write as negatively about China or Pakistan as is commonly done about India. The end result is a complete lack of a sense of proportion, for example, grave concern about alleged discrimination against the minorities in India even when the situation of the minorities in Pakistan is much worse by any standard, violent indignation at the alleged Hindu plans for a "Hindu state" but acceptance as a matter of course of the actually existing "Islamic state" in Pakistan and Bangladesh.

India, and with it Hinduism, is paying for its broad-mindedness and tolerance, while China and Pakistan are being rewarded for their intolerance. This situation presents obvious parallels with the Cold War: in the West, you could freely demonstrate against the ruling power ("Nixon murderer!"), but in the Soviet Bloc, there was no such freedom. Judging from the decibels of slogan-shouting, you would have concluded that the Western system was about to be overthrown from within while the Soviet system was secure. However, the outcome of the Cold War has proven the long-term superiority of free societies tolerant of criticism. In South Asia too, India's climate of freedom is certainly the right policy, yielding better results even for India's national self-interest in the long run. Only, for us it means that we have to remain aware of its temporary distortive impact on the information and opinion flow.

A PRACTICAL CONCLUSION

In this study, the Hindu revivalist programme and position on the challenges of Islam and secularism will be presented in considerable detail. An evaluation of what is said (sometimes also of what is conspicuously left unsaid) is attempted to the extent that this is feasible. Of course, when the argument is about fundamental questions like whether God exists, no quick decision will be hazarded. On the other hand, in some cases, such as the debate about the anti-Hindu discriminations in the Constitution, the facts can be traced and stated definitively; where a simple factual analysis can put an end to ongoing quarrels, it would be an act of laziness and irresponsibility to present a matter of fact relativistically as a matter of opinion. Finally, there are cases where the issues can be settled provisionally, to the extent of separating the wildly unreasonable from arguments which deserve a further hearing on some future occasion.

My position vis-à-vis the heavy bias which pervades most secondary literature is that it can largely be ignored in a study of primary sources. I will not take it as a guideline nor let it prejudice my own interpretation of the material. The problem is also lessened by the fact that a lot of the ground I will cover has never been covered before. About the Hindu nationalist organizations, I will borrow some hard data painstakingly gathered by certain colleagues, and on occasion, I will enter into a discussion with the apparent consensus in India-watching circles. But my overriding concern will be, to do justice to my subjects-matter, the ideological developments in the Hindu revivalist movements as attested in the writings of its legitimate spokesmen.

Historical Survey

The purpose of this chapter is merely to give a factual framework of historical data concerning the protagonists of Hindu revivalist politics and ideology, a framework in which to situate the ideological statements and debates studied in subsequent chapters. It is not to give a full account of the history of any given organization or personality. On some of the personalities and organizations mentioned, exhaustive studies have been published, which I will not seek to reproduce or improve upon. Only those personalities on whom nothing has been published so far will receive a more detailed treatment in this chapter.

As this study wants to be a history of ideas rather than a political history, the space given to different movements and personalities is proportionate not to the numerical strength of their support base, but to their input of genuine ideas into the debate on the status of Hinduism in India and the legitimacy of Hinduism vis-à-vis the challenges thrown by secularism and Islam.

THE HINDU RENAISSANCE

"Hindu Renaissance" is the name given to a mild reassertion of Hinduism in British India, mostly in its oldest province, Bengal. This trend was definitely related to the Orientalist fashion in the West: Hindus were trying to incorporate the best things from the West, but while some were trying to make a clean break with their own heritage, others tried to preserve and revive their heritage in an adapted form, partly because they felt encouraged by the appreciation which cultured Westerners extended to things Hindu.

The Brahmo Samaj

The first organized attempt of Hindus to come to terms with the twin challenge of Christianity and modernity as brought home to them by the European colonization was the *Brahmo Samâj*, founded in Calcutta in

1828 by Raja Rammohun Roy (1772-1833).[1] Its main ideological thrust was to transform Hinduism in the mould of Christianity. It assumed that Hindu society could only be healed of its social evils by adopting Christian (Protestant) taboos on polytheism and idolatry.

In Rammohun Roy's days, Christian writing on India was full of invective against "the evils of Hindu society", meaning such practices as the prohibition of widow remarriage (at least among the higher castes), the self-immolation of widows (*satî*, then commonly spelled *suttee*), and of course caste discrimination. In response, some Hindu reformers including Roy made these criticisms their own and started working for the abolition of the said "evils". Roy's major claim to fame from a Western angle was his campaign for the prohibition of *satî* until Governor-General Lord William Bentinck enacted it in 1829.[2]

This interiorization of outside criticism of Hindu society took place not only among low-caste reformers (e.g. the so-called *non-Brahmin movement* of the secularist Jotirao Phule in Maharashtra, an early "product" of Christian education)[3] but also in the elite circles in Bengal whence the Brahmo Samaj had emerged. The Brahmo position was indeed very defensive, and its ideologues imbibed quite a bit of Christianity (particularly its Unitarian form) along with some Deism of the European Enlightenment. The third-generation Samaj leader Keshub Chandra Sen (1838-1884) professed a Christian-like veneration of Jesus of Nazareth and interiorized the Christian concept of man's profound sinfulness.[4]

---

[1]See e.g. M.C. Kotnala: *Raja Rammohun Roy and Indian Awakening*; J.N. Farquhar: *Modern Religious Movements in India*, Ch.2.1; D. Kopf: *The Brahmo Samaj*; and Spencer Lavan: "The Brahmo Samaj: India's first modern movement for religious reform", in R.D. Baird, ed.: *Religion in Modern India*, pp.1-25.

[2]However, Jeevan Kulkarni, in his Writ Petition (1989) to the Supreme Court challenging (in vain) the constitutional validity of the *Commission of Sati (Prevention) Act*, 1987, pp.4-5, translates the Bengali poem *No Fear* by the most famous Brahmoist, Rabindranath Tagore (from *Ravîndra Rachanâvalî*, vol.5, p.441), which turns out to contain an unabashed *glorification* of *satî*; as Kulkarni points out, present anti-*satî* legislation makes the public reading of this poem a punishable offence.

[3]See D. Keer: *Mahatma Jotirao Phule, Father of Indian Social Revolution*. The Government of Maharashtra has published the *Collected Works of Mahatma Jotirao Phule* (1991-92).

[4]Like Christianity, Hinduism rejects utopian views of man as "naturally good" and is aware of man's intrinsic limitations and sinfulness. But unlike in Christianity, this sinfulness is seen as only the superficial debris which obscures the profounder divinity of the Self, to be achieved through yoga, a point made by Ramakrishna Paramahansa in reaction to Sen's alleged obsession with sin (Mahendranath Gupta and Swami Nikhilananda: *The Gospel of Sri Ramakrishna*, p.138).

In a half-intended way, the Brahmo accommodation of certain Christian ideas including a certain veneration for Jesus Christ did blunt the sword of the Christian mission in the most effective way possible under the circumstances. It made Jesus acceptable to urban Hindus as a venerable teacher of ethics, possibly even an *Avatâr* (incarnation of Vishnu), i.e. in roles known to Hindu tradition, but not as the unique Saviour which he was claimed to be in the missionaries' preachings. This domesticated version of Jesus propagated by Brahmoists has caught on among English-educated Hindus till today: more than Mohammed, Jesus is accepted as a genuine spiritual teacher. With hindsight, we can say that this did more to avert further Christian inroads into educated Hindu circles than the open and systematic polemics marginally produced by a few nineteenth-century Pandits.[5]

Often this enlistment of Jesus in the Hindu pantheon was subsequently enriched with mystery stories propagated by the Theosophical Society, a spiritualist society of Westerners fascinated by the Orient. Thus, claims are abroad that Jesus had been trained as a yogi, or that he came to India after the Resurrection and died at age 115 in Srinagar (where an actual grave is venerated as Jesus' grave by the Ahmadiya Muslim sect). Many yoga authors targeting the anglicized Hindu and the Western public started arguing that Jesus' message was all about yoga, as if to permit their readers to practise yoga without rejecting Christianity.[6] At any rate, this Hinduization of Christ has worked as a very Hindu way of rendering Christianity harmless without really attacking it.

In terms of numbers, the Brahmo Samaj remained marginal, but it exerted a strong influence on most Bengali Hindu leaders of the colonial age, including Swami Vivekananda and the poet and educationist Rabindranath Tagore, whose father Debendranath Tagore had been the Brahmo Samaj's leader in the mid-nineteenth century. Among its lasting contributions, we must mention the now-popular notions of an underlying unity of all religions and of a universal and "scientific" religion, free from the doctrines of Revelation and Incarnation.

---

[5]See Richard F. Young: *Resistant Hinduism. Sanskrit Sources on anti-Christian Apologetics in Early Nineteenth-Century Hinduism*, about three Pandits writing little-read tracts against Christianity. Their degree of effectiveness can be deduced from the fact that one of them ended up converting to Christianity. By contrast, a public debate between Sinhalese Buddhists and Jesuits in 1873 was decisive in restoring confidence among the Buddhists in Sri Lanka.

[6]E.g. Sri Yukteswar: *The Holy Science*, and Paramahansa Yogananda: *Autobiography of a Yogi*.

The Arya Samaj

The first truly public and sustained polemical attack on Christianity and Islam was mounted by Swami Dayananda Saraswati (1824-1883)[7] and the organization which he founded in 1975 in Mumbai (though the heartland of the movement was Panjab), the *Arya Samâj*.[8] This was by any standard the most influential Hindu reform movement in the colonial period. Its foundational scripture was the *Satyârtha Prakâsh* ("Light of Truth"), of which the definitive version was published shortly after his death. This book contains a polemical chapter against Christianity, one against Islam, one against Buddhism and Jainism, and several against allegedly degenerative trends in Hinduism.

The attempt to provide a detailed critique of Islam was a new element in the Hindu position vis-à-vis Islam. Because of its anti-Islamic Chapter 14, the *Satyârtha Prakâsh* was a constant irritant to militant Muslims. An Arya Samaj biography of Swami Dayananda claims that because of his public criticism of Islam, he was attacked by Muslims while meditating on the Ganga riverside.[9] The offending chapter was banned in some Muslim-dominated princely states and in 1944 also in the Muslim-dominated province of Sindh.

That being the negative part, the positive message of the *Satyârtha Prakâsh* was the return to the Vedas, the pristine purity of the tradition of which modern Hinduism was but a cruel caricature. Contrary to the Brahmo Samaj, which considered all scriptures as fallible, the Arya Samaj was a *fundamentalist* movement in the true sense of the word. Though both movements were reformist, the Arya Samaj presented its reforms as a return to the pristine Vedic tradition rather than as a selective adoption of

---

[7]About Dayananda, see N.B. Sen, ed.: *Wit & Wisdom of Swami Dayananda*; Vandematharam Veerabhadra Rao: *Life Sketch of Dayananda*; and K.C. Yadav, ed.: *The Autobiography of Dayananda Saraswati*.

[8]For Arya Samaj self-presentations, see e.g. Lala Lajpat Rai: *The Arya Samaj*; D. Vable: *The Arya Samaj*, and *The Arya Samaj, the Most Revolutionary Reform Movement of India*; or Mahatma Narayan Swamy: *What is Arya Samaj?* The leading study by an outsider is Kenneth W. Jones: *Arya Dharm*. A good attempt to systematize Arya doctrine is Acharya Vaidyanath Shastri: *The Arya Samaj, Its Cult and Creed*.

[9]Vandematharam Veerabhadra Rao: *Life Sketch of Swami Dayananda*, p.13. According to Rao, Dayananda was thrown into the water and saved himself because his *prânâyâma* (breathing exercises) practice allowed him to stay under water until his attackers left the site, assuming he had drowned.

Western ideas and standards.[10] The question is, of course, to what extent the Arya Samaj understanding of Vedic culture was historically authentic; like most fundamentalist movements, it shaped the past Golden Age after ideals which had developed in the intervening and the contemporary period. Thus, it favoured a ban on cow slaughter, while the ancient Vedic sacrifice seems to have taken the lives of cows on many occasions.

In some cases, however, the Arya Samaj was simply right in claiming that Vedic norms were much closer to modern standards than to those of nineteenth-century Hinduism. Thus, caste oppression and untouchability are not mentioned in the Veda Samhitas. Similarly, the status of women in Vedic society was probably somewhat more equal with that of men, and their relations more relaxed, than in Hindu society of the Victorian age.[11] When you consider certain cruel and wasteful Hindu rules of conduct, such as the prohibition of widow remarriage (often affecting child widows), or the loss of all proportion in the obsession with purity as expressed in the practice of untouchability, it is hard not to sympathize with the Arya Samaj project of returning to the Vedic outlook, which had at least been much closer to human common sense. The Vedic seers (some of them female) were adventurous and creative, while the Hindu of recent centuries was continually inhibited by fear of trespassing against a million scriptural rules, astrological warnings and the opprobrium of purity-conscious fellow-castemen.

The Arya Samaj generally blames the decline of Hindu civilization on purely Hindu factors, most notably "Brahminical priestcraft", a scapegoat borrowed straight from Christian missionary anti-Brahminical polemic. This anti-Brahminism was, moreover, cast in the mould of Protestant anti-Popism, i.e. it was conceived as a restoration of the original divinely revealed doctrine against the distortive accretions of "tradition" and its wily guardians, the institutionalized priesthood.

Later Hindu polemicists propose that Islamic rule was a major factor in the aggravation of caste discrimination and of the declining status of

---

[10]A detailed analysis of the "fundamentalist" quality of Arya Samaj thought is J.E. Llewellyn: *The Arya Samaj as a Fundamentalist Movement. A Study in Comparative Fundamentalism* (1993).

[11]The decline of women's status in the post-Vedic age is documented in A.S. Altekar: *The Position of Women in Hindu Civilization.* Altekar's own drive to prove this point was typical of the widespread effort, pioneered precisely by the Arya Samaj, to demonstrate the consonance of Vedic and modern values. See also L.K. Tripathi: *Position and Status of Hindu Women in Ancient India.*

women.[12] If the Arya Samaj has not explored this line of thought, it may be due to limitations of the available historical knowledge and perspective, or to the as yet largely defensive psychology of the pioneers of Hindu Revival, or to a no-nonsense attitude of reformists who want to set their own house in order without laying any of the freshly assumed responsibility at the door of outsiders.

The Shuddhi movement

A central concern of the Arya Samaj was *Shuddhi*, "purification", i.e. giving the Vedic initiation to non-Hindu or low-caste Hindu people. With this ritual, originally devised for Brahmins who had lost their caste purity (e.g. by travelling abroad), two different problems were sought to be solved in one stroke: intra-Hindu inequality and the historical or ongoing conversion of Hindus to Christianity or Islam. The biggest problem for the *Shuddhi* movement was to get newly initiated ("twice-born") Untouchables accepted by caste Hindus; sometimes the Shuddhi performers themselves were expelled by their native caste for polluting themselves by their communion with Untouchables.

The great success story of this movement was the conversion of almost half a million Malkana Rajputs, who were accepted as Hindu Kshatriyas by the All India Kshatriya Sabha, meeting in Agra in 1922. The enthusiasm waned when the Malkana Rajputs found that many a Hindu-born fellow Rajput was still reluctant to give his daughters in marriage to them. In fact, the operation had almost backfired dramatically: the Hindus initially went back to sleep after passing the resolution accepting the Malkanas as Hindu Rajputs, which had alerted Muslim preachers to start their first great *Tablîgh* ("propaganda") campaign to keep the Malkanas in the Muslim fold; only an all-out effort by Arya Samaj activists narrowly saved the Shuddhi project.[13]

In order to motivate the Indian Muslims to convert (or "reconvert") to Hinduism, the Shuddhi workers argued that their ancestors had been pressured or forced into Islam, and that after the demise of Muslim rule, there was no reason left to continue this enforced pretence of believing in the religious doctrines of the erstwhile conquerors. One of the most important contributions to this line of thought was Pandit Lekh Ram's

[12]E.g. K.S. Lal: *The Legacy of Muslim Rule in India*, Ch.7, and K.S. Lal: *Growth of Scheduled Tribes and Castes in Medieval India*.

[13]Related in Swami Shraddhananda: *Hindu Sangathan*, pp.121 ff.

Risâla-i-Jihâd ya'ni Dîn-i-Muhammadî kî bunyâd, "Treatise on Holy War, or the Basis of the Mohammedan religion" (Lahore 1892).[14] It documented the violence of the Muslim conquests and listed cases of forced conversions. The bottom line was a call to the Indian Muslims to undo their past islamization: "Dear Brethren! Let us remove hatred and jealousy from our hearts, sit in an atmosphere of love and unity and worship the one God. Let us purify our hearts through the Vedic way of worship. The doors of penance of your return to the fold of your former real faith are wide open to let you in. Shed the burden put on your necks by force and under compulsion. Befriend the truth and help us in spreading the truth, because God helps those who help themselves."[15]

Pandit Lekh Ram's *Risâla-i-Jihâd* was the object of a lawsuit, in which Muslims demanded that the book be banned. After several rounds in court, they lost definitively in 1896. But the matter did not end there, for Lekh Ram was murdered in March 1897. Some Muslims, including Mirza Ghulam Ahmad (1838-1908, pretender to prophethood and founder of the Ahmadiya sect of Islam),[16] openly applauded the murder: "Mirza Ghulam Ahmad published a tract in which he thanked God for the fulfillment of his prophecy that Lekh Ram would die a violent death. ... Individuals reported receiving threatening letters, and mysterious notices appeared on the wall throughout the province. 'All Hindus are warned to remember the

---

[14]Literature on Lekh Ram's arguments in *Risâla-i-Jihâd* is extremely scarce. Kenneth W. Jones devotes five whole pages to the Arya-Muslim conflict provoked by the book, but hardly one page (*Arya Dharma*, p.150) concerns the actual contents of its polemic. Jones does not evaluate the historical accuracy of Lekh Ram's position, but merely expresses his own contempt for this "infamous pamphlet" which "fitted well into Hindu prejudice". The book itself is very hard to find now, and most living Arya Samajis have never seen it; I myself was told at the *Sarvadeshik Arya Pratinidhi Sabhâ* (All-India Arya Representative Council) office that unfortunately they could not find a copy. Is it the present secularist climate which makes the Arya Samaj shy about its past stand against Islam?

[15]Lekh Ram: *Risâla-i-Jihâd*, p.55.

[16]Whether Ahmadiyas are Muslims at all is disputed, because Ahmad's claim to prophethood is incompatible with Mohammed's status as "seal of the prophets". After Partition, the Pakistani (not the Indian) Ahmadiyas revised Ahmad's status to that of *Mujaddid*, "Renewer", but the Ulema were not convinced. The *Khâksar* militia, founded by Allama Mashreqi in the mould of the Nazi *Sturmabteilung* (Mashreqi had returned from Germany in the 1930s), terrorized the Ahmadiyas with open encouragement from Maulana Abul-Ala Maududi (who was tried and sentenced to death for this in 1953, but soon released). In 1974, the Pakistani Government ruled that Ahmadiyas would no longer be considered Muslims, so that their entry in mosques is forbidden, while their own places of worship can no longer be called mosques.

Islamic prophets and believe in them; otherwise they will be murdered like Lekh Ram. The members of the Shuddhi Sabha and the Arya Samaj should consider themselves dead men. (sd.) A well-wisher of the nation.'"[17] Twenty thousand people attended Lekh Ram's funeral rites, and Lala Munshi Ram (later ordained as Swami Shraddhananda) started a newspaper called after Lekh Ram's nickname *Arya Musâfir*, "Arya traveller".[18]

The Shuddhi movement undeniably contributed to the ongoing Hindu-Muslim polarization. Riots and mutual economic boycotts followed the rising tide of rumours of the enemy community's master-plans for genocide. Islamic *Tablîgh* (propaganda) workers understood that a more thorough indoctrination in Islamic religion and a more complete acculturation into Islamic customs would immunize Muslim communities against the overtures of Shuddhi campaigners, for instance: "In 1921 new problems arose when Arya preachers resolved to reconvert the Indian Muslims to their ancestral religion. ... The solution to this problem was to impart to them religious education so that they did not yield to any malign influence."[19] A race started between *Shuddhi* and *Tablîgh* workers for the souls of these borderline Muslims, susceptible to rehinduization because of their enduring cultural closeness to the Hindus.

Thus, the Muslims of Mewat, forcibly converted in punitive expeditions by the Delhi Sultanate against their guerrilla (fourteenth century), had remained culturally Hindu and became a promising target for the Shuddhi campaign. So, one Maulana Ilyas in Mewat set up Islamic schools there.[20] The results greatly satisfied the Tabligh strategists: "We can now help our young men to acquire a religious education side by side with a secular one; Tabligh provides a religious environment where they can be indoctrinated in religious beliefs and practices without this in any way being an obstacle to their studies."[21] This way, the Tabligh campaign threw up a solid defence against the attempts by Shuddhi workers to seduce Muslims back into their ancestral religion.

---

[17]Kenneth W. Jones: *Arya Dharm*, p.196, with reference to *Tribune*, 24.3 and 7.4.1897, and *Panjâb Samâchâr*, 10.4.1897.

[18]As J.E. Llewellyn (*Arya Samaj as a Fundamentalist Movement*, p.105) explains, the nickname referred to the travelling which the Pandit had done while preparing a biography of Swami Dayananda, viz. to interview all the people who had personally known him.

[19]Wahiduddin Khan: *Tabligh*, p.9.

[20]Wahiduddin Khan: *Tabligh*, p.9.

[21]Wahiduddin Khan: *Tabligh*, p.61.

The Shuddhi ritual was not only meant for Muslims but also for Untouchables who wanted to become equal-ranking Hindus. In 1922, as an extension of the Arya Samaj's anti-caste drive, Bhai Parmanand (1875-1947)[22] and other Arya Samajis founded the *Jât Pat Torak Mandal* ("Association for Breaking Caste"), which was to be a spearhead of social reform in the next two decades. Swami Dayananda had condemned Untouchability and had fought caste as it existed in the modern age but, like Mahatma Gandhi after him, he had not radically repudiated the principle that society should be divided into hereditary groups. He had at least left sufficient ambiguity to allow some conservative Arya Samajis to defend the status-quo and to act as a dead weight hampering the anti-caste drive of the more radical faction, an attitude which Bhai Parmanand had bitterly denounced at the anniversary celebration of the Lahore Arya Samaj that same year. By contrast, "the Jat Pat Torak Mandal stood for nothing short of the abolition of caste".[23] For this reason, it attracted the sympathy of important non-Arya Hindu activists, most notably the later Hindu Mahasabha leader Vinayak Damodar Savarkar.

The limits of the *Mandal*'s view of social reform became visible in 1936, when it invited Dr. Bhimrao Ramji Ambedkar, the most prominent leader of the Untouchables, to speak at its annual conference. However, its leadership developed second thoughts when it received the text of Ambedkar's proposed speech: he intended to declare that caste could only disappear if the scriptures on which the institution was based were discarded, and planned to announce that this was to be his last speech as a Hindu, because Hinduism was incurable unless it ceased to be Hinduism. This position was contrary to the Mandal's very *raison d'être*, which was precisely to cure Hinduism. Therefore, Dr. Ambedkar was disinvited.[24] The Arya Samaj position was precisely that the truly fundamental texts of

---

[22]Parmananda's statue still adorns the steps to the HMS Bhavan (on Mandir Marg, Delhi), which he founded, partly with donations from the Birla family, which was also Mahatma Gandhi's sponsor. See also Indra Prakash: *A Prophet of Modern Times*, and Shive Saran: *Life Sketch of Devtaswarup Bhai Parmanand*.

[23]Related in J.E. Llewellyn: *Arya Samaj as Fundamentalist Movement*, pp.102-03.

[24]Dr. Ambedkar's undelivered speech, *Annihilation of Caste*, is included in his *Writings and Speeches*, but has also been republished separately (Arnold Publ., Bangalore 1990) with a foreword by the Communist novelist Mulk Raj Anand and a reprint of the correspondence between Ambedkar and the *Jât Pat Torak Mandal*.

Hinduism, the Vedas, did not institute caste but actually contained a fairly egalitarian view of society.

The Arya Samaj in the freedom movement

Many Arya Samajis were active in the freedom movement, the most well-known among them being Lala Lajpat Rai (1865-1928), Congress president in 1920.[25] Though the Indian National Congress, founded in 1885, was not strictly a Hindu movement, it was predominantly manned by Hindus, both reformists and traditionalists. Most notable among the latter was Bal Gangadhar Tilak (1856-1920), who was the first to connect Hindu symbolism with the freedom struggle.[26] Tilak also interpreted the Bhagavad Gita in terms of political activism.[27] In both respects, he prefigured typical traits of his successor Mahatma Gandhi's policies as Congress leader.

The Arya Samaj's most remarkable ideologue after Dayananda, Swami Shraddhananda, had participated in Congress work, but after being released from prison for his role in the Non-Cooperation and Khilafat agitation of 1919-1922, he became known as a sharp critic of the Congress.[28] The feeling was mutual: Congress leader Mahatma Gandhi repeatedly denounced the Arya Samaj as fanatical, though it had been Shraddhananda who first called Gandhiji *Mahâtma*, "Great Soul" (when for a few months in 1915, he kept Gandhiji's children in his Vedic school).[29] From then onwards, we find Arya Samajis among the leaders of the Hindu nationalist parties (Hindu Mahasabha, Jana Sangh) and among their activists till today. Thus, one Arya Samaji who made a distinctive Arya mark as a BJS politician was O.P. Tyagi, who proposed the anti-missionary *Freedom of Religion Bill* under the Janata Government in 1978.

---

[25]See Purushottam Nagar: *Lala Lajpat Rai. The Man and His Ideas*, and Feroz Chand: *Lala Lajpat Rai, Life and Work*.

[26]About Tilak, see e.g. D. Keer: *Lokamanya Tilak*, and S. Wolpert: *Tilak and Gokhale*.

[27]B.G. Tilak: *Gîtâ-Rahasya*, "The Secret of the Gita" (1914).

[28]See Swami Shraddhananda's booklet *Inside the Congress*, a collection of 26 articles published by him in his weekly *The Liberator* between 1 April and 28 October 1926.

[29]In his defence speech (1948), Gandhiji's murderer Nathuram Godse (*Why I Assassinated Mahatma Gandhi*, pp.53-4) accused Gandhiji of having provoked the murder of Shraddhananda by a Muslim in 1926.

On the other hand, some Arya Samajis emphasized social more than religious reform and joined the Left parties, e.g. in recent years Swami Agnivesh, who advocates "Vedic socialism".[30] In fact, like the Brahmo Samaj and the Gandhian movement, it became one of the main recruiting-fields for the Left.

Meanwhile, the organization's defiant stand against Islam was increasingly reaping the whirlwind. The polemical candidness pioneered by the Arya Samaj had emboldened other sections of Hindu society to speak their minds about Islam as well, but this triggered a drama in Kohat (North-West Frontier Province). A pamphlet of the local *Sanâtana Dharma Sabhâ*, written by its secretary Jiwan Das in reply to a Muslim pamphlet disparaging Sita, contained an anti-Islamic poem. Frightened by the first Muslim protests, the Hindu minority convened and passed a resolution "regretting their error and requesting pardon". To appease the Muslim protesters, the authorities arrested Jiwan Das and kept him in prison for a week. Nevertheless, on 9 and 10 September 1924, Muslim mobs raided the Hindu neighbourhood, killing dozens of Hindus; the rest had to be escorted to safety by the army.[31]

The most outstanding Arya Samaji of the twentieth century, Swami Shraddhananda, was killed by one Abdul Rashid on 23 December 1926 as he was lying sick in bed. He was soon followed into martyrdom by another prominent Arya Samaji, Lala Nanakchand. Next, Mahashay Raj Pal, signatory of the pamphlet *Rangîla Rasûl* (approximately "Playboy Mohammed"), which contained some petty backbiting about Mohammed's sex life, was killed in his shop by one Ilamdin in April 1929. The murderers were apprehended by the British authorities and duly sentenced. When Abdul Rashid was hanged for murdering Swami Shraddhananda, Muslim clerics all over India held prayer-meetings for his martyred soul. Dr. Ambedkar, the later Minister of Law, testifies: "The

[30]Agnivesh stood as a Janata Dal candidate in the 1991 elections (which did not keep him from protesting, in Brian Barron's BBC *Assignment* documentary on Hindutva, May 1991, that the *sâdhus* of the Vishva Hindu Parishad "mix religion with politics") and is known internationally as a campaigner against debt slavery. See about him e.g. Rudi Rottier: *Kinderen van de krokodil* (Dutch: "Children of the crocodile", on bonded labour), pp.18-19, and Catherine Vuylsteke: "Subversieve swami", *De Morgen*, 9.2.1994. However, when he signs as an office bearer of the "Arya Samaj", it should be kept in mind that his is a breakaway faction, not the organization founded by Swami Dayananda.

[31]R.C. Majumdar: *Struggle for Freedom*, pp.428-33.

leading Muslims, however, never condemned these criminals. On the contrary, they were hailed as religious martyrs."[32]

In 1933, another Arya Samaji, Nathuramal Sharma, was taken to court for publishing a similar pamphlet as Lekh Ram's, and he lost his case under Art.295-A of the Indian Penal Code (enacted in 1898, a move partly triggered by the murder of Lekh Ram), which forbids any form of insult against religions, calculated or reasonably expected to arouse hostility. In September 1934, Sharma went to court to plead his appeal against the sentence, and in the courthouse itself he was murdered by one Abdul Qayum. According to Dr. Ambedkar, "Mr. Barkat Ali, a barrister of Lahore who argued the appeal of Abdul Qayum ... went to the length of saying that Qayum was not guilty of murder of Nathuramal because his act was justifiable by the law of the Koran."[33]

This spate of killings of Arya Samajis in retaliation for their critique of Islam and for their reconversion efforts had the predictable effect of isolating the Arya Samaj from Hindu society. Intimidated by the murders, few people were willing to stand up and say that the Arya Samaj's policy was the correct one. The Arya Samaj got slightly unnerved by the murders and subsequent street riots, against which the police had proven unwilling or unable to protect them. This led to the creation, in 1927, of the *Arya Vîr Dal*, "Arya heroes' group", which took up training in physical self-defence, in an exact parallel with the contemporaneous RSS initiative to include martial training in its daily schedule. These Arya self-defence squads played a central role in the peaceful protest movement (*Satyâgraha*, in the then-common Gandhian term) in 1939 which forced the Nizam, the Muslim princely ruler of Hindu-majority Hyderabad, to adopt political reforms and lift the ban on the *Satyârtha Prakâsh*.[34] And in 1948, they were very active in the struggle with the Muslim *Razâkâr*

---

[32]B.R. Ambedkar: *Writings and Speeches*, vol.8, p.156.

[33]Related by Dr. B.R. Ambedkar: *Writings and Speeches*, vol.8, p.156. Reference is apparently to the same Quran verses as were cited in defence of the death sentence on Salman Rushdie, viz. Q.6:10 ("Mocked were many Messengers before thee; but the scoffers were overpowered by the object they mocked"), Q.13:32 ("Mocked were Messengers before thee, but I gave respite to the Unbelievers and finally I punished them: then how was My chastisement!") and Q.33:57 ("Those who insult Allah and His Messenger—Allah has cursed them in this world and in the Hereafter, and has prepared for them a humiliating punishment").

[34]See J.E. LLewellyn: *Arya Samaj*, p.107.

militia which terrorized the Hindus in a bid to prevent the incorporation of the Nizam's domain into India.[35]

From *c.* 1930, the importance of the Arya Samaj gradually declined, and the 1947 loss to Pakistan of its West Panjab heartland including its nerve centre in Lahore, the Dayananda Anglo-Vedic College campus, definitively demoted it to the back benches of India's social and cultural development. After Independence, the new state ideology of secularism was unfavourable to progressive projects based on religion, and even more to the reconversion campaign. If its activists were no longer martyred, part of the reason was that its stand had become much less bold. None the less, it continues to do meritorious work in education and in the self-organization of overseas Hindus.[36]

Bankimchandra Chatterjee

Hindu Revivalism was and is a widespread ferment only partly channeled by established organizations. Individual writers have pioneered it and only later their thought has been incorporated in the ideology of Hindu organizations.

One of these individuals was Bankimchandra Chatterjee (1838-1894), the Bengali writer. He had received an English education and made his mark as a promotor of Western science. His first novel, *Rajmohan's Wife*, was in English, but for the rest of his work he reverted to Bengali. His religious and philosophical ideas have been expressed in an explicit form in *Dharmatattva* ("Essentials of Dharma", first published as a serial, 1884-85) and *Krishnacharita* ("Life of Krishna", 1885); for the rest, novels carried his message. Women play a central part in his writings ("Woman is the crowning excellence of God's creation ... Woman is light, man is

---

[35]The Arya Samaj leadership in the 1948 struggle in Hyderabad was in the hands of the brothers Vandematharam Veerabhadra Rao and Vandematharam Ramachandra Rao, whom I interviewed in his capacity as *Sarvadeshik Arya Pratinidhi Sabhâ* president in 1995. Prominent Congressman K.M. Munshi, who as Agent General saw to the administrative integration of Hyderabad, said: "The part played by Vandematharam brothers wa accompanied with great risks. I am surprised to see them alive today" (quoted in Mahatm Narayan Swamy: *What is Arya Samaj*, p.50; see also Kranti Kumar Koratkar: *A Gloriou Chapter*).

[36]See e.g. Kumari Saraswati Pandit: *A Critical Study of the Contribution of the Ary Samaj to Indian Education*; and Nardev Vedalankar & Manohar Somera: *Arya Samaj an Indians Abroad*.

shadow")[37], and the Motherland is revered as a Mother Goddess in his most famous and most political novel, *Ananda Math* ("Abbey of Bliss").

The *Ananda Math* story is set in the eighteenth century, when a group of warrior-monks mount a guerrilla was against Muslim rule. The activists of the freedom movement understood this as a metaphor for the struggle against British rule, though in the last chapter, Chatterjee explicitly attributes a historical role to the British in the long-term Hindu revival. The idea that Muslim rule could be considered as a type of colonial rule on par with (or even worse than) British rule is nowadays considered outrageously communal, but at the time, it seemed evident.

Chatterjee's most conspicuous contribution lies in the poem *Vande Mâtaram*, "Hail Mother(land)", which became the battle-song of the 1905 Swadeshi movement against the Partition of Bengal, and of the Indian National Congress.[38] Set to music by Jadunath Bhattacharya, it was first sung at the 1896 session of the Congress.[39] These lyrics became the object of a still unresolved communal controversy because many Muslims consider the song idolatrous, a thinly-veiled hymn to the tigerborne goddess Durga. To placate the Muslims and Jawaharlal Nehru, the Constituent Assembly rejected it as national anthem in favour of Rabindranath Tagore's *Jana Gana Mana*.[40] Justice to *Vande Mâtaram* remains one of the symbolic demands of the Hindu Nationalist movement.

Swami Vivekananda

Another Bengali who made a lasting impression was Swami Vivekananda (1863-1902, civil name Narendranath Dutta). After going through the

---

[37]From B.C. Chatterjee's novel *Krishnakanta's Will*, quoted in William J. Jackson's preface to the Orient Paperbacks English translation by Basanta Koomar Roy of B.C. Chatterjee's *Ananda Math*, p.8.

[38]First given in B.C. Chatterjee: *Ananda Math*, Ch.10, or pp.37-9 of B.K. Roy's translation.

[39]S.B. Bhattacherjee: *Indian Events & Dates*, p.A-124.

[40]*Jana Gana Mana* itself is controversial because Tagore had allegedly written it in honour of the King of England, George V, the *jana gana mana adhinâyak*, "master of the people's minds", and the *Bhârata bhâgya vidhâtâ*, "shaper of India's destiny", mentioned in the opening line. There is a lot of circumstantial evidence for this, and there is no convincing alternative explanation for the said opening line. In his 1911 Delhi *darbâr* (royal court session), George V had annulled the Partition of Bengal, conceding a nationalist demand, and that could give this glorification of the king a nationalist twist; but in general, Tagore was quite pro-British, which is what made him eligible for a Knighthood and the Nobel Prize (1913).

standard English school curriculum, he became a pupil of Sri Ramakrishna Paramahansa (1836-86), an ecstatic devotee of Goddess Kali who, though a married layman, acquired the aura of a great religious visionary. With his limited grounding in traditional religious training, Swami Vivekananda's understanding of Hindu tradition as laid down in his handful of books on yoga is sometimes criticized as distorted and superficial.[41]

Swami Vivekananda gave Hindu self-confidence a boost with his successful lecture tour in Western countries, particularly his widely applauded speech on behalf of the Hindu religion at the Parliament of Religions in Chicago, 1893. Strictly speaking, the official representative of Hinduism was a Brahmo Samaji, Protap Chunder Mazumdar. Vivekananda had been sent by wealthy South Indian sponsors who objected to the idea of being represented by a heterodox Brahmoist.[42]

In 1897 he established the Ramakrishna Mission, a society of monks and laymen who do social and educational work in the spirit of Ramakrishna and Swami Vivekananda. Though Swamiji became world-famous as a "Hindu" monk and launched the still-popular slogan: *Garv se kaho ham Hindû hain* ("Say with pride: we are Hindus"), in the 1980s the Ramakrishna Mission tried to deregister itself as Hindu and get recognition as a non-Hindu religious minority.[43]

The doctrinal position of Vivekananda and his order may be summed up as follows: "The Ramakrishna Mission order ... disseminates Vivekananda's vision of Hindu modernism as Neo-Vedanta: that there is an essential unity to Hinduism underlying the diversity of its many forms. Whereas Christianity accepts only itself as the truth, claimed

---

[41]In his book *The Light at the Center* (pp.153-55), the Austrian indologist and Hindu monk Swami Agehananda Bharati ridicules Vivekananda's writings on yoga as hasty and simplistic. Particularly his *Râja Yoga* is dismissed as a "dangerous" book which has caused "more harm than good".

[42]See Spencer Lavan: "The Brahmo Samaj", in R.D. Baird: *Religion in Modern India*, p.19. According to Spencer Lavan, Vivekananda just happened to be around and was invited on the mistaken assumption that he belonged to Shankaracharya's *Dashanâmî* ("of the ten names", after its branches *Giri*/mountain, *Saraswatî*/river, *Aranya*/forest, *Tîrtha*/ford, etc.) order of monks, the backbone of Hinduism's religious establishment. In those days, real Dashanamis refused to travel abroad for fear of the pollution it brings, so Vivekananda could step in and take their place.

[43]About the RK Mission's defection from Hinduism, see Ram Swarup: *Ramakrishna Mission in Search of a New Identity*. The said slogan is a favourite hate object in secularist circles, e.g. after the Babri Masjid demolition (6.12.1992), anti-Hindutva demonstrators turned it into: *Sharm se kaho ham Hindû hain*, "Say with shame: we are Hindus".

Vivekananda, Hinduism is pluralistic and accepts all religions as aspects of the one truth. This message had great popularity among India's emergent English-educated middle classes, along with Vivekananda's stress on Hinduism as a 'scientific' religion ... While this view of Hinduism tends to override the differences within Hindu traditions (let alone between world religions), and has been criticized as leading to a kind of woolly thinking ... it nevertheless provides a strong ideology to link into Indian nationalism on the one hand, and the construction of Hinduism as a world religion on the other. ... The vision of Hinduism promoted by Vivekananda is one generally accepted by most English-speaking middle-class Hindus today."[44]

Swami Vivekananda's political statements were mostly made during speeches, many of them improvised. These have been published in Vivekananda's *Complete Works*, but also in separate booklets selecting excerpts from a specific ideological angle, whether spiritual or do-gooder, nationalist or Marxist.[45] Indeed, the Marxist Government of West Bengal has invested a lot in recuperating the popular Swami for its own cause, presenting him as a socialist and secularist. Conversely, the polemical passages against Islam in his work have been republished separately by Hindu nationalists in a similar effort at recuperation of Vivekananda's authority.[46] During the twentieth century, Vivekananda has served as an all-purpose authority.

Sri Aurobindo

Sri Aurobindo Ghose (1872-1950), internationally known as a writer on yoga and related subjects, was a revolutionary activist in Bengal during the Swadeshi movement, which aimed at undoing the Partition of Bengal (1905-11). His medium in this period was *Bande Mâtaram*, a paper founded in August 1906 by Bipin Chandra Pal (1858-1932), leader of the "Extremist" faction in the Indian National Congress, then dominated by

---

[44]Gavin Flood: *Introduction to Hinduism*, p.259.

[45]For a nationalist selection, see e.g. Vivekananda: *To the Youth of India*, or Swami Tapasyananda, ed.: *The Nationalistic and Religious Lectures of Swami Vivekananda*. Leftist samples include Vivekananda: *Caste, Culture and Socialism*; Vivekananda: *Proletariat, Win Equal Rights*; and Binoy K. Roy: *Socio-Political Views of Vivekananda*.

[46]J.M. Jagtiani: *Swami Vivekananda on Islam*. I am not aware of a separate publication of his statements on Christianity, but his polemical exchanges with the missionaries have been presented from a Hindu revivalist angle in S.R. Goel: *History of Hindu-Christian Encounters*, Ch.13.

the Moderates. Already by November 1906 he was the controlling editor of the *Bande Mâtaram*, a position which made him one of the leading spokesmen of the Extremist faction. He was arrested in May 1908 as a suspect in the Alipore Bomb case, but was acquitted and released in 1909; on that occasion, he delivered his famous Uttarpara Speech, one of the founding statements of Hindu nationalism (discussed below). In 1910 he retired from active politics, but through his writings he remained in touch with political developments.

In recent biographies and selections of his sayings published by his followers, the revolutionary and Hindu-nationalist aspects of his career are usually minimized in favour of his purely spiritual and universalist dimension. It has been observed that: "His role as a leader of revolutionary terrorists is less well known and its nature uncertain. This is due in large measure to the inadequacies of the secondary literature. Aurobindo's memory is mainly in the keeping of persons interested chiefly in his spiritual accomplishments. ... They concede that Aurobindo was not opposed to violent revolution in principle but never present him as promoting much less taking part in violent acts. He is depicted in these treatments as a dynamic revolutionary leader who had nothing to do with the revolutionaries' deeds."[47]

At least one researcher claims that a perusal of Aurobindo's published writings and diaries shows a gradual development from sympathy for the armed struggle to actual involvement; then to doubts and misgivings after his stay in prison, when he remained in contact with a group of terrorists led by Motilal Roy without trying to restrain them; and finally, by 1914 at the latest, to revulsion. This ultimate rejection was partly out of sympathy for the victims and partly out of the realization that the kind of terrorism then practised in Bengal was a ridiculous conspiratorial game which led its practitioners to the gallows, but not India to Freedom.[48]

Sri Aurobindo's father had chosen to educate his sons like true Englishmen. In England, Aurobindo became proficient in the modern European languages, while also winning prizes in Latin and Greek composition along the way. When at age twenty he decided to give up his

[47]Peter Heehs: "Aurobindo Ghose and Revolutionary Terrorism", *South Asia*, 1992/2, pp.47-69, p.47, with reference to A.B. Purani: *The Life of Sri Aurobindo* (Pondicherry 1978) and K.R.S. Iyengar: *Sri Aurobindo: a Biography and History* (Pondicherry 1985).

[48]Peter Heehs: "Aurobindo Ghose and Revolutionary Terrorism", *South Asia*, 1992/2, pp.67-8.

studies and career prospects in the colonial establishment and serve the cause of India's Freedom instead, he was as estranged from Indian culture as a born Indian could possibly be. The effect of this thorough Westernization is that Aurobindo's attitude to his ancestral culture is clearly coloured by Western concepts, as exemplified by his disdain for "superstitious" ritualism and his concomitant attempt to discard ritualistic explanations of Vedic texts.[49]

The most important example of the Western (including Theosophy's) impact on Aurobindo's understanding of Hinduism is probably his incorporation of the then-recent notion of *evolution* in his theory of yoga (somewhat parallel to Teilhard de Chardin's attempt to integrate evolution into a Christian view of man). In the traditional view, the yogic state is very simple, unchanged since the first yogi stumbled upon this state, forever perfect and beyond progress. Moreover, it is a strictly individual experience: one has to retire from intercourse with the rest of humanity and direct consciousness inward. Aurobindo, by contrast, sees a collective march towards a higher consciousness as a gradual incarnation of the Supermind in mankind. This doctrine, in various forms, has acquired a large following in the past few decades, to the point of being a central idea of what is loosely known as *New Age* thinking. The same assumption of a collective evolution towards spiritual awakening underlies Maharishi Mahesh Yogi's programme (since 1992 also propagated by a worldwide political party, the *Natural Law Party*) of social and political improvement by means of the "good vibrations" emanating from thousands of yogis practising together.[50]

After his retirement from politics to an *ashram* in the French enclave of Pondicherry, Sri Aurobindo did make a few more public statements on current politics. In 1942, he sent a message to the Congress leaders

---

[49]E.g., Aurobindo dismisses the classical commentator Sayana's ritualistic understanding of the Vedas as "the working of a mind ignorant of the meaning of the text and compelled to hammer out a meaning in harmony with tradition and ritualistic prepossessions": *Secret of the Veda*, p.499. This observation may well be right and I tend to agree with it; but the Western influence behind the sudden popularity of this view in India is undeniable.

[50]The idea is that if some thousands of yogis practise together, they create a mental force field which changes people's behaviour for the better, e.g. the crime rate goes down (as Maharishi publications claim to have demonstrated under scientific supervision), and potential enemies would refrain from attacking, see e.g. Mahesh Yogi: *Invincibility to Every Nation through Transcendental Meditation and the TM-Siddhi Programme*, 1978.

(through his secretary Anil Baran Roy who went to see Nehru), urging them to accept the Cripps Mission proposals, i.e. to openly support the British war effort against the Axis powers in exchange for a promise of autonomy after the end of the war. His position, reiterated in a number of letters and talks, was that this was a war of light against darkness, and that the Allied cause was a good cause worth supporting, more even on principle than as a bargaining chip for future negotiations on independence.[51]

In 1949-50, Aurobindo's associate K.D. Sethna edited a fortnightly paper *Mother India*, of which the editorials were subjected to Aurobindo's consent.[52] Through this medium, the aging Aurobindo gave as his opinion that the Chinese occupation of Tibet was an attack on India, and he warmly supported the UN/US war effort in Korea ("The Americans should give the Communists a sound beating").[53] When Hindus reacted angrily to pogroms against the Hindus of East Bengal and to Nehru's passive complicity in the plight of the minorities in Pakistan generally, and particularly when Dilip Kumar Roy, inmate of his ashram, wrote to Aurobindo that he felt like slapping Nehru, Aurobindo made a statement that one should not make too much of the troubles in Pakistan, and that Partition "must and will go". In the 1950s, spokesmen of his Ashram even claimed that he had said that the Partition was bound to be short-lived and India would be reunited in the near future, "within ten years".

One cannot say that Aurobindo's post-*sannyâs* statements have made any impact on Indian political thinking. He had by then been marginalized into a Guru of an increasingly foreign band of yogic disciples who loathed politics, and Hindu politics even more than secular politics. Though

---

[51]Aurobindo's telegram to C. Rajagopalachari, his letter to Sir Stafford Cripps and another letter explaining the same position are partly reproduced in Sri Aurobindo: *India's Rebirth*, pp.228-30. Gandhi's only comment (quoted *ibid.*, though other sources attribute the comment to Nehru) was: "He has retired from political life, why does he interfere!"

[52]After Aurobindo's death on 5 December 1950, the paper soon became irrelevant to politics, though it continued to exist as a monthly controlled by followers who prefer to ignore the political aspect of Aurobindo's thought. K.D. Sethna later wrote some interesting books on ancient Indian history, especially *Karpâsa* ("cotton", about the far-reaching chronological implications of the archaeological and literary evidence concerning cotton, 1981) and *The Problem of Aryan Origins* (1980, 2nd ed. 1992).

[53]For Aurobindo on Communist expansionism, including his prediction in June 1950 that China would invade Tibet (as it did five months later, to Nehru's apparent surprise), see Aurobindo: *India's Rebirth*, pp.244-45; and *Sri Aurobindo on Himself*, pp.416-17.

everything they teach and practise (at Auroville, his followers' model town in Pondicherry, and elsewhere) is taken from Hindu sources, and though their Guru never renounced his commitment to Hindu tradition, his disciples shy away from the word "Hindu".[54] Rather than influencing their surroundings in a pro-Hindu sense, the Aurobindoites followed the spirit of the times in its post-Independence anti-Hindu drift.

The Hindu Renaissance in Bengal was closely linked with the Orientalist fashion in the West. Hindus living in the shadow of British rule acquired some renewed self-respect from the incoming information about the veneration for India among nineteenth-century Westerners like Friedrich Schlegel, Arthur Schopenhauer and Friedrich Max Müller. When by the time of World War 1, this fashion died down, and Aurobindo retired from public life, Hindu Renaissance thought died as well, soon to be replaced by the emerging new fashion from the West, Marxism.

THE HINDU MAHASABHA

Congress and Muslim League

The Indian National Congress was from the beginning (1885) a movement manned and led mostly by Hindus, though not a Hindu movement. By contrast, Muslims were conspicuous by their absence, much to the desperation of the Congress leadership. The attempt to attract and show off Muslim participants was intensified after the creation of the All-India Muslim League in 1906. This organization was directly opposed to the anti-colonial programme which had in the mean time been adopted by the Congress, and was explicitly loyal towards the British Empire.

Indeed, in his inaugural address at the founding session of the Muslim League, Viqar-ul-Mulk had declared that the League would work for the Muslim community's interest "without prejudice to the traditional loyalty of the Mussalmans to the Government".[55] Again, the meeting of the Council of the All-India Muslim League on 31 December 1912, presided over by the Aga Khan, passed a resolution defining the aims of the Muslim

[54]Still, a few lone voices among them have taken up the thread of Hindu awakening where their Guru had left it, notably at the Mira Aditi Centre in Mysore and its European partner, the *Institut de Recherches Evolutives* in Paris, which published the already-quoted selection of Aurobindo's political statements, *India's Rebirth*.

[55]Dhaka, 30.12.1906; see B.N. Pandey, ed.: *The Indian Nationalist Movement 1885-1947*, p.18.

League, the first of which was: "To promote and maintain among Indians feelings of loyalty towards the British Crown".[56] It should admittedly be kept in mind that the Indian National Congress had likewise been started on a loyalist platform, as a harmless debating society. But the much-resented Partition of Bengal in 1905 definitively set Congress on an independentist course. This in turn triggered the formalization of British-Muslim rapprochement in 1906.

The pro-British position of the first all-India Muslim political forum was partly the result of a deliberate British policy of ruling India with the help of privileged enclaves within the native society (most conspicuously the Sikhs). But it is quite naïve to blame the British for the opposition of the Muslim elites to the Freedom Movement, and rank sentimentalism to claim that without this British "divide and rule" policy, the Indian Muslims and Hindus would have co-operated in a spirit of brotherhood and common national feeling. The British only used the opportunity which Indian communal realities had offered them.

In 1906, the same situation prevailed all over India which the historic Muslim League president Mohammed Ali Jinnah was to describe in 1940 as follows: "The differences in India were far greater than those between European countries and were of a vital and fundamental character. ... The Muslims had a different conception of life from the Hindus. They admired different qualities in their heroes; they had a different culture based on Arabic and Persian instead of Sanskrit origins. Their social customs were entirely different. Hindu society and philosophy were the most exclusive in the world. Muslims and Hindus had been living side by side in India for a thousand years but if one went into any Indian city one would see separate Hindu and Muslim quarters."[57]

Upon quoting this famous passage, historian R.C. Majumdar rightly comments: "It is impossible to deny that there was a great deal of truth in Jinnah's assessment of Hindu-Muslim relationship, which a patriotic Indian may regret, but can ignore only at his peril."[58]

To be sure, there was plenty of Hindu-Muslim syncretism. At the mass level, many Muslim communities had been islamized only superficially. When the first census (1881) showed that the Muslims constituted the majority in Bengal, this came as a big surprise, because most of them

---

[56]Included in B.N. Pandey: *Indian Nationalist Movement*, p.19.

[57]R.C. Majumdar: *Struggle for Freedom*, pp.729-30.

[58]R.C. Majumdar: *Struggle for Freedom*, p.730.

didn't *look* like Muslims outwardly (till today, many Bengali Muslim women wear saris, denounced by clerics as un-Islamic and typically Hindu). At the elite level, many Hindu princes had adopted the styles and language of the Muslim courts. Nevertheless, the sense of communal identity was nearly universal in the urban centres where politics was practised, and the existing syncretistic phenomena were to be combated with remarkable success in the subsequent decades, especially by the Tabligh movement, which sought to weed out un-Islamic customs and practices among nominal Muslims. It is in addition to this existing religious cleavage of society that the institutional fact of communal politics, formally started with the founding of the Muslim League, was to force its own logic upon the consciousness of Hindus and Muslims.

Congress tried its utmost best to attract Muslims and become a truly representative body. At the same time, the officially unacknowledged Hindu identity of Congress members was being explicitated in the political agitation of the Congress among the masses. Gopal Krishna Gokhale gave the slogan: "Spiritualize politics!"[59] Bal Gangadhar Tilak turned the Freedom Movement into a mass movement at least at the local level of his native Maharashtra by giving a nationalist dimension to the traditional *Ganesh Chaturthî* festival. Mohandas Karamchand Gandhi (1869-1948) was to extend this approach to the national level. But when the Muslim League started its communal politics, defending sectional rather than national interests, Congress did not respond by espousing Hindu interests, but by maintaining its national outlook and pretending to be as representative of Indian Muslims as of the Hindus.

The Hindu Sabha

Not all Congressmen were satisfied to see a Muslim party defend Muslim interests at the expense of Hindu interests without creating a Hindu counterweight. In response to the creation of the Muslim League in 1906, within months provincial *Hindû Sabhâ*s were founded in Panjab (the Arya Samaj heartland) and then in other provinces. Already in 1910, an *All-India Hindû Sabhâ* (headquarters in Allahabad) was created as a common platform of local Hindu Sabhas, at least on paper.

This is the testimony of the leading Congressman Motilal Nehru (1861-1931, Congress president in 1919 and 1928), writing to his son

[59]Quoted in D. Keer: *Lokamanya Tilak*, p.xix.

Jawaharlal about the Congress session held in the last week of December 1910: "The Congress passed off successfully in the sense that there was no row. The Hindu-Mohammedan Conference brought about by Sir W.W. [William Wedderburn] went off successfully too, in the same sense. They called each other 'brothers', 'cousins', and so on. There were a few gushing speeches and the function ended by the appointment of a Committee of eight Hindus and eight Mohammedans with Gokhale as the 17th member nominated by the Aga Khan. It is certain that this Committee will either never meet or come to no conclusion whatever.

"Another new feature of the Congress week has been that it has given birth to an All India Hindu Sabha which in my opinion will not only minimize all chance of the Hindu-Mohammedan Committee doing any good but sap the foundation of the Congress itself. I opposed the formation of this Sabha as strongly as I could and had the satisfaction of bringing round to my view men like B.N. Bose and S.N. Banerjee, but the great majority of the so-called leaders in Upper India, specially those of the Panjab, all worked themselves into a high pitch and could not be made to listen to reason. Bombay, Madras and Central India were not even consulted and yet the name given to the new organization is the All India Hindu Sabha. I have refused to join it."[60]

As Motilal Nehru's testimony confirms, this All India Hindu Sabha was originally a forum of Congressmen, i.e. of men committed to the cause of India's Freedom (then not necessarily understood as full independence outside the British Empire). This is in diametrical contrast with the Muslim League, which was started as a counter-weight against the freedom movement, an embodiment of Anglo-Muslim cooperation.

While opposing the Muslim League, the Hindu politicians who founded the Hindu Sabha were also imitating it in at least one important respect, viz. its attempt to unite all sections of the community on a single platform in order better to defend its interests (though it was never remotely successful in this endeavour, much less than the League). In the words of Sir Shadi Lal, then president of the Panjab Hindu Sabha, in 1912, "events of the past four or five years proved beyond the shadow of doubt that with a body which could speak with the authority of the entire Hindu community behind its back and resist the aggressive action of the Moslem League, the Hindus would not have been in the plight in which they find

[60]Letter to Jawaharlal Nehru, dated 6 January 1911; included in B.N. Pandey, ed.: *The Indian National Movement 1885-1947, Select Documents*, pp.18-19.

themselves at present."[61] In its initial phase, then, the Hindu Sabha was a purely reactive phenomenon, an attempt to counter Muslim communal organization for the furtherance of Muslim interests by means of Hindu self-organization for the defence of Hindu interests.

The Hindu Mahasabha

The All-India Hindu Sabha was never very active: "The objects and rules of the Sabha were settled and the office-bearers were elected but owing to diverse reasons, no practical steps could be taken to make the organisation a reality", mostly because "Hindu lethargy was a hard nut to crack".[62] The initiative to turn the loose confederation of Hindu Sabhas into an effective political organization at the national level was taken by the conservative Pandit Madan Mohan Malaviya (1861-1946, Congress president in 1909 and 1918), otherwise best known for founding *Benares Hindu University* in 1916. Significantly, this Hindu institution never became a very effective centre of Hindu mobilization the way Aligarh Muslim University became the locomotive of the Pakistan movement; though it did play a role in the freedom movement and especially in the promotion of Hindi.[63]

Contemporary Hindu Mahasabha (hereafter HMS) documents mention 1915 as the year of its formal foundation, but in fact it was a gradual process. The first issue to mobilize the Hindu Sabhas and whip some life into their new national forum was the Lucknow Pact of 1916 between Congress and the Muslim League, in which the Congress leadership had conceded the principle of communal electorates (i.e. separate electorates for Hindus and Muslims, with Muslim candidates being answerable only to Muslim voters) and weightage in representation (one-third of the seats in the Central Assembly for the 22% Muslims).

This upset the Hindus because they objected to the principles of communal electorates and communal weightage (unknown in the only model of modern democracy they knew, Great Britain), but most of all

---

[61]Quoted in Indra Prakash: *Hindu Mahasabha, Its Contribution to India's Politics*, p.12. It is not clear what "plight" of the Hindus is referred to; the long-standing Hindu demand that the Partition of Bengal be undone had just been conceded.

[62]Indra Prakash: *Hindu Mahasabha*, p.13.

[63]The Marxist fortnightly *Frontline* ("Confrontation at BHU", 4.4.1997) concedes this much: "The Benares Hindu University has an important place in modern Indian history. ... Students and teachers of the University ... were involved in the freedom movement, and the resistance by campus-based organisation to the Emergency in 1976-77 was notable. The movements invariably brought students and teachers together and the campus was known for a certain democratic spirit."

because they saw it as a trendsetter for similar future developments, as proof that the Congress leadership was on the slippery ground of conceding anything the Muslims demanded. As if to confirm these fears, the Muslim leader Muhammad Ali related later about the Lucknow talks: "When at Lucknow, in 1916, some Hindus complained to my late chief, Bal Gangadhar Tilak Maharaj, that they were giving too much to the Musalmans, he answered back like a true and far-seeing statesman, *'You can never give the Musalmans too much'*."[64] And Tilak was a staunch Hindu, still a revered name in the Hindutva account of the freedom struggle. If he could make such concessions, the HMS saw reason to fear that others might go even farther in the policy which would later be called "Muslim appeasement".

However strong the HMS's dismay with the compromise policies of the Indian National Congress, its opposition could never be very effective with leading HMS men also being Congress office-bearers. This was even more painfully clear in 1920, when the Congress leadership decided on a mass movement of Non-Co-operation in support of the pan-Islamist agitation for the restoration to the Turkish Ottoman Caliph of his empire and at least of the guardianship of the Islamic sacred sites in Palestine and the Hejaz. *Khilâfat* concerns had already provided the background to the Lucknow Pact of 1916: the Muslim League had only been willing to make a deal with the Congress when it developed an anti-British grievance of its own, viz. over the British war effort against the Ottoman Empire, an ally of Germany, in World War 1. Now that the Ottoman Empire had been reduced to its Turkish rump, Indian Muslims felt they had to start a life-and-death struggle to preserve the gravely threatened *Khilâfat*.

This Muslim concern about the Caliphate was understandable, but it was much less evident that the Indian National Congress ought to support the Caliphate cause. Later HMS writings denounce the 1920 decision in its support as a Himalayan blunder, but the fact is: among the signatories we notice HMS leader M.M. Malaviya and others who now belong to the Hindu nationalist pantheon, such as Lala Lajpat Rai. One of the highlights of the *Khilâfat* agitation was when another HMS pioneer, Arya Samaj

---

[64]Md. Ali: speech delivered at the annual session of the Indian National Congress at Coconada in 1923, quoted in V.P. Varma: *Modern Indian Political Thought*, pp.438-39; emphasis mine.

educationist Swami Shraddhananda, spoke at the Jama Masjid to the Muslims of Delhi in support of the *Khilâfat* cause.

But this Hindu-Muslim honeymoon was to be short-lived. When Gandhiji called off the Non-Co-operation campaign after the killings of some policemen by his own followers in Chauri-Chaura, the Muslim Khilafatists felt let down and soon turned against the Hindus. It was the Hindu-Muslim riots of 1921-24 which whipped the HMS into becoming a real political force. Two of the most important HMS leaders, Bhai Parmananda and Balkrishna Shivram Moonje (1872-1948, founder of the Bhonsle Military School in Nasik), cited their horror at the massacres of Hindus in Kohat and Malabar as their personal reason to throw their full weight behind the HMS.[65]

The escalation of Muslim and Hindu self-organization for an ongoing confrontation was now in full gear: "Later in the year [1923] the Muslims started a definite communal movement called *Tanzeem* and *Tabligh* in order to organize the Muslims as a virile community. All this had a great repercussion upon the Hindu Mahasabha which, among other things, sought to strengthen the Hindu community by admitting the depressed classes to the rights and privileges of the higher classes. Corresponding to the Tanzeem and Tabligh of the Muslims, a *Sangathan* movement sprang up among the Hindus."[66] From this time onwards, *Hindû Sangathan* (Hindu self-organization) became the most important focus of Hindu revivalist activity.

Save the dying race

The Hindu Mahasabha had appeared on the scene at a time when among Hindus, the drive towards independence was growing at the cost of the commitment to social reform. In the Congress, it was Bal Gangadhar Tilak who represented this shift most explicitly: a radical in demanding independence, he also opposed raising the minimum marriage age (pleading that a foreign government has no right to legislate for the Hindus) and observed caste discrimination in his private life even when

---

[65]Indra Prakash: *Hindu Mahasabha*, p.17 and p.22.

[66]R.C. Majumdar: *Struggle for Freedom*, p.425. *Tanzîm/tanzîmat* = reorganization (as a reform policy in the Ottoman Empire, which was essentially right but "too little too late", it is sometimes translated, with reference to a similarly desperate but belated attempt at reform in recent history, as *perestroika*); *tablîgh* = propaganda; *sangathan* = organization.

signing some mild anti-caste resolutions in public.[67] The early Hindu Mahasabha too was inclined towards the orthodox and conservative line, in spite of the presence of Arya Samaj reformists like Lala Lajpat Rai, because it saw itself as a pan-Hindu platform open to the conservatives as well.

In 1923-25, the Arya Samaj leader Swami Shraddhananda strongly pleaded the ethical as well as the political necessity of social reform. He was disappointed with the slackness of the HMS on the vital question of ending the discriminations against Untouchables. The dead-weight impact of conservatives on the social reform drive of the likes of Shraddhananda was to trouble the party at least until Vinayak Damodar Savarkar became the party's president in 1937, and then it only moved out of sight because the communal escalation was absorbing all the attention. (An idea of the increasing hold of conservatives on the HMS can be deduced from the fact that in 1933, Shri Bharati Krishna Tirtha, the Puri Shankaracharya, condemned the HMS for working against caste,[68] and that in 1936, the same man was elected HMS president.)

During the post-Khilafat Hindu-Muslim conflict, Swami Shraddhananda got a copy of a pamphlet which was being spread among the Muslim elites, with a view to mobilizing them all for a grand strategy of conversion of low-caste Hindus to Islam. The pamphlet, *Daî-i Islâm* (Urdu: "Invitation to Islam") by Khwaja Hasan Nizami, had been written as the foreword to a larger book, *Fâtamî Dawat-i Islâm*, (Urdu: "Islamic Conversion Work"), which laid out detailed plans for securing a Muslim majority in India by means of large-scale conversions, all the while impressing on its readers the need to keep the operation a secret.[69] Its message was that all Muslims, from princes to prostitutes, should each make their contribution to the project of penetrating Hindu communities and converting Hindus.

Alarmed by this pamphlet, Shraddhananda lost his last illusions about Hindu-Muslim unity. With an increased sense of urgency he took up

---

[67]See D. Keer: *Lokamanya Tilak*, Ch.5. Reform often being associated with the European Enlightenment, hence with colonialism, the leaders of the decolonization process were sometimes spokesmen for barbaric native customs, e.g. in his independence speech, Jomo Kenyatta of Kenya announced that the native custom of female circumcision would be restored.

[68]Shri Bharati Krishna Tirtha: *Secret of India's Greatness* (a collection of lectures given in 1933), p.111.

[69]Discussed in J.T.F. Jordens: *Swami Shraddhananda, His Life and Causes*, p.148. Abdul Rashid, who killed Shraddhananda, had been inspired to this act by Hasan Nizami.

Shuddhi work. After his retirement from active politics, he summarized the strategic assessment of the problems before Hindu society which he had developed over the years, along with the outline of a solution, in his most influential book, *Hindu Sangathan, Saviour of the Dying Race* (1926), undoubtedly a milestone in the history of Hindu revivalism.

In this book, Shraddhananda argues at length that the Indian Muslim community is the result of forcible conversions of Hindus. He finds his evidence largely in the details of a book which seeks to prove the exact opposite, *The Preaching of Islam* by T.W. Arnold (1913). In episodes which Arnold cites as voluntary conversion, Shraddhananda detects indications of forms of social pressure and indirect threats which do not amount to brute force but which could only be labelled "voluntary" with considerable cynicism. The whole point of this argument is to show that Indian Muslims are not "really" Muslims, and that it is best for them to undo the forcible conversion of their ancestors by returning to the Vedic fold.

A second point is the way Hindu social customs contribute to the growing strength of Islam in India, e.g. how the prohibition on widow remarriage was forcing many pubescent widows (there were hundreds of thousands of them, married in childhood and losing their "husbands" to childhood diseases etc.) into prostitution or into marrying Muslims. This, then, is the over-all message of the book: the close interconnectedness between the ongoing struggle with Islam and the struggle against social evils in Hindu society.

One of the highlights of Shraddhananda's book was a diagnosis of the competition between Hindus and Muslims for the numbers: "while Muhammadans multiply like anything, the numbers of the Hindus are dwindling periodically".[70] The Swami quoted from the 1911 Census Report to show the reasons why the Muslim population was growing faster than the Hindu population: "The number of Muhammadans has risen during the decade [1901-11] by 6.7 per cent as compared with only 5 p.c. in the case of Hindus. There is a small but continuous accession of converts from Hinduism and other religions, but the main reason for the relatively more rapid growth of the followers of the Prophet is that they are more prolific."[71] Follow a number of social customs which encourage

[70]Shraddhananda: *Hindu Sangathan*, p.99.

[71]Shraddhananda: *Hindu Sangathan*, pp.18-19.

the Muslim birth rate, for example, fewer marriage restrictions and common remarriage of widows, absence of a celibate monkhood, and the Muslim insistence that the children of mixed marriages be brought up as Muslims.

In 1909, on the basis of demographic trends visible in the census results, Colonel U.N. Mukherji had projected the rate of Hindu decline into the future in a strictly linear fashion, and calculated logically (if simplistically) that it would take less than 420 years for the Hindu race to disappear completely from the face of India. The series of articles in the *Bengalee* of 1909 in which Mukherji proposed his analysis was titled: "Hindus, a Dying Race".[72] One of Mukherji's concluding sentences, "They count their gains, we calculate our losses", became the title of a Hindu Mahasabha pamphlet as late as 1979.[73]

The Hindu suspicion that Islam is using demography to increase its strength is a constant theme in Hindu Revivalist writing till today. The rhetoric is often shrill and exaggerated, for example, a variation on the official birth-control slogan, *"we are two, our [children] are two"*, is the following: "For the Hindu the slogan is: *We are two, and we have two*. The slogan for a Moslem is: *We are five and we have twentyfive*."[74] Sometimes, outside authorities (the BBC, the WHO) are falsely claimed as confirming the Hindus' worst fears: "The United Nations census projections have indicated that the uncontrolled birthrate of the Moslems of India coupled with huge infiltrations will turn India into a Moslem majority country before the year 2000 AD."[75]

It is, therefore, no surprise that the *Economist* ridicules these demographic doomsday scenarios: "Hindu militants are talking nonsense by predicting that chunks of the country will gain Muslim majorities and then secede".[76] There is no doubt that some of the rhetoric is nonsense, but it doesn't follow that the proportional decline of the Hindus is mere

[72]See also P.K. Datta: "'Dying Hindus'—Production of Hindu communal common sense in early 20th century Bengal", *Economic and Political Weekly*, 19.6.1993, p.1307; and C. Jaffrelot: *Hindu Nationalist Movement*, p.24. Typically, both exclusively discuss the presumed sociological determinants and other externals of Mukherji's analysis, not its degree of accuracy.

[73]Indra Prakash: *They Count Their Gains, We Calculate Our Losses.*

[74]S.K. Bhattacharyya: *Genocide in East Pakistan/Bangladesh*, p.159. In the Hindi original: *Ham do hamâre do—Ham pânch hamâre pachîs*. The saying is sometimes accompanied by a cartoon showing the Government poster (father, mother, boy, girl) plus its alleged Muslim variant: a man with goat-beard and four veiled wives surrounded by a sea of children.

[75]S.K. Bhattacharyya: *Genocide in East Pakistan/Bangladesh*, p.151.

[76]*The Economist*, 7.11.1992.

fantasy. The *Economist* itself acknowledges the numerical gains of the Indian Muslim community, and explains that, apart from a lower infant mortality rate (Muslims are more concentrated in the cities where medical care is better), Muslims are less willing to use birth control.

Because of the time lapse, the present generation is in a position to evaluate these predictions. In truncated India, the Muslim population has grown 2.69 per cent in forty years (from 9.91 per cent to 12.60 per cent in 1951-91)[77], though Muslim leaders claim that the true figure of the Muslim population in the Indian Republic is about 3 per cent higher.[78] Even without these alleged unregistered millions, it is hardly exaggerated to say that in the Indian Republic, ever since 1951, "the proportion of Muslims has been gradually but steadily increasing every decade by roughly one percentage point".[79] By contrast, the Hindu category (which includes the pre-Independence "animist" category) declined from 84.98 per cent to 81.54 per cent. It is conceded by all sides that as per the census results, the Muslim percentage has kept on increasing every decade in British India, independent India, Pakistan and Bangladesh.[80] The Muslim percentage in the subcontinent has grown from 19.97 per cent in 1881 to 24.28 per cent in 1941 and to 29.92 per cent.[81] The Hindu percentage

---

[77]Table of census data in K.R. Malkani: *The Politics of Ayodhya and Hindu-Muslim relations*, appendix 4. In the absence of actual census data for Jammu and Kashmir, an extrapolation is used for that state, see Ashish Bose: "1991 Census data: Muslim rate of growth", *Indian Express*, 9.9.1995, and Syed Shahabuddin: "Census 1991, Muslim Indians and Sangh Parivar", *Muslim India*, September 1995, p.386. This estimate is based on the assumption of a constant ratio between the religions, which understates the Muslim percentage by ignoring the higher Muslim birth rate and the massive Hindu emigration from the state.

[78]In a letter published in *Organiser*, 15.6.1997, Syed Shahabuddin opines that the Indian Muslims may well be "the largest Muslim community in the world", i.e. larger than the Indonesian Muslim community.

[79]Ashish Bose: "1991 Census data: Muslim rate of growth", *Indian Express*, 9.9.1995.

[80]The only *seeming* exception is Pakistan between 1971 and 1981, owing to the official declaration of Ahmadiyas, at 3%, as non-Muslims in 1974; I include them in the Muslim category, as they themselves also do.

[81]Figures for British and Independent India are reproduced in appendix 4 in K.R. Malkani: *The Politics of Ayodhya and Hindu-Muslim relations*. The figure for Bangladesh (86.8% of 108,760,000) is based on *Encyclopaedia Brittannica, Book of the Year 1992*, entry *Bangladesh*, official figure for 1991. Figure for Pakistan (97.0% of 126,406,000) is based on UNO estimate for religion-wise percentage given in *Jaarboek 1996* of *Winkler Prins-Encyclopedie* (the 1991 census did not take place); the *Encyclopeadia Brittannica* yearbooks 1991-96 only give the 1981 figure: 96.7%. Estimated total for 1991 is 29.92% of 1,081,515,050, or about 323,657,480 Muslims in the subcontinent.

declined from 77.66 per cent to 71.72 per cent (or from 75.09 per cent to 69.46 per cent if the "animist" category is excluded), and to 65.15 per cent in 1991.[82] Mukherji's calculations implied that the Hindu percentage in the sub-continent would fall to 54 per cent by 1991, so he has clearly exaggerated.

Secularist observers have admitted that "it is true that the growth rate amongst Muslims is higher than amongst Hindus", and have calculated that "if both the communities continue to grow at the same rate, ... it will take 316 years for Muslims to outnumber Hindus".[83] Though less dramatic than Mukherji's prediction, this too implies that demography leads India straight to a Muslim majority. However, like Mukherji's, this projection is a strictly linear extrapolation of the Hindu-Muslim differential in the recent past (i.e. in the decade 1971-1981), while the demographic evolution is not linear. The Muslim percentage has not only increased, but the rate of increase itself has increased. This is very clear when we take a long-term perspective: in the *fifty* years between 1941 and 1991, their percentage has risen 5.64 per cent, substantially more than the 4.31 per cent gain in the *sixty* years between 1881 and 1941. On the Hindu side too, we see a long-term acceleration of the observed trend: a decrease of 5.94 per cent in the sixty years between 1881 and 1941, and a larger decrease of 6.57 per cent in the shorter period of fifty years between 1941 and 1991.

At the subcontinental level, Muslims were increasing and Hindus decreasing by less than 1 per cent before 1941, and by more than 1 per cent after 1941. Moreover, the cumulative effect of the larger Hindu participation in birth control since the 1960s in the birth rate of the next (proportionately smaller) Hindu generation is only just beginning to show in the 1991 census, but this factor, unforeseen by Shraddhananda, is bound to have a larger effect in the next decades. So, the observed trends are accelerating, and unless the tide is turned, Muslims will need far less than 316 years to outnumber the Hindus in India.

This means, from the Hindu revivalist angle, that time is running out, though at a pace slow enough to allow for counter-measures. These were outlined by Swami Shraddhananda as essentially two: *Shuddhi* (reconversion of Indian Muslims to Hinduism) and *Sangathan*: "self-organization". It was to this task of Hindu Sangathan that the historic leaders of Hindu revivalist associations would apply themselves.

---

[82]This assumes the *Encyclopaedia Brittannica* figure for the 1991 Hindu percentage in Bangladesh, viz. 11.9%, which is probably too high.

[83]N. Bhandare, L. Fernandes, M. Jain: "A pampered minority?", *Sunday*, 7.2.1993.

Swatantryaveer Savarkar

In 1934, HMS leader Bhai Parmananda decided to change his organization from an intra-Congress lobby group into a separate political party. This was partly in response to pressures from Congress Leftists who insisted that dual membership in HMS and Congress be disallowed. Soon after, the HMS acquired a more distinctive ideological identity thanks to the rise of Vinayak Damodar Savarkar (1883-1966) on the political firmament. At that time, V.D. Savarkar was already a big name in India as a hero and martyr of the armed faction of the freedom movement.

In 1899, the young Savarkar had founded the *Mitra Melâ* ("Friends' Assembly"), later known as the *Abhinava Bhârat* ("Young India") Society. The latter name was an explicit adaptation of *Giovine Italia*, "Young Italy", the activist group founded by the nineteenth-century Italian nationalist Giuseppe Mazzini, whose liberal-nationalist ideas and revolutionary example were to influence Savarkar as much as Hindu tradition did. Mainly consisting of college students, the group promoted traditional forms of exercise and popularized nationalist ballads to spread the message among the masses.[84] It counted armed struggle among the legitimate methods for throwing off the foreign yoke. Working as a secret society, the group established links with its Bengali counterpart, the *Anushîlan Samiti*, to co-ordinate revolutionary activity.[85] However, consisting of middle-class intellectuals, these groups failed in their attempts to reach the masses.

Meanwhile, these "revolutionary terrorists" did manage to create an atmosphere of danger and unwelcomeness for the colonial administrators, especially in Bengal after the Partition of that province in 1905.[86] Even in England itself they struck terror with murder attempts on retired colonial officials. It was in connection with one such (successful) attempt, that Savarkar, shortly after his graduation from the Law Faculty, was arrested in March 1910 (his registration for qualifying as a barrister had already been cancelled because of his seditious activities). He had not personally participated in the murder of Sir William Curzon-Wyllie, but he had

[84]W. Andersen and S. Damle: *Brotherhood in Saffron*, p.17.

[85]The *Anushîlan Samiti*, more or less "Devoted Practice Committee", was named after the guerrilla group in Bankimchandra Chatterjee's novel *Ananda Math*, a case of life imitating art.

[86]About the revolutionaries, especially the martyred ones, see Pandit Bakhle, ed.: *Heroes of the Freedom Struggle*.

provided the murderer, Madanlal Dhingra, with the revolver. He was tried in a London court and deported for trial in the Nasik Conspiracy case.

Savarkar was being transported from Britain to India when he made use of the ship's anchoring in the harbour of Marseilles to make his spectacular escape. He was caught by the French police and handed over to his British pursuers on French soil, in violation of international law. The case was taken to the International Court at The Hague, but after a well-publicized trial, the Court ruled in favour of the British. At that time, Savarkar had already been sentenced in India and incarcerated in a penal colony on the Andaman Islands. He stayed there until 1921, when he was moved to Ratnagiri prison near Mumbai. By that time, his release was being demanded in many forums, especially after earlier amnesty decrees following the British victory in the Great War, and in 1923 even the Indian National Congress passed a resolution demanding his release. On 6 January 1924, he was released, after signing a promise that he would stay in the Ratnagiri district and refrain from politics for five years.

It was during his stay in Ratnagiri prison, in 1922, that he wrote his influential book *Hindutva* ("Hindu-ness"). The text was smuggled out and published under a pseudonym. The highlight of the book was his definition of the term *Hindu*: "one for whom India is both Fatherland and Holyland". Swami Shraddhananda was among those who expressed their enthusiasm for the book: "It must have been one of those Vedic dawns indeed which inspired our seers with new truths that revealed to the author of *Hindutva* this Mantra, this definition of Hindutva."[87]

In 1937, shortly after being freed from all constraints on his movements and political involvement, Savarkar was elected as President of the HMS. His speeches given in that capacity at the annual meetings, bundled in the book *Hindû Râshtra Darshan* ("Vision of the Hindu State"), constitute another important formulation of Hindutva ideology. In 1943 he retired from the HMS presidency for health reasons. In 1948 he was dragged to prison as a co-accused in the Mahatma murder case, but he was acquitted.

Veer Savarkar died in 1966. He fasted unto death after it had become clear that he had no chance of recovering a decent state of health.[88] This self-chosen death confirmed him in his role as the antipode of Mahatma

---

[87]Quoted in Dhananjay Keer: *Veer Savarkar*, p.162.

[88]About Savarkar, see D. Keer: *Veer Savarkar*; V. Grover, ed.: *V.D. Savarkar*; Jagjit Singh, ed.: *Savarkar*.

Gandhi, who "fasted unto death" a dozen times without ever dying except by a bullet.

The murder of the Mahatma

In the months after the Independence and Partition of India on 15 August 1947, Hindu public opinion in truncated India was angered by the sight of massive waves of refugees from the new state of Pakistan, and turned against the Congress leadership which had won the December 1945 elections by promising to prevent Partition; or, as the HMS would have it, by "stealing the HMS campaign platform". This was, after all, not the independence of a united Motherland, which Mahatma Gandhi and millions of Hindus had been fighting for, but the independence of a truncated India and of an intrinsically hostile neighbour carved out of her, Islamic Pakistan. Now that Congress had broken its promise by negotiating the Partition of India, the HMS was in a position to make spectacular gains among the Hindu electorate. But just when the political wind seemed finally to be blowing the HMS way, the party was reduced to an insignificant fringe group overnight.

As millions of Hindu refugees kept pouring in from newly-created Pakistan, there was a public outcry against the politicians who had not been willing or able to ward off the Partition, especially against the main champion of Hindu-Muslim unity, Mahatma Gandhi. Cries of *Gândhî murdâbâd* ("death to Gandhi", usually to be interpreted as a softer "down with Gandhi", but on that occasion often intended literally) were the order of the day during Hindu-Sikh protest demonstrations. It got worse when Gandhi forced the Government to pay Rs. 550 million to Pakistan as its share in the British-Indian treasury, in spite of the occupation of a part of Kashmir (and the wholesale elimination of the Hindu and Sikh minorities there) by Pakistani troops. In this climate, a small group of Hindu Mahasabhaites could not control their anger, and decided to murder the Mahatma. A clumsy collective attempt on 20 January failed, but on 30 January 1948, when Gandhiji came out for his public prayer session in the garden of Birla House in New Delhi, Nathuram Godse, editor of the Pune-based HMS-leaning Marathi paper *Hindû Râshtra*, fired the fatal shots at the Mahatma.[89]

[89]For factual accounts of the murder intrigue, see Tapan Ghosh: *The Gandhi Murder Trial*, and Manohar Malgonkar: *The Men who Killed Gandhi*; for a more popular but biased and occasionally inaccurate account, see Larry Collins and Dominique Lapierre: *Freedom at Midnight*, chapters 16-20.

In the subsequent trial, party ideologue Veer Savarkar was acquitted and the party itself cleared of all suspicion of complicity in the murder, but the actual conspirators were convicted. Nathuram Godse and his closest associate Narayan Apte were hanged, three others including Godse's brother Gopal were given long prison sentences. However, the trial was the occasion of Nathuram Godse's defence speech (published first as *May It Please Your Honour*, more recently as *Why I Assassinated Gandhi*), which is a remarkable critique of the Mahatma's policies, a handy summary of all the pre-1948 Hindu invective against Gandhiji for his "appeasement policy" vis-à-vis the Muslims.[90]

The post-1948 HMS

The Mahatma murder case was the end of the HMS as a political alternative to the Congress. Immediately after the murder the party was banned, its offices closed down (if not burnt down by mobs), its workers arrested. Less well-known is that the followers of the apostle of non-violence murdered an unknown number of Brahmins, especially Chitpavan Brahmins, the caste to which the murderer belonged.[91] It was the same type of collective revenge as the one wrought on the Sikh community of Delhi (killing several thousands) by Congress activists after the murder of Indira Gandhi by her Sikh bodyguards in 1984. The house of party president L.B. Bhopatkar, another Chitpavan Brahmin, was burnt down. But more definitive than the material destruction was the political damage.

After the Court had ruled that the party as such had not been involved in the conspiracy, the ban was lifted. However, the HMS was totally discredited and condemned to a shadowy existence. Shyama Prasad Mookerjee, its main leader apart from the sickly Savarkar, left the party first to join the Congress, then to lead the newly-founded *Jana Sangh*. After 1948, the HMS has occasionally managed to get one to three candidates elected to the Lok Sabha. Its last MP so far was Mahant Avaidyanath, elected from Gorakhpur in 1989, but in subsequent elections he campaigned on an *ad hoc* "United Hindu Front" ticket, under the umbrella of the rival *Bhâratîya Janatâ Party* (BJP).

---

[90]The latest edition of Nathuram Godse's speech, *Why I Assassinated Mahatma Gandhi*, was published with a lengthy introduction and appendices by co-conspirator Gopal Godse; see also the latter's own account: *Gandhiji's Murder and After*.

[91]The official death toll was 8; the *New York Times* of 31.1.1948 counted double that number in Mumbai alone, while eye-witnesses told me (admittedly after a lapse of half a century) of "at least fifty in Pune alone".

The reason for Avaidyanath's seeming defection is that in 1992 (as already foreseen by Avaidyanath in the 1991 election campaign) the Election Commission decided to de-register the HMS as a political party, on the ground that it "mixes religion with politics". When given the choice to either scrap the word "Hindu" from its name and constitution or face deregistration, the HMS chose to stay true to its explicitly Hindu identity. However, in 1996 the HMS won its appeals trial against this deregistration. None the less, its chances of returning to Parliament seem bleak. Formally, the party still has an organized presence in twelve states, but it is not very active.

Ideologically as much as politically, the HMS became a fringe group. A small band of HMS men gather every year to commemorate Nathuram Godse's "sacrifice". The party supports attempts to "rewrite Indian history", which unfortunately are not limited to the legitimate decolonization of Indian historiography. Thus, it propagates P.N. Oak's efforts to show that the Taj Mahal, the Red Fort and even the contentious Babri Masjid in Ayodhya were not built by Muslims but by Hindus.[92] Otherwise, the party maintains the classical Hindu nationalist positions defined half a century ago.

The HMS constitution

The Constitution of the "All-India Hindu Great-Assembly" or *Akhil Bhârat Hindû Mahâsabhâ* (as amended at a meeting of its All-India Committee held at New Delhi on 9 September 1990), includes, apart from purely organizational arrangements, the following politically important passages.

"2. Jurisdiction. The jurisdiction of the Hindu Mahasabha shall extend to the whole of India or Bharat as it existed before August 14, 1947."[93] Born in the struggle against Muslim separatism, the HMS has not reconciled itself to the fact of Pakistan (including the former East Pakistan, now Bangladesh) and tries to maintain the notion of a united India ("*Akhand Bhârat*") at least in its own functioning. For all practical purposes, this passage is without effect as there is no HMS activity in Pakistan or Bangladesh.

"3. Aim. The aim of the Hindu Mahasabha is to establish a really democratic Hindu State in Bharat, based on the culture and tradition of

[92]See the *Annual Research Journal* of the *Institute for Rewriting Indian and World History*, Pune, of which INA veteran P.N. Oak is the editor.

[93]HMS: *Constitution, Aims, Objects and Rules*, p.1.

Hindu Rashtra, and to re-establish Akhand Bharat by all constitutional means."[94] The emphasis on democracy is, apart from a matter of political principle, also a reminder of the struggle against Muslim separatism, which fought the full democratic play of numerical majorities by wresting separate electorates and finally a separate state from its Congress and British partners.

"3-A. Akhil Bharatiya Hindu Mahasabha bears faith and allegiance to the Constitution of India as established by Law and to the principles of socialism, secularism and democracy and would uphold sovereignty, unity and integrity of India."[95] The reference to socialism and secularism is an echo of the inclusion of the same two terms in the preamble of the Constitution of India in 1976; it confirms that the HMS is not as far removed from the political mainstream as is sometimes believed.

"4. Objects. The objects of the Hindu Mahasabha are:

"(a) To remove all forms of inequalities and disabilities and thus to establish an order in which all nationals will enjoy equal opportunities to serve the State."[96] Evidently modern and egalitarian, this seeming platitude which could have been copied from any mainstream party manifesto in any democratic country in the world, contains an implicit demand for a Common Civil Code, actually a very controversial issue in India.

"(b) To assure to each national full freedom of thought, expression, association and worship not inconsistent with the national interest.

"(c) To make Bharat militarily strong and self-reliant in defence.

"(d) To promote the glorious ideals of Aryan womanhood and to establish Ashrams for the protection, education and vocational training of women and children."[97] True to the conventions of electoral propaganda (where it is important not to alienate any segment of the targeted constituency), the expression *"glorious ideals of Aryan womanhood"* is neatly ambiguous, catering to both the traditionalist and the reformist audiences: to the former, it means chaste women who know their places and serve their husbands and children, while the latter may read a reference to the supposedly more emancipated Vedic women into it, as a

---

[94]HMS: *Constitution, Aims, Objects and Rules*, p.1.

[95]HMS: *Constitution, Aims, Objects and Rules*, p.1.

[96]HMS: *Constitution, Aims, Objects and Rules*, p.1.

[97]HMS: *Constitution, Aims, Objects and Rules*, p.1.

good non-Western model for the process of women's emancipation in modern India.[98]

"(e) To make Bharat politically, economically, morally and materially strong and self-reliant.

"(f) To remove gross inequalities in the distribution of wealth, to assure a decent standard of living to each national and to secure to the workers and peasants their rightful share in the economy of the country and to promote class co-ordination instead of class conflict.

"(g) To reclaim all those who have left the Hindu fold and welcome others into it.

"(h) To promote protection of cow and its progeny and to ban cow slaughter.

"(i) To establish Sanskritised Hindi as the National Language and Devnagari as the National Script, with due regard to national languages."[99] According to the Constitution, sanskritized Hindi already is India's national language, but in practice English remains the dominant language and in many institutions including state television, "Hindustani" or persianized Hindi is promoted.[100] Conversely, proper (*shuddh*, "pure") or sanskritized Hindi is neglected if not disparaged and ridiculed.

"(j) To cultivate friendly relations with other nations with a view to maintain internal and international peace and progress.

"(k) To ameliorate the economic, social and political conditions of the so-called Scheduled Castes and Scheduled Tribes as well as the Backward Classes, so as to bring them at par with other nationals of the country as early as possible. ..."[101] Like the other social clauses in this list, this last point is a standard item in the programmes of practically all Indian political parties.

---

[98]See A.S. Altekar: *Position of Women in Hindu Civilization*, and L.K. Tripathi: *Position and Status of Women in Ancient India*.

[99]HMS: *Constitution, Aims, Objects and Rules*, pp.1-2.

[100]Hindustani is really a synonym (or, before Hindu audiences, a euphemism) for Urdu, witness the title of a grammar written *in tempore non suspecto* by John T. Platts: *A Grammar of the Hindustani or Urdu Language* (1878). Only, it may (as Gandhiji envisaged) be written in both the Arabic and the Devanagari script; but that too is a point in common with Urdu, with Urdu newspapers increasingly switching to the Devanagari script because numerous young Muslims have gained literacy through Hindi medium schools.

[101]HMS: *Constitution, Aims, Objects and Rules*, p.2.

5. Membership.

(a) Primary members. Any Hindu of 18 years and over who accepts in writing the Aims and Objects of the Hindu Mahasabha is entitled to become a primary member of the Hindu Mahasabha on payment of Re 1/ per year. A Hindu means a person who regards this land of Bharatavarsha from the Sindhu to the seas as his Fatherland as well as his Holyland and professes any religion of Bharatiya origin. ..."[102] This clause effectively excludes Muslims and Christians as members, and was the main reason for a 1992 decision of the Election Commission to exclude the HMS from contesting elections, a decision which was overruled by Court order in 1996.

"(c) Active members. A primary member may be enrolled as an active member of the Hindu Mahasabha if he is of the age of 21 or over and has been a primary member for consecutive two years and pays an additional annual subscription of Rs. 10 and fulfils any two of the following conditions: ... (3) Maintains a cow in his house. (4) Has produced original literature of approved worth on Hindu ideology. (5) Has suffered imprisonment in the cause of the Hindu Mahasabha. (6) Works on Shuddhi front. ..."[103]

Only real, practising Hindus are welcome in the membership ranks of the HMS, as could be expected from the Hindu vanguard party. In that sense, it could certainly be called a "communal" party: it seeks to *represent* only the Hindu community, or rather the "Hindu nation". Of course, one should not confuse private arrangements with programmes for public policy: anyone has the right to join or set up a club which recruits only in a specific segment of the population (which is why the Election Commission decision to bar the HMS from contesting the elections, could not be upheld).[104] Formally, the question is only whether the party

---

[102]HMS: *Constitution, Aims, Objects and Rules*, p.3.

[103]HMS: *Constitution, Aims, Objects and Rules*, pp.3-4.

[104]Many Indian political parties explicitly represent sectional interests: Dravida Munnetra Kazhagam (Tamil Nadu), Shiv Sena (Maharashtra), Samajwadi Party (Uttar Pradesh) and Rashtriya Janata Dal (Bihar) defend the interests of the middle castes of their respective areas (the latter two also of the Muslims), while the Republican Party and Bahujan Samaj Party seek to represent specifically the Scheduled Castes. The Akali Dal is a Sikh party, while the Muslim League (Kerala) and the *Majlis-i-Ittihâd-ul-Muslimîn* (Hyderabad) are Muslim parties. However, even for them it is uncommon to formally exclude from membership people who don't belong to their privileged constituency (e.g. the Shiv Sena also has Brahmin, Scheduled Caste and Muslim members). The Bahujan Samaj Party has made it known (at the time of its breakthrough, *c.* 1990) that it was not taking upper-caste people as members, on the plea that the Dalits had to speak up for themselves at last rather than be represented by upper-caste paternalists.

spokesmen would include such discrimination in its policies after taking public office. On that count, the HMS's intention, at least on paper (see point 4:a above), is to abolish all religion-based discriminations if ever it comes to power.

An HMS manifesto

A recent HMS manifesto (1995) is quoted below in its entirety, with brief comments on the more interesting or puzzling points.

"Hindu Mahasabha declares:

"1. Post-Partition Hindusthan belongs to those who regard this land as their fatherland, motherland and holyland." This is an obvious reference to Savarkar's definition of "Hindu".

"2. Hindusthan belongs to one nation. To the other Pakistan had been given.

"3. Hindu Mahasabha gives a solemn promise that when returned to power it would stop the use of the terms *majority* and *minority* for the Hindus and the Muslims.

"4. In conformity with the Constitution all citizens, men and women, will be treated as equals before the law.

"5. Both Radha and Rashida will be entitled for maintenance allowance from their husbands."[105] Explanation: Muslim women ('Rashida'), unlike Hindu women ('Radha'), are not entitled to maintenance after having been repudiated by their husbands, as became dramatically clear with the Shah Bano case in 1985. This discrimination in favour of Muslim men (as compared both with Hindu men and Muslim women) has since become the symbol of the allegedly privileged position of Muslims (meaning Muslim men) in India, hence also of the need to abolish the separate religion-based Personal Law systems. This demand may therefore be interpreted as a call to enact a Common Civil Code and abolish the validity of the Sharia-based Muslim Personal Law.

"6. If necessary, there will be a law for family planning applicable to all irrespective of religion." Implicit reference is to the allegedly unequal receptivity to family planning campaigns among Hindus and Muslims.

"7. Antinationals engaged in riots will be dealt with severely. That will save a huge burden of expenditure on the police force." Comment: like the subsequent points 13 and 17, this is tough language, and it is remarkable that the strongest language in this manifesto is not used for religious but for typically nationalist concerns.

[105]Shiv Saran (HMS president), ed.: *Join Hindu Mahasabha*, pp.1-2.

"8. Expenditure on Ministers, Members of Parliament and Legislators will be drastically cut down.

"9. There shall be a moratorium for five years on taking foreign loans and payments thereof.

"10. Every effort will be made to increase the food production and for the remunerative prices to the farmers. There will be security of job and full employment.

"11. Untouchability will be rooted out. There will be full economic and social justice to all." Comment: contrary to the very common allegation that the Hindutva forces intend to restore the caste system, the anti-caste and especially the anti-Untouchability stand has always been a prominent plank in the platform of the HMS, as also of the BJS-BJP. At the same time, it must be admitted that several Hindu nationalist organizations including the HMS were created by reformists and then joined by the not-so-creative conservatives who infused a dead-weight policy to stem the reformist momentum.

"12. There will be full protection to the Cow and no effort will be spared to improve its breed and population.

"13. Strict vigil will be maintained on the borders and infiltrators will be shot down." Reference is to the problem of illegal Bangladeshi immigration, or "infiltration" in Hindutva parlance.

"14. New national education policy will provide compulsory and free education up to eighth standard.

"15. There will be no hegemony of English. Hindi and regional languages will be developed to replace English in every walk of life and every sphere of learning." This is merely the implementation of the Constitutional provision on language policy, for Article 343 lays down that Hindi will be the official language of the Union, and that English will be phased out by 1965. The implementation of this provision was prevented by the Nehruvians in combine with Tamil regionalists, but it is still on the Statute Book.

"16. Corruption will be rooted out and morality will be brought in social and political life of the country.

"17. Bangladeshi Muslim infiltrators who were deeply involved in Bombay and Calcutta riots in Dec. '92 and Bombay and Calcutta bomb blasts thereafter are not only a danger to the security and law and order in the country but also a burden on the food resources and employment potential of the country, will be scared away to their native places.

"18. Borders with Pakistan and Bangladesh will be completely sealed. Ex-army men will be rehabilitated on Kashmir borders. Article 370 will be removed." Explanation: Art.370 of the Constitution accords a special, semi-sovereign status to Kashmir, the only Muslim-majority state in India; populating the Kashmir border zone with army pensioners would be a way of relatively decreasing the Muslim majority and of geographically isolating Kashmiri separatists from their Pakistani support base.

"19. Election rules will be amended so as to make elections—the root cause of corruption—non-expensive." Remark: the clumsy English wording should not suggest that elections as such are considered a reprehensible thing; what is meant is that the rising expenditure of election campaigns is one of the main reasons for politicians to start taking bribes.

"20. Amongst all Hindus—Sanatanists, Arya Samajists, Jains, Sikhs, Buddhists, Lingayats, backwards and elite, awareness will be created against the hovering dangers to the country, and spirit of sacrifice will be inculcated to face collectively and unitedly all dangers to the physical and political freedom of the country.

"Only Hindu Mahasabha promises the respectable life for the Hindus and all others and will do everything possible when in a position to do it.

"Only Hindu Raj can save the country."[106] This is one of the rare occasions where a Hindutva manifesto uses the term "Hindu Raj" (Hindu rule), on the model of "British Raj", an infelicitous connotation. The more usual term is "Hindu rashtra" (Hindu state). Unlike the Jana Sangh and BJP, the HMS has never been ambiguous about its commitment to the creation of a Hindu state.

THE SANGH PARIVAR

Doctor Hedgewar's RSS

The most powerful Hindu organization to emerge in post-Independence India has no doubt been the *Râshtrîya Swayamsevak Sangh* ("National Volunteer Association").[107] It was founded by Keshav Baliram Hedgewar (1889-1940) in Nagpur, then capital of the Central Provinces, on the Vijayadashami festival day of 1925.

---

[106]Shiv Saran, ed.: *Join Hindu Mahasabha*, pp.2-3.

[107]An inside story of the RSS is H.V. Seshadri: *RSS, a Vision in Action*; another is K.R. Malkani: *The RSS Story*. A hostile account is D.R. Goyal: *Rashtriya Swayamsevak Sangh*. The classic study is Walter Andersen & Shridhar Damle: *The Brotherhood in Saffron*.

Its very first unit acted as a vigilante group to protect Hindus against Muslim rioters during the post-Khilafat tension, who, in the perception of the Hindus, had been given a free hand by the police in Nagpur. That, along with Hindu martial tradition, is how stick-fighting became an element of the RSS daily training routine, which it has remained even after the militant wings of other religions have taken to more dangerous weaponry. In general, however, the RSS defines its goals as "character-building", "instilling patriotism and the spirit of sacrifice for the Motherland", and "humanitarian service".

Since childhood, Hedgewar had been a great admirer of the Maratha freedom fighter Shivaji. As a student, he was an avid reader of B.G. Tilak's nationalist weekly *Kesarî* and a follower of the Nagpur-based Congress and HMS leader B.S. Moonje. It was at Moonje's request that in 1910, Hedgewar went to Calcutta to study medicine,—and to establish links with the Bengal revolutionaries.[108] During his six years in Calcutta, he came into contact with the *Anushîlan Samiti* and learnt their technique of attracting young men by organizing sports activities, chiefly *lâthî* (stick) training. On his return to Nagpur in 1916, he disappointed his family by renouncing any prospects of marriage and a medical career, opting for full-time activism instead.

Hedgewar joined Congress in 1919, but quit in 1928: "The withdrawal was from factional politics of the Congress, not from its programmes, as the RSS cadres and leaders participated in all subsequent movements of the Congress."[109] He also applauded the 1928 Congress resolution in favour of complete independence.

Dr. Hedgewar was a man of action, not a thinker and writer. He has left us very few writings, but that in itself is indicative of an important choice which the RSS has made since the beginning and to which it has remained true: a disdain for intellectual work. Hedgewar was of the opinion that Hindu society already had everything to succeed in the struggle for survival and freedom, except for a single prerequisite: organization. So, he wanted no more time to be wasted on reading and writing, and all energy to be devoted to organizing the Hindus.

The local Hindu group which he had started in Nagpur in 1925 was given the name *Râshtrîya Swayamsevak Sangha* only in 1927. Gradually,

---

[108] W. Andersen and S. Damle: *Brotherhood in Saffron*, p.31, with reference to Appaji Joshi, "perhaps Hedgewar's closest confidante".

[109] Rakesh Sinha:"Not a negative role", *Hindustan Times*, 5.9.1997.

the association expanded, first in Maharashtra, then in the rest of India. It took until 1939 before there were *shâkhâs* (branches) in cities in every province of British India; even now, the RSS is only sparsely implanted in areas like Tamil Nadu and the North-east, and the expansion into the North-Indian countryside has only begun in right earnest with the Ayodhya movement of *c.* 1990. Though Hedgewar and many other volunteers individually joined the Gandhian agitations against colonialism, he kept the organization as such out of politics, partly for safety reasons, not to endanger the young sapling, and partly because he had a metapolitical project in mind.

Guru Golwalkar

The single most articulate ideologue of the RSS was no doubt its second *Sarsanghchâlak* ("chief guide of the association"), Madhav Sadashiv Golwalkar (1906-1973), usually referred to as *Gurûjî*.[110] Golwalkar studied Biology in the newly-founded Benares Hindu University, and stayed on to teach there. He then chose a spiritual career. RSS sources claim that he was about to be nominated as *Shankarâchârya* when he received Doctor Hedgewar's insistent invitation to take office in the RSS leadership. Hedgewar designated him as his successor, and he held the RSS top office from 1940 until his death in 1973. He left the most decisive mark on the ideological outlook of RSS workers till today, and was responsible for the expansion of RSS-affiliated organizations into all domains of society. In spite of an interruption after the Mahatma murder (1948-49, when Golwalkar was imprisoned and the RSS was banned though it could not be connected to the murder), Golwalkar's RSS grew increasingly strong.

Shortly before Golwalkar was nominated as Hedgewar's successor, he wrote the booklet *We. Our Nationhood Defined*, completed in November 1938. Its stated project was to define nationhood and apply this concept to Hindu society, and also to explore the borders of this nation and define the position of semi-Hindu and non-Hindu groups in India. In style and contents, it was just a rambling pamphlet, and it contained careless statements which are still used against the RSS.[111] In 1948, Golwalkar

[110]See e.g. Ritu Kohli: *Political Ideas of M.S. Golwalkar.*

[111]See e.g. Sitaram Yechury (CPM Politburo member): *What is this Hindu Rashtra?*, also included in P. Lahiri: *Selected Writings on Communalism*. For an in-depth discussion of Golwalkar's *We*, see K. Elst: *The Saffron Swastika*, Ch.2.

himself decided to withdraw it from circulation. His main doctrinal work is *Bunch of Thoughts* (1964). Some interviews with him have been collected in *Spotlights* (1972).

Golwalkar was very anti-political, and unlike Hedgewar, he did not encourage his volunteers to participate in anti-British activities. This led to great frustration among his cadres, and to the still-common allegation that the RSS stood aloof from the freedom movement.[112] Its standing as a defender of Hindu interests also went down: "The lukewarm response of the RSS to the Hindu Mahasabha's political agenda led the latter to form its own volunteer organisations—the Hindu Militia and the Ram Sena. The RSS was increasingly seen by many Hindu organisers including Savarkar and Moonje as too ineffectual to counter Muslim aggressiveness. Thus, a large number of [non-RSS-related] volunteer organisations, for instance the Mahavir Dal and Agni Dal in UP and Punjab, Hindu Rashtra Dal in Pune, Hindu Rashtra Sena in Bhopal, Mukteshwar Dal and Rashtriya Swayamsevak Mandal in the CP, Shakti Dal in Jabalpur and Hindu Rashtriya Sena in Giridih in Bihar, were formed to fight 'Muslim domination'."[113]

The dissolution of the RSS by the Government during the crackdown on Hindu nationalism in 1948 (in connection with the Gandhi murder, from which the RSS was officially cleared) forced the imprisoned Sarsanghchalak to comply with Government demands. One of these was to endow the RSS with a constitution, thus ending its "secret society" working-style. After its unbanning, the RSS kept a low profile (except through its political front, the Jana Sangh) but worked very hard. It earned some recognition for its volunteer work during the Chinese invasion in 1962, so that Nehru gave the RSS a place in the 1963 Republic Day parade: "Given the spirit, even the lathi could successfully face the bomb."[114]

---

[112]The allegation is countered by Rakesh Sinha: "Not a negative role", *Hindustan Times*, 5.9.1997. He lists instances of RSS involvement in the freedom struggle, but these are all taken from the period of Hedgewar's tenure. After Golwalkar took over, that involvement in politics was actively discouraged.

[113]Rakesh Sinha: "Not a negative role", *Hindustan Times*, 5.9.1997. He also claims that in 1934, a Muslim member of the Central Provinces (CP) Council, M.S. Rahman, exonerated the RSS of the charge of communalism.

[114]Quoted in J.P. Mathur: "A saga of faith, conviction and commitment", *BJP Today*, 16.8.1997.

The RSS constitution

At first, the RSS had no written constitution. In 1949, after having been banned for more than a year in the aftermath of the murder of Mahatma Gandhi by an ex-swayamsevak, the RSS adopted a constitution, in compliance with the Government requirements imposed as conditions for the organization's unbanning. After studying a draft constitution written by Guru Golwalkar in prison, the Congress Government under Nehru had extracted from him a promise to, *inter alia*, "make the loyalty to the Union Constitution and respect for the National Flag more explicit in the Constitution of the RSS", to "provide clearly that persons believing in or resorting to violent and secret methods will have no place in the Sangh", and to work "on a democratic basis".[115] The following are the programmatically relevant parts of the RSS Constitution:

"Whereas in the disintegrated conditions of the country it was considered necessary to have an Organisation

"(a) to eradicate the fissiparous tendencies arising from diversities of sect, faith, caste and creed and from political, economic, linguistic and provincial differences among Hindus;

"(b) to make them realise the greatness of their past,

"(c) to inculcate in them a spirit of service, sacrifice and selfless devotion to the Hindu Samaj as a whole;

"(d) to build up an organised and well-disciplined corporate life; and

"(e) to bring about an all-round regenration of the Hindu Samaj; ...

"The Rashtriya Swayamsevak Sangh hereby adopts the following constitution: ..."[116]

Considering that the RSS Constitution was written under duress, one can always argue that its wording need not be taken seriously: since Golwalkar and his lieutenants merely wanted the RSS to be unbanned, they were willing to make all the right noises which could convince the Government of the organization's harmlessness. This has in effect been the attitude predominant among Hindutva-watchers: to assume that an RSS man who says something unobjectionable must be lying.[117]

---

[115]Government communiqué dd. 11 July 1949, reproduced in D.R. Goyal: *RSS*, p.205.

[116]Reproduced in D.R. Goyal: *RSS*, pp.206-08.

[117]During the plenary discussion on the 1996 elections at the South Asia Conference in Madison, Paul Brass rejected the view that the BJP is a party like any other, among other reasons because, through its link with the RSS, it is "secretive and dishonest".

"Article 3. The Aims and Objects of the Sangh are to weld together the diverse groups within the Hindu Samaj and to revitalise and rejuvenate the same on the basis of its Dharma and Sanskriti, that it may achieve an all-sided development of the Bharatvarsha.

"Policy. Article 4.

"(a) The Sangh believes in orderly evolution of the Society and adheres to peaceful and legitimate means for the realisation of its ideals.

"(b) In consonance with the cultural heritage of the Hindu Samaj, the Sangh has abiding faith in the fundamental principle of tolerance towards all faiths. The Sangh, as such, has no politics and is devoted purely to cultural work. The individual swayamsevaks, however, may join any political party, except such parties as believe in or resort to violent and secret methods to achieve their ends; persons owing allegiance to such parties or believing in such methods shall have no place in the Sangh.

"Flag. Article 5. While recognising the duty of every citizen to be loyal to and to respect the State Flag, the Sangh has as its flag the 'Bhagwa Dhwaj', the age-old symbol of Hindu culture.

"Swayamsevaks. Article 6.

"1. (a) Any male Hindu of 18 years or more, who subscribes to the Rules and Regulations of the Sangh and takes its pledge, set out in Appendix (a), can be registered as a swayamsevak."[118]

Like the HMS, and in contrast with the BJS and BJP, the RSS restricts its membership to Hindus. Under the Janata Government, due to pressure from the Socialist coalition members, the RSS briefly considered throwing open its membership to non-Hindus as well, but when the Government collapsed, nothing came of it.

The pledge mentioned in the RSS Constitution 6:1-a is the following, as fixed in 1939:

"Before the All-Powerful God and my ancestors, I most solemnly take this oath, that I become a member of the Rashtriya Swayamsevak Sangh in order to achieve all-round greatness of Bharatvarsh by fostering the growth of my sacred Hindu Dharma, Hindu culture and Hindu society. I shall perform the work of the Sangh honestly, disinterestedly, with my heart and soul, and I shall adhere to this oath all my life. Victory to Mother India."[119]

---

[118]Reproduced in D.R. Goyal: *RSS*, pp.206-08. *Samâj*: society; *bhagva dhvaj*: the saffron flag.

[119]Given in D.R. Goyal: *RSS*, pp.200-01.

Golwalkar's successors

The third Sarsanghchalak was "Balasaheb" Madhukar Dattatreya Deoras (1914-1995), designated by the dying Guru Golwalkar as his successor in 1973. Formally, the Sarsanghchalak's successor is democratically elected by the whole elected RSS leadership, but so far, the latter has never taken any major decision which went against the Sarsanghchalak's wishes. Remark also that whereas Golwalkar acceded to the post at age 34, Deoras was already 59; the RSS was becoming (and has since remained) a gerontocracy.[120]

Deoras had been involved in the RSS since its first beginnings in Nagpur. In an RSS account: "In 1927, the local Muslims created riot conditions on the Diwali day in Nagpur. Muslims planned disturbances targeting Hindus in the lanes of Mahal area. Sensing trouble, Balasaheb (with [his brother] Bhaurao in tow) and other associates challenged them for the first time and taught them a lifetime lesson."[121]

The first decade of his term in office coincided with the apogee of socialism in world politics. The Soviet sphere of influence reached its greatest expansion with the conquest of Indochina, the Portuguese colonies and Ethiopia. In the West, even nominally conservative parties opted for socialist policies ("We're all socialists now"). In India too, the time of Deoras' accession to the RSS top office saw the expansion of Leftist power throughout the public sector. The Indian Communists pursued an "entryist" policy, viz. massively joining the Congress Party and influencing its policies from within. Rajni Kothari is one of the very few to have briefly described "the determined bid for power from the Left of the Congress Party in which sections of the CPI leadership also played a role. ... It started after the 1969 split of the Congress after which Indira Gandhi had to depend on communist support for survival. ... a

[120]In spite of the traditional respect for elders, gerontocracy is against the Hindu tradition, which expects people to retire into *vanaprasthâshrama*, the "life stage of the forest-dweller". The Deendayal Research Institute, an RSS front, has a "Vanaprastha scheme" for involving retired citizens in service and educational work (see DRI: *Towards a New Horizon*, p.45). Both facts, that the RSS top leaders never retire (except when forced by ill-health) and that it has elderly citizens "retire" into something "socially useful", indicate that the RSS has lost the Hindu emphasis on interiority (to which a householder should devote himself once he has brought up his children) in favour of the Christian emphasis on charitable work. The old spirit is that cultivating interiority is a priceless service to mankind in itself.

[121]Shrikant Joshi: "Remembering Balasaheb Deoras", *Organiser*, 7.12.1997.

number of former card-carrying members of the Communist Party made their way into the Congress with the hope of penetrating its core both in the government and in the party. ... As it turned out, Indira Gandhi was nobody's fool and she seems to have used them, rather than the other way around. But they did make a major effort at influencing not just the polity but also a number of scientific and educational institutions, a variety of government and semi-government committees, inner councils of the party and Parliament, a considerable cross-section of the mass media as well as important journals which they came to control. After all, in the Stalinist view of things the intellectual-scientific domain is extremely important. ... Meanwhile, the country also drifted more and more into the Soviet dragnet which had its local networks of individuals, research institutions and funding agencies which gradually forced many intellectuals and bureaucrats to fall in line."[122]

So, Indira Gandhi's political secretary P.N. Haksar and education minister Nurul Hasan manoeuvred Communists in all manner of power positions and set up a number of institutions manned by committed Marxists *ab initio*, most importantly the Jawaharlal Nehru University, intended to be India's Harvard.[123] While Indira's father Jawaharlal Nehru, an open sympathizer of Communism, still had to reckon with an influential conservative section within the ruling Congress, Indira herself, though much less ideologically committed to "progressive" causes than her father, presided over a party and a political establishment with a far more decidedly Leftist orientation. (In July 1975, Sanjay Gandhi took the Communists by surprise and threw them out of Congress: he had realized that the Communists, who were setting up "street committees" to enforce

[122]Rajni Kothari: "Dangers to democracy. The challenges from within", *Times of India*, 22.9.1995. Kothari adds in the present tense: "Even today some of these influence-peddlers are around though under Rajiv Gandhi and then under Narasiṃha Rao their fortunes have declined." Testimonial glimpses of the Indian Leftist scene in this period can be found in Raj Thapar: *All these Years*. Though the Communist influence on Indira Gandhi's policies in 1966-77 changed the face of India, most political histories of India hardly even hint at it. Paul Brass (*Politics of India since Independence*, p.79) doesn't get any closer than this: "The CPI ... has favored a strategy of alliance with the Congress or at least with 'progressive elements' within the Congress".

[123]P.N. Haksar (d.1998) had started publishing his autobiography, *One More Life*, in instalments; though vol.1 (1913-29) was already published by OUP Delhi in 1990, his testimony about the period under consideration is still awaited and probably never materialized.

the Emergency in every corner, were trying to take over. But he did not touch the Communist hegemony in the cultural sector, not being sensitized to the importance of cultural power.)

It is typical, and arguably not unwise, that the RSS just moved with the dominant wind of socialism. Balasaheb Deoras has left no major doctrinal writings, but many of his speeches have been published as pamphlets, and in these, the focus is on the RSS commitment to social justice and equality. The most pressing concern was the struggle against caste discrimination and the inclusion of the Scheduled Castes and Scheduled Tribes as equals in a rejuvenated Hindu society.[124] They also contain repeated assurances that the RSS is "secular" in outlook and innocent of the communal violence which rocked India with increasing frequency during Deoras's term.[125]

Organizationally too, the RSS reached out to the Backward castes, for example: "The RSS is accused of being a brahmin-dominated organisation, but in Kerala the opposite is the case. Most of the swayamsevaks come from the lower middle class, the working classes and the scheduled castes. The hold of the RSS on the lower classes is so strong, leaders of the CPI(M) and other Left parties have started panicking."[126]

At the same time, the RSS-affiliated political party, the Jana Sangh, now dominated by Atal Behari Vajpayee (1926), was also in the process of liquidating its ideological distinctiveness and moving to the Left. On the bright side, this made it easier for the movement to co-operate with the Socialists led by Jayaprakash Narayan in combating the Emergency dictatorship imposed by Indira Gandhi in 1975. Together, RSS men, disaffected Congressmen and Socialists formed the Janata Party and, after winning the elections, the first non-Congress Government at the Centre in 1977.[127]

Towards the end of his term, Deoras led (by remote control) the Hindu

---

[124]E.g. Deoras: *Social Equality and Hindu Consolidation*, and: *The Malady & the Remedy* (1980).

[125]E.g. Deoras' *Speech in Jamshedpur* (April 1979), published afterwards to refute the common allegation that this speech had triggered the communal riots that had taken place in the subsequent days. See also the BJP report on the matter: *Jamshedpur Riots: the Truth Unmasked* (1981).

[126]Suresh Kumar: "March of the RSS", *Surya India*, Aug. 1989.

[127]For Hindu nationalist accounts of the Emergency, see L.K. Advani: *A Prisoner's Scrap-Book*; K.R. Malkani: *The Midnight Knock*; and P.G. Sahasrabuddhe and M.C. Vajpayee: *The People vs. the Emergency*.

movement for the liberation of Rama's supposed birthplace in Ayodhya, the "largest mass movement in India since Independence. At its height, more people were detained by the police than during the course of the Salt March and the Quit India movement combined."[128] On December 6, 1992, the movement culminated in the demolition of the Babri Masjid, a mosque (used as a temple since 1949) standing in the way of the reconstruction of a Rama temple at the contentious site in Ayodhya, presumably Lord Rama's birthplace (*janmabhûmi*). The RSS was banned a third time (after the Mahatma murder and the Emergency), but unbanned five months later by Court order.[129]

Upon retiring in 1994, Deoras appointed Rajendra Singh, commonly known as Rajju Bhayya, as his successor. At the time of writing, a few speeches of his are in print, which simply reiterate the well-known Hindu nationalist positions. The same is true of K.S. Sudarshan, who succeeded Rajju Bhayya, bedridden with diabetes, as Sarsanghchalak in 1999. Under their terms, the BJP acceded to power at the centre. At the same time, they were confronted with the problem of depleting ranks: all the while the shakhas kept on increasing in number and striking roots in the South and in the villages of the North, attendance at the shakhas declined. Modern youngsters felt visibly less attracted to the quaint boy-scout-like discipline of the RSS.

Apart from the Sarsanghchalaks, the most productive top leader of the RSS in terms of ideological statements has been general secretary H.V. Seshadri. He wrote *The Tragic Story of Partition*, representative of the RSS understanding of the forces and processes which resulted in the partition of the Motherland. Seshadri's books *The Way* and *RSS: a Vision in Action* are two important self-presentations of the RSS.

The Sangh Parivar

The RSS has generated a large array of organizations active in all domains of social life: education, labour, women, religion, politics, uplift of underprivileged groups, material welfare, etc. The whole array is usually called the *Sangh Parivâr*, the "family of the [Râshtrîya Swayamsevak]

---

[128]Edward A. Gargar: "Peril to the Indian state: a defiant Hindu fervor", in Arvind Sharma, ed.: *Our Religions*, p.55.

[129]See "Another setback" [i.e. for the Narasimha Rao Government], editorial in *Indian Express*, 5.6.1993.

Sangh".[130] Some of the more important members of the Sangh Parivar are the following.

* The *Akhil Bhâratîya Vidyârthî Parishad* ("All-India Student Council", 1949) is India's largest student organization. Significantly, it includes teachers as well as students.

* The political party *Bhâratîya Jana Sangh* ("Indian People's Association"), later reconstituted as *Bhâratîya Janatâ Party*, which will be discussed below.

* The *Vanavâsî Kalyân Ashram* ("Forest-dweller Prosperity Centre", 1952) works among the tribal populations, mostly in central India; attempts to penetrate the North-eastern tribal belt have so far been less successful. It seeks to organize them, instil self-confidence, develop skills, and especially to keep alive their cultural traditions under an essentially Hindu aegis. Its main ideological plank is that India's tribal populations are segments of the larger Hindu society, and that their cultural traditions are tributaries to Hindu culture, even if they have not gone through the same evolution on some points.[131] The VKA boasts that in many areas it has managed to stop conversions to Christianity and even to reconvert many christianized tribals.[132] While verification of this claim is outside the purview of this study, we may just mention that even people who are generally skeptical of the RSS and its claims of sterling services to the Hindu cause, admit that the VKA is fairly successful. On the other hand, it is doubtful that the VKA can keep up with its non-Hindu competitors, for Christian (especially Evangelical) preachers are penetrating ever-new corners of India's interior.[133]

---

[130]In the Indian context, it is what comes closest to what Flemish and Dutch people know as a *zuil*, a "pillar". This is a structure centred along one "vertical" or ideological (e.g. Catholic, Socialist) axis, consisting of units at every "horizontal" level of society: trade-union, broadcasting foundation, schools' network, political party, cultural organizations.

[131]This claim is hotly contested by the Christian missionaries, who insist that "tribals are not Hindus". Yet, whenever tribals misbehave, e.g. by attacking Christian mission posts, Christian and pro-Christian media invariably report that "*Hindu* fanatics attack missions".

[132]E.g. about the Jashpur area (Madhya Pradesh): "Over twenty thousand 'tribals' to return to Hindu fold", *Organiser*, 1.1.1995. These reconversion ceremonies (*ghar-wâpasî*, "home-coming") have been described to me by preacher-lady Prema Pandurang, who led a few. She laughed off the Christian claim that these are empty festivals in which tribals merely participate for the attendant meal and merry-making.

[133]See e.g. M.G. Vaidya's article on mushrooming missions in rural Maharashtra: "Conversion assumes alarming proportions", *Organiser*, 2.3.1997.

* The *Bhâratîya Mazdûr Sangh* (BMS, "Indian Workers' Association") was started in July 1955 at the initiative of the Jana Sangh's labour department, and given a formal constitution in August 1959. At the time of writing, it is the largest Indian trade-union in terms of *active* membership (having been part of an oppositional political family for decades, it could not attract purely careerist memberships). Its approach to labour relations and economic policy is roughly that of the Christian-Democratic trade-unionists in Europe: opposed to the Marxist idea of class struggle, aiming at the advancement of the workers' condition through constructive negotiations. Its founder-president Dattopant B. Thengadi, author of the books *Third Way* and *Nationalist Pursuit*, has been the *Sangh Parivâr*'s chief ideologue on socio-economic policy for decades.[134]

The *Vishva Hindû Parishad* ("World Hindu Council") is a religious organization founded at Guru Golwalkar's advice in 1964. It seeks to create a common platform of Hindu religious personalities, and to represent Hindu religious viewpoints and interests in international forums. One of its most remarkable achievements is that it has been able to unite most of the ever-quarrelling *sâdhu*s on a common platform of the defence and reform of Hindu society, with the effective abolition of Untouchability as top priority. As a result of the VHP's efforts, even known arch-conservative clerics have come around to verbally supporting the programme of social reform.[135] The VHP is also mildly active on the *Shuddhi* front, its greatest success being the reconversion of the superficially islamized Meherat Rajput community in the Udaipur and Ajmer districts of Rajasthan.[136] Its women's wing is called the *Durgâ Vâhinî* ("Brigade of the Tiger Goddess"), its youth wing the *Bajrang Dal* ("Team of Hanuman", Rama's valiant helper).

The *Deendayal Research Institute* was founded by Jana Sangh leader Nana Deshmukh in 1972. Supposedly the RSS "think tank", it is hardly performant in the intellectual domain. Apart from books celebrating

---

[134]See also Prof. M.G. Bokare (an ex-Marxist): *Hindu Economics*, with a foreword by D.B. Thengadi.

[135]Some of the achievements of the VHP have been discussed by Prof. Edmund Weber: "Moderne Hindukultur", reproduced in the conference book of the 1992 *European Hindu Conference* in Frankfurt, pp.164-69.

[136]"Conversion Convulsions", *India Today*, 30.6.1986: "Over the last five years, the VHP has been bringing the Meherat into the Hindu fold. 40,000 Meherat Muslims have reconverted." *Hinduism Today* (Honolulu, January 1993) reports on another 48,000 Muslims accepted into Hinduism thanks to the VHP's efforts.

Sangh Parivar stalwarts, its publications are not more than a handful. Its periodical *Manthan* is a meritorious publication, e.g. in regularly publishing collections of historical texts useful as background to particular debates, but it is rarely on the edge of these debates. On the other hand, the DRI plays a key role in the co-ordination of many types of developmental and social work.[137]

Sevâ Bhâratî, the RSS "Service organization" (1979) works among slum dwellers and in Scheduled Caste *bastî*s and in the countryside. Apart from this formal organization, RSS workers in general have an impressive record of relief work during earthquakes, floods and the like.[138] When RSS men say that India has no need for a Mother Teresa, it is not purely a matter of envy or sectarian spite. Unlike their Marxist academic critics, they have personal experience of such work, and they consider their own record in social service as no less deserving of a Nobel prize.

Founding of the Jana Sangh

The *Bhâratîya Jana Sangh* ("Indian People's Association", BJS) was founded in 1951 as an initiative of RSS activists.[139] The RSS had grown into a nationwide Hindu network (though only thinly implanted in the South and East), but emphatically refrained from political activities, devoting its attention to "character-building" and socio-cultural organization instead. When the RSS was suppressed after Mahatma Gandhi was murdered by Nathuram Godse, who was a former RSS member, no politician came forward to defend it, and this experience convinced many activists of the need to start a political party of their own. Other reasons were that after the achievement of independence, the Congress lost its role of common nationalist platform and became an ordinary political party increasingly dominated by Nehru, and that the

---

[137]For a survey of the developmental and educational schemes initiated and co-ordinated by the DRI, see the DRI brochure *Towards a New Horizon*.

[138]An illustration of media bias is the total silence about this service aspect of RSS work. Thus, after the plane crash near Delhi in November 1996, the Marxist weekly *Frontline* published pictures of the relief work, on which the Hindi-speaking reader can recognize RSS banners, but the captions are strictly silent about the RSS participation. The Western media have duly noted that the Islamists in Turkey and Egypt have built themselves a respected position with their social work, but the corresponding information about the RSS is systematically withheld.

[139]See Craig Baxter: *Jana Sangh*; and Bruce Graham: *Hindu Nationalism and Indian Politics. The Origins and Development of the BJS*.

HMS had been marginalized by its alleged association with the Gandhi murder.

The initiative was taken in January 1951 by a group of RSS men from Panjab, Delhi and U.P., including Vasant Krishna Oke, Hansraj Gupta, Bhai Mahavir, Balraj Madhok, Yodhraj and Balraj Bhalla, and Deendayal Upadhyaya, and by non-RSS man Pandit Mauli Chandra Sharma (son of a former HMS president). RSS supremo Guru Madhav Sadashiv Golwalkar, who was sceptical regarding party politics, described Vasant Krishna Oke's desire to set up a political party as "a liking for political work to a degree uncommon and undesirable for a Swayamsevak".[140] Reluctantly, he consented to the enrichment of the Hindu movement with a political party, reportedly with the words: "All right then. After all, a house also needs a lavatory."[141] This distrust of party politics was in keeping with Golwalkar's (and earlier Hedgewar's) view of the nature of RSS work as essentially metapolitical.

Before the 1952 elections, the party was still being organized at the provincial level and took shape as a national party only just in time for participating. The RSS announced that it would remain neutral rather than work for the candidates of the HMS or the new party: "In the coming elections the RSS will not back the Hindu Maha Sabha or any other party in particular. In the drama of elections we shall be mere spectators. The Swayamsevaks are free to do as they please."[142] I surmise that one factor in this hesitation to support the Hindu Nationalist opposition parties was the grudging sympathy for the Congress machine (in spite of Nehru then still a predominantly Hindu party) as an effectively national organization, implanted in every village and thereby an embodiment of national unity.

The Jana Sangh was in some ways a continuation of the HMS, which ceased to be a viable party after its member Nathuram Godse killed Mahatma Gandhi. The first Jana Sangh president, law scholar Shyama Prasad Mookerjee (1901-53), had been elected to the Bengal Legislative Council in 1929 as a Congressman.[143] Under Mahatma Gandhi's directive to boycott the councils, he resigned in 1930 and started concentrating on

---

[140]Golwalkar's memoir concerning his relations with S.P. Mookerjee, in *Organiser*, 25.6.1956, quoted by Craig Baxter: *Jana Sangh*, p.69.

[141]According to the then general secretary and eye-witness Eknath Ranade, who told Sita Ram Goel, who told me.

[142]*Organiser*, 29.10.1951, quoted in Baxter: *Jana Sangh*, p.74.

[143]More details about Mookerjee's career in C. Baxter: *The Jana Sangh*, pp.62-74.

his academic career; in 1934-38, he was the youngest person ever to hold the office of Vice-Chancellor of Calcutta University. In 1937, he was elected as an independent from the University constituency (there was a corporatistic element in British-Indian democracy, with separate representation of certain professional groups), and in 1939 he joined the HMS. In 1941-42, he was Finance Minister in Fazl-ul-Haq's Government of Bengal, which did not save him from being imprisoned, along with Savarkar, during a British crackdown on the Bhagalpur session of the HMS.

In the elections of 1945-46, he was one of only three HMS candidates in India to be elected. He was also elected to the Constituent Assembly of India. On Independence Day, Nehru included him in his Cabinet as Minister of Industries and Supplies, clearly a move to prevent the HMS from actively opposing the government all the while effectively sidelining its representative in an ideologically inconsequential post. After the Gandhi murder (30 January 1948), Mookerjee stayed on as Minister and did not resign his HMS membership until December 1948. Along with another Bengali, K.C. Neogy, he resigned from the Cabinet on 8 April 1950 in protest against the Nehru-Liaqat Pact, an "unequal treaty" in which Nehru promised Pakistani Prime Minister Liaqat Ali Khan not to interfere in the treatment of the minority Hindus across the border, even while the latter were suffering large-scale atrocities in East Bengal (Liaqat's counter-promise not to interfere in India's dealings with its Muslim minority was without object, a stable communal cease-fire having descended on India on the day of the Gandhi murder).

In 1951, Mookerjee was a leader without a party, while the prospective party which some RSS activists wanted to set up, was in need of a leader of national stature. Though the BJS's ideological orientation owes a lot to the HMS's historic leader V.D. Savarkar, Mookerjee no longer considered the HMS as a good vehicle for the Hindu nationalist ideology; after some hesitation, he accepted the offer to lead the Jana Sangh. One of his conditions for acceptance was that the new party would have an open membership, as opposed to the HMS and RSS which enrolled only Hindus; this demand was immediately conceded.

The most important difference between the HMS and the new party (a difference which would go on increasing in subsequent decades) was that the HMS was more radical, more outspokenly Hindu, more defiant vis-à-vis the official dogma of secularism, while the BJS was more equivocal.

Essentially for this reason, HMS president N.B. Khare refused to dissolve his party into the new party when Mookerjee made this request.[144] The HMS has criticized the BJS for "professing secularism".[145] The difference between the two parties is all summed up in the difference between their names: the HMS calls itself "Hindu", while the BJS/BJP always shuns the term, preferring the vaguer and essentially secular alternative "*Bhâratîya/* Indian".[146]

To an extent, the shift from "Hindu" to "Indian" was not due to conviction but to fear, to the shock which the Hindu nationalist movement had received during the crackdown following the murder of Mahatma Gandhi. Nehru never made a secret of his deadly hostility to the Hindu Nationalists. Once he told Mookerjee: "We will crush you!" (Mookerjee, always more polite than Nehru, replied: "We will crush this crushing mentality.")[147]

In 1953, Shyama Prasad Mookerjee led an agitation against the separate status of Kashmir, where non-Kashmiri citizens could only enter with a permission from the Kashmiri state government. He was arrested for crossing the Kashmiri border, and died in prison of a heart attack.[148] Though even top Congress leaders "demanded a judicial inquiry into the circumstances of his death", the inquiry was never held, so that "the obstinate refusal of Pandit Nehru to concede the demand for inquiry deepened the mystery and created widespread doubts regarding the real nature of his death".[149] At least in Sangh Parivar circles, it is common to refer to Mookerjee's death as his "martyrdom".[150] Many BJP offices are still adorned with his photograph.

---

[144]For some details about Mookerjee's talks with Guru Golwalkar and with N.B. Khare, see B. Graham: *Hindu Nationalism*, pp.26-7.

[145]V.P. Varma: *Modern Indian Political Thought*, p.622.

[146]I have met activists of the Bajrang Dal, another RSS-affiliate, who have preferred to join the HMS rather than the RSS-affiliated BJP, which they find too goody-goody.

[147]Recalled by A.B. Vajpayee: "Victory will be ours", *BJP Today*, 16.8.1997.

[148]See e.g. Jawaharlal Kaul: "The fountainhead", *Indian Express*, 23.6.1990. A laudatory biography of S.P. Mookerjee is Balraj Madhok: *Portrait of a Martyr* (1969). From Mookerjee's own diary notes a selection was published: *Leaves from a Diary* (1993).

[149]M.R. Varshney: *Jana Sangh, RSS and Balraj Madhok*, p.9.

[150]A less romantic account was given by Gurudatt Vaidya, a prominent Arya Samaji, Jana Sanghi, Hindi writer and friend of Sita Ram Goel, who related it to me. In the Kashmiri prison cell which Vaidya shared with Mookerjee, the latter was provided with medical care; the doctor gave him an injection and told him not to eat chicken, but he ate two, hence the heart attack.

Commitments of the BJS

The summary given in the *Bhâratîya Jana Sangh* Constitution under the heading "Aims and Objectives in Brief", a programme to which all BJS party members pledged their loyalty, is as follows (we give it in its entirety, but change the order so as to group the different points under headings of our own making).

The BJS formulates its cultural nationalism in these points:

"Political, social and economic reconstruction of the country on the basis of Bharatiya Sanskriti and Maryada.

"Protection and promotion of the cow.

"Use of Hindi and other Pradesh languages as official languages in their regions.

"Changes in the judicial system to suit the genius of India and fit in with present-day conditions."[151]

While not very detailed, this contains the typical points of concern of Hindu Nationalism. Further items of political nationalism are the following:

"The establishment of a unitary government and decentralisation of political and economic power.

"Establishment of Akhand Bharat.

"Complete integration of Kashmir.

"Liberation of territory occupied by China and Pakistan.

"A foreign policy based upon enlightened self-interests of the country.

"Modern-most military armaments."[152]

This is a far more aggressive stance on reconquest of lost territories than the present-day BJP wants or dares to take. A very important though not too controversial point to note is the combination of centralization and decentralization: against Nehru's policy of economic and political centralization, the BJS took the Gandhian line of decentralization and revaluation of the villages; but it also warned against the decentralization of loyalties which seemed implicit in regionalist movements, at that time mostly in the agitation for linguistic states.

---

[151]Reproduced in BJS: *Party Documents 1951-1972*, vol.1, p.222. *Sanskrti*: culture; *maryâdâ*: "limit", self-control, dignity, ethics; *pradesh*: province, state.

[152]BJS: *Party Documents 1951-1972*, vol.1, p.222.

The following points form the BJS's social policy:

"Protection of the fundamental rights of the individual and the promotion of interests of the Society.

"Guarantee of the fundamental right to work and livelihood.

"Upholding establishment and protection of the tiller's right to ownership of land.

"Ceiling on agricultural land and redistribution of land.

"Eradication of untouchability.

"Elimination of corruption.

"Free education up to middle class.

"Facilities for medical care and social security."[153]

This is a social-democratic programme, though certain phrases are open to interpretation. Thus, the "right to work" could be read as a threat to the "right to strike"; though such a line was never taken by the BJS, some would certainly surmise as much by sheer deduction from the common description of the BJS as "Rightist". The juxtaposition of the "interests of Society" (often invoked during the Cold War by Soviet apologists to counter Western-individualist insistence on "human rights") with the "rights of the individual" is a typically centrist position, wary of both collectivism and wild individualism, quite like the general outlook of the Christian-Democrats and the democratic Socialists in Europe.

The BJS's economic policy is summed up in these points:

"Encouragement to small mechanised and rural industries.

"Nationalisation of basic industries.

"Curbing monopolistic tendencies in the economic sphere.

"Determination of minimum and maximum expendable income.

"Worker's participation in the profit and management of the industries.

"Stabilisation of prices."[154]

This is by no means a "Rightist" programme. Ever since, the BJS and BJP have always included distinctly Leftist items in their social and economic programmes. Thus, the 1989 Manifesto with its anti-multinational slogans was interpreted as "an attempt to disown the 'rightist' label stuck on the BJP".[155] In 1995, the BJP, as a partner in the

[153]BJS: *Party Documents 1951-1972*, vol.1, p.222.

[154]BJS: *Party Documents 1951-1972*, vol.1, p.222.

[155]"The BJP manifesto", editorial in the *Hindustan Times*, 10.11.1989.

Maharashtra state government, was in a position to implement its anti-multinational programme by cancelling a deal with Enron, an American energy producer. The deal was saved in the end, on terms more favourable to India, but the BJP's reputation as anti-multinational sloganeers was made: "The knickerwallahs follow an economic policy that is now so Leftist that their campaign has received warm-hearted support from a whole variety of Leftist intellectuals, even in the press, who have been bereft of causes and ideas for some years now."[156] What we learn from this manifesto, is that this Leftist element was present in the Hindu Nationalist programme since 1951; then already, it was shaking off the "'rightist' label".

And not just in theory. The fledgling BJS refused to compromise on its social agenda even at the cost of alienating influential potential supporters: "The Jana Sangh also ignored the possibility of mobilising support from influential sections of society in Rajasthan, where it did not hesitate to alienate Rajput landlords. As the 1951-52 elections approached, associations of landowners were looking for a political mouthpiece to reinforce their opposition to Congress, which had just announced the abolition of the *zamîndârî* and *jâgîrdârî* systems. They first opted for the Jana Sangh; then the Kshatriya Mahasabha (which was dominated by Rajput landowners) sponsored the formation of a Samyukta Dal (Party of Unity) in association with the Ram Rajya Parishad and Hindu Mahasabha. The Jana Sangh refused to join the Samyukta Dal so as to remain faithful to its position on agrarian reform."[157] Those Rajput landlords which had already joined the BJS and were elected, "abandoned the party when it appeared that it was not likely to amend its stand on the question of land reform".[158]

Undeniably, the BJS showed a commitment to principle by deliberately alienating important potential supporters who opposed the party programme. And they opposed it because it contained classical Leftist promises. The party even paid a financial toll: "Handicapped all

---

[156]Tavleen Singh: "Twisted Version of Nationalism", *Indian Express*, 11.6.1995. *Knickerwallah*: one who wears knickers, part of the RSS uniform (originally the uniform of Congress volunteers during a Congress session in Nagpur, shortly before Dr. Hedgewar founded the RSS there), hence a nickname of RSS swayamsevaks.

[157]C. Jaffrelot: *The Hindu Nationalist Movement*, p.152. *Zamîndârî*: landlordism, as opposed to the "land to the tiller" principle. *Jâgîrdârî*: feudality, absentee landlordism.

[158]C. Jaffrelot: *The Hindu Nationalist Movement*, p.152.

through the 50s by a crippling lack of financial resources, its small achievements look all the more impressive when viewed against the background of the irresistible financial power of both the Congress Party and the CPI."[159] Whatever else may be said of the BJS, it genuinely functioned on pure idealism.

Deendayal Upadhyaya

After S.P. Mookerjee's demise, the BJS was effectively dominated by its RSS-trained cadres, among whom Deendayal Upadhyaya was the coming man. The actual presidents, Mauli Chandra Sharma (1953-54), Prem Nath Dogra (1954-56), Deva Prasad Ghosh (1956-60), Pitambar Das (1960-61), Avasaralu Rama Rao (1961-62), Raghu Vira (1962-63, died in a car crash), and Bachhraj Vyas (1963-65), were weak figureheads. Not weak in every sense, e.g. Raghu Vir was a renowned scholar, an expert on China (this was the time of the Chinese invasion, autumn 1962), a bridge-builder with other opposition parties, and the best possible spokesman for a language policy of national self-respect against the pro-English policy of the Nehru Government.[160] But the ideological orientation of the party was firmly in the hands of RSS men, first of all of Deendayal Upadhyaya, who was the BJS general secretary for a long time before formally becoming the party president in December 1967. Sharma had stepped down in protest against this RSS interference.

Undeniably, the RSS presence laid the foundation for the party's future success as a cohesive and well-organized party that could count on dedicated cadres, all the more needed in the absence of sizable financial backing from big business or other sources. In electoral terms, however, this policy of close RSS involvement in the BJS made the party less adaptable and insufficiently capable of attracting the mainstream Hindu vote, which remained with the Congress Party or went to the rival Swatantra Party.

Like S.P. Mookerjee's and Raghu Vir's, Deendayal's presidency was cut short by his dramatic death. And like Mookherjee's, his death

[159]Amaury de Riencourt: *The Soul of India*, p.394.

[160]Raghu Vira, who had been a Congressman for long, is famous for his bulky *Comprehensive English-Hindi Dictionary*, in which many pure Hindi alternatives for English terms were presented, some of them invented by Raghu Vira himself (not that they always caught on). His son Lokesh Chandra, the well-known art historian, has been a Rajya Sabha member for Congress under Indira Gandhi; in late 1997, he joined the BJP.

(11 February 1968) became the object of a controversy. He was standing at the door of a train coming from Delhi and approaching Moghulserai railway station, just outside Varanasi. The next thing we know is that he was found lying beside the railway track a mile west of the station, with a five-Rupee note in his hand.[161] In his compartment, all his belongings were missing, and the RSS decided that this could not have been an accident but a "murder most foul".[162] Even Bruce Graham writes that he was "apparently murdered".[163]

In principle, we ought to stick to the rule that *"entia non sunt multiplicanda sine necessitate"*, we should not presuppose entities which are not necessary for explaining the available data. For all we know, the wounds on Deendayal's body were not different from what one would expect if someone simply falls out of the train. Of course it is thinkable that someone had pushed him out, but the subsequent investigation found no clue in that direction. Even if it was murder, it could simply have been a case of robbery by excessive means. Since the investigation was carried out by officers who owed their job to Congress authorities, one can always claim that under orders from a corrupt Congress leadership, they have withheld the truth. Many *Sangh* people say that Deendayal was murdered by the security services acting on orders of the ruling party.

On the other hand, an intra-party intrigue has also been suggested: Balraj Madhok has alleged that BJS leaders A.B. Vajpayee and Nana Deshmukh were behind it, and that Indira Gandhi used this information to blackmail them into toeing a secular-Leftist line.[164] I fear that this is merely one of the numerous attempts of Hindutva activists to comprehend ideological positions in purely *paurusheya* (related to the individual, non-ideological) terms. It is of the same order as the allegation, common among Hindutva hard-liners, that bachelor Vajpayee is an alcoholic and has a mistress and child in the US.

Such petty gossip is widely indulged in as a substitute for proper ideological analysis. Vajpayee's and Deshmukh's "secularist" and "leftist" position can perfectly be understood from a well-known

---

[161]In the Deendayal Research Institute, just across from the RSS Delhi headquarters, there is a permanent exhibition on Deendayal Upadhyaya and his "martyrdom".

[162]"Murder most foul of Pt Deendayal", *Organiser*, 22.2.1968.

[163]B. Graham: *Hindu Nationalism*, p.91.

[164]Balraj Madhok's thesis is presented in M.R. Varshney: *Jana Sangh/RSS and Balraj Madhok*, Ch.6.

ideological power equation, viz. that secularism was the official and prestigious doctrine, while Hindutva had a bad name. Introducing a superfluous cloak-and-dagger story to explain something which is not a mystery at all, looks like an attempt to avoid facing the facts which provide the true explanation—and which are unpleasant to face, because they imply that the Hindutva movement itself has been slack and ineffective in developing its own ideology and impressing it on its own elected representatives.

Deendayal Upadhyaya's main contribution to Hindu Revivalism is the concept of *Ekâtmatâ-Mânavavâd*, "Integral Humanism", which became the official party doctrine in 1965, and which we will discuss more closely later on in this book.[165]

Balraj Madhok

The strongest BJS party leader in the 1960s was undoubtedly Balraj Madhok (1921), who taught History in Delhi University. He organized the civilian defence of Srinagar against the invading Pakistani irregulars in 1947-48 and co-founded the RSS student wing ABVP. In 1961 he was the first to raise the Ayodhya issue in Parliament: during the debate on "emotional integration", he argued that a heartfelt national unity could not come about when one community occupied or laid claim to the sacred places of another. As a Panjabi Hindu (born in the Panjabi-speaking part of Jammu & Kashmir), he led the unsuccessful opposition to the partition of East Panjab into a Panjabi-speaking and a Hindi-speaking part (Panjab and Haryana), as demanded by many Sikhs and conceded in 1966. Widely respected as a foreign policy specialist, he was president of the Indo-Israeli Friendship Society in 1967-74, and more recently of the Indo-Tibetan Society.

After the figurehead presidents of 1953-65, Balraj Madhok was again a president of substance (1965-67), both within the party's own policy-making and in the national political arena. He led the BJS to its best electoral score in its history: 9.4 per cent of the votes in the 1967 Lok Sabha elections, yielding 35 seats, up from 3 seats in 1952, 4 in 1957, 14 in 1962, and better than the 22 seats obtained in 1971.[166] Madhok was a

[165]Explained in four lectures published together as D. Upadhyaya: *Integral Humanism* (1965); the BJS statement *Principles and Policies* (1965, in *Party Documents 1951-1972*, vol.1, pp.1-43) is a more concrete formulation.

[166]Figures in Paul Brass: *Politics of India Since Independence*, pp.76-7.

committed anti-Communist and this brought him in conflict with the more Left-leaning party leaders, who sought to form "unprincipled" alliances with the Left parties in states where this could ensure a non-Congress majority and an "opposition government" (as non-Congress governments were then called).

Later, Madhok explained as follows the episode of "the *Samyukta Vidhâyak Dal* [SVD, United Legislative Team] after the general election of 1967. The Congress was reduced to a minority in many states. Ram Manohar Lohia gave a call for unity of the opposition parties on the basis of non-Congressism to wrest power from the Congress. Power-hungry politicians of almost all parties including the Jan Sangh welcomed this move. Since the Jan Sangh had emerged as the main opposition party in these states, its concurrence was vital. As president of the BJS, I opposed this plan. I felt that the SVD governments would not last long. They would fall under their own contradictions leading to mid-term elections which would enable the Congress to stage a come-back. ... SVD governments were formed in Punjab, Haryana, UP, Bihar and Madhya Pradesh and crashed within two years."[167]

Out of more than 30 books Madhok wrote, the following are the most relevant to the present study:

India's Foreign Policy and National Affairs (1969, a collection of his speeches in Parliament);

Indianisation (1970);

RSS and Politics (1986);

Case for Hindu State (1989);

Rationale of Hindu State (1992);

Kashmir, Storm Centre of the World (1992).

After Deendayal Upadhyaya's demise, the party was increasingly controlled by Atal Behari Vajpayee, Nana Deshmukh and their "Leftist" faction, to which Madhok developed an open hostility. When he failed to win a seat in the 1971 Lok Sabha elections, he alleged that Congress had rigged the elections by means of ballot-papers produced in Moscow and treated with invisible ink; this conspiracy theory made him the butt of uncharitable jokes.[168] In 1973, Balraj Madhok was expelled from the party

[167]Balraj Madhok: "Learn from history", *Indian Express*, 28.5.1996.

[168]The relevant correspondence between Madhok and the party leadership, including an argument about the "invisible ink", is published as appendix in M.R. Varshney: *Jana Sangh, RSS and Balraj Madhok*.

because of "anti-party activities". After the BJS had been dissolved and then reconstituted as the BJP in 1980, Madhok re-founded the BJS, but without the RSS cadres behind him, he never got very far with it.

The Emergency and the Janata Government

The Jana Sangh became the main opposition party in the early 1970s: "Its membership jumped, according to its own statistics, from 2,75,000 in 1960-61 to two million in 1973. Even if that figure were divided by two, it remained a substantial force, with far greater discipline and cohesiveness than most of its rivals, including those on the Left. It is, therefore, not too difficult to grasp how it became the organisational mainstay of the JP movement",[169] i.e. the neo-Gandhian mass agitation led by JP/ Jayaprakash Narayan.

In 1975, Indira Gandhi cracked down on the JP movement by declaring a state of Emergency. The opposition leaders, Socialists as well as Hindu nationalists, were imprisoned and civil freedoms suspended. The movement against the Emergency led to the creation of an alliance into which other parties including the BJS merged their separate identities: the Janata Party. Unexpectedly, this party won the 1977 elections and formed the first non-Congress Central Government in independent India.

Though the vast majority of jail-goers under the Emergency had been RSS/BJS men, and though the underground resistance which had prepared the way for the Janata take-over had been manned mostly by RSS workers, the RSS would quickly become the black sheep of the Janata Party. At the initiative of Madhu Limaye, the Socialists in the Janata Party, who owed their chairs in large measure to the sweat and blood of RSS activists, raised the so-called "double membership" issue.[170] The RSS members in the government were given a choice between renouncing their Janata Party membership (or government post) and renouncing their RSS membership. Alternatively, the RSS was given the option of renouncing its Hindu identity and becoming the multi-religious mass organization of the Janata

[169] T. Ali: *The Nehrus and the Gandhis*, p.198.

[170] Madhu Limaye had earlier disrupted the (admittedly not too vital) Praja Socialist Party from within, a Leftist but anti-Communist party. When he also wrecked the Janata Government, which had replaced Indira Gandhi's Moscow-friendly regime, and which included veteran anti-Communists like Morarji Desai, Limaye was called the "one-man demolition squad" and people wondered aloud if he was in the pay of Moscow. In India, the role of foreign money is a reality, and while such rumours should be kept between brackets until tangible proof is forthcoming, they should not immediately be laughed off either.

Party. Fortunately for the RSS, the dilemma was aborted by the fall of the Janata Government.[171]

Being on the defensive like this, the BJS members exerted no substantial influence on government policy. Lal Krishna Advani (1927) was a meritorious Information Minister, but did not press any specific Hindu reforms, except for two harmless and peripheral innovations: a daily recitation from Tulsidas' *Râmcharitmânas* on All-India Radio (which still continues) and recitation on Tuesdays of the *Hanumân Châlîsâ* (discontinued when Indira Gandhi returned in 1980).[172] The Janata government did not realize a single point that had been a distinctive concern of its BJS component. On the contrary, on several points, Foreign Affairs Minister A.B. Vajpayee (1925) out-Nehrued the Nehruvians. On a visit to China, he formally expressed India's acceptance of China's claim that Tibet is an integral part of China, a position diametrically opposed to the one stated in the BJS election manifestoes.[173] Not surprisingly, China's leader Li Peng was one of the first to congratulate Vajpayee when he briefly assumed office as Prime Minister in May 1996.

Vajpayee also inducted the diplomat Syed Shahabuddin into the Rajya Sabha, presenting him as a model Muslim and a progressive alternative to obscurantist leaders like the influential Imam Bukhari of Delhi's Jama Masjid; however, Shahabuddin was to become an articulate spokesman of Muslim radicalism. Finally, Vajpayee also made it much easier for Pakistani citizens to travel to India, a facility which is hard to disconnect from the recent boom in espionage and sabotage acts which Hindu nationalists routinely impute to Pakistani agents inside India.

In the case of Vajpayee, all this is hardly surprising when one looks past his label as an "RSS man" and focuses on the positions he has actually taken.[174] This leader of a supposedly anti-Nehruvian movement was

---

[171] An inside account of the Janata experience and its premature end is L.K. Advani: *The People Betrayed.*

[172] *Râmcharitmânas*: the Hindi biography of Rama, popular counterpart of Valmiki's Sanskrit *Râmâyaṇa*, written by Goswami Tulsidas (1532-1624). *Hanumân Châlîsâ*: forty couplets in praise of Râmâyana hero *Hanumân*, to whom Tuesday is dedicated.

[173] Mentioned in Avinash Jaiswal: "The Glory and the Shame", *Organiser*, 21.7.1996.

[174] During the discussion on the 1996 Lok Sabha elections in the subsequent South Asia conference in Madison, Paul Brass cut short musings by some panelists about Vajpayee's "moderate views" with the curt reminder that "Vajpayee is a dyed-in-the-wool RSS man". This is quite right, but the question is: should this make us suspect Vajpayee's "progressive" statements, or should it make us rethink our frozen views about RSS "Rightism"?

always an outspoken admirer of Nehru. The chapter on Vajpayee in Janardan Thakur's skeptical report on the Janata Government is titled: "Atal Behari—'A New Nehru'". Thakur writes: "Vajpayee had been a great admirer of Jawaharlal Nehru, and had supported the basic concepts of his foreign policy. ... 'The sun has set!', Vajpayee said in his eloquent tribute to Nehru when he died."[175] Subramaniam Swamy, the renowned economist who was with the BJS in the 1970s, commented that "Vajpayee is as wishy-washy as Nehru was. I don't think he has any ideology."[176] Much more recently, Nehru admirer Mani Shankar Aiyar called Vajpayee "a Nehruvian in drag".[177]

The only Hindu-sounding stir created by a Jana Sangh politician was the Freedom of Religion Bill, moved by O.P. Tyagi, which proposed to outlaw conversion by force or fraud. Unobjectionable as that proposal might seem, the Christian missionaries launched a worldwide campaign against its alleged implication of outlawing proselytization altogether. The non-BJS section of the Government thwarted its adoption. Similar laws had none the less been adopted at the state level by *Congress* governments in Madhya Pradesh, Orissa and Arunachal Pradesh.

In the Janata interregnum (1977-79), former BJS members constituted the largest faction in the Janata Party parliamentary representation, *c.* 95 out of 295. Yet, this did not in the least lead to any kind of "hinduization" of the polity: they did not influence policy in proportion to their numerical strength (one in three), nor even to the extent of one half or one tenth or one percent of their strength. It remains puzzling that all manner of India-watchers have painted grim doomsday scenarios about "Hindu theocracy" in case of a Hindu nationalist majority, when the historical experience of the Janata regime tells such a radically different story.

---

[175]Janardan Thakur: *All the Janata Men*, pp.136-37.

[176]Quoted in Y.K. Malik and V.B. Singh: *Hindu Nationalists in India*, p.39. The statement does injustice to Nehru, who was passionate and articulate about ideology.

[177]M.S. Aiyar: "Trampling on a tradition", *Indian Express*, 6.10.1998. There is also a persistent rumour that in his student days, Vajpayee had been a Communist, but this has been laid to rest by his Kannada biographer, Vishweshwar Bhat, according to a summary by K.S. Dakshina Murthy: "Vajpayee was never a Communist, claims book", *Hindustan Times*, 14.4.1999. The explanation given is that as a student union leader, he was always in the company of colleagues who happened to be Communists.

The BJP

In 1980, when Indira Gandhi returned to power, the Janata Party split and many former BJS members of the Janata Party founded a new party: the *Bharatiya Janata Party* (BJP).[178] Where BJP and BJS positions differ, generally by a softening of the BJP position vis-à-vis the BJS original, it is still useful to know the latter because it often represents the lingering heartfelt opinion of at least a part of the BJP cadres and constituency. Only in 1991-92 was the BJP led by an acknowledged hard-liner, nuclear physicist Murli Manohar Joshi (1934); otherwise the presidency has been swapped between the soft-spoken gentleman Lal Krishna Advani ("really one of the most able, cool-headed, courteous and clean politicians left today")[179] and the popular orator Atal Behari Vajpayee. Often described by secularists as "the right man in the wrong party", Vajpayee is also a Hindi poet, and Narasimha Rao, Congress Prime Minister and something of a litterateur himself, has declared that in poetry: "Atalji is my guru."[180]

The BJS/BJP is formally totally independent of the RSS, but most of its leaders and active members, including its latest presidents Kushabhau Thakre (1998-2000) and Bangaru Laxman (2000-), have an RSS background. The RSS weeklies *Organiser* and *Panchjanya* often provide a look into the concerns and opinions of the BJS-BJP constituency, even when they go against the official party line.

Nevertheless, we should not ignore the differences between the RSS and the BJP, resulting from the constraints which political practice imposes, as well as from the fact that the BJP increasingly includes people without RSS background. Through the normal procedures of intra-party

---

[178]Not all of them, e.g. the brainy but maverick economist Subramaniam Swamy stayed in the Janata Party rump and remained an implacable critic of the RSS and BJP until the 1998 elections.

[179]According to Khushwant Singh, quoted in Y.K. Malik and V.B. Singh: *Hindu Nationalists in India*, p.42. He adds: "I am pretty certain that he will never be unfair to Muslims if he becomes minister." See also the sympathizing portraits by Gulab Vazirani: *Lal Advani, the Man and His Mission* (1991), and Atmaram Kulkarni: *The Advent of Advani* (1995).

[180]"PM releases Vajpayee's book", *Organiser*, 29.10.1995. Suzanne Goldenberg gives this a hateful twist ("Nationalists get chance to rule India", *The Guardian*, 16.5.1996): in her version, Vajpayee, a nationally acclaimed poet, "fancies himself a poet".

democracy, these people also make their presence felt. Being the only major party in India with an effectively democratic party structure ("the BJP was one of the rare parties where the internal elections were held regularly")[181] the BJP's policies are partly those of its non-RSS membership.[182] The softening of the BJP's positions when compared with those of the BJS is partly due to an ideological softening in the RSS itself, and partly due to a greater input of non-RSS members.[183]

Thus, economic policy is one field where differences between the BJP and the RSS have surfaced. In the last couple of years, the RSS and several of its affiliates, most particularly the *Swadeshi Jagaran Manch* (Front for National Self-Reliance Awakening) led by S. Gurumurthy, have been campaigning for economic *Swadeshi*. This notion of national self-reliance dates back to the nationalist agitation in Bengal in 1905, when British goods were boycotted and replaced with native, *Swadeshi* ones.[184] Many businessmen and economists inside or in the orbit of the BJP shrug at this old and quaint-sounding slogan. Therefore, the BJP has tried to redefine *Swadeshi* in such a way as to make room for the more internationalist interests of this constituency: liberalization combined with a dose of protectionism.[185]

For a more fundamental doctrinal example, the BJP espouses "genuine secularism" or "positive secularism". It will carefully avoid using the term *Hindu Râshtra* ("Hindu state"), which spokesmen of the

---

[181]Gérard Heuzé: *Où va l'Inde moderne?*, p.53. I am not denying that the Congress Party formally has a democratic structure; but the normal democratic procedures have been put aside by Indira Gandhi and never fully restored. The Communist parties, of course, have "democratic centralism" as their principle. The centre-Left (now essentially casteist) parties which come and go, have mostly had a feudal style of functioning centred around autocratic leaders like Charan Singh, Mulayam Singh Yadav, Laloo Prasad Yadav, and Kanshi Ram, a pattern also in evidence in the Shiv Sena.

[182]The same is true for the VHP, which has attracted clerics who are foreign to the RSS discipline and sometimes embarrass the leadership with statements that are in conflict with the RSS-VHP philosophy. Starting in 1991, a handful of these Sants have been elected on a BJP ticket and have thereby been subjected to the BJP party discipline in Parliament.

[183]A pro-BJP biography of the party is: Gurdas M. Ahuja: *BJP and Indian Politics* (1994).

[184]See e.g. C.K. Saji Narayana and Manhar Bhai Mehta: *Multi-Nationals, Anti-Nationals* (1992, a critique of Finance Minister Manmohan Singh's policies); K.S. Sudarshan, Nikhil Chakravarthy and S. Gurumurthy: *Restructuring India's Polity the Swadeshi Way*; and S.R. Ramaswamy: *In the Woods of Globalisation* (1995).

[185]See BJP: *Humanistic Approach to Economic Development (A Swadeshi Alternative)*, 1992, and *The GATT Treaty, a Total Surrender*, 1994.

RSS (and of Hindu organizations outside the Sangh Parivar, especially the HMS) freely use, albeit with the obligatory addition that "throughout history, Hindu states have always been secular". At the height of the Ayodhya temple/mosque controversy, the VHP published advertisements titled: "Hindu India, secular India". But the BJP will not go beyond stating that "India should not betray its essentially Hindu personality" (as BJP President L.K. Advani is wont to say),[186] or that, vaguely, "Hinduism is the answer".[187] In their official statements, the notion of a "Hindu state" is entirely absent: "I do not want India to be the Hindu version of Pakistan."[188]

The BJP cannot take the support of the Sangh organizations for granted. During local elections in autumn 2000 in Uttar Pradesh and Gujarat, the VHP expressed its disapproval of BJP governance (which failed to realize any specific Hindu demand) by refusing to lend a hand in the campaign. In both states, the BJP was routed. When power at a more consequential political level is at stake, such move to teach the BJP a lesson is less likely, yet it has been done once when the BJP could not dream of coming to power anyway.

The BJP defeat in the 1984 elections (2 Lok Sabha seats, an all-time low, down from an already disappointing 4 in 1980) was partly due to the fact that the RSS workers gave their support to Indira Gandhi. She had committed herself to the defence of Hindu interests in Jammu and Kashmir, where they complained of discrimination by the local Muslim majority. After she was murdered, they shifted their temporary allegiance to her son Rajiv, perceived as the best guarantee for India's unity under the circumstances (the Khalistan movement for a Sikh state, emanating from a breakaway Hindu minority, was deemed a more profound threat than Muslim separatism). By 1989, however, the adoption of the Ayodhya cause by the BJP ensured it of full RSS support, which helped the BJP to a spectacular breakthrough.

The BJP constitution

In its *Constitution and Rules*, the BJP defines its ideology as follows.

"Article II: Objective. The party is pledged to build up India as a strong and prosperous nation, which is modern, progressive and

[186]Talking to Brian Barron, BBC Assignment, May 1991; and on many other occasions.

[187]Preacher-lady Uma Bharati, later elected as MP for the BJP from Khajuraho, talking to Smriti Vohra, *Times of India*, 21.12.1989.

[188]L.K. Advani, quoted in A. Kulkarni: *Advent of Advani*, p.249.

enlightened in outlook and which proudly draws inspiration from India's ancient culture and values and thus is able to emerge as a great world power playing an effective role in the comity of Nations for the establishment of world peace and a just international order.

"The party aims at establishing a democratic state which guarantees to all citizens irrespective of caste, creed or sex, political, social and economic justice, equality of opportunity and liberty of faith and expression.

"The party shall bear true faith and allegiance to the Constitution of India as by law established and to the principles of socialism, secularism and democracy and would uphold the sovereignty, unity and integrity of India."[189] Perhaps this is all perfunctory, but it is at least there, in cold print.

"Article III: Basic Philosophy. Integral Humanism shall be the basic philosophy of the Party.

"Article IV: Commitments. The Party shall be committed to nationalism and national integration, democracy, Gandhian Socialism, Positive Secularism, that is 'Sarva Dharma Samabhav', and value-based politics. The party stands for decentralisation of economic and political power."[190]

Upon joining the party, every BJP member makes the following pledge:

"I believe in Integral Humanism which is the basic philosophy of Bharatiya Janata Party.

"I am committed to Nationalism and National Integration, Democracy, Gandhian Socialism, Positive Secularism (Sarva Dharma Samabhava) and value-based politics.

"I subscribe to the concept of a Secular State and Nation not based on religion.

"I firmly believe that this task can be achieved by peaceful means alone.

"I do not observe or recognize untouchability in any shape or form.

"I am not a member of any other political party.

---

[189]BJP: *Constitution and Rules*, p.19.

[190]*Constitution and Rules (as amended by the National Council at Gandhinagar, Gujarat, on 2 May 1992) of the Bharatiya Janata Party*, pp.3-4. *"Sarva-Dharma-Samabhâva"* is a Gandhian slogan meaning "equal respect for all religions".

"I undertake to abide by the Constitution, Rules and Discipline of the Party."[191]

The letter and spirit of this pledge is widely at variance with the impression of BJP "fundamentalism" fostered in much of the secondary literature.

The Ayodhya controversy

The VHP shot to prominence (or notoriety) with the campaign for the liberation of the Hindu sacred sites in Ayodhya, Mathura and Kashi. This issue had been on its agenda since its foundation in 1964, but became a priority in 1986. That was when a major concession to Muslim pressure on an issue of the separate Muslim Personal Law (the Shah Bano affair) forced the Rajiv Gandhi government to make a compensatory gesture to Hindu sensibilities.[192] In that climate, a polite suggestion from the sadhus was enough to make the government order the removal of the locks on the Babri Masjid, a mosque-structure built on Rama's supposed birthplace. In this building, idols of the god-king Rama and his companions had been installed in 1949, but Hindu worshippers had only had limited access to it.

After the opening of the locks, Muslim militants founded the *Babri Masjid Action Committee* and the rivalling *Babri Masjid Movement Co-ordination Committee* to campaign for the restoration of the mosque status of what had effectively become a Hindu temple. Marxist academics came to the rescue of the BMAC and BMMCC by floating the *ad hoc* theory that there had never been a temple at the disputed site. Talks on the historical evidence for the past existence of a Hindu temple at the site yielded important new findings (confirming its existence) but no consensus.[193] In 1994, the Supreme Court rejected a request from the Narasimha Rao Government to express an opinion on the historical question. At any rate, most Muslim claimants insist that even undeniable evidence that the mosque had been built in forcible replacement of a

---

[191]BJP: *Constitution and Rules*, p.19.

[192]See e.g. the comment with the self-explanatory title by Ramakrishna Bajaj (editorially introduced as "a leading industrialist and veteran Gandhian"): "Implications of Ayodhya. The Hindu aggressiveness witnessed today is a reaction against minority appeasement", *Observer of Business and Politics*, 25.12.1992.

[193]See VHP: *The Great Evidence*, also published, with some relevant appendices, by Voice of India as *History vs. Casuistry*; and R.S. Sharma (who led the BMAC-mandated team) *et al.*: *Historians' Report to the Nation*.

temple does not invalidate their claim. So, the litigation which started in 1950 has continued, with little promise of a satisfactory verdict.[194]

Meanwhile on the streets, the long-drawn-out Hindu-Muslim confrontation with various marches and agitations kept India under tension for several years. On the BJP side, the main event was L.K. Advani's car procession from the Somnath temple in Gujarat (a famous temple repeatedly destroyed by Muslim iconoclasts and rebuilt again, last just after Independence) to Ayodhya. This Rath Yatra may not even have been the BJP's own initiative. At the time itself, I was told at the BJP office that Prime Minister V.P. Singh had suggested to Advani that he create some public opinion pressure on the Government concerning Ayodhya. That way, V.P. Singh (who rejected the claim that the disputed building was a "mosque") could explain to his Muslim supporters that in the face of such mighty pressure, he would be unable to keep his promise to give them the disputed Ayodhya site. So, possibly that is how the BJP decided to have the Rath Yatra.

It was much to the BJP's own surprise that Advani received a stormy welcome by unprecedentedly large crowds. The BJP had not been aware of the groundswell of Hindu consciousness and of the mass enthusiasm for the Ayodhya temple until it was confronted with this response. And even then, it has refused to believe its own eyes, for its policy ever since has been to push the Ayodhya issue into the background. Indeed, it was in reaction to the BJP leadership's pussyfooting on Ayodhya that ordinary Hindutva activists took matters into their own hands.

The agitation culminated in the demolition of the disputed building on 6 December 1992. The demolition was a strange event. While participants deny that there had been any preparation at all, other Hindu activists claim that it had been prepared by a small group of volunteers led by a professional engineer, and that once this core group took the initiative, the crowd joined in. At any rate, appeals by RSS leader H.V. Seshadri, VHP leader Ashok Singhal and BJP leader L.K. Advani to maintain the discipline and refrain from vandalism were ignored by the defiant and exuberant rank and file.

---

[194]A secularist afterthought on the Ayodhya affair is found in Nilanjan Mukhopadhyay: *The Demolition*, and likewise Pradeep Nayak: *Politics of the Ayodhya Dispute*. One from the Hindu angle is Jitendra Bajaj, ed.: *Ayodhya and the Future India*. See also the Vigil anthology: *The 5 Hours and After: the English Press on Ayodhya after Dec. 6, 1992*.

The provincial security forces refused to intervene (the film of the event shows a commander shouting at his men, who quietly refuse to act), and the Central Government refused to send troops until it was too late. Most Muslims have accused Prime Minister Narasimha Rao of deliberately allowing the demolition to take place, and I believe rightly.

Consider the matter from his viewpoint: as long as the "mosque" (for the BJP, the "disputed structure"; for commentator Girilal Jain, the "non-mosque") was standing, the BJP could use it as a rallying-point, a visible "sign of national humiliation imposed by the invader Babar" kept in place by the "pseudo-secularist" Congress Government. On the other hand, if the building was demolished in a BJP-related action, this could be used against the BJP and the whole Hindu movement, viz. as a reason to dismiss the BJP state governments and ban the Hindu mass organizations. This is at any rate what effectively happened: the Ayodhya theme was killed as a BJP vote-getter, and the BJP's march to power was temporarily reversed.

Another strange aspect of the affair is that nobody seemed interested in finding the culprits.[195] It took me only a very small effort to find out who actually took the lead of the operation, at least according to one group of Kar Sevaks, others claiming that the whole affair had been totally spontaneous. I cannot be equally definitive about which Hindutva *leader*, if any, may have patronized it against his own colleagues. At any rate, a cover story of the type: "This man [photograph] demolished the Babri Masjid", would have been the scoop of the year. Yet, no editor put his investigative journalists to work on this. The reason is that pro-Hindutva media didn't want to cause these activists any trouble, while the dominant anti-Hindutva media wanted to cast the net of guilt as widely as possible, especially so as to include the BJP leadership.

When the demolition started, BJP leader L.K. Advani (along with H.V. Seshadri and Ashok Singhal) pleaded in vain for sticking to the planned programme and had tears in his eyes when seeing this breakdown of RSS discipline. The secularist media want us to believe that this was mere theatre, when all inside sources confirm that Advani's surprise was quite genuine. By contrast, Sadhvi Ritambhara exhorted the *kar sevak*s with the famous words: *"Ek dhakkâ aur do, Bâbrî Masjid tor do!"* (*"Give*

---

[195]Except initially and without insistence, e.g. "Have you any clue?", *Sunday*, 24.1.1993.

one more push, destroy Babar's mosque!"). No, the Sangh Parivar is not a monolith; a radical faction knew very well that it could not trust the main leaders to put an end to the Babri Masjid stalemate, so it went its own way. But to keep the pressure on the BJP leadership up, the media were willing to ignore these facts and forgo the scoop of the year.

Only immediately after the event did a few journalists make an attempt to find out more precisely. For what it is worth, Rajat Sharma reported: "The high and mighty in the RSS were shell-shocked when the Kar Sewaks defied the high command and demolished the structure. A baffled Sunder Singh Bhandari told the press in New Delhi soon after the Ayodhya episode that the Shiv Sena had done it. L.K. Advani was at a loss for words. Rajendra Singh wanted to consult colleagues before making a statement. The two top RSS leaders, H.V. Seshadri and K.S. Sudarshan who were present in Ayodhya on December 6 were angry for the breach of organisational discipline. ... They were stunned when repeated appeals in several languages had no effect on the *kar sewaks*. ... In fact during the first two days after the demolition of the structure the RSS-BJP leadership was down and demoralised. On the one hand they were trying to find excuses to save face in public and on the other an internal inquiry was on to identify the culprits."[196]

Sharma's own feeling was that the *Panchjanya* adviser Bhanu Pratap Shukla and former BJP president Murli Manohar Joshi were behind it; the latter was the only BJP leader present who started cheering when the walls came tumbling down. At any rate, most top leaders opposed the "anarchy", but failed to stop it. Even Communist observer Manini Chatterjee writes: "On December 6, 1992, when thousands of *kar sevaks* descended on Ayodhya, the leaders had long surrendered all capacity to lead."[197]

Secularist sources have uniformly decried the Babri Masjid demolition on 6 December 1992 as a terrible drama, but far from being a neutral scholarly judgement, this was actually one extreme of the opinion spectrum, with other responsible intellectuals describing the same event as a symptom of "a new, historical awakening".[198] Others have pointed out its

---

[196]Rajat Sharma: "Is the Ayodhya whodunnit solved?", *Sunday Observer*, 20.12.1992.

[197]Manini Chatterjee: "The BJP: political mobilization for Hindutva", *South Asia Bulletin*, 1994/1, p.22.

[198]V.S. Naipaul, interviewed by Dileep Padgaonkar: "An area of awakening", *Times of India*, 18.7.1993. Likewise, Nirad C. Chaudhuri, *Times of India*, 8.8.1993; remark that earlier in their careers, both authors were scathing denouncers of Hinduism.

cathartic effect: after a decade full of communal riots, the post-demolition conflagration strangely opened a period free of riots, in spite of regular bomb attacks (by fringe groups, not involving the masses) against Hindu targets. When comparing, in terms of death toll, the five years before mid-January 1993 (when the post-demolition fervour had spent itself) with the five subsequent years, one finds a contrast of thousands vs dozens. One cannot deny that among the unforeseen effects of the demolition, the best surprise was a salutory psychological shock which made people reconsider the Hindu-Muslim polarization. This can hardly be counted as a "merit" of the demolishers, but all the same, it ought to cool tempers when the demolition is evaluated in retrospect.

The VHP's "Hindu agenda"

One RSS-affiliated organization which has been in the limelight a lot in the past decade is the Vishva Hindu Parishad. Though not a political organization, it chose to present its charter of demands before all political parties contesting the 1996 Lok Sabha elections, promising support to the party which takes up this agenda. Some of these demands are at variance with the BJP's positions, though most are not. The VHP's 40-point "Hindu Agenda", drafted at its National Meeting in Mumbai, December 1995, is as follows:[199]

"Vishwa Hindu Parishad presents this Hindu agenda before the political parties to salvage Bharat and the Hindu nation unfortunately surrounded by inimical forces and innumerable difficulties to ensure just human rights to the vast community of 80 crore in their homeland. It is the duty of every political party in the country to promise to safeguard the interests of the national mainstream, i.e. Hindu Samaj (Sanatan, Bauddha, Jain, Sikh panth, etc.). In the forthcoming elections we want the parties to promise the following agenda:

"1. Hindutva and nationalism in Bharat are synonymous. Hindu Samaj is undisputably the main current of Bharat. Hindu interest is the national interest. Therefore, the honour and the interests of Hindus will be protected in every manner.

---

[199]Published in *Organiser*, 4.2.1996, under the heading: "By presenting Hindu agenda VHP tells the political parties to *respect the Hindu sentiments*". Remark the somewhat pitiable focus on "sentiments": this is the language of a supplicant (begging for goodwill rather than pleading a case which can stand on merit), not of a pretender to the seat of power.

"2. Every nation has a constitutional denomination. Only 'Bharat', which has ancient glorious and historical connotations will have constitutional recognition." The reader has understood that in this case, *denomination* does not mean 'religious denomination' but simply 'name'.

"3. The patriotic Hindus all over the world aspire to construct a magnificent temple at Sri Ram Janmabhoomi in Ayodhya in accordance with the model approved by the revered saints. The Janmabhoomi complex will be immediately handed over to Shri Ramjanmabhoomi Nyas, which is in the forefront of Shri Ramjanmabhoomi awakening and is recognised as such by Hindus all over the world." This means that the existing VHP-approved platform of sadhus (the *Râm Janmabhûmi Nyâs*/ Trust), rather than one newly constituted by the Government, should oversee the construction of the projected Ram temple.

"4. The holy campuses of Shri Krishna Janmasthan at Mathura and Shri Kashi Vishvanath temple, Gyanvapi at Varanasi, which were desecrated and remodelled by foreigners, will be immediately handed over to the Hindu samaj by enacting a suitable legislation.

"5. Slaughter of cow and its progeny shall be completely banned throughout the country by enacting an effective legislation and made a rigorously punishable offence.

"6. Gau-seva [cow-service] ministries will be formed at the Centre and in the States to protect the environment, natural ecology and agro-economy, for establishment of self-reliant village-oriented economy, to foster and develop the national species of cow and its progeny, for production of natural and organic manure and to enhance the production of milk, butter, ghee and yoghurt, etc., and to utilise the tremendous ox-power in national interest.

"7. The anti-national activity of religious conversion of Hindus by force, fraud or false propaganda by exploiting the innocence and poverty of backward communities will be strictly banned.

"8. All foreign remittances to non-Government agencies, social, religious or service organizations or individuals will be stopped, so that the money and material so received is not misused for religious conversion and other divisive conspiracies.

"9. A uniform civil code will be promulgated throughout the country to check inequality, imbalance, injustice, atrocities on women and to stop the malpractice of polygamy.

"10. Abortion and female infanticide which promote immorality and female persecution will be banned. More stringent penal provisions will be made against rape and kidnapping of women. Firm steps will be taken to check the scourge of the dowry system." People from a Christian background may expect the demand to prohibit abortion as a minimum requirement for a movement to be "fundamentalist". Though Hindu scriptures are as outspoken in condemning abortion as the Catholic Church is, the point is rarely taken up by Hindutva activists due to the national concern about controlling population growth by all means; but here, at last, it is.[200]

"11. Article 370 of the Constitution, which smacks of a separate Balkanised identity of Kashmir from the rest of the country will be scrapped. The restriction on sale and purchase of property in Kashmir to Bharatiya citizens will be abolished.

"12. The Kashmiri migrants will be honourably rehabilitated. Their properties will be restored and the deprived families will be compensated. Adequate arrangements for their security will be made." Remark that even the VHP has adopted the secularist term 'migrant' when referring to the Hindu refugees from Kashmir.

"13. Secessionist demands and propaganda in Kashmir or anywhere else in the country or indulging in violent activities will be ruthlessly suppressed. Secessionist demand will be a strict penal anti-national offence.

"14. Terrorism results in untold sufferings to the people of the country. Therefore, the very source, whether internal or external, will be uprooted by determined action of the Government.

"15. The special rights and privileges granted to the minorities will be made available to all sections of the society to end inequality." This point refers to a string of constitutional, legal and political inequalities between Hindus and non-Hindus, best represented by Article 30 of the Constitution, which grants the minorities the right to set up and administer (after their own principles and in their own interest) their own state-subsidized schools. Unlike the BJP election manifestoes of 1996 and 1998, which merely promise to "amend Article 30", this VHP manifesto

---

[200] About the Hindu scriptural condemnation of abortion, see H.G. Coward, J.J. Lipner, K.K. Young: *Hindu Ethics: Purity, Abortion and Euthanasia.*

specifies in which direction Article 30 should be amended and equality achieved: the privileges of the minorities should not be taken away, but should be extended to the Hindu majority.

"16. Universally recognised, well developed and scientific language, Sanskrit, will be made a compulsory subject of study throughout the country." This is a very mild proposal in the light of the fast-spreading enthusiasm for "spoken Sanskrit" (promoted not only by the RSS but also by private organizations)[201] and the re-emerging opinion among Hindu intellectuals that Sanskrit should be made the link language of India, instead of Hindi or English. This proposal is not as outlandish as it may seem to some, and was made not only by Hindu Revivalists like Swami Vivekananda and Sri Aurobindo, but is actually being revived by contemporary Muslim progressives, Saeed Naqvi (who refers to the revival of Hebrew to counter the unfeasibility objection) and Ansar Hussain Khan.[202] Considering that there is merit in the argument against giving an unfair advantage to Hindi speakers by elevating their mother tongue to link language status, the choice of Sanskrit surprisingly emerges as the best alternative to the dominance of English.

"17. Mother-tongue will invariably be the medium of primary education.

"18. Teaching of Bharatiya culture and dharma will be made compulsory.

"19. The status of second official language accorded by certain States to Urdu in foreign script will be withdrawn.

"20. The distorted presentation of modern, social and cultural history of Bharat will be rewritten by honest, patriotic and learned historians and archaeologists. The teaching syllabus shall be accordingly reformed.

"21. Singing of *Vande Mataram* everyday will be compulsory in all educational institutions.

"22. Pooja, archana and religious construction activities of maths, mandirs and ashrams will be deemed charitable activity and will be entitled for exemption from income-tax."[203]

---

[201]I was introduced to the Spoken Sanskrit movement by N.S. Rajaram; like with other scientists (e.g. Subhash Kak), his enthusiasm for Sanskrit is at least partly based on the presumed scientific merits of Sanskrit grammar.

[202]S. Naqvi: *The Last Brahmin Prime Minister of India*, pp.20-1; and A.H. Khan: *The Rediscovery of India*, p.315.

[203]*Pûjâ*: a ritual of worship; *archanâ*: a ritual of worship.

"23. A specified portion of Government revenue shall be earmarked for various dharmic, charitable objects of the tax-payers.

"24. Efforts will be made at Governmental level to spread and develop Ayurveda and other indigenous medical systems.[204]

"25. Government interference and control on pilgrim centres, maths, mandirs and ashrams will be removed and they will be made autonomous for proper management."[205]

"26. Pilgrimages shall be made tax-free. Ministries shall be established at the Centre and in the States to restore the glory of pilgrim centres and to develop them as also to facilitate and encourage pilgrimage.

"27. Drinking and non-vegetarianism will be discouraged by the Government. All meat export from the country will be banned. All big mechanical abattoirs will be closed." This, then, is truly a demand which subordinates economics to culture. It is a reversal of fifty years of "development" in which culture was pushed aside as a useless relic in favour of notions of progress often directly dictated by foreign development organizations, e.g. the implantation of fisheries in areas where vegetarianism used to be the norm.

"28. Vigorous efforts will be made for immediate expulsion of all those who have infiltrated into Bharat after January 1, 1970. Country's borders will be impregnably guarded and sealed. Identity cards will be issued to the residents of bordering areas.

"29. Pervasive arrangements will be made for the cleanliness, piety and glory of religious centres and rivers."[206]

"30. Terrorist and anti-national activities will be ruthlessly crushed by appropriate legal provisions.

"31. Any denigration of or disrespect to any faith including Hindu

---

[204]This demand is always present in BJP manifestoes, e.g. *Election Manifesto 1998*, p.22. However, Krishna Kumar (Coimbatore), swayamsevak and manager of a network of Ayurvedic clinics, told me that the BJP doesn't mean business on this point, as on many others. In 1991, at the request of BJP President Murli Manohar Joshi, he had formulated a detailed plan for the promotion of Ayurveda; at the next National Executive meeting where this plan was to be tabled, members hadn't even received copies of his text, and nothing came of it, not even a commitment on paper.

[205]*Math*: Hindu abbey; *mandir*: temple; *âshram*: hermitage.

[206]My thanks to Veer Bhadra Mishra (BHU), convenor of the *Swacha Ganga* campaign, who showed me around the (as yet incomplete) realizations of this desperate effort to save the Ganga river from impending biological death. Needless to say, such efforts to save the sacred river are frequently denounced as "communal".

culture, belief or tradition or any venerated character, by audio-visual, written or spoken means will be a penal offence and strictly enforced.

"32. National economic policy will be based on Swadeshi and self-reliance.

"33. It shall be the moral duty of the Government to protect the religious and cultural rights of non-resident Bharatiyas living in neighbouring and far-off countries and to develop their dharmic, cultural and social relations.

"34. Non-resident Bharatiyas will be treated as Bharatiya citizens." This would formally put them in the uncomfortable position of "dual loyalty", precisely what Hindu nationalists hold against the Indian Muslims.

"35. The old and glorious historical names of towns, roads and places will be restored." This alludes to renaming Allahabad as *Prayâg*, Delhi as *Indraprastha*, Ahmedabad as *Karnâvatî*, etc. No BJP State Government has ever done anything about it, only the BJP-SS Government in Maharashtra has implemented the SS promise to rename *Bombay* as *Mumbai*.

"36. Prominent Hindu festivals will be declared national holidays.

"38. In view of the unimpeachable historical literary and archaeological evidence, the Places of Worship (Special Provision) Act, 1991, shall be suitably modified/repealed." This refers to a 1991 law freezing the religious status of places of worship as on 15 August 1947, prohibiting the conversion of mosques into temples even where there is evidence that the mosque had forcibly replaced a temple.

"37. The rights and privileges accorded to Scheduled Castes and Scheduled Tribes will be withdrawn on their conversion." This is in reaction to Christian attempts to extend the special benefits for SC members to Christian converts from these communities (as is already the case for ST members).

"39. Minority commission and similar partisan institutions will be abolished." Strictly speaking, this is a secularist demand for the abolition of a communal institution, viz. a commission constituted on the basis of religion and by definition excluding the Hindus.

"40. Recruitment in armed, paramilitary and police forces on communal lines will not be permitted." This is in reaction against Muslim demands that a minimum percentage of army and police personnel be recruited from among the Muslim community, reminiscent of communal recruiting in the British period.

The BJP's march to power

The BJS/BJP's percentage of votes had been consistently between 7 per cent and 12 per cent for more than three decades until and including 1989. Of course, the first-past-the-post electoral system made for swings in its tally of seats totally out of proportion with the limited swings in vote percentage. Thus, the rise of the BJP from 7.4 per cent in 1984 to 11.4 per cent in 1989 translated into a rise from 2 seats to 86 seats, largely because in 1989 it had made seat adjustments with other parties in the broad anti-Congress front led by Congress defector Vishvanath Pratap Singh (Janata Dal). In 1991, when the BJP was back on its own, the BJP's percentage of votes shot up to 20.2 per cent, good for 119 seats, only to climb even higher in 1996: about 23 per cent and 161 seats.

The breakthrough in 1989 and 1991 was definitely due to the BJP's apparent return to its Hindu roots. The party had abandoned Vajpayee's secular and socialist rhetoric for some sturdy Hindu issues, chiefly the Common Civil Code (against Muslim "separatism" in Personal Law highlighted in the 1985-86 Shah Bano affair), the struggle against Khalistani and Muslim Kashmiri secessionism, and the Ayodhya controversy. In 1989, the party involved itself in the VHP campaign for the "liberation" of the Ram Janmabhoomi site in Ayodhya, and this brought it rich electoral dividends. After a very difficult electoral start, the party's history was one of spectacular growth, only weakly interrupted by the Government crackdown after the demolition of the Babri Masjid in 1992. On that occasion, its four state governments (elected in early 1990 in Madhya Pradesh, Himachal Pradesh, Rajasthan and Uttar Pradesh) were dismissed by the President under advice from P.V. Narasimha Rao's Congress Government; in the next state elections there, the BJP did poorly.

In 1996, the long-standing division of the Indian political spectrum in Congress and the non-Congress parties gave way to a new polarization between the BJP (with its smaller allies, Shiv Sena and in 1996 also the socialist Samata Party, the Haryana Vikas Party and the Akali Dal (Badal)) and the anti-BJP alliance including Congress. In the 1996 elections, the BJP emerged as the largest party; in contrast with the two preceding elections, this victory was explained as being due to a *softening* of the BJP's Hindu profile, people being a bit tired of the "communal" issue after the Ayodhya demolition of 6 December 1992.

As the largest party, the BJP formed a Government headed by Atal Behari Vajpayee. He was sworn in on 15 May, but the anti-BJP alliance remained firm and announced its refusal to condone this Government in a vote of confidence. Vajpayee used all his charms to win MPs over, including a speech in Tamil to counter Dravidian misgivings about his image as a champion of Hindi.[207] He countered allegations against the RSS by reading out an old newspaper article in which Deve Gowda, prime-ministerial candidate of the United Front had praised the RSS as a "spotless" organization.[208] But all to no avail: on 28 May, he chose to step down rather than face an unwinnable vote of confidence.

In the second half of 1996 and in 1997, India was governed by the "United Front", a coalition of 13 Leftist and regionalist parties, led first by Deve Gowda, then by Inder Kumar Gujral. The UF was supported from outside by Congress and the CPM, all united in the overriding concern to keep the BJP out of power, confirming the new polarization in Indian politics after decades of "Congress vs the opposition". The BJP used the occasion to consolidate its position, profile itself as a coherent party which can guarantee stability (in contrast with the sorry sight of permanent infighting in the anti-BJP coalition), and build bridges with a few more regional parties.

However, in 1996 the BJP also faced a major internal crisis: the break-away of a large section of its powerful Gujarat unit, which managed, with Congress support, to replace the BJP State Government. It was a fairly typical Indian defection drama: leader Shankarsingh Vaghela (an RSS man for 30 years)[209] trusted his followers so little that he spirited them away in a plane to Khajuraho, out of reach of BJP negotiators who might entice them back into the mother party. He also made big promises of

---

[207]As Foreign Minister in the Janata Government, Vajpayee's most spectacular (and only Hindu Nationalist) act was to give a speech in the United Nations in Hindi. India had to make special arrangements for the simultaneous translation, for this third most spoken language of the world is not even an official UNO language. Vajpayee is also an accomplished Hindi poet; on this count, Congress Prime minister P.V. Narasimha Rao once called him "my Guru".

[208]"Uproar in LS over Vajpayee's remark", *Indian Express*, 29.5.1996.

[209]Details about Vaghela (1940) in Angana Parekh: "Will wily Vaghela win?", *Indian Express*, 18.8.1996.

lucrative posts to each individual MLA to ensure his "loyalty". Proof was established that even in political morality, BJP men (well, ex-BJP men) are not all that different from the average politician. Vaghela formed a state government, but his *Râshtrîya Janatâ* Party was completely routed during the 1998 Lok Sabha polls.

By contrast, the BJP obtained 178 seats and along with its by now numerous allies and some independents, it could form a Government at the Centre and win the confidence vote in March 1998. Like in 1977, the Hindu Nationalists had to compromise with their allies, so that the Government's "National Agenda" did not contain the hard points of the BJP programme. None the less, this time at last, the BJP was definitely the dominant partner in the Government. From that point onwards, a new chapter in the history of Hindu revivalism started, one that is outside the scope of the present study.

The BJP's 1998 manifesto

The 1998 elections brought the BJP to power, by any standards a watershed in modern Indian political history. Let us now look into the ideologically important parts of the BJP's 1998 election manifesto:

"This ageless nation is the embodiment of the eternal values enshrined in the concept of 'Sanatana Dharma' which, according to Maharishi Aurobindo, is synonymous with Indian nationalism.[210] This ancient nation evolved a world-view based on the motto *'Loka samasta sukhino bhavantu'* (Let the entire world be happy) thousands of years before any League of Nations or United Nations was thought of to avoid global strife. The Indian nation evolved this grand vision not by marching its armies and conquering the rest and offering peace;[211] but by the inner-directed pursuit of universal values by the Rishis living in the forests and mountains of India."[212]

"The Bharatiya Janata Party is a proud inheritor of this tradition while all other political parties have branded everything associated with this

[210]Reference is to Sri Aurobindo: *Uttarpara Speech*.

[211]Reference is apparently to the British Empire, which was presented as a *Pax Brittannica* imposed by force of arms but justified as a beneficial imposition well worth the initial battles because of the resulting order, peace, progress and rule of law. In a famous anecdote, Viceroy Lord G.N. Curzon (1899-1904) rebuked a lieutenant who claimed that India was won by the sword and would be retained by the sword: the Empire's philosophy, as Curzon pointed out, was that India would be retained by British *justice*.

[212]BJP: *Election Manifesto 1998*, p.1.

great tradition as sectarian, unworthy of being followed. The post-Independence tendency to reject all ancient Indian wisdom in political life led to all pre-Independence values and symbols—be it the idea of spiritual nationalism expounded by Swami Vivekananda, or the concept of Ram Rajya articulated by Mahatma Gandhi, or the soul-stirring 'Vande Mataram' song by Bankim Chandra—being discarded as unsecular and unacceptable. The BJP rejects this attitude and idea of disconnecting from the past."[213]

The BJP believes in a profound and time-tested national unity: "The unique cultural and social diversity in India is woven into a larger civilizational fabric by thousands of years of common living and common and shared values, beliefs, customs, struggles, joy and sorrow, as well as symbols of high degree of unity without uniformity. Our nationalist vision is not merely bound by the geographical or political identity of Bharat but it is referred by our timeless cultural heritage."[214]

But the BJP's understanding of cultural nationalism has room for diversity: "Diversity is an inseparable part of India's past and present national tradition. The BJP not only respects but celebrates India's regional, caste, credal, linguistic and ethnic diversity, which finds its true existence and expression only in our national unity. This rich tradition comprises not only the Vedas and Upanishads, Jainagamas and Tripitaka, Puranas and Guru Granth Sahib, the Dohas of Kabir, the various reform movements, saints and seers, warriors and writers, sculptors and artists, but also the Indian traditions of the Muslims, Christians and Parsis."[215]

Hence, for example, the promise to look after Urdu as well as Sanskrit: "Encourage the enrichment, preservation and development of all Indian languages, including Sanskrit and Urdu".[216] This is definitely a departure from the anti-Urdu positions of the BJS.

All this diversity talk is very nice, but what does this mean for a controversial issue like Ayodhya? The BJP thinks there need not be a conflict between the law and the project of building the temple: "The BJP is committed to facilitate the construction of a magnificent Shri Ram Mandir at Ram Janmasthan in Ayodhya where a makeshift temple already exists. Shri Ram lies at the core of Indian consciousness. The BJP will

---

[213]BJP: *Election Manifesto 1998*, pp.1-2.
[214]BJP: *Election Manifesto 1998*, p.4.
[215]BJP: *Election Manifesto 1998*, p.1.
[216]BJP: *Election Manifesto 1988*, p.23.

explore all consensual, legal and constitutional means to facilitate the construction".[217]

It is reassuring to the mass of liberal or non-militant Hindus that the BJP commits itself to exploring "consensual, legal and constitutional" ways of achieving the goal of building the temple. It is also a matter of relief to Hindu activists that the temple has remained on the BJP agenda, for contrary to what many foreign observers have claimed, the BJP's enthusiasm for Ayodhya has been very low ever since the issue had yielded its electoral fruits in 1991 and especially since the embarrassment of the Babri Masjid's demolition (6 December 1992). In autumn 1996, BJP spokeswoman Sushma Swaraj even dismissed any further investment of energy into the Ayodhya issue with a laconical: "You cannot cash a cheque twice", as if to confirm the suspicion that Ayodhya had never been anything except an electoral tactic for the BJP.

Another classic of Hindu politics is the demand that cow-slaughter be banned, or in legal terms, that the "directive principle" to ban cow-slaughter laid down in Article 48 of the Constitution be implemented:

"The BJP regretfully observes that, despite Article 48 of the Constitution, millions of cows and cow progeny are slaughtered every year, most of them for export, thereby causing irreperable harm to agriculture and villages. Keeping in view Article 48, the BJP will:

"1. Impose a total ban on the slaughter of cows and cow-progeny, including bulls and bullocks, and prohibit all trade, including export (state as well as private) in beef.

"2. Create a policy that will result in improved cattle breeding.

"3. Exempt the income of Goshalas and Pinjrapoles from tax."[218]

This is unexpectedly clear language, quite different from the BJP's equivocation on minority-related issues such as its policy vis-à-vis the Bangladeshi "infiltrators" (the BJP dropped its earlier promise of sending the illegal immigrants back to their country of origin, limiting its promises to the prevention of future infiltration).[219] The BJP does plan to turn a Hindu taboo into secular law.

The inevitable populist element is summed up in a promise to fight the four B's: "The BJP shares, embodies and energizes the vision of every

---

[217]BJP: *Election Manifesto 1998*, p.4.

[218]BJP: *Election Manifesto 1998*, p.28. *Goshâla* or *pinjrâpol*: cow-tending centre, cow asylum.

[219]BJP: *Election Manifesto 1998*, section "Illegal infiltration", p.33.

patriotic Indian to see our beloved country emerge as a strong, prosperous and confident nation, occupying her rightful place in the international community. It is a vision to see our Motherland freed from the scourge of *bhûkh* (hunger), *berozgârî* (unemployment), *bhay* (fear) and *bhrashtâchâr* (corruption)."[220]

On corruption, the BJP has earned a certain credit, e.g. in 1992, its UP government introduced legislation against a very popular form of corruption: copying during exams. The next Government, headed by Mulayam Singh Yadav, championed the Backward Castes cause and denounced this law as "anti-Backward" and immediately abrogated it upon coming to power in 1993.[221] In 1998, the BJP reintroduced it again.[222] However, a survey of the BJP state governments' record regarding corruption is beyond the scope of this study; suffice it to say that such lofty promises are not always easy to keep once a party comes to power.

Against the said B scourges, the BJP asserts the four S's plus Hindutva: "The five-fold concept of *Shuchitâ* (probity in public life), *Surakshâ* (security), *Swadeshî* (economic nationalism), *Samâjik Samarasatâ* (social harmony) and *Hindutva* (cultural nationalism) will constitute the core content and ideological pillars of the BJP."[223]

The BJP promises "housing for all" and "health for all" by 2003.[224] Of course, why settle for less? These are obviously not the distinctive elements of the BJP programme, but worn-out items from most Indian party programmes for decades. The BJP also knows all the latest buzz-words in the field of social engineering. It wants to "empower"[225] the Scheduled Castes and Scheduled Tribes and "generate awareness on gender issues".[226] As to contents, here again, the BJP is echoing the standard promises of all Congress and Janata manifestoes since Indira Gandhi's 1971 slogan *Gharîbî hatâo* ("destroy poverty").

---

[220]BJP: *Election Manifesto 1998*, p.2.

[221]Readers who are not familiar with Indian political parlance may be shocked to read crude terminology like "backward"; this is, however, the standard term for the combined "Scheduled Castes" (Dalits, former Untouchables) and "Other Backward Castes", as opposed to the upper or "Forward" castes.

[222]"Anti-copying Act re-imposed in UP", *Organiser*, 29.3.1998.

[223]BJP: *Election Manifesto 1998*, pp.2-3.

[224]BJP: *Election Manifesto 1998*, p.21.

[225]BJP: *Election Manifesto 1988*, p.34.

[226]BJP: *Election Manifesto 1988*, p.38.

A remarkable element of the 1998 BJP Manifesto is its stand on women's issues. Under the heading "Nari Shakti: Empowerment of Women", the BJP makes all sorts of promises to women, such as "1) Provide free education to women up to graduation, including professional studies like medicine and engineering."[227] One of the reasons for this eagerness to push women on to the job market, apart from egalitarian principles, is that it is a very effective incentive to family planning, still a top priority in India. Indeed, "the BJP will put population-related issues, including family planning, back on the national agenda" and to this end it will "promote women's education, employment and empowerment".[228]

Probably the most sensational item of BJP feminism is: "2) Immediately seek the passage of the Bill reserving 33 per cent seats for women in all elected bodies, including the Lok Sabha and State Assemblies."[229] A Bill to this effect had been discussed in the Lok Sabha in 1997, but nothing came of it, partly because it would be difficult to organize (should it be done through "reserved constituencies" where only women can be candidates?), partly because all the casteist parties feared it would interfere with caste-based reservations. Undaunted, the BJP wants to go ahead with it. One could speculate that the BJP expects women to be led more by religious sensibilities.[230] The context suggests that the link between women's rights and the Common Civil Code issue has been a major factor in the BJP's conversion to feminism.

Indeed, the BJP promises to:

"3) Actively promote the legal and economic rights of women which must be equal to those of men and not subject to the debilitating clauses of personal laws."[231] Hindu Law has been reformed in an egalitarian sense in

---

[227]BJP: *Election Manifesto 1998*, p.38.

[228]BJP: *Election Manifesto 1998*, p.40. Population control became a taboo issue after Sanjay Gandhi's coercive policies of sterilization under the Emergency; indeed, procreation was one way of protest against the Emergency, which is the stated reason why Laloo Prasad Yadav (then student leader, more recently Chief Minister of Bihar) has nine children.

[229]BJP: *Election Manifesto 1998*, p.38.

[230]Likewise, in Belgium between 1920 and 1948, the Christian-Democrats championed the extension of voting rights to women, while the Socialists opposed it, precisely because both parties assumed that women are more religious, hence more inclined to vote for a "religious" party.

[231]BJP: *Election Manifesto 1998*, p.38.

the 1950s; though this reform was effected by Nehru and against BJS opposition, the relatively progressive guidelines of Hindu Law are now an asset to the Hindu Revivalists, for traditional Christian and Islamic Personal Law, which no secular Parliament has dared to touch, are much less egalitarian. What this BJP promise means in effect, is that some clauses of Islamic and Christian Personal Law should be overruled by secular and egalitarian clauses.

The BJP specifies these reforms:

"4) Entrust the Law Commission to formulate a Uniform Civil Code based on the progressive practices from all traditions. This Code will:

"a) Give women property rights;

"b) Ensure women's right to adopt;

"c) Guarantee women equal guardianship rights;

"d) Remove discriminatory clauses in divorce laws;

"e) Put an end to polygamy;..."[232]

This reform is sure to generate an Islamic agitation, for it is directly in conflict with Islamic Law, and by replacing religious law with secular law, it would also undermine the power position of Islamic clerics within the Muslim community. Nevertheless, from a secular and egalitarian viewpoint, it is hard to object to such a reform.

Among the BJP's other promises to women, let us note the following:

"6) Enact and enforce an anti-sexual-harassment code;

"7) Enforce the principle of equal wages for equal work.

"18) Amend laws that deal with molestation, rape and dowry, to provide for in-camera trial, swift justice and tough deterrent punishment as well as rehabilitation for the victims of these crimes;

"19) Amend the Prevention of Immoral Traffic Act to make clients as culpable as commercial sex-workers.

"24) Rapidly induct more women into the police force and appoint women to senior positions.

"27) Strictly enforce the exising laws that prohibit unethical practices like pre-natal sex-determination tests, female foeticide and infanticide.

"31) Set up a national-level apex women's development bank to cater to the financing needs of women entrepreneurs and the vast number of

---

[232]BJP: *Election Manifesto 1998*, p.38.

self-employed women."[233] This last point is obviously inspired by the Grameen Bank in Bangladesh, which has played a crucial role in women's economic "empowerment".

All in all, this is a very mainstream social programme, not excelling in originality, but not confirming the BJP's reputation as a reactionary Rightist party either. This programme was of course written with an eye on the formation of a coalition, and deliberately kept out controversial points. In the 1999 elections, the BJP didn't even issue a manifesto of its own but joined the common programme of the coalition, under the name of National Democratic Alliance (NDA). This was an apt completion for a decade of what Hindu hardliners criticized as a continuous process of programmatic self-effacement.

RELATED PARTIES

In profile and ideology, the BJS-BJP can be distinguished from smaller parties located in roughly the same corner of the political spectrum: the Hindu opposition to the Nehruvian system.

The Ram Rajya Parishad

The political Hindu movement has almost entirely emanated from reform-oriented sections of Hindu society. The reality of modernization and the rise of the Backward Castes made any attempt at traditionalist politics a non-starter. The major exception to the rule was the *Râm Râjya Parishad*. The RRP was founded in 1948 by the prominent renunciate Swami Karpatri (1905-1980).[234] Born in Pratapgarh (U.P.) as Har Narayan Ojha, he was married and the father of a baby daughter when he left home at age 17 to seek ordination as a *sannyasin*. After his years of learning, including three years in icy caves in the Himalaya, he was ordained as Swami Hariharananda Saraswati, but his ascetic nickname *Karpâtrî* ("he who uses his hand as a food vessel") stuck.[235]

The Ram Rajya Parishad won 3 Lok Sabha seats in 1952, none in

---

[233]BJP: *Election Manifesto 1998*, pp.38-9.

[234]A personal testimony on Swami Karpatri is given in Alain Daniélou: *Le chemin du labyrinthe*, pp.150-52. His year of birth is not altogether certain, because he strictly adhered to the rule that a *sannyasin* never speaks about his pre-*sannyas* life.

[235]About Karpatri's career, see T.C. and R.K. Majupuria: *Sadhus and Saints of Nepal and India*, p.304.

1957, 2 in 1962 (of whom one would defect to the Swatantra Party and the other to the Jana Sangh), and none in 1967. In 1952, 1957 and 1962, it also won several dozens of Assembly seats, all in the Hindi belt, mostly in Rajasthan.

In so far as the Swami's thought gave the party its identity, the RRP was the most orthodox Hindu party. Its 1952 election manifesto was replete with Sanskrit verses and theological argumentation, almost obscuring its status of a political party. Unlike the HMS and the RSS, the RRP advocated the continuation or restoration of the caste system, including the system of untouchability. It had the dubious generosity of offering to the untouchables high posts in their own traditional sectors, like the sanitation department and the leather industry.[236]

However, in practice, most candidates of the RRP didn't care too deeply for Swami Karpatri's programme, and acted more as representatives of the landholders' class interests than as champions of traditionalist Hindu causes. Many of these candidates had no problem crossing over to the more promising Swatantra Party. Apart from bouts of prominence during the agitation against the reformist Hindu Code Bill in the mid-fifties and the several campaigns against cow-slaughter, the RRP never exerted any influence on India's political agenda. After the unruly cow-protection agitation of 1966, the aging Swami Karpatri was virtually left alone with his traditionalist party.

The importance of Swami Karpatri's participation in politics is that it served to highlight some characteristics of the mainstream Hindu movement by sheer contrast. Repeated attempts to merge or forge an alliance with the Jana Sangh and the Hindu Mahasabha failed because of (apart from personal differences, as in 1953) ideological incompatibilities, especially the retention or abolition of caste (in 1962) because: "Karpatri objected not only to Muslim membership but also to Harijan membership. He also wanted the constitution of the party to be based on the shastras. The Jana Sangh could have gone along with some of the communal demands of the Mahasabha but the obscurantist program of the Ram Rajya Parishad was too much."[237]

In pamphleteering publications about the Hindutva movement, it is often alleged that it is an "upper-caste" ploy to retain caste privileges, and that it is a retrograde fundamentalist movement which wants to restore the

---

[236]More on Ram Rajya Parishad in Craig Baxter: *Jana Sangh*, pp.78-80.

[237]C. Baxter: *Jana Sangh*, p.132.

Shâstras as the basis of legislation (on the model of the *Shari'a* in Islamic states), disregarding the fact that from an upper-caste initiative, the movement has become mainly a low-caste affair in some states.[238] Paul Brass' claim that BJS/BJP "manifestoes emphasized the maintenance of traditional Hindu institutions of family, caste structure and law" would apply to the RRP, but is simply untrue for the BJS/BJP as far as "caste structure" is concerned.[239]

The Ram Rajya Parishad was the voice of traditionalist Hinduism, while the BJS/BJP became the voice of reform Hinduism. The genuine defenders of caste hierarchy were well-placed to be arbiters in the matter, and they were dismayed at the Sangh's "betrayal" of Hindu tradition. Swami Niranjan Dev Tirth, just retired as Puri Shankaracharya, said he was in "cent per cent agreement" with his late friend Karpatri who had "exposed the conspiracy" in his book *RSS and Hindu Religion*, which lashes out against the RSS rejection of caste hierarchy.

Indeed, "one of the former Shankaracharya's main complaints is that the RSS does not believe in *varnashram* (caste system). The former Shankaracharya's remarks are significant because it explains why the vast majority of leaders of different Hindu sects have not personally involved themselves in the Ram Janmabhoomi [movement] even though many of them have expressed moral support."[240] Moreover: "'The RSS does not believe that the Ganga is holy or that Ram and Krishna are gods. Guru Golwalkar wrote that it was a mistake to raise them to the status of deity. The RSS is against our Shâstras. I oppose it in all my meetings. I will oppose any interference with our Shâstras', he said."[241] This is obviously a continuation of the traditionalist argument against the Brahmo Samaj and Arya Samaj.

The RRP fitted the stereotype of a "fundamentalist" party in all its

---

[238]This is conspicuously the case in Kerala, where the upper castes are with the CPM and Congress. About the RSS in Kerala, see K. Jayaprasad: *RSS and Hindu Nationalism*.

[239]Paul Brass: *Politics of India*, p.84.

[240]Saibal Dasgupta: "RSS tampering with 'Shâstras', says Sankaracharya", *Times of India*, 5.1.1993. None the less, the Shankaracharya also declared: "Whatever else you write about this interview, you must also write that I fully support the demolition in Ayodhya. It was a Hindu temple and Hindus have demolished it. The Muslims have no reason to complain."

[241]Saibal Dasgupta: "RSS tampering with 'Shâstras', says Shankaracharya", *Times of India*, 5.1.1993. Likewise, Anikendra Nath Sen ("Periphery to the fore", *Times of India*, 11.1.1993) quotes the retired Shankaracharya as denouncing the Sangh Parivar as "revisionists" who "consider our *Shâstras* outdated" and "do not believe in *varnâshram*".

colourful medievalism, e.g. during the Chinese invasion in 1962, Swami Karpatri announced that with his spiritual power, his body would not be hurt by Chinese artillery (he is not known to have put his boast to the test).[242] By contrast, the BJS/BJP is simply a modern party.

The Swatantra Party

The Swatantra Party was founded in 1959 by business interests and defenders of free entreprise, at the initiative of the Parsi business family the Tatas. The Tatas had been Jawaharlal Nehru's sponsors until 1954, when he embarked on a policy of turning India into a socialist economy. The party's political leader was Minoo Masani (1905-1998), a Parsi lawyer who had been a co-founder of the Congress Socialist Party in 1934. He was to retain cordial contacts with the Socialists, particularly with Jayaprakash Narayan, but turned against socialism. In 1950, he collaborated with Home Minister Sardar Patel in setting up an anti-Communist think-tank.

Masani briefly served as India's ambassador to Brazil, but after an alleged scandal (taking bribes and being rude to his personnel) he fell out with Prime Minister Nehru. At that point, he started planning the creation of a political party. In the 1957 Lok Sabha elections, 30 candidates for the prospective party stood as independents under various umbrellas. One of them, Sita Ram Goel, was on the BJS ticket, others were with the HMS or local parties, and Masani himself was on a Jharkhand Party ticket (Jharkhand being a mining and industrial area where the Tata family as the largest employer was very influential). Masani had hoped that a few prospective Swatantra spokesmen could already be elected as independents, but he himself was the only one among them to win a seat. In 1959 the party was formally constituted, and it managed to attract one of the historic Congress leaders, C.R. Rajagopalachari (1879-1972), as its charismatic spokesman. In the 1962 elections, the party got 18 Lok Sabha seats, 44 seats in 1967, and 8 in 1971.[243]

Compared to the BJS, its positions were more diametrically opposed to those of the Soviet-oriented Congress Party, at a time when communal issues were less in focus while economic reforms like the attempted collectivization of agriculture and the nationalization of the banks were the order of the day. One political scientist even claims that the SP "had

[242]Witnessed by Kedar Nath Mishra (BHU).

[243]Figures in Paul Brass: *Politics of India*, pp.76-7.

come into existence to oppose co-operative farming".[244] The SP sought an alignment with the West in the Cold War, and was articulately anti-Communist. In the Vietnam War it supported South Vietnam, and it demanded an initiative to go and liberate Tibet. A telling point of difference with the BJS is that the SP welcomed the continued use of English as India's link language, as against the BJS's advocacy of its replacement with Hindi (as mandated by the Constitution). To sum up: "The only authentic party of the traditional Right, as that term would be understood in Europe, was the Swatantra party, a coalition of urban big business and rural aristocratic and landlord elements in which the latter were dominant. ... During its heyday, Swatantra was the leading secular party of the Right offering a full-scale critique of the Congress policies of centralized planning, nationalization of industries, agrarian reform, and non-alignment."[245]

On the other hand, the SP did go with the BJS, at least part of the way, in recognizing the legitimate role of religion in public life: "It fully declared its intrinsic ideological commitment to the rule of law as an essential element in democracy but over and above the juristic theory of the rule of law, it recognised the overwhelming significance of the Rule of Dharma or 'a God-oriented inner law. ... The Swatantra stated that democracy would cease to be the tyranny of the majority or the dictatorship of a dominant party only, when it would be suffused with the chastening and transforming spirit of Dharma. ... The Swatantra thinks that the restoration of religion to its legitimate place would serve to moralize democracy by emphasizing the ethical presuppositions and governing norms of correct and proper political conduct."[246]

The SP's anti-socialist positions were unacceptable to the socialist-leaning wing of the BJS. For this reason, Balraj Madhok's attempt to arrange a merger between the two parties for the 1962 elections was rejected by his own party; only an electoral alliance materialized in 1967. The SP remained an elite party without a mass base, which could only acquire a modest presence in Parliament by allying itself with the BJS and its well-organized cadre and mass base. On the other hand, the support of many princely families gave it disproportionate clout; the legendary

[244]V.P. Varma: *Modern Indian Political Thought*, p.613.
[245]P. Brass: *Politics of India*, pp.82-83.
[246]V.P. Varma: *Modern Indian Political Thought*, pp.615-616.

princess Gayatri Devi won the Jaipur seat with an unprecedented majority on a Swatantra ticket.

The open princely support for the leading opposition party was the most important reason for Indira Gandhi to abolish the princes' privileges in violation of the promises made to them at the time of their accession to the Union of India. By depriving the princes of a large part of their income, she also cut into the financial support base of her political adversaries. The unwinnable confrontation of the opposition forces linked to Swatantra with Indira Gandhi in 1970, aggravated by the death of C.R. Rajagopalachari, proved to be the SP's swan song: from being the largest opposition party in 1967, it fell back to a handful of seats in 1971. In 1974, its remains disappeared into Charan Singh's liberal-populist conglomerate, the *Lok Dal* ("People's Group"), and thence into the Janata alliance of 1977.

The Shiv Sena

The Shiv Sena was founded in Mumbai in 1966. Its name refers to the seventeenth-century Maratha freedom fighter Shivaji as well as to the god Shiva. The popular base of the party was first the Maratha caste and more generally the middle castes (now known as "Other Backward Castes"), upwardly mobile at the expense of the Brahmins. In a symbolic sense, this process was a revenge for the take-over of Maratha power by the Brahmin Peshwas ("Prime Ministers") from Shivaji's heirs in the early eighteenth century. It is important to keep in mind that the Shiv Sena is at once a pro-Hindu and an anti-Brahmin party. This fact incidentally jeopardizes the neat explanation of Hindu revivalism as a Brahmin conspiracy, or the claim that "the objective of Hindu nationalists all along has been to preserve and perpetuate the hegemonic interests of the upper castes".[247] Like the Arya Samaj and like many individual Hindu revivalists, Sena spokesmen have even blamed the Brahmins for the defeats suffered by Hindu society in centuries past. Bal Thackeray told me that in his young days, he had briefly joined the RSS, but left it "because I saw all these Brahmins around me".[248]

At the same time, the Shiv Sena championed the cause of the poor Maharashtrians of all (and especially the low) castes against the

---

[247]Badrinath K. Rao: "Mobilisation strategies", *Frontline*, 13.6.1997, with reference to C. Jaffrelot: *The Hindu Nationalist Movement*.

[248]Interview at Bal Thackeray's headquarters, November 1993.

immigrants from other parts of the country, most of all against South-Indian Brahmins fleeing casteist discrimination in Madras and seeking new opportunities in the metropols.[249] For twenty years, it was most of all a regionalist, "sons of the soil" party, a platform which already made it the second strongest party in Mumbai by 1969. The party made Hindu concerns its priority in the 1980s, and this made it the strongest party in the entire state of Maharashtra.[250] It controlled the Mumbai City Corporation in 1984-92, with Chhagan Bhujbal as mayor, and its alliance with the BJP won a majority in the Maharashtra Legislative Assembly in 1995. However, it will hardly figure in our discussion of ideology and polemics, for it is a purely action-oriented party which practically dispenses with the formalities of doctrinal statements, under the motto: "Our actions are our programme". Its positions on current affairs can best be followed in the Marathi paper *Sâmnâ*, "Confrontation".

Come the age of the internet, the Shiv Sena had to put some kind of manifesto on its home page, and given its laconical brevity, we can reproduce it in its entirety: "Aims and objectives. We are Hindustanis and therefore, Hindu is the belief of our party. We love Hindustan more than we love ourselves. Therefore, Shivsena's fight against anti-national forces shall be ceaseless. Shivsena shall encourage youth to struggle for their rights and struggle for national cause. Shivsena believes that service of the people and unity of the people are the only ways of social development. Therefore, Shivsena believes more in social activities than in active politics. Shivsena does not believe in petty differences like caste, creed, religion or language. It preaches that nobody should be under the spell of such differences. Shivsena believes that the youth should get education in the official state language. The youth should also master Hindi, the National language, and English, the international language."[251]

The Shiv Sena (SS) is a populist party deeply rooted in Maharashtrian popular culture, and representing popular creativity, popular sentiment and also popular anger. According to V.S. Naipaul, the SS has been a very

---

[249]Because of anti-Brahmin discrimination in Tamil Nadu, Tamil Brahmins are highly over-represented among expatriate Indian communities (as also among India's top scientists).

[250]See e.g. Jayant Lele: "Saffronisation of Shiv Sena", *Economic and Political Weekly*, 24.6.1995; included in expanded form in S. Patel and A. Thorner: *Bombay, Metaphor for Modern India*.

[251]www.shivsena.org, downloaded on 20.4.1999.

constructive social force in Mumbai's slum areas, even before ever coming to power.[252] It has also developed a very effective trade-unionist wing, and Marxists claim that this was in fact the reason why industrialists (including the veteran Gandhian Ramakrishna Bajaj) had welcomed and probably financed the budding Shiv Sena: to keep the working class outside the Communist sphere of influence.[253]

The Shiv Sena's founder-leader Bal Thackeray, a former cartoonist, has occasionally caught the attention with his unabashed and sometimes ill-inspired rhetoric. In the world of facts, however, the Sena's terms in office in the Mumbai City Corporation and in the Maharashtra State Government have not been characterized by less democracy, more communal violence or more corruption than Congress governments (which does not amount to denying that its administration has been quite corrupt). The great waves of communal violence in Greater Mumbai took place in about 1980 and in 1992-93, when both the city and the state governments were in Congress hands.

The SS got a lot of bad press when it reacted in strength against a series of Muslim attacks on Hindus in early January 1993. After three days of Muslim rioting (6 to 8 January), Bal Thackeray's activists took the law into their own hands. The result was a large-scale conflagration killing at least 557 people, a majority of them Muslims.[254] Even six years later, no SS spokesman is apologetic about this operation: they see it as a necessary intervention in a Muslim attempt to take over the city with street terror. On the other hand, the Sena refrained from taking the violence beyond the "normal" magnitude of street riots: when some 300 Hindus were killed in Muslim bomb attacks (12 March 1993) against Hindu or predominantly Hindu targets, including a failed one against the SS headquarters, the SS did not react, and preferred to avoid further escalation.

During the last several elections, the BJP and the SS formed an

---

[252]V.S. Naipaul: *A Wounded Civilization*, p.64.

[253]Marxist accounts of the Shiv Sena include S.G. Sardesai: *Fascist Menace and Democratic Unity* (1970); Sampradayikta Virodhi Committee ("Committee Against Communalism"): *Shiv Sena Menace*, *c.* 1969; most specifically about the SS's impact on organized labour; CPI-Maharashtra: *Shiv Sena: the Fascist Menace behind the Pseudo-Maharashtrian Mask*, *c.* 1970; and finally a published Ph.D. dissertation from JNU, Dipankar Gupta: *Nativism in a Metropolis: Shiv Sena in Bombay*, 1982.

[254]Figure given in C. Jaffrelot: *The Hindu Nationalists*, p.552. For an admittedly partisan (anti-Sena) account of the January 1993 riots, see Dilip Padgaonkar: *When Bombay Burned*.

alliance, much in contrast with the early years, when the Sangh Parivar denounced this regionalist party as a threat to national unity.[255] Over the years, however, the SS evolved from an anti-immigrant party to a structure which helps the endless stream of newcomers to integrate into the Mumbai metropolis: "People from Tamil Nadu, to a lesser degree Kerala, began early to vote for the Shiv Sena and sizeable groups of them entered the organization during the seventies. They have only to accept simple principles, especially the Maharashtrian nature of Bombay, and the importance of Shivaji."[256] Even Muslims have found a place in the SS: "There are several ghata pramukhs (sub-branch organizers) of Bombay, and at least one shakha pramukh (branch organizer) of Pune who are Muslim."[257]

At the cultural level, the difference between BJP and SS is conspicuous: BJP men try to speak chaste Hindi and propagate Sanskritic culture, while the SS uses the idiom of regional-Maharashtrian popular culture. The BJP cannot conceal its occasional embarrassment with its SS ally, known for its less polished working-style and underworld connections. In this respect, the SS is by no means exceptional: Congress, Janata Dal, Samajwadi Party and some of the regional parties have been at least as much involved in violence and underworld activities. This is not even punished by the voters: most politicians representing sectional interests can safely count on their support base regardless of their criminal record. But the BJP prides itself on its clean hands, and this makes its relation with the SS rather uneasy.[258]

The relation between the SS's Hindutva and its Mafia character is one

[255]Guru Golwalkar "has rushed to condemn Shiv Sena and asked its leaders to wind up shop", according to Sampradayikta Virodhi Committee: *Shiv Sena Menace*, p.6.

[256]Gérard Heuzé: "Cultural populism: the appeal of the Shiv Sena" (doubtlessly the best recent presentation of the real-life sociology of the SS), in S. Patel and A. Thorner: *Bombay, Metaphor for Modern India*, p.234. Incidentally, the editors' obstinate refusal to use the official name *Mumbai*, accepted by all mature international media (say, the London *Economist*), can be read as an anti-SS political statement.

[257]Gérard Heuzé: "Cultural populism: the appeal of the Shiv Sena", in S. Patel and A. Thorner: *Bombay, Metaphor for Modern India*, p.234.

[258]An incident which highlighted the difference between the Sangh Parivar and the Shiv Sena was the controversy between Bal Thackeray and the anti-corruption activist Anna Hazare, who has often worked with RSS cadres (and who was given a spirited defence by Arun Shourie). Secularists have, none the less, amalgamated SS and RSS, and presented Anna Hazare as an anti-Hindutva activist; see Dilip Karambelkar: "Anti-Hindutva elements hijack Anna Hazare", *Organiser*, 2.2.1997.

of inverse proportionality: on a number of occasions, the SS called off Hindu nationalist agitations in exchange for money. The SS support to the Indira Gandhi's Emergency dictatorship should be seen in the same light; it was the only "communal" organization not to be banned. By its very nature, this type of Mafia activity is hard to document, but at least Thackeray's reputation in this respect is very solid: even the Sena's otherwise laudable vigilance preventing anti-Sikh violence in Mumbai after the murder of Indira Gandhi in 1984 is usually explained in terms of Sikhs paying "protection money".

As one independent Hindu revivalist puts it: "Thackeray is a Don whose protection can be bought. One tactic of his is to announce agitations and cancel them on being suitably recompensed. The most notorious [instance] was during the Shah Bano incident. When the Rajiv Gandhi government passed the Muslim Women's Bill ... Thackeray announced a programme of rallies ... at the venue of the Congress centenary celebrations [1885-1985] scheduled to be held a month or two later. Foreign journalists would have been present, and the pseudo-secular activities of the Congress would have been fully exposed before the international media. However, at the last minute, he was called for a meeting with the Chief Minister, and then he cancelled the agitation without any explanation."[259]

The difference in radicalism between the BJP (or the Sangh Parivar) and the SS can be illustrated with the reactions of the two parties after the Ayodhya demolition on 6 December 1992. Bal Thackeray, when shown press allegations that his Shiv Sainiks had participated in the demolition, owned it up at once: "If my boys have done it, I am proud of them." One of his MPs, Moreshwar Save, attained "notoriety for claiming to have led the demolition squad at Ayodhya".[260]

By contrast, BJP President L.K. Advani, who had led the Ayodhya movement in 1989-92, and who was there on the spot for what was meant to be an inconsequential ceremony, could not contain his tears when the youngsters pushed the elderly leaders aside and started the demolition work. Back in Delhi, he made a mild statement in which he did not own up

---

[259]Shrikant Talageri: "A General Picture of the Shiv Sena", unpublished paper, 1996, p.2.

[260]Faraz Ahmad: "Thackeray knocks out another rising star", *Pioneer*, 19.2.1995. The piece was written when Thackeray had just expelled Save from the party; like Indira Gandhi, he does not like an alternative leadership to emerge within his party.

the demolition but merely pointed out the double standards of the secularists who remained silent when Muslim terrorists destroyed Hindu temples in Kashmir a few years earlier. Most national-level BJP leaders have tried to avoid talking about the Ayodhya demolition altogether. BJP leader A.B. Vajpayee immediately condemned the demolition outright, and during the 1996 election campaign, he even called it a "Himalayan blunder" which "ruined everything". It was only at the demolition's third anniversary that a lone BJP MP, Vijay Kumar Malhotra, came forward to say in the Parliamentary Committee for Home Affairs that he, too, was proud of this historical event.

Because of the BJP's perceived softness, small local Shiv Senas have been set up in Panjab, Uttar Pradesh and other parts of India.[261] Though mostly independent from the Mumbai SS, they profess to emulate Bal Thackeray's toughness in preference to the *safedposh* ("white shirt", afraid of getting tainted) behaviour of the BJP. The election results of 1996-98 suggest that the Shiv Sena is not catching on in areas outside Maharashtra where the BJP is well-established. Even in Maharashtra, the Shiv Sena tally for the Lok Sabha in 1998 fell back from 15 to 6, clearly in reaction to its corrupt goovernance at the state level.

The reconstituted BJS

Among alternative Hindu parties, we should also mention the existence and activity *c.* 1990 of a reconstituted Bharatiya Jana Sangh. This was a late result of an intra-BJS conflict between Balraj Madhok and other party leaders, particularly Atal Behari Vajpayee and Nana Deshmukh. Apart from a clash of personalities, the initial issue was the latter's willingness to make alliances with the Communist parties at the provincial level, after the opposition gains in the 1967 elections. Madhok, a principled anti-Communist and critic of Islamic politics was fed up with the fact that, in his opinion, BJS politics vis-à-vis the enemies of Hinduism had been watered down into "appeasement", hardly distinguishable from Nehru's politics. After several more quarrels, he was expelled from the party in 1973 on grounds of "anti-party activities".

When the BJS was reconstituted as the BJP in 1980, Madhok floated a revived BJS, virtually a one-man party. Still, in the 1989 Lok Sabha elections, he seemed to have a good chance of winning the Lucknow seat,

[261] Maria Abraham: "Sena goes national", *The Week*, 3.12.1995.

and local RSS-BJP activists wanted to support him rather than the candidate of the Janata Dal, with which the BJP had an electoral alliance. Atal Behari Vajpayee personally intervened to force the activists back in line, and the neo-BJS was thwarted in its only real chance of entering parliament.

Among Hindu radicals, Vajpayee has never been forgiven for his action against Madhok. An NRI paper reports on a lecture by Vajpayee: "In his fulminations against Jan Sangh president, Mr. Balraj Madhok, Mr. Vajpayee said that Mr. Madhok had done immense harm to his party. And when someone asked if that was why he went to the Lucknow elections where Mr. Madhok had been winning and started to lose as soon as Mr. Vajpayee came in with his hordes to sabotage the elections of another Hindu, Mr. Vajpayee denied the charge but did not convince anyone present."[262]

Next to the HMS and the SS, the reconstituted BJS is another proof that the BJP can hardly be called "extremist". Most politically conscious Hindus find the BJP rather wishy-washy, though many concede that in the present political configuration, a really straightforward and articulate Hindu party is hardly possible. For one thing, the mentality of the Hindu masses themselves is wishy-washy as far as specifically Hindu problems are concerned. They are easily aroused by spectacular incidents of Hindu-Muslim conflict and "Muslim appeasement", such as the Shah Bano case. But they are hardly aware of more fundamental issues, nor of events which are no longer in the news, e.g. the massacre of Bengali Hindus by the Pakistani army in 1971 is not the object of any literature or films or even Hindutva pamphlets. Moreover, most people prefer peace to riots, and they don't mind the post-Demolition BJP combining a basically pro-Hindu line with a pragmatic approach to controversial issues. The BJP is in tune with the Hindu electorate to a large degree when it takes a soft line.

INDEPENDENT HINDU AUTHORS

One of the grossest misconceptions about the Hindu movement, is that it is an artificial creation of political parties like the BJP and the Shiv Sena. In reality, there is a substratum of Hindu activist tendencies in many corners of Hindu society, often in unorganized form and mostly lacking in intellectual articulation. To this widespread Hindu unrest about the

---

[262] "Atal Behari Vajpayee's visit to the United States", *Young India*, July 1990.

uncertain future of Hindu culture, a discursive expression has been given by a small but growing group of independent writers.

Ram Swarup as an anti-Communist

In the long run, Ram Swarup will probably prove to have been the most influential Hindu thinker in the second half of the twentieth century. He has, at any rate, been a crucial influence on most other Hindu Revivalist authors of the last couple of decades.

Born in 1920 as the son of a "*raîs* and banker" in Sonipat, Haryana, Ram Swarup (gotra: *Garg*, belonging to the merchant *Agrawâl* caste) earned a degree in Economics from Delhi University in 1941. He joined the Gandhian movement and acted as the overground contact ("postbox") for the underground activists including Aruna Asaf Ali during the Quit India agitation of 1942.[263] He spent a week in custody when a letter bearing his name was found in the house of another activist, the future homeopath Ram Singh Rana. In 1942-44, he worked as a clerk in the American office in Delhi which had been set up in the context of the Allied war effort against Japan.

In that period, his wit made him quite popular in progressive circles in the capital. He was a declared socialist, a great fan of Aldous Huxley and a literary imitator of George Bernard Shaw. In 1944, he started the "Changers' Club", alluding to Karl Marx's dictum that philosophers have interpreted the world instead of changing it. Of course, it was never more than a discussion forum for a dozen young intellectuals, including the future diplomat L.C. Jain, the future Planning Commission member Raj Krishna, future *Times of India* editor Girilal Jain, and historian Sita Ram Goel. At that time, Ram Swarup was a committed atheist, and in the Changers' Club manifesto he put it in so many words: "Butter is more important than God." In 1947, the club disbanded because its members plunged into real life, e.g. L.C. Jain became the commander of the largest camp for Partition refugees, organizing the rehabilitation of Hindu refugees from the North-West Frontier Province in Faridabad, Haryana.

[263]Aruna's husband Asaf Ali was seemingly a freedom fighter but unbeknownst to his comrades, he was in fact a British agent inside the Congress Working Committee, which was collectively imprisoned on the first day the agitation started. When the British left, they forgot a few files by mistake, and one of these revealed Ali's espionage. Ali, already sent to Washington as India's first ambassador there, was recalled and sidelined as Governor of Orissa, though Mahatma Gandhi intervened to spare him an overt fall from grace.

Just around the time of Independence, Ram Swarup developed strong opinions about the ideology which was rapidly gaining ground among the intelligentsia around him: Communism. When the CPI defended the Partition scheme with contrived socio-economic arguments, he objected that the Partition would only benefit the haves among the Muslims, not the have-nots. He moved in a direction opposite to the ideological fashion of the day, and became one of India's leading anti-Communists. His first books, *Let Us Fight the Communist Menace* (1949) and *Russian Imperialism: How to Stop It* (1950), were published by *Prâchî Prakâshan*, an anti-Communist a publishing house which he and Sita Ram Goel had set up in Calcutta, then as now the centre of Indian Communism. Financial help was provided by Hari Prasad Lohia.

The books drew attention in high places. In 1949, Home Minister Sardar Vallabhbhai Patel decided to found a think-tank specifically devoted to monitoring Communism, the Democratic Research Service, which was formally started in November 1950.[264] It was sponsored by the industrialist Birla family, and initially led by Morarji Desai, who passed the job on to Minoo Masani. It was as secretary of the DRS that Ram Swarup prepared a *History of the Communist Party of India*, which Masani published in his own name. A lot of bad blood developed between them, and Ram Swarup quit the DRS to join Sita Ram Goel in Calcutta and establish the *Society for the Defence of Freedom in Asia*.[265] Meanwhile, the DRS continued to be operative, but beyond publishing the meritorious periodical *Freedom First*, it never became very dynamic.

There was yet another anti-Communist centre in India, the *Congress for Cultural Freedom*, an international network with chapters in most countries of the free world. In India, it published the periodical *Quest* (Calcutta) and, for the Chinese public, *China Report* (New Delhi).

---

[264]Related in Minoo Masani: *Against the Tide*, p.54. Apart from its stated objective, the DRS was part of Patel's strategy against Nehru. Patel even intended to throw Nehru out of Congress, which is why Nehru asked his lieutenants Rafi Ahmed Kidwai and Acharya Kripalani to leave Congress and prepare a new party, the *Democratic Front*, which was dissolved again when Patel suddenly died in December 1950 and Nehru's position in Congress became unassailable.

[265]In his memoirs about the anti-Communist struggle, *Against the Tide*, Masani does not even mention Ram Swarup or Sita Ram Goel, much less acknowledge Ram Swarup's hand in the *History of the CPI*.

However, it lost all credit when, in 1966-67, it was found out to be financed by the CIA.[266]

The most authentic and effective Indian centre of fact-finding and consciousness-raising about the Communist menace was undoubtedly the *Society for the Defence of Freedom in Asia*. Though routinely accused of being lavishly financed by the CIA, this organization started with just Rs.30,000, half of which was brought in by Goel personally, and continued its work with the help of donations by friends, its budget seldom exceeding Rs.10,000. It published some important studies, which were acclaimed by leading anti-Communists in the West and Taiwan, and on one occasion vehemently denounced in the *Pravda* and the *Izvestia*. Until its closing in December 1955, the centre was the main independent focus of ideological opposition to Communism in the Third World.

Ram Swarup's main books on Communism are:

Let us Fight the Communist Menace (1949);

Russian Imperialism: How to Stop It (1950);

Communism and Peasantry: Implications of Collectivist Agriculture for Asian Countries (1950, but only published in 1954);

Gandhism and Communism (1954);

Foundations of Maoism (1956).

His *Gandhism and Communism*, which emphasized the need to raise the struggle against Communism from a military to a moral and ideological level, was brought to the attention of Western anti-Communists including several US Congressmen, and some of its ideas were adopted by the Eisenhower administration in its agenda for the Geneva Conference in 1955.[267]

Later, Arun Shourie wrote about Ram Swarup's struggle against Communism: "Ram Swarup, now in his seventies, is a scholar of the first rank. In the 1950s when our intellectuals were singing paeans to Marxism, and to Mao in particular, he wrote critiques of communism and of the actual—that is, dismal—performance of communist governments. He

---

[266]Strictly, it *had* been financed by the CIA but since early 1966, the Ford Foundation was its only financier. See K. Vanden Berghe: "Het Congres voor de Vrijheid van de Cultuur", *Onze Alma Mater* (Leuven), 1997/2, pp.193-211; and Frances Stonor Saunders: *The CIA and the Cultural Cold War*.

[267]According to the biographical note in Ram Swarup's recent publications, e.g. *Hinduism vis-à-vis Christianity and Islam*.

showed that the 'sacrifices' which the people were being compelled to make had nothing to do with building a new society in which at some future date they would be heirs to milk and honey. ... He showed that the claims to efficiency and productivity, to equitable distribution and to high morale which were being made by these governments, and even more so by their apologists in countries such as India, were wholly unsustainable, that in fact they were fabrications. Today, anyone reading those critiques would characterise them as prophetic. But thirty years ago, so noxious was the intellectual climate in India that all he got was abuse, and ostracism."[268]

Ram Swarup as a Hindu revivalist

Initially, Ram Swarup saw Gandhism as the alternative to Communism, and he has never really rejected Gandhism. In a small pamphlet written after the Gandhi murder, *Mahatma Gandhi and His Assassin* (1948), he argued that martyrdom was only befitting a man of Gandhiji's greatness. He showed no interest in murderer Nathuram Godse's motives, but he did appreciate that the urge to exact some punishment somewhere, though misguided (and in targeting Gandhi, misdirected), was a sign that Hindu society was not entirely dead, for suffering a calamity like the Partition and swallowing it without reaction would be a sure sign of virtual death.

In 1948-49, Ram Swarup briefly worked for Gandhi's English disciple Mira Behn (Miss Madeleine Slade) when she retired to Rishikesh to edit her correspondence with Gandhiji, a project which was not completed. He continued to explore the relevance of Gandhism to real-life problems, e.g. in his booklet *Gandhian Economics* (1977). But gradually, he moved from the Gandhian version of Hinduism to a more comprehensive understanding of the ancient Hindu tradition.

By the late 1970s, his focus had turned to religious issues. Apart from a large number of articles published in *Hinduism Today* (Honolulu), *Organiser*, and some mainstream dailies (in the 1980s the *Telegraph*, the *Times of India* and the *Indian Express*, in recent years mostly the *Observer of Business and Politics* and the Birla family's paper *Hindustan Times*), Ram Swarup's contribution to the religious debate consists of the following books:

[268]"Fomenting reaction", in A. Shourie: *Indian Controversies*, p.293, written on the occasion of the ban on Ram Swarup's book *Understanding Islam through Hadis*.

Buddhism vis-à-vis Hinduism (1958, revised 1984);

The Hindu View of Education (1971, text of a speech given before the convention of the RSS student organization ABVP);

The Word as Revelation: Names of Gods (1980, on the rationale of polytheism);

Hinduism vis-à-vis Christianity and Islam (1982, revised 1992, also in Hindi: *Hindu Dharma, Isâiat aur Islam*, 1985);

Christianity, an Imperialist Ideology (1983, with Major T.R. Vedantham and Sita Ram Goel);

Understanding Islam through Hadis (1983);[269]

Foreword to a republication of D.S. Margoliouth's *Mohammed and the Rise of Islam* (1985, original in 1905);

Hindu-Sikh Relationship (1985);

Ramakrishna Mission in Search of a New Identity (1986);

Cultural Alienation and Some Problems Hinduism Faces (1987);

Foreword to Anirvan: *Inner Yoga* (1988, reprint 1995);

Foreword to the republication of Sardar Gurbachan Singh Talib, ed.: *Muslim League Attack on Sikhs and Hindus in the Punjab, 1947* (1991), also separately published as *Whither Sikhism?* (1991);[270]

Foreword to a republication of William Muir's *The Life of Mohammed* (1992, original in 1894);

Hindu View of Christianity and Islam (1993, a republication of the above-mentioned forewords to books on Mohammed by Muir and Margoliouth plus an enlarged version of *Hinduism vis-à-vis Christianity and Islam*);

Woman in Islam (1994);

Pope John-Paul II on Eastern Religions and Yoga: A Hindu-Buddhist Rejoinder (1995);

On Hinduism: Reviews and Reflections (posthumously published, 1999).

Meditations: Yogas, Gods, Religions (posthumously published, 2000).

---

[269]First published in the USA by Arvind Ghosh, Houston; Indian reprint by Voice of India, 1984.

[270]The original had been published in 1950 by the Shiromani Gurdwara Prabandhak Committee, Amritsar. Remark how the Sikhs did take the trouble of more or less cataloguing the atrocities which the Pakistanis had committed on them as well as on the Hindus; the Hindu nationalist organizations failed to make any serious effort in this direction.

In October 1990, the Hindi translation of *Understanding Islam through Hadis* was banned, followed by the English version in March 1991; and in 1993, Syed Shahabuddin, who had managed to get Salman Rushdie's *The Satanic Verses* banned (September 1988), made an attempt to get Ram Swarup's *Hindu View of Christianity and Islam* banned as well. A prompt reaction by Arun Shourie in his weekly column and a petition of intellectuals led by K.S. Lal contributed to the defeat of this attempt.[271] People had not forgotten the result of Shahabuddin's earlier book-banning endeavour, and even the secularists who had supported Shahabuddin on that occasion were in no mood for a repeat performance: they simply looked the other way.

Ram Swarup died unexpectedly on 26 December 1998 during his afternoon nap.[272] He was a quiet and reflective type of person. He never married, never went into business, hardly ever had a job, never stood for an election. When I first met him in 1990, he lived in a rooftop room in the house of the late industrialist Hari Prasad Lohia, a sponsor of a variety of Hindu sages (including even Bhagwan Shree Rajneesh). He had been living with the Lohia family in their Calcutta or Delhi property since 1949; only in his last years did he move to his deceased brother's house. At any rate, his biography was not very eventful apart from daily yoga practice and his pioneering intellectual work.

Sita Ram Goel as an anti-Communist

Sita Ram Goel was born in 1921 in a poor family (though belonging to the merchant *Agrawâl* caste) in a village in Haryana. As a schoolboy, he got acquainted with the traditional Vaishnavism practised by his family, with the *Mahâbhârata* and the lore of the *Bhakti* saints (especially Garibdas), and with the major trends in contemporary Hinduism, especially the Arya Samaj and Gandhism. He took an M.A. in History at Delhi University, winning prizes and scholarships along the way. In his school and early university days he was a Gandhian activist, helping a Harijan Ashram in his village and organizing a study circle in Delhi.

In the 1930s and 40s, the Gandhians themselves came in the shadow of the new ideological vogue: socialism. When they started drifting to the

---

[271]See S.R. Goel, ed.: *Freedom of Expression*.

[272]Having just arrived in India, I was to meet Ram Swarup for dinner that very evening. Instead, I got to attend his cremation the next morning.

Left and adopting socialist rhetoric, S.R. Goel decided to opt for the original rather than the imitation. In 1941 he accepted Marxism as his framework for political analysis. At first, he did not join the Communist Party of India, and had differences with it over such issues as the creation of the religion-based state of Pakistan, which was actively supported by the CPI but could hardly earn the enthusiasm of a progressive and atheist intellectual. He and his wife and first son narrowly escaped with their lives in the Great Calcutta Killing of 16 August 1946, organized by the Muslim League to give more force to the Pakistan demand.

In 1948, just when he had made up his mind to formally join the Communist Party of India, in fact on the very day when he had an appointment at the party office in Calcutta to be registered as a candidate-member, the Government of West Bengal banned the CPI because of its hand in an ongoing armed rebellion. A few months later, Ram Swarup came to stay with him in Calcutta and converted him as well as his employer, Hari Prasad Lohia, out of Communism. Goel's career as a combative and prolific writer on controversial matters of historical fact can only be understood in conjunction with Ram Swarup's sparser, more reflective writings on fundamental doctrinal issues.

Much later, in a speech before the Yogakshema society, Calcutta, 1983, he explained his relation with Ram Swarup as follows: "In fact, it would have been in the fitness of things if the speaker today had been Ram Swarup, because whatever I have written and whatever I have to say today really comes from him. He gives me the seed-ideas which sprout into my articles. ... He gives me the framework of my thought. Only the language is mine. The language also would have been much better if it was his own. My language becomes sharp at times; it annoys people. He has a way of saying things in a firm but polite manner, which discipline I have never been able to acquire."[273]

S.R. Goel's first important publications were written as part of the work of the *Society for the Defence of Freedom in Asia*.

World Conquest in Instalments (1952, an annotated reprint of chapters 3 and 7 of Josef Stalin's *Foundations of Leninism*, 1924);

The China Debate: Whom Shall We Believe? (1953);

Mind Murder in Mao-land (1953);

China is Red with Peasants' Blood (1953);

---

[273]S.R. Goel: *The Emerging National Vision*, p.1.

Red Brother or Yellow Slave? (1953);

Communist Party of China: a Study in Treason (1953);

Conquest of China by Mao Tse-tung (1954, an annotated reprint of some of Mao's writings on strategy);

CPI Conspire for Civil War (1954).

Netaji and the CPI (1955);

Nehru's Fatal Friendship (1955);

Goel also published books on Communism by other authors, including *Blowing up India: Reminiscences of a Comintern Agent* by Philip Spratt (1955), who, as an English Comintern agent, had founded the Communist Party of India in 1926. After spending some time in prison as a convict in the Meerut Conspiracy case (1929), he had come under the influence of Mahatma Gandhi, and ended as one of the best-informed critics of Communism.

Then, and all through his career as a polemical writer, the most remarkable feature of Sita Ram Goel's position in the Indian intellectual arena was that nobody even tried to make a serious rebuttal to his theses: the only counter-strategy has always been, and still is, "strangling by silence", simply refusing to ever mention his name, publications and arguments.

An aspect of history yet to be studied is how such anti-Communist movements in the Third World were not at all helped (in fact, often opposed) by Western interest groups whose understanding of Communist ideology and strategy was just too superficial. Most US representatives starkly ignored the SDFA's work, and preferred to enjoy the company of more prestigious (implying: fashionably anti-anti-Communist) opinion makers. Goel himself noted in 1961 about his Western anti-Communist contacts like Freda Utley, Suzanne Labin and Raymond Aron, who were routinely dismissed as bores or CIA agents: Communism was "opposed only by individuals and groups who have done so mostly at the cost of their reputation. ... A history of these heroes and their endless endeavour has still to be written."[274]

Sita Ram Goel and the RSS

In the 1950s, Goel was not active on the "communal" battlefield: not Islam or Christianity but Communism was his priority target. Yet, under Ram Swarup's influence, his struggle against Communism became

[274]S.R. Goel: *Genesis and Growth of Nehruism*, p.212.

increasingly rooted in Hindu spirituality, the way Aleksandr Solzhenitsyn's anti-Communism became rooted in Orthodox Christianity. He also co-operated with (but was never a member of) the Bharatiya Jana Sangh, and he occasionally contributed articles on Communism to the RSS weekly *Organiser*. In 1957 he contested the Lok Sabha election for the Khajuraho constituency as an independent candidate on a BJS ticket, but lost. He was one of the thirty independents fielded as candidates by Minoo Masani in preparation for the creation of his own Swatantra Party. Masani had selected him for being one of the rare men deemed able to stand up to Nehru in parliamentary debate.

In that period (1952-60), apart from the topical books in English, Goel wrote and published 18 titles in Hindi: 8 titles of fiction and 1 of poetry written by himself; 3 compilations from the *Mahâbhârata* and the *Tripitaka*; and Hindi translations of these 6 books, mostly of obvious ideological relevance:

The God that Failed, a testimony on Communism by Arthur Koestler, André Gide and other prominent ex-Communists;

Ram Swarup's *Communism and Peasantry*;

Viktor Kravchenko's *I Chose Freedom*, another testimony by an ex-Communist;

George Orwell's *Nineteen Eighty-Four*;

Satyakâm Sokratez ("Truth-lover Socrates"), the three *Dialogues* of Plato centred round Socrates' last days (*Apology*, *Crito* and *Phaedo*);

Shaktiputra Shivâjî, a history of the seventeenth-century Hindu freedom fighter, originally *The Grand Rebel* by Denis Kincaid;

There is an RSS aspect to this publishing activity. RSS secretary-general Eknath Ranade had asked Goel to educate RSS workers about literature, and to produce some literature in Hindi to this end. The understanding was that the RSS would propagate this literature and organize discussions about it. Once Goel had set up a small publishing outfit and published a few books, he had another meeting with Ranade, who gave him an unpleasant surprise: "Was the RSS created to sell your books?" Fortunately for Goel, his friend Guru Datt Vaidya and son Yogendra Datt included Goel's books in the fund of their own publishing-house, Bharati Sahitya Sadan. This is Goel's own version, and Ranade is not there to defend himself; but Goel's long experience in dealing with the RSS leadership translates into a long list of anecdotes of RSS petty-mindedness, unreliability and lack of proper manners in dealing with fellow-men, especially fellow Hindu activists.

In May 1957, Goel moved to Delhi and got a job with a state-affiliated company, the Indian Co-operative Union, for which he did research and prospecting concerning cottage industries. The company also loaned him for a while to the leading Gandhian activist Jayaprakash Narayan, who shared Goel's anti-Communism at least at the superficial level (what used to be called "anti-Stalinism": rejecting the means but not the ends of Communism).

During the Chinese invasion in 1962, some leftist politicians including P.N. Haksar, Nurul Hasan and the later Prime Minister I.K. Gujral, demanded Goel's arrest. But at the same time, the Home Ministry invited him to take a leadership role in the plans for a guerrilla war against the then widely-expected Chinese occupation of eastern India. He made his co-operation conditional on Nehru's abdication as Prime Minister, and nothing ever came of it.

In 1963, Goel had a book published under his own name which he had written in 1961-62 as a series in *Organiser* under the pen name *Ekâkî* ("solitary"): a critique of Nehru's consistent pro-Communist policies, titled *In Defence of Comrade Krishna Menon*.[275] In it, he questioned the current fashion of attributing India's Communist-leaning foreign policy to Defence Minister Krishna Menon, and demonstrated that Nehru himself had been a consistent Communist sympathizer ever since his visit to the Soviet Union in 1927. Nehru had stuck to his Communist sympathies even when the Communists insulted him as Prime Minister with their unbridled scatology. Nehru was too British and too bourgeois to opt for a fully authoritarian socialism, but like many European Leftists he supported just such regimes when it came to foreign policy. Thus, Nehru's absolute refusal to support the Tibetans even at the diplomatic level when they were overrun by the Chinese army ("a Far-Eastern Munich"),[276] cannot just be attributed to circumstances or the influence of his collaborators: his hand-over of Tibet to Communist China was quite consistent with his own political convictions.

While refuting the common explanation that the pro-Communist bias in Nehru's foreign policy was merely the handiwork of Minister Krishna Menon, Goel also drew attention to the harmfulness of this policy to

[275]An annotated edition of this book was published in 1993: *Genesis and Growth of Nehruism*.

[276]This comparison with the British abandonment of Czechoslovakia in 1938 was made by Minoo Masani: *Against the Tide*, p.45.

India's national interests. For all its pertinence and depth, the article serial in *Organiser* was discontinued after sixteen instalments because Ranade and Vajpayee feared that if any harm came to Nehru, the RSS would be accused of having "created the climate", as in the Gandhi murder case.

Goel's critique of Nehru's pro-China policies was eloquently vindicated by the Chinese invasion in October 1962, but it cost Goel his job. He withdrew from the political debate, went into business himself and set up *Impex India*, a company of book import and export with a modest publishing capacity.

In 1964, RSS general secretary Eknath Ranade invited Goel to lead the prospective Vishva Hindu Parishad, which was founded later that year, but Goel set as his condition that he would be free to speak his own mind rather than act as a mouthpiece of the RSS leadership; the RSS could not accept this, and the matter ended there. Goel's only subsequent involvement in politics was when he was asked by the BJS leadership to mediate with the dissenting party leader Balraj Madhok in a last attempt at conciliation, which failed; and when he worked as a member of the think-tank of the Janata alliance before it defeated Indira's Emergency regime in the 1977 elections (though he was under watch and his correspondence was censored, he managed to stay out of the Emergency jails).

As a commercial publisher, he did not seek out the typical "communal" topics, but none the less kept an eye on Hindu interests. That is why he published books like Dharampal's *The Beautiful Tree* (on indigenous education as admiring British surveyors found it in the nineteenth century), Ram Swarup's apology of polytheism *The Word as Revelation* (1980), K.R. Malkani's *The RSS Story* (1980) and K.D. Sethna's *Karpâsa in Prehistoric India* (1981; on the chronology of Vedic civilization, implying decisive objections against the Aryan Invasion Theory). It may also be said that he thrived as a businessman and earned considerable wealth, an asset which was to make possible the next step.

Sita Ram Goel as a Hindu revivalist

In 1981 Sita Ram Goel retired from his business, which he handed over to his son and nephew. He started the non-profit publishing house *Voice of India* with donations from sympathetic businessmen, and accepted *Organiser* editor K.R. Malkani's offer to contribute some articles again, articles which were later collected into the first *Voice of India* booklets.

Goel's declared aim was to defend Hinduism by placing before the public correct information about the situation of Hindu culture and society, and about the nature, motives and strategies of its enemies. For, as the title of his book *Hindu Society under Siege* indicates, Goel claims that Hindu society has been suffering a sustained attack from Islam since the seventh century, from Christianity since the fifteenth, and from Marxism in the twentieth, and all three have carved out a place for themselves in Indian society from which they besiege Hinduism. The avowed objective of each of these three world-conquering movements, with their massive resources, is diagnosed as the replacement of Hinduism by their own ideology, or in effect: the destruction of Hinduism.

Apart from numerous articles, letters, contributions to other books (for example, Devendra Swarup, ed.: *Politics of Conversion*) and translations (for example, the Hindi version of Taslima Nasrin's Bengali book *Lajja*),[277] Goel has contributed the following books to the inter-religious debate:

Hindu Society under Siege (1981, revised 1992);

Story of Islamic Imperialism in India (1982);

How I Became a Hindu (1982, enlarged 1993);

Defence of Hindu Society (1983, revised 1987);

The Emerging National Vision (1983);

History of Heroic Hindu Resistance to Early Muslim Invaders (1984);

Perversion of India's Political Parlance (1984);

Saikyularizm, Râshtradroha kâ Dûsrâ Nâm (Hindi: "Secularism, another name for treason", 1985);

Papacy, Its Doctrine and History (1986);

Preface to *The Calcutta Quran Petition by Chandmal Chopra* (a collection of texts alleging a causal connection between communal violence and the contents of the Quran; 1986, enlarged 1987 and again 1997);

Muslim Separatism, Causes and Consequences (1987);

Foreword to *Catholic Ashrams, Adapting and Adopting Hindu Dharma* (a collection of polemical writings on Christian inculturation; 1988, enlarged 1994 with new subtitle: *Sannyasins or Swindlers?*);

History of Hindu-Christian Encounters (1989, enlarged 1996);

Hindu Temples, What Happened to Them (1990 vol.1, enlarged 1999; 1991 vol.2, enlarged 1993);

Genesis and Growth of Nehruism (1993);

---

[277]Published in instalments in *Panchjanya*, summer 1994.

Jesus Christ: An Artifice for Aggression (1994);

Time for Stock-Taking (1997), a collection of articles critical of the RSS and BJP;

Vindicated by Time. The Niyogi Committee Report on Christian Missionary Activities (1998, reprint of the full report from 1956);

Pseudo-Secularism, Christian Missions and Hindu Resistance (1998), the separately available editorial foreword to *Vindicated by Time*.

Goel's writings are practically boycotted in the media, both by reviewers and by journalists and scholars collecting background information on the communal problem. Though most Hindutva stalwarts have some *Voice of India* publications on their not-so-full bookshelves, the RSS *Parivar* refuses to offer its organizational omnipresence as a channel of publicity and distribution. Since most India-watchers have been brought up on the belief that Hindu activism can be identified with the RSS *Parivar*, they are bound to label Sita Ram Goel (the day they condescend to mentioning him at all, that is) as "an RSS man". It may, therefore, surprise them that the established Hindu organizations have so far shown very little interest in his work.

It is not that they would spurn his services: in its Ayodhya campaign, the Vishva Hindu Parishad has routinely referred to a "list of 3000 temples converted into or replaced by mosques", meaning the list of nearly 2000 such cases in Goel, ed.: *Hindu Temples, vol.1*. Goel also published the VHP argumentation in the government-sponsored scholars' debate of 1990-91 (titled *History vs. Casuistry*), and he straightened and corrected the clumsily drafted BJP White Paper on Ayodhya. But organizationally, the Parivar is not using its networks to spread Ram Swarup's and Sita Ram Goel's books and ideas. Twice, in 1962 and 1982, the RSS intervened with the editor of *Organiser* to have ongoing serials of articles by Goel, on Nehru on Islam, halted (the second time, the editor himself, the long-serving arch-moderate K.R. Malkani, was sacked as well). And ideologically, it has always turned a deaf ear to their analysis of the problems facing Hindu society.

Arun Shourie

After Ram Swarup and Sita Ram Goel started an intellectual Hindu awakening separate from the propaganda channels of the Sangh Parivar, others have joined them or followed their example. One of them is a towering personality in India's print media: Arun Shourie, who gained fame in India as the crusading editor of *Indian Express*. Arun Shourie was born in Jalandhar in 1941 in a Panjabi Saraswat Brahmin family as the son of a famed civil servant and later founder of Common Cause (a public-interest juridical pressure-group), H.D. Shourie. He earned a Ph.D. in Economics from Syracuse University (New York), then worked for the World Bank.

Back in India in 1976, Shourie was to work for several leading dailies. He met newspaper owner Ramnath Goenka when staying at the *Indian Express* guest house in Bangalore: "Ramnath Goenka started the transformation to today's Arun Shourie, the roots of which date back to 1976. 'What are you doing?', Goenka asked. 'I am writing a book', said Shourie. 'Nobody will read your book', said Goenka, 'you come and work for me'."[278] Goenka made him executive editor of *Indian Express* but sacked him a few years later. In 1982 he joined the *Times of India*, with the understanding that he would succeed Girilal Jain as editor, but Jain went back on his word and had Shourie sacked in 1983. Then Goenka took him back, and Shourie made history as editor of *Indian Express*.

Shourie made a name for himself by his fearless criticism of Indira Gandhi's dictatorial methods (see his books *Symptoms of Fascism* and *Mrs. Gandhi's Second Reign*), his lucid observation of the Janata interregnum (*Institutions in the Janata Phase*) and more generally by his crusades against falling moral standards in public life. He played a decisive rcle in Rajiv Gandhi's electoral defeat in 1989 with the revelations about the Bofors arms deal (see his book *These Lethal, Inexorable Laws: Rajiv, His Men & His Regime*).

As a high-profile dissident, Shourie was blacklisted by a number of criminal and extremist groups, and became a regular recipient of death threats (and of journalistic and other prizes, for example, the Magsaysay Award and the International editor of the Year Award), entitling him to the dubious privilege of round-the-clock police protection. In late 1990, he was again sacked as *Indian Express* editor and since then, he has established himself as a syndicated columnist and independent self-publishing writer. His books on religion-related issues and on questions concerning national unity, mostly reworked compilations of his columns, are the following:

Hinduism, Essence and Consequence (1979, a rationalist critique of Hindu scripture);

---

[278] "Hook, line and thinker", *Sunday*, 17.10.1993.

Religion in Politics (1987, enlarged 1989);

Individuals, Institutions, Processes: How One May Strengthen the Other in India Today (1990, application of Gandhian principles to India's current political life);

'The Only Fatherland': Communists, 'Quit India' and the Soviet Union (1991, a historical study of Communist treason against the freedom movement);

The State as Charade: V.P. Singh, Chandra Shekhar and the Rest (1992; not in itself about religion, but the issues which troubled the Government periods studied happened to be casteism and Ayodhya);

Indian Controversies (1993);

A Secular Agenda (1993);

Missionaries in India (1994, an elaborated version of a speech given on 5 January 1994 before the Golden Jubilee meeting of the Catholic Bishops' Conference of India);

Arun Shourie and His Christian Critic (1995; the record of a debate in Hyderabad subsequent to the *Missionaries* book);[279]

The World of Fatwas, or the Shariah in Action (1995);

Worshipping False Gods. Ambedkar, and the Facts Which Have Been Erased (1997);

Eminent Historians. Their Technology, Their Line, Their Fraud (1998);

Harvesting Our Souls. Missionaries, Their Design, Their Claims (1999).

The first book, *Hinduism, Essence and Consequence*, is sometimes quoted by anti-Hindu polemicists, because it actually debunks much of the pious self-flattery commonly found in anglicized-Hindu books on religion. It points out the contradictions and circular reasoning in basic texts of Hinduism including the Upanishads and the Bhagavad Gita. Because of its strongly secular-humanist outlook, this first book has paradoxically enhanced Shourie's later credibility as a spokesman for Hinduism.

In 1999, his enemies heaved a sigh of relief upon hearing that Shourie had been included in Vajpayee's government. He was to oversee the

---

[279]Weeks after the frank but cordial exchange of opinions at the CBCI meeting, a rather polemical correspondence ensued between the CBCI Secretary, Father Augustine Kanjamala, and Shourie, hence the postscript volume. After that, another Christian author, Vishal Mangalwadi, also wrote a bulky reply to Shourie's arguments: *Missionary Conspiracy: Letters to a Postmodern Hindu* (1996).

implementation of the Plan, i.e. controlling what actually happens with those billions of rupees earmarked for all manner of projects by the Planning Commission. For a crusader against corruption, this should be a plum job as well as a fierce challenge. But it put an end to his weekly column.

Arun Shourie is an embarrassment to the critics of Hindu revivalism. With his high intellectual qualifications, his well-known record of struggle for democracy and for morality in politics, and with his fortitude in his private life (he is a caring father of a handicapped son), he can hardly be dismissed as one of those monsters which the "Hindu fundamentalists" are supposed to be.

Writers and journalists

In English-language Indian journalism, there has been a considerable migration of reputable secularists into the Hindu revivalist fold. Two well-known examples are Girilal Jain and Swapan Dasgupta.

Girilal Jain, a long-time confidant of Indira and Rajiv Gandhi, was *Times of India* editor in the 1980s. After being dismissed there in 1989 for his increasing sympathy towards the BJP, he continued writing as a syndicated columnist until his death in 1993. M.J. Akbar, who, as a Muslim secularist, had been on the other side of the political battlefield, wrote in his obituary: "He dared you with Olympian majesty and, whether dispensing Royism or Advanism, tossed out his formulations with a merciless disregard for sentiment. ... during the final phase of his long career ... he began to champion a cause totally alien to virtually everything that Girilal Jain had stood for previously."[280]

A selection of his columns was posthumously published under the title *The Hindu Phenomenon* by his daughter, political scientist Meenakshi Jain.[281] By the time he died, his other daughter Sandhya Jain was making her name as a combative pro-Hindu columnist.

---

[280]M.J. Akbar: "This tongue had bones. Girilal Jain's passionate espousal of causes was part of his intense nationalism", *Telegraph*, 25.7.1993. The title refers to an Armenian saying, "the tongue has no bones", meaning that it can move in any direction. *Royism*: the "Radical Humanist" (non-Communist Leftist) doctrine of former CPI pioneer M.N. Roy, fairly popular among intellectuals in the 1950s.

[281]Meenakshi Jain herself became fairly well-known with a series of *Indian Express* columns (summer 1990) about casteism and anti-Brahminism, during that newspaper's campaign against V.P. Singh's decision to implement the Mandal Commission recommendations, viz. to extend caste-based reservations (constitutionally allotted to the Scheduled Castes and Tribes) to the so-called Other Backward Castes.

Swapan Dasgupta has been a regular columnist for several dailies and periodicals, including *Indian Express*, *Times of India*, *Sunday* and *India Today*. Like BJP economist Jay Dubashi, he combines a modernist no-nonsense attitude to politics and economics with a belief in the beneficial effect of cultural rootedness. He is often reminded of having once been a Trotskyite, as was evident one last time in his insightful obituary of Belgian Trotskyite economist Ernest Mandel, a name which even India's Communists (who are Stalinists) would mostly ignore.[282]

Jain and Dasgupta changed camp when it was difficult and required courage to do so. But as the BJP grew in strength and increasingly looked like the wave of the future, more and more "fairweather friends" started joining the Hindu camp, not just in politics but also in the media. We need not bother about these late converts here, for so far they have not contributed many original thoughts to Hindu revivalist discourse.

Meanwhile, younger Hindu voices were given a forum in the newspapers (sometimes under pressure from their commercial departments),[283] the most articulate example being Varsha Bhosle, a sharp critic of not only the anti-Hindu forces but also of the Hindu slackness in the BJP. We should also not forget the journalists who openly affiliate themselves with the Sangh Parivar without necessarily ceasing to be perceptive columnists or fearless investigators, such as veteran editor M.V. Kamath, Dina Nath Mishra and others.

In 1993, when the Hindu side was under fire for its alleged responsibility in the Demolition of the Babri Masjid in Ayodhya, famous NRI authors Nirad C. Chaudhuri and V.S. Naipaul, who had little to gain or fear in India, have also contributed to Hindu revivalist polemic, most of all in their interviews in mid-1993.[284] On that occasion, Naipaul made waves with his assessment that "what is happening in India is a new historical awakening". The concise and occasional nature of their interventions is easily compensated for by their international standing and, for credibility, by their earlier anti-Hindu positions.[285] For this reason, they are

[282]In 1995-96, Dasgupta was *Indian Express* correspondent in London, where I met him in April 1996.

[283]An extreme example of a paper changing its line because of the changing mood and concomitant expectation pattern of the readers, was the Mumbai weekly *Blitz*, which turned from red to saffron in a matter of months in 1992-93.

[284]See Dileep Padgaonkar's *Times of India* interviews with V.S. Naipaul (18.7.1993) and Nirad C. Chaudhuri (8.8.1993).

[285]E.g. V.S. Naipaul: *An Area of Darkness*; and Nirad C. Chaudhuri: *Thy Hand, Great Anarch*, and to an extent, *Hinduism*.

very eagerly quoted as arguments of authority in numerous Hindutva pamphlets.

Historians

As a lot of the polemic between Hindu revivalism and its opponents concerns history, it is no surprise that we find several professional historians among the main contributors to the Hindu Revivalist debating position. Kishori Saran Lal (1920) taught history at the universities of Delhi, Jodhpur and Hyderabad. Before entering the "communal" arena, Lal had already gained some fame as a historian, with his shiny illustrated book *The Mughal Harem* (1988) adorning many a parlour table. He was first accused of "Hindu communalism" after the publication of *Growth of Muslim Population in India* (1973). As he told me, he noticed he was no longer being invited to certain conferences, and upon inquiring was told that he had painted an intolerably negative image of Islamic rule in India.[286] He says he hadn't suspected that his findings (for example, a sharp decline in the Indian population during the Sultanate period 1206-1526) could be considered as showing any "communal" animus. In the subsequent years, he was inconspicuously reaccepted into the mainstream and could have forgotten about the ideological struggle had he chosen to.

After his retirement, however, he associated openly with Hindu revivalism. Thus, he chaired the *Historians' Forum*, a group of scholars who supported the temple thesis in the Ayodhya debate. A week after the demolition of the Babri Masjid on 6 December 1992, it was he who, along with VHP-affiliated archaeologist Dr. S.P. Gupta and with Dr. Sudha Malaiya, presented the decisive evidence which came to light during the demolition: a stone inscription declaring in so many words that the building of which it was part was a temple dedicated to Rama.[287] The following are his scholarly contributions to the Hindu revivalist argument on Islam:

Indian Muslims, Who Are They? (1990);
Legacy of Muslim Rule in India (1992);
Muslim Slave System in Medieval India (1994);

---

[286]Interview, December 1992, Delhi.

[287]I was present at this press conference, which ended on a dramatic note when the police came in to arrest Dr. S.P. Gupta, a known member of the RSS, which had just been banned because of the demolition; Gupta managed to escape and absconded for several weeks, until it became clear that the Government did not mean business with the ban.

Growth of Scheduled Tribes and Castes in Medieval India (1995), a large part of which is devoted to the role of the Islamic regime in the marginalization of certain classes of Hindu society;

Theory and Practice of the Islamic State (1998).

Another historian of impeccable repute who joined the Hindu revivalist circle of scholars was the late Harsh Narain (1922-95), a scholar of Sanskrit, Persian and Arabic, who taught at five Indian universities including BHU and AMU. He was a member of the team of scholars mandated by the VHP during the Government-sponsored historians' debate in 1990-91. The following books of his are pertinent to our topic:

Jizyah and the Spread of Islam (1990);

The Ayodhya Temple-Mosque Dispute. Focus on Muslim Sources (1991);

Myths of Composite Culture and Equality of Religions (1991).

Three amateur historians should also be mentioned. Suhas Majumdar (1937-96) was a mathematician who started taking an interest in Islamic doctrine after reflecting on how he had narrowly escaped the Noakhali slaughter of 1946. In this context, one title of his which must be considered is: *Jihâd, the Islamic Doctrine of Permanent War* (1994).

Another mathematician to join the polemic is N.S. Rajaram, engineering researcher at the University of Houston and NASA adviser. After retirement, though a US citizen, he chose to live part of the year in his native Bangalore. He has contributed several books to the ongoing debate, notably:

The Politics of History (1994);

Secularism, the New Mask of Fundamentalism (1995);

Vedic Aryans and the Origins of Civilization (1996);

Profiles in Deception: Ayodhya and the Dead Sea Scrolls (2000).

Bank employee Shrikant Talageri (b.1958) from Mumbai has authored two books of considerable genius, which deal with ancient history but bring in some ideas on the contemporary Hindu-Muslim and Hindu-secularist confrontations too:

Indian Nationalism and Aryan Invasion Theory (1983);

The Rigveda, a Historical Analysis (2000).

Apart from these authors who have openly associated themselves with Hindu revivalist causes, we shall complete the picture with some contributions of people who have not formally entered into polemics, though they did defend Hinduism and specific Hindu viewpoints in their works, as if to convince an unidentified devil's advocate, typically a representative of Western opinions (or misunderstandings, or prejudice). While they were nobody's ghost-writer, their work has exerted an often unacknowledged influence on the Hindu revivalist world-view.

One such independent historian who deserves mention here is Ram Gopal Misra, who taught at Meerut University. Important in the present context is his book *Indian Resistance to Early Muslim Invaders upto 1206 AD* (1983), which counters the belief shared by Indian Muslims and Hindus that there was no effective Hindu defence against the Islamic invasions.

For the earlier part of the twentieth century, we should mention a few influential scholars whose views were less controversial then than they were to become in the decades of secularist-Marxist hegemony, and who are now regurlarly quoted in Hindu revivalist polemic. One of the most lucid exponents of Hindu tradition in this century was definitely Ananda Kentish Coomaraswamy (1877-1947). He was a Tamil Brahmin born in Colombo, Sri Lanka, who studied Geology in England and worked in the USA, where he was to remain for most of his life. His understanding of Hindu philosophy and religion was quite precise, and his comparative perspective is still nearly unequalled; his "works provide virtually a complete education in themselves".[288] In the more high-brow debates, notably on the exact relation between Hinduism and Buddhism, his input is decisive, even though it is now referred to only by some BHU professors, rarely by print media like *Organiser*.

Another art historian thoroughly at home in the Vedic worldview, and meriting mention in this survey, is the late Professor V.S. Agrawal of BHU, if only for his countering, in his collection of articles *India, a Nation* (from the period 1943-1970), the colonial-cum-Marxist position that India is an artificial state without ethnic or historical legitimacy. Finally, established historians like Sir Jadunath Sarkar and R.C. Majumdar, and anthropologists like G.S. Ghurye, while by no means involved in polemics

[288]Coomaraswamy's most important philosophical essays have been compiled in the Princeton's Bollingen Series volume *Metaphysics*, edited by Roger Lipsey. The quote is from its biographical note on the cover.

or politics, have also published the kind of findings which earned them the label "Hindu communalist".

Civil servants

Two civil servants should be mentioned as committed participants in the Hindu revivalist side of the debate. One is a retired police officer, Baljit Rai (1928), a privileged witness to the state's neglect of urgent security issues, and author of:

Islamic Fundamentalism in the Indian Subcontinent (1991);

Demographic Aggression against India: Muslim Avalanche from Bangladesh (1993);

Is India Going Islamic? (1994).

The other civil servant in our list is Abhas Kumar Chatterjee (1942). Like his old class fellow at Saint Stephen's College, Arun Shourie, he built himself a reputation as a crusader against corruption in the administration, again to the embarrassment of the detractors of Hindu revivalism. He actually practises the anti-caste and anti-dowry social reforms which others only preach: as a born Brahmin he married an Oraon (tribal) woman, and he has always refused to attend weddings if he is aware that a dowry (*dahej*) has been paid.

In 1992, he tendered his resignation in protest against the all-devouring corruption in the state of Bihar. He was involved with the Ramakrishna Mission for a while, but was never connected to (and actually an outspoken critic of) the Sangh Parivar. None the less, he participated in the gathering of evidence for the VHP during the Government-sponsored scholars' debate on Ayodhya. Here, we shall pay attention to his book: *The Concept of Hindu Nation* (1993).

To conclude this chapter, I would like to draw attention to the fact that Hindu revivalism is not a movement with membership rolls. Some people openly profess that this is where they situate themselves politically, but quite a few arguments supporting the Hindu revivalist viewpoint have been made by people normally not classified as such. On some points, nationalist Congress leaders Lokamanya Tilak, Mahatma Gandhi and Sardar Patel, as well as anti-nationalist social leader Dr. Bhimrao Ambedkar, have been spokesmen and agents of the same ideals which declared Hindu revivalists profess. Ram Swarup and Sita Ram Goel started as Gandhians, and it is even said that: "In modern India it was primarily Mahatma Gandhi who sought such a Hindu revival. It is his ideas (however attenuated), particularly on the economy, which continue to resonate in the minds of the Hindu revivalists and are (at least rhetorically) embodied in their current policy programs."[289]

Here and there, we shall come across such instances where a Congressman or other formal outsider to the movement took the stand which Hindu revivalists also took (or would have taken if present). It will not do to separate the Hindu revivalist movement from Hindu society as a whole: there is a definite continuity between them, as there is between a tree and its roots.

---

[289]Deepak Lal: "The economic impact of Hindu revivalism", Martin Marty and Scott Appleby: *Fundamentalisms and the State*, p.411.

Ideology and polemic in the organized Hindu movement

Before addressing the subject of Hindu revivalism's ideological positions regarding Hinduism, nationalism and secularism, I first want to give an outline of the peculiar place of ideology as such, especially within the organized Hindu nationalist movement as contrasting with a number of independent authors. There is of course a large section of the electorate which votes for Hindu parties without being motivated by ideological considerations, e.g. because the BJP looked less prone to corruption. Even among the Sangh Parivar activists, a simple devotion to the Motherland or to Hinduism may be sufficient motivation, not needing a sophisticated political analysis. The fact is that the ideological aspect of this movement has for long been remarkably underdeveloped.

THE SANGH'S ANTI-INTELLECTUALISM

Too busy to think

A first perusal of the literature of the organized Hindutva movement, particularly of the *Sangh Parivar*, the "RSS family" including the BJP, will leave the reader with the impression of an unusual intellectual poverty. First of all, relative to the age and membership of this family of organizations, its literary output is quite small. Secondly, what little is available is often very elementary and repetitive. A movement with literally millions of activists, in existence for more than seventy years, and operating in a country where opinions are free and publishing is cheap and easy, has little excuse for its very limited achievements in the intellectual processing of the situation and challenges before it. As we shall see, it does not even want an excuse, for it has deliberately chosen the non-intellectual mode of functioning. If it hadn't been for the efforts of some independent (non-Sangh) Hindu Revivalist authors, there would be little Hindu argumentation to discuss here.

As the most direct manifestation of the Sangh Parivar's anti-intellectualism, the situation on the ground is that RSS men are always on the move. As a US-based Hindu leader reported: "When I make a phone call to an RSS office-bearer in India, he will most often not be in the Delhi office, not in Nagpur or another town, but somewhere on the way."[1] And the wife of a BJP leader observed: "Being on the way from one place to another is a status symbol among RSS men."[2] With all this physical movement, little time and occasion is left for concentrated mental work. One visible effect is the poor state of health of RSS office-bearers, whose bodies are exhausted by all this locomotion.

One reason for this is the RSS's original preference for "secret society" methods as a consequence of Keshav Baliram Hedgewar's association with the armed fringe of the Freedom Movement. Thus, after returning to Nagpur from his medical studies in Calcutta in 1916, Hedgewar formed a "Revolution Group" (*Kranti Dal*), and "over 150 volunteers enrolled themselves with the Kranti Dal. Greatest attention was bestowed on maintaining absolute secrecy. No new recruits were admitted without a thorough scrutiny. ... All communications were sent through messengers, and invariably in coded language."[3] Till today, the RSS leadership prefers to communicate with the local branches through personal visits.

The contemporary justification for all this locomotion is that Hindu society has been lacking in communal solidarity, and that face-to-face contact in regular meetings at the *shâkhâ* (branch) level and in regular visitations by regional and national office-bearers is a substantial factor in kindling the community spirit.

The RSS think-tank

There is not much of a think-tank culture in India, much less in the organized Hindu movement. There is a *Deendayal Research Institute* (DRI) in Delhi, founded in the 1970s by Nanaji Deshmukh, and led by BJP ideologue K.R. Malkani, later by Devendra Swarup, and most recently by L.S. Bhide. One of the financial sponsors of the DRI was Deshmukh's

---

[1]Raj Dave, then president of the VHP-Chicago, talking to me in October 1995.

[2]Mrs. Madhuri Sondhi, wife of M.L. Sondhi and a lucid philosopher in her own right (co-author of the book *Hinduism with a Human Face*), talking to me in December 1992, Delhi.

[3]H.V. Seshadri, ed.: *Dr. Hedgewar, the Epoch-Maker*, p.39.

friend Nusli Wadia, a Parsi industrialist and the son of M.A. Jinnah's daughter. Its activities were always very limited, it published only a handful of books, half of them hagiographies of Hindutva stalwarts like RSS founder K.B. Hedgewar and BJS ideologue Deendayal Upadhyaya. As a Hindu critic of the Sangh Parivar notes: "In 25 years of its existence the Deendayal Research Institute inspired by the Sangh has published hardly anything that can be called a work of solid Hindu scholarship."[4] Of its seven-storey building, a large part is rented out because the RSS thinkers cannot put it to some good use themselves.

The pinnacle of the DRI's career was when it collected some scholars from outside the Sangh Parivar and prepared the intellectual defence of the Hindu (VHP) claim to the disputed Ayodhya site. This resulted in an ostensible victory during the Government-sponsored historians' debate (winter 1990-91) with the group of Marxist and Muslim historians mandated by the Babari Masjid Action Committee.[5] After that, however, it was back to the normal unexciting pace.

More recently, the DRI's intellectual activity has been further dismantled after the return in 1994 of Nanaji Deshmukh, who had started professing a Nehruvian belief in "development" rather than this "sterile" ideological work. The DRI periodical *Manthan* ("churning") is decent but it has lost the polemical edge which it still had when edited by Devendra Swarup. In the polemical arena, it is no match for its Marxist counterparts.

The result of this lack of intellectual alertness is that Sangh Parivar leaders, including most BJP parliamentarians, are quite uninformed even about the specific issues which their organization wants to take up. On the eve of a Lok Sabha debate about infiltration from Bangladesh, a classic theme in Sangh Parivar propaganda, several BJP MPs telephoned Dr. Sujit Dhar for information. Dr. Dhar from Calcutta is one of the few real brains I ever encountered in Hindutva circles, a top office-bearer of the VHP, and

---

[4]A. Chatterjee in S.R. Goel, ed.: *Time for Stock-Taking*, p.71.

[5]The argumentation of the VHP-mandated scholars was published by the VHP as a book, *The Great Evidence of Ram Janmabhhomi Mandir* (1991), and again (with appendices) by Voice of India as *History vs. Casuistry* (1991). The BMAC team's case was published as R.S. Sharma *et al.*: *Historians' Report to the Nation* (1991). The only Sangh Parivar member in the VHP-mandated team was archaeologist Dr. S.P. Gupta; the others were Harsh Narain, B.P. Sinha, B.R. Grover and A.K. Chatterjee. At a later stage (after archaeological findings in Ayodhya in 1992), a "Historians' Forum" was founded, which included the same scholars as well as K.S. Lal (its president) and Dr. Sudha Malaiya, as well as DRI manager Devendra Swarup.

certainly one of the best-informed people about the situation in the North-East, including the problem of illegal immigration from Bangladesh.[6] But he is also a busy medical practitioner and consequently not in the centre of VHP policy-making. He told the BJP men: "What can I tell you? If you want to deal with such an important matter, why such amateurish improvization?"[7]

In fairness, it must be conceded that for all its anti-intellectual bias, through its dedicated investment in grass-roots work involving enormous personal effort of several millions of activists, the Sangh Parivar has unmistakably succeeded in establishing an impressive presence among the common people. Also, it must be said that some RSS leaders, particularly its fourth *Sarsanghchâlak*, Rajendra Singh, seem to have understood the folly of this anti-intellectual prejudice, and now vaguely exhort their workers to do some reading. At the margin of the Sangh, some local groups have started to process information and disseminate ideas through well-produced booklets and internet newsletters, most notably the *Vigil* group in Chennai and the *Hindu Vivek Kendra* in Mumbai.[8] But the consequences of this long-standing policy of mindless activism are bound to run their course for some more years.

No need for ideology

The Sangh has a basic commitment to India and to Hindu culture, but beyond that, its ideological position is hazy and undeveloped. As Sangh workers are wont to say: "It doesn't take any learning to love your mother", meaning in this case the Motherland. The result is that the Sangh's political line is malleable in the hands of ideologically more articulate forces. It has been more influenced by dominant political currents and intellectual fashions, often emanating from its declared enemies, than one would expect from an "extremist" movement.

Like in the Congress and Janata parties, quarrels within the BJP are rarely about ideology. As ex-insider Balraj Madhok wrote in a comment on the quarrels (and ultimate split) within the Gujarat BJP of 1995-96:

---

[6]See the booklets by Sujit Dhar: *Scourge of Infiltration, Gravest Threat to Our National Security* (1986), and *Bangladesh Islamised—What Next?* (1988).

[7]Interview, Calcutta, November 1993.

[8]A similar ferment exists among NRIs, e.g. the Californian Federation of Hindu Associations, see: "FHA organizes first Hindu think tank meet", *India Journal*, 26.1.1996.

"Personal differences rather than ideological factors lie at the root of the rifts within the Sangh Parivar."[9]

To an extent, the BJP has its lack of ideological sophistication in common with all non-Communist parties, most of all with Congress. A few recycled old slogans, a picture of its long-dead leaders, some material presents for the voter (*ad hoc* food subsidies, writing off farmers' loans), and there you have a Congress election campaign. *Mutatis mutandis*, the same is true for most parties. The simple slogans on the outside are not the summary of a profound and complicated programme too esoteric to trouble the voters with (as in the case of the Communists). The surface is all there is to it, at least as far as ideology is concerned.

This ideological hollowness is merely the application to politics of a more general superficiality afflicting India's public discourse. Sri Aurobindo already said it: "I believe that the main cause of India's weakness is not subjection, nor poverty, nor a lack of spirituality or Dharma, but a diminution of thought-power, the spread of ignorance in the motherland of Knowledge. Everywhere I see an inability or unwillingness to think—incapacity of thought or 'thought phobia'."[10] The great ailment of India today is the decline in thinking power. India was once the cradle of great pioneers in abstract and social sciences (e.g. Panini in linguistics, Baudhayana in mathematics, Aryabhatta in astronomy), and it is already recovering some of its ancient greatness in economics and the exact sciences. But this hopeful trend has not yet reached the centres of Hindutva ideology.

To the general atmosphere of intellectual sloppiness, the RSS has contributed its own wilful anti-intellectual prejudice. The perception from which Dr. Keshav Baliram Hedgewar started his RSS project was that Hindu society essentially had everything, even the best of everything, certainly also in intellectual culture, and that the only thing it lacked was *organization*. It is debatable whether lack of organization was a factor in the historical defeat of Hindu princes by Muslim invaders and British colonizers, but for the interbellum period with its communal escalation, this analysis possibly had its merits.

While the Muslim vanguard had its party, the Muslim League, and its

---

[9]B. Madhok: "A Question of Power", *Indian Express*, 29 October 1995.

[10]Spoken in April 1920; quoted in Abhas Chatterjee: *Concept of Hindu Nation*, p.67.

thought centre, Aligarh Muslim University, most politically active Hindus were members of the pluralist Indian National Congress, and the newly founded (1916) Benares Hindu University never played a role comparable to that of AMU for the Muslim community. Quite apart from formal organizations, the Muslims showed a much stronger commmunal solidarity, whereas the Hindus were more fragmented on caste, sect, class and ideological lines. And so, the RSS put all its eggs in the single basket labelled Hindu *sangathan*/"organization", hence its weekly's name *Organiser*.

To RSS ideologues, organization is more than a practical way of doing things, it is a near-metaphysical category. Organization is not done for the sake of a particular goal to be achieved, it is a goal in itself. I once heard RSS trade-unionist Dattopant Thengadi explain: "What shall we do when, by organizing, we have achieved our objectives? Organize."[11] Rewording founder Hedgewar's thoughts, an RSS man explains: "in the individual's case if the dictum is health for health's sake, in the case of society it is organisation for organisation's sake".[12] It is merely saying the obvious: that life forms, including collective life forms such as a human society, are characterized by self-organization. But then, sometimes it may be useful to remind oneself of such basics.

However, modern history teaches that organization and numerical strength cannot prevent movements from failing if they don't develop a good analysis of the situation they are facing.[13] Consider the fortunes of Gandhism and Communism. Gandhi was immensely popular, and he appealed deliberately to people's emotions, while the Communists were a fringe group, but they worked on people's minds. Now, who won? In the 1940s, while Gandhi was still alive, the Gandhians imbibed ever-larger doses of Marxist ideas and phraseology, and started saying: "We, too, are

[11]Dattopant Thengadi speaking at the European Hindu Conference in Frankfurt, August 1992.

[12]Ranga Hari: "Organisation for organisation's sake", *Organiser*, 13.4.1997.

[13]For this insight, I acknowledge a debt to the Maoist perception that peasant revolts in China have always failed until in Marxism they found an ideological compass to guide them to lasting victory. Though this was an entirely false explanation of the Communist victory in the Civil War of 1945-49 (which was not a peasant revolt), it is none the less attractive and may apply elsewhere.

socialists."[14] This was simply untrue, at least to the extent that they were real Gandhians still: the anti-modernist Mahatma believed in a voluntarist moral effort of *people* ("change of heart"), not in social structures. The Marxists were not getting influenced by Gandhi, on the contrary, they denounced him and his ideas left and right. By 1950, Gandhism had become the province of a few marginal activists like Vinoba Bhave, while Marxism was being promoted by the Prime Minister and dictating economic policy. Gandhian do-good emotions proved to be no match at all for Marxist intellectual work.

Moreover, the ideological prism through which a movement sees the world has to be propagated. Once the thought has been firmly implanted in people's minds, it can move (or jump over) organizational mountains. To take an example from India's immediate post-Independence history, the conservative wing of Congress was deeply rooted in Indian society and controlled the party apparatus, yet it lost out to Nehru. Many Congress Leftists had left the party and joined the Socialists and Communists. As the party's top Leftist, Jawaharlal Nehru was in a minority position, so the conservative wing (Sardar Vallabhbhai Patel, Govind Ballabh Pant, Purushottamdas Tandon) thought they could control Nehru with all his "loose talk". "Loose" or "foolish talk", that is how simple nationalists understood Nehru's fiercely ideological statements.

Nehru concentrated entirely on deciding policy and made it clear that Congressmen could get all the posts they wanted, but that they should leave it to him alone to make policy statements: "Patel might win on personalities and postings; [Nehru] would win on issues."[15] While the Congress bosses were sitting in their offices, Nehru was on the airwaves or being filmed during international meetings, busy creating public opinion in his own favour and instilling his own worldview. Nehru in person was

---

[14]Mahatma Gandhi's great-grandson Tushar Gandhi stood for the Lok Sabha elections in 1998 in Mumbai as a candidate of the Samajwadi (= Socialist) Party, and explained to Flemish interviewer Lucas Vanclooster (VRT Radio 1, *De Wandelgangen*, 30.1.1998) that "Mahatma Gandhi was a socialist". In fact, when alive, Gandhi was systematically denounced by the Left as an agent of the trader community, "the cleverest bourgeois scoundrel", because, as Alain Daniélou (*Histoire de l'Inde*, p.364) remarks, "his social reforms always ended up benefiting the merchant bourgeoisie".

[15]Rajmohan Gandhi: *Patel*, p.526.

responsible for the popularization of buzz-words like "secularism" and "progressive". During his first term as Prime Minister, Nehru was still afraid of being thrown out of the party by Patel. This is why he had his friends Rafi Ahmed Kidwai and Acharya Kripalani establish a new party, the *Democratic Front*, as a new platform for himself in case he could no longer dispose of Congress. But within a few years, he could put the conservatives in a corner, and their supposed control of the Congress party machine could not save them.

Thus, in 1951 Nehru demanded the abdication of the democratically elected party president Purushottamdas Tandon ("an old Hindu communalist and bigot")[16] by threatening his own abdication as Prime Minister.[17] Nehru objected to Tandon's championing Hindi as link language and to his involvement in the rehabilitation of Hindu refugees from East Bengal, though Patel had argued that Tandon had a restraining influence on this "communalized" constituency. In Tariq Ali's account, Nehru "forced Tandon to resign, thus weakening Patel's grip over the party machine."[18] This account is chronologically wrong, for Patel had already died at the end of 1950, but the point is that the Patelite conservative mainstream of the Congress party was indeed swiftly sidelined.

People's behaviour is ultimately determined by what they think and believe, more than by organizational structures. In modern politics, public opinion is important, not the "silent majority" which the RSS claims to represent, but vocal public opinion which influences the views of the silent majority. It is no use controlling an institution, when that institution is recruiting among people whose convictions are largely borrowed from the hostile dominant ideology. Just like other movements and political parties, the RSS always tries to put its people in place to "control" institutions. But once they are there, all they do (if I may be permitted a sweeping generalization) is to oversee the working of that institution, all the while leaving it to its secularist personnel to decide its ideological direction, which the RSS men often don't understand properly.

---

[16]Assessment by Tariq Ali: *The Nehrus and the Gandhis*, p.82.

[17]Nehru's anti-Tandon intrigue is related in C. Jaffrelot: *The Hindu Nationalist Movement*, pp.98-101. Jaffrelot correctly explains (p.100): "Nehru had inherited from Gandhi a moral ascendancy ... Here he used this asset in the same way as Gandhi, who had not hesitated to violate a basic rule of democracy, that of numbers, by calling on his personal authority to bring erring majorities back to the right path."

[18]Tariq Ali: *The Nehrus and the Gandhis*, p.83.

That is why every single organization ever floated by RSS activists (least perhaps the VHP, because it recruits among Sadhus who have a very distinct intellectual horizon of their own) has always been unable to launch an alternative ideological fashion even within its own ranks. A few emotional patriotic slogans were the only immunizer which the RSS could offer its own men to shield them from imbibing the dominant Nehruvian paradigm. From the 1948 ban on the RSS until at least the BJP's accession to power in 1998, the Sangh Parivar has largely played by the rules set by its enemies, and looked at the world through the glasses its enemies had put on its nose.

Golwalkar's advice

Dr. Hedgewar's successor Madhav Sadashiv Golwalkar, *Sarsanghchâlak* in 1940-73, though having worked as a university teacher in Biology, despised intellectual pursuits. When he saw RSS people reading books or newspapers, he would ask them if they had "nothing useful to do for the Sangh?"[19] When I mention this to RSS activists, they protest that there are many doctors, engineers and scientists in the RSS, and some of them recount as their personal experience that Golwalkar had encouraged them in their studies.[20] It is true that Golwalkar saw the usefulness of having RSS sponsors with academic or professional prestige, but that is not the same thing as valuing their learning: Golwalkar's approach to academics was (and the RSS approach still is) status-oriented rather than thought-oriented.

However, to take the said protests into account, let me rephrase my understanding of Golwalkar's anti-intellectualism. Golwalkar, who had been trained as a biologist, shared with many people from the exact sciences a dismissive incomprehension for the humanities, the disciplines which have no technical use but which practise critical thinking. Secondly, he shared with many spiritual-minded people a skepticism of the power of the intellect as compared to that of supposedly deeper layers of consciousness. Thirdly, he shared with many activists a distrust of sterile cerebration and its tendency to paralyse people's power to act. And fourthly, he shared with many Hindus a disgust with the traitorous role of

[19]As testified by K.R. Malkani, interview, December 1990.

[20]E.g. child psychiatrist Dr. Manohar Shinde, top Sangh office-bearer in the USA (interview at his home, Los Angeles, March 1993), told me that after getting his first medical degree, he had been advised by Guruji not to return to RSS volunteer work but to pursue his education to "top-notch" level.

the Communists, intellectuals all of them, in the British suppression of the 1942 Quit India movement and the Partition of India. Hence the rhetorical question of many RSS people: "What good was ever done by intellectuals?"

Meanwhile, the actual careers of the doctors and scientists who had been encouraged into academic pursuits by Golwalkar, hardly refute my thesis of Golwalkar's anti-intellectual bias. After all, they themselves, though becoming success stories in lay society, remained as not more than peripheral well-wishers in the RSS, without much influence on RSS policy; while those who stayed on for a career within the RSS hierarchy, are the ones who obeyed Golwalkar's strictures against bookish pursuits. It is generally not the bright but the mediocre minds who man the higher échelons of the RSS. The fact is that under Guruji, even phases of spectacular growth of the Sangh were not accompanied by any intellectual development worth mentioning, so that its literary output never exceeded a handful of repetitive and poorly written pamphlets per year.

It is a tragi-comical sight: such a huge network of organizations as the RSS *parivar* with such small influence on politics and public discourse. As a result of its leaders' boy-scout attitude of preferring mindless action to "sterile" intellectual work, the Sangh Parivar provides the pitiable spectacle of "a big dinosaur with a small brain".[21]

RSS people often tell you the well-known story of the pandit who crosses the river and asks the boatman if he ever studied philosophy: "No? Then half your life is wasted!" But when the boat starts to sink, it is the boatman's turn: "Panditji, have you studied swimming? No? Then all your life is wasted!" And then they have a good laugh, satisfied at having proven how useless intellectual effort is.

But the fact is: in the modern world, the equivalent of "swimming" in the above story, the skill necessary to disentangle yourself from the impasse and reach the goal, is not the physical locomotion at which RSS officials are so good. Among the skills needed for successful social and political action in the modern age, we should include the art of collecting and analysing information, and the art of formulating and publicizing viewpoints. Not the intellectuals, but the RSS itself acts like the pandit in

[21]The expression came up during my discussion with Balbir Poonj (*Observer of Business and Politics*) and Dina Nath Mishra (syndicated columnist close to the RSS) in 1992. The latter's practical conclusion was: the thing to do is not to build up an alternative organization, but to "infuse some brain into the dinosaur".

the story who had spurned mastering the art of swimming. The RSS attitude of spurning the intellect and denouncing the intellectuals has worked as a self-fulfilling prophecy: since they left the intellectual field entirely to their enemies, the available intellectuals would not be "of any use to the nation", meaning not sympathizing to the RSS programme. The political Hindu movement has paid a heavy price for this silly anti-intellectual prejudice.

Where is the RSS taking Hinduism?

When you bring up the matter of the Sangh's poor intellectual performance, the answer you mostly get from Sangh leaders is that they have such a neat scheme of character-building, such a fine organization, so many well-trained and dedicated cadres, such a wide range of activities and front groups. But they will have little to say about the direction which this vast machinery is taking except in hazy sloganesque terms, "a strong nation" and the like. As we shall see, even the central concept of *Hindû Râshtra* has never been properly outlined.[22]

This attitude reminds me of a Chinese story about a man who equipped himself for a journey to the south. He took the road to the north. Stopping at an inn, he met someone who explained to him that he would never reach his southern destination by going north. In disbelief, he started boasting about what a good chariot he had, and what fine horses, and what a first-class charioteer, and how such excellent equipment could obviously get him to any destination he wanted. Undaunted by the stranger's insistent advice to reconsider the direction he was taking, he drove off on his intended route—and never reached his destination.[23]

RSS rhetoric is full of the glorious future of Hinduism: "The twenty-first century will be the century of Hinduism", and the like. But it has very little idea of where it is taking Hinduism. Without a proper analysis of the situation, without an ideological compass, this vast network of RSS branches and front organizations may get lost along the way.

But then again, as K.R. Malkani told me in defence of his movement, people can also make up their compass as they proceed. As long as the Sangh Parivar was in the opposition, a precise blueprint wasn't necessary.

[22]For the best attempts, see Balraj Madhok: *Rationale of Hindu State*, and Abhas Chatterji: *Concept of Hindu Nation*.

[23]The story can be found in the 1980 official Beijing manual of Chinese, *Elementary Chinese Readers*, vol.3, pp.184-86.

As election campaign managers the world over know: ideas only divide the people, whereas simple emotive slogans unite them. Also, its actual achievements at the grass-roots level constituted a programme in itself, and devotion to the Motherland was a sufficient policy criterion. As late as 1988, the movement's stay in opposition reasonably seemed bound to last forever; nobody had foreseen that the BJP would become the largest opposition party in 1991, the largest party in 1996, and the ruling party in 1998. And somehow, as if by God's grace, that great leap forward coincided with the induction into the movement of a new generation of educated professionals, who may take care of the intellectual needs of a movement at the helm of the world's largest democracy.

So, that is the more optimistic reading of the Sangh's long-standing amateurism in improvisation in ideological matters. Only time will tell if it is right.

CONSEQUENCES OF THE SANGH PARIVAR'S ANTI-INTELLECTUALISM

Borrowing the opponent's glasses

The two most important consequences of the anti-intellectual prejudice animating the Sangh are, first, the stunted development of the Sangh Parivar's own intellectual grip on the world, and secondly, an extreme ineptness at public relations. In their political analysis, Hindutva activists often use the categories developed by their enemies and they become the prisoners of these categories. For example, first they let their enemies lay down the norm of *secularism*, and then they try to live up to this norm and prove that they are better secularists than others, hence BJP "positive secularism" vs. Nehruvian "pseudo-secularism". This way, they constantly have to betray their own political identity and try to fashion themselves a new ("genuinely secular") identity which their enemies have defined but are not willing to concede to them.

For another example, in a Doordarshan (Indian national TV) debate between VHP leader Giriraj Kishore and Janata Dal Scheduled Caste leader Ram Vilas Paswan, the latter objected to the *Mahâbhârata* episode in which the archery teacher Drona rejects the tribal boy Ekalavya as a pupil, as an illustration of how deeply ingrained caste prejudice is in Hindu tradition. Kishore could have explained that within the story, this attitude of Drona was not a matter of caste prejudice at all, nor did Ekalavya see it that way: Drona's job was to make the *Pândava* brothers into the best archers in the land, and so he didn't want to train anyone, of any caste, who might become their rival at a later stage. Instead, the VHP leader, hopelessly on the defensive, hastened to disclaim Drona ("We do not recognize him as an *âchârya*") with a typical readiness to lop off from Hindu tradition any and every part to which the opinion establishment objects.

This tendency to try and live up to standards set by one's declared enemies has been common Hindu practice in the modern age. Thus, the Christian and Muslim emphasis on monotheism and condemnation of idol-worship has been interiorized by Hindu reform movements even as the latter were trying to reconvert Indian Muslims and counter Christian power in India. Instead of defending Hindu polytheism against the missionary vilification of "idolatry", the Brahmo Samaj and Arya Samaj movements claimed that monotheism was indeed right and polytheism was indeed wrong, but that Hinduism, properly understood, is more monotheistic than Christianity and Islam. As Shrikant Talageri has remarked: "This was rather like accepting or adopting the European prejudice which treats white-skinned people as superior to dark-skinned people, and then trying to show that Indian skins are whiter than European skins!"[24]

Such hopeless exercises in trying to defeat an opponent after first borrowing his thought categories and value judgements are understandable as a result of the inferior position in which Hindu society has found itself for centuries, always trying to live up to standards set by victorious enemies. In an inertial hold-over of this psychology, today's Hindutva activists have an inferiority complex and value nothing so much as being accepted by respected people, meaning secularists. That is why they always offer their platforms to people with status, including people who despise them, such as the Janata Dal politician Inder Kumar Gujral (the later Prime Minister) and the Sikh secularist writer Khushwant Singh, to name just two whom I have seen scheduled as guests of honour at functions of the RSS student organization *Akhil Bhâratîya Vidyârthî Parishad*. Thought or opinion is not what the Sangh values, but status, and in the Nehruvian dispensation, status would imply contempt of Hindutva.

---

[24]S. Talageri: *The Rigveda, a Historical Analysis*, p.406.

The experience of 1975-79

For an example of how the Sangh Parivar is forced to play by the rules set by its enemies, consider the period 1975-79. The vast majority of people jailed and tortured under the Emergency were RSS men, or what Indira Gandhi called "fascists" (the "threat of fascism" had been the declared reason for imposing the Emergency). It is on their sweat and blood that in 1977 all kinds of Socialists climbed to power. But under the Janata regime, the same Socialists (Madhu Limaye giving the lead) raised the "double membership" issue: they objected to the combination of Janata office with RSS membership, and prepared to hound out the RSS members. The latter took it lying down; in fact, to comply with the "anti-communal" standards set by their enemies, they were about to scrap all references to Hinduism from the RSS constitution. Fortunately for their credibility, the fall of the Janata Government in 1979 put an end to the whole controversy. When looking at the meekness of the RSS before secularist pressure, one cannot help remarking that "fascism" should be made of sterner stuff.

The RSS was helpless because of the ideological power equation. Socialist secularism was the dominant ideology, while Hindu nationalism counted as politically incorrect. Those who swore by socialist secularism could afford to kick its alleged opponents around at will.

The contrast with the Communists is striking. The Communists stood exposed as traitors in 1942-47, when they informed the British government (a Soviet ally) about Quit India activists and served as a mercenary intellectual vanguard for the Muslim League by propagating economic and other secular-sounding arguments for Partition; once more in 1948-50, when they supported the separatist *Razâkâr* militia in Hyderabad and subsequently started an armed uprising of their own; and yet again in the run-up to the Chinese invasion of 1962, when they clamoured that "China's chairman is also India's chairman" and accused India of having started the war with China. But they were always back on top within a short time, fully respected members of the democratic political spectrum. Better still, they managed even to make other parties implement much of the Communist agenda, from the nationalization of the banks to an unnecessary degree of hostility to the West, upheld by Congress and Janata governments alike. Such are the results when you make it your priority to control the ideological air space, rather than the ground level of work among the masses.

Even worse (at least from a Hindu nationalist viewpoint) than the treatment which the Hindu nationalists received, was their own record as policy-makers. Instead of removing the anti-Hindu discriminations from the Constitution, they co-fathered the Minorities Commission, an official institution with at least advisory capacities (given a statutory status in 1992), but from which members of the Hindu majority were by definition excluded. Their Foreign Minister Atal Behari Vajpayee facilitated the entry of Pakistani citizens ("infiltrators", in Hindutva parlance), condoned the continued Chinese occupation of Tibet (Hindutva spokesmen had always denounced Nehru's passive complicity in it), and inducted Foreign Service bureaucrat Syed Shahabuddin into politics, supposedly a "nationalist Muslim" who soon proved to be a much sharper and abler spokesman for Islamic causes than the existing past-oriented clerical Muslim leadership.

Instead of offering an alternative political agenda on the basis of their own party doctrine (Integral Humanism), the BJS men were trying very hard to live up to the standards set by their enemies, begging them for a certificate of good conduct, calling themselves "socialists" (even if qualified as "Gandhian socialists") and "secularists" (even if qualified as "positive" or "genuine" secularists). Briefly, they were dancing to the tune of the dominant ideology because they had never projected a credible ideological alternative.

BJP rides with the tide

Hindu critics of the BJP allege that in its eagerness to be progressive and acceptable, the party simply abrogates its own natural Hindu identity. To start with a controversial example, when the *Commission of Sati (Prevention) Act* of 1987 made the existing *Satî-sthal* temples (commemorating the self-immolations of widows on their husbands' funeral pyres) illegal, HMS member Jeevan Kulkarni made an unsuccessful attempt to have the Supreme Court declare the Act unconstitutional.[25] The only politician of a major party to protest against the law was the late Kalyan Singh Kalvi, a Rajasthani member of the Rajput caste, the one most affected by the Act; far from being a Hindutva activist, he belonged to the militantly secularist Janata Dal. The BJP, by contrast, fully supported the new legislation.

[25]Jeevan Kulkarni: *Writ Petition (Civil) No. 587 of 1989*, filed in the Supreme Court of India.

Kulkarni commented: "Congress and the BJP have succeeded where even Aurangzeb failed: to prevent the Hindus from honouring their heroines who braved death itself and provided inspiration for the Hindu warriors riding to their probable deaths in desperate struggles against the Muslim armies."[26]

The BJP's motive in supporting this legislation may be analysed as follows. Part of it is a genuine belief that the prohibition of honouring *satî* women is a necessary component of the prohibition of *satî* itself (there is a native Hindu tradition of opposing *satî*, for example, its prohibition in parts of the Maratha confederacy decades before it was prohibited in British Bengal in 1829). The greater part, however, is the fear that the party would be branded pro-*satî* if it didn't support the crackdown on the *satî-sthal* category of Hindu temples. Nothing determines the BJP position as predictably as the fear of being associated with anything of which the secularist establishment disapproves.

The BJP has also gone along with the rising tide of caste-based reservations. In L.K. Advani's *Rath Yâtra* to Ayodhya in 1990 (which was entirely peaceful),[27] the only incident was some stone-pelting by students who were angry because Advani didn't support their action against Prime Minister V.P. Singh's implementation of the recommendations of the Mandal Commission Report, viz. the extension of caste-based reservations in recruitment and college enrolment (till then confined to the Scheduled Castes and Scheduled Tribes, 22.5 per cent of the total population and of the jobs concerned) to the middle or so-called Other

---

[26]Speaking to me at the time of his court proceedings (1992), at his lawyer's office on *Tîs Hazârî* court; his Writ Petition is a remarkable document on Sati, at times cranky but also providing little-known hard information.

[27]The reader may be surprised to learn that Advani's 1990 *Rath Yâtra* was bloodless, for the opposite is said in most secularist references to the event. The allegation is based on the synchronicity between Advani's tour and large-scale rioting in Uttar Pradesh and Hyderabad, places where the procession did not pass through. Thus, in Colonel Ganj, UP: "When slogans in support of the Ram temple were shouted, Muslims responded by throwing stones and petrol bombs. The riot spread to the Scheduled Caste area and then to neighbouring villages—the death toll was around 100" (C. Jaffrelot: *The Hindu Nationalists*, p.419, based on *Frontline*, 27.10.1990). The riots were often Ayodhya-related, but the pomp and ceremony of the car procession had a very positive effect on the Hindu masses, and the police was deployed beforehand, so that on Advani's itinerary at least, Ayodhya enthusiasm did not turn violent.

Backward Castes (OBCs, about 46 per cent).[28] Though some Hindu revivalist intellectuals vehemently opposed this proliferation of reservations, the BJP's criticism of reservation schemes has never gone beyond points of detail. In 1991, the BJP government in Uttar Pradesh was the first to fully implement the Mandal recomendations.[29] In its 1996 and 1998 election manifestoes, the BJP even proposed a 33 per cent reservation of seats in parliament for women, a demand not actively supported by public opinion, nor for that matter by the RSS.[30]

Remark the contrast with the Shiv Sena, "the only organized political group to take sides clearly against the conclusions drawn by the commission":[31] as a party recruiting mainly among the so-called Other Backward Castes, the beneficiary of the Mandal Commission's recommendations, the Shiv Sena flatly rejecting the Mandalite reservations for OBCs. At the height of the Mandal agitation, SS president Bal Thackeray spoke to a mass gathering in Mumbai, and declared his rejection of the reservation scheme for OBCs. He asked the OBC members in the audience to raise their hands; most people raised their hands. Then he challenged them: who will support the SS in its opposition to reservations for OBCs? A massive roar of applause was the response to Thackeray's defiant preference for Hindu unity over the caste interests of his own constituents.[32] The BJP, by contrast, has maintained a low profile in this matter, and cannot be counted upon to reverse the trend towards more quota.

---

[28]As C. Jaffrelot mentions (*The Hindu Nationalists*, p.416), on 20 September 1990, five days before the *Rath Yâtra* started, Advani and Madan Lal Khurana (leader of the BJP's Delhi unit) were attacked when they tried to visit one of the students who had set himself on fire in protest against the new casteist quota policy. Fellow protestors objected to this cheap politicians' gesture when the BJP was refusing to give effective political support to the anti-quota movement.

[29]This does not keep experts (e.g. Sandria B. Freitag in D. Ludden, ed.: *Making India Hindu*, p.226) from declaring that "mandalization" is the BJP's biggest enemy, and that the Ayodhya campaign (which pre-dated 1990 by years) was merely a diversionary tactic to minimize the impact of Mandal. There is no doubt that *some* Sangh leaders opposed the principle of caste quota, but the BJP has accommodated the quota wave without hesitation.

[30]Thus, in the RSS weekly *Organiser* (3.11.1996), Ushatai Chati of the RSS women's wing *Râshtra Sevikâ Samiti* says: "Reservation for women is unnecessary. With equal rights and duties one should progress on one's own."

[31]Gérard Heuzé in A. Bonner: *Democracy in India*, p.164.

[32]Reported to me by eye-witness Shrikant Talageri.

"I am a Hindu communalist"

A symptom of the ideological power equation is the Sangh Parivar's permanent checkmate in the "war of the words". The Sangh is at the mercy of the meanings which its enemies allot to important terms, such as "communalism".

The *Oxford Dictionary* (1986) defines *communal* as "of or for the or a community, for the common use". It also has an entry *communalism*, defined as "principle of communal organization of society", and calls the Paris *Commune* a "communalistic government in Paris in 1871". Indian journalists going abroad find to their initial disbelief that no one in the West or anywhere else ever uses or even understands this swearword "communalist". If asked for a guess, few non-Indians would say that the word might have a pejorative meaning. The magic charm "communalism" which has put the whole Indian political scene in a mood of graveness and militancy for half a century, is a provincial and distorted usage exclusive to India's English-speaking elite.

Originally (at least in Indian politics), "communal" was the term by which the British labelled political arrangements, such as separate electorates and quota-based recruitment, which took the religious community as the operative unit rather than the individual or the family or the region or the nation. The term was never hurled at people who rejected these arrangements, but was quite sincerely accepted by the people who proposed the "communalization" of the polity: the British and the Muslim League openly advocated "communal" electorates and "communal" quota in the services. The Congress became a party to the "communal" principle through the Lucknow Pact (1916), which conceded "communal" electorates to the Muslim League. When in the early 1930s the British proposed the Communal Award, its beneficiaries never thought of treating "communal" as a dirty word and throwing it at the Communal Award's opponents.

The main opposition to the unapologetic communalism of the British and the Muslim League came not from Congress (except initially), but from the Hindu Mahasabha. The Hindutva movement was born in the struggle *against* communalism; that struggle was its very *raison d'être*. The HMS's stated programme was to *abolish communalism* and make India an unalloyed democracy without separate electorates or recruitment by communal quota.

Congress, embarrassed by its own compromise with communalism, tried to cloud the debate by misapplying the term "communal" to the HMS on the analogy of the Muslim League. It falsely posited a symmetry between the Muslim League and the Hindu Mahasabha, obscuring the antisymmetry between the League's adherence and the HMS's opposition to the communal principle.[33] Very quickly, accurate usage of the term "communal" was eclipsed by muddled usage. Today, the mores of public discourse have sunk to the level where politicans and journalists and scholars systematically and exclusively apply the term to a movement which never used it as a description of its own positions, and which has always opposed those very policies which were described by their own proponents as "communal". And where the term does apply, as in the co-existence of separate religion-based Personal Law systems (which the BJP *opposes*), it is studiously avoided.

The Sangh people, after having been battered and beaten for decades on the words front, could have decided to hit back. They might have chosen to proudly carry the name with which they are stuck anyway, frankly telling every interviewer: "I am a Hindu communalist." They might perhaps have tried to restore the word to its pre-secularist or even its pre-colonial dictionary meaning. They might have turned the tables on their opponents by being creative with terminology. Instead, they have meekly accepted the semantic inversion imposed by their opponents and desperately tried to shake off the "communal" label which had been stuck on to them.

Counterproductivity of being nice

When dealing with fellow politicians, BJP men tend to remain friendly and co-operative even when they are being insulted. They were loyal partners in the Janata Government even though their nominal allies in that Government were pestering them with the "double membership" issue. The same attitude was in evidence in the short-lived BJP-BSP coalitions in Uttar Pradesh (mid-1997): BSP president Kanshi Ram and BSP Chief Minister Mayawati would insult the BJP no end ("a cobra on one occasion and a vulture on another"), but the BJP put up with it all, to the extent that the *Hindustan Times* compared it with the fighting between a mongoose

[33]This false symmetry is still propagated by the likes of Mani Shankar Aiyar, who once called the BJP the "Hindu chapter of the Muslim League".

and a cobra: the cobra may otherwise be fierce and frightening, but a mongoose can bite it and bleed it and reduce it to helplessness.[34]

During the thirteen-day tenure of the first-ever BJP Government (May 1996), as on many other occasions, Prime Minister A.B. Vajpayee and other BJP leaders were pleading that the BJP is the most secularist of all. From a hard Hindutva viewpoint, this amounted to crawling before the secularist opinion masters and begging them for a certificate of good secularist conduct,—which they were determined never to concede to the BJP. This approach proved to be counterproductive, and if the Hindutva strategists had it in them to learn from the feedback they get from reality, they might have given it up long ago and opted for a bolder profile. Thus, in spite of all the assurances of the BJP's secularism by Vajpayee, not a single MP belonging to the Congress or National Front crossed the floor to support his government in the 1996 vote of confidence. Seeing the BJP's envy of their own unassailable power position, the secularist parties behaved like spoiled children: the sight of beggars merely made them laugh.

The BJP's overdoing the secular and progressive thing does not convince the party's critics. No matter how much it may champion the cause of the OBCs or of women, it is still branded as "reactionary" and the like.[35] No matter how much it may dilute its naturally Hindu character and go out of its way to accommodate the Muslims, it is not rewarded with even a tiny bit of Muslim sympathy. Consider this reading of the BJP's friendly face by Islamic scholar Ausaf Vasfi : "Mr. L.K. Advani has gone to the extent of saying that the BJP is not anti-minority. ... For the sake of power he has not hesitated to dilute his party's very *raison d'être* ... it would have been far more upright morally had Mr. Advani plainly admitted his party's Hindu character and constituency. But he wants to have the best of both worlds. It is sheer hypocrisy."[36]

Vasfi may be right, but the typical BJP reply is that the irreconcilable Muslim critics whose published commentaries I can quote, belong to the

[34]"Cobra and mongoose", *Hindustan Times* editorial 5.9.1997. Remark that in the person of Mayawati, it was the BJP which first brought a Dalit woman to the rank of Chief Minister, verily a first in emancipation.

[35]A trend-setting book about Hindutva's "sexist" secret agenda (about the Hindu nationalist way of "gendering the history of Partition" etc.) is certainly Tanika Sarkar and Urvashi Butalia: *Women and the Hindu Right*.

[36]S. Ausaf Vasfi: *Radiance*, 18.8.1996, reproduced in *Muslim India*, March 1997.

intellectual elite, which is a small minority. The increasing presence of ordinary Muslims in the BJP organization would seem to confirm the wisdom of the BJP's liberal and multicultural posturing.

Fruits of being nice

In spite of the irreconcilable hostility in secularists which no compromise position of the BJP could soften, developments in democratic politics seem to confirm the rightness of the BJP's soft line. In the 1996 Lok Sabha elections, several smaller parties (Samata Party, Akali Dal [Badal], Haryana Vikas Party) ignored the secularist embargo and allied themselves with the BJP. In the run-up to the 1998 Lok Sabha elections, the BJP's untouchability was terminated: local parties in Tamil Nadu, Orissa and other states also joined the BJP in a national alliance, and many anti-BJP intellectuals became much friendlier. It is very unlikely that that development would have taken place if the BJP had not cultivated a softer, "secular" image.

So, from the BJP viewpoint, something can be said in favour of this soft line. The rising middle class, at any rate, wants a soft BJP.[37] For example: "Well-known writer Kamala Das, though traditionally a Congresswoman, is veering towards the BJP ...: 'I am fed up with the Congress. I am beginning to prefer the BJP to the Congress, because the Congress is now more communal than the BJP, despite Ram Janmabhoomi. It is the Congress which evolved the Muslim vote-bank. ... In comparison, I prefer the BJP as an alternative, because it is less corrupt. The BJP at least loves the country. But I wish the BJP does not stress redundant issues like the Ram Janmabhoomi or other places of worship. It is not relevant to the thinking mind. Such talk will only invite rejection and inflame passion. I don't think that a thinker like Vajpayee will spout such sentiments.'"[38]

The electoral successes following the BJP's soft-pedalling of the Ayodhya issue confirm that the hard line is not necessarily the one which yields the most tangible results. Sailors have to make use of adverse winds sometimes, without altogether abandoning the course toward the chosen destination, and that is what the Sangh Parivar, when confronted with hard-liner criticism, claims to be doing in softening its Hindu image. But

---

[37]V.A. Pai Panandiker: "Soft Hindutva's appeal", *Indian Express*, 20.5.1996.

[38]Leela Menon: "Guest chair: Kamala Das", *Indian Express*, 12.5.1996.

even inside the Sangh Parivar, the question is raised whether the BJP is indeed true to its Hindu destination or whether its "opportunistic" choice to ride with the tide has made it forget why it was ever created in the first place.[39]

Public relations failures: the Ayodhya disaster

One of the Sangh Parivar's persistent failures has been its ineffectiveness in getting its message across to outsiders, whether Indian non-Hindus or foreign observers. To an extent, these were not failures because there was no attempt at success in the first place. For a long time, the RSS cultivated a stark non-interest in the opinions of outsiders. That is no longer the case, but the demonization which has widely caught on in past decades, is still making its effects felt.

An example of the RSS weakness on public relations is the staggering failure of the campaign reclaiming Ayodhya to communicate its case to the world. At a time when Native Americans, New Zealand Maoris and Aboriginal Australians were frequently (and often successfully) going to court to reclaim sacred sites and other heritage items, it shou'd not have been too difficult to explain to the international public the reasonableness of Hindus claiming a Hindu sacred site, all the more so because the contentious building with mosque architecture was already in use as a Hindu temple since 1949 (with restrictions until, and without restrictions after 1986). Yet, the net result was the exact opposite: the whole of world opinion, to the extent that it took interest in a presumed backwater like India, was solidly behind the Muslim claim and decried the Hindus as "fundamentalists", "fascists" and what not.

In other conflicts (say, the Gulf War), world opinion will always contain vocal supporters for *both* sides, not in equal measure, but at least even the less popular party will not be entirely bereft of support. In the case of the Ayodhya controversy, *nobody* who cared to pronounce an opinion and had the media at his disposal to do so, has come out in support of the Hindu side. The single exception I know of was François Gautier, India correspondent of the French conservative daily *Le Figaro*, who described the reactions of his colleagues as "such pompous, overblown,

---

[39]See e.g. Shreerang Godbole: *Time for Stock-Taking* (1997), a swayamsevak's second thoughts about the Sangh Parivar's compromising discourse and policies.

sanctimonious, holier-than-thou, atrocious, ridiculous, sly and totally undeserved outrage".[40] It is not really exaggeration to say that the BJP's Ayodhya campaign was the public relations disaster of the century.

Some smaller Ayodhya-related PR disasters resulted not from the Sangh's traditional disdain for PR, but from its ineptness at handling information. On 20 February 1991, the VHP released a list of 50 names of people allegedly shot dead by the police during Kar Seva in late October, early November 1990. However, it turned out that many of the people listed were still alive or had died at other places, whether in other riots or of natural causes. One boy from Mathura had made a trip to Calcutta, and when he came back home, his relatives, who had seen his name in the VHP list and given him up, took him for a ghost.[41] When I inquired about this at the VHP office in Delhi, I was told that many Kar Sevaks had not been known by their names, since they came from all over India. Even if that is true, it is not a valid excuse for just making up a list, which is neither honest nor appropriate in a situation where subsequent scrutiny is certain.

In the same period, BJP office-bearer K.L. Sharma floated a so-called "Mahatma Gandhi formula" to solve the Ayodhya dispute, viz. that Muslims should voluntarily hand over the sites of demolished temples. Secularists could easily show that the cited reference to a specific issue of Gandhi's weekly *Young India* wasn't right, and that for all we know, Gandhi never said or wrote such a thing (though he did say: "Muslims must realize and admit the wrongs perpetrated under the Islamic rule.").[42] So, here was a top leader going public with a historical claim which he knew was going to be challenged, yet he didn't even take the trouble to verify it. Consequently, he became an easy target for accusations of "Goebbelsian lies"[43] (a comparison that is unfair to both men: Sharma wasn't evil and Goebbels wasn't stupid). However, after this painful experience of what the RSS culture of going by rumours can lead to, no gaffes that silly have been heard of.

---

[40]F. Gautier: *Rewriting Indian History*, p.106.

[41]S.P. Singh and Venkitesh Ramakrishnan: "When the 'dead' came back. *Frontline* investigation exposes bodycount hoax", *Frontline*, 11.5.1991.

[42]This was on 25.12.1947 in reaction to a post-Partition Urdu poem protesting against the planned rebuilding of the Somnath temple and calling for "a new Ghaznavi to avenge the renovation of the Somnath temple"; quoted by Rajmohan Gandhi: *Revenge and Reconciliation*, p.237.

[43]E.g. Sankar Ray: "Goebbelsian tactics", *Statesman*, 24.11.2000.

No need for media

Possibly the RSS leadership was satisfied with the support it received in a section of the vernacular press and refused on principle (viz. nationalist pride) to be concerned with the comments in the foreign and the "foreign-oriented, anti-national" secularist media. At the same time, however, one cannot miss the sloppiness or inertia or unconcern which kept the Sangh from verifying whether its message came across, and from devising ways to deal with the hostile climate in the national media and among India-watchers. On the contrary, the RSS has always cultivated a haughty unconcern for what the media write. In 1925, the media were admittedly far less important than they are today, but the RSS kept on favouring a Gandhian type of "living in the past", keeping up the pre-modern ways. Instead of relying on the media, the RSS believed in direct mass contact at the ground level rather than in raining viewpoints on the people from the media air space.[44]

In the RSS view, the "air space" of the public arena, the media and the whole realm of public discourse controlled by the secularist "chattering classes", is nothing but a paper tiger before the strength of the Hindu masses as soon as they get organized. The electoral breakthroughs of the BJP since 1989 would seem to prove the point, and the Janata (i.e. partly BJS) victory in the 1977 elections seems to prove it even more decisively. As Nana Deshmukh explained it to me: "What do we need media for? In 1977 we defeated Indira Gandhi who held all the media on a leash, we came to power without the benefit of any media support at all."[45]

It is undeniable that several men with an RSS background became Cabinet Ministers in 1977-79; but the point is that they played entirely by the rules laid down by their secularist opponents inside and outside the Government, and added not one ounce of Hindutva contents to the Government's policies. The general opinion climate was such that they would have needed a lot of courage and adroitness to insinuate any Hindutva plank into the Janata Government's platform. To a large extent, that opinion climate was created precisely by those media for which RSS stalwarts claimed to have no use. The personal career of politicians associated with Hindutva may not have been impeded by the hostility of

---

[44]In the 1970s, the RSS did publish a daily paper, *Motherland*. Apart from being harassed by Indira Gandhi's men, the paper was also mismanaged; K.R. Malkani told me in 1992 that they were still paying off debts incurred by *Motherland*.

[45]Brief interview at the Deendayal Research Institute, March 1990.

the dominant media, but the implementation of the Hindutva programme certainly was.

Lethal consequences of media absence

One of the effects of Hindutva's absence in the important media is that it has prevented the Hindu revivalists from forming friendships with possible allies abroad. There is a lot of talk in Hindutva circles about the West and India having a common interest in the containment of Islam, so it would be natural if contact were made with like-minded people in the West. Yet, it is highly unlikely that someone like Samuel Huntington, whose theory of the "clash of civilizations" is quite familiar to Hindu revivalists (Girilal Jain, for one, already wrote to that effect during the Ayodhya controversy in 1990-92),[46] would agree to being photographed in the company of RSS stalwarts, simply because the latter have been given such a bad reputation worldwide by the media.

Meanwhile, the destruction which a media bombardment with hostile opinion can work among the support base of a movement is enormous. So many Hindu intellectuals I have talked with were reluctant to come out in the open with their Hindutva sympathies because they felt intimidated by the secularist opinion constraints. During the Ayodhya crisis this went as far as pronouncing secularist opinions in the presence of a third person, only to retract those opinions as soon as we had the room to ourselves. Many potential Hindutva activists or sympathizers were exposed to the daily battering of the Hindutva movement in the media with hostile stories and opinions and ended up developing doubts about the rightness of the Hindutva cause.

What is more, sometimes the effects of a generalized anti-Hindu and anti-India bias get physical. Thus, a lot of the killing of Hindus and of Indian defence personnel in Panjab, Kashmir and the North-east was made possible by the diplomatic or indirect material support which the separatists there were receiving from foreign countries; and this support, in turn, was made possible by an anti-Hindu or anti-India tilt in Western media opinion.[47] Why is American military aid to Pakistan not made conditional on the termination of Pakistani involvement in Kashmiri

---

[46]See e.g. G. Jain: *The Hindu Phenomenon*, Ch.1: "The civilizational perspective".

[47]E.g.: "US questions Kashmir's status as part of India", *The Hindu*, 30.10.1993; or "Kashmir disputed, says US", *Times of India*, 30.10.1993: "In a highly provocative statement, the Clinton administration yesterday specified that the United States does not recognise the 1947 Instrument of Accession by which Kashmir became a part of India."

terrorism? Why is Western development aid to Bangladesh not made conditional on the termination of the country's hospitality to separatist militias? Largely because no public opinion is created on these issues by a press which has otherwise amply proven that it can whip up public indignation in any direction desired (for example, to prepare NATO interventions in Iraq or ex-Yugoslavia). This means that Hindus and others have been killed as a consequence of the absence of the Hindu or even just a neutral perspective in the international media, whose reporting is based entirely on the most partisan English-language Indian media.

Thus, if due publicity had been given to the expulsion of around 200,000 Hindus from Kashmir in early 1990 by the Muslim separatists, or to the instant expulsion of 50,000 Hindus from Kabul immediately after the Islamic conquest of the city in April 1992, this might have influenced world opinion in a pro-India and pro-Hindu sense.[48] Now, most Westerners have never heard about the Hindu refugee problem, for most journalists including reputed India hands have simply kept it out of the picture.[49] Where it was at all mentioned, it was given a vicious twist, for example: "The BJP ... has told the Hindus to leave Kashmir, so that the Army could enter."[50] While refugees are normally the object of pity, *The Economist* called the Hindu refugees "cowards".[51]

Sometimes Western commentators have their own pro-Pakistani agenda (particularly British and American ones, because of the long-standing alliance of their countries with Pakistan), but mostly they get their inspiration from Indian opinion makers. Consider for example the ludicrous claim that Jagmohan, Governor of Kashmir in the winter of

---

[48]A rare survey of the multi-faceted Hindu refugee problem is "The Hindu as refugee", *Sunday*, 5.7.1994. One caption reads: "Thousands of displaced people stream in. Their only crime is that they are Hindus."

[49]This is true of most Western papers, in which the expulsion of the Kashmiri Hindus was never mentioned for years after the event, even in survey articles of the problem. A particularly crass case is the review article of four Kashmir-related books (including Jagmohan: *My Frozen Turbulence in Kashmir*, which contains enough hard information about the expulsion) by the former India correspondent for *Time* magazine, Edward Desmond: "Himalayan Ulster", *New York Review*, 4.3.1993.

[50]Marc Colpaert, speaking on *Radio Trottoir*, BRTN-1 (Flemish Radio, Brussels), 5.8.1995.

[51]*The Economist*, 10.4.1993. A reply dated 13.4.1993 by the Kashmiri Pandits Association was not published. The article casts the same aspersions on the Hindu refugees from Pakistan 1947, the specific target being K.R. Malkani, a refugee from Sindh.

1989-90, had herded the Hindus out: "The Kashmiri Pandits left the Valley in droves in 1990 because they were corraled and herded out like cattle by the cowboy-Governor of the day."[52] This is in disregard of the numerous testimonies of the refugees themselves, who were glad enough that Jagmohan had sent troops to escort them to safety, and most of whom had horror stories about relatives murdered by once-friendly Muslim neighbours; not to speak of the testimony provided by hundreds of actual dead bodies of Kashmiri Hindus. In keeping with this scenario of Hindus voluntarily leaving their homes just to please a whimsical Governor, the Indian media have systematically referred to the refugees with the euphemism "Kashmiri *migrants*", and the foreign correspondents didn't find the news of a mere "migration" spicy enough to trouble their information consumers with.

However, these Kashmiri refugees have made their own contribution to Hindu nationalist polemic. Hindutva authors have published some interesting books on the Kashmir problem, but not through publishing-houses which reach beyond the circle of already-convinced Hindus.[53] In 1991, under the impact of the Pakistani "proxy war" in Kashmir, refugees in Jammu started a newsletter, *Kashmir for Kashmiriat*, which developed into a full-fledged Pakistan-watching medium reporting on narco-terrorism, sectarian violence in Pakistan's cities and Northern Areas, atrocities on women, the oppression of Pakistan's Hindu, Christian and Ahmadiya minorities, the Afghan civil war, and of course all aspects of Pakistani involvement in Kashmir and other hot spots in India.[54] Its sources of information include direct testimonies, the Pakistani press (*Dawn*, *Herald et al.*), and reports of Western agencies and parliamentary committees. But again, this meritorious attempt to disseminate information remains marginal and has little impact on the broader process of opinion-making.

---

[52]Mani Shankar Aiyar: "Kashmir is not Bangladesh", *Sunday*, 17.10.1993. For contrast, Arun Shourie wrote ("A disastrous retreat", *Indian Express*, 26.5.1991): "It is Mr. Jagmohan ... who saved the Valley for India. He slowly re-established the authority of the State. He put the terrorists on the run."

[53]E.g. Rajendra Singh: *Our Kashmir*; Utpal Kaul: *Agony of Kashmir*; Anil Maheshwari: *Crescent over Kashmir*; and Balraj Madhok: *Kashmir, Storm Centre of the World*.

[54]Their example has meanwhile been emulated by Arun Shourie, who in the spring of 1998 published a serial of probing syndicated columns (e.g. in *Observer of Business and Politics*) on ethnic and communal relations and policies in Pakistan.

The Sangh's responsibility

The reason for the *Kashmir for Kashmiriat* initiative was the alleged blinkered vision of professional human rights bodies which only noticed army atrocities on poor hapless Kashmiri Muslims including terrorists, but not the atrocities which these victims themselves committed on the Hindus.[55] At least one human rights organization subsequently adjusted its position and released a report on human rights violations by the terrorists.[56] A similar initiative in Panjab during the (equally Pak-supported) separatist violence, *Human Rights for All*, was started for the same reason, witness its headline: "The roll-call of horror. Let us shed at least a few tears for them, since the Amnesty International won't". The ensuing list of killings of civilians is concluded with this comment: "And it goes on. Without Respite. Like an unending nightmare. Like a Greek tragedy. Without a tear being shed. Neither by the Amnesty International; nor by any of the other organisations which pride themselves as champions of human rights, the human rights of the perpetrators of terror and slaughter. The so-called violations of their human rights have been documented by these organisations—diligently, thoroughly, with all the resources and expertise at their command. But, who is going to document the violations of the human rights of these unknown martyrs who were, in cold blood, deprived of the most fundamental of their fundamental human rights—the right to live?"[57]

Note that these initiatives do not emanate from the established Hindutva organizations. They are *ad hoc* initiatives by people who became conscious of the problem facing the Hindu minority in Kashmir, Panjab and the North-East after having suffered in person. Thus, K.N. Pandita, the secretary of the *Friends of Kashmir* who showed me around some refugee camps, and some of the refugee spokesmen to whom he

---

[55]A cartoon in the cover story of *Human Rights for All*, June 1992, "Amnesty (Selective) International", shows the shadow of a terrorist who just shot someone down, and a Western-looking *human-rightswallah* stepping over the dead body, saying: "You poor, poor assassin! I hope you won't be unduly harassed for this."

[56]*Asia Watch*: "Violation of Human Rights of Innocent Civilians by Extremists", released on 30.6.1993. Also, a fairly objective Kashmir-watch newsletter is published by the *Belgische Vereniging voor Solidariteit met Jammu en Kasjmier* (Belgian association for solidarity with JK), Beveren.

[57]*Human Rights for All*, 6.4.1992.

introduced me, have a Marxist past.[58] The *Kashmir for Kashmiriat* newsletter occasionally betrays that secular-Marxist view of religion, viz. by associating religion itself with backwardness.

Whether it is the Kashmiri refugee crisis or the terrorizing of the minorities in Bangladesh or the horror stories brought along by Hindu refugees from Afghanistan in 1992, the organized Hindu movement shows a haughty unconcern for collecting the actual data of these events.[59] Rumours headed for oblivion take the place of properly processed information.

The Sangh likes to attack Indian and international human rights activists for their alleged anti-India and anti-Hindu bias (for example: V.M. Tarkunde, Kuldip Nayar, B.G. Verghese),[60] but to the extent that the allegation is justified, the Sangh itself cannot disown part of the responsibility. Even the most critical and independent-minded India-watchers or Amnesty International volunteers cannot avoid being influenced by the general opinion climate and the actual flow of information. In this case, the flow of information is highly selective, with only one version coming through. If the press correspondents in Delhi would get a reasonable proportion of intelligently written formulations of the Hindu viewpoint, not just in party organs like *BJP Today* but in the quality newspapers, this would not fail to have a corrective impact.

---

[58]An important contribution to Kashmiri historiography by K.N. Pandita, a scholar of Persian and Central Asian History at Srinagar University, is *Bahâristân-i-Shâhî, a Chronicle of Mediaeval Kashmir*. His guest column "Destroyed legacy: Kashmir has lost its pluralist character" (*Pioneer*, 27.10.1993) represents the secularist (rather than a specifically Hindu) outcry against "theo-fascism".

[59]A very partial exception is provided by V.P. Bhatia's weekly column in *Organiser*, e.g.: "Thrown to the wolves. Bangladesh—a concentration camp for minorities", *Organiser*, 14.4.1996.

[60]E.g., the BJP statement, "The truth about the temples in Kashmir" (April 1993) accuses B.G. Verghese of falsely certifying that Hindu temples in Kashmir were undamaged (e.g. in his columns in *Indian Express*, 8.5.1991 and 11.6.1991) though the BJP investigation team already found 24 temples burnt down and 24 others desecrated in 1990. On the same issue, see also Dina Nath Mishra: "Anatomy of a lie", *Observer of Business and Politics*, reproduced in *Organiser*, 7.3.1993. Likewise, V.M. Tarkunde's *People's Union for Civil Liberties* was attacked for its allegedly anti-India position on Kashmir by A.C. Vasishth: "A poser to PUCL", *Indian Express*, 5.6.1990, and by Virendra Kumar: "PUCL report: a political pamphlet", *Indian Express*, 18.6.1990. On the other hand, when Verghese defended the Army against Tarkunde's and other human rights groups, Anil Maheshwari applauded him: *Crescent over Kashmir*, p.138.

Until a decade ago, most observers and even enemies of Hinduism were prepared to concede to it a certain harmlessness and benevolent tolerance as quintessentially Hindu qualities; today, even that little credit has been taken away. Hindus used to take great pride in Swami Vivekananda's triumphal speech at the Parliament of Religions (Chicago 1893), but the celebration of its 100th anniversary in Washington DC was embarrassing because the Ayodhya demolition was generally considered to have disproven Vivekananda's description of Hinduism as tolerant.[61] Hinduism is now never discussed without mentioning the existence of "Hindu fundamentalism", at best to disclaim this phenomenon as part of genuine Hinduism, but more often to prove that Hinduism is just as conducive to fanaticism as Islam and Christianity are. The credit for this additional blot on the fair name of Hinduism must go to the Sangh Parivar, not because it has taken up Hindu causes, but because it has handled them in such a mindless way.

Information has an impact on people's behaviour, and opinions have consequences, sometimes even lethal ones. Therefore, it was irresponsible for the leaders of a political movement to spurn some of the available ways of spreading pertinent information and influencing public opinion.

HINDU CRITICISM OF THE SANGH PARIVAR

If anything proves that there is something seriously wrong with Hindutva studies in India as well as in the West, it is the puzzling fact that nobody has cared to notice the existence of a strong dissatisfaction with the Sangh Parivar among supporters of Hindu revivalism. I noticed this Hindu criticism of established Hindutva already during my first meetings with Hindu activists inside and outside the Sangh Parivar, but somehow the acclaimed experts have failed to see it.[62] Is it because most established experts base their studies purely on written texts without ever actually meeting the activists, or because these activists don't speak their mind to interviewers suspected of profound hostility?

At any rate, Hindu dissatisfaction with the Sangh Parivar has become much more accessible thanks to the publication of a collection of Hindu

[61] See the VHP (USA) conference brochure *World Vision 2000*.

[62] What comes closest is Gérard Heuzé's remark (*Où va l'Inde moderne?*, 1993, p.124) that the younger cadres and sympathizers "openly mock the aged leaders of the RSS, BJP, VHP and even of the Shiv Sena (Bal Thackeray is 66)". The gerontocracy which especially the RSS has become symbolizes its ideological sclerosis.

comments on the Sangh's performance. In October 1996, after some fruitless correspondence with RSS top leaders about his misgivings, Dr. Shreerang Godbole, a physician from Pune and an RSS member for seventeen years, decided to circulate an eight-page brochure: *Time for Stock-Taking: A Swayamsevak Speaks*. The supportive comments which he received were subsequently put together by Sita Ram Goel into a sizable volume published under the title *Time for Stock-Taking: Whither Sangh Parivar?* Most of the comments and of the brochure itself deal with the confused attitude of the RSS and BJP towards the "Muslim problem"; some of them will be discussed below.

A history of failure

One of the contributors to the Goel-Godbole volume is Abhas Chatterjee, who co-operated closely with the Sangh in 1989-92. He writes: "Secularists of every hue also keep proclaiming the RSS to be a radical militant Hindu organisation and a majority of the Hindu society appears to believe so. But conscious, perceptive Hindus cannot but see that the RSS has proved a paper tiger. All its bombastic pronouncements have been 'sound and fury signifying nothing'. Whether on Ayodhya or on Kashmir, on Article 30 or Article 370, on infiltration of Bangladeshi Muslims or enactment of common civil laws, on Sanskrit or Urdu, on *Vande Mâtaram* or cow-slaughter—the RSS has always taken a step forward only to take two steps backwards.[63] Rather, it has made one appropriate noise and then retreated into its hole. On no issue has the RSS been able so far to mount a campaign resulting in successful protection of Hindu causes. ... On issue after issue, the RSS starts with a roar, then shrinks into a whimper, then grovels and finally gives up, defeated but careful to save its face by inventing excuses. ... Lack of a clear ideological vision is the hurdle on which the RSS flounders again and again."[64]

Whatever Chatterjee's explanation for it, the fact itself certainly deserves to be noted: from 1952 to 1997, the BJS/BJP cannot boast of a single policy decision which the Indian state has made under its influence. The fact that the party was in the opposition most of the time is no excuse: in most democracies, skilful opposition politicians can occasionally make deals with the ruling parties or enter their own themes on to the national

[63]Cf. the pamphlet by maverick NRI publisher Arvind Ghosh: *BJP's One-step-forward/Two-steps-back Policy Will Lead Nowhere* (1997).

[64]A. Chatterjee in S.R. Goel, ed.: *Time for Stock-Taking*, pp.49-50.

agenda by creating public opinion. The best example is the Ayodhya controversy: at least until its electoral defeat in late 1989, the Congress Party was certainly amenable to a compromise allotting the disputed site to the Hindus in exchange for some concession of a different type to the Muslims (Rajiv Gandhi had the temple-mosque thrown open for Hindu worship in 1986 and permitted the *Shilânyâs*, the laying of the first brick, in 1989), so if the BJP had cultivated that avenue, the definitive Rama temple might have been built already.

However, as Chatterjee correctly points out: whether by political compromise, by mass agitation or by any other means, the BJS-BJP has not succeeded in pushing its agenda even once. Or as Arvind Ghosh puts it with some hyperbole, it is the Sangh Parivar's strategy to "snatch defeat from the jaws of victory", to ruin projects which were bound to bring success if only they were pursued with firmness and conviction.[65]

Perhaps, achieving goals is not even the movement's main interest any more. According to Chatterjee: "Organisations generally reach a stage when the organisation itself becomes more important than the idea it was supposed to promote. The vehicle becomes more important than the goal. The RSS too has reached that stage."[66] That the RSS spends all its energies on itself is in fact an old criticism, dating to the time when Golwalkar kept his volunteers out of politics; Savarkar is often quoted as having commented that "the epitaph of an RSS man will be: *he was born, went to shâkhâ, and died*."[67] Others would limit this criticism to the Sangh *leadership*, and confirm that in spite of the legitimacy of Chatterjee's criticism, the Sangh still consists largely of dedicated activists who really want to serve Hindu society.[68]

By the year 2000, however, the situation had further aggravated in the direction outlined by Chatterjee. Thus, a group of swayamsevaks from Karnataka issued a pamphlet titled *Save RSS from BJP: an SOS to Sarsanghchalak*[69]. They lamented the decline in discipline and commitment, aggravated by the entry of corruption with the BJP's accession

[65]A. Ghosh: *Sangh Parivar's Strategy: Snatch Defeat from the Jaws of Victory*.

[66]A. Chatterjee in S.R. Goel, ed.: *Time for Stock-Taking*, p.73.

[67]E.g. Shridhar Damle, personal communication, 1993; and Vikram Savarkar (grandson of Veer Savarkar's brother and former HMS president), personal communication, December 1995.

[68]E.g. Mayank Jain, personal communication, December 1997.

[69]Reported by Rajesh Ramachandran: "Unhappy Sangh members begin pamphlet war: a guide on how to save RSS from BJP", *Times of India*, 30.11.2000.

to power: "In our own neighbourhood two regular shakhas of 20 years of nourishing have become Sunday shakhas, that too if there is nothing else to do. Even when we gather, we only talk about how BJP men have degraded and why we fools are wasting our lives in 'nikkars'", meaning knickers, part of the RSS uniform. To many, particularly to those who have an interest in the RSS's image as fanatical and dangerous, this came as a revelation; but it had already been in evidence for a whole decade.

Ayodhya, a case study in confusion

Chatterjee describes in some detail some of the climbdowns performed by the Sangh Parivar after striking militant postures initially, e.g.: "The ideological muddle of the RSS was starkly exposed by its ambivalent conduct of the Ayodhya movement. ... A clear national vision would have told the RSS that the Babri mosque had no business to stand on the *Râma Janmabhûmi* and its demolition was a rightful aspiration of the Hindu nation. But the RSS never developed this conviction. It soon started talking of 'making a new temple on RJ' instead of 'liberating' it. ... It avoided facing the basic issue—no temple can be built unless the original site is liberated and restored to the Hindus. Soon the Sangh Parivar was taking recourse to new subterfuges. They said that the mosque was not a mosque at all but a temple (!), that they wanted to 'renovate' it and not pull it down, that they wanted to do so because it was a temple, and that it should be called a 'disputed structure' instead of Babri mosque, and other such nonsense."[70]

Where in the whole of journalistic and scholarly literature on the Ayodhya affair, with its competition in superlatives to label the movement as the *neç plus ultra* in fanaticism, can you find the observation that the movement was in fact confused, shy, eager to appease its opponents? On this point, Chatterjee is quite factual and confirms what I have seen and heard time and again when discussing the Ayodhya matter with Sangh Parivar stalwarts in 1990-93: as the months passed, their Ayodhya rhetoric became woollier, and after the 1991 electoral breakthrough, the BJP definitely started soft-pedalling the issue, ostensibly calculating that the issue's electoral potential had been exhausted.[71]

---

[70]A. Chatterjee in S.R. Goel, ed.: *Time for Stock-Taking*, p.68.

[71]In November 1996, BJP spokeswoman Sushma Swaraj said about the Ayodhya issue: "You cannot cash a cheque twice."

According to Chatterjee: "As time passed, the Sangh Parivar was hedging further. ... They talked of acquiring the site through legislation, building a temple without damaging the mosque, 'relocating' the mosque with respect and Muslim co-operation, making construction only on surrounding land (77 acres) and so on. Stalwarts of the Sangh Parivar were also giving undertakings in courts and political fora that they would protect the Babri mosque! The president of the VHP proclaimed the nonsense that Babar was a tolerant ruler who did not demolish temples, that it was his general Mir Baqi who built the Babri mosque without Babar's knowledge, and that 'offering *namâz* on a disputed site is forbidden in Islam'. The Sangh Parivar tried to fool the Muslims, and begged that RJ be handed over by Muslims as 'a gesture of goodwill'."[72]

It would not be unfair to say that here, Chatterjee is rebuking the BJP for not being sufficiently fanatical. Whereas the BJP hopes to settle the Ayodhya affair by legal means, Chatterjee calls for a revolutionary gesture disregarding the law and the institutions of the State. This has to do with a fundamental assessment of the character of the Indian State from a Hindu nationalist viewpoint. For Chatterjee, the "Nehruvian" state is an imposition like the Islamic and British regimes, and the declaration of India as a Hindu state constitutes a revolution; for the Sangh, Hindu society is largely responsible for the Indian state as it exists, and it should take control of the state and gradually reform it in accordance with the genius of Hinduism. The Indian state as it exists is indeed largely a creation of Hindus, perhaps insufficiently committed Hindus, but at least not non-Hindus, and consequently, Hindus should indeed assume responsibility for the good and bad points of the state, implementing reform where necessary. Chatterjee is mistaken in condemning the BJP's attempt to stay on the right side of the law, even from the Hindu nationalist viewpoint.

A valid point made by Chatterjee is: "The Sangh Parivar tried to *fool* the Muslims". It is an apt description of the RSS attitude towards its declared enemies: it tries to deny that there is a conflict, to have its way without a fight, by misrepresenting the stakes in the conflict and hoping that the opponents will grant its wishes. Of course, this tactic has never

---

[72]A. Chatterjee in S.R. Goel, ed.: *Time for Stock-Taking*, p.69. RJ: *Râm Janmabhûmi*, "Rama's birthplace".

worked; those who tried to fool others have only fooled themselves. Thus, the RSS insisted that Ayodhya was not a religious conflict between Hindu and Muslim, but a secular conflict between the foreigner Babar and the Indians, both Hindu and Muslim: "Babar came to India as an aggressor and defeated the joint force of Hindus and Muslims. ... to cause a rift between the Hindus and Indian Muslims, he demolished the Rama Janmabhoomi temple and built a masjid in its place."[73]

The anti-Babar "Indian Muslims" referred to must be the Afghans: the Lodi dynasty of Delhi which fought Babar but was defeated by him, and then the Bengal-based Suri clan, who fought Babar's son Humayun and grandson Akbar. The Suri clan employed a Hindu general, Himu (who got captured and was beheaded by Akbar), which is what the RSS spokesman describes as Hindu-Muslim unity. All the same, from a Hindu nationalist viewpoint, the fact that the Afghans fought the Moghul invaders and took the help of Hindus in their desperation does not nullify the fact that the Afghans themselves were foreign occupiers in the first place. The RSS man also fails to pinpoint just how the demolition of the Babri Masjid interfered with this instance of Hindu-Muslim unity, a scenario unsupported by any evidence and obviously made up for the sake of presenting a "secular" case against the Babri Masjid. Faced with this kind of casuistry, absolutely no one in the Muslim or secularist camp has conceded the RSS claim that Ayodhya was a "national" rather than a "Hindu" concern.

Chatterjee continues: "When the fateful day of 6th December 1992 came, the Sangh Parivar was in a state of pathetic self-contradiction. The assemblage of Hindu youth fired with nationalist zeal was not prepared any more to play the RSS game of merry-go-round on RJ. As they started bringing down the offending structure, the RSS arrayed its volunteer corps who tried their best to resist the Hindus and protect the mosque! Luckily, they failed. As Babar's mosque was demolished, Hindus rejoiced while ... the Sangh Parivar started hiding its face behind excuses. They disowned the act and the heroes who had performed it. ... And that was the end of the Ayodhya movement. The Sangh Parivar simply dropped a movement which they had promised would be the greatest mass movement in human

[73]Rajendra Prasad Jain: "How Hindu Resistance to Babri Masjid Got Recorded in 1850", *Organiser*, reproduced in A.A. Engineer: *Babri Masjid Ram Janmabhoomi Controversy*, p.92.

history. They meekly agreed to surrender to a secularist judiciary the right to decide whether the RJ belonged to the Hindus at all."[74]

Here again, Chatterjee, a law-abiding citizen, criticises the principle of recognizing the legitimacy of existing institutions. In Chatterjee's view, the capitulation of the BJP before the Nehruvian state is no small matter, worse even than the abandonment in 1967 of the anti-cowslaughter agitation:[75] "The midstream jettisoning of the Ayodhya movement has been the most severe blow to Hindu interests since the Partition. It has demoralized Hindus, confused them and created doubts in their minds about the legitimacy of their aspirations. It has left the Hindu society even more directionless and less self-confident than ever before. ... The RSS betrayal of the Hindu society was complete."[76]

Of course, we don't have to share Chatterjee's indignation about the allegedly soft stance of the RSS-BJP. Dr. Walter Andersen, one of the rare Western Hindutva-watchers who have seen through the image of the RSS as a tough "private militia",[77] recommends the conciliatory RSS position as a welcome alternative to the purist position upheld by a Sita Ram Goel or an Abhas Chatterjee.[78] The RSS, meanwhile, congratulates itself for bringing the BJP to power with its alternating doses of radicalism and moderation.

RSS opposition to thought

Abhas Chatterjee tries to trace RSS confusion to its root: "Why has the RSS landed itself in such a pathetic hole? The answer is straightforward—the organisation lacks an intellectual base. When Dr. Hedgewar laid stress on organisation in 1925, he may have been right. But his successors got so obsessed with *sangathana* (organisation) that they totally neglected scholarship and intellect."[79]

---

[74]A. Chatterjee in S.R. Goel, ed.: *Time for Stock-Taking*, pp.69-70.

[75]About the 1966-67 agitation against cow-slaughter, see B. Graham: *Hindu Nationalism*, pp.147-57.

[76]A. Chatterjee in S.R. Goel, ed.: *Time for Stock-Taking*, p.70.

[77]Secularists sometimes label the RSS as "the world's largest private militia" and the RSS considers itself a formidable force, but Gérard Heuzé (*Où va l'Inde moderne?*, p.122) stays closer to the facts when he points out that "the way in which the RSS was overwhelmed by a thousand determined youngsters on 6 December 1992 is telling. The sect is worthless in street combat. ... Its manifestations remind us more of the boy-scouts than of mass politics".

[78]I talked with Dr. Andersen (author, with Shridhar Damle, of *The Brotherhood in Saffron*) at his office in the State Department, Washington DC, October 1996.

[79]A. Chatterjee in S.R. Goel, ed.: *Time for Stock-Taking*, p.70.

The organizational culture of the RSS may be the direct cause of RSS anti-intellectualism: "Freedom of intellect was probably seen as an obstacle in the way of obedience and discipline (just as in Islam) and therefore detrimental to organisation. RSS meetings generally include what they call a *bauddhik* (an intellectual discourse) and have *bauddhik pramukh*s at different levels to conduct them, but their lectures are generally quite hackneyed, superficial and uninspiring. More significantly, it is forbidden in the so-called intellectual sessions to ask questions at the end of the lectures."[80]

And this, Chatterjee continues, is the result: "Suspicious of liberty of thought, the RSS thus produced a generation of 'uneducated' leadership. ... These leaders know next to nothing either about Hinduism or about prophetic monotheism, about the psyche that has guided this nation or its enemies, the ethical values that India stood for and those its invaders sought to impose on her. Hardly anything of notable scholarship has been produced by the RSS *'bauddhik'* brigade. ... For the overwhelming majority in the Sangh Parivar, including most of its bigwigs, the intellectual equipment remains limited to some layman perceptions which are either too superficial to help formulate ideological convictions, or too much at variance with realities to help explain emerging events."[81] This is correct.

Such leadership is obviously unable to counter the dominant ideology with an articulate Hindu alternative: "The RSS, suffering from intellectual impoverishment, was unable to counter the Gandhi-Nehru onslaught or equip the Hindus to reject its ideas. Instead, the Sangh was sucked into the thought-stream of a perverted secularism. Since then they have largely obeyed the secularist track-rules, except for making occasional noises to the contrary."[82] This is in agreement with my own findings outlined above.

A different aspect of the matter is that this uninspired leadership ultimately damages the organisation itself: "For all its boasting about being the largest voluntary organisation in the world (500,000 swayamsevaks, 40,000 shakhas and all that), the RSS is now virtually a dead institution unable to force the secularist system to bend to the Hindu viewpoint on a single issue. ... It is like a lifeless monster of enormous proportions rather than a throbbing little bee with a sting. ... an utter lack of

[80]A. Chatterjee in S.R. Goel, ed.: *Time for Stock-Taking*, p.70.

[81]A. Chatterjee in S.R. Goel, ed.: *Time for Stock-Taking*, pp.70-1.

[82]A. Chatterjee in S.R. Goel, ed.: *Time for Stock-Taking*, p.71.

inner strength, conviction and commitment characterizes all its activities. Having seen the working of the VHP, Bajrang Dal, Vanavasi Kalyan Kendra and the like from close quarters, I found only a massive form without any content, a yawning void behind a lofty façade. Programmes are launched with fanfare, there is hectic activity to get media publicity, but the office-bearers mereiy go through the motions without any commitment, and the end result is zero."[83]

In Chatterjee's rather dramatizing view, this demoralization spells the doom of the Sangh: "Talk to them in private, and you will know that the cadre of swayamsevaks is deeply frustrated. Bright idealistic young men who had sacrificed lucrative material careers and joined the Sangh out of genuine nationalist urge, feel cheated. ... Some of them get disillusioned and quit, others carry on with the rituals and wonder what it is all about."[84] But then came the 1998 elections, which boosted Sangh morale. Whether this is the start of a long-term upswing remains to be seen.

An orphaned society

Even when thinkers of calibre are available, the Sangh Parivar will not provide them with a proper platform. In 1964, when the VHP was being founded, RSS general secretary Eknath Ranade asked Sita Ram Goel to become the general secretary of the new organization. Goel agreed on one condition: that he would be allowed to speak his own mind. This was unacceptable to RSS general-secretary Eknath Ranade, who said: "You have to manage the organization's affairs. If statements have to be made, we will do that." On such conditions, Goel was not interested in the nomination.[85]

In 1991, after the BJP became the second-largest party in the Lok Sabha and was in a position to nominate some eminent citizens to the Rajya Sabha, L.K. Advani suggested nominating Arun Shourie. Shourie wanted to consider it on condition that they really wanted Shourie in the Rajya Sabha, and not just another party-line loudspeaker. But this was unacceptable to a majority of the party high command, for would it not be unfair to allot a seat to some pen-pusher who never did any work for the party, rather than to a dedicated party activist? At the very least they

---

[83]A. Chatterjee in S.R. Goel, ed.: *Time for Stock-Taking*, p.71.

[84]A. Chatterjee in S.R. Goel, ed.: *Time for Stock-Taking*, p.72.

[85]Interview with K.R. Malkani and S.R. Goel, March 1990.

insisted that Shourie become a party member and compromise with the party discipline, and so he declined the honour (in 1998-99, when the winning party had a few seats to spare, he did get his chance at last).[86] The party bureaucrats in the Hindutva offices just don't value thought.

For the period under consideration, Hindu society could be described as *an orphaned society*. It has no recognized intellectual leadership. Whereas the Christians, the Muslims and the Communists (and likewise on a smaller scale the Sikhs, Buddhists and Jains) have plenty of institutions to further their respective causes, there is no university or professional think-tank wedded to the Hindu cause. All there is, is an organization vaguely professing its attachment to Hinduism and the Motherland, relatively well-meaning but quite incompetent; apart from an array of self-centred little sects whose awareness of Hindu tradition is eclipsed by the fixation on their own guru. Numerous idealists who feel they want to do something for Hinduism turn to the Sangh Parivar, because it happens to be around, it is big, and its enemies always call it Hindu (though it prefers to call itself *Râshtrîya*/national or *Bhâratîya*/ Indian, safely secular terms). But their energy is at least partly wasted, because the Sangh fails to provide intelligent leadership.

Abhas Chatterjee argues that the presence of a false guardian of Hindu interests is worse than the total absence of Hindu self-organization, because in the latter case at least, people would be aware of the defect and start building up a stalwart Hindu organization: "Secularists of every hue continue to spread the lore that the RSS is a powerful, radical Hindu organisation, and most Hindus keep believing it. ... Just as Savarkar failed to get Hindus behind him because of Mahatma Gandhi, so small pockets of wakeful Hindus are today unable to gather wider support because the public continues to believe that RSS is there to protect their interests. ... Continued Hindu faith in the RSS has forestalled the emergence of a genuinely Hindu alternative, whereas the Sangh Parivar has started imaging itself as the rightful guardian of the Hindu society and views the

[86] Arun Shourie, interview, December 1992. He had also been offered a Rajya Sabha seat by V.P. Singh in 1989, when they were both fighting Prime Minister Rajiv Gandhi over the Bofors arms deal corruption case, but he fell out completely with V.P. Singh when the latter, as Prime Minister, implemented the Mandal Commission recommendations on reservations for the Other Backward Castes in mid-1990. Shourie's passionate opposition to Mandal would have been an embarrassment for the BJP too in the general scramble for the OBC vote.

possible emergence of a 'competitor' with unease. At the same time, Hindus continue to be taken for granted and the ground continues to slip from under their feet, week after week, month after month, year after year. ... the Hindu society under its care is reduced to 'blind men led by the blind'."[87]

A similar point is made by Shrikant Talageri: "Congress secularism can only succeed in subverting the consciousness and morale of the *general* Hindu public. The more conscious Hindus remain unmoved by it. Similar secular propaganda by the Sangh Parivar, however, directly targets these sections of Hindu society, and can succeed in effectively and completely neutralising Hindu sentiments, Hindu reactions and Hindu activism."[88] This means that the Sangh Parivar is channelling Hindu revivalist energy among the masses away to the achievement of goals of a much less Hindu calibre.

Common origins of Hindus and Muslims

One of the arguments used to minimize the seriousness of the Hindu-Muslim conflict is that Hindus and Indian Muslims have a common ancestry. This is a Sangh favourite though its weakness has been exposed long ago. V.D. Savarkar disagreed with those Hindus who expected much from the recognition of the common origin of Hindus and Indian Muslims: "Some well-meaning but simple-minded Hindus amuse themselves with the thought ... that inasmuch as the majority of Indian Moslems also are in fact allied to us by race and language ... they could easily be persuaded to acknowledge this homogeneity and even blood relation with the Hindus and merge themselves into a common National Being if but we only remind them of these affinities and appeal to them in their name. ... As if the Moslems do not know it all!! The fact is that the Moslems know of these affinities all but too well: the only difference [is] that while the Hindus love these affinities which bind the Hindu to a Hindu...—the Moslems hate the very mention of them and are trying to eradicate the very memory of it all. Some of them fabricate histories and genealogies to connect their origin with Arabians or Turks [and] are bent on widening the cleavage deeper and broader by removing every trace which may remind them of having once [had] something in common with the Hindu stock."[89]

[87]A. Chatterjee in S.R. Goel, ed.: *Time for Stock-Taking*, p.76.

[88]S. Talageri in S.R. Goel, ed.: *Time for Stock-Taking*, p.223.

[89]Savarkar: *Hindu Rashtra Darshan*, p.80.

Savarkar's reference is to the anti-"idolatrous" impact of Islam in general and of the *Tablîgh* movement in particular: from *c.* 1920 to the present, this movement has worked to eradicate Hindu elements from the culture of the Indian Muslims, and has definitely succeeded in widening the gap between the two communities.

Among the "well-meaning but simple-minded Hindus" who take the line which Savarkar has criticised, we must first of all think of Mahatma Gandhi, who often used the argument of a common ancestry in his plea for Hindu-Muslim unity. But, in more recent times, the main RSS ideologues also fall in this category. A follower of Savarkar, Dr. Shreerang Godbole, criticizes the chummy *Hindû-Muslim bhâî-bhâî* positions taken by Sangh Parivar stalwarts K.S. Sudarshan, M.M. Joshi, Dattopant Thengadi, K.R. Malkani, S. Gurumurthy, Devendra Swarup, Muzaffar Hussain, P. Parameswaran and M.G. Vaidya at a seminar held in Pune on 27-28 July 1996, one of these positions being summarized as: "If Muslims are told of their common ancestry, they will unite with Hindus."

Godbole comments: "How foolish! As if Muslims are not aware that their forefathers were converted to Islam. However, for Muslims, pre-Islamic period is a period of darkness (*jâhilîya*). Prophet Mohammed is himself reported to have said that his mother and beloved uncle were sent to Hell because they were non-Muslims."[90] Savarkar's and Godbole's position is that while the Indian Muslim community has been cut out of the flesh of Hindu society and should ultimately be brought back to its ancestral religion, it is no use denying that the Muslim leadership is hostile to Hinduism, known to be their ancestral religion. More generally, they consider it necessary to take the challenge of Islamic doctrine and its "separatist" impact seriously, rather than spirit it out of sight with a clever little explanation about common ancestry.

The BJP flag

A significant symbol of the BJP's eagerness to curry favour with the Muslims is the party flag. The BJS flag was plain saffron with a blue lamp on it. When the BJP was founded, a new flag was devised: "two vertical colours, saffron and green, in the ratio of 2:1, with the election symbol of the Party [lotus flower] in blue colour in the middle of the saffron portion

[90] Shreerang Godbole: "Time for Stock-Taking", included in S.R. Goel: *Time for Stock-Taking*, p.iv.

equal to half its size. The green portion will be near the mast."[91] Why the green part? When questioned, more than one BJP spokesman will try to conceal the simple truth, for example, by arguing that this was the flag of the unified Janata Party of 1977-79, of which the new BJP had claimed the heritage.[92] In reality, the Janata Party had its colours in horizontal instead of vertical juxtaposition (green with a saffron strip on top), and no lotus flower, so the BJP flag was definitely a newly designed flag.

The presence of the green colour in the Janata flag was meant to represent greenery and agriculture, the "people's party" being largely a peasants' party. In the BJP flag, it is obviously included as the colour of Islam, which means that to prove its secularism, the BJP thinks it necessary to do that which on other occasions it calls "Muslim appeasement". Whether one applauds or deplores it, the actual facts are that the BJP, like the pre-Independence Congress, goes out of its way to put some token Muslims (or in this case, Muslim symbols) on display.

This choice of flag has naturally received a lot of criticism from the rank and file. Consider Shrikant Talageri's comment: "*The very first thing, in my opinion, is that the Sangh Parivar should see to it that the BJP changes its flag from saffron-green to saffron.* This is only a symbolic change, but it *symbolizes everything*."[93]

Talageri brings in George Orwell to clarify his point: "In [George Orwell's] *Animal Farm*, it must be remembered, the Animals realize the full extent of the betrayal only when they hear the sheep (who are utilised by the leaders to drown out murmurs of dissent with their loud and continuous slogan-chanting), who have all along been chanting 'four legs good, two legs bad', suddenly start a cacophony of 'four legs good, two legs *better*'. The viewpoint of the Sangh Parivar, even if not precisely expressed in the form of a slogan, was always 'saffron flag good, saffron-green flag bad'. H.V. Seshadri ... castigates the Congress for introducing a green strip in the national flag 'for the sake of pampering the communal Muslim mind' He calls it a betrayal of 'the most adored and shining symbol of a Nation—of its ideals and aspirations, its history and traditions, the endless sacrifices and sufferings of its martyrs, the prowess and

---

[91] BJP: *Constitution and Rules*, p.4.

[92] This was the explanation given in 1990 by the RSS *Baudhik Pramukh* (overseer for intellectual development) for Maharashtra to Shrikant Talageri (personal communication, December 1995).

[93] S. Talageri in S.R. Goel, ed.: *Time for Stock-Taking*, p.225; emphasis in the original.

penance of its heroes and saints.' However, it has been quite some time since the Sangh Parivar's viewpoint appears to have changed to 'saffron flag good, saffron-green flag *better*'."[94]

In Talageri's view, this petty symbolic issue reveals a lot about the supposedly Hindu or "saffron" character of the BJP: "The flag of a party is its *own* prerogative. No one can legitimately question the BJP if it changes over to the saffron flag. The fully green flag of the Janata Dal gets countless Hindu votes; and as recent trends in Mumbai (e.g. in the Muslim stronghold of Behrampada in the recent Municipal Corporation elections) show, the saffron flag of even a rabidly Hindutva-spouting party like the Shiv Sena can effectively garner staunch Muslim votes, if *that* is to be any consideration in deciding the colour of the Sangh Parivar's political flag. The only thing preventing the BJP from having a saffron flag is its own leadership. And here lies a fundamental question: is it even within the realms of possibility that this party which does not even have the guts to paint the colour of its *own* flag saffron, could ever have the guts to paint the colour of the national polity saffron?"[95]

This debate reveals at least how far the BJP has moved away from its origins in order to make itself acceptable to the Muslims and live up to the standards set by the secularists. Contrary to a common perception, the BJP is not an extremist party.

RSS reaction to criticism

Hindu activists criticize the Sangh Parivar leadership; what is the latter's reaction? This is Abhas Chatterjee's experience: "Meet some RSS bigwigs, and you would find them talking about what happened in the Sangh meeting somewhere, how a family was drawn to it, how Guruji said what to whom and how Deorasji responded, how the Sangh Parivar is a well-knit family, and so on. An unwillingness to face the failures or to objectively discuss unpleasant realities cannot be missed. On the contrary, point out the failures, and pat comes the reply: 'Aren't we alone doing *something* for the Hindus? Who else is doing anything at all?'"[96] A very limited interest in the feedback they get from reality is indeed a mentality

[94]S. Talageri in S.R. Goel, ed.: *Time for Stock-Taking*, p.225, with reference to H.V. Seshadri: *Tragic Story of Partition*, pp.122-24; emphasis in the original.

[95]S. Talageri in S.R. Goel, ed.: *Time for Stock-Taking*, pp.225-26; emphases in the original.

[96]A. Chatterjee in S.R. Goel, ed.: *Time for Stock-Taking*, pp.73-4.

problem afflicting the higher rungs of the RSS machinery. This may be a more general Hindu problem, witness for instance, how Mahatma Gandhi persisted in a policy of total accommodation towards the Muslim League for thirty years even when the results continued to be negative.[97]

Shrikant Talageri has the same experience, and takes a grim view of it: "If the Sangh leadership refuses to take stock of the situation, or responds with the usual evasionist squeals—'We know all these things, we do not require *you* to tell us ... why don't *you* do something instead of doling out advice to us ... we are doing everything that is required to be done, but in the *proper* way as only *we* know how ... you will find out in good time, trust us'—then only 'God' can help us."[98]

Perhaps it is no use waiting until the aged RSS leadership (and tomorrow its by then equally aged successors, etc.) learns the lessons from the feedback which it is receiving from reality. There is, at any rate, a more optimistic prognosis. At the turn of 1998, a number of Hindu activists summed it up as follows: "The Sangh is so confused because it has been pushed around for so long, the BJP has been in the opposition for too long. What they should do is to make any compromise needed to come to power, and then savour the invigorating feeling of being at the helm. In their first term, they don't even need to do anything specifically Hindu, their agenda can wait. First they have to develop self-confidence. It is just like the position of India on the world scene: when India becomes strong politically and economically, the increased national self-confidence will automatically lead to a revaluation of Indian culture."[99]

Wages of the soft line

The RSS has made a choice for action and emotion (devotion to the Motherland) and against intellectual work in circumstances which no longer obtain. From a semi-secret society thrown up by the struggle for freedom, it has grown to become independent India's largest mass movement, carrying important social responsibilities. In the 1990s, its

[97]Even Gandhi admirer B.R. Nanda (*Gandhi and His Critics*, p.94) admits that "from the acceptance of separate electorates in the Lucknow Pact in 1916 to the acquiescence in the Communal Award in 1933, and finally to the Cabinet Mission Plan in 1946, it was a continual retreat in the face of Muslim pressure".

[98]S. Talageri in S.R. Goel, ed.: *Time for Stock-Taking*, p.231.

[99]These are the words of Mayank Jain, but other activists have spoken to the same effect.

political wing, the BJP, also accepted political responsibilities at the state and even at the central level. The anti-intellectual prejudice which Guru Golwalkar instituted as an RSS policy, has become a serious anachronism, even assuming that it ever had any specific merits. With the influx of modern and well-educated people in the BJP, the demise of this policy is a foregone conclusion, and the Sangh Parivar will have to start to develop its intellectual wing as well. In the preceding sections, we have taken stock of the results of this policy in the past decades.

One of the results has been that ideologically, the Sangh has been at the mercy of its opponents, imbibing their outlook even when criticising them. This has put it in a very weak position in the political arena. It has also prevented the establishment of working relations with potential allies abroad and limited co-operation with other tendencies in India to a co-operation on terms entirely imposed by the latter. Witness the Sangh Parivar's choice for "Gandhian socialism" in the wake of RSS participation in the Gandhian-cum-socialist JP movement. In its own functioning, the Sangh has often been reduced to reliance on rumours and on a political analysis of an abysmally simplistic quality, and to inconsistencies which gave it a reputation of dishonesty.

In its analysis of and polemic against rival religions and ideologies, we find the Sangh Parivar spokesmen invariably avoiding the more complex and more genuinely controversial issues, reducing everything to a question of loyalty or disloyalty to India. By contrast, non-Sangh Hindu revivalist thinkers have developed a serious discourse on Islam, Christianity and Communism, sometimes in line with Western sources of inspiration, sometimes quite original, if not always with the necessary nuances. While the Sangh avoids criticism of Islam but gets entangled in conflicts with Muslims none the less, these non-Sangh authors concentrate on the challenge of Islam as a doctrine.

The contrast between this fairly solid Hindu tradition of debate as applied to contemporary ideological challenges and the poverty and monotony of Sangh discourse, as well as the resultant inconsistencies in the Sangh's policy, have provoked an increasingly vocal dissatisfaction among the educated rank and file. They are particularly piqued at the unprincipled policy of "Muslim appeasement" which, in their view, is being pursued by the leadership, in emulation of long-standing Congress policies. On the other hand, the leadership can undeniably boast of tangible results: the "unprincipled" policy of compromise with secularism and of courting the Muslim community has lessened communal tension, contributed to a pro-India shift in Muslim opinion, and convinced many fence-sitting Hindu voters that the BJP is a force of stability rather than a factor of communal crisis.

POLEMIC AGAINST CHRISTIANITY

In the following sections, we shall consider the Hindu polemical spirit in action, viz. against Christianity, Marxism and Islam. This is important as an explicitation of the Hindu understanding of the ongoing conflicts with these systems of thought or belief, but also as an illustration of the difference in approach between a string of independent authors on the one hand, and the spokesmen of the organized Hindutva movement on the other. The former address issues and appeal to the whole intellectual reservoir of both Hindu civilization and the recent inputs from Western ideology and scholarship, while the latter reduce each and every matter to a simple conflict between "national" and "anti-national". It will become apparent that the former continue the mainstream of the revival movement started by Dayananda, Bankimchandra, Vivekananda, Aurobindo and Shraddhananda, while the latter, in spite of their organizations' numerical and political weight, are most properly understood as an aberrant branch. The Sangh Parivar has, in this respect, strayed from the mainstream into a dead end of monodimensional nationalism.

Christianity as a threat to Hinduism

The first concern of Hindu revivalism is to prevent Hinduism from dying off any further, from being killed in places where it is still alive. In this context, military terms like "attack", "defeat" and "killing" may shock some readers attuned to the project of "interreligious dialogue", but in studying conflicts we should not be inhibited by sentimentalism. Most Hindu revivalists feel that Hinduism is involved in a life-and-death struggle, besieged by enemies who are after its skin and who have already conquered quite a bit of Hindu territory, both geographically and psychologically. Ever since a serial in the RSS weekly *Organiser* was titled "Hindu society under siege", commentators have been saying that Hinduism is suffering from a "siege mentality", implying that it is a purely subjective affair.[100] The Hindu perception is that "residues" of past

[100]The article series by Sita Ram Goel was published as a pamphlet: *Hindu Society under Siege*, 1981; I have used the revised edition of 1992. I surmise that M.J. Akbar's book *India: the Siege Within* (1988) alludes to the same phrase.

imperialisms which colonized India have stayed on and continue to attack Hindu society even after Independence.

The most direct threat is the conversion of Hindus. Even though the success of Islamic and Christian missionaries in India has been very limited when seen in relation to the vast efforts in man-power and finances expended for the purpose, the very fact that an impressive apparatus is at work to take Hindus out of Hinduism is a major irritant.[101] In the Hindu view, this is like having a snake inside the house, waiting around for a chance to strike.

Of course, *every* religion is under siege in the sense that preachers from other religions may be on the prowl, that Liberal and Communist authorities propagate atheism through the schools, and that the media spread crass godless hedonism. Still, the deliberate effort to lure people away from their ancestral religion is perhaps nowhere as serious in magnitude as in India, partly because the country puts no substantial hurdles in the way of internal and foreign missionaries, as opposed to most of its neighbours.

The magnitude of the conversion effort is a decisive aspect to consider. Roman Catholicism in Belgium or Spain or Poland is not "threatened" by the activities of Jehovah's Witnesses: the former has not only inertial loyalty of the population on its side but also institutional power and the education system, while the latter are beggars with nothing to offer except the energy to peddle their message from door to door. By contrast, the missionary religions in India, along with Marxism, have a tremendous organizational advantage over Hinduism, being well-entrenched in political and/or educational institutions and in the media sector, and often enjoying lavish foreign funding. If any comparison can be made, it is with the well-funded US-based Protestant mission in Latin America, against which the Pope protested during his visit to Guatemala, pleading that the people there had been Catholics "for centuries".[102] In a letter to the editor, Mumbai VHP president Ashok Chowgule commented that this is a case of double standards, for Hindus have been Hindus "for centuries" too, yet the Pope is not cancelling the Catholic mission project among Hindus.

---

[101]Though not always strong at fact-finding, Hindu revivalist authors regularly report statements and figures about the Christian mission effort, easy to obtain through Christian publications, e.g. Ram Swarup: *Hindu View of Christianity and Islam*, app.1; B.D. Bharti: *Christian Conversions*; Devendra Swarup, ed.: *Politics of Conversion*.

[102]"Protesting against Protestants", *Observer*, Mumbai, 8.2.1996.

The vigilance of Hindu revivalists is directed mostly against Islam and against Nehruvian secularism; Christianity is only a distant third. In 1939, Veer Savarkar made a distinction in the non-Hindu population between Muslims and others: "The Parsees have ever been working shoulder to shoulder with the Hindus against the English domination. ... Culturally too they are most closely akin to us. In a lesser degree the same thing could be said about the Indian Christians. Although they have yet done but little to contribute any help to the national struggle, yet they have not acted like a millstone round our neck. They are less fanatical and are more amenable to political reason than the Muslims. The Jews are few in number and not antagonistic to our national aspirations. All these minorities of our countrymen are sure to behave as honest and patriotic citizens in an Indian state."[103]

Meanwhile, for more recent history, it should be kept in mind that the power of the Churches in India is totally out of proportion to the numbers of Indians they represent. The Catholic Church by itself is among the biggest owners of real estate, publishing-houses, print media and educational establishments; the situation of the Baptists and other Protestant Churches is, in relative figures, similar. Christians are on the average among the more affluent communities, and have a strong presence in the administration, especially in the two southernmost states.[104] In quarrels between the Hindutva forces and the Muslims or the secularists, the Christian institutions and media are invariably on the anti-Hindu side. Conversely, in some of the polemics between Hindus and Christians which we shall discuss, the secularist media are generally also on the Christian side. There are also Christian armed separatist movements in Nagaland and Mizoram.

Non-Sangh polemic against Christianity

As Christianity still constitutes a very real challenge to Hinduism, Hindu revivalist authors, most notably non-Sangh authors Ram Swarup, Sita Ram Goel, N.S. Rajaram, Arun Shourie and Ishwar Sharan, have produced

---

[103]V.D. Savarkar: *Hindu Rashtra Darshan*, p.23.

[104]One of my contacts, the Canadian-born Swami Devananda, who lives in an ashram near Chennai, claims he was temporarily forced to leave the country as a result of machinations of Christians in the Tamil Nadu administration who fear the influence of anti-Christian Westerners as these are better equipped to argue against Christianity than most Hindus are.

a handful of polemical works against the Christian missionaries. A first and easy target is of course the Churches' alleged record of cultural destruction in India and in other parts of the word, as exemplified by some church buildings in South India standing on the debris of Hindu temples.

This literature includes S.R. Goel: *Catholic Ashrams—Sannyasins or Swindlers?* (1988, 1994), and Arun Shourie: *Missionaries in India*, which, after unexpected hostile reactions from his former Christian dialogue partners, received a sequel: *Arun Shourie and His Christian Critic*, and one more after the media commotion on Hindu-Christian clashes in 1998-99: *Harvesting Our Souls*. Likewise sections of Ishwar Sharan: *The Myth of Saint Thomas and the Mylapore Shiva Temple*, and of N.S. Rajaram: *Secularism, the New Mask of Fundamentalism*, about the strange collusion between the Indian secularists and Church interests against their common enemy, Hinduism.[105] In this respect, anti-Christian polemic is a variation on the better-established tradition of anti-Islamic polemic.

Secondly, Hindu authors have imported the Western secular critique of Christianity and of the Bible into India. Some of this polemic is harsh and implacable, e.g. Goel's book *Jesus Christ, an Artifice for Aggression* contains chapter titles like "Jesus is junk", and "Christianity is a big lie", while his introduction to *Vindicated by Time*, the reprint of the Niyogi Committee Report (see below), contains the allegation that the Nazi Holocaust was the logical outcome of centuries of Christian anti-Jewish indoctrination.[106] Some of it is purely scholarly, e.g. Goel's *Papacy, Its Docrine and History*, documenting an institution and the influence it has exercised. But whether in moderate or harsh tones, this whole line of argument is in essence a transfer to India of the anti-Christian polemic

---

[105]By contrast, Ananda Coomaraswamy always used to draw attention to the similarities (in ethics, philosophy, ritual, art) which Christianity and Hinduism had developed in spite of their different origins, see especially his *Metaphysics* and *The Dance of Shiva*. Simply by virtue of being religions, Christianity and Hinduism had to go through parallel developments, but that doesn't nullify their doctrinal antagonism.

[106]Though few people even inside the Christian Churches would deny that Christian anti-Semitism was a contributing factor to the Holocaust, at least three other, *modern* factors must be taken into account, viz. quasi-Darwinist *race* theory, *envy* against the successful emancipated Jews who had come out of the ghettoes where they had lived separately in the Christian age (of the same type as the envy of the Chinese in Indonesia or of the Indians in Africa), and finally *Communism*, which opened up new horizons in mass-murder but had wrongly been identified as a "Jewish" movement in propaganda writings including the notorious *Protocols of the Elders of Zion*. These factors cannot be reduced to Christian influence.

which has animated Western intellectual circles from the eighteenth century till today.[107]

Indeed, Goel, Rajaram and Sharan profusely quote Western critics of Christianity, such as Thomas Jefferson, Mark Twain and Bertrand Russell. In Arun Shourie's dialogue with Catholic bishops (recorded in his book *Missionaries in India*), this most prominent Hindu revivalist thinker repeatedly challenges the bishops to inform their flock of the findings of modern scholarship on the Bible and the genesis of Christianity. N.S. Rajaram was the first to present to the Indian public the story and relevance of the Dead Sea Scrolls and the doubts they cast on certain unicity claims of Christianity (for example, the celebration by a Jewish sect of a Last Supper rite decades before Christ's birth should indicate that the Last Supper was but a dramatization of an existing practice, not its origin).[108]

He has also reiterated all the allegations from the Western Leftist press about Vatican intrigues in Italian politics, the *Banco Ambrosiano* scandal, the strange death of Pope John-Paul I, rumoured links with the Mafia, the controversial role of *Opus Dei*, the alleged cover-up of the Dead Sea Scrolls, all rendered more relevant to India by the warning that Sonia Gandhi may be an agent of this Popish Plot.[109] It is remarkable that the so-called Hindu Right has adopted all the rationalist and Leftist arguments against Christianity, highlighting its imperialism and connivance with colonialism and secular exploitative regimes, its miracle-mongering reliance on people's gullibility, its oppression of Pagans and women, etc. Conversely, it is totally ignorant of or uninterested in the Rightist critique of Christianity (as being sentimental, feminine, plebeic, egalitarian) developed by a Friedrich Nietzsche or a Julius Evola.

A third line of polemic is more specifically Hindu, and has been developed by Ram Swarup.[110] It is a spiritual critique, and questions the spiritual value of conversion, e.g.: "Regarded from a deeper angle, Christian proselytising is an arrogant idea, a denial both of God and of

[107]E.g. the multi-volume catalogue of alleged Christian wrongdoings by Karl-Heinz Deschner: *Kriminalgeschichte des Christentums*, "Crime history of Christianity".

[108]N.S. Rajaram: *Profiles in Deception. Ayodhya and the Dead Sea Scrolls*.

[109]Serial by N.S. Rajaram in *Organiser*, March 1998, largely reproduced in Frawley and Rajaram: *Crusade in India*, pp.27-36.

[110]Chiefly Ram Swarup: *Hindu View of Christianity and Islam* (1992) and *Pope John-Paul II on Eastern Religions and Yoga, a Hindu-Buddhist Rejoinder* (1995).

one's neighbour; it denies God, denies His working in others, denies the many ways in which He fulfils Himself. It helps neither the missionaries nor the converts."[111]

Ram Swarup attacks the principle of "proxy religions", meaning religions in which contact with the Divine is established through privileged intermediaries, the Prophet or God's Only-Begotten Son, as opposed to religions of direct experience. Though to my knowledge no formal rebuttal of Ram Swarup's positions has ever been attempted, one could argue that (like Swami Vivekananda) he reduces Hinduism to its spiritual component, disregarding more problematic aspects, i.e. the common reliance on ritualistic mediation by a monopoly-holding priesthood which is, in a sense, also a "proxy". To be sure, this could at worst only be a mirror-image of the more common reduction of Hinduism to only its problematic aspects, its caste oppression and widow-burning and all the other classics of drain inspection.[112]

The myth of Saint Thomas

A special point in the Hindu-Christian debate concerns the myth of the apostle Thomas coming to India to bring Christianity there in AD 52. This would make Christianity in India older than in Europe and thus form a strong argument against the association of Christianity with colonialism. The case against it has been argued by Ishwar Sharan in his *Myth of Saint Thomas and the Mylapore Shiva Temple*. He points out that even Christian

---

[111]Ram Swarup: "The ethics of conversion", *Organiser*, 8.9.1996. He cites, for the 1970-85 period, 1.47 million converts per year in Africa, and 44.000 in South Asia, as well as an example, courtesy *Hinduism Today*, of the type of faith involved in conversion: "In 1993, a new convert in Fiji burned a Hindu temple to the ground to 'see if the God could save it'. Put to this kind of test, Jehovah and Allah would fare no better."

[112]Chetan Bhatt (*Liberation and Purity*, p.156) laments the fact that Western spiritualists always focus on Hindu philosophy and disregard the evil social and political aspects of Hinduism. If true, this provides only the mirror-image of the selective vision which is fairly common among Hindutva-watchers, viz. to reduce Hinduism to "social injustice" and "caste calculus". But those spiritualists are not bound by any deontology to remain objective and balanced; the academic experts, by contrast Ishwar Sharan (*Myth of Saint Thomas*, p.162, seconding S.R. Goel: *Papacy*) cites "distinguished scholars like R. Garbe, A. Harnack and L. De la Vallee-Poussin" as well as bishop Stephen Neill (*History of Christianity in India*, Cambridge University Press 1984) as having "denied credibility to the *Acts of Thomas*, on which the whole story is based"; on pp.38-9, he lists more sceptics, including Jacques Basnage, Maurice Winternitz, Arnold Toynbee *et al.*

historians in the West have become sceptical of this story, and that they favour the account of Christianity being brought to India by Syrian refugees from the Persian empire in AD 345.

For one thing, the legend's textual basis, the apocryphal *Acts of Thomas*, is ambiguous at best.[113] Its setting of the story indicates Arsacid Iran (several Persian names, "a desert country") more than India, and its use of the term *India* should be seen in its context: in the pre-colonial age, "India" often meant "Asia" from Yemen to Japan, e.g. when Columbus thought he had landed in Cathay/China or Zipangu/Japan, he called the natives "Indians". Furthermore, if the Church relegated the *Acts of Thomas* to the apocryphal dustbin, it was not without reason: the text paints an unflattering picture of both Thomas and Jesus.

First of all, Thomas is called Jesus' twin-brother, so what with Jesus as "God's only-begotten son"? Thomas is also said to be sold as a slave by his brother Jesus (the redeemer!), then to have made a career as an unscrupulous magician who had a boy killed by magic for not serving him quickly enough, and who lured women away from their families. Finally, Thomas's "martyrdom" came about when he arrogantly refused to heed the request to leave, a request made by the king who had protected him against the anger of the people yet found it impossible to do so any longer given the apostle's persistent anti-social behaviour. Can such a problematic text be upheld by Christians just because it supports their claim to an Indian sojourn of an apostle?

At any rate, Indian and missionary Christians continue to invest heavily in defending the Saint Thomas story. This is understandable; less so is the support they are getting from the secularists, who are always full of contempt for religious myths such as those pertaining to Rama's Ayodhya. It is a standard phrase in political speeches (by Nehru, by presidents Rajendra Prasad and S. Radhakrishnan)[114] as well as newspaper columns by secularists that Christianity was brought to India in its very first years. Ishwar Sharan's book started as an article written in reply to an article by Christian author C.A. Simon, affirming the Thomas legend.[115]

---

[113]In the 1980s, in the course of "Theology of Non-Christian Religions" taught at the Katholieke Universiteit Leuven, Frank de Graeve s.j. repeatedly told us that the Saint Thomas story was highly apocryphal indeed, and that Christianity more probably arrived in India only in the fourth century.

[114]Quoted in Ishwar Sharan: *Myth of Saint Thomas*, p.74.

[115]C.A. Simon: "In memory of a slain Saint", *Indian Express* (Madras), 30.12.1989.

Simon's article had been published in the Madras edition of *Indian Express*, which refused to publish Sharan's reply except in truncated form as a "letter to the editor". He and several of his friends tried to get the true story across to the *Indian Express* readers, but to no avail: the esteemed paper's pages were open to Christian legend, not to Hindu scholarship. Instead, the editor, along with his colleague at *The Hindu*, chose to greet the first edition of Ishwar Sharan's book with a renarration of the legend (but not *as* legend) on the children's page. It is that kind of incident which convinces Hindus that secularism is but a euphemism for Hindu-baiting: secularist values like rationalism are laconically dropped the moment they threaten to support a Hindu cause or to undermine the cause of an anti-Hindu party.

Another aspect of the Thomas legend is that it contains blood libel against the Hindus, particularly the Brahmins. According to the *Acts*, Thomas was killed twenty years after his arrival, in AD 72, by king Mazda's soldiers, in punishment for his "sorceries" and "evil deeds" and after the king had exercised "long patience with thee".[116] He was killed *be ruhme*, Syriac for "with a spear". Centuries later, these consonants (Syriac usually writes no vowels) were reinterpreted as rendering *brahma*, "(by) a Brahmin". No location for the execution is given, but the sixteenth-century Portuguse colonizers decided that it was on the Mylapore beach outside Madras, where a Jain and a Shaiva temple were demolished to make way for the San Thomé cathedral in commemoration of the apostle's martyrdom.

One could say to this: "So what? The European landscape is studded with churches containing false relics of false saints to whom false martyrdom is attributed." But look at it from the Hindu angle: Hindus had the good grace to give asylum to the Christian refugees in AD 345, allowing them to maintain their separate identity in full freedom for seventeen centuries, and now the thanks they get for it is that visitors of the San Thome cathedral are told about fanatical Brahmins murdering the noble founder of Indian Christianity. And then the secularist establishment makes it worse by blocking the public's access to the scholarly view and continuing to instil the blood-libel legend. It is highly significant for the power equation in India that this state of affairs is possible at all.

---

[116]The concluding part of the *Acts of Thomas* is given in its entirety by Ishwar Sharan: *Myth of Saint Thomas*, p.27.

Is there a conversion strategy?

A strange element in the Indian conversion debate is that secularists and even some Christian spokesmen deny the existence of a conversion programme. In the case of the secularists, this is a purely opportunistic position: they perforce have to deny whatever the Hindu revivalists say, and they have to take the position which best serves the interests of the latter's enemies. In the case of Christians, we are dealing with double-speak, though usually honest in the sense that they themselves really believe in it: they claim that conversion work somehow isn't really conversion work, that "only the Holy Spirit can work conversion" so that the missionary's work must be something else, say "bringing the Pagans in touch with Jesus Christ's liberating message", which is, *not* the same thing as converting people (an example follows).

However, that the goal of converting *the* (i.e. all) Hindus and other non-Christians still animates the missionaries, has been ascertained by Hindu authors (and can be ascertained by anyone) from Christian sources.[117] Even the general media could not keep such first-hand testimonies out of view altogether. In autumn 1999, the synod of the Southern Baptists (USA) reiterated the classical Christian position that Hindus live in darkness and are in need of Jesus Christ, and a few weeks later the Pope came to Delhi to say in so many words that the Church wants to "reap a rich harvest of faith in Asia". The secularists felt badly let down by the Pope, because they had been dismissing as paranoid hate propaganda the Hindu misgivings about Church designs on the Hindu soul. To all those, secularist or Christian, who wanted to blur the issue, the Pope's unambiguous statements came as a most unkind cut.

Now for an example. To limit the damage caused by the Pope's speech, Christian theologian Ambrose Pinto hurried to explain, in a fine example of convoluted apologetics, that "there is Christian jargon in the

[117]Summaries of evangelical reports, reproductions of pamphlets and correspondence with a number of missionaries including Bede Griffiths are included in S.R. Goel: *Hindu-Christian Encounters* and Ram Swarup: *Hindu View of Christianity and Islam.* A recent document by the Pope on Asian religions is discussed in Ram Swarup's *Hindu-Buddhist Rejoinder to Pope John-Paul II.* For a Western reminder that conversion is still Church policy, and that the Third World Christians still support this policy, see V. Neckebrouck: *De stomme duivelen. Het anti-missionair syndroom in de Westerse Kerk* (Dutch: "The mute demons. The anti-missionary syndrome in the Western Church").

document and exclusivist language... But to interpret such language without proper knowledge of Christian theology is dangerous and misleading." What the Pope really meant was that he wants Asians to "follow the inspiration of Jesus Christ to provide a better quality of life to their people especially the poor and the disadvantaged among them".[118] But the difference between becoming a Christian and "following the inspiration of Jesus Christ" is not explained.

Next, as a Liberation theologian, Pinto stoops to making his religion subservient to socialism: Christians in Asia should "move away from religious practices and charitable works to works of change of social structure". Yet, even then he doesn't lose sight of the propagation of Christianity: the Church should "align itself with the larger secular forces that believe in the tenets of social change, socialism and egalitarianism to make Christ known all over Asia". So, even when trying to soften the Pope's naked announcement of further conversion campaigns, this Church spokesman cannot bring himself to denying or concealing the plan "to make Christ known all over Asia".

Pinto also gives new flesh to the myth of the apostle Thomas coming to India: "Since among the countries of Asia *Christianity is the oldest in India*, the Pope decided to promulgate the document from India."[119] As if the Pope had the choice to promulgate it in any other Asian country (except the Catholic Philippines, where he had made the same statement about a rich harvest of faith in Asia a few years earlier). Christianity was brought to India by Syrian Christians from Iran, but could the Pope have made his statement in Damascus or Teheran? Or Islamabad or Kabul or Rangoon or Beijing, for that matter? The Pope could not go and make his statement in Teheran or Beijing: as long as Islam and Communism (and in some countries, Buddhism) prevent Christian proselytizing in their domains, the conversion of Asia essentially means the conversion of India, which may then function as a base for further expansion once the rest of Asia becomes more accommodating.

But the main point here is that the Pope's Hindu critics were absolutely right in identifying the conversion of Hindus to Christianity as the main goal of Christian activity in India. That Christians must spread

---

[118]Ambrose Pinto: "Not a call for conversion", *Hindustan Times*, 14.12.1999.

[119]Ambrose Pinto: "Not a call for conversion", *Hindustan Times*, 14.12.1999; emphasis added.

the faith can be ascertained from the basic texts of Christianity. As Saint Paul said: "Woe to me if I do not preach the Gospel!"[120] It has also been certified from official Christian sources, and the Pope himself has come to the land of the Hindus to say it to their faces. For those who are in the habit of dubbing every claim made by Hindu revivalists as "lies", here is a very clear-cut case where Hindu spokesmen along with the Pope were speaking the verifiable truth, while some of their Christian and most of their secularist opponents were saying something else.

Conversion and "dialogue"

The Ram Swarup school writes against Christian efforts from a love for Hinduism itself: every conversion means that a person abandons the practices which make up Hindu tradition. In the present situation, this concern implies first of all vigilance against the more subtle new ways of enticing Hindus out of their native traditions, particularly under the cover of "dialogue".

One might be tempted to wonder: considering newer approaches like "acculturation", "dialogue" and "*fulfilment* (of native religiosity) through Christ", can conversion still be described as an "attack" on the converts' former religion? The Hindu answer is simple: yes, because conversion, if successful on a large scale, means that the abandoned religion is left to die for want of practitioners. The empirical argument that "enough Hindus still remain" is rejected: it is not said in any official Islamic or Christian publication that conversion should stop halfway, that it should stop at this border or that percentage. The intention is and remains the complete conversion of the Hindu population, which amounts to the final death of Hinduism.[121] One theatre in this war is the dialogue front.

From 1980 to 1995, Sita Ram Goel was the treasurer of the Abhishiktananda Society, a Christian platform for Hindu-Christian dialogue, which included big names like Raimundo Panikkar and Bettina

---

[120]1 Corinthians 9:16.

[121]The Church in the West has become so mild that many of its members see no use for a conversion effort anymore. For a reminder that conversion is still Church policy, and that the Third World Christians still support this policy, see V. Neckebrouck: *De stomme duivelen. Het anti-missionair syndroom in de Westerse Kerk* (Dutch: "The mute demons. The anti-missionary syndrome in the Western Church"). In the case of Islam, there is no doubt at all. Even I have been sollicited for conversion to Islam quite a number of times.

and Odette Bäumer, and James Stuart, along with Ram Swarup.[122] Though Goel ultimately quit when he found its Christian members were backbiting against him or avoiding him, but never confronting him, he had certainly proven his willingness to engage in dialogue. All the more reason for him not to accept any compromise on this point of conversion and its new strategies. His experiences made Goel especially sceptical of the recent theologies of "acculturation" and "fulfilment". Less experienced Hindus may have a less solid scepticism, but usually also less of an interest in comparative religion, so the dialogue wing of the Church has a hard time finding valid Hindu partners in the first place.

The "theology of fulfilment", which admittedly presents a welcome "change from calumny to expressions of empathy",[123] teaches that Pagan spirituality has "prepared" the Pagans for Christianity, and now only a small addition is needed to bring the religious evolution to its fulfilment, to turn the hidden "unknown Christ" contained in their ancestral religion into an "acknowledged Christ".[124] Thus, the Indian tribals are told that they have been "monotheists" all along, almost-Christians with only the Gospel information on the historical Christ missing. Similarly, the Upanishads are searched for uplifting and potentially monotheistic or Salvation-oriented statements ("Lead us from death to immortality"), so that Sanskritic Hinduism can equally be presented as a natural preparation of the Pagans for Christ.[125]

Against this focusing on the continuity between a convert's former and new religion, Hindu revivalists point out that conversion, if successful on a large scale, still means that the abandoned religion of the converts is left to die for want of practitioners. And the fact itself of dialogue and

---

[122]In his own version, Goel resigned from the society when it turned out that its Christian members, who were always friendly to his face, were backbiting against him; he thought this was an odd form of "dialogue". At any rate, he was described as a "fanatical Hindu fundamentalist" by Abhishiktananda Society member Vandana Mataji: "Formation in Ashrams", *Studies in Formative Spirituality* (Pittsburgh), November 1990.

[123]A. Shourie: *Missionaries in India*, p.228.

[124]The terms are from the titles of Raimundo Panikkar: *The Unknown Christ of Hinduism*, and M.M. Thomas: *The Acknowledged Christ of the Indian Renaissance*.

[125]In 1988, I attended the Christmas eucharist in Nagwa, Varanasi, and was surprised to hear that the first readings were from the Upanishads. This seems to be fairly common, as part of the Church's "acculturation" policy, though it goes beyond what the Church leadership in Rome would explicitly condone.

similar gentle-sounding concepts being conceived as instruments of conversion, is ascertained from primary sources. A Vatican document of 1990, *Redemptoris Missio* ("The Redeemer's Mission") confirms that "dialogue" is still a means of conversion rather than a meeting between equals. Winand Callewaert, a prominent Catholic Indologist (and in spite of religious and political differences, a friend of Ram Swarup) summarized *Redemptoris Missio* (RM) thus:

"The Church is by definition missionary. ... For our subject, it is important to note that RM strongly emphasizes the need of missionary activity in Asia. For this mission, 'dialogue' and 'inculturation' are recommended as the best strategies. The challenge consists in tuning that dialogue to the primordial goal, viz. evangelization. ... After all, [RM declares:] 'the obvious road to salvation is the Church, which alone is entrusted with the fulness of the instruments of salvation.' ... RM continues to assert that 'Christ is the only redeemer of all men', 'the only mediator between God and men'."[126]

In spite of secularist attempts to blur issues, Hindu revivalists conclude that this one is crystal clear: as per the official Christian sources: the goal of the missionaries in India is to convert every non-Christian to Christianity. This means that if Hinduism chooses to survive, it finds itself in a life-and-death struggle with missionary Christianity. That need not imply the inevitability of armed struggle, but a no-nonsense scepticism would be a minimum.

A different aspect of this matter pointed out by Ram Swarup is that the syncretistic practices of the "Christian Swamis" and other acculturationists (an Om sign on a Cross, saffron robes, talk and practice of meditation) is not approved by Church authorities in the Vatican, nor by many Indian Christians.[127] Indeed, his book *Pope John-Paul II on Eastern Religions and Yoga: a Hindu-Buddhist Rejoinder* (1995) was occasioned precisely by one of the Pope's statements (*Crossing the Threshold of Hope*, 1994) condemning the incorporation of yogic practices in the spiritual discipline of Christian clerics and laymen.

It is, incidentally, a little disappointing that as the former mastermind of Indian anti-Communism, Ram Swarup fails to acknowledge the crucial role of this Pope in the fall of Soviet Communism. While an opponent in

---

[126]W. Callewaert: "Christenen in India", *India* (Brussels) June 1995, pp.17-20.

[127]See e.g. Victor J.F. Kulanday: *The Paganization of the Church in India* (1988).

the religious sphere, it should be reckoned important enough that he has also acted as an ally in the political sphere. Further, the whole Hindu argument against the acculturationist tendency does not stop to acknowledge the sincerity with which many Christians profess this new approach. They may be self-deluded about the possibility of Hindu-Christian syncretism, but in most cases they are not animated by an intention to deceive others. On the contrary, many dialogue-prone Christians are genuine admirers of Hinduism.

The fate of Paganism

For the long-term effects of conversion, reference is frequently made to the fate of Pagan religions in now-Christian countries, considering the "great similarity between old European Paganism and Hinduism".[128] Thus, the searching of Greek philosophy for elements which could be reinterpreted by the Church Fathers as a "preparation" for Christianity, prefigured a similar exercise with the Upanishadic, Bhakti and tribal traditions. The Church Fathers managed to incorporate the Old Testament as the preparation of the Jews for Christ, and Plato as the preparation of the Greeks for Christ, so now it is simple enough to reinterpret Hindu philosophy as the appropriate Hindu form of preparation for Christ.

When Christianity converted Europe, it already "acculturated" and adopted a lot of Pagan lore: the Yuletide became Christmas, ancient gods were turned into Saints, Virgil was still read as a matter of Latin language training for clerics, etc. It is therefore no surprise to see "Christian swamis" dress up as Hindu swamis, use Hindu or tribal symbols in their church interior, if possible locate churches on pre-Christian sacred sites (common in the colonial period, still done in tribal villages), incorporate Vedic one-liners in the peripheral parts of their liturgy.

But from the Pagan viewpoint, these elements of continuity were and are small consolation. The decisive change in Europe was that the sacred fires on the altars to Vesta, Zeus, Lug or Wodan were extinguished, their hymns forgotten, their worship suspended. Like Latin, Pagan mythology became a dead language. Conversion also meant that Aristotle and the

[128] Ram Swarup: *Hindu View of Christianity and Islam*, p.49. He reports Nigel Pennick's speech at a neo-Pagan conference, to the effect that "their old religion was part of a larger religious system which once prevailed in other parts of the world as well" and that "Hinduism represented the Eastern expression of this universal tradition" so that "Hindus might come to accept Europe's Pagans as a European branch of Hinduism".

Stoics were banished and forgotten for a thousand years because their teachings were in conflict with Christian dogma. True, some argumentative techniques and metaphysical concepts of the philosophers were incorporated into nascent Christian theology. But the fundamental spirit of philosophy, its radical doubt, its fearless inquisitiveness, was curtailed by the basic Christian attitude of *faith*, or what Ram Swarup calls "proxy" religion. Only marginal Pagan doctrines and practices remained alive among the illiterate masses, increasingly distorted, unrespectable ("superstition", "witchcraft"), and finally disappearing as well. It is that very fate which Hindus with an attachment to their tradition want to avoid.

The comparison between the known fate of European Paganism and the missionaries' designs for Hinduism is even more apt than the Hindu authors realize, for more parallels can be found than have hitherto been pointed out. The modernmost trends in Christian mission policy in India were already in evidence in the christianization of Europe. Thus, the association of Christianity with the most advanced civilization of the day, material as well as intellectual, was and still is used as a trump card in effecting *voluntary* conversions. The Russian elite converted after it was impressed by the brilliance and artistic perfection of Byzantine liturgy. The Germanic tribes were impressed by the technical know-how and organizational efficiency of the Roman Empire, appropriated by Christianity (which had had no merit in their development). For an Old Saxon as much as for a contemporary Santhal or Naga, the great civilizational step of first learning to read was cleverly fused with indoctrination in the Christian religion. This way, a general association of Paganism with backwardness and Christianity with progress played a role in both early medieval Europe and British India, and even in the backward areas of independent India.

The parallel between the fate of European Paganism and the threat to Hinduism is developed in some detail by Ram Swarup in his book *The Word as Revelation: Names of Gods*, but he concludes on a constructive note: "Hindu India has a sense of continuity with its past which other nations that changed their religion at some later stage, lack. It is also known that the Hindu religion preserves many old layers and forms. Therefore, its study may link us not only with its own past forms but also with the religious consciousness, intuitions and forms that prevailed in the past in Europe, in Greece, in Rome, in many Scandinavian and Baltic countries, amongst the Germanic and Slavic peoples and also in several countries of the Middle East. In short, the study may reveal a fundamental form of spiritual consciousness which is wider than its Hindu expression."[129]

Nationalism is totally out of the question here: Ram Swarup evokes a world-wide struggle between proselytizing Christianity and Islam on the one hand, and all the traditional native religions on the other. He does not accept the purely defensive attitude of the many Hindus who (in the footsteps of Mahatma Gandhi) consider all religions equally valid. In particular, he is skeptical of that Hindu nationalist attitude which considers it perfectly right if someone is a Christian, but which objects to this if that Christian is a convert from Hinduism. From a critique of conversion, he proceeds to a critique of Christianity itself, both from the Enlightenment angle and from a specifically Hindu spiritual angle. Consequently, he invites all Christians to rediscover their spiritual heritage, long eclipsed by the conquering religion.

Sangh polemic against Christianity

In the Sangh Parivar literature, it will be hard to find one sentence criticizing Christianity. Shripaty Sastry, RSS leader of the key state of Maharashtra, affirms: "I revere Christ. One of the reasons why I do so is that I am a Hindu. There is much to admire in Christianity—the life-story of Jesus Christ, sayings of the prophets, educative parables and the ideals presented therein."[130] This position is very common among modern Hindus, both villagers and urban sophisticates.

Sastry generalizes his own respect for Christ and Christianity to the Sangh as a whole: in the RSS literature of the last fifty years, "I challenge anyone of you to point out a single derogatory word or expression towards Jesus Christ, Biblical teachings, Prophets of the Bible, Mohammed Paigambar or Koran, or pilgrimage to the Holy Land Jerusalem or Mecca, or about anything which is purely religious. RSS has nothing against the above; it just cannot even afford to be so for the simple reason that within the Hindu fold numerous religions flourish. Religion is not the concern of the RSS at all."[131]

---

[129]Ram Swarup: *The Word as Revelation*, p.108.

[130]S. Sastry: *Christianity in India*, p.5.

[131]S. Sastry: *Christianity in India*, p.18. On pp.21-2, he claims to know a good many Christian RSS members who have "subordinated all other considerations of life to the supreme interest of the nation like any other Hindu of the RSS". One Christian author who wrote favourably about the RSS was Anthony Elenjimittan: *Philosophy and Action of the RSS for Hind Swaraj* (1951).

If it contains no criticism of Christian religion, Sangh literature contains all the more criticism of Christian people. Thus, Jay Dubashi off-hand rejects the view that the religious fanaticism of the Portuguese colonizers was an intrinsic trait of the Christian religion: "What the Christians did in Goa, the Muslims did in the rest of India. They were all foreigners, and the fact that they were Christians or Muslims is immaterial. ... The Portuguese vandalised Hindu temples in the territories they had occupied by force, just as the marauding Moghuls did. They did so because they wanted to humiliate the Hindus, not because they were good Christians or good Muslims."[132] In this approach, the religion of Portuguese temple-demolishers is not important, only their foreignness is. Which leaves unexplained why the Enlightened British foreigners did not demolish temples, nor why native converts like Malik Kafur did.

In general, this literature ignores Western scholarship and the Enlightenment criticism of Christianity, and focuses exclusively on the role which the missionaries have played or are playing in India, especially their political role. A typical example, discussing records of conversion and the missions' international sponsoring, is Brahma Datt Bharti: *Christian Conversions* (1980). The Sangh's Deendayal Research Institute has also contributed one substantial book to this literature, viz. Devendra Swarup, ed.: *Politics of Conversion* (1986). However, the classic in this genre is not an individual write-up, but an official report commissioned by the (Congress) State Government of Madhya Pradesh in the 1950s: the *Niyogi Committee Report*.[133]

The single most frightening moment for the Christian missions in independent India was in the mid-1950s, when the Bharatiya Jana Sangh was hardly in the picture as a political force. Not the BJS but the Congress governments of Madhya Pradesh and Madhya Bharat (a state now merged with Madhya Pradesh) ordered investigations of allegedly fraudulent conversions through social pressure and material inducement by Christian missionaries in the tribal belt. At that time, Congress was still a largely

---

[132]Jay Dubashi: "'The Goa Inquisition'", *Organiser*, 13.10.1991, a review of A.K. Priolkar: *The Goa Inquisition*.

[133]The *Niyogi Committee Report*, formally the *Report of the Christian Missionary Activities Enquiry Committee*, is republished in 1998 by Voice of India. Committee chairman B.S. Niyogi, far from being a Hindu fanatic, was one of the most prominent converts to Buddhism during the 1956 mass conversion ceremony led by Dr. Ambedkar.

Hindu party, with an important Hindu revivalist section holding out in the provinces against Nehru's increasing grip on the party. The power equation was such that Nehru could not prevent the state governments from commissioning the Report, but they, in turn, could not make Nehru take any action on the basis of the Committee's findings.[134]

On the sidelines, the BJS supported the implementation of the recommendations concluding the report, especially for a much stricter control of missionary activities and finances. The BJS 1957 election manifesto stated: "The recommendations of the Niyogi Committee and Rege Committee will be implemented to free the Bharatiya Christians from the anti-national influence of foreign missionaries."[135] Remark the language used: it sounds as if the BJS wants to protect the *Christians* against the missionaries. Then already, it apparently felt the need to cloak its concern for Hindu interests in an ostensible concern for the minorities.

Surprisingly, many Sangh Parivar stalwarts, at least in their public statements, do not see conversion to Christianity as a problem, and when they do, they still try to put it in a Christian-friendly way, e.g. Swami Ranjeet invokes Jesus Himself as an argument against conversion: "Christ never ordered conversion. He was a reformer of his own religion—Judaism. He lived and died a Jew".[136] If they go out of their way to attack the missionaries, it is usually about the *way* in which conversion is effected, rather than against the right to convert itself. Thus, Guru Golwalkar said: "We have nothing against the Christians except their methods of gaining converts. When they give medicines to the sick or bread to the hungry, they should not exploit the situation by propagating their religion to those people."[137]

It seems to me that from a Hindu angle, focusing on the *methods* of conversion misses the point. To be sure, the use of service and material incentives for conversion purposes can again be certified from Christian sources, e.g. Protestant missionaries in Pakistan (not Hindu fanatics, they) allege that the conversion of thousands of Protestant converts to

---

[134]There is also a Christian reply to the Niyogi Report, viz. A. Soares, ed.: *Truth Shall Prevail. Reply to the Niyogi Committee Report.*

[135]BJS: *Party Documents*, vol.1, p.82. The Rege Committee was the Madhya Bharat counterpart of the Niyogi Committee.

[136]Swami Ranjeet: "An honest crusade", *Organiser*, 17.3.1996.

[137]M.S. Golwalkar: *Spotlights*, p.56.

Catholicism on the occasion of famines was first of all the result of relief supplies: "Partition in 1947 left the Christian community financially poor and economically insecure, because many of their Hindu and Sikh landlords had fled the country. Severe floods devastated the Punjab in 1950, 1954, 1955 and 1959, destroying the homes and crops of thousands of Christians. Church World service and Catholic relief organizations poured in badly needed supplies. When the emergency situation was over, Church World Service diminished its supplies and later discontinued them altogether. ... The Catholic Church continued to receive massive relief supplies. These were distributed to Catholic school children and church members. In order to be eligible to receive regular relief goods, thousands of nominal Protestants became members of the Roman Catholic Church."[138]

So there you have it: material incentives are used to gain and retain converts. This also came to light after the murder of missionary Graham Staines in late 1998: in spite of his family's refusal to hand over copies of their despatches to the homefront bulletin *Tidings* to the police investigators, a few were traced elsewhere and turned out to monitor the harvest in souls gradually being reaped as a result of the missionary's investment in material gifts and social service.[139] That service was not purely altruistic, it was meant as a bargaining chip in order to get the natives to accept the missionary's message. And indeed, every Christian parishioner the world over knows that the money he donates to the Church serves, among other purposes, to give some material flesh to the Good News propagation of the missionaries.

Yet, if Christianity were the true religion, the exclusive road to Salvation, this tricking of materially deprived people into the faith by means of material incentives would be a very small matter. Against this background, the fuss over the methods used becomes petty and sterile: either Christianity is true, and then the converts should be grateful for being tricked into it, or Christianity is false, and then the focus should be on proving its falsity. Also, one cannot deny that those who leave their comforts and career behind to live among tribals in a jungle do have a genuine idealism, and are at least subjectively being altruistic when they

---

[138]Frederick and Margaret Stock: *People Movements in the Punjab*, p.316.

[139]Reported and quoted in some detail in Arun Shourie: *Harvesting Our Souls*, pp.15-19.

render services not in order to "win" the tribal souls for themselves, but on the contrary to "give" to them the Way, the Truth and the Life. Whether these missionaries are vampires trying to deprive the tribal of his soul, or altruistic saints who sacrifice a lot in order to *save* the tribal's soul from Pagan darkness, entirely depends on whether Christianity is true or not. But in the whole Sangh Parivar literature, I have never (or it would have to be in Dr. Rajaram's guest columns in *Organiser*) come across a single line arguing against the truth claim of Christianity.

Hindutva media prefer to pay attention to more superficial data, such as Hindu-Christian clashes: "Karungal, a Christian-dominated village in Kanyakumari district of Tamilnadu was the latest scene of Christian vandalism, when a Ganesha idol was smashed to pieces by a gang of Christian fundamentalists."[140] Or the Christian expulsion of the non-Christian Reang tribals in Mizoram, one of whom is quoted as saying: "If we embrace Christianity, we can settle down freely. This is what the Mizo terrorists want."[141] Or, of course, the cases of Christian separatism in the North-East, mostly in Nagaland and Mizoram, which have occasionally attracted international media attention.[142] Older publications in this tradition include Thanulinga Nadar: *Unrest at Kanyakumari* (1983), and Major T.R. Vedantham: *Christianity, a Political Problem* (1984). The core message invariably is that Christianity encourages separatism, whether social (pitting converts against Hindus) or political-territorial.

A case study in Sangh polemic against Christianity

The official position of the Sangh, repeated very consistently in many forums (though it is hard to believe that it is a heartfelt conviction) is that conversion from one cult to another is a purely individual matter to which no Hindu could object. The problem only starts when conversion also has a political dimension, viz. by changing the convert's political loyalty. The only thing which the Sangh officially holds against the Christian

---

[140]"Christian fundamentalists destroy idol", *Organiser*, 11.12.1994.

[141]Pramod Kumar: "Non-Christian Reang tribals forced to leave Mizoram", *Organiser*, 21.12.1997.

[142]"The most important Naga group brandishes the motto 'Nagaland for Christ', which doesn't keep them from massacring the equally Christian Kukis", according to Freddy De Pauw: "Toenemende etnische onrust in noordoosten van India" (Dutch: "Increasing ethnic unrest in India's North-East"), *De Standaard*, 27.7.1994.

missionaries is their alleged role in "anti-national activities", making people disloyal to India and fomenting separatism among the tribals, who have been redefined as the "indigenous people of India".

This insistence on the status of the tribals as "indigenous" has specific political implications: it brings the Indian tribals in the same category as the "indigenous peoples" of America and Oceania, and for them, the World Council of Churches has a declared policy of political separatism, laid down in the Darwin Declaration of May 1989, in which "the Churches confess to having been part of the problem and rise to become part of the solution, in keeping with the principles of the Gospel". As a spokesman of the RSS tribal organization *Vanavâsî Kalyân Ashram* pointed out to me, this declaration includes the following political programme: "...(4) Indigenous peoples strive for and demand the full spectrum of autonomy available in the principle of self-determination, including the right to re-establish our own nation-states, independent of the jurisdiction of our invaders and their accompanying political structures. (5) Indigenous peoples shall control our own institutions of government, our economies and our social and legal structures."[143]

Nothing can spur an RSS man to action like a whisper about separatism. So, 99 per cent of RSS writings about the missionaries deal with their alleged involvement in "anti-national activities". RSS author Bhanu Pratap Shukla starts his diagnosis with the typical RSS attention to matters of national identity: "To the majority of Indians, especially the Hindus, proselytisation means only a change of faith or way of worship and as such they do not take it very seriously, because they think that a faith or a way of worship is an individual's relationship with his creator and as such every man should be free to have his own ideas in these matters. But Christian proselytisation is not that innocent. It not only affects a change of faith or way of worship but also tries to give them a separate nationality."[144]

In other words: we don't mind if you convert Hindus, even all Hindus, as long as it is only a "change of faith" and not a "change of nationality", as long as they remain loyal to India. Turn India into a Christian state if you want, as long as you keep it united and independent. Formulated this radically, it will of course be rejected by RSS men, but it is none the less

---

[143]Published in *Link*, the bimonthly newsletter of the WCC's "programme to combat racism", 1989/4; shown to me at the DRI by a North-Eastern delegation of the *Vanavâsî Kalyân Ashram*.

[144]B.P. Shukla: *What Ails India's Northeast?*, p.26.

the logical implication of Shukla's position. Ths same implication is present in VHP spokesman Giriraj Kishore's statement: "The pope should withdraw all foreign missionaries from our soil. Indian Christian missionaries are competent to do their job."[145] So, is conversion of Hindus to Christianity all right as long as it is done by Indian missionaries?

Shukla builds up his evidence for Christian separatism by borrowing from Christian sources an enumeration of ethnic groups who, as Christians in non-Christian-majority states, had started separatist movements, e.g.: "When Indonesia became independent, the Ambonese, most of whom were Christians, revolted against their own government. When Burma went out of the British Commonwealth, a good number of the leaders of Karen who revolted against the state of Burma were Christians. Today some of the agitators for an independent Naga State apart from India are also Christians. ... These facts have reinforced the suspicion that Christianity alienates the Asian from loyalty to his own country."[146]

So far, so good. The claim that being Christian and being separatist coincide in the case of some ethnic groups can be verified, notably for the Mizos and Nagas in the North-East. In the case of the Naga tribals, it is well-documented that they were purposely delivered to the influence of the missionaries by the colonial government: "The British, who had a policy of transforming the border regions into a protective cordon of the empire, 'discovered' the Nagas in about 1830 but prohibited the entry in this area to anyone without official or military capacity, which curiously did not exclude the Christian missionaries! ... One might say that it was the administrators, and in their wake the ethnographers and missionaries who, by a need of rational classification and order, *invented* the Naga tribes and consequently Naga nationalism. ... In a concern to protect the tea plantations of Assam (from, among other things, the Naga incursions), the British pursued a long process of pacification, administration and christianization, deeper and deeper into the hill country. The Nagas vigorously resisted this expansion; the response to their rebellions consisted of punitive expeditions and the 'civilizing'

---

[145]Quoted in: "Pope lands to protests by Parivar", *Deccan Chronicle*, 6.11.1999.

[146]Quoted from Joint East Asia Secretariat of the International Missionary Council of Churches: *Christianity and Asian Revolution* (read out at the World Council of Churches conference in Evanston 1954), p.77 and p.215; in B.P. Shukla: *India's Northeast*, p.27. On p.30 Shukla notes the synchronicity between the Evanston conference and the creation of the South-East-Asian Treaty Organisation.

missions..."[147] In that case, christianization was used as an instrument by a secular agency, viz. the colonial government.[148]

However, while Christian separatism is indeed a reality in the small and peripheral states of the North-East, in most tribal areas both native and foreign-missionary Christians have definitely accepted the fact of India: even most tribal "separatisms" allegedly supported by missionaries, such as the Jharkhand movement in Chhotanagpur, merely demand a redrawing of provincial boundaries and the creation of smaller provinces tailored to the size and circumstances of smaller communities (a project actually supported by the BJP).[149]

But before (even instead of) attempting to show a causal connection between Christianity and separatism, Shukla muddles his own argument by bringing in a third factor: the Western powers which are allegedly using the missions as pawns in their own neo-colonial strategy. He writes: "The Church acts as 'sappers and miners' of the Western army. ... the Church is not merely a medium for propagation of Christian faith but is an instrument of the Western powers in their global strategy. The world Ecumenical movement itself was the result of the concern of the Western powers to consolidate their strength in the world at large."[150]

Shukla sidetracks his own attack on Christianity by alleging the subordination of Christianity to a purely political conspiracy by foreign states. So now, the problem is not Christianity, but the political designs of the secular powers which stand behind the Christian missions. This is the RSS mind typically at work: reducing an ideological confrontation between religions to a purely political confrontation between nations.

This clumsy "reasoning" results in part from an intellectual inferiority feeling: rather than facing the difficult challenge of properly preparing for a debate on the intricacies of religious doctrines, it is easier and safer to

---

[147]Hélène Willemart: "Les Naga, montagnards entre l'Inde et la Birmanie", *India* (Brussels), June 1992.

[148]Likewise, the militantly secularist Third Republic in France promoted Christianization in its colonies as a means of strengthening the bonds between the natives and the French.

[149]According to the BJP's *Election Manifesto 1998* (p.5): "The BJP will carve out Uttaranchal, Vananchal [= Jharkhand], Vidarbha and Chhattisgarh as separate States." In the year 2000, the BJP government fulfilled this promise regarding Uttaranchal, Jharkhand and Chattisgarh; Vidarbha proved a more difficult proposition as a result of the opposition from the Shiv Sena, which favours a big Maharashtra including all Marathi-speaking areas.

[150]B.P. Shukla: *India's Northeast*, pp.27-8.

hide behind the rhetoric of patriotism versus foreign intrigue, for few people would want to be seen as unpatriotic and agents of a foreign power. In a variation on Dr. Samuel Johnson: patriotism is the last refuge of duffers.

It may also be part of the Sangh Parivar's charm offensive towards the minorities: explicitly accepting their religious identities and concentrating on severing their alleged extra-territorial loyalties. One of the first statements of K.S. Sudarshan upon becoming RSS Sarsanghchalak in 2000 was that the Church should "Indianize" itself, severing its links with the Vatican or other Western centres of authority (recalling, *mutatis mutandis*, the Chinese People's Republic's toleration of the "Patriotic" Catholics but suppression of those Catholics who remain loyal to the Pope).[151] Finally, it is in part a matter of intellectual inertia: in anti-colonial rhetoric, we often find that time has stood still, and that scenarios which were real enough in the colonial period (such as the British effectively using the missions to "pacify" the Nagas), are projected on to the present, where such scenarios have become impossible.

At any rate, Shukla's focus is not on the religious concern that Hindu or tribal traditions are finished off when their practitioners are converted, but on the political concern that converts to Christianity allegedly become susceptible to separatist tendencies. We shall see it on a number of occasions: the RSS is more a nationalist than a religious Hindu movement. This is read by Hindu radicals as a sidetracking of a Hindu organization from its original goal of serving Hinduism to the secondary, seemingly less controversial and more respectable, more "secular" goal of serving India.

The BJP and Christian history

In Hindu-Muslim relations, a large part is played by historical memories, often accompanied by pseudo-historical stories. Thus, the Ayodhya controversy pertained to the history of Islamic iconoclasm in India. In the history of Hindu-Christian relations, similar sources of potential friction exist, though on a much smaller scale. Is there any chance of the Hindu nationalists raking up some old temple demolition story involving a Christian church?

In 1994, the BJP made its position absolutely clear on the occasion of

[151]Farzand Ahmed: "Missionary imposition", *India Today*, 23.10.2000.

a very small incident in the Chennai area. After reading Ishwar Sharan's book *The Myth of Saint Thomas and the Mylapore Shiva Temple*, which argued that a number of South-Indian churches including the one commemorating the alleged martyrdom of Saint Thomas had been built on destroyed Shiva temples, a back-bench member of the RSS-affiliated Tamil organization Hindu Munnani decided to restore the Hindu sanctity of at least one of these shrines.[152] Equipped with the paraphernalia for *pûjâ*, he went to the Velankani Cathedral of Pondicherry, built by French Jesuits in forcible replacement of the Vedapuri Iswaran temple (AD 1748), and inquired where the Shivalingam was, so that he could worship it. Immediately, the Catholic Church was alarmed and warned that the Hindu fundamentalists were trying to create a second Ayodhya affair.[153]

The Hindu Munnani then held a small demonstration near the church (as close as the police allowed it to go) to draw attention to the Catholic Church's record in the destruction of Hindu temples in South India. However, it did not let the controversy escalate any further, not least because the BJP had immediately disowned the agitation. When I mentioned this incident to some leading BJP members, none of them expressed any sympathy for the Hindu Munnani's initiative, which could only disturb the BJP's post-Demolition charm offensive towards the minorities. BJP ideologue K.R. Malkani laughed it off and said that "we have no quarrel with the Christians".

In May 1998, it was exactly 500 years ago that missionary Christianity arrived in India with Vasco da Gama landing on the Malabar Coast. This was the exact counterpart of Christopher Columbus' landing in America: the start of a campaign to win "pepper and souls", to exploit and christianize. Due to very different power equations, the results were very different in scale, but only in scale, for the Portuguese intentions in India were exactly the same as those of the Spanish in America.[154] The 500th

---

[152]Other, older books about the anti-Hindu policies of the Portuguese missionaries and colonial administrators in India, have recently been republished: A.K. Priolkar: *The Goa Inquisition* (1991, original 1961), including an annotated edition of two testimonies from 1684 and 1808, and K.M. Panikkar: *Malabar and the Portuguese* (1997, original 1929).

[153]"'Ayodhya-type situation won't be allowed in T. Nadu'", *The Hindu* (international ed.), 12.3.1994. The words quoted are by Home Minister S.B. Chavan.

[154]In the Treaty of Tordesillas of 1994, the Pope divided the world in two halves, one for Spain and the other (including Africa and India) for Portugal, on condition that they use their power to promote the spread of Christianity.

anniversary of Columbus' landing was commemorated with a lot of soul-searching in essays and symposia, films and novels, and formal apologies to the Natives including one by the Pope during his visit to the Dominican Republic.[155]

It was to be expected that Hindu nationalist organizations would organize similar events, albeit on a proportionately smaller scale, to commemorate Vasco da Gama's landing in India. They could even have issued a demand for apologies from the Pope: no demolition, no riots, just *words*. Yet, even this much was too much for the "Hindu fanatics" of the BJP, who took no initiative at all, neither as a private organization nor as ruling party. No native American individual or organization has been denounced as "fanatical" for commemorating the destruction which started with Columbus' landing, nor for demanding apologies from institutions associated with that history. Yet, so scared was the BJP of negative reactions to a similar initiative, or so little interested in historical commemoration, that it let the occasion pass.

Likewise: "In Goa, where RSS man Manohar Parrikar is chief minister, the parivar is moving cautiously. Even though the VHP has been raising disputes about some churches built by the Portuguese, including the one on Diwar island off the Goa coast, the saffron brigade is unlikely to raise the issue as long as Parrikar is at the helm."[156] The Hindutva brigade is not all that eager for avoidable confrontation. Under BJP rule, India will remain the safest country for Christians on the Asian mainland.

POLEMIC AGAINST MARXISM

Early HMS polemic against Marxism

In the 1930s, some Hindu Mahasabha leaders were aware that a new enemy of Hinduism was in the ascendant: Marxism. The *Congress Socialist Party*, an intra-Congress faction founded in 1934, brought Marxism close to the future seat of power. In 1936, after the election of the foremost Leftist, Jawaharlal Nehru, as Congress president, HMS leader B.S. Moonje warned: "But a greater calamity is impending, nay, has practically almost fallen on the Hindu religion and culture, by the

---

[155]See e.g. Mario Coolen: *Tussen God en Goud* (Dutch: "Between God and Gold"), an example of Christian soul-searching concerning the role of the Church in the colonization of the Americas.

[156]Frederick Noronha *et al.*: "Searching for new Ayodhyas", *The Week*, 3.12.2000.

Congress leaders having enthroned socialism-communism in the Congress, by making room for Pandit Jawaharlal Nehru, to be elected President, unopposed, of the Congress for the next year. ... This further means that Pandit Jawaharlal Nehru will, with authority and the prestige of the Congress, preach for abolition of religion and for instituting Russian sociology and morality in place of Indian religions and cultures. Of course, he cannot preach it amongst the Musalmans, because if he were to do so, he won't survive for twenty-four hours. As for Christianity, it has got the support of the mighty strength of the British Empire and the missionaries —all combined together spend about three crores of rupees every year for converting the lower classes of the Hindus. Pandit Jawaharlal Nehru cannot affect them. The only people who I fear will fall an easy victim will be the Hindus who have no leaders to guide them and stabilize them."[157]

This statement against Marxism implicitly contains the essence of the post-Independence critique of the new state ideology, *secularism*, undoubtedly a component of Marxism. For Moonje, the problem with Marxism was not its economic doctrine, but its hostility to religion. Marxists themselves like to name "Capitalism" as their enemy, and invariably insinuate that those who oppose them are agents of Capitalism. In reality, the history of anti-Communism in the Cold War shows that, apart from a few economists like Friedrich von Hayek, anti-Communists rarely focused on the economic aspects of Communism; their concern was with democracy and civil freedoms, most notably freedom of religion. Indeed, many critics of Communism, like Aleksandr Solzhenitsyn and Pope John-Paul II, have also criticized Capitalism as merely another face of materialism, which matches Marxism in its reduction of man to his dimension of producer and consumer of material goods. B.S. Moonje, too, belonged to this mainstream of non-economist anti-Communism.

Sangh polemic against Marxism

Moonje's embryonic critique of Marxism was never followed up with a more in-depth critique, at least not within organized Hindu nationalism. On the contrary: in 1938, Guru Golwalkar wrote that "socialism is modern Russia's religion. ... For the Russians, their prophet is Karl Marx and his opinions are their Testament. ... The Russian Nation adheres with religious

[157]Letter of B.S. Moonje to M.M. Malaviya, 29.11.1936, reproduced in B.N. Pandey, ed.: *The Indian Nationalist Movement 1885-1947, Select Documents*, p.116.

fervour [to Marxism]."[158] I don't think many Russians could agree with that; Communism was imposed on them by ruthless force, but Golwalkar described it as their fervently practised religion. Later on, Golwalkar became a declared anti-Communist, but to judge from his writings, he never deepened his knowledge of the subject.

Sangh polemic against Communism was and remained nothing but an endless repetition of the allegation of Communist disloyalty to India, documented in K.L. Sharma: *The Great Betrayers*. According to the BJP, the Communist parties "have a hideous history of betrayal of the national interest at every critical juncture".[159] Here again, we see an ideological issue being reduced to a purely national issue: Communism is bad because its focus of loyalty is *foreign*. The more promising title *Collapse of Communist Oligarchy* by S.V. Seshagiri Rao turns out to offer only a countrywise recapitulation of the events which constituted the revolution of 1989, the collapse of Communism in the Soviet empire; not bad as ready reference, but not adding anything to a specific Hindutva analysis of this process nor of Marxism in general.

The only exception of sorts is BJP economist Jay Dubashi, who has often linked criticism of Soviet Communism with criticism of Nehruvian secularism. His columns in *Organiser* in the crucial period 1988-91 carried self-explanatory titles like "Blood-soaked Beijing", "The Marxist gang", "The Marxist god is dead", "Decline and fall of Marxism".[160] Not to be unfair, I should also mention an author of a special category: Sudhakar Raje, who has been writing the satirical column of *Organiser* under the pen name *Satiricus* for more than fifty years, has always been a lively lambaster of Communism. For the rest, Marxism to the Sangh Parivar was but a nameless face in the crowd of "anti-national forces".

The BJS on Communism

From the fact that the Indian Communist parties have always been the most virulent opponents of the BJS-BJP, and from journalistic descriptions of the BJS-BJP as "right-wing", many people deduce that the BJS-BJP is anti-Communist. This is simply not true.

The BJS did occasionally make anti-Communist statements, or at least some of its spokesmen did, in particular Balraj Madhok. He advocated an

[158]M.S. Golwalkar: *We*, p.37.

[159]BJP: *Election Manifesto 1998*, p.55.

[160]Collected in J. Dubashi: *The Road to Ayodhya*.

abandonment of the effectively Soviet-aligned policy of "non-alignment", and an open alignment with the West to contain Communism. In India, the only party ever to espouse an explicitly pro-Western line was the Swatantra Party. Madhok also opposed any coalitions at the regional and local levels between the BJS and the Communists. However, when the gains of the opposition parties in the 1967 elections created the occasion to form non-Congress provincial governments, on condition of opposition unity against Congress, Madhok's tirades against these "opportunistic" coalitions with the Left parties failed to convince the office-bearers of his own party. This was not merely because the prospect of office was so enticing for many Jana Sangh politicians, but just as much because few Jana Sangh activists had ever bothered to study Communist ideology and to form an opinion about it. Their judgement of Communism was mostly limited to two elementary observations: the Communists felt no loyalty towards India, and they hated the Jana Sanghis.

The first problem, however, had been somewhat diminished in importance by the Chinese Invasion of 1962, when in the teeth of public opinion anger, the Communists had been forced to eat their earlier pro-Chinese slogans ("China's chairman is also India's chairman"), and had refrained from actively supporting the invaders or sabotaging India's defence. With the mobilization of Indian public opinion against China, the increasing hostility between the Soviet Union and China, and the American military presence in Pakistan and Indochina, the chances of a Communist take-over seemed to have receded. At heart the Communists certainly might have remained disloyal, but this was no longer feared as an acute threat. As for the second problem, the Jana Sanghis did not intend to reciprocate contempt with contempt: it was neither the first nor the last time that the BJS/BJP people, with their inferiority complex and their shopkeeper mentality, would bend and crawl to curry favour with people who despised them.

With the BJS approaching the Communist problem in terms of national security and of its own standing, it failed to do anything about, or even to seriously take notice of, the increasing Communist hold on India's cultural sector, where "a number of former card-carrying members of the Communist Party ... did make a major effort at influencing not just the polity but also a number of scientific and educational institutions, a variety of government and semi-government committees, inner councils of the

[Congress] party and Parliament, a considerable cross-section of the mass media as well as important journals which they came to control."[161]

As already explained (and given the general neglect of this crucial event, it bears repetition), the key moment in this development was the power position which entryist Communists gained around Indira Gandhi *c.* 1970. This was when in the words of Indira's erstwhile adviser D.P. Mishra, "Communists have a field day", and Indira's loyal Congress socialists (the so-called Young Turks, like Chandra Shekhar) "were being overshadowed by the Communists both inside the Congress organization and the Congress Parliamentary Party".[162] Sanjay Gandhi, supported by the purely careerist and opportunist section of Congress, thwarted the Communist designs of a take-over of the party from within, but neglected to do anything about the stranglehold on the cultural and educational establishment which the Communists had acquired in the meantime. Later those circles were to provide a storm centre of the struggle against Hindu nationalism, as in the Ayodhya controversy.

The BJS called itself "a centrist party", which has been "assailed" by "protagonists of complete freedom in the economic sphere" as "being worse than communists".[163] Though in a 1958 manifesto, it gave "expression to people's feelings on national questions, e.g. ... opposition to co-operative farming and state trading in food grain"[164] and similar Soviet-oriented policies, it had also supported a number of anti-feudal and anti-capitalist demands. Thus, the BJS had "all along stood for abolition of *Zamîndârî* [= landlordism] and the principle 'land to the tiller', for measures to prevent concentration of economic power in the hands of a few individuals, for the imposition of curbs on profiteering, and for the adoption of fiscal and taxation steps to remove the vast disparities in incomes of various sections".[165] In socio-economic policies, there was a lot of common ground with the Communists, especially after the latter were constrained to adopt a social-democratic strategy instead of their own revolutionary programme.

The Jana Sangh summed up its objectives in its Constitution, and these

---

[161]Rajni Kothari: "Dangers to democracy. The challenges from within", *Times of India*, 22.9.1995.

[162]D.P. Mishra: *The Post-Nehru Era*, p.134.

[163]BJS: *Party Documents 1951-1972*, vol.1, p.v.

[164]BJS: *Party Documents 1951-1972*, vol.1, p.123.

[165]BJS: *Party Documents 1951-1972*, vol.1, p.iv.

included the following: "Guarantee of the fundamental right to work and livelihood. Upholding establishment and protection of the tiller's right to ownership of land. Ceiling on agricultural land and redistribution of land. Eradication of untouchability. Free education up to middle class. Facilities for medical care and social security. Encouragement to small mechanised and rural industries. Nationalisation of basic industries. Curbing monopolistic tendencies in the economic sphere. Determination of minimum and maximum expendable income. Worker's participation in the profit and management of the industries. Stabilisation of prices."[166] By Western standards at least, this would count as a socialist programme.

In 1977, BJS leader Atal Behari Vajpayee became Foreign Minister in the Janata government. Before he met Soviet Prime Minister Andrei Kosygin, there was great concern in Leftist circles that Vajpayee, as a member of an "anti-Communist" party, might do serious harm to Indo-Soviet friendship. Afterwards however, Kosygin said that Vajpayee was more progressive than his own Communist comrades back home, and Indo-Soviet relations flourished. When Vajpayee presided over the founding of the BJP, he made the party adopt "Gandhian socialism" as its official ideology. For the sake of continuity, and because no one was able to unite Gandhism with socialism conceptually, it was decided afterwards that "integral humanism", the name of the official party doctrine of the erstwhile BJS, meant the same thing as "Gandhian socialism": a measure of the party's lack of ideological *sérieux*. Since then, "Gandhian socialism" has been quietly moved into the background; but the point is that the BJP was eager to pledge its loyalty to some kind of "socialism", even if qualified as "Gandhian".

The BJP on Communism

In April 1981, the newly founded BJP passed its first resolutions on foreign policy, and made it clear in passing how little it had to do with any conscious anti-Communism. To be sure, the BJP condemned the Soviet occupation of Afghanistan, and aptly remarked that "the claim of certain nations that the Soviet Union was a 'natural' ally of the non-aligned countries has been proved hollow by Soviet action in Afghanistan".[167] But then the BJP affirmed that nevertheless, it "would like to see further

[166]Reproduced in BJS: *Party Documents 1951-1972*, vol.1, p.222.

[167]BJP: *Foreign Policy and Resolutions*, p.9.

strengthening of Indo-Soviet ties", and referred to the time when "the Janata Government [1977-79, with Vajpayee as Foreign Minister] had succeeded in deepening and strengthening the bonds of Indo-Soviet friendship".[168] And again: "The BJP is appreciative of the commonality of ties with USSR. We would work towards further strengthening of these ties on the basis of equality and mutual benefit."[169]

The fledgling BJP also condemned the occupation of Cambodia by Soviet ally Vietnam in very mild terms. Here again, the choice of terminology is revealing: the expression "the heroic struggle of the people of Vietnam, Laos and Kampuchea against American intervention in Indo-China"[170] feigns to ignore the Cold War dimension of this struggle, and assumes unquestioningly that the Communist armies which took control of Cambodia and South Vietnam really represented "the people", a position which no anti-Communist would readily accept.

The expression of antipathy for "the tyrannical Pol Pot regime"[171] pretends by implication that the Cambodian genocide was the idiosyncratic handiwork of an individual "tyrant", as if the ideology motivating Pol Pot's regime had nothing to do with it. The horrors of Pol Pot's killing fields were a central piece in anti-Communist writing at the time, and a powerful trigger of massive defections from the Communist camp among Western intellectuals, yet the BJP throws away this occasion to score at least a rhetorical point against Communism.

American attempts to contain the Communist menace did not get the sympathy of the BJP: "From Turkey through Saudi Arabia to Pakistan, the USA is creating a 'cordon sanitaire' in its attempts at containment of USSR. The BJP has already rejected such theories."[172] Since the BJP offered no alternative to the American strategy against Commmunism, we may have to conclude that it didn't see Communism as a threat.

In 1994, when the RSS-affiliated *Swadeshi Jagaran Manch* ("Self-reliance Awakening Front") joined hands with the Communists in a demonstration against the GATT/WTO treaty, some RSS/BJP spokesmen proved fully equal to the Communists in venting a crude anti-Americanism. Sangh Parivar stalwarts like Dattopant Thengadi and K.N.

---

[168]BJP: *Foreign Policy and Resolutions*, p.10.
[169]BJP: *Foreign Policy and Resolutions*, p.14.
[170]BJP: *Foreign Policy and Resolutions*, p.10.
[171]BJP: *Foreign Policy and Resolutions*, p.10.
[172]BJP: *Foreign Policy and Resolutions*, p.15.

Govindacharya have for long imbibed and relayed quite a bit of Marxism themselves.[173]

And what strikes you in the following passage from a 1995 BJP publication? "With China our relations have been on a see-saw ever since the liberation of China. Now there is an opportunity to put the relationship on a firm footing of friendship and co-operation. For this purpose it is essential to solve the border question in a fair and equitable manner."[174] That the nationalist BJP renounces its explicit demand of full restoration of Chinese-occupied Indian territory to India is sensational enough: in the BJS days, this demand was always made very explicitly, even by other parties (a parliament resolution demanding 100% restitution, voted after the Chinese invasion in 1962, has never been withdrawn). But the truly shocking part is that the "anti-Communist" BJP describes Mao's military conquest of China as a "liberation". One might argue that "Liberation" has become a proper name rather than an evaluation of the event, but in that case, a capital L should have been used. And no genuine anti-Communist would concede this merely conventional use of a value-laden term like "liberation" anyway. The BJP has always been a non-Communist but never an anti-Communist party.

The BJP and the implosion of Soviet Communism

The fall of Communism in the Soviet Bloc was the cause of some euphoria in Hindu nationalist circles. After the VHP had laid the first stone of the Ayodhya temple on 9 November 1989, Jay Dubashi wrote somewhat pompously that "on the very same day the first brick of the Ram Shila foundation was being laid at Ayodhya, the Berliners were removing bricks from the Berlin Wall. While a temple was going up in Ayodhya, a communist temple was being demolished five thousand miles away in Europe. If this is not history, I don't know what is."[175]

The link between the European and the Indian revolution seemed just too good to be true. About the Nehruvians and Indian Communists with their opposition to the Ayodhya movement, this is Dubashi's verdict: "These men are elitist by nature and for them any *popular* movement, no matter how democratic and mass-based, is almost *ipso facto* suspect, if it

[173]About Govindacharya's Leftist sympathies, see Ajay Singh: "K.N. Govindacharya: seeing red clothed in saffron", *Pioneer*, 7.9.1997.

[174]BJP: *Foreign Policy and Resolutions*, p.3.

[175]J. Dubashi: "From 'Shilanyas' to Berlin Wall", *The Road to Ayodhya*, p.18.

does not meet their prejudiced convictions. This is Stalinism of the worst kind, the kind that led to the building of the Berlin Wall, one of the ugliest structures in the world. ... They belong to the same class as Stalin in Soviet Russia and Hitler in Nazi Germany, who presume to know what is good for you and me, the ordinary mortals. And these men will go the same dusty way as the tyrants whose bodies are now being exhumed all over the Soviet empire and thrown to the vultures. ... The post-Nehru era began at Ayodhya on November 9 [1989], and it will gather momentum in the years to come, like the post-communist era in Europe and elsewhere."[176] To keep up the morale of a movement, it is certainly helpful to create the feeling of being on a historic mission echoed by history itself from the far corners of the earth.

However, neither Dubashi nor any other BJP official hazarded a more in-depth critique of Soviet Communism. In September 1991, the BJP declared: "The end of communism and the advent of democracy in the SU are welcome developments."[177] But no effort was ever made to analyse the implosion of the Soviet Union in terms of the BJP's own ideology, e.g. by trying to pinpoint the role of factors like the democratic opposition, minority nationalism, Great-Russian cultural nationalism combined with religious revivalism, if not the American containment policy and the economic effects of the arms race.

In 1996, BJP president L.K. Advani lambasted the Communists thus: "How ridiculous, indeed, do these dinosaurs of Indian politics get in their efforts to hide their own obsolescence! Our communists here, who for seven long decades used to dutifully hold aloft the umbrella whenever it rained in their Fatherland, were celebrating ... the 79th anniversary of the 'Great' Russian Revolution, which even the Russians have now put behind them."[178]

But this was followed by a warning against the new direction in Indian Communist politics: "But an alarming situation is developing in national politics. These communists who called India's Independence in 1947 'sham independence', who supported India's partition and projected the Soviet Union to be the ideal model of national integration until its sudden implosion in the early '90s, who still revere Lenin and Stalin but do not

---

[176]J. Dubashi: "From 'Shilanyas' to Berlin Wall", *The Road to Ayodhya*, pp.19-20.

[177]BJP: *Foreign Policy and Resolutions*, p.31.

[178]L.K. Advani: "Inaugural address", in BJP: *Resolutions Adopted at National Executive Meeting, Jaipur, November 15-17, 1996*, p.5.

give the same status to Gandhi or Subhash Chandra Bose or Jayaprakash Narayan or any of the other Indian towering figures, have today become the brain behind the ruling establishment in India. Since history ... has disrobed them of all pieces of their ideological attire—be it anti-capitalism, anti-imperialism, dictatorship of the proletariat and other such absurdities—they have now invented anti-BJP-ism as the last and the only fig-leaf to hide their irrelevance. The recent spurt in Marxist violence against BJP, RSS and ABVP cadres in Kerala is also a manifestation of their pique."[179]

The BJP leaders must have been aware of the Communists' role as the "brain behind the ruling establishment" since the late 1960s; there was nothing new in that. But they had a point in observing that the Communists' "proximity to power and opinion-making structures has increased to a level that is totally disproportionate to their stagnant or shrinking electoral base."[180] It should be added, though, that the intensity and purity of the Marxism animating influential intellectuals and media people in the mid-1990s was inevitably diminishing under the impact of the fall of Soviet Communism. Many Marxists, though continuing to think within the Marxist framework, would no longer publicly call themselves Marxists, or would only go public with soft Marxist concerns (practical benefits for the poor) rather than with its doctrinal hard core (dictatorship of the proletariat etc.).

But this softening of the revolutionary fervour went hand in hand with a hardening of Marxist hostility to the BJP. The struggle against Hindutva had been promoted from a secondary role to the central mission of the Indian Communist movement in the 1990s: "The most pernicious communist influence on Indian polity is today manifest in the way the BJP is sought to be isolated in the name of fighting communalism. The communists are prepared to go to any length—I repeat, to any length—in their bid to grab and retain power ... even if the BJP has to be as good as illegally gagged out of existence."[181]

It should not be forgotten that the BJP's accession to power in 1998

[179]L.K. Advani: "Inaugural address", in BJP: *Resolutions Adopted at National Executive Meeting, Jaipur, November 15-17, 1996*, p.5.

[180]L.K. Advani: "Inaugural address", in BJP: *Resolutions Adopted at National Executive Meeting, Jaipur, November 15-17, 1996*, p.6.

[181]L.K. Advani: "Inaugural address", in BJP: *Resolutions Adopted at National Executive Meeting, Jaipur, November 15-17, 1996*, p.6.

was preceded by attempts to keep even eleceted BJP representatives and majorities from exercising their mandates, and even to bar the BJP from contesting elections or to dissolve the party. At the level of discourse, this tendency was probably at its strongest in 1993, after the Babri Masjid demolition, when Human Resources Minister Arjun Singh proposed to organize Maoist-style "people's committees" to enforce the ban on the RSS. Two Bills were introduced in the Lok Sabha in 1993, the Constitution (80th Amendment) Bill and the Representation of the People (Amendment) Bill, which would have excluded parties which mix religion and politics from contesting elections, the obvious aim being to exclude the BJP and Shiv Sena (the Bills were defeated largely because to many in the Janata and regional parties they were eerlily reminiscent of the Emergency).

There were also attempts to annul the election of BJP and Shiv Sena candidates on grounds of appealing to religion during their campaigns, attempts mostly struck down by the courts.[182] There were several cases where BJP state governments were removed from power by procedures bordering on the unconstitutional, starting with the removal of the BJP governments of Rajasthan, Madhya Pradesh and Himachal Pradesh in December 1992 though they were unconnected with the Ayodhya demolition and had kept communal peace in their states far better than the non-BJP governments in Andhra Pradesh and Bihar. In 1996, *Indian Express* had to comment on the ruling "United Front's decision to give the installation of an elected government in Uttar Pradesh a go-by", that "when anti-BJP-ism involves disregarding all established conventions and Constitutional propriety, it becomes a threat to the very survival of democracy".[183] The crucial turning point had been President K.R. Narayanan's refusal in late 1997 to impose President's rule in Uttar Pradesh in lieu of BJP rule.

In the willingness of Congress and the then National Front (Janata plus regional parties), between 1991 and 1997, to explore unconstitutional means of keeping the BJP from power, one can easily recognize the influence of the Communists. They were always the most enthusiastic

[182]This to the dismay of Brenda Cossman and Ratna Kapur: *Secularism's Last Sigh? Hindutva and the (Mis)Rule of Law*, a discussion of these verdicts generally upholding the right of politicians and political parties to champion Hindutva.

[183]"Constitutional massacre. Is the system safe in these hands?", editorial, *Indian Express*, 19.10.1996.

promoters of such attempts, having chosen Hindutva over capitalism as their newly favoured enemy. Having lost credibility on the economic front, they just had to redirect their energies to new battlefields. This way, the collapse of the Soviet Union had made the nuisance of Communism for the Hindutva movement not less but more intense.

SDFA polemic against Marxism

In the early fifties, when concern about Communist expansionism was at its highest, the real work of studying Communism and producing informed criticism was left to the non-Sangh *Society for the Defence of Freedom in Asia* of Ram Swarup and Sita Ram Goel. The stated aim of the SDFA's publications was to expose the lies that formed the backbone of Communist propaganda, many of which had entered popular belief. Thus, in *The China Debate: Whom Shall We Believe?*, Goel compared the economic figures in official Chinese publications with the statements made by Indian delegations to China, and showed how they contradicted each other.

In *Conquest of China*, Goel demonstrated that Mao Zedong's victory against Jiang Jieshi (Chiang Kai-shek) was not determined by the level of popular support, but rather by hard military factors such as the supplies which Mao received from the Soviets (including lots of American weapons given to the Soviet Union for a war against Japan which it only declared when Japan was already defeated) and which Jiang did not receive from the US, first because of the American prioritary concern for Europe at the expense of the Chinese front, later (1946-48) as a result of an American arms embargo against "both parties in the Chinese Civil War". Any man of action would hold it as self-evident that a war is won by the party which is militarily the strongest, but in academe the belief has caught on that the Chinese Civil War was a victory of proletarian enthusiasm over bourgeois-reactionary fire-power.[184] To quite an extent, Goel's critique, solitary and therefore looking like a querulous oddity next to the flood of pro-Mao literature, has recently been vindicated in Steven Mosher's study

[184]This belief is propagated or taken for granted in most publications on the Chinese Civil War by Western China-watchers, from Edgar Snow's infamous *Red Star over China* to Jonathan Spence: *The Gate of Heavenly Peace* (1981), not forgetting Barbara Tuchman's *Notes on China* (1972); a good critique of the Mao myth as cherished by Western intellectuals is given in Michel Korzec: *Het voelen van de draak* (Dutch: "Feeling the Dragon"), and in Steven Mosher: *China Misperceived*.

of China reporting, *China Misperceived: American Illusions and Chinese Reality.*[185]

In general, the SDFA publications have stood the test of time: the collapse of the Soviet system and the subsequent opening of the Kremlin archives have given a clear (if belated) verdict in the polemic between the SDFA and the Communists. How many old Communists would like to go public today with what they wrote in the 1950s and 60s in praise of Stalin or the Chinese Cultural Revolution? By contrast, the SDFA veterans now claim with satisfaction that "the numerous studies published by the [SDFA] in the fifties exist in cold print in many libraries and can be consulted for finding out how the movement anticipated by many years the recent revelations about communist regimes".[186]

While the SDFA was toiling away, the RSS took little interest in the SDFA's work. Many RSS men actually suspected the SDFA scholars of being American agents, exactly what the Communist propaganda against the SDFA had been saying.[187] In reality, the SDFA was sceptical of American anti-Communist policies (as opposed to the work of private American anti-Communists) and was shunned by American officials in India.

In a paper written in 1956, Goel criticises the underlying philosophy of the American containment policy against Communism. It is in the form of a story, the protagonist being a young renunciate in whom one can easily recognize Ram Swarup. His opening observation is certainly original: "The singular sin of the United States, he said, was Dialectical Materialism."[188] This Marxist philosophy is shown to underlie American anti-Communist policies in the Third World, in this sense that the US expected the masses to reject Communist ideology if only favourable material conditions were created—a change in mental outlook

---

[185]Steven Mosher: *China Misperceived: American Illusions and Chinese Reality.* Mosher's own troubles with his university (Stanford) after this book was published shows that it still takes courage and sacrifice of career prospects to criticize the Chinese Communist system and its supporters in the West.

[186]Back cover of Sita Ram Goel: *Hindu Temples, What Happened to Them*, vol.2.

[187]Sita Ram Goel told me that before the 1957 elections, Deendayal Upadhyaya approached him with a request for brokering some American funding for the BJS, on the assumption that the Americans would be interested in supporting the only sizable non-Left party in India, and that Goel was an American agent. If Goel's information is correct, it would be quite embarrassing for the RSS-BJP with its current anti-American posturing.

[188]S.R. Goel: *Genesis and Growth of Nehruism*, p.208.

automatically resulting from a material change: "The US has an idea. Democracy. She has practised it for long, and has prospered on it. ... Her one ambition is to share it with every other country. ... What does she do? She proclaims that democracy can be distilled from the standard of living. So let every country improve its agriculture and industry, and develop schools, cinemas, railways, ... Let everyone have fruit juice for breakfast, wear a silk hat, ride a Mercedes, and giggle at Marilyn Monroe. And democracy will develop to the detriment of all other ideas."[189]

In pursuing this policy, the Americans are not interested in whether people are pro- or anti-Communist. They support people like Nehru "who can push through plans for industrialization. ... She turns a deaf ear to the denunciations they daily hurl at her. Dip them with another darned good dose of dollars, and in due course they shall deliver democracy." By contrast, in a bitter hint at the treatment which Indian anti-Communists received from the US: "The US cannot bother about blighters who believe (!) in democracy, and who write and fight for it. ... She cannot afford to provoke people in power for a pack of funny friends, hated and hunted by their own people."[190] After all, in this approach, convictions are not important.

The sage concludes: "Now, all this is exactly what we know as Dialectical Materialism. In the universe presided over by this deity, consciousness oozes out of matter like oil from sunflower seeds, ideas are concomitants of material changes. ... It is a universe of objective and subjective necessities, in which there is no freedom and, therefore, no place for faith."[191]

But if the US believes in Dialectical Materialism, it shares the philosophy of the Soviet Union, doesn't it? Should this not offer hope for a reconciliation between the superpowers? Not at all: "The Soviet Union only sells Dialectical Materialism to those she wants to defeat and destroy. As for herself, she stands for what in philosophy we call Idealism. ... The Soviet Union too has an idea. Totalitarianism. ... And she also spends billions to ... secure it in every corner of the world. What does she do? She propounds that the standard of living and much more follow from faith in totalitarianism. She elaborates the idea in an unending stream of books,

---

[189]S.R. Goel: *Genesis and Growth of Nehruism*, p.208.
[190]S.R. Goel: *Genesis and Growth of Nehruism*, p.208.
[191]S.R. Goel: *Genesis and Growth of Nehruism*, pp.208-209.

pamphlets, posters, handbills and films, produced in every language. ... She employs an army of men and women to retail this idea on a mass scale in order to convert or corrode as many people as possible, and to ultimately impose it with force of arms in true crusading fashion. The material conditions may differ from Czechoslovakia to Albania to Tibet. But they are all equally ripe for totalitarianism. The triumphal march of an idea does not and should not depend on any material preparation. The idea cannot and should not wait for slow and stupid material changes. What the idea needs is human minds, their craving for it."[192]

The result, in Third World countries, is a division of labour: "The United States is trying to take care of our bodies. ... The Soviet Union is taking care of our heads. The US builds schools and spreads literacy among the peasants. The Soviet Union provides them the newspapers they read. The US erects factories in which the workers earn a livelihood. The SU bands them into trade unions, trains their leaders. ... The US gives scholarships to promising students for studies abroad. The SU equips them with political glasses through which they can survey the world. ... The US spends on library premises. The SU stocks the shelves within with her own choice of literature."[193]

Not material conditions but convictions are what matters. While the Americans avoid people with the right convictions but without prestige, the Communists *create* prestige for the people with the right convictions: "Nor does the Soviet Union seek for any credentials of power or prestige in choosing her friends. All she cares for is their convictions. Let the convinced ones be obscure and unknown. She makes them famous overnight by powerful publicity. ... If you can turn a phrase, you can be turned into a world-famous author. ... People everywhere will be informed by the Soviet network that your wonderful works are under translation. ... All you have to do is to believe in and seek for totalitarianism, and all the rest will be added unto you."[194] The reference is obviously to a string of Leftist writers in India whose literary qualities were inversely proportional to the publicity they received.

At any rate, not material conditions but "consciousness-raising" is what the Communists count on to create the right climate for

[192]S.R. Goel: *Genesis and Growth of Nehruism*, p.209.
[193]S.R. Goel: *Genesis and Growth of Nehruism*, p.210.
[194]S.R. Goel: *Genesis and Growth of Nehruism*, p.209.

the Revolution.[195] In philosophical terms: "This is not Dialectical Materialism. This is Idealism, according to which consciousness converses with consciousness as one lamp is lighted by another. ... In this universe, the ill-fed and ill-clad underdogs have as much capacity as their more privileged fellow-beings. For, this is the universe of freedom, and of faith."[196]

It is not enough to make catalogues of Communist wrongdoings, it is also necessary to investigate its philosophical assumptions. This is a level of intellectual work rarely found among the Pentagon containment strategists and never in the Sangh Parivar publications. Yet, in the larger scheme, it is one contribution of which India has reason to be proud.

POLEMIC AGAINST ISLAM

According to R.C. Majumdar, the Muslim occupation of the larger part of India was as much and as certainly a *colonization* as British paramountcy has been. Islamic conquerors turned India into an exploitation colony and in some parts also into a settlement colony. The steepest inequality between colonizing ruling class and colonized underclass prevailed. True, there were concessions for some collaborating enclaves (Jain financiers, Rajput vassal princes), but that too formed an exact parallel with British colonial policy, which depended on the Sikhs, the Muslim League, Indian civil servants and other collaborator enclaves of the native society. There were also differences between the two systems, of course, and internal evolutions in both, surely, but in this essential respect they were similar: they were colonial systems and reduced the Hindus to colonial subjects.

Yet, notes Majumdar, this glaring fact is hushed up by the post-Independence elite: "It is an ominous sign of the time that Indian history is being viewed in official circles in the perspective of recent politics. The

[195]Historically, this approach must be attributed not to Marx but to Lenin, whose "Revolution" took place in a country in which the economic conditions were not sufficiently "advanced", in Marxist terms, for the Revolution. The reliance on convictions and will-power (extended in the form of fire-power) in defiance of material conditions, and the subsequent cult and glorification of will-power (as in the model proletarians Stakhanov and Lei Feng), are among the profound common traits of Communism and Fascism; they are also of one piece with the cult of the Leader (Conducator, Great Helmsman etc.) as the embodiment of the collective Will, another common trait of Fascism and the really existing Socialism.

[196]S.R. Goel: *Genesis and Growth of Nehruism*, pp.209-10.

official history of the freedom movement starts with the premise that India lost independence only in the eighteenth century and had thus an experience of subjection to a foreign power for only two centuries. Real history, on the other hand, teaches us that the major part of India lost independence about five centuries before, and merely changed masters in the eighteenth century."[197]

To Hindu revivalists, Islam is certainly one of the occupying powers from which India had—and partly still has—to liberate itself. Their polemic against Islam has consequently been quite thorough. Because of its political importance for the present and the future, the Hindu revivalist view of Islam will be discussed in considerable detail in the following sections.

Arya Samaj's philosophical polemic against Islam

Islam challenged Hinduism by force of arms a mere four years after the Prophet's death, in "AD 636. The first recorded Arab expedition to India was by a naval enterprise under Uthman-ath-Thakafi, Governor of Bahrain. It plundered the west coast of India during the rule of Caliph Omar bin Khattab".[198] Muslim invasions continued until 1761, when Ahmad Shah Abdali from Afghanistan responded to the invitation of the well-known Sufi Shah Wali-Allah to teach the infidel Marathas a lesson (which he did in the Third Battle of Panipat). Alternatively, one could say that they continued until at least 1999, when the Pakistani Army staged an invasion in the Kargil sector of Jammu and Kashmir. Islamic invasion has at any rate been a constant for more than a thousand years and has profoundly affected the Hindu psyche.

Yet, a Hindu critique of Islam that went beyond a curt dismissal of Islam as barbarism perpetrated by "the wicked *Mlechchhas*", was only written more than twelve centuries after the first invasion: the fourteenth

---

[197]R.C. Majumdar: *History of the Freedom Movement*, vol.1, p.xii-xiii; also quoted with approval in N.S. Rajaram: *Profiles in Deception*, p.183. The one thing that could be objected is that Majumdar, along with Muslim chauvinists, overlooks the very real collapse of Muslim power in the eighteenth century well before the British were in a position to take over, the factual sovereignty of the Marathas, Rajputs, Jats and Sikhs. Then again, the fact that the Marathas failed to depose the powerless Moghul and declare Hindu sovereignty shows that mentally they were indeed still the subjects of the Moghul sovereign.

[198]S.B. Bhattacherje: *Encyclopaedia of Indian Events & Dates*, p.A-13.

chapter of the *Satyârtha Prakâsh* (*Light of Truth*), completed in 1875 by Swami Dayananda Saraswati, founder of the Arya Samaj.[199] This critique is not very sophisticated but it attacks the very heart of Islam. Its paragraphs are organized as commentaries on quotations from the Quran (without reference to any secondary literature whatsoever), in Quranic order.

Many of them concern alleged contradictions in the Quranic worldview. Thus, the Quran says: "Whichever way ye turn, there is the face of God".[200] True enough, says Dayananda, but in that case, "why [do] the Mohammedans turn their face towards Qibla (i.e. the sacred mosque at Mecca)?"[201] The objection that the special status of the *Ka'ba* in Mecca amounts to a form of idolatry is an old one, which even Chengiz Khan brought up when a preacher explained Islam to him: why go on pilgrimage to Mecca when God is omnipresent?[202] Islam abolished all forms of pilgrimage, except for the (originally Pagan) pilgrimage to Mecca, which thereby got invested with even more sanctity. In a comment on another Quranic injunction to "turn thy face towards the sacred Mosque [= the *Ka'ba*]",[203] Dayananda concludes: "Now is this trivial idolatry? We should think it is the crudest form of idolatry."[204]

The questions of the Qibla (direction of prayer) and of the pilgrimage to Mecca are troubling because these are typically Pagan practices in the heart of Islam. Any Islamic attempt to justify them could promptly be adopted by Pagans in their own defence against Islamic denunciations of their "idolatry": if the Black Stone in Mecca's *Ka'ba* can represent Allah,

[199]Though a lot has been written and published on the Arya Samaj, the specific criticisms of Islam are seldom enumerated, and never properly discussed. It is not even mentioned in home-made Arya Samaj histories, D. Vable: *The Arya Samaj*, and Vaidyanath Shastri: *The Arya Samaj*. The Arya Samaji freedom fighter Lala Lajpat Rai only mentioned it in passing (*The Arya Samaj*, p.150), in the haziest terms imaginable: Swami Dayananda "found that in Christianity and Islam, Hinduism had formidable rivals". In his standard introduction, outsider Kenneth W. Jones devotes hardly one page (*Arya Dharma*, pp.145-46) to Swami Dayananda's highly influential 74-page critique of Islam.

[200]Q.2:115/109. The double verse numeration tries to accommodate both the the so-called Kufa c.q. Basra numerations, as both given in J.H. Kramers: *De Koran* (Dutch translation, 1956) and explained in its introduction.

[201]*Satyârtha Prakâsh* 14:26; *Light of Truth*, p.662.

[202]Quoted in M. Habib & K.A. Nizami: *Comprehensive History of India*, vol.5, *The Delhi Sultanate*, p.81.

[203]Q.2:144/139.

[204]*Satyârtha Prakâsh* 14:30; *Light of Truth*, p.663.

why should not the 360 statues in the *Ka'ba* which Mohammed and his nephew Ali destroyed also be legitimate representations of the Divine? Why not the Shiva Lingam in the Somnath temple which Muslim armies destroyed time and again as a "den of idolatry"? Dayananda challenges the Muslims: "They too, whom you call image-worshippers, do not regard the image as God. They profess to worship God behind the image. If you are image-breakers, why do you not break that big image called Qibla (the sacred Mosque)?"[205] This question strikes at the very heart of the iconoclastic tradition.

Dayananda also rejected the jump from the infinite to the finite, from eternity to time, which is implied in the doctrine of creation and in the doctrine of everlasting reward or punishment for choices made in this finite human life: "As the soul is finite, its deeds—good or bad—cannot be infinite. It cannot, therefore, be sent to an everlasting hell or heaven. ... Human deeds being finite, their fruits—reward or punishment—cannot be infinite."[206]

Even the whole idea of a finite creation starting at a certain point in time by an infinite and eternal God is questioned: "The Mohammedans believe that the world has been in existence for less than seven or eight thousand years. One should like to know if God was sitting idle before Creation and will do the same after the day of judgement. These are all childish things, because God is ever active".[207] Most India-based philosophies including Buddhism and Jainism assume that the universe is eternal; in antiquity, Jainism has probably developed the most elaborate and explicit affirmation of the world's eternity.[208] From the existence of causality within the world, they do not deduce that the world itself must also be the causal result of an earlier act, viz. the act of creation by an extra-cosmic God.

Dayananda was not above taking cheap shots at the Prophet's sexual morality through the Quranic references to his arrangements with his many wives. The most explicit Arya Samaji propounder of this scandal-mongering line of polemic was Mahashay Rajpal, who in the 1920s

---

[205]*Satyârtha Prakâsh* 14:30, *Light of Truth*, p.663.

[206]*Satyârtha Prakâsh* 14:16; *Light of Truth*, p.659.

[207]*Satyârtha Prakâsh* 14:16; *Light of Truth*, p.659.

[208]As Paul Dundas (*The Jains*, p.77) summarizes: "The *loka* [= world] is without beginning or end in time and was not brought into existence through the agency of any divine being."

signed as the writer of the pamphlet *Rangîlâ Rasûl* (roughly "Playboy Mohammed"). Though the book had been ghost-written by an employee of his, it turned Rajpal into a Salman Rushdie *avant la lettre*, except that he did not go underground in time: he was murdered in 1929. It is a rather petty-minded description of the Prophet's sex life, admittedly adapted from impeccably Islamic sources, and a tirade against the alleged licentiousness condoned and inculcated by Islamic law.[209] It was part of an escalation in which "some communal propagandists—Arya, Hindu and Muslim—resorted to vile slander, vicious insinuation and sexual satire".[210]

As for its contents, it was of course no news that even by Islamic standards, Mohammed had a few wives too many; but then what? How could this detail about his lifestyle decide the basic question whether his claim of receiving divine revelations was true or false? And conversely, what about Krishna's frolicking with the *gopîs* (cow-girls), including women married to other men? What about Draupadi's polyandry with no less than five men? This type of scandal-mongering discourse on Islam misses the point completely. Even so, it has retained a certain popularity on the fringes of the Hindutva movement.[211]

A more fundamental criticism of Muslim ethics concerns the Quranic doctrine of predestination, which is rejected as implying an utterly unjust, loveless and whimsical God. Thus, Allah, Who punishes people with eternal hellfire for their unbelief, has first determined Himself who shall be an unbeliever: "There is an infirmity in their hearts and God hath increased that infirmity; Allah through the continuous manifestation of

---

[209]Two similar scandal-mongering pamphets were published by other Arya Samajis in the same period, viz. Pandit Kalicharan Sharma and Devi Sharan Sharma, as reported by J.E. Llewellyn: *Arya Samaj as a Fundamentalist Movement*, p.106.

[210]J.T.F. Jordens: *Swami Shraddhananda*, p.175.

[211]A recent example is P.N. Oak: *Islamic Havoc in Indian History* (1996). Oak, an Indian National Army (Subhash Bose's collaborationist army in 1943-45) veteran who, in his Marathi books, "proves" that the Taj Mahal, Fatehpur Sikri and the Red Fort in Delhi were originally Hindu buildings, is frequently used by Marxist polemicists as a straw figure in whom they can attack "Hindu history-rewriting" without risking a competent rebuttal. Unlike his other books, this one is based on serious sources, and though unabashedly tendentious, it deals in real facts of history; but its distinguishing feature is the inordinate attention it pays to episodes of cruelty and debauchery in the history of the Delhi Sultanate courts, which it relates in full detail, with drawings.

His signs causes their infirmity to grow worse. For them there is a painful punishment because of their lying."[212] Allah declares that it is He Himself, rather than their own free will, who has hardened the hearts of the unbelievers and thus condemned them to the promised punishment. Dayananda comments: "Is not this act more devilish than that of the Devil? To seal their hearts and to increase their infirmity could never be the work of God inasmuch as the increase of infirmity is the result of one's own sinful actions."[213]

This pertains to the whole problem of evil, for which some theologies (Christian, Zoroastrian) have developed complex explanations which, from an Islamic viewpoint, detract from their monotheism. For Islam, the simple and straightforward religion, there is only one Creator, and it accepts the consequence, viz. that He is responsible for evil as well. Man's predestination, even for evil, is the necessary implication of God's being All-Powerful: there cannot be anything which God has not willed.

Similarly, the Quran is quoted as saying: "But God will show His special mercy to whom He will."[214] Here, Dayananda argues, predictably, that this divine predestination makes the whole idea of ethical effort useless: "Does God show His special mercy to those who do not deserve it? If He does, He works great mischief, for all men will become indifferent to the practice of virtue."[215] The role of ethics after the acceptance of a principle of divine love or divine mercy is a point of dispute not merely between Hindus and Muslims (as here), or between Catholics and Calvinists, but also within the theistic schools of Hinduism. There is also a parallel with the intra-Hindu debate between theories of Salvation, viz. between Salvation by divine grace and by one's personal effort.[216] These are interesting and legitimate religious questions, but have little specific relevance to the Hindu-Muslim conflict, which did not arise

---

[212]Q.2:10/9.

[213]*Satyartha Prakash* 14:6; *Light of Truth*, p.654.

[214]Q.2:105/99.

[215]*Satyârtha Prakâsh* 14:24, *Light of Truth*, p.661.

[216]Thus, in Ramanuja's *Shrî-Vaishnava* school of philosophy, there is the well-known debate between "the way of the kitten", in which the soul is being saved by divine grace (the way a kitten is picked up by its mother), and "the way of the baby monkey", in which the soul liberates itself through its own effort (the way a baby monkey grabs its mother with its own hands); see Gavin Flood: *Introduction to Hinduism*, p.137.

as a consequence of philosophical differences of opinion.

Holy war

We get closer to the Hindu-Muslim conflict when we consider the Arya Samaj writings on *jihâd*. A central concept in Islam, and one prominently featuring in debates on Islam worldwide, is *jihâd fî sabîl Allâh*, "effort in the way of Allah", the technical term for "armed struggle against the unbelievers". Swami Dayananda introduces this subject by drawing attention to the non-universality of the Quranic message: a book "which is so full of partiality and favouritism, cannot be the word of God".[217] God's attitude towards believers widely differs from His treatment of the unbelievers, e.g. by promising the earth in this life and paradise in the afterlife to the believers: "The earth will be inherited by My servants",[218] and on Judgment Day, "the God-fearing ones ... will say: praise to God who fulfilled His promise to us and has made us inherit the earh".[219]

Dayananda comments: "The truth is that only the good and the virtuous will enjoy happiness, while the wicked will be subjected to pain and suffering, whichever faith they may belong to."[220] If at all there is a kind of retribution after death, it stands to reason that it would depend on universal criteria like "virtue", rather than on sectarian criteria such as "belief" in the particular claims of this or that prophet. In the same spirit, Dayananda rejects the fundamental Islamic notion that unbelievers are enemies of God, as in: "The curse of God is on the infidels",[221] or in: "God

[217]*Satyârtha Prakâsh* 14:4; *Light of Truth*, p.653.

[218]Q.21:105.

[219]Q.39:73-4. Summarizing the data collected by Dayananda and later authors, we find that the believers are kept out of hell in 44:56, 52:18, except if they refrain from participating in *jihâd*, 8:16. Hell is mentioned with unspecified purpose in 81:12, 102:6. The unbelievers are promised hellfire in 2:24/22, 4:56/59, 5:37/41, 6:70/69, 8:50/52, 9:73/74, 10:4, 21:98, 22:19/20, 26:91, 29:54, 37:23, 37:38/37, 37:55/53, 37:64/62-68/66, 37:97/95, 37:163, 38:27/26, 38:57-61, 39:71-72, 40:6-7, 44:43-50, 46:34/33, 55:44, 56:42/41, 56:54, 56:93-94, 66:9, 69:31, 72:15, 73:12, 78:25, 79:36-39, 82:14, 83:16, 96:18, 98:6/5. Moreover, punishment in the afterlife without specifying hell or hellfire is promised to the unbelievers in Q.2:6-8, 2:16-17, 2:20, 3:85/86, 22:57/56, 25:11/12, 25:19/21, 68:33. Hell is promised to the Jews in Q.59:2-3, 2:80/74, 3:24/23, and to the Christians in Q.5:72/76.

[220]*Satyârtha Prakâsh* 14:8; *Light of Truth*, p.655.

[221]Q.2:88/83.

[222]Q.2:98/92.

[223]*Satyârtha Prakâsh* 14:21; *Light of Truth*, p.661.

is an enemy to infidels".[222] He argues that "God is an enemy to none".[223] He denounces the Quranic division of mankind into two sections, Muslims and non-Muslims, having a radically different status both in this world and in the next.

Highlighting militant verses in the Quran has remained a key element in non-Sangh polemic, even from the mild Swami Vivekananda, for example: "The Mohammedan religion allows Mohammedans to kill all who are not of their religion. It is clearly stated in the Koran, 'Kill the infidels if they do not become Mohammedans.' They must be put to fire and sword."[224] The claimed verse is not to be found anywhere in the Quran, but certain verses come close to the injunction "quoted" by Swamiji, like: "Make war on them until idolatry does not exist any longer and religion belongs to Allah alone."[225]

The late Suhas Majumdar has presented a detailed survey of the jihadic verses in the Quran and the major *Hadîs* collections and biographies of the Prophet. He deduces that Allah "enjoins perpetual war for ... the abolition of all non-Islamic religions the world over".[226] Writing for an urban Hindu audience brought up on either Gandhism or secularism, Suhas Majumdar addresses their probable question: "Is this war allegorical? Since Mahatma Gandhi's allegorical explanation of the Kurukshetra war, it has been the fashion in India to consider all types of religious wars as wars against the baser passions of the human mind. The contagion has not spared even Muslim scholars who are sometimes heard giving a non-violent interpretation of *jihâd*. But such interpretation is clearly contrary to Koranic verses."[227]

We might add that it is also contrary to actual usage: from the Prophet down to contemporary *mujahedîn*, Muslims have always consistently used the term *jihâd* for a specific type of warfare. This usage is not abrogated by an occasional metaphorical use of the same term, just as the metaphorical

---

[224]Swami Vivekananda: *Complete Works*, vol.2, p.335.

[225]Q.2:193/189, also 8:39/40.

[226]S. Majumdar: *Jihad*, p.11. In summary, the Quran exhorts the believers to *jihâd* in at least 22 Quran passages: Q.2:193/189, 3:200, 4:76/78, 4:84/86, 5:33/37, 8:12, 8:39/40, 8:60/62, 8:65/66, 9:5, 9:14, 9:29, 9:41, 9:73/74, 9:111/112, 9:123/124, 25:52/54, 37:22-23, 47:4, 48:29, 66:9. Only in the first one is *jihâd* depicted as defensive. Nine verses glorify participation in *jihâd* and condemn abstention from *jihâd*: Q.2:216/212, 3:142/136, 3:157/151-158/152, 4:74/76, 8:15-16, 9:20, 9:39, 9:111/112, 49:15.

[227]S. Majumdar: *Jihad*, p.12. Kurukshetra, "field of the Kuru clan", near Delhi, is where the decisive battle of the *Mahâbhârata* war was fought.

slogan "war on poverty" does not abrogate the primary meaning of the word *war*. Follow some verses in which the allegorical subtlety is hard to seize, like: "Let those fight in the way of Allah who sell the life of this world for the other. Whoso fighteth in the way of Allah, be he slain or victorious, on him we shall bestow a vast reward."[228] The reference to the chance of being "slain" shows that no allegorical war is meant, but a physical confrontation with winners and losers, martyrs and killers.

Majumdar concludes that *jihâd* generally meant offensive warfare, and that Islamic theology never bothered to hide behind a defensive justification: "Far from being an act of non-aggression, it could not even count as compensatory retaliation by any stretch of the imagination. ... The theory of *jihâd* as defensive war must, in the circumstances, be rejected as a figment of the modern apologist's imagination."[229] At this point, it is a pity that Suhas Majumdar has not taken into account the work of Islamic jurists who have genuinely tried to rethink *jihâd*. It would be interesting to see what proponents of the theory that *jihâd* as offensive war against the infidels is completely intrinsic to Islam, have to say about authentic efforts by Islamic jurists to fit a new interpretation of *jihâd* into an equally new theory of international relations which accepts peace (rather than expansion of the Caliphate) as the norm, even with non-Islamic states, and which reinterprets *jihâd* as "just war", a radical innovation.[230]

The violent verses

In the 1980s, the polemic against the Quran, highlighting its enmity-promoting verses, was taken to the popular level. At the same time, it was taken to the courts, in the form of a petition to ban the Quran.

In India, it is not uncommon that books critical of Islam are banned, for example, R.M. Eaton's published Ph.D. thesis, *Sufis of Bijapur* (1984), which in a few marginal sentences casts an unfavourable light on the Sufi tradition, and Arvind Ghosh's *The Koran and the Kafir*, yet another annotated enumeration of Quranic injunctions which may adversely affect the relations between Muslims and unbelievers. The official motivation

---

[228]Q.4:74/76.

[229]S. Majumdar: *Jihâd*, pp.98-9.

[230]See the Harvard reader on *jihâd*, R. Peters, ed.: *Jihâd in Classical and Modern Islam*, especially the treatise on *jihâd* by the progressive Al-Azhar Rector (1958-63) Mahmud Shaltut. About *jihâd* theory through the centuries, see Alfred Morabia: *Le Gihad dans l'Islam Médiéval*.

for this banning of books is that they have been maliciously intended to create enmity between communities or to hurt the religious feelings of a community (Article 153A and Article 295A of the Indian Penal Code). Under section 95 of the Criminal Procedure Code, the executive power must take action against such books.

In 1984, Himangshu Kishore Chakraborty, a refugee from East Bengal, filed a petition with the Secretary of the Home Department of the West Bengal Government to ban the Quran in accordance with the said articles. He added a list of 37 Quran verses which "preach cruelty, incite violence and disturb public peace" (to use the terminology of the Penal Code), 17 verses which "promote, on grounds of religion, feelings of enmity, hatred and ill-will between different communities in India", and 31 verses which "insult other religions as also the religious beliefs of other communities".

When the West Bengal authorities gave no reply to Chakraborty's petition, one Chandmal Chopra, a Jain, took the matter to the Calcutta High Court, where he filed a petition asking the Court to direct the West Bengal Government to issue a ban on the Quran. He added a list with controversial verses from the Quran: 29 passages from the Quran (1 to 8 verses in length) which "incite violence" against unbelievers, 15 which "promote enmity", 26 which "insult other religions".

Some typical examples cited are: "Mohammed is Allah's apostle. Those who follow him are merciless for the unbelievers but kind to each other."[231] Or: "We break with you; hatred and enmity will reign between us until ye believe in Allah alone."[232] Or: "The Jews and Christians and the Pagans will burn forever in the fire of hell. They are the vilest of all creatures."[233] On this basis, Chandmal Chopra stated in his writ petition: "The cited passages in the Quran ... arouse in Muslims the worst sectarian passions and religious fanaticism, which has manifested itself in murders, massacres, plunder, arson, rape and destruction or desecration of sacred places both in historical and in the contemporary period, not only in India but in large parts of the world."[234]

The petition created a lot of furore in Calcutta and abroad, including riotous Muslim demonstrations in Dhaka (12 killed in police firing),

---

[231]Q.48:29.

[232]Q.60:4.

[233]Q.98:6/5.

[234]S.R. Goel, ed.: *The Calcutta Quran Petition*, p.143.

Ranchi and Srinagar.[235] On 17 May 1985, Justice Bimal Chandra Basak delivered his verdict. He observed that Article 295 of the Indian penal Code *protects* books like the Quran against insults, so that it would be absurd to *ban* the same book under Article 295-A. He dismissed the petition on this ground: "This book is not prejudicial to the maintenance of harmony between different religions. Because of the Quran no public tranquillity has been disturbed upto now and there is no reason to apprehend any likelihood of such disturbance in the future."[236]

Beside Chakraborty's and Chopra's petitions, a third text which pointed to the Quran as a source of religious violence was a poster published in Delhi (1986) by Indra Sain Sharma and Rajkumar Arya, prominent members of the Hindu Mahasabha. The poster carried the caption: "Why do riots break out in this country?" It showed 24 combative Quran verses, such as: "Fight the unbelievers in your surroundings, and let them find harshness in you"[237], and: "Kill the unbelievers wherever ye find them, capture and besiege them and prepare them every kind of ambush".[238] Both publishers were arrested and brought to trial, but they were acquitted. The judge ruled that they had made a "fair criticism", for: "With all due respect to the holy Quran, an attentive perusal of the verses shows that these are indeed harmful and preach violence and have the potential to cause conflicts between the Muslims and the others."[239] The Government did not file an appeal against this judgement and when it did, the appeal was dismissed as time barred.

A basic assumption in such arguments is that unlike the writings of an occasional pamphletteer, the Quran verses are taught as God's own words, repeated in grave tones by mullahs and instilled in children's minds. But then, precisely because the Quran is considered a sacred book, many people take it *less* literally than secular texts. Most Muslims have unbelievers living in their surroundings, yet they do not go out and fight them. Of sacred books, it is easily assumed that they have an esoteric meaning, and that we should await the judgment of competent scholars before acting upon scriptural injunctions. This way, few people act out

---

[235]S.R. Goel, ed.: *The Calcutta Quran Petition*, p.17-18, referring to the *Statesman*, 13/14.5.1985 and to the *Telegraph*, 14.5.1985.

[236]Goel, ed.: *The Calcutta Quran Petition*, pp.160-61.

[237]Q.9:123/124.

[238]Q.9:5.

[239]Quoted in S.R. Goel: *The Calcutta Quran Petition*, p.7.

Krishna's model behaviour of seducing large numbers of cowgirls, or Jesus' model behaviour of turning the other cheek and walking on water; or indeed the jihadic injunctions of the Quran.

Secular apologists of Islam tend to dismiss polemics centred on Islamic scripture as anachronistic and irrelevant; as if any Muslim worth his salt would dismiss the Quran as an "old book" which is no longer valid. Conversely, it could be said that Hindu polemicists err by going to the other extreme, viz. reading Islamic scripture as if it were a faithful rendering of contemporary Islam. In spite of the attempt by Muslims to emulate the Prophet, certain profound changes have nonetheless crept into Islam. Thus, slavery was approved of by Mohammed and the Quran; it was the cornerstone of the Muslim economy from the seventh till the nineteenth century, and when it was abolished by the French and British (in West Africa and India) or under their pressure (in the Ottoman Empire) in the mid-nineteenth century, the move was fiercely opposed by the guardians of orthodoxy.[240] Yet today, no "fundamentalist" who preaches a return to the pure Islam of the Prophet advocates reintroducing the slave-trade; on the contrary, Islam is advertised among American blacks as a religion which has consistently opposed slavery. While this is crudely unhistorical, it does at least show to what extent Muslims have interiorized the un-Islamic rejection of slavery. This way, living Islam cannot be entirely reduced to its Quranic origins.

Mohammed's own holy wars

Context is the key to the meaning of a text, and the jihadic verses in the Quran are part of the justification of actual warfare in which the Prophet and his companions engaged. It is nonsense to discuss "contemporary Indian Islam" as a subject in its own right without reference to the life and works of Prophet Mohammed in the seventh-century Arabia, for there simply is no Islam without the constant invocation of Mohammed's mission and example, no Islamic Law without permanent reference to Mohammed's model behaviour. The real meaning of and intention behind the concept of *jihâd* can best be checked at the very source where Islamic scholars learn the alpha and omega of their religion: the traditions concerning the words and deeds of the Prophet, or *ahâdîs* (singular *hadîs*).

---

[240]On Islamic slavery, see Bernard Lewis: *Race and Slavery in the Middle East*; Murray Gordon: *Slavery in the Arab World*; and specifically from a Hindu angle, K.S. Lal: *Muslim Slave System in Medieval India*.

Suhas Majumdar claims that the purely aggressive nature of *jihâd* can be verified in the *Hadîs* literature: "Very many verses of the Koran and the whole of the *Hadîs* literature breathe the spirit of unqualified aggression. ... not a single *ghazwah* ... of the Prophet, barring that of Uhud (AD 625) and Ahzâb (AD 627), can by any stretch of the imagination be reckoned defensive war. In other words, 24 out of 26 *ghazwahs* of the Prophet were aggressive in intent as well as execution."[241]

It is Ram Swarup's stated view that the Prophet brought a new ethics of warfare, a "total war" more ruthless than what the Arabs had known till then, and that one after another, he broke all the existing taboos which limited the scope of warfare in Pagan Arabia, like the prohibition to kill kinsfolk, the prohibition on warfare in the sacred months (the ones before, during and after the annual Pagan pilgrimage to Mecca), and the prohibition on cutting the scarce useful vegetation. This goes against the common apologetic claim that if Mohammed's Islam was sometimes characterized by violence, it was due to the violent nature of Arab society, which was then gradually *tempered* by Islam.

Ram Swarup also discusses the Prophet's major raids and battles, and his policies vis-à-vis the non-Muslims, for example his warning to the Jews who were unwilling to accept Islam: "You should know that the earth belongs to Allah and His apostle, and I wish that I should expel you from this land", and his announcement to his lieutenant Umar: "I will expel the Jews and the Christians from the Arabian peninsula and will not leave any but Muslims".[242] Ram Swarup connects the destruction of Arabia's multicultural society by Mohammed with the doctrine of monotheism: "Pagan Arabia accepted Jews and Christians but rejected their God for itself; Muslim Arabia accepted their God but rejected His people."[243] The testimony of stray cases of intolerance by non-monotheistic religions is rejected: "Religious intolerance was there before, but it was not supported by a theology. It was with the coming of Christianity and Islam that

---

[241]S. Majumdar: *Jihâd*, p.64. *Ghazwa* (Arabic, whence Italian *razzia*): raid. For the count of Mohammed's raids (26 led by the Prophet himself and 56 by his lieutenants, according to the most common version, others not differing much), see *Sahîh Muslim* 2283 and 4464-4469, discussed in Ram Swarup: *Understanding Islam through Hadis*, p.108.

[242]Ram Swarup: *Understanding Islam*, p.110, with reference to *Sahih al-Muslim*, 4363 and 4366.

[243]Ram Swarup: *Hindu View of Christianity and Islam*, p.39.

religious arrogance descended on the earth on a large scale and with a new power."[244]

Predictably, he pays detailed attention to the Prophet's mass execution of about 700 Jews belonging to the *Banû Quraiza*, the last remaining Jewish tribe in Medina.[245] Other paragraphs are devoted to the conquest of Mecca, with its iconoclasm in the Ka'ba, and to the assassination (before the conquest) or formal execution (after the conquest) of about a dozen of the Prophet's critics. Ram Swarup argues, in a summary of the scriptural references given to the same effect by two Islamic scholars, that Ayotallah Khomeini's death sentence against Salman Rushdie was nothing but the emulation of Mohammed's model behaviour.[246] This way, a critical look at Mohammed remains the key to understanding the problems which Islam poses today.

A Hindu look into Mohammed's mind

The Hindu revivalist school connects the nature of Mohammed's leadership with the nature of his status as prophet. The basis of Islam is the belief that Mohammed heard a voice dictating Allah's own words. This is understood to have been a constant process of "revelation" from AD 610 (when Mohammed was 40) until his death in AD 632. The compilation of these "divine revelations" is the Quran. As Hindu students of Islam point out,

---

[244]Ram Swarup: *Hindu View of Christianity and Islam*, p.41.

[245]Ram Swarup: *Understanding Islam*, pp.110-14. The historicity of this "Arabian holocaust" is questioned by Barakat Ahmad: *Muhammad and the Jews*, pp.68-94. If he is right, it would exonerate Mohammed, but it would also undermine the very basis of the entire edifice of Islamic law, viz. the accuracy of the testimonies concerning Mohammed's model behaviour which has precedent value in setting standards of what is lawful for Muslims. Islam being a self-described "seamless garment", the falseness of one tradition would render every other tradition questionable as well.

[246]Ram Swarup: "Swords to sell a god", *Telegraph*, 16.6.1992, with reference to Maulana Mohsin Usmani Nadwi: *Ahânat-i Rasûl kî Sazâ* (Urdu: "Punishment for Criticizing the Prophet"), and Maulana Majid Ali Khan: *Muqaddas Ayat* (Urdu: "The Sacred Verses"), both Delhi, 1989, and both written in defence of Khomeini's death sentence. Specifically directed against apostates like Rushdie is: "If they turn away from you, catch them and slay them wherever ye find them" (Q.4:89/91). This is supported by a *hadîs* (Bukhari 88:2): when Ali had some apostates killed on the pyre, his lieutenant Ibn Abbas protested that the Prophet had prescribed a different punishment: "Do not punish with God's punishment [i.e. fire, as in hell], but him who changes his religion, kill him with the sword."

many of Mohammed's contemporaries were skeptical of his recipiency of divine messages: "The Meccans stood firm by their gods; their faith in the gods was not at all shaken by Muhammad's attacks. Allah reports: 'When it was said unto them, There is no God save Allah, they were scornful, and said: Shall we forsake our gods for a mad poet?'[247] 'And they marvel that a warner from among themselves had come. They say: This is a wizard, a charlatan.'"[248-49] Some modern Western and even some Muslim-born scholars have diagnosed the process of revelation as a case of paranoid delusion.[250] Others classify Mohammed as a kind of Shamanic medium, which still undermines his claim to a unique status as the final prophet.[251] The specifically Hindu contribution to this perspective on Quranic revelation is to bring in the yogic experience.

As an example of how yogic practice can go wrong, warning against the dangers of experimenting with yoga without competent guidance, Swami Vivekananda mentioned none other than Mohammed: "The yogi says there is a great danger in stumbling upon this state. In a good many cases, there is the danger of the brain being deranged, and, as a rule, you will find that all those men, however great they were, who had stumbled upon this superconscious state without understanding it, groped in the dark, and generally had, along with their knowledge, some quaint superstition. They opened themselves to hallucinations. Mohammed claimed that the Angel Gabriel came to him in a cave one day and took him on the heavenly horse, Burak, and he visited the heavens.

"But with all that, Mohammed spoke some wonderful truths. If you read the Koran, you find the most wonderful truths mixed with superstitions. How will you explain it? That man was inspired, no doubt, but that inspiration was, as it were, stumbled upon. He was not a trained

---

[247]Q.34-36/35.

[248]Q.38:4/3.

[249]S.R. Goel: *Hindu Temples*, vol.2, p.334.

[250]See e.g. Maxime Rodinson: *Mohammed*, pp.78-9; and for the most systematic analysis, Herman Somers: *Een Andere Mohammed* (Dutch: "A Different Mohammed"). Reportedly, a similar view is developed in Abdullah Kamal: *A Psychological Analysis of Prophets* (in Arabic, first published as a serial in the Egyptian magazine *Rose al-Youssef* in early 1996), as reported by Reuters (e.g. *De Standaard*, 15.7.1996), which adds that Shaykh Mohammed al-Tantawi of *al-Azhar* issued a *fatwa* calling the book "blasphemous" and had its stock confiscated.

[251]E.g., G. Feuerstein: *Holy Madness* (a book on the interface between religion and altered mental conditions), p.15.

Yogi, and did not know the reason of what he was doing. Think of the good Mohammed did to the world, and think of the great evil that has been done through his fanaticism! Think of the millions massacred through his teachings, mothers bereft of their children, children made orphans, whole countries destroyed, millions upon millions of people killed! ... So we see this danger by studying the lives of great teachers like Mohammad and others. Yet we find, at the same time, that they were all inspired. Whenever a prophet got into the superconscious state by heightening his emotional nature, he brought away from it not only some truths, but some fanaticism also, some superstition which injured the world as much as the greatness of the teaching helped."[252]

Most yoga manuals emphatically warn against wrongly practising the techniques of *Hatha Yoga*, which are very powerful whether used properly or in disregard of the concomitant rules. Yogic masters can relate anecdotes of pupils or colleagues who spurned the precautions and practised dangerous forms of *prânâyâma* ("breath control" or "control of the vital energies") till they impaired their nerve systems.[253] Many mystic phenomena the world over come about as cases of stumbling upon certain states of consciousness, which may lead to some kind of "enlightenment" but also to serious delusions (most typically megalomania, witness the self-importance of the assorted messiahs in the modern cult scene). Hindu yogis claim to have left these dangerous mind games behind because their forebears have developed a safe and sound method laid down in such classics as Patanjali's *Yoga Sûtra*. Ram Swarup argues that the methodical and systematic "science of yoga" has a substantial qualitative edge over other forms of mysticism or mediumism.[254] From this angle, it is unfair (even if fashionably in tune with the "equal truth of all religions" doctrine) to put yoga in one class with the experiments of Shamans taking

[252]Vivekananda: *Complete Works*, vol.1, p.184. The passage is from the book *Raja Yoga*, Ch.7: "Dhyana and Samadhi". Mental disturbance as a consequence of meditative experiments had already been named as the cause of the Quranic revelations by Gisbertus Voetius, a seventeenth-century Calvinist theologian from Utrecht (Netherlands) who trained missionaries for conversion work in Indonesia; discussed in Karel Steenbrink: *Dutch Colonialism and Indonesian Islam*.

[253]One written testimony is given in Gopi Krishna: *Kundalini*. Arya Samaj leader V.R. Rao told me of one case involving a friend of his who inflicted brain damage on himself and died of a stroke as a consequence of improper *prânâyâma* practice. Likewise, Taoist *Qigong* comes with the same warning and anecdotes.

[254]Ram Swarup: *Hindu View of Christianity and Islam*, pp.45-6.

hallucinogenic plants, or with the uninvited voice-hearing experiences of Mohammed.

In recent years, Ram Swarup and Sita Ram Goel have further developed Swami Vivekananda's position on the nature of Quranic revelation.[255] They conclude that the Pagan Arabs had every right to reject Mohammed's claims, born from a deluded consciousness but propagated on a war footing, but that they made the one mistake which history does not forgive, viz. the mistake of being defeated. However, "the fact that they failed to understand the ways of Mohammed and could not match his mailed fist in the final round, should not be held against them. It was neither the first nor the last time that a democratic society succumbed in the face of determined gangsterism. We know how Lenin, Hitler and Mao Tse-tung succeeded in our own times."[256]

As far as I can see, the foregoing constitutes the single most radical criticism of Islam available in the world. Christian critics, no matter how fierce, usually appreciate at least Mohammed's monotheism, which does not impress these Hindu authors. Though "irreverent" and "demythologizing" are among the most specious words of praise in the review columns of modern newspapers, few people have the stomach for something as irreverent and demythologizing as the Hindu revivalist analysis of the Prophet's mission.[257] Most spokesmen of the organized Hindutva movement, at any rate, stay as far away from it as possible.

Holy war in Indian history

Swami Dayananda had based his polemic against Islam purely on Islamic scripture. His follower Pandit Lekh Ram (1858-97) brought in another type of evidence against Islam, viz. Islam's actual history. In his *Risâla-i-Jihâd ya'ni Dîn-i-Muhammadî kî Bunyâd* (Urdu: "A Treatise on Holy War, or the Basis of the Mohammedan Religion", Lahore 1892), Lekh Ram argues that Islam has always been intolerant and aggressive compared to all other religions, and that it is incapable of peaceful co-

---

[255]Ram Swarup: *Hindu View of Christianity and Islam*, p.107; S.R. Goel, ed. *The Calcutta Quran Petition*, p.103 ff.; with reference to A. Guillaume: *Life of Muhammad*, pp.104/150-107/154.

[256]Goel: *Hindu Temples*, vol.2, p.272.

[257]In the case of other prophets, this psychopathological critique is not that uncommon, e.g. Gershom Scholem (*Sabbatai Zwi, der mystische Messias*, p.150) calls the seventeenth-century Jewish self-styled messiah Sabbatai Zwi a manic-depressive neurotic. In *Jesus Christ, an Artifice for Aggression*, Sita Ram Goel lists a whole series of Western scholars and medics who have made a similar diagnosis of Jesus.

existence except as a matter of temporary truce in the ongoing struggle to turn the whole world into an Islamic state.

The context of Lekh Ram's argument was the tendency in late-nineteenth-century Islamic apologetics to downplay the importance of *jihâd* in Islam. After the enthusiastic participation of Muslims in the 1857 Mutiny (which was largely an attempt to restore the Moghul empire), the emerging class of modernist Muslims led by Sir Sayyid Ahmad Khan (1817-1898, a civil servant who remained loyal to the British during the 1857 Mutiny) adapted their discourse in order to assuage British suspicions about the political and military programme of Islam. They repudiated the nominal loyalty which Indian Muslims owed the Caliph in Istanbul and affirmed that they were loyal subjects of the British Government.[258]

The reinterpretation in a purely moral or pacifist sense of the term *jihâd* was part of this charm offensive, though it also showed the genuine influence of the newly dominant Enlightenment mentality, which favoured pluralism and abhorred the use of force in the service of religion. Pandit Lekh Ram observed: "Since then some naturalist Mohammadis are trying, rather than opposing falsehood and accepting the truth, to prove unnecessarily and wrongly that Islam never indulged in Jihad and the people were never converted to Islam forcibly."[259] Lekh Ram countered this new line in Muslim apologetics by quoting at length from Muslim accounts of self-described *jihâd* in Indian history, featuring conquerors like Mahmud Ghaznavi, Mohammed Ghori, Timur, Alauddin Khilji and Aurangzeb.

Recent variations on this approach are the books by Sita Ram Goel: *Story of Islamic Imperialism in India*, and, focusing specifically on the aspect of temple destructions: *Hindu Temples, What Happened to Them*. The backbone of this class of books essentially consists in a list of quotations from Muslim sources describing the destruction of Hindu lives and Hindu culture. As to facts, the view of history presented by them, though obviously selective, is not really controversial; we encounter the

---

[258]Rajmohan Gandhi: *Understanding the Muslim Mind*, p.26.

[259]Lekh Ram: *Risâlâ-i-Jihâd* (Aror Bans Press, Lahore 1892), p.1, quoted in K.W. Jones: *Arya Dharm*, p.150. Lekh Ram had a rather simplistic view of "conversion by force". Many conversions took place under social pressure, e.g. people converted to escape the *jizya* (poll-tax levied on non-Muslims), to achieve legal equality with a Muslim opponent in a lawsuit, or to lawfully marry a Muslim girl. Such conversions were not the result of a religious conviction and would not have taken place but for their tangible advantages, yet they were not the same thing as conversions at swordpoint.

same facts in standard history books by Western authors, even by those who sympathize with Islam.

Thus, French Indologist Louis Frédéric, who emphasizes in his introduction that the Muslims in India created an "original civilization, combining Hindu and Muslim influences", frequently mentions forced conversions, massacres and temple demolitions: "Mohammed Ghori had the Hindu temples of Ajmer demolished and ordered the construction of mosques and Quran schools on their ruins. ... He plundered Kanauj and Kashi and destroyed their temples" while his generals "destroyed in passing the remaining Buddhist communities of Bihar and destroyed the universities of Nalanda".[260] Bakhtiar Khilji "established a Muslim capital in Lakhnautî (Gaur) on the Ganga and destroyed, in 1197, its basalt temples. In Odantpurî, in 1202, he massacred two thousand Buddhist monks."[261] Meanwhile, back in Delhi: "This Quwwat-ul-Islam (Might of Islam) was built in a hurry using the debris, chiefly sculpted pillars, of twenty-seven dismantled Hindu temples."[262] Thirty years later, "Iltutmish did not forget that he was a Muslim conqueror. He showed himself to be very pious, never forgetting to do his five devotions daily. ... He likewise showed himself totally intolerant vis-à-vis the Hindus who refused to convert, destroying their temples and annihilating Brahmin communities".[263]

However, in India a literature has developed which denies, minimizes or whitewashes this history.[264] For Goel as for Lekh Ram, the stated motive for collecting and publishing primary evidence is indignation at the contrast between the negationist claims of modern Islamic apologetics (often adopted by leading secularists)[265] and the testimony of historical

---

[260]L. Frédéric: *L'Inde de l'Islam*, p.42.

[261]L. Frédéric: *L'Inde de l'Islam*, p.44.

[262]L. Frédéric: *L'Inde de l'Islam*, p.45.

[263]L. Frédéric: *L'Inde de l'Islam*, p.49.

[264]Two classics in the effort to justify the Muslim conquest and minimize its atrocities are Mohammed Habib: *Introduction* to the 1951 reprint of vol.2 (on the effective Muslim conquest, twelfth-thirteenth century) of H.M. Elliot and J. Dowson: *History of India as Told by Its Own Historians*; and M. Habib and K.M. Nizami: *A Comprehensive History of India*, vol.5, *The Delhi Sultanate*.

[265]Trend-setting publications promoting a positive perspective on the Islamic conquest of India include the Report by the Indian National Congress' Committee of Enquiry into the Cawnpore (Kanpur) Riots, written mostly by Bhagwan Das and Pandit Sunder Lal in 1932-33, and reproduced in its entirety in N.G. Barrier: *Roots of Communal Politics*; secondly M.N. Roy (founder of the CPI): *Role of Islam in History* (1939); and thirdly Jawaharlal Nehru: *The Discovery of India* (1946).

records no less Islamic: "There was a time, not so long ago, when the exponents of *jihâd* minced no words and pulled no punches. They were brutally frank in spelling out what *jihâd* really meant. But times have changed. ... Standards of moral judgements have increasingly tended to become universal, and no statement of faith can escape scrutiny simply because it is made in a book hailed as holy by some people. Defenders of *jihâd* have been forced to develop an apologetics. They are now trying to protect by means of scholarship a doctrine which has so far been sustained by means of the sword."[266]

The view of Islam represented by authors from Lekh Ram down to Sita Ram Goel is widespread in Hindu society. Swami Vivekananda (who, unlike Lekh Ram and Goel, also had some nice things to say about Islam) merely voiced the *communis opinio* when he wrote that "the Mohammedans used the greatest violence",[267] and when he asserted: "You know that the Hindu religion never persecutes. It is the land where all sects may live in peace and amity. The Mohammedans brought murder and slaughter in their train, but until their arrival peace prevailed."[268]

Hindu and Muslim ethic of warfare

The self-perception of Hindus as essentially non-violent, and in contrast with Muslims, has been widespread during most of the twentieth century, especially after being greatly encouraged by Mahatma Gandhi (who even read pacifism into the *Bhagavad-Gîtâ*, actually an exhortation to hero Arjuna to participate in battle). However, war was common enough in pre-Muslim India, as should be clear from the epics *Râmâyana* and *Mahâbhârata*; though the contenders in both stories shared the same religion, their purely secular conflicts of interest provided ample cause for waging wars. At most it could be said that peace prevailed between different religions or sects as such; but for the victims of the wars which did take place, it may not have mattered much whether they were killed for the true religion or for some more mundane reason.

---

[266]S.R. Goel in foreword to S. Majumdar: *Jihâd*, p.v. A Western scholar of religion, Jonathan Riley-Smith ("Reinterpreting the Crusades", *The Economist*, 23.12.1995, p.75), has summed up the debate thus: "Some Muslims now maintain that the *jihâd* should be interpreted merely as a battle against evil. But in its traditional form, it was a war for the extension of Islamic territory. Some Muslims still seem to envisage the use of force, not only to counter perceived threats to their way of life, but to bring about world reformation on their own terms."

[267]Vivekananda, *Complete Works*, vol.8, p.217.

[268]Vivekananda: *Complete Works*, vol.5, p.190.

On the other hand, Hindu apologists have a point when they assert that Hinduism knows of no *jihâd* or "holy war" concept. The "corresponding" Hindu concept of *Dharma-yuddha* means "war according to a chivalrous deontology", not war for religion but war subject to "religious" or at least dharmic rules. This much is a fact, that Hindu scriptures do prescribe strict rules of chivalry, e.g.: "One should not kill the enemy who is lying unconscious, who is crippled, devoid of weapon, or is stricken with fear and also who has come for shelter (asylum). A strong and brave warrior should not chase and kill any fleeing enemy, who is stricken with fear."[269] And: "The person who is asleep, who is in a drunken state, who is devoid of clothes or weapons, the lady, the minor, the helpless, the afraid one who deserts the battlefield should not be killed."[270]

This tradition of chivalry is often contrasted with the allegedly more barbarous Muslim style of warfare, for example Golwalkar cites an application of these rules to prove Hinduism's moral superiority: "The famous instance of Shivaji who sent back honourably and laden with presents the beautiful daughter-in-law of the Muslim Subedar of Kalyan captured in war (though it appears exceptional in the eyes of the foreign, especially Muslim, historians) is a very ordinary instance of the sublime culture of this land."[271]

On the other hand, this chivalry is also blamed for the most decisive Hindu defeat against a Muslim invader in the second battle of Tarain in 1292: a year before, at the same site and against the same army led by the same Mohammed Ghori, a victorious Prithviraj Chauhan "could now have easily consummated his victory by chasing and annihilating his routed enemy. But instead, he allowed the defeated Muslim army to return unmolested."[272] The Hindus made the same strategic mistake as the Pagan Arabs during the *Ridda* ("return" to Paganism, apostasy) war just after Mohammed's death: they defeated Abu Bakr's Muslim army but failed to pursue the fleeing Muslims, so that the latter could regroup and return victorious.

It remains an interesting topic for research to what extent the scriptural code of chivalrous warfare was a reality or merely an ideal. It certainly had

[269]*Dhanurveda* 3:41-42, tra. Purnima Ray: *Vasistha's Dhanurveda Samhitâ*, pp.64-5.

[270]*Dhanurveda* 3:64, tra. Purnima Ray: *Vasistha's Dhanurveda Samhitâ*, pp.74-5.

[271]Golwalkar: *Bunch of Thoughts*, p.163. *Sûbedâr*: provincial governor.

[272]R.G. Misra: *Indian Resistance*, p.92. A popular variation (probably stemming from confusion with Ghaznavi's raids, often estimated as numbering 17) is that Prithviraj offered pardon to a defeated Mohammed Ghori no less than 17 times.

its limitations. No less a person than Krishna used, and advised others to use, deceit and below-the-belt strikes at critical moments in the *Mahâbhârata* war (at least against people to whom no moral appeal proved possible), apparently assuming the doctrine that the end justifies the means. Thus, Karna was killed while he was pulling his chariot up when it got stuck.[273] The justification given was that the enemy side had proven so treacherous that against them, a *dharma-yuddha* (war which follows the code of chivalry) was impossible. It stands to reason that many a Hindu general in history must have considered his enemy equally unworthy of chivalrous treatment.

The mirage of Hindu-Muslim unity

A number of Arya Samajis have written pamphlets against Islam, others have cursorily made critical remarks about it. The most famous example of the latter type is probably Lala Lajpat Rai's letter to C.R. Das on the theme of Hindu-Mohammedan unity, after the 1922 Khilafat riots: "I have devoted most of my time during the last six months to the study of Muslim history and Muslim law and I am inclined to think, it [= *Hindu-Muslim unity*] is neither possible nor practicable. Assuming and admitting the sincerity of the Mohamedan leaders in the non-cooperation movement, I think their religion provides an effective bar to anything of the kind. ... I am also fully prepared to trust the Muslim leaders, but what about the Quran and the Hadis? The leaders cannot override them."[274]

Swami Vivekananda is likewise sceptical: "Mohammedans talk of universal brotherhood, but what comes out of that, in reality? Why, anybody who is not a Mohammedan will not be admitted into the brotherhood; he will more likely have his throat cut."[275]

An important part of the Congress view of the Hindu-Muslim conflict was that it had been created (rather than just exploited) by the British. Aurobindo ridiculed this as escapist myth-making. When a disciple said that "it is because of the British divide-and-rule policy that we [Hindus and

[273]A list of examples of Krishna's less than chivalrous conduct is given in W. Callewaert: *India, betoverende verscheidenheid*, p.140.

[274]This letter is frequently referred to or republished in Hindutva publications, e.g. Indra Prakash: *Life of Savarkar*, and B.N. Jog: *Threat of Islam*, pp.166-67; also quoted with approval in Dr. Ambedkar: *Pakistan* (vol.8 of his *Writings and Speeches*) pp.275-76.

[275]Vivekananda: *Complete Works*, vol.2, p.380; possibly alluding to Q.48:29: "Mohammed is Allah's apostle. Those who follow him are merciless to the unbelievers but kind to each other."

Muslims] can't unite", Aurobindo replied: "Nonsense! Was there unity in India before the British rule?"[276]

He believed that the Hindu-Muslim conflict had deeper roots than British machinations, and consequently rejected any expectations of imminent Hindu-Muslim reconciliation as a result of Gandhi's policies: "You can live amicably with a religion whose principle is toleration. But how is it possible to live peacefully with a religion whose principle is 'I will not tolerate you'? How are you going to have unity with these people? Certainly, Hindu-Muslim unity cannot be arrived at on the basis that the Muslims will go on converting Hindus while the Hindus shall not convert any Mohamedan."[277]

Though Aurobindo himself was never personally involved in the Hindu-Muslim conflict, he did countenance the possibility that the Hindus would have to fight against the Muslims: "I am sorry they are making a fetish of this Hindu-Muslim unity. It is no use ignoring facts; some day the Hindus may have to fight the Muslims and they must prepare for it. Hindu-Muslim unity should not mean the subjection of the Hindus. Every time the mildness of the Hindus has given way. The best solution would be to allow the Hindus to organize themselves and the Hindu-Muslim unity would take care of itself, it would automatically solve the problem."[278] This last statement put Aurobindo squarely in the camp of *Hindû Sangathan*, "Hindu self-organization", a project launched by Swami Shraddhananda and taken up systematically by the RSS.

V.D. Savarkar did not believe the Congressite assurance that the Hindu-Muslim conflict was merely the result of British machinations: "These well-meaning but unthinking friends take their dreams for realities. That is why they are impatient of communal tangles and attribute them to communal organizations. But the solid fact is that the so-called communal questions are but a legacy handed down to us by centuries of a cultural, religious and national antagonism between the Hindus and the Muslims."[279]

---

[276]Aurobindo (1940): *India's Rebirth*, p.221.

[277]Aurobindo: *India's Rebirth* (a collection of sayings partly selected from the *Evening Talks*; 23.7.1923), p.161. The larger context is the controversy on the Arya Samaj's Shuddhi campaign, which Mahatma Gandhi opposed.

[278]Sri Aurobindo (18.4.1923): *India's Rebirth*, p.160.

[279]Savarkar: *Hindu Rashtra Darshan*, p.24. Reference is at least partly to the Congress report on the Kanpur riots, a seminal text which argues at length that the communal problem was created by the British.

The view of Hindu-Muslim hostility as profound and ultimately intrinsic to the very nature of Islam has been articulated most sharply by Sita Ram Goel, and could be summarized as follows.[280] Islam started as a movement to destroy the traditional religion of Arabia, a pluralistic and polytheistic religion typologically similar to Hinduism. The Islamic war against Hinduism waged by a long series of invaders (AD 636 to 1761) was nothing but a continuation of the war waged by Mohammed himself against Arab Paganism. This explains Islam's fiercer and more intolerant policy vis-à-vis Hinduism as compared with Christianity and Judaism.

Due to the demographic magnitude of Hindu society and the resultant power equation, Muslim rulers, who frequently had to contend with palace revolutions by fellow Muslims, were forced to compromise with the Hindus, using the model already instituted in the "toleration" of Christians and Jews in West Asia (including the payment of the *jizya* or toleration tax), and even incorporating semi-independent Hindu princes as vassals in the imperial command structure under Akbar (1556-1605). But the spirit of uncompromising hostility remained alive among the clergy; it was reinstalled as state doctrine by Aurangzeb and revived on a smaller scale on numerous occasions during the colonial and post-colonial periods. According to Goel, a basic awareness of this implacable hostility to Hinduism has lingered in the Indian Muslim mind due to Quranic indoctrination, and it is this mentality which explains phenomena like the Partition of India (1947) and the Bangladesh genocide (1971).

In praise of Islam?

At the turn of 1993, the year in which Swami Vivekananda's 1893 trip to America and speech before the Parliament of Religions in Chicago was to be commemorated, the CPI, CPM and various militant secularists were brandishing Swami Vivekananda's name in their campaign against the Hindutva movement.[281] They claimed that Swamiji had been a "secularist"

---

[280]See esp. S.R. Goel: *Muslim Separatism, Causes and Consequences*, and his preface to S.R. Goel, ed.: *The Calcutta Quran Petition*,

[281]See the debate in *Sunday* between A.B. Bardhan (CPI) on the one hand and Arun Shourie and Dina Nath Mishra on the other: Shourie: "Myths about the Swami", 31.1.1993, and "Quotable Quotes", 7.2.1993; Mishra: "Visions of a Hindu India", 2.5.1993; Bardhan: "Of Shourie and Vivekananda", 28.3.1993, and "The many faces of Vivekananda", 8.8.1993. See also the debate in *Blitz*: Bardhan: "RSS can't hijack him", 14.8.1993; S. Gurumurthy: "He can't be desaffronised", 14.8.1993; Madhu Dandavate: "Don't communalise him", 14.8.1993.

(a concept which was simply non-existent in Vivekananda's India), and in particular that he opposed the aversion for Islam common among Hindus and allegedly cultivated by the contemporary Hindutva movement.[282] When Arun Shourie challenged these claims, they tried to back them up with a selection of quotations.[283]

These show that on occasion, Swami Vivekananda was undeniably full of praise for Islam, e.g.: "Mohammed married quite a number of wives afterwards. Great men may marry two hundred wives each. The characters of the great souls are mysterious, their methods past our finding out. We must not judge them. Christ may judge Mohammed. Who are you and I? Little babies. What do we understand of these great souls? Mohammedanism came as a message for the masses. The first message was equality. There is one religion—love. No more question of race, colour, [or] anything else. Join it! That practical quality carried the day. ... The great message was perfectly simple: believe in one God, the creator of heaven and earth."[284]

The Marxist fortnightly *Frontline* did not have great difficulty in finding a Swami willing to defend its own thesis that Swami Vivekananda was a "secularist": Kundrakudi Adigalar, the 45th head of the *Kundrakudî Tiruvannamalai Adhînam* in Tamil Nadu. The Adigalar does have a point when he argues that Vivekananda also said some nice things about Islam: "Swami Vivekananda also has said: 'The Mohammedan conquest of India came as a salvation to the down-trodden, to the poor. That is why one-fifth of our people have become Mohammedans. It was not the sword alone that did it all.'"[285] It is undeniable that Vivekananda has on occasion spoken in favour of Islam.

The Adigalar, along with the CPI, CPM and their press, also repeats the famous *"Vedanta brain, Islam body"* quotation: "On the other hand, my experience is that if ever any religion approached to this equality in an appreciable manner, it is Islam and Islam alone. Therefore I am firmly persuaded that without the help of practical Islam, theories of Vedantism,

[282]To be on the safe side of secularism, the Ramakrishna Mission is trying to sanitize Vivekananda by censoring out some of his statements critical of Islam in recent popular editions of his works; that, at least, is disclosed by Arun Shourie: *A Secular Agenda*, p.71.

[283]See, for the quotations plus Shourie's comment, A. Shourie: "Read before You Quote", included as Ch.37 of A. Shourie: *A Secular Agenda*.

[284]Vivekananda: *Complete Works* vol.1, p.482.

[285]Reference is to Vivekananda: *Complete Works*, vol.3, p.294.

however fine and wonderful they may be, are entirely valueless to the vast mass of mankind. ... For our own Motherland a junction of the two great systems, Hinduism and Islam—Vedanta brain and Islam body—is the only hope."[286] It is typical of modern religious-polemical discourse in India that this statement by Vivekananda is quoted again and again without anyone properly reflecting on it. After all, contrary to what its quoters imply, this statement is hardly even-handed between Hinduism ("Vedanta") and Islam. Though it accepts "Islam body", meaning social equality, the guiding light remains Hindu, the "Vedanta brain".

Moreover, a grimmer version of Vivekananda's view of the relation between Islam and the Hindu problem of inequality is also available: "If you grind down the people, you will suffer. We in India are suffering the vengeance of God. Look upon these things. They ground down those poor people for their own wealth, they heard not the voice of distress, they ate from gold and silver when the people cried for bread, and the Mohammedans came upon them slaughtering and killing; slaughtering and killing they over-ran them."[287] This is Biblical language down to the details of style, but the most Biblical element, in almost literal imitation of the great prophets, is its claim about "the vengeance of God".

While ostensibly agreeing with the present-day Muslim claim that conversions were related to injustice in Hindu society, Vivekananda's position can hardly be called sympathetic to Islam: he considers its progress as a divine *punishment*. Secular psychologist Sudhir Kakar aptly warns the secularist Vivekananda quoters: "Swami Vivekananda, too, I am afraid, belongs to the Hindu nationalist camp as far as the Muslim question is concerned."[288]

Likewise, Kakar cautions against the incorporation of Sri Aurobindo into the secularist pantheon on the basis of a stray Muslim-friendly quotation: "In his *Evening Talks*, Sri Aurobindo's evaluation of Muslim rule is uniformly negative."[289] The *Evening Talks* contain Aurobindo's stray comments on politics after he had formally retreated into a life of yoga; during his political and especially his revolutionary period (up to

---

[286]Swami Vivekananda: *Complete Works*, vol.4, pp.415-16.

[287]Swami Vivekananda: *Complete Works*, vol.7, p.279. It goes without saying that this purely negative view of pre-Islamic caste society is rejected by a number of Hindu scholars, e.g. K.S. Lal: *Growth of Scheduled Tribes and Castes in Medieval India*.

[288]Sudhir Kakar: "Disdain behind Hindu tolerance", *Times of India*, 25.8.1993.

[289]Sudhir Kakar: "Disdain behind Hindu tolerance", *Times of India*, 25.8.1993.

1909), Aurobindo made little distinction between Hindu and Muslim, as was common in the revolutionary movement. He is frequently applauded for saying that "the Mussalman domination ceased very rapidly to be a foreign rule ... even the foreign kings and nobles became almost immediately wholly Indian in mind, life and interest".[290] This statement is at variance with the refusal of all Muslim rulers until the eighteenth century to learn an Indian language, the court language being Persian; but its inaccuracy does not stand in the way of proving young Aurobindo's "secularism".

To counter the impression created by this single line, Kakar quotes the following passage: "The Mohamedan or Islamic culture hardly gave anything to the world which may be said to be of fundamental importance and typically its own; Islamic culture was mainly borrowed from others. Their mathematics and astronomy and other subjects were derived from Greece. It is true they gave some of these things a new turn, but they have not created much. Their philosophy and their religion are very simple and what they call Sufism is largely the result of gnostics who lived in Persia and it is the logical outcome of that school of thought largely touched by Vedanta. [Except for Indo-Saracenic architecture], I do not think it has done anything more in India of cultural value. It gave some new forms to art and poetry. Its political institutions were always semi-barbaric."[291]

Kakar's point is that even when advocating tolerance, Aurobindo and Vivekananda didn't hide their disdain for Islam. An instance which he does not cite but which aptly proves his point, is this letter by Aurobindo to a Muslim disciple: "You have insisted on my writing and asked for the Truth and I have answered. But if you want to be a Mussalman, no one prevents you. If the Truth I bring is too great for you to understand or to bear, you are free to go and live in a half-truth or in your own ignorance."[292] Aurobindo's (and most Hindus') attitude of tolerance regarding Islam is conceived as the condescending tolerance of an adult for the juvenile follies of a teenager, not the respect due to an equal.

Hindu stagnation under Islam

According to Swami Vivekananda, the Hindu effort to resist Islam entailed a stagnation of Hindu culture in most other respects: "Of course, we had to stop advancing during the Mohammedan tyranny, for then it was not a

[290] Aurobindo: *Foundations of Indian Culture*, pp.377-78.

[291] Aurobindo (12.9.1923): *India's Rebirth*, p.162.

[292] Aurobindo (23.10.1929): *India's Rebirth*, pp.184-85.

question of progress but of life and death."[293] This is a sweeping statement, proposing a single state of affairs over centuries and in a large area. It is not implausible, in this sense that wartime does not favour the subtler cultural pursuits. I am at least not aware of discoveries, inventions and other objectively optimizing innovations made in India under Muslim rule. (The replacement of one building style, literary fashion etc. by another does not by itself constitute objective progress.) Ancient India was famous for certain scientific advances, but no trace of creativity in those fields is in evidence in medieval India, a condition quite like the collapse of scientific progress in China (which had made such promising strides in the preceding Sung period) under the Mongol occupation in the thirteenth-fourteenth century.

Till today, this is a frequent Hindu criticism of Islam, e.g. N.S. Rajaram writes: "Here is one telling statistic that should help give a true picture of Medieval India. ... Pre-Islamic India was renowned for its universities. Great centres of learning like Nalanda, Vaishali, Sarnath, Vikramashila, Takshashila and many more—they attracted students from all over Asia and the world. Following the Islamic invasion of India, all these universities were destroyed. In the centuries following, not a single university was established by any Muslim ruler. This was a Dark Age darker than the one that overtook Europe."[294]

However, the impression exists that Hindu civilization had already entered a stage of sclerosis before the Muslim invasions. Thus, the ancient Hindus had been great astronomers, but when Albiruni visited India at the time of Mahmud Ghaznavi's incursions, he found Hindu astronomers unable to point out in the sky the constellations which they knew from their astronomical tables.[295] Possibly the temporary dominance of Buddhism with its anti-worldliness had diminished Indian inquisitiveness,

---

[293]Vivekananda: *Complete Works*, vol.4, p.373.

[294]N.S. Rajaram: *From Harappa to Ayodhya*, p.14. Remark, however, that the said universities taught philosophy and related subjects rather than exact sciences, and the same could be said for the theological academies which the Muslim rulers patronized. Though the destruction of universities is an eloquent symbol of barbarism (remember the propagandistic use which the British made of the destruction of the library of the *Université Catholique de Louvain* by the Germans in World War 1), in India's case it is not identical with the destruction of science. But it could still be argued that Buddhist philosophy and psychology were more scientific (even though not dealing with physical reality) than the revelation-based Islamic theology and casuistic Islamic jurisprudence.

[295]Albiruni describes the "confused notions" and "mistakes" he encounters among Hindu scientists at every turn, e.g. Edward Sachau ed.: *Alberuni's India*, vol.1, p.393 (end of Ch.45) and vol.2, p.86 (Ch.66).

but the matter deserves deeper investigation. It also seems that in the period under consideration, scientific progress and creativity were as conspicuous by their absence in the Hindu empire of Vijayanagar in South India as they were in Muslim-dominated North India. So, India's stagnation cannot entirely be blamed on Islam.

Another example of the Hindu criticism of Islam's non progressiveness is this statement by Sangh Parivar author S. Gurumurthy: "From the earliest times, Islam has proved itself incapable of producing an internal evolution; internally legitimized change has not been possible since all change is instantly regarded as an act of apostasy. Every change was—and is—put down by bloodshed. In contrast, the Hindu ethos changed continually. ... It is the changelessness of Islam—its equal revulsion towards dissent within and towards non-Islamic thoughts without—that has made it a problem for the whole world."[296] The revulsion of Islam to dissent, chiefly to challenges to Mohammed's prophetic status (and such a challenge is implied in any proposed amendment to Islamic Law, ultimately based on Quranic revelation or on the Prophet's model behaviour), is indeed a serious problem, as much for Muslims as for non-Muslims.

Reconversion

In a hint at the need to reconvert the Indian Muslims, Vivekananda traces their origins: "What is called the Mohammedan invasion, conquest or colonization of India means only this, that under the leadership of Mohammedan Turks who were renegades from Buddhism, those sections of the Hindu race who continued in the faith of their ancestors were repeatedly conquered by the other section of that very race who also were renegades from Buddhism or the Vedic religion and served under the Turks, having been forcibly converted to Mohammedanism by their superior strength."[297] In other words: Muslim are not *really* Muslims, the Muslim identity was imposed on them, it is a mere surface layer, and it can be scratched off.

This point was made much more explicitly by the Arya Samaj which started an organized effort to convert or "reconvert" Indian Muslims to Vedic Hinduism. The Hindu Mahasabha and the Vishva Hindu Parishad

---

[296]S. Gurumurthy: "Semitic monotheism: the root of intolerance in India", *New Perspectives Quarterly* (LA), spring 1994, p.52.

[297]Vivekananda: *Complete Works*, vol.7, p.395.

have continued the effort on a limited scale, and though no solid figures are available, the total of reconverted Muslims in the twentieth century may amount to several hundred thousand. To my knowledge, no systematic follow-up study of their subsequent integration in Hindu society (or "relapse" into Islam) has ever been done, certainly not by the Hindu reconversion agencies themselves, this in significant contrast with the intense survey work which Christian mission agencies do (or commission) as preparation and follow-up to their conversion campaigns.

However, the modern-educated Hindus who do the intellectual homework of Hindu revivalism are, precisely because of their modern outlook, not too comfortable with the whole idea of running after people and trying to sell them some message. In fact, neither the modernist nor the traditional Hindu outlook is easily compatible with the conversion project. Rather, conversion is seen in a negative way: Muslims have to be "liberated from the mental prison-house of Islam", as Ram Swarup and Sita Ram Goel are wont to say, or in Abhas Chatterjee's words: "The goal is to bring our minorities back into our nation after destroying the deadly intoxication of these ideologies", meaning Christianity and Islam.[298] After this "deprogramming", the ex-Muslims will have to find out for themselves, somewhat like the millions of modern Westerners who have abandoned Christianity and are now groping around for new spiritual sustenance. With Hinduism being all around them, many Indian ex-Muslims will then naturally turn to old or new forms of Hindu ritual and spirituality to fill up what Salman Rushdie called the "God-shaped hole" left behind by the apostasy from Islam.[299]

Both the modernist critics and the Shuddhi campaigners insist that their problem is not with Muslims, but with Islam. I have yet to see the first study or critique of the Hindu revivalist movement which manages to seize

[298] A. Chatterjee: *Concept of Hindu Nation*, p.45.

[299] Rushdie himself is only one of many South-Asian Muslims who have "outgrown" Islam. Others include Taslima Nasrin, "Ibn Warraq" (pseudonymous author of *Why I Am Not a Muslim*), and Shabbir Akhtar, formerly an apologist of Islam (see his *Be Careful with Mohammed! The Salman Rushdie Affair*, 1989), who explains his disappointment with the lack of intellectual freedom in Muslim universities and his subsequent retreat from the faith in: "Ex-defender of the faith", *Times Higher Education Supplement*, 22.8.1997, included in S.R. Goel, ed.: *Freedom of Expression*. One who has moreover found the way back to Hinduism is Anwar Shaikh, author of *Eternity* (1990) and target of a death-sentence *fatwa* (1994) for apostasy. All these apostasy stories are exactly what Ram Swarup and Sita Ram Goel have in mind as the course for Muslims to follow.

this crucial distinction; most inaccurately allege that Hindu revivalism is "anti-Muslim". And this is not because the Hindu spokesmen have failed to explicitate the distinction. As Sita Ram Goel writes: "The most malevolent of these residues [of bygone imperialisms] is Islamism, the residue of the Muslim invasion of India spread over several centuries. ... Let it be clear that the reference here is not to our Muslim brethren who are our own flesh and blood, except for that microscopic minority which takes pride in the purity of its Arab, Persian or Turkish descent. Instead of being the proponents of Islamism, the Muslims are its victims whom it is trying to use as vehicles of its poisonous virulence. The vast majority of Indian Muslims were converted to Islam by force or allurements. ... The Muslims of India, therefore, have to be freed from rather than accused of Islamism."[300]

It is, of course, a different matter whether the Indian Muslims are all that eager to be "freed from Islamism". This is, in the Hindu view, a matter of consciousness-raising, of exposing them to the flaws of the Islamic religion and, more constructively, to the values of Hindu tradition. As Ram Swarup puts it, "there is no doubt that once Hinduism comes into its own and begins to speak for itself, those who were forced to leave it under very special circumstances will return to their old fold."[301]

None of this critical rejection of Islam as such is in evidence in BJP thinking on Hindu-Muslim relations. Quite to the contrary, during the BJP climbdown from Ayodhya after the Demolition, BJP leader L.K. Advani proved his Islam-friendly disposition by presiding over the *Nikâh* (Islamic wedding) ceremony of his niece, who married into a Muslim family and converted from Hinduism to Islam. The BJP and the dominant section of the RSS (and its new Muslim-oriented front, the *Sarva Panth Samâdar Manch*, "Respect for All Religions Front") envision the integration of the Indian Muslims *as Muslims* into the "national mainstream". Even Guru Golwalkar already rejected the reconversion drive: "Let Muslims be more devout Muslims. We will help them to be more devout."[302] Contrary to the wild image of "Hindu fanaticism" projected by most India-watchers, most Hindutva activists have interiorized the sugary Gandhian notion of the "equal truth of all religions".

---

[300]S.R. Goel: *Hindu Society under Siege*, p.7.
[301]Ram Swarup: *Hindu View of Christianity and Islam*, p.53.
[302]Golwalkar: *Spotlights*, p.48.

Savarkar on Islam

The Hindutva view of Islam is characterized by a progressive softening from V.D. Savarkar through M.S. Golwalkar down to the present BJP. And even Savarkar was not uniformly the hawk he is always made out to be. In general, the organized Hindutva movement has never produced a very sophisticated discourse on Islam, merely a few sweeping generalizations whether in a hostile or in a flattering sense. In the founding statements of the RSS, there is no trace of a fundamental critique of Islam, nor is there any in the books and speeches of its leaders.

In his prolific writings, HMS ideologue Veer Savarkar developed only little criticism of Islamic doctrine, except for endlessly reiterating a few generalizations about Muslim behaviour in India. In his first book, *The Indian War of Independence* (1909), he extolled Hindu-Muslim cooperation during the 1857 Mutiny.[303] However, during most of his career, Muslims figure in his writings as obviously the enemy of the Hindus. Savarkar took Muslim hostility for granted, and diagnosed failure to face this fact of Muslim hostility as the cause of confusion and of the increasing helplessness of the Gandhian Congress in facing Muslim League pressure: "It is this political lunacy which has affected the Congressite Hindu mind that constitutes the real cause of our present helplessness".[304]

However, Savarkar never wrote an analysis of Islamic doctrine beyond a simple equation of Islam with violent self-righteousness, as here in his influential book *Hindutva* (1923), written during the wave of communal violence unleashed by the failure of the *Khilâfat* movement: "Religion is a mighty motive force. So is Rapine. But where Religion is goaded on by Rapine and Rapine serves as a handmaid to Religion, the propelling force that is generated by these together is only equalled by the profundity of human misery and devastation they leave behind them in

---

[303]Most observers consider the Mutiny as predominantly a Muslim attempt to restore the Moghul Empire, e.g. T. Metcalf: *The Aftermath of the Revolt*, p.298, or R.C. Majumdar: *British Paramountcy* (*History and Culture of the Indian People*, vol.9), p.616. A few minor Maratha princes also participated, but all the important ones remained neutral, and some factions (most prominently the Sikhs) openly supported the British, partly because they had tasted the strength of British arms and considered rebellion useless, partly because they refused to make common cause with Muslim revivalism.

[304]Savarkar: *Hindu Rashtra Darshan*, p.133.

their march. Heaven and Hell making a common cause—such were the forces, overwhelmingly furious, that took India by surprise the day that Mahmud Ghaznavi crossed the Indus and invaded her. Day after day, decade after decade, centuries after centuries, the ghastly conflict continued and India single-handed kept the fight morally and militarily."[305]

Marxist historian Bipan Chandra quotes this passage as a self-evident proof of Savarkar's rabid anti-Muslim prejudice.[306] By contrast, Hindu polemicists from Swami Dayananda and Pandit Lekh Ram to Ram Swarup and Suhas Majumdar cite scriptural references as justifying "rapine" in Islam.[307] Savarkar's own position on Islam can be summed up thus: rather than being brothers belonging to a single nation, naturally inclined to unity, Hindus and Muslims are separated by an old and profound cleavage, though not on equal terms: Hindus are just Hindus regardless of their views of Islam, while Muslims are ex-Hindus in whom an artificial hostility to Hinduism had been fostered as a necessary component of their loyalty to Islam. Remove that hostility, and Muslims would naturally gravitate back to their Hindu mother society.

Golwalkar on Muslim disloyalty

The leading Marxist critic of Hindu Nationalism, Bipan Chandra, admits that the really nasty anti-Muslim attitude which is routinely attributed to the Hindutva movement cannot be found in its official statements: "it is not easy to document the more rabid and vicious examples of communal propaganda since it was carried on orally."[308] However, the central anti-Muslim allegation can amply be documented from the writings of the most influential Hindutva ideologue, Guru Golwalkar. Though Golwalkar's published speeches and writings run into many hundreds of pages, only a few dozen of these pages deal with Islam. His image in the secularist press was that of an "anti-Muslim fanatic", yet the interest he took in the

---

[305]Savarkar: *Hindutva*, p.35.

[306]B. Chandra: *Communalism in Modern India*, pp.223-24.

[307]Ram Swarup: *Understanding Islam through Hadis*, pp.101-08, e.g. after the expulsion of a Jewish clan from Medina, the Quran says: "And He has made you inherit their land and their dwellings and their property" (Q.33:27); Arabs who hesitate to follow this new ethical code, are reassured that enjoying plunder is all right: "But (now) enjoy what ye took in war, lawful and good" (Q.8:69/70).

[308]B. Chandra: *Communalism in Modern India*, p.217.

"Muslim problem" was very limited and never motivated him to a serious study of the subject.[309] His utterances invariably revolved around the alleged Muslim disloyalty to India.

Golwalkar routinely referred to Muslims as foreigners who treat India as a *sarai*.[310] He neglected to provide evidence even for the subjective sense of foreignness among the Muslim elites, though other authors have collected such evidence from the writings of educated Muslims, e.g. in the closing line of Mohammed Iqbal's poem *Shikwa* (1909): "No matter if my idiom is Indian, my spirit is that of Hejaz", i.e. of Mecca and Medina.[311] A decade earlier, Hali had expressed "his pessimism about the prospects of India's Muslims under democracy"[312] as follows: "Farewell to thee, o ever-green garden of India. We foreigners have stayed long in this country as your guests."[313]

Pakistan's official self-history squarely identifies it as the successor state of the Moghul Empire and considers the "subcontinental Muslims" for whom Pakistan was created as the cultural if not the biological progeny of the foreign Islamic invaders. This was illustrated by its 1998 missile test featuring the *Ghaurî* missile, named after Mohammed Ghori, who forced the decisive Muslim breakthrough into India in 1192. (At this point, we must emphasize the distinction between the masses of native Muslim converts, and the elites which traced their ancestry at least partly to the Turkish and Iranian invaders: the sense of foreignness was quite real among the latter, much less among the former.)

In his 678-page book *Bunch of Thoughts*, Golwalkar devotes just one 15-page chapter plus a handful of brief passages to Islam. His main objection is that Islam makes its adherents less loyal to India: "Conversion of Hindus into other religions is nothing but making them succumb to

---

[309]Because he wrote so little about Islam at his own initiative, interviewers tended to focus on the subject, and most quotations which follow are from interviews, published partly or wholly, and with overlappings, as an appendix in *Bunch of Thoughts*, in *Spotlights* and as separate pamphlets: *Guruji on the Muslim Problem* and *Shri Guruji Meets Delhi Newsmen*.

[310]Golwalkar does so "almost on every page of *We*", according to an exaggerating Bipan Chandra, *Communalism*, p.218.

[311]Muhammad Iqbal: *Shikwa & Jawab-i-Shikwa*, translation by Khushwant Singh, p.58. Khushwant Singh translates it less literally as: "What if the song be Indian, it is Hejazi in its verve."

[312]Rajmohan Gandhi: *Muslim Mind*, p.15.

[313]Quoted in Rajmohan Gandhi: *Muslim Mind*, p.15.

divided loyalty in place of having undivided and absolute loyalty to the nation. It is dangerous to the security of the nation and the country. It is therefore necessary to put a stop to it."[314] As a full-blooded nationalist, he expected people to have a total and exclusive loyalty to the nation and did not consider for a moment that people can and do have loyalties at many levels, both larger and smaller than the nation.

In history, there have been cases of Muslim disloyalty to their Hindu employers at critical moments, the most consequential occasion being the battle of Talikota, on 23 January 1565, which broke the back of the Vijayanagar empire, the last Hindu stronghold against the southward advances of the confederacy of Islamic states including Bijapur and Golkonda: "At first the Hindus fought with success and nearly won the battle; but the issue was decided by the desertion of two Muslim commanders of Rama Raya's army, each in charge of seventy to eighty thousand men."[315]

But Golwalkar never took the trouble of looking up historical anecdotes to buttress his argument (much less to discuss anecdotes which might contradict it), except for one large-scale event which took place during his own lifetime: the secession of Pakistan. The Partition of the Motherland in 1947 provided Golwalkar with a vivid proof of the disloyalty of the Muslims, many of whom had none the less remained behind in truncated India:

"It has been the tragic lesson of the history of many a country in the world that the hostile elements within the country pose a far greater menace to national security than aggressors from outside. ... Is it true that all pro-Pakistani elements have gone away to Pakistan? It was the Muslims in Hindu majority provinces led by UP who provided the spearhead for the movement for Pakistan right from the beginning. And they have remained solidly here even after Partition. ... In those elections [1945-46] Muslim League had contested making the creation of Pakistan its election plank. The Congress also had set up some Muslim candidates all over the country. But at almost every such place, Muslims voted for the Muslim League candidates. ... It only means that all the crores of Muslims who are here even now, had en bloc voted for Pakistan."[316]

---

[314]Golwalkar: *Bunch of Thoughts*, p.225. The book's title is aped from Nehru's collection *Bunch of Old Letters*, disregarding that *bunch* connotes "unrelated, scattered, stray", whereas *thought*, by definition, seeks order and coherence.

[315]Nilakantha Shastri: *History of South India*, pp.294-95.

[316]Golwalkar: *Bunch of Thoughts*, pp.233-35.

It is a fact that in the 1945 elections, the Congress claim to also represent the Indian Muslims was completely defeated by the Muslim electorate, of which 86.6 per cent voted for the Muslim League and its one-point programme: Pakistan. B.N. Jog, a contemporary RSS author argues that even the 1937 elections, though often mentioned as proof that the Muslim electorate was largely "secular" because of the poor results for the Muslim League, had already disproven this Congress claim: most Muslim votes had gone to other Muslim-dominated parties, chiefly the Unionist Party of Sir Sikandar Hayat Khan in Panjab and the Krishak Praja Party of Fazlul Haq in Bengal.[317] Even the supposedly defeated Muslim League had won 108 of the 492 Muslim-reserved seats in 1937, against 26 for Congress. So, Jog concludes, the Muslim vote was largely motivated by sectional interests rather than by commitment to the national struggle.

Golwalkar and Jog overlook the fact that many Muslims had not voted for Pakistan simply because they had been excluded from voting under the census system. Though one cannot say that the non-voting Muslim masses ever expressed a determined opposition to the Pakistan scheme in any way, the historical fact remains that we will never know how the non-enfranchised Muslims would have voted if given a chance. Golwalkar also overlooks the fact that a part of the Muslim elites in U.P. and East Panjab who spearheaded the Pakistan movement *did* move to Pakistan. They are known as the *Mohajirs*, "migrants", those who made the *hijra* to Pakistan on the model of Mohammed's migration/*hijra* from heathen Mecca to the more Islam-friendly city of Medina. The fact that the Mohajirs' integration in Pakistani society was not too successful, and that they feel seriously discriminated against in the country of their own creation, is often cited by Hindus as a case of just desserts.

In Golwalkar's view, the creation of Pakistan has not removed the problem of "disloyal Muslims", on the contrary: the "enemy within" has become doubly dangerous, for now he possesses a base beyond the control of the national Government. Golwalkar's distrust of the Muslims inside India is total: "It would be suicidal to delude ourselves into believing that they have turned patriots overnight after the creation of Pakistan. On the contrary, the Muslim menace has increased a hundredfold by the creation of Pakistan which had become a springboard for all their future aggressive designs on our country."[318] And again: "The Muslim looks upon Partition

---

[317]Discussed in detail in B.N. Jog: *Threat of Islam*, pp.224-25.

[318]Golwalkar: *Bunch of Thoughts*, p.235.

only as a springboard for further aggression."[319] And so: "From the day the so-called Pakistan came into being, we in Sangh have been declaring that it is a clear case of continued Muslim aggression."[320]

Golwalkar calls Muslim pockets in India "miniature Pakistans": "Such 'pockets' have verily become centres of pro-Pakistani elements in this land."[321] His evidence is not very hard, though: from the fact that Pakistani radio mentioned a Hindu-Muslim riot in Mumbai "within a few hours", he deduces that "there must be some pro-Pakistani gentleman with a pro-Pakistani transmitter and he must be in constant touch with Pakistan".[322] The striking feature of this chapter of Guruji's worldview is not its rightness or wrongness, but the way it is based on stray impressions and vague rumours. This man passed as the great ideologue of the largest mass movement in India, yet he never bothered to give a decent factual and conceptual basis to his view of urgent matters such as the Hindu-Muslim conflict. As to contents, his entire discourse on Islam boils down to raising suspicions that the Indian Muslims are a fifth column of world Islam as incarnated in the state of Pakistan.

In practice, there has been no substantial collusion of Indian Muslims with Pakistan in the wars of 1965 and 1971. Secularists never fail to point this out, but some RSS people remain unconvinced. In November 1965, just after the war with Pakistan, pressmen in Bangalore asked Guru Golwalkar to comment on this observation: "In the recent war with Pakistan, Muslims have been loyal to us." Golwalkar replied: "That is because they were afraid. I told once that if there was a major defeat to our army, there would have been an upsurge by these people in our country. Fortunately, there was no defeat. Our army is marching from victory to victory. Seeing that it would be very dangerous for them if they revolt, they have shown discretion and kept quiet. Not only that, out of sheer fear, they have also begun to loudly express their loyalty to this country."[323]

This way, even professions of loyalty are neutralized as mere expressions of fear. That, then, was Golwalkar's most notorious contribution to Hindu-Muslim relations: to solidify the suspicion that all Muslims are agents of an enemy state.

---

[319]Golwalkar: *Spotlights*, p.45.
[320]Golwalkar: *Bunch of Thoughts*, p.235.
[321]Golwalkar: *Bunch of Thoughts*, p.243.
[322]Golwalkar: *Bunch of Thoughts*, p.244.
[323]Golwalkar: *Spotlights*, p.63.

Other voices on Muslim disloyalty

The theme of Muslim disloyalty frequently reappears in Hindu nationalist writing. In Vivek's satirical column in *Organiser*, a reader asks: "Should not Indians who praise Pakistan be called Non-Resident Pakistanis?" His reply: "They should be called upon to become Resident Pakistanis."[324] A cruder variation is the slogan from Partition days: *Mussalmân ke do hî sthân, Pâkistân yâ Qabrastân*, "for Muslims there are only two places, Pakistan or the graveyard".

In support of this view of Muslim disloyalty, a number of facts are mentioned. One of these is the deliberate adoption of foreign elements by the Indian Muslims, starting with their names. Many native converts to Islam cultivate imaginary genealogies connecting them with the Prophet and his companions or with the Turkish conquerors of India. It is often alleged that Hindu nationalists claim that Indian Muslims are foreigners, but exactly the reverse is the case: it is Muslims themselves who claim foreign descent, while Hindus try to remind them of their Indian roots. K.R. Malkani writes: "I will give here just one example of these grand illusions. In the 1872 census, Bengal had a Muslim population of 17.5 million; 2,66,000 (i.e. less than 1.5 per cent) of them claimed to be persons of foreign origin. In the census of 1909, out of a Muslim population of 21.5 million, as many as 19.5 million (i.e. over 90 per cent) claimed to be persons of foreign origin! Fact is that not even one per cent of Muslim population is immigrant; and even this one per cent has been too completely Indianised over centuries of residence and intermarriage to have any 'foreignness' about them."[325]

A secularist journalist expresses his sympathy for Indian Islam, yet acknowledges that Hindus may get the impression that Islam's loyalty is conditional on its perceived chances of seizing power, in the sense that weak Muslim minorities espouse secularism and multiculturalism but drop these minority-protecting values as soon as the lure of Muslim majority power looms on the horizon: "Indeed it is Indian Islam which has the greatest potential to emerge as a model where faith and culture and nationalism form a harmonious continuum. If this model does not emerge, then in view of much of what is happening in the Islamic world many non-

[324]Vivek: "Indraprastha calling", *Organiser*, 29.3.1998.

[325]K.R. Malkani: "Looking at the future", *Hindustan Times*, 17.1.1993.

Muslims in India will be well within their rights to ask whether Indian Muslims espouse secularism only because they are not in a majority and, no less important, not in power."[326]

Then there are the statements of Muslim leaders, e.g. at the First Asian Islamic Conference at Karachi in July 1978, leading Indian Muslim cleric Ali Mian said: "Muslims all over the world including those of India were hopefully looking up to Pakistan for help and guidance and whatever happened in Pakistan or any other Muslim country cast its shadow on the Indian Muslims also. The Pakistani debacle of 1971 had caused immense grief to Indian Muslims."[327]

Another point of reference is the occasional statement by international Muslim leaders that peace with non-Muslims is only a temporary ploy to build up strength for a future showdown, e.g. by Yasser Arafat. On 10 May 1994 in Johannesburg, Arafat "called for jihad to liberate Jerusalem" and "the Palestinian leader put himself in the shoes of Prophet Mohammed who in 628 concluded a peace treaty with the Quraish and violated it two years later with the conquest of Mecca. Yasser Arafat said in Johannesburg that the treaty signed by Prophet Mohammed was equally non-binding as the treaty which he himself concluded with Israel."[328] Such statements are cited as nourishing the impression that under Islamic law, the Muslim *ummah* is permanently at war with the rest of humanity, with peace treaties only serving to bridge periods of Muslim weakness in preparation of future victories.

It also disturbs Hindus that Muslim spokesmen apparently cannot bring themselves to condemn the foreign Muslim conquerors of yore: "the Indian Muslims should shout this out aloud and dissociate themselves from the idol-breaking and destruction of temples carried out by Mahmud of Ghazni and Aurangzeb".[329] Nor to reciprocate Hindu syncretism: "The Hindu is willing to say, 'Ram Rahim ek hai'; is the Muslim also prepared

[326]Dileep Padgaonkar: "Men in dark times", *Times of India*, 13.12.1992.

[327]Quoted by Arun Shourie: "What Ali Mian had said in 1978: 'Muslims ... were looking to Pakistan for help'", *Organiser*, 22.1.1995.

[328]"Rabin eist schriftelijke belofte van Arafat over naleving akkoorden", *De Standaard*, 24.5.1994. The precedent value of Mohammed's Treaty of Hudaibiya with the Pagan Meccans (which he unilaterally rescinded when he felt strong enough to subdue Mecca) is discussed in detail by Daniel Pipes: "Lessons from the prophet Mohammed's diplomacy", *Middle East Quarterly*, September 1999, pp.65-72.

[329]Quoted with approval from a letter by Ansar Hussain Khan to Jamia Millia University, pleading for Muslim abandonment of all claims to the Ram Janmabhoomi site, by M.V. Kamath: "Indian history: a new approach", *Organiser*, 28.1.1996.

to say it? Gandhiji had said: 'There is in Hinduism room enough for Jesus, as there is for Mohammed, Zoroaster and Moses.' Does Islam in India have room enough for Ram—as Islam in Indonesia has room enough for Rama?"[330]

Finally, public figures who did not belong to the Hindu "communalist" parties have been cited as witnesses to Muslim disloyalty. In a speech in Lucknow in 1948, Sardar Patel complained about the Indian Muslims' silence over Kashmir: "It should not surprise Muslims if doubts were entertained about their loyalty. They could not ride on two horses."[331] He "was also concerned to reduce the influence and numbers of Muslims in the police".[332] Even apolitical Hindus sometimes innocently refer to Muslims as "Pakistanis".

And yet, many Indian Muslims I have talked with are definitely not "Pakistani patriots", but tend to speak rather scornfully about Pakistan, a failed state if ever there was one, a terror-ridden clerico-feudal narco-state kept together by Kashmir-obsessed gun-and-moustache men. Even the *Mohajirs*, the Uttar Pradesh Muslims who clamoured loudest for Partition, but who have been at the receiving end of ethnic violence in Sindh, have voiced their disillusionment in their self-made Promised Land.

Pakistanis have had to accept that Pakistan is not very popular among the Indian Muslims for whom the state was created: "On a recent visit to India, a young Pakistani writer Sameen Tahir Khan discovered to her dismay that anti-Pakistan sentiments abound among Indian Muslim youth."[333] Ms. Khan quotes an Indian Muslim as saying: "I think our future over here is brighter than yours in Pakistan." A young student is quoted: "In the past, our grandfathers used to live in India but their heads belonged to Pakistan. I don't believe in that. I was born here and I love India. In fact, I don't even like Pakistan. I find it a hypocritical country." Ms. Khan comments: "I was impressed by the spirit of nationalism among Indian Muslims. I felt envious and wished we in Pakistan could learn a lesson from them."[334]

---

[330]K.R. Malkani: "Looking at the future", *Hindustan Times*, 17.1.1993.

[331]Rendered thus in *Hindustan Times*, 7.1.1948, quoted in B.D. Graham: *Hindu Nationalism*, p.10.

[332]Lance Brennan: "The state and communal violence in UP: 1947-1992", *South Asia*, vol.17, special issue 1994, p.21.

[333]"Indian Muslims have nothing nice to say about Pakistan", *Observer of Business and Politics*, 31.12.1995, courtesy *Dawn*, Lahore.

[334]"Indian Muslims have nothing nice to say about Pakistan", *Observer of Business and Politics*, 31.12.1995.

Therefore, enthusiasm for Pakistan among Indian Muslims is low, and in that sense, there is no reason to mistrust the self-description of modernist Indian Muslims like journalist M.J. Akbar as "nationalist Muslims".[335] Enlightened Indian Muslims find Pakistan a pitiable state: "Pakistan ... fought wars with us; it assisted secessionism in Punjab and Kashmir; it raised the Kashmir issue in international fora; time and again it tried to embarrass us in the Organization of Islamic Conference. In brief, it set itself up as a state in opposition to us in perpetuity. But wasn't this what Pakistan was supposed to be? After all, it came into being on the basis of the two-nation theory, that Hindus and Muslims were two separate states, that Hindus and Muslims could not live together. We are because we cannot live with *them*. That was Pakistan's *raison d'être*. Supposing by some black magic they converted to another way of thinking: we are even though we could have lived with them, Pakistan would collapse. Therefore one of the planks of Pakistani statecraft was to keep reminding its people and the world at large of that mantra of survival: we are because we cannot live with *them*."[336]

Among the Indian Muslims, the 1990s have witnessed an acceleration in the acceptance of their Indianness. This has been at least partly the result of the refocusing of national attention on liberalization, modernization and informatization. Here was a non-communal development offering hope and perspective to all young Indians regardless of their religious background, which suddenly looked like being just that—a mere background to the real facts of life.

Consider the following testimony about the reaction to a cricket match (which, in the RSS rumour mills, has become the standard test for Muslim loyalty to India, disproven if Muslims cheer for a Pakistani victory): "Time, too, does its work, and the young generations of the *millat*, unlike their elders, are not so sensitive concerning Pakistan. We have recently seen a highly symbolic and revealing demonstration of the new behaviour: during the cricket world cup games in March 1996, young Muslims of the old city of Delhi have enthusiastically celebrated India's victory against Pakistan in the quarter finals. Sweets were distributed. Such a thing had

---

[335]Thus in the biographical note on the author in M.J. Akbar: *India, the Siege Within*, in which he argues that because of its secular democracy, India has proved the experts wrong by staying together, while Pakistan, because of its enforced uniformity, has already fallen apart once and is still in a permanent state of crisis.

[336]Saeed Naqvi: *Reflections of an Indian Muslim*, p.13.

not been seen since Partition."[337] Reality is having its effect on the imaginary foreign identity of Indian Muslims.

Golwalkar on Muslims vs. Islam

In Guru Golwalkar's opinion, the pluralism which exists within Hinduism should simply be extended to include Islam as well: "There are so many people in the Hindu dharma who do not believe in the Divine Incarnation of Rama and Krishna. But they believe that they are great personalities, worthy of emulation. So what does it matter if Muslims do not believe that God incarnated Himself? Why should they not consider such personalities as their national heroes? According to our ways of religious belief and philosophy, a Muslim is as good as a Hindu. It is not the Hindu alone who will reach the ultimate Godhead. Everyone has the right to follow his path according to his own persuasion."[338] Indeed, when speaking of Islam, Golwalkar effectively espoused the belief in the equality of all religions: "Give people true knowledge of Islam. Give people true knowledge of Hinduism. Educate them to know that all religions teach man to be selfless, holy and pious."[339]

It is extremely important to understand that Golwalkar's position, which has remained the RSS and BJP position till the time of this writing, is a deviation from the Hindu revivalist position established by the Arya Samaj, maintained by the Hindu Mahasabha, and kept alive today by some sections of the VHP as well as by independent authors like Abhas Chatterjee. What Golwalkar says, is: Islam is all right, the problem lies with the Muslims.[340] The view of Hindu revivalists from Dayananda to Ram Swarup is exactly the opposite: the problem is not Muslims but Islam, Muslims are simply "our estranged countrymen" who have to be liberated from the mental stranglehold of Islam. Remark how Golwalkar's refusal to criticize Islam (and preference to foment suspicion against Muslims as Pakistani agents instead) led to more, not less, hatred of the Muslim community.

---

[337]Violette Graff: "L'islam indien à la croisée des chemins" (French: "Indian Islam at the crossroads"), *Relations Stratégiques et Internationales*, p.120, n.6.

[338]Golwalkar: *Bunch of Thoughts*, pp.640-41.

[339]Golwalkar: *Spotlights*, p.55.

[340]Ram Swarup and Sita Ram Goel reported the following statement by Golwalkar during a speech in Delhi in 1958: "I hold the Quran in as great esteem as our Vedas. Mohammed was a great Prophet, as great as our Rishis. Islam is a great religion. But the Muslims are *pâjî*/scoundrels!"

This is the view which most modernist Hindus (including the Sangh Parivar membership) cherish: the true Islam as conceived by the founder is impeccable, the only problem is that some followers misunderstood him, or that purely nominal Muslims with little interest in the true Quranic message falsely used the label "Islam" as justification for their un-Islamic selfish acts. Thus, VHP treasurer Anand Shankar Pandya exonerates Mohammed of all the problematic aspects of Islam: "According to scholars, after the passing away of prophet Mohammed, power-hungry leaders made many anti-Islamic changes in Shariat and Hadis, and in the name of Islam, looted the weak and raped women."[341] Though a good many Hindutva ideologues are anti-Muslim at heart, the point to note is that they are not *anti-Islamic* at all. Even when attacking Muslims, they invariably hasten to exonerate Islam as such from the alleged misbehaviour of its votaries.

Indeed, all kinds of cheap stories about Islam are abroad in Hindutva circles. Here is K.R. Malkani's attempt to reconcile Islam with Indian nationalism: "Fortunately, the Prophet of Islam had a very positive view of India. He once said to his wife Hind, 'May Allah bless the country after which you are named.' That is something to build on."[342] Mohammed never said this, and Hind was not his wife but his fiercest opponent. Malkani also discovered (and this one may be true but also quite irrelevant): "According to scholars, the Prophet of Islam carried flags of different shades, including, on one occasion, Bhagva, but he never carried a green flag."[343]

In the Ayodhya controversy, it was standard Sangh Parivar rhetoric that the demolition of the Hindu temple at the disputed site had been an un-Islamic act motivated by some purely secular intrigue: "Muslims are still intransigent on rebuilding the temple, which was admittedly demolished by Babar—*contrary to the tenets of the Quran—thus a non-Islamic action.*"[344] It was claimed that this was not a religious conflict between Hindu and Muslim, but a secular conflict between the foreigner Babar and

---

[341] A.S. Pandya: *Role of Hinduism in 21st Century*, p.21.

[342] K.R. Malkani: "Legacy of hate. Hindus and Muslims must endeavour to undo partition", *Indian Express*, 15-8-1994.

[343] K.R. Malkani: "Looking at the future", *Hindustan Times*, 17.1.1993. *Bhagva*: ochre or saffron, the colour of Hinduism.

[344] Anand Prakash Singhal: "Genesis of intolerance", *Organiser*, 18.10.1998; emphasis added.

the Indians, both Hindu and Muslim: "Babar came to India as an aggressor and defeated the joint force of Hindus and Muslims ... to cause a rift between the Hindus and Indian Muslims, he demolished the Rama Janmabhoomi temple and built a masjid in its place."[345] But how should a rift between the Hindus and the "Indian Muslims" (meaning the Pathan occupation forces) get caused by a temple demolition wrought by the Moghuls, whose identity was not "Muslim" (in common with the India-based Muslims) but "foreign"? If the RSS thought it could fool its opponents with this kind of casuistry, it should have noticed later on that absolutely no one in the Muslim or secularist camp has conceded the RSS claim that Ayodhya was a "national" rather than a "Hindu" concern.

Golwalkar's view of Islam as good and Muslims as bad is the direct explanation for the paradoxical twin fact that the RSS has produced no anti-Islamic polemic worth mentioning, but that its rank-and-file regularly gets embroiled in Hindu-Muslim street-fighting. His de-ideologization of the Hindu-Muslim conflict, reducing it to a conflict between two tribes rather than two worldviews, has proven to be a consequential mistake. A certain amount of Hindu-Muslim violence was probably unavoidable, but things might have looked much less tense if Golwalkar had trained his following in a mature intellectual attitude which distinguishes between a doctrine and the people who are conditioned by that doctrine to a greater or lesser extent.

Blaming British mischief

In contrast with Aurobindo and Savarkar, Golwalkar supported the Gandhian and secularist view that the Hindu-Muslim conflict in 1921-47 culminating in the Partition was purely a British machination unrelated to the political doctrine of Islam as such. To the question what would happen to Hindu-Muslim relations if India reconquers Pakistan, and whether the Hindu-Muslim problem would continue, Golwalkar said: "No, it will not. This so-called Hindu-Muslim problem is only a political problem. When the whole country becomes one, the problem will be solved as there will be no power to support the separatist Muslim tendency. It is only the British who gave a fillip to the Muslim communal frenzy. Before they came, there was the process of their identification with the mainstream of our national

[345]Rajendra Prasad Jain: "How Hindu Resistance to Babri Masjid Got Recorded in 1850", *Organiser*, reproduced in A.A. Engineer: *Babri Masjid Ram Janmabhoomi Controversy*, p.92.

life. Now that the British have left, that process can be resumed provided we prove ourselves to be the masters of the situation."[346]

This view is still very common in Sangh Parivar circles, e.g. in 1994 Gurdas Ahuja writes: "Religious riots were almost unknown to Indian history before the advent of the Britishers, who systematically developed a 'Divide and Rule' strategy to strengthen their regime."[347] BJP party ideologues K.R. Malkani and K.N. Govindacharya have also expressed themselves in the same sense, e.g. Malkani, while surveying the irritants in Hindu-Muslim relations, writes: "The Hindu, in turn, has many grievances against the Muslims. By far the biggest is that the Muslim League insisted on Partition and the bulk of Indian Muslims voted for it. Actually the British had much more to do with Partition."[348] Since this view is so widespread, both in secularist and in Hindutva circles, we might as well take the trouble of evaluating it briefly.

This much is probably true, that Hindu-Muslim violence in the pre-British period was far more a matter of oppression of the Hindus by Muslim armies, largely consisting of foreign-born mercenaries and conscripts, than of street riots between Hindu and Muslim commoners. Considering the persistent Muslim-Hindu demographic differential, the Muslim masses must have been relatively much less numerous in the seventeenth than in the twentieth century, and more importantly, most of these converts were still very close to their non-converted neighbours in their daily way of life. In those circumstances, Hindu-Muslim animosity must have been a much smaller problem at the mass level than it has been in the twentieth century; but that is not the same thing as the Hindu-Muslim *friendship* which Ahuja suggests, nor is it proof that the modern boom in Hindu-Muslim riots was due to British intervention.

For all their "divide and rule" tactics at the diplomatic level, especially in their dealing with princes and top clergy and office-holding native lawyers (Gandhi, Jinnah, Ambedkar, Nehru), the British never encouraged communal rioting. It is a plain fact that in the period of unchallenged British power, between 1859 and 1919, communal riots were far fewer and less serious than in the subsequent period of native self-assertion, both

---

[346]Golwalkar: *Spotlights*, p.62.

[347]G.M. Ahuja: *BJP and Indian Politics*, p.281.

[348]K.R. Malkani: "A treaty to heal Hindu-Muslim rift", *Times of India*, 8.2.1993.

before and after Independence.[349] Indeed, when counted in deaths caused by violent confrontations between Hindus and Muslims, those sixty years were definitely far more peaceful than any other sixty-year period between 1192 and the present.

The lingering popularity of anti-Britishism in divergent corners of India's political spectrum is at least partly due to the perfect comfort and safety of blaming a party which has left the scene more than fifty years ago. It is, for instance, much simpler than elaborating a balanced assessment of the conflictual role of Islam in Indian history, which avoids both scapegoating today's Muslim community and wilful blindness to unpleasant historical facts. On this point, the Sangh Parivar is largely on the secularist wavelength, viz. dismissing the Hindu-Muslim conflict as a false and artificial conflict manipulated by non-religious vested interests.

The disagreement is only about pinpointing the clever conspirator who managed to turn this artificial conflict into a persistent reality—depending on the speaker, it may be the British, or the Hindu communalists, or Congress vote-bank politics, but never the fighting people themselves (the "people" being a holy cow of socialism/populism), nor their religious convictions (Hinduism and the minority religions being holy cows of the Sangh Parivar). A recent addition to this line of rhetoric is blaming the Americans for the Indo-Pakistani conflict because of their sales of weapons to Pakistan. At any rate, from Golwalkar to Vajpayee, the Sangh Parivar has studiously kept Islam itself strictly outside its range of targetable scapegoats.

Indianization

Guru Golwalkar drew attention to the cultural estrangement of Muslims from India: "As a matter of fact, in no other country in the world, where Islam has spread, their original dress, language, view of life etc., have remained the same. But in our country everything, even thinking also, is

[349] And the communal riots which did take place, or which the British reported as having taken place, were often wrongly interpreted as such, at least according to a now-popular secularist theory, which may well be correct in some instances. The central evidence given by secularist historian Gyanendra Pandey (in his book *The Construction of Communalism in Colonial North India*) in support of his thesis that "communalism" was a "construct" of colonial perception, is precisely that many social conflicts were *misinterpreted* as Hindu-Muslim conflicts by the British.

changed. If this change was not there, there would have been no Muslim problem at all. It has cut them off from the main national current of life."[350] And if conversion estranged them from the national mainstream, they had to revert to the old national ways: "The Muslims must realise that we are all one people and it is the same blood that courses in all our veins. They are not Arabs or Turks or Mongols. They are only Hindu converts."[351]

And if the Muslims do re-identify with India, Golwalkar assures them that they need not fear for their position in Hindu India: "History bears testimony to the fact that Bharat is the cradleland of religious generosity. It has always welcomed and assured all religious groups a free, honourable and secure life. Even in the Hindu Empires of Vijayanagar, Maharashtra and Punjab which rose to defend our national freedom from Muslim onslaughts, Muslims were in some of the highest positions of trust and responsibility."[352] To Golwalkar, it didn't matter what citizens believed in, as long as the system as a whole would be Hindu. Apparently, the recent well-publicized cases of Indian Muslims cheering an Indian sports victory against Pakistan would fulfil the Sangh Parivar criteria of "indianization".

Most Sangh Parivar people, starting in the 1960s with Guru Golwalkar and BJS leader Balraj Madhok, have suggested that the Hindu-Muslim conflict can be solved by "indianization": *Islam has to "Indianize" itself.*[353] Madhok drew attention to this notion in a speech at a symposium in Delhi concerning the 1969 Rabat Conference of Heads of Islamic States, where Indira Gandhi had tried to get herself invited on the plea that India should also count as an Islamic state because its Muslim population was the third largest in the world (after Indonesia and Pakistan). Madhok's

---

[350]M.S. Golwalkar: *Bunch of Thoughts*, p.647.

[351]M.S.Golwalkar: *Spotlights*, p.43.

[352]M.S. Golwalkar: *Spotlights*, p.66.

[353]As late as 1993, Madhok still repeated this exact sentence to me as his formula to solve the Hindu-Muslim problem. The classic statement of this doctrine is Balraj Madhok's booklet *Indianisation* (1970). This book came back into the news when a Muslim, Dr. Abid Reza Bedar wrote a belated reply to it, *Sîmâ kî Talâsh* (Urdu: "In Search of the Border"), which earned him a *fatwa* urging a social boycott against him for declaring that Hindus are not *Kâfir*s and thereby blurring the Islamic distinction between believer and unbeliever; see *Frontline*, 31.7.1992. The incident showed again that, in spite of RSS perceptions of a monolithic and fanatical Muslim community, the latter also has its share of people seeking a soft solution to the Hindu-Muslim conflict, some of them even using for this purpose the typically Hindu device of manipulating terminology, "addressing practical problems with theoretical solutions".

point was that instead of India seeking to integrate itself into the Muslim world, the Indian Muslims should seek integration in India.

"Indianization" has remained the Sangh Parivar's *final solution of the Muslim problem in India*: Muslims should not be expelled or exterminated, they should not even be assimilated into Hindu society, they should simply "identify with India". Or as the *Organiser* once put it: "Let Muslims look upon Ram as their hero and the communal problems will be all over."[354]

But can Muslims look upon Rama as "their" hero without ceasing to be Muslims? Guru Golwalkar used to answer this question by taking a leaf from the book of the Iranian Muslims: "Some Muslims say that Rustom is their national hero. But Rustom was a Persian hero. He has nothing to do with them. He was born long before Islam. If he could be considered a hero by the Muslims, why not Sri Rama?"[355]

But what exactly is this Indianization? The term "Indianization" was already in existence: it had been used during the Freedom struggle in the sense of "replacement of Englishmen by Indians in the civil service". The term appears to have first been used in the sense intended by Madhok in Jawaharlal Nehru's book *Discovery of India*, from which Madhok quotes a passage about the Muslim invasions: "It was a continuous long drawn out conflict, and while the struggle was going on, the other process of absorption and *Indianisation* was also at work, ending in the invaders becoming as much Indians as any one else."[356]

Madhok's book on the subject starts with a 21-page chapter "Indianisation: What?" But there, unfortunately, we find little except for the well-known arguments about how not India but the Muslim world had benefited from the contact, how India had been pluralistic since Vedic times, and how the Indian Muslims "are mainly converts and not foreigners".[357] The latter point at least provides a clue: "The change of way of worship under duress or for other reasons has not changed their forefathers

[354]*Organiser*, 20.6.1971, quoted in Tapan Basu *et al.*: *Khaki Shorts, Saffron Flags*, p.12.

[355]Golwalkar: *Bunch of Thoughts*, p.640.

[356]Quoted from Nehru: *Discovery of India*, p.154, in B. Madhok: *Indianisation*, p.19. Nehru's reference is explicitly to Akbar, "the great representative of the old Indian ideal of a synthesis of differing elements and their fusion into a common nationality. Because he identified himself with India, India took to him although he was a new-comer."

[357]B. Madhok: *Indianisation*, p.27.

or their culture. Culture is associated with a country and not with a religion."[358]

In my opinion, this last sentence is an escapist device, a way to deny the Hindu-Muslim conflict by positing an over-arching unity based on culture based in turn on common territory. It is, at any rate, incorrect. Modern American culture is much more akin to European culture, also in religion, than to the country-based Native-American culture. Indian Muslim culture has remained fairly close to Hindu culture due to inertia, but has distanced itself from it as the impact of Islam grew stronger, and has always *tried* to be more like Arab Muslim than like Indian Hindu culture.

It is true that in some pockets, Hindu culture has remained quite alive among Muslim converts, e.g. *Organiser* reports how a childless Meo Muslim (from Mewat, south of Delhi) has donated 7 acres of his land for setting up a Goshala (cow-shelter), a very Hindu thing to do. He explained that "his ancestors and those of other Meos were Rajputs who did not eat beef. Even today a large number of Meos do not take beef. Beef-eating and even slaughter of cows in Mewat, he said, was introduced by Tablighi Muslims and Deoband Maulvis coming from U.P., only in the last ten years or so. Shri Ismail also pointed out that Meos solemnised their marriages in the Hindu style. ... They recited Mewati Ramayan and Mahabharat morning and evening. But under the influence of Muslims coming from outside, he said, everything is changing."[359]

This example illustrates how the lingering attachment of Muslim converts to ancestral Hinduism is an unstable situation, a mid-way station on the way to either full Islamization or reconversion to Hinduism; this unstable mix can hardly be the basis of India's cultural unity. It also shows how change of religion does entail change of culture, at least in many important respects: marriage customs, food habits and taboos, reverence of cows and Hindu epics, and likewise dress, script, language.

Even so, for the Sangh since Golwalkar, "Indianization" does not mean Hinduization through conversion: "'Indianization' does not mean making all people Hindus. Let us realise and believe that we are all children of the soil coming from the same stock, that our great forefathers were one, and that our aspirations are also one. This is all, I believe, the

[358]B. Madhok: *Indianisation*, p.27.

[359]*Organiser*, 9.4.1995, reproduced in *Muslim India*, May 1995, p.234.

meaning of 'Indianisation'. ... The main reason for Hindu-Muslim tension is that the Indian Muslim is yet to identify himself fully with India, its people and its culture. Let the Indian Muslim feel and say that this is his country and these are his people, and the problem will cease."[360] In this view, Indian Muslims should "become" Indians, not Hindus. Once again, the Sangh Parivar proves to be a nationalist rather than a Hindu movement.

The Sangh wooing the Muslims

Wherever Hindus have a real or imagined problem with Muslims or Islam, they tend to vote BJP except if they have tougher alternatives, most notably the Shiv Sena (though even the latter has made overtures to the Muslim electorate and included a Muslim in its Maharashtra Government in 1995).[361] Yet, the record does not bear out the deduction that the BJP must be an anti-Muslim party.

It is easy to establish that the Sangh Parivar is not preparing but rather avoiding any confrontation with Islam. The BJP goes out of its way to assure everyone that it has no bad feelings towards Islam as such, for example: "To oppose Islamic fundamentalism does not mean to oppose Islam, which like all other major faiths is a religion of love, peace and brotherhood."[362] This is not empty rhetoric: the BJP enlists as many Muslims as it can get, and has even created a "Minority Cell" for them.

As a Leftist critic observes: "When in Opposition, the BJP lost no opportunity to castigate the Congress (I) for providing a subsidy in the matter of the air fare for the Haj pilgrimage, which in its eyes was a symbol of minority appeasement. Today, the BJP proudly advertises its decision to increase the subsidy given to the pilgrims."[363] Indeed, once the BJP came to power, it proved everything its Hindu critics had been alleging since 1992 (when the party started wobbling about Ayodhya), especially that it was, as Abhas Chatterjee put it to me, the "Congress B-team", trying to be all things unto all people. Secularist editor Vir Sanghvi remarked that

[360]M.S. Golwalkar: *Bunch of Thoughts*, pp.645-46.

[361]Radhya Rajadhyaksha: "Muslim Shiv Sainik: a suitable Hindutvawadi. Sabir Shaikh, the only Muslim in the Maharashtra Government", *Muslim India* (courtesy *Times of India*), May 1995, p.234.

[362]*Foreign Policy Resolutions*, p.5 (1995).

[363]V. Venkatesan: "The Laxman line", *Frontline*, 29.9.2000, p.7. Alongside is BJP president Bangaru Laxman's defence of his pleas for wooing the Muslims, in an interview given to V. Venkatesan: "In defence of a pro-Muslim strategy".

"as any fool can see, the current BJP bears no relations to Advani's Hindutva BJP" of pre-Demolition days, and he started wondering: "Whatever happened to Hindutva?"[364]

Contrary to certain impressions created in the media, the BJS-BJP and RSS leaders have a heartfelt desire to woo the Muslims. Especially after the Ayodhya Demolition, there have been numerous Hindutva fraternization meetings for Muslims, e.g. "Four thousand Muslims attended BJYM Conference"[365], or events indicating "Growing Muslim support for BJP".[366] Muslim columnist Sultan Shahin confirms that after the Demolition, the Muslims "discard[ed] their communal as well as professional secularist leadership" and "took the first avilable opportunity to open a line of communication with the forces of Hindutva", many of them even "voting for the BJP and the Shiv Sena".[367] *Organiser* claimed to know that "the Muslims are not anti-BJP", and quoted the Mumbai Urdu daily *Inqilab* as questioning five Muslim readers about the BJP, with four of them declaring that the BJP should be given an opportunity to form the government.[368]

Observers have acknowledged the BJP's systematic and nationwide effort to assure and win over the Muslims: "Having realised that it cannot afford to alienate the Muslims, the BJP is making subtle efforts to win them over by restoring their confidence. ... To convince Muslims that they will be safer under a BJP Government, party leaders are cashing in on the fact that BJP-ruled states were largely free of communal riots and tension and the BJP governments did not discriminate against Muslims or any other community. ... The West Bengal BJP put up 1,600 Muslim candidates—including 400 women—in the panchayat elections and a sizable number of them won. ... In Madhya Pradesh, over 96 lakh people have signed the BJP's appeal for construction of the Ram temple at Ayodhya. Of them, one lakh are Muslims."[369]

The Muslim presence in the Lok Sabha rose by one in the 1998 elections, "due to the one prestigious win at Rampur by a BJP candidate, Mukhtar Abbas Naqvi against Begum Nur Bano of the ex-ruling house of

---

[364]Vir Sanghvi: "Whatever happened to Hindutva?", *Rediff on the Net*, 6.5.1999.

[365]*Organiser*, 30.11.1997. BJYM: *Bhâratîya Janatâ Yuvâ Morchâ*, "Indian People's Youth Front", the BJP youth organization.

[366]Muzaffar Hussain in *Organiser*, 18.5.1997.

[367]Sultan Shahin: "For a grand reconciliation", *Hindustan Times*, 23.8.1995.

[368]Muzaffar Hussain: "Growing Muslim support for BJP", *Organiser*, 18.5.1997.

[369]Shyam Khosla: ""Courtship of convenience", *Indian Express*, 5.9.1993.

Rampur State in UP".[370] No wonder RSS chief Rajendra Singh said that "there was a slight, but encouraging, change in the attitude of the minority community".[371] The present official position of the RSS (and *a fortiori* of the BJP) is, more than ever, that Muslims are our brothers, that Islam itself is quite all right, and that only fundamentalism is wrong.

Even in the RSS weeklies, while the case against Islamic "fundamentalism" inside and outside of India is documented and argued week after week, criticism of Islam itself is extremely rare. Indeed, the RSS goes out of its way to blunt the sword of those who do try to criticize Islam. When in the 1980s Sita Ram Goel filled a weekly column in *Organiser* arguing that "fundamentalism" is the essence of Islam rather than a deviation, RSS General Secretary H.V. Seshadri intervened to have the column discontinued and the editor, the arch-moderate K.R. Malkani, sacked. The reason given for the discontinuation was that "otherwise, with such attacks on Islam, the Muslims will not join us".[372] The same reason had already been given by the BJS leadership when asking Balraj Madhok to leave the party, in 1973, "on the grounds that since Muslims had become allergic to me they would not join the party".[373] Contrary to a widespread impression, the Sangh Parivar tries to minimize Hindu animosity against Islam.

Even when addressing Muslim-related issues, BJP spokesmen bend over backwards to avoid any communal colouring. Thus, in its 1996 Election Manifesto, the BJP warns that because of Bangladeshi infiltration, "various demographic entities are bound to come in conflict" as a result of "an alarming growth of a section of the population"; already, "a section of the population has grown by almost 100 per cent" in certain northeastern areas.[374] This is so faithful to the rules of secular reporting on communal problems (where "Muslims" become "members of a particular community"), that it almost reads like a parody. At any rate, the whole issue of sending the Bangladeshi immigrants back has been removed from the BJP programme in the 1998 electoral campaign.

On the other hand, even the sanitized wording of the 1996 Manifesto

---

[370]V.P. Bhatia: "How the Islamic 'Qurbani' for secularism is proving counter-productive", *Organiser*, 29.3.1998.

[371]"Muslim attitude encouraging: RSS chief", *Indian Express*, 1.5.1995.

[372]Interview with K.R. Malkani, December 1992.

[373]That at least is Madhok's own version, see Balraj Madhok: "A Question of Power", *Indian Express*, 29.10.1995.

[374]BJP: *Election Manifesto 1996*, p.39.

betrays an acute uneasiness about the fast-growing Muslim presence in India, and that is the more fundamental mind-set of the BJP core constituency regardless of the fashions in terminology. The whole Sangh Parivar really has a problem here: unable to conceptualize Islam as a problem and constrained to strike Muslim-friendly postures, the Hindu nationalists are nonetheless uncomfortable with Muslims. On this point, I must agree with secularist perceptions about RSS insincerity: at least in some cases, anti-Muslim feelings are hiding just beneath the surface of Muslim-friendly statements.

The Sangh's Muslims

Unlike the HMS, the Sangh Parivar, in particular the BJP, actively seeks to befriend Muslims and even to enlist them as members. It is always useful to claim the assent or quote the approving statements of Muslims when defending yourself against Muslim or secularist spokesmen who claim to safeguard the Muslim interests.

The best-known case is that of Freedom Fighter and BJP office-bearer Sikander Bakht. Mr. Bakht struck me as being a thorough gentleman, but his main value for the BJP is that he is a born Muslim.[375] Thus, the 13-day BJP Government of 1996 could demonstrate its "secularism" by including one Muslim Minister, viz. Sikander Bakht. In 1998 he was included again, along with a young Shiite Muslim, Mukhtar Abbas Naqvi, who had led a Muslim support group for the Ayodhya temple.[376]

Sikander Bakht was often shown off as the party's token Muslim, but just as often, angry Muslims would write letters to the editor to explain that Mr. Bakht is not a Muslim at all.[377] They say that he actually converted to Hinduism on the occasion of his marriage to a Hindu woman, and that his children were raised as Hindus. And how else could we interpret Bakht's own statement: "I am a Ram bhakt first"?[378] The fact is that he strongly identifies with the Hindu viewpoint, witness his pamphlet "Why

[375]I met Mr. Sikander Bakht at the 1992 European Hindu Conference in Frankfurt.

[376]Ashis Nandy *et al.* claim (*Creating a Nationality*, p.35) that the BJP's claim of Muslim support in the person of Mukhtar Abbas Naqvi was "untrue"; it was true enough, and Naqvi was rewarded for his services with a junior minister post in Vajpayee's 1998 cabinet.

[377]E.g. letter by Tariq Alavi from Lucknow in *Indian Express*, 27.12.1993.

[378]Pradeep Kaushal: "I am a Ram bhakt first, says Sikandar Bakht", *Indian Express*, 4.4.1991. *Bhakta*: "devotee".

Hindus in the Dock?", which gives the classic Hindu case against the anti-Hindu bias of "pseudo-secularism".[379] He also protested when during L.K. Advani's 1997 *Swarna Jayanti Rath Yâtra* (Golden Jubilee car procession), Advani and Uma Bharati cancelled the singing of *Vande Mâtaram* at interreligious functions in order not to offend Muslim sensibilities, precisely the kind of "appeasement" which the BJP had always attacked when it was practised by Congress.

Apart from actual Muslim members, the Sangh Parivar has Muslim friends. Balraj Madhok's book *Indianisation* (1970) includes as annexures statements by a number of "nationalist Muslims", including M.C. Chagla and Hamid Dalwai. M.C. Chagla had been an assistant to Jinnah (a Khoja Muslim like himself), Bombay High Court Judge, Education Minister under Indira Gandhi, and Ambassador to Washington. In a Rajya Sabha speech, he said: "I appeal to the Muslim community and other minority communities also to join the national mainstream. ... What we want is that all of us, the Hindus, Muslims and Christians, should ... feel and think as Indians and should not get into separate compartments".[380]

The Sangh Parivar notion of Muslims as "Mohammedi Hindus" was endorsed by M.C. Chagla: "In the true sense, we are all Hindus although we may practise different religions. ... It is the distinction between Hindus and non-Hindus that has created all the trouble in this country and has even led to the partition of our motherland. ... If the distinction were to go then there will be no conflict between Hindus and non-Hindus."[381] Chagla even said: "I am a Hindu because I trace my ancestry to my Aryan forefathers."[382] He gave a guest speech at the BJP's first plenary session in 1980, full of praise for Vajpayee and Advani.[383]

---

[379]Included in the unsigned booklet (published by RSS publisher Suruchi Prakashan) *"Angry Hindu!"—Yes, Why Not?* (1988)

[380]In B. Madhok: *Indianisation*, p.150.

[381]Quoted from *Bhavan's Journal* (27.8.1978), in the foreword to the 1980 edition of Golwalkar: *Bunch of Thoughts*, p.vii. Chagla was not rewarded by Indira Gandhi for his exemplifying the "nationalist Muslim" type. As another nationalist Muslim, Hamid Dalwai (*Muslim Politics*, p.77), testifies: "The unceremonious exit of Mr. M.C. Chagla from her Cabinet and the relaxation of the rule prohibiting polygamy among Muslim employees of the Central Government are but two examples of the concessions she is making to Muslim communalism."

[382]Thus quoted by H.P. Sharma: "This land of Aryans", *Pioneer* (Varanasi), 21.12.1989, who hurries to add the explanation: "Aryans and Hindus are synonymous to each other, one and the same."

[383]M.C. Chagla: "BJP, the only alternative", *BJP Today*, 16.8.1997.

The late Hamid Dalwai, then introduced by Balraj Madhok as "the young pioneer of modernization of Islam in India", and denounced in the Jamaat-i-Islami weekly *Radiance* as a "Sanghist Muslim",[384] was regularly quoted as saying the very things about the Indian Muslim mentality which Hindus could only say at the cost of being decried as "communal". Here, he counters the usual secularist claim that Islamic separatism is the province of only a small and non-representative minority among the Muslims: "In post-partition India no significant differences now exist between western-educated and orthodox Muslims. The *Muslim Majlis Mushâwarat*, which is the united front of Muslim organizations in India, includes in its fold educated Muslims like Dr. A.J. Faridi at one extreme and orthodox Muslims like Maulana Nadvi at the other. The election manifesto of the Mushawarat at the time of the last general election contained a 9-point charter of demands which can only be interpreted as asserting that Muslim Indians constituted a 'sovereign' society. Since the Mushawarat represents practically all the Muslim organizations in Indian politics, it is reasonable to infer that most Muslim Indians subscribe to this view."[385]

Hamid Dalwai goes on to sum up a few signs of Islamic separatism, and he warns against worse to come: "The creation of Pakistan is not the end of this problem. H.S. Suhrawardy said in 1946 that Pakistan was 'not the last but only the latest demand' of Indian Muslims. ... He recommended the creation of a number of 'Muslim-majority pockets' in India. The birth of the Mallapuram district is therefore only a sign of further demands to come. ... The relaxation, on the eve of a mid-term poll, of the service rules enjoining monogamy on Central Government servants whose religion permitted polygamy was effected by the Government of India under the pressure of these organizations. ... The leftists have gone even further by conceding the demand for a Muslim-majority Mallapuram district and by supporting Mushawarat demand for the recognition of Urdu as a second official language in States [in none of

[384]Quoted by Dalwai himself: *Muslim Politics*, p.80.

[385]From a guest column by Hamid Dalwai in *Times of India*, 17.5.1970, in B. Madhok: *Indianisation*, p.144. In the Sangh's post-Demolition charm offensive, such quotation would preferably not be reproduced in *Organiser*, for the approach has more than ever become, to distinguish between the Muslim masses and the allegedly unrepresentative "communalist" leadership.

which] the constitutional requirement for such recognition is satisfied."[386] This is the standard Hindutva complaint against "Muslim appeasement".

According to Hamid Dalwai: "Leaders of secular parties ... have so far made no serious effort to understand the true nature of Muslim politics in India."[387] In particular, Hindu-born secularists systematically join hands with Muslim communalists in bewailing the precarious position of Muslims in a Hindu-majority country, and explaining Muslim separatism as a reactive phenomenon against the "Hindu threat". This, Dalwai argues, is completely mistaken: "That this understanding was wrong was made clear by no less a person than Mr. Liaqat Ali Khan himself. According to *The Hindu* of April 18, 1946, he declared that the demand for Pakistan today is not based on the fear of a Hindu majority at the Centre. ... it is the urge of a nation to mould its own ideals and culture and cannot be satisfied without having a full sovereignty which necessarily implies full control over all departments of state without exception."[388] In other words, the Muslim desire for sovereignty is a necessary implication of the present-day Muslim self-perception as a separate nation, regardless of whether the Muslims find themselves "in danger" or in a comfortable majority position.

Dalwai briefly endorses a whole catalogue of RSS demands: "We have to check Pakistani expansionism and protect our borders. ... We have to support Muslim modernism in India. We have to insist on a common personal law for all citizens of India. ... Religious conversion should not be allowed, except when the intending convert is adult and the conversion takes place before a magistrate. ... Government should have control over the income of all religious property. ... The special status given to Kashmir should be scrapped. All Indian citizens should be free to visit Nagaland. There should be opportunities for the development of Urdu. ... However,

---

[386]Quoted in B. Madhok: *Indianisation*, pp.145-46. Mallapuram is a "gerrymandered" district in Kerala, carved out of other districts so as to unite Muslim pockets into a Muslim-majority district. H.S. Suhrawardy was the Muslim League Chief Minister of Bengal in 1946, and politically responsible for (if not the actual mastermind behind) the "Great Calcutta Killing" of August 1946, a slaughter of Hindus which provoked a Hindu retaliation against Muslims, neatly calculated to convince Muslim opinion that co-existence with the Hindus was impossible, and also to convince the British and the Congress leadership that any further opposition to Partition would lead to disaster.

[387]Quoted in B. Madhok: *Indianisation*, pp.145-46.

[388]Quoted in B. Madhok: *Indianisation*, pp.145-46.

the demand for giving Urdu the status of the second official language of a state should be firmly resisted. ... The purdah should be legally banned. ... Family planning should be made compulsory for all."[389] This was an RSS man's dream of how a Muslim should be. Dalwai had not renounced Islam, and could consequently serve as a genuine Muslim who is none the less a nationalist. At the same time, he legitimized the standard Hindutva complaints about Muslim attitudes by endorsing them from a non-Hindu angle.

Among the latest crop of Hindutva-friendly Muslims, we must note Maulana Wahiduddin Khan, an ideologue and leader of the *Tablîgh* movement, the object of which is to "purify" Muslim culture of Hindu influence. He is regularly presented in *Organiser* as an enlightened alternative to Islamic fanaticism, especially since he counselled Muslims to abandon their claim to the controversial Ayodhya site.[390] He is also applauded for admitting that most riots are started by Muslims.[391] In July 1994, he presided over the RSS function at which the *Sarva Panth Samâdar Manch* ("Respect for All Religions Front") was founded, more or less an RSS front working among the minorities. The RSS, in its eagerness to find some kind of approval in the enemy camp, wilfully ignores Wahiduddin Khan's fundamental *Tablîghî* hostility to Hinduism, somewhat like the US Government which ignored the intense anti-Americanism in Pakistan when it built up that country as an outpost against the Soviet Union and Iran.

The rationale behind the *Tablîgh* movement is the following: Muslim power weakens when Muslim commitment to pure Islam weakens; when Muslims turn or return to pure Islam, they will be able to restore Islamic power.[392] One would think it would be the enemy par excellence of the Hindutva movement, as it was of the Arya Samaj in the 1920s. But the RSS eagerly accepts what little amount of positive attention an acclaimed secularist is willing to give to it.

---

[389]H. Dalwai: *Muslim Politics*, pp.106-08. *Pardâh*: "curtain", seclusion of Muslim women.

[390]Maulana Wahiduddin Khan: *Indian Muslims. The Need for a Positive Outlook* (1994), pp.109-30. See also, in the same spirit, Wahiduddin Khan: "Muslim leadership has failed them", *Times of India*, 17.5.1995.

[391]V.P. Bhatia: "Muslims start the riots, says Waheeduddin Khan", *Organiser*, 7.3.1993.

[392]See Maulana Wahiduddin Khan: *Tabligh Movement* (1986).

Re-evaluation of Partition

The Sangh is also enthusiastic about Ansar Hussain Khan, whose book *The Rediscovery of India* shows him to be a modernist Muslim who seeks an exit from the Islamic worldview.[393] The Sangh does not seem to notice that the actual *ideas* formulated by Ansar Hussein Khan are, on closer consideration, not really supportive of Hindu interests. Most importantly, A.H. Khan pleads for undoing the Partition, entirely in agreement with similar pleas by K.R. Malkani and other Sangh stalwarts.[394] Thus, M.V. Kamath supports Ansar Hussain Khan's call for a "confederation" of India, Pakistan and Bangladesh.[395]

In order to win Muslims over to the idea, some even adopt the Congress delusion that Partition never was what Muslims wanted, that the British had foisted it upon India against the will of the Indian people, Muslims included: "Partition was a folly and a crime. It has hurt Muslims as much as the Hindus. The real villain here was the Briton—Perfidious Albion—and not the Momin."[396] In reality, Viceroys Lord Wavell and Lord Linlithgow had opposed the Partition plan, being proud of the state their predecessors had created and intending to keep it in one piece even if it had to be released from the Empire. It was only because Lord Mountbatten was presented with the accomplished fact of massive communal violence by the Muslim League that he gave in to its demand of Partition. The blame lay squarely with the Muslim League, and other parties including Congress and the British can only be blamed for acquiescing in the Partition, not for desiring or imposing it.

Of course, the better part of Hindutva activism has been directed against the Pakistan movement and subsequently against the state of Pakistan, but that should not stand in the way of a re-evaluation of

---

[393]Ansar Hussein Khan: *The Rediscovery of India. A New Subcontinent*. The book contains a thorough deconstruction of the entire Congress version of the Freedom Struggle and the Partition machinations.

[394]See e.g. "Deendayal-Lohia plea for Indo-Pak Confederation", in K.R. Malkani: *The Politics of Ayodhya*, pp.180-81.

[395]Quoted with approval from a letter by Ansar Hussain Khan to Jamia Millia University, pleading for Muslim abandonment of all claims to the Ram Janmabhoomi site, by M.V. Kamath: "Indian history: a new approach", *Organiser*, 28.1.1996.

[396]K.R. Malkani: "Looking at the future", *Hindustan Times*, 17.1.1993. *Mo'min*: "believer", viz. in Islam.

Partition from a Hindu perspective, viz. as the lesser evil. If we accept the Hindu Revivalist notion of a "besieged" Hinduism, Partition has proved to be a blessing in disguise for Hinduism, a last chance to survive. When you consider that before Independence, the Hindu Congress stalwarts were taken for a ride by the determined Muslim leadership though the Muslims represented less than one-fourth of the population and there were practically no Islamic states to support them, how would the Hindus fare in a united South Asia in which the Muslims now constitute nearly one-third of the population and receive support from a string of rich and well-armed Islamic states?

As Hamid Dalwai has remarked, non-Partition would not have been all that pleasant for the Hindus: "It is quite true that partition far from proving to be a solution to the Muslim problem has only aggravated it. But it is simply not true that there was a happy solution waiting round the corner only if partition had been avoided. For the Muslims demanded parity as the price for remaining in a politically united India and surely this was an impossible demand."[397] The last offers made to Jinnah to make him abandon his Partition plans included 50% reservations for Muslims at all levels and an effective predominance of the Muslims in the government. What Jinnah gave up by refusing the offer was a *Muslim-dominated Akhand Bhârat*, an unassailable country with the highest population in the world, a Muslim superpower.

It is no coincidence that all Indian Muslim intellectuals now openly deplore Partition: they realize that Indian Islam lost badly on Partition. The Muslim community has been split into three roughly equal parts; compared with the emerging superpower India, Pakistan and Bangladesh are uninspiring backwaters; and the Muslims in India cannot entirely free themselves of the Partition stigma. It is now clear that from the viewpoint of Islamic interests, the pro-Partition school (based in the more modernist Aligarh Muslim University) was wrong and the anti-Partition school (centred on the theological academy Dar-ul-Uloom of Deoband) was right: Islam in India should not have settled for a part of the country, but should have aimed for control of the whole country. In Bangladesh the idea of a South-Asian confederation is very popular because it would formalize the *de facto* permeability of the Indian border for Bangladeshi migrants. Akhand Bharat is now high on the Islamic agenda, and

---

[397]H. Dalwai: *Muslim Politics*, p.113.

calculating Islamic strategists (among whom I would not count A.H. Khan) are welcoming and encouraging RSS daydreaming about reunification.

By contrast, Girilal Jain, always a pleader for *Realpolitik*, dismissed the sentimental yearning for reunification as contrary to Hindu interests: "The importance of partition in 1947 for Hindus has been completely missed by the proponents of secular nationalism and Hindu rashtra alike. Though partition did not settle the civilizational contest that began with Muslim rule first in Sindh and then in much of North India, it facilitated the task for Hindus since they now have a well-organized and powerful pan-Indian modern state of their own. ... I have often said, half in jest and half in seriousness, that Muhammad Ali Jinnah was the greatest benefactor of Hindus in modern times ... partition was the best thing that could have happened for Hindus in the given situation ... partition had finally ended [the old civilizational stalemate] in favour of Hindus in three-fourths of India".[398]

Even a more neutral observer like K.D. Prithipaul records a discussion with an Iranian colleague, who "argued that the partition of India was a disaster for the Muslims as it split the community into three parts. I observed that the partition has been a boon for India, for the majority Hindus, after nearly forty years of non-violent struggle, would have been no match for the violence of the Muslim League and its lust for power."[399] But again, the RSS has apparently never thought of this aspect of the matter.

Islam, the Arab national movement?

Another fresh arrival from the Muslim side in the Hindutva camp is Anwar Shaikh. He was a 19-year-old Muslim in Lahore when the Partition took place. After witnessing the arrival of a train full of dead Muslims slaughtered by the Sikhs in Amritsar station, he killed three Sikhs with his own hands. In the 1950s, he settled in Britain and became a successful businessman. Since the 1980s, he has been writing on religion and visibly distancing himself from Islam. In 1990, he published *Eternity*, a meditation on religions in general with the pride of place given to Vedic Hinduism. He also publishes a bilingual (English-Urdu) quarterly *Liberty*,

---

[398]G. Jain: *The Hindu Phenomenon*, pp.56-7.

[399]K.D. Prithipaul: "Reason, law and the limits of Indian secularism", *International Journal of Indian Studies*, 1992, p.21.

in which he has developed a systematic critique of Islam. In 1994, Anwar Shaikh published a book which endeared him in a definitive way to the Sangh Parivar: *Islam, the Arab National Movement*, which we will discuss in this section.[400]

The review of Anwar Shaikh's work in *Organiser* was titled "Muslim proud of his Aryan ancestry", but this title was untruthful.[401] It is true that Anwar Shaikh has rediscovered the "Aryan" (i.e. Vedic) heritage which his great-grandfather had abandoned by converting to Islam, but the consequence of this rediscovery was precisely the opposite of what the *Organiser* title suggests: he *quit Islam*, becoming a "non-Muslim proud of his Aryan ancestry".[402] The message which *Organiser* sought to convey was that Indian Muslims should follow Anwar Shaikh's example: remain Muslim all the while rediscovering their Aryan heritage (i.e. "Indianizing" themselves). This was a replay of the Freedom Movement's notion of the "nationalist Muslim", one for whom Islam and Indianness are not incompatible.

But if anything, the case of Anwar Shaikh pointed in the opposite direction: by rediscovering his Hindu heritage, a Muslim loses his Muslim identity. Islamic hardliners are wholly aware of this phenomenon, which is why they try to nip it in the bud, for instance, by prohibiting Hindu religious music on Pakistani radio. From the Hindu viewpoint as pioneered by the likes of Swami Shraddhananda, the message of the *Organiser* should have been: "Indian Muslims, follow Anwar Shaikh's example, rediscover your Vedic heritage, and abandon Islam."

In his book *Islam, the Arab National Movement*, the apostate author Anwar Shaikh has accurately documented how islamization has meant external Arabization (names, clothes, script) for most converted populations, but has wrongly inferred that Islam is a form of Arab

[400]For a non-Hindutva introduction to Anwar Shaikh's thought, see his talk with Tariq Ali: "Publish and be damned", *Observer* (*Review*), 8.10.1995.

[401]T.H. Chowdary: "A Muslim proud of his Aryan ancestry", *Vande Bhârathmâtharam* (Hyderabad), November 1994, subsequently reproduced in *Organiser*. See also H.V. Seshadri: "Why dread a mere writer?", *Organiser*, 30.7.1995, and an interview with Shaikh taken by Ranjit Kumar, *Organiser*, 6.10.1996.

[402]The story of his apostasy is told in Anwar Shaikh: *Eternity*, and in various issues of his quarterly *Liberty*. In April 1994, a British-Pakistani Mufti issued a fatwa sentencing "the apostate Anwar Shaikh" to death, but with the caveat that British Muslims should not take the law into their own hands, and that the execution should only be performed by a duly consituted Court in an Islamic state.

nationalism or Arab imperialism.[403] It is generally correct that islamization of non-Arab populations has meant their progressive Arabization: their names, script, vocabulary, dress and marriage customs all tend to create the impression of a community frozen in seventh-century Arabia. But his conclusion is less uncontroversial: that Islam was a kind of Arab nationalism. We may compare Mohammed's conquest of Arabia with Mao's conquest of China: the real nationalists trying to preserve national culture and identity were his opponents, but his own imported ideology (prophetic monotheism, Marxism) pushed out the national mainstream by winning the war.

As against Shaikh's thesis, Sita Ram Goel has argued that "the Arabs were the first victims of Islam" (though he too had written, in his first publication on communal issues, that "Islamism is only another name for Arab imperialism which had, at one stage of its history, pillaged and populated with its own progeny many foreign lands and which even today keeps many non-Arab nations spiritually enslaved").[404] Nevertheless, if any movement in seventh-century Arabia can count as "the Arab national movement", it was undoubtedly the so-called *Ridda* ("return" to god-pluralism) uprising against the Islamic state after Mohammed's death, in which the Arabs tried to shake off Islamic rule and restore their pluralistic culture. Even A.A. Engineer admits that "the war of *ridda* (apostasy) was a general insurrection throughout Arabia".[405] Within a year, Caliph Abu Bakr put the uprising down and definitively plunged the Arabs into Islam.

For the Sangh, the thesis that Islam is but Arab nationalism is doubly welcome: it recasts the Islam problem in the familiar, safely secular-sounding terms of nationalism, and it legitimizes Islam ("See we're not against Islam?") all the while limiting Islam's legitimate geographical domain to Arabia, so as to exclude India from it. This yields a neat scheme: Hinduism is Indian nationalism, and Islam is Arab nationalism. This is certainly clever, though it only establishes an imaginary deal with the Indian Muslims, who are bound to reject the reduction of their universal religion to an Arab nationalism. Most of all, the Sangh Parivar's fondness for this reduction of religions to nations and nationalisms confirms

[403] A. Shaikh: *Islam, the Arab National Movement*, 1994.

[404] S.R. Goel: *Hindu Society under Siege*, p.11. This is also the message of V.S. Naipaul: *Beyond Belief* (1997), about the arabization and consequent cultural self-alienation among the Muslims of Iran, Pakistan and South-East Asia.

[405] A.A. Engineer: *The Origin and Development of Islam*, p.131.

again that theirs is more a nationalist than a religious "fundamentalist" movement.

Reproach to Westerners and Christians

Suhas Majumdar berates Western intellectuals for their refusal to face facts concerning the aggressive designs of Islam: "Thanks to the money-power of the oilrich Arab countries, Islam has spread its tentacles to the farthest corners of the globe, and is making known its intention of world-domination in no uncertain terms. The intellect of the West looks at the spectacle, benumbed and fascinated, sometimes breaking into loud acclamations as to the glory that is Islam, and sometimes mumbling incoherent protests against its 'fundamentalism'. As Nirad C. Chaudhuri has pointed out, this division of Islam into two variants—the one fundamentalist and the other Liberal—is the result of 'either ignorance or repulsive hypocrisy'."[406]

The West's "colossal intellectual failure" regarding Islam has already led to serious policy mistakes, according to Majumdar: "It is against the background of this failure that a great many contemporary events have to be judged: the West's prevarication with the events in Bosnia or in Kashmir; its impatience with Israel in its life-and-death struggle in surroundings where a single false step could spell its destruction; and, coming to a lower plane, the Prince of Wales's breaking out into singing the glory of Islam from a public platform."[407]

It is true that Western politicians and foreign policy experts dismiss suspicions of Islam's ambitions of conquest as paranoid or at any rate anachronistic, for example, a Belgian expert claims: "Western politicians who worry excessively about political Islam, are years behind on the facts."[408] The same view is propagated by leading Islamologists like Gilles Kepel, Olivier Roy and many others.[409] Dutch Minister Jan Pronk has spoken out in favour of an Islam-friendly cultural relativism: "It is a

[406]S. Majumdar: *Jihâd*, p.66; no source is given for Nirad C. Chaudhuri's comment, but talking to me, the veteran writer confirmed that this was his considered opinion.

[407]S. Majumdar: *Jihâd*, p.67; remark that Prince Charles's paean to Islam is part of a broad multiculturalist discourse which has also made him applaud Hinduism, as on the opening of the Swaminarayan temple, Neasden, in 1995.

[408]Rik Coolsaet: "De islam, een politieke bom?", *De Standaard*, 19.6.1997, with reference to British Middle-East-watcher Michael Field..

[409]See e.g. Olivier Roy: *The Failure of Political Islam*.

Western misconception that the Taliban are really violating human rights. These Afghan warriors in some cases apply a different type of human rights. ... Some human rights are applied in a different manner on the basis of a different philosophy."[410]

As for the Christian missionaries, "their latter-day flirtation with Islam is probably the stupidest thing these worthies have done. ... Apparently this flirtation is aimed at peaceful conversion of the pagan peoples of Asia and Africa in some sort of active collaboration with the Islamic zealots".[411] In the past at least, they "did not fail to see *jihâd* for what it was—a code of murder and rapine disguised under a thin coating of religious verbiage" and they "knew that their greatest adversary in the business of proselytization was Islam", even when they were "enamoured of the Koran's full-throated pagan-bashing".[412]

Now and in the future, "the toothless Christianity of the twentieth century, preached by means of fraud and bribery and a prodigious establishment of social service, will certainly prove no match for Islam when the latter sets out to declare full-fledged *jihâd* against the converts which Christianity has gained by years of hard labour and a mind-boggling expenditure of money. ... Christian missionaries should take lesson from the fate of the Christians under the Ottoman Empire and, for the matter of that, under its Kemalist successors. Slowly and surely, Turkey has been denuded of the Christian element of its population, with the Western powers looking on in blissful unconcern.[413] There is no reason to believe that the same fate does not await the new converts to Christianity in Asia and Africa."[414]

India already provides some examples of conflict between Christian converts and Muslims. In 1964, the mostly christianized Garo tribals were massacred and expelled from East Pakistan, resulting in large-scale violence between tribals and Muslims in the adjoining tribal belts of India: "In early 1964, there were bloody riots once more in East Pakistan

[410]"Pronk vraagt begrip voor Taliban" (AFP), *De Standaard*, 21.2.1998.

[411]S. Majumdar: *Jihâd*, p.67.

[412]S. Majumdar: *Jihâd*, p.67.

[413]About the gradual expulsion of Christians from southeastern Turkey, see the proceedings of the symposium *Chrétiens du Sud-Est de la Turquie*, Brussels, 16-17 March 1991; and Bat Ye'or: *Chrétiens d'Orient entre Jihad et Dhimmitude* (French: "Christians of the Middle East between Jihad and Zimmi Status").

[414]S. Majumdar: *Jihâd*, p.68.

between the majority and the minorities. The past six, seven years, the Muslims had been pestering the *Adibâsî*s ... a stream of refugees had ensued ... a mad anti-Hindu propaganda egged on the Muslims in East Pakistan, also against the Christians. It was the first time that Christians were systematically chased out from there."[415]

In the 1980s and 90s, there have regularly been clashes between Bangladeshi settlers and christianized tribals in India's North-East, chiefly in Meghalaya and Tripura, most gruesomely in Nelli (1983): "Nelli was an unknown little village till over three thousand people were slain in one orgy of killing. It was Bangladeshi refugees killing Bengalis and Assamese; Assamese and Bengalis kiling each other; tribals killing non-tribals; Muslims killing Hindus and Christians; Christians killing Hindus."[416] No common Abrahamic monotheism or joint participation in the Minorities' Commission could keep the Muslims from expropriating the lands of the Christians, nor the Christians from fighting back.

Majumdar's message to the Christians is that they had better join hands with the Hindus against Islam.[417] This vision of an expanding Islam necessitating a joint Christian-Jewish-Hindu front, reminiscent of Samuel Huntington's thesis of a "clash of civilizations", is very common in Hindu revivalist circles. The underlying assumption is that the hour of truth has struck for Islam: for the first time, the issue is nothing short of world supremacy, and Mohammed's dream of converting or fighting the unbelievers "until religion belongs to Allah alone"[418] is about to be realized—or broken forever.

However, that is not the vision propagated by the Sangh Parivar. Especially the 1990s have seen a sharp shift away from concerns about pan-Islamic expansion and towards animosity against American hegemony. Symptomatic in this regard was the BJP's (very low-profile) support to the Gulf War giving way very quickly to a vocal rejection of the American-imposed UN embargo against Iraq. In the mid-1990s, i.e. before the BJP in government started making friends with the US, anti-

[415]Robert Houthaeve, in his biography of Father Herman Rasschaert (who died while trying to save Muslims): *Recht, al Barstte de Wereld*, p.276.

[416]Khushwant Singh: *Many Faces*, p.29. "Bangladeshi refugees" is the secularist term for Bangladeshi illegal immigrants, or what Hindutva authors call "infiltrators".

[417]This position is also part of the reason for the BJP's support to the candidacy of the North-eastern Christian tribal G.G. Swell for the presidency of India in 1992.

[418]Q.2:193/189, 8:39/40.

Americanism was a more forecefully articulated theme in *Organiser* than anti-Islamism. Part of the reason may have been India's growing self-confidence, which dismissed as demeaning the old quarrel with the much weaker neighbour Pakistan, and assumed India's new status as a member of the top league along with the European Union, China and the US. But part of the reason certainly was the Sangh Parivar leadership's getting tired of the exhausting conflict with the Muslims, which had yielded nothing except a bad image. Indeed, the Sangh leaders had genuinely embraced the belief that Indian Muslims and Hindus are just compatriots sailing in the same ship and condemned to some kind of mutual agreement.

THE CHALLENGE OF "EGALITARIAN" ISLAM

In this section, we move on to a line of polemic where independent authors totally leave the Sangh brigade behind: the polemic concerning Islam's claim of moral superiority regarding the value of social equality. According to a now-common belief, this is the one trait about Islam which is most attractive, most responsible for the conversion of Hindus past and present to Islam: its egalitarianism. It is a key element in the psychology of the colonial underling that he starts justifying to himself his own lowly position and the supremacy of his master. In this case, we get a back-projection of a modern value, viz. egalitarianism, on to an age when that value was not in focus, in order to retro-actively justify the successes of the Islamic invaders to the detriment of the Hindus. We shall see that some Hindu thinkers had some difficulty in freeing themselves from this newly propagated belief, in the sense that they kept on assuming it even when trying to refute it. But we shall also see that recent authors have countered it very thoroughly.

Swami Shraddhananda against Hindu social evils

The book *Hindu Sangathan, Saviour of the Dying Race* (1926) by Swami Shraddhananda, Arya Samaj educationist and a leader of the Hindu Mahasabha, was a true milestone in the development of Hindu revivalism. Within the Arya Samaj, it marks a shift from doctrinal debates about the rightness or wrongness of Hinduism and other religions to a reflection on the social and political conditions for the very survival of Hinduism. There is also a shift from Christianity to Islam as the most worrying threat, which may reflect an awareness of the decline of British power in India and of the prospect that the Hindus would soon be left alone to face their Muslim fellow-countrymen rather than the British-Christian intruders.

In particular, Shraddhananda makes a diagnosis of the competition between Hindus and Muslims for the numbers, which was developing to the disadvantage of the Hindus. He discusses the problems of conversion to Islam and of the demographic differential all the better to introduce a neat solution: Hindu *Sangathan*, "self-organization". Both the HMS and the Sangh Parivar see themselves as the organizing force which is implementing Shraddhananda's mission to salvage Hinduism. For a proper evaluation of the performance of those organizations, it is necessary to understand and to verify Shraddhananda's analysis, which we will take as the starting-point in this chapter.

The first chapter of *Hindu Sanghatan, Saviour of the Dying Race* tries to depict the situation of Hinduism in the pre-Muslim period as distinctly better from the Hindu viewpoint, though not necessarily a Golden Age. In Swami Shraddhananda's view, until the death of Harsha of Kanauj (AD 647), i.e. until about the time of the first Muslim invasions, Hindus had never been converted to other religions. Whichever invader populations had settled in India, had all soon been assimilated into Hindu society. Apart from the controversial question of the status of Jainism and Buddhism vis-a-vis Hinduism (not discussed in *Hindu Sangathan*), this generalization seems fair enough, and we need not take issue with it.

The chapter concludes: "Up to the death of Emperor Harsha, foreigners had not got any permanent foothold on the Indian soil, foreign invasions had been frequently beaten back and if partially successful for a time were obliged ultimately to beat retreat, there was no non-Aryan community in residence and if any non-Aryans came, they were absorbed by the Hindu community."[419] So, why did Hinduism fail to solve the problem posed by the Muslim invasions in a similar way?

According to Swami Shraddhananda, the development of the caste system is largely to blame. In Harsha's time, on the eve of the Muslim invasions, the caste system had roughly the same divisions as in the early twentieth century, but not the proliferation of sub-castes, while inter-

---

[419]Shraddhananda: *Hindu Sangathan*, p.10. It is obvious that "Aryan" is not used in contradistinction with "Dravidian", but as a synonym of "native Hindu".

marriage was still more accepted: "there were only three upper castes i.e. Brahmans, Kshatriyas and Vaishyas among whom no subcastes then existed, intermarriages among these principal castes were of frequent occurrence, among the Shudras there were probably subcastes according to the different services which they rendered and lastly there were the so-called untouchables or Panchamas who were forced to live outside the habitations."[420] This was, in Shraddhananda's opinion, much better than the state of the caste system in his own day, but already a degeneration.

The theme of the Golden Age is quite common in Hindu writings. Imagining an ancient Golden Age is by no means a modern device of the Hindutva ideologues but an ancient Hindu tradition, which saw the world declining from a perfect Satya Yuga down to a strife-ridden Kali Yuga. But the characteristics which each author attributes to his Golden Age is dependent on his own ideological position. While traditionalists identify the Golden Age with the full flourishing of the caste system and the Ages of Decline with an increasing incidence of "mixing of castes", modernizers like Shraddhananda say that the caste system didn't exist then, or wasn't rigid, or wasn't hereditary, or wasn't cruel. In Shraddhananda's book, the purpose of this vision was to connect the Hindu losses under Muslim rule with the degeneracy of Hindu culture itself, implying that a regeneration of true Vedic culture will make Hindu society immune to Islamic inroads and capable of winning the lost members back into the fold.

Some of the social evils prevalent among Hindus in the colonial period were part of the degeneracy which made the defeat against Islam possible. Others, however, only came about after and as a result of the establishment of Muslim rule. Thus, "during the reign of Harshavardhana, some 1300 years ago ... early marriage was unknown. ... But when the Muhammadan invaders ... conquered the disorganised Hindu hosts, and Hindu young women began to become a prey to the lust of some of the conquerors, the custom of early marriage and the unnatural *purdah* were introduced by the degenerate Hindus of Northern India as refuge against the inroads of Muslim Ghazis in Hindu homes."[421]

Vedic society did not practise child marriage, and the Hindu medical

---

[420]Shraddhananda: *Hindu Sangathan*, p.10.

[421]Shraddhananda: *Hindu Sangathan*, p.95.

classics warn against conception before the ages of sixteen for the woman and twenty-five for the man, because this causes the child to be weak.[422] Yet, some historians argue that it came about as a native development predating the Muslim period, for example, A.S. Altekar traces it to the *Yajnavalkya Smriti*, which he dates to AD 200, and which justifies prepubertal marriage with the natalist argument that otherwise a lot of occasions for impregnation are wasted.[423] Even so, the Muslim period certainly did have an impact, as for example in introducing the seclusion of the women of wealthier families inside the house (*pardah*, "curtain") and, for a minor but very telling example, the conducting of wedding ceremonies at midnight rather than in broad daylight (as was the ancient custom), out of fear for Muslim attacks on the festive gatherings.

In Shraddhananda's thesis, however, the role of Islam in degrading Hindu mores is only an aside. His main point is that Hindu society was already on a downward slope, and that it had to pull itself up, back to the Vedic level, if it was to have a chance of survival. Unlike many other Hindu pamphleteers, Shraddhananda was not playing a blame game, not given to endless wailing about the injustice inflicted by others. At the same time, the Swami did see the end of Muslim rule as the golden opportunity for healing Hindu society, but found the Hindus too static to seize it: "The despotic tyrannical Mohammadan rule is a thing of the past, conditions for the removal of social evils, which are eating into the vitals of the Hindu society, have been favourable for the last 80 years, but custom-ridden Hinduism is still stagnant and refuses to move, child marriage still prevails, in the remotest corners of India, among Hindus."[424]

This is suicidal for Hindu society, for the combination of child marriage with the prohibition of widow remarriage (another entirely native "social evil") leads to the existence of a large class of very young widows. Shraddhananda quotes census figures indicating that their number in 1921 was 736,248, "an appalling figure! Out of these 7¼ lakhs of child-widows, there are thousands who lead a life of strict chastity, and it is perhaps due to their Tapasya that the Hindu society still ekes out its

---

[422]In a typical bid to bring in scriptural authority, Shraddhananda (*Hindu Sangathan*, p.98) quotes the Ayurveda classic *Sushruta Samhitâ* (10:47-48) to support his position that child marriage "has made the Hindus a community of weaklings". Swami Vivekananda expressed the same opinion (*Our Women*, p.20).

[423]A.S. Altekar: *The Position of Women in Hindu Civilization*, p.56.

[424]Shraddhananda: *Hindu Sangathan*, pp.95-6.

existence. But an overwhelming majority consists of those who are compelled to leave their homes on account of the brutal tyranny and lustful attacks of their female and male relatives, and to seek shelter under Muhammadan roofs or to add to the numbers of the daughters of shame. In this way, by reducing the numbers of Hindus, they add to the numerical strength of beef-eating religious societies."[425]

This way, Swami Shraddhananda links all the defects of Hindu society to the threat of rival religions which are besieging it. Like the misery of young widows, the ill-treatment of Untouchables chases Hindus of that category towards Christianity or Islam. In the circumstances, Hindus simply cannot afford to tolerate the social evils of their society any longer, for they add to the strength of the enemies of Hinduism day by day.

Acceptance of the Islamic equality thesis

If social evils pertaining to marriage customs caused conversion to Islam, this had to be all the more true for the most outstanding social evil of Hinduism, caste oppression. Swami Shraddhananda surveys the Muslim populations in different parts of India and mentions some specificities of their conversion stories. Thus, the Muslims of Bengal, 36 per cent of the Subcontinental Muslims, had originally "professed a debased form of Buddhism", had "never been fully Hinduised", and had therefore been "spurned by the high-class Hindus as unclean". The result was that they "listened readily to the preachings of the Mullahs who proclaimed that all men are equal in the sight of Allah, backed as it often was by a varying amount of compulsion".[426]

It is remarkable that the Swami believed in the emerging Muslim claim that the Hindu masses had been swayed by the "Islamic message of equality". As we shall see in the next sections, this claim is disputed for most of Islamic history, though it has a certain validity for Islamic conversion campaigns in the twentieth century, which have specifically targeted India's lower classes. In his own day, Swami Shraddhananda must have been aware of the use of social reform arguments by Islamic preachers in imitation of Christian missionaries, but he shows no historical testimonies or research data in support of the claim (then spreading fast,

---

[425]Shraddhananda: *Hindu Sangathan*, pp.97-8. *Tapasyâ*: "self-abnegation, ascetic practice", thought to give strength, hence Shraddhananda's half-serious suggestion that widows have saved Hindu society with their *tapasyâ*.

[426]Shraddhananda: *Hindu Sangathan*, p.17.

now virtually universal) that egalitarianism had been a decisive factor in converting Hindus to Islam. Within the Hindu spectrum of opinion, this claim could be used in support of the reformist Arya Samaj position: if inequality had driven people away from Hinduism, then only the Arya Samaj programme of social equality could save Hinduism.

The Swami stresses that "the Muhammadan population is by no means wholly of foreign origin".[427] Even in Panjab, where almost two out of twelve million Muslims claimed descent from Pathan, Baluch, Sheikh, Sayyid and Moghul invaders (often in spite of having "very little foreign blood in their veins"), he finds that "ten million showed by the caste entry (such as Rajput, Jat, Arain, Gujar, Mochi, Turkhan and Teli) that they were originally Hindus".[428] This may seem obvious, but it is worth emphasizing in view of later allegations that Hindu revivalists consider Muslims as foreigners. For Swami Shraddhananda, the Hindu origin of the Indian Muslims settles the question for good: of course they are not foreigners. They are not very different from Hindus, and ought to be brought back to Hinduism.

Forced conversion

The next chapters of Shraddhananda's book "take up one by one the causes of Hindu deterioration" and "examine the remedies which Hindu reformers have from time to time tried to apply for the amelioration and revivification of the race".[429] First of all, Shraddhananda quotes profusely from the book *The Preaching of Islam* by T.W. Arnold. The position developed in this book may be guessed from the reason given for its recent re-publication: "Hitherto Islam has suffered from the image of being a faith imposed by the sword. To help dispel this grossly unfair interpretation, this objective study, now reprinted, will be a singular contribution."[430]

---

[427]Shraddhananda: *Hindu Sangathan*, p.17.

[428]Shraddhananda: *Hindu Sangathan*, pp.17-18. In today's India, the Muslim masses, when speaking to Hindu or foreign questioners, often pretend to have no caste, in conformity with the official line that the Muslim community is egalitarian; by contrast, Pakistani Muslims will freely tell you: "I am a Jat Muslim", "I am a Rajput Muslim", and the like (as I found out after a hint from Shridhar Damle). Some Muslim scholars openly discuss the reality of caste among Indian Muslims, notably in Imtiaz Ahmad, ed.: *Caste and Social Stratification among Muslims in India*.

[429]Shraddhananda: *Hindu Sangathan*, p.19.

[430]Back cover of the 1990 reprint (of the "second, enlarged edition" of 1913) from Low Price Publications, Delhi.

According to Shraddhananda, Arnold is "a European writer who beats even Muslim original historians in his partiality towards the Muhammadans of India."[431] Yet, even in this book which supposedly disproves the violent character of the Islamic conversion drive, Shraddhananda digs up considerable testimony proving, at least to his own satisfaction, the reality of forcible conversions.

Thus, Arnold writes about the invader Mahmud Ghaznavi's encounter with a Hindu chieftain (*râi*), Hardatta, who realized he had no chance to hold out against the impressive strength of the invading army: "So he reflected that his safety would best be secured by conforming to the religion of Islam, since God's sword was drawn from the scabbard. ... He came forth, therefore, with ten thousand men, who all proclaimed their anxiety for conversion and their rejection of idols."[432] Shraddhananda comments: "If this is not a forcible conversion, then it would be idle to search for forcible conversions in Islam."[433]

Likewise, Arnold quotes a testimony from the North-West Province (presently Uttar Pradesh): "Muhammadan cultivators ... assign the date of their conversion to the reign of Aurangzeb, and represent it as the result sometimes of persecution and sometimes as made to enable them to retain their rights when unable to pay revenue."[434] This would be a testimony from the horse's mouth, given *in tempore non suspecto*, and therefore hard to dismiss as hostile Hindu propaganda.

After describing forced conversions from the period of the early Muslim incursions (most notably by Mahmud Ghaznavi), Arnold claims: "These new converts probably took the earliest opportunity of apostatizing presented to them by the retreat of the conqueror—a kind of action which we find the early Muhammadan historians of India continually complaining of."[435] As convincing proof, he cites a lineal descendant of the said forced convert Hardatta whose name, Chandrasen, betrays his Hindu identity. But this type of automatic reconversion must have become a lot more difficult as soon as Muslim invaders were no longer pushed back, when they managed to establish an empire in India. The Islamic

---

[431]Shraddhananda: *Hindu Sangathan*, p.37.

[432]T.W. Arnold: *Preaching of Islam*, p.257.

[433]Shraddhananda: *Hindu Sangathan*, p.33.

[434]Quoted from the *Gazetteer of the North-West Province*, vol.xiv, part iii, p.47; in T.W. Arnold: *Preaching of Islam*, p.260.

[435]T.W. Arnold: *Preaching of Islam*, p.257.

punishment for apostasy is death, and even when this was not taken literally, it is to be expected that a Muslim Government would exert serious pressure against such reconversions.[436]

Indeed, Arnold's only later example of such return to Hinduism of forced converts to Islam concerns precisely a case where Muslim rule had lapsed and no danger attached to reconversion any more: in 1789 Tipu Sultan "issued general orders that 'every being in the district without distinction should be honoured with Islam, that the houses of such as fled should be burned ...'. Thousands of Hindus were accordingly circumcised and made to eat beef; but by the end of 1790 the British army had destroyed the last remnant of Tipu Sultan's power in Malabar, and this monarch himself perished early in 1799 at the capture of Seringapatam. Most of the Brahmanas and Nayars who had been forcibly converted, subsequently disowned their new religion."[437]

Arnold also describes a number of mass conversions to material inducement, ranging from presents given to converts by the sultan in person to the threat of confiscation of a community's land and the perennial burden of the *jizya* and other disabilities imposed on the non-Muslims.[438] This is not forced conversion *stricto sensu* but at least it is conversion under tangible pressure. To Shraddhananda, the reality of this type of conversion, like that of conversion at swordpoint, was useful in demonstrating the altogether insincere motives underlying the genesis of the Indian Muslim community. In practical terms: twentieth-century Indian Muslims should feel no guilt in abandoning Islam, for their ancestors had never embraced it out of conviction.

To complete his argument for the insincerity of the entry of certain Indian communities into Islam, Shraddhananda discusses some of the traditions narrated by these communities themselves concerning their ancestors' conversion. Thus, according to a tradition of the Bachgoti clan of the Ayodhya region, its ancestor Tilok Chand's beautiful wife was kidnapped by the Moghul emperor Humayun, but when he released her

---

[436]About apostasy, the Quran says: "When they turn away from you, seize them and put them to death wherever you find them." (4:89/91)

[437]T.W. Arnold: *Preaching of Islam*, p.262. Interestingly, in one of his proclamations announcing his policy of mass conversion, Tipu cites as his motive his revulsion for what he perceived as female "promiscuity" and "polyandry" among the matriarchal Hindus of Malabar.

[438]T.W. Arnold: *Preaching of Islam*, pp.257-60.

again, both Tilok Chand and his wife converted to Islam "in gratitude" for this generous gestue.[439] *Gratitude* to a man who kidnaps your wife, merely for dumping her afterwards? Most people heave a sigh of relief when a loved one is finally released by kidnappers, but "gratitude" is not the word, nor would they describe the religion of the kidnappers as one which "taught such generous purity", as the Bachgoti clan purportedly did.

Apparently the story has a historical core but has gradually been twisted by the second or third generation of converts who had to put Islam, the religion they were born into, in a more favourable light. Shraddhananda may have a point when he comments that in its present form, this "legend, on the very face of it, appears absurd."[440] Indeed, Arnold himself also mentions a second tradition, viz. that Tilok Chand was imprisoned by Humayun's father Babar, and only released on condition of becoming a Muslim.[441]

T.W. Arnold concedes that "some Muhammadan rulers may have been more successful in forcing an acceptance of Islam on certain of their Hindu subjects" but maintains that "Islam has gained its greatest and most lasting missionary triumphs in times and places in which its political power has been weakest, as in Southern India and Eastern Bengal".[442] This statement is patently untrue. There is a distinct proportionality between the percentage of Muslims in a given area of India and the duration of Muslim rule in that area, e.g. Bengal (and likewise the areas which now make up Pakistan) with its large proportion of Muslims was firmly under Muslim domination for centuries. In South India (as in the forest areas of Himachal Pradesh, Orissa and Madhya Pradesh), Muslim "political power has been weakest", but there, Islam has definitely not "gained its greatest and most lasting missionary triumphs", for it has a low percentage of Muslims. None the less, Swami Shraddhananda is willing to "patiently examine" Arnold's assertion.

It so turns out that many conversion narratives are untrustworthy, partly because they depend on miracle stories. Thus, Shraddhananda dismisses the miracle by which one Baba Fakhruddin converted the Dunde-Kula community (he and a Hindu priest were both tied in sacks

[439]T.W. Arnold: *Preaching of Islam*, pp.259-60.

[440]Shraddhananda: *Hindu Sangathan*, p.37.

[441]T.W. Arnold: *Preaching of Islam*, p.259.

[442]T.W. Arnold: *Preaching of Islam*, p.263, quoted by Shraddhananda: *Hindu Sangathan*, p.50.

filled with lime and thrown into the water; only the Baba reappeared, by being miraculously transported to a hill outside the town), with the predictable argument that such miracles only happen in the past or at a distance, where nobody can verify them, but fail to happen in modern India, though Muslim Babas are as eager as ever to make converts.[443]

In other narratives, particularly those pertaining to Muslim-ruled areas, the language used may well be euphemistic, if not sarcastic, e.g.: "During the three centuries of Arab rule there were naturally many accessions to the faith of the conquerors. Several Sindian princes responded to the invitation of the Caliph Umar b. Abd-al-Aziz to embrace Islam."[444] But what is the reality to which the courteous phrase "responded to the invitation" corresponds? Shraddhananda questions the voluntary nature of these conversions: "Of course Arnold calls all these conversions voluntary, but compulsion does not always consist of open threat of death."[445] At any rate, Arnold's assertion that there were "*naturally* many accessions to the faith of the *conquerors*" is in contradiction with his own thesis that Islam scored its greatest missionary successes in areas where it did not wield political power.

After relating some more miracle stories which Muslim communities pass on to explain their ancestors' conversions, Shraddhananda blames the Hindus along with the Muslim preachers for this superstitious type of conversion: "But the chief reason is to be sought in the credulity and blind superstition of the Hindus of that period. It is needless to multiply examples of fraud practised by Muhammadan missionaries for converting Hindus to Muhammadanism during the reign of the Muslim Emperors and kings. My only purpose, in giving lengthy extracts from historians who are partial to the Muslims, was to show that it was mere credulity, superstition and intolerant tyranny of so-called higher-caste Hindus, rather than any merit and appreciation of the faith, which drove millions of low castes into the fold of Muhammadanism."[446]

This conclusion does not fit in logically with the preceding list of data borrowed from T.W. Arnold's book. From the episodes of conversion discussed by Shraddhananda, it is possible to derive an impression of

---

[443]Shraddhananda: *Hindu Sangathan*, pp.53-4.

[444]T.W. Arnold: *Preaching of Islam*, p.272; quoted in Shraddhananda: *Hindu Sangathan*, p.56.

[445]Shraddhananda: *Hindu Sangathan*, p.56.

[446]Shraddhananda: *Hindu Sangathan*, pp.60-1.

appalling gullibility among the converts regarding Sufi "miracles", but the alleged "intolerant tyranny of so-called higher-caste Hindus" is nowhere in evidence. Shraddhananda brings it in at the last moment without connecting it with the historical material which he has just presented. The reason apparently is that this just happened to be one of the main planks in the reformist platform of the Arya Samaj: the upper castes have damaged Hindu society with their caste discrimination (which few will dispute), *ergo* they must also be blamed for the apostasy of lower-caste people (which does not follow from the data presented). At this point, Shraddhananda muddles his own argument against the sincerity of conversions to Islam by forcing an extraneous pet concern of his own into it.

Shraddhananda's main line of argument, however, is quite strong. It could have been more broad-based than the refutation of just one (albeit authoritative and influential) book, but we should make allowance for a number of practical limitations under which the Swami had to operate. He has shown that even in cases mustered as proof for the purely voluntary and religious reasons for conversion to Islam, physical or social pressure did play a crucial role. Those who support T.W. Arnold's position may come up with new evidence, but at least this particular round of the debate has definitely been won by Shraddhananda.

The jizya

If Islam gained converts among Hindus, it was not because of the equality it brought, but on the contrary because of a specific form of inequality which it instituted, viz. inequality between Muslim and non-Muslim. Thus argues Harsh Narain, and many Hindus with him. Once the Muslim rulers were safely in power and in a position to reward and encourage conversion by means of tax discrimination, legal discrimination (win the dispute with your neighbour if you convert), favouritism in employment and similar incentives, more and more Hindus started to convert to Islam. A typical element of discrimination was the *jizya*, the tax levied on the non-Muslims in exchange for "toleration" of their religious practices, and this became probably the most important motivator for Hindus and other non-Muslims to accept Islam, certainly in peacetime when purely forcible conversions were rare.

Harsh Narain, one of the rare Hindu scholars fluent in Arabic beside Persian and Urdu, has written a brief study (with a high density of Arabic references) about the Islamic treatment of the non-Muslims: *Jizyah and the Spread of Islam.* The main thrust of his argument is that steep inequality between Muslims and non-Muslims is an intrinsic feature of Islamic doctrine, and was applied in the Islamic world until the emergence of non-Muslim powers forced its formal (if not always its effective) abolition. In 1717, the tottering Moghul Empire had to abolish the *jizya* in the face of ever-stronger Hindu opposition, and in the Ottoman Empire, the emancipation of the non-Muslims (equality before the law) was decreed under Western pressure in 1855, after Britain and France had saved the Turks against the superior military power of Czarist Russia in the Crimea War. However, the newly emerging Muslim states of the post-colonial era have not failed to re-instate this inequality, albeit in different degrees of intensity.[447]

Harsh Narain inquires into the sources and scriptural justification of the inequality between Muslims and others. The starting-point is the belief that Muslims ought to rule the world, in preparation of the conversion of all mankind to Islam, as laid down in Quran, Sunna and later theological writings. Narain quotes Mohammed as saying that "the whole world belongs to Allah and His Prophet";[448] Ibn Taymiya as saying that "conquest in *jihâd* simply restores lands to the Muslims", who enjoy a kind of Divine right over them; and Mohammed Iqbal as saying that "every land belongs to us because it belongs to God".[449]

The next component of the doctrine of Muslim-Kafir inequality cited is that the idol-worshippers are "unclean" (*najas*), and should therefore be kept at a distance from Muslims and sacred places, and certainly not be befriended.[450] Narain quotes some minor theologians to the effect that if an unbeliever falls into a well, all the water has to be drawn out and rejected as unclean (not unlike India's former Untouchables). Even Ayatollah Khomeini is quoted as listing the unbelievers among the unclean things: "Eleven things are unclean: urine, excrement, sperm, blood, a dog, a pig, bones, a non-Muslim man and woman, wine, beer, perspiration of the

---

[447]For a description of the plight of these *kâfirs* and *zimmis*, see e.g. Bat Ye'or: *The Dhimmi* and *Les Chrétiens d'Orient entre Jihad et Dhimmitude* (French: "Christian communities of the Orient between *jihâd* and *zimmi* status"). Bat Ye'or is practically the only Western author to appear in the references in Harsh Narain's *Jizyah*.

[448]*Sahîh al-Bukhârî* 2:406.

[449]H. Narain: *Jizyah*, p.1.

[450]Q.3:28/27, 3:118/114, 4:144/143, 5:51/56, 5:57/62, 5:80/83, 9:16-17, 9:23. 9:28.

camel that eats filth. The whole body of a non-Muslim is unclean, even his hair, his nails, and all the secretions of his body. A child below the age of puberty is unclean if his parents and grand-parents are not Muslims."[451]

Harsh Narain traces Mohammed's career, including the occasions on which Mohammed's successors have based their policy vis-à-vis the unbelievers. It is obvious that Mohammed's goal was the conversion of everyone to Islam. Yet, when he had Arabia in his power, he gave only the Pagans the choice between death and conversion, while Jews and Christians could remain Jews and Christians (though not in Arabia), on condition of accepting some humiliating conditions and paying a heavy toleration tax. The precedent is the treatment of the Jews of Khaybar, who were allowed to stay (not as a matter of right, but as a unilateral favour which Mohammed could and, after a few years, did revoke) on condition of paying him half their income.

For Hindus, the important question here is whether non-monotheists could also be "tolerated" on this model. A crucial clue is the following verse, apparently in AD 631, a year after the capture of Mecca, when tribe after tribe was submitting to the Prophet, who set his sights on the complete conquest of Arabia and beyond: "Fight against such of those who have been given the scripture as believe not in Allah nor in the Last Day, and forbid not that which Allah hath forbidden by His messenger, and follow not the religion of truth, until they pay the tribute readily, being brought low."[452]

Understood this way, the verse only pertains to the non-Muslim "people of the Book", viz. Jews and Christians. That is why three of the four Sunni schools of jurisprudence assume that this toleration can be accorded to Jews and Christians alone, while Pagans have to choose between conversion and death. Though this was not always implemented literally, the long-term result confirms this uneven treatment of monotheists and "idol-worshippers": while Christian and Jewish communities in the Muslim world have survived until the twentieth century, the presence of Buddhists, Zoroastrians and Manichaeans in Iran and Central Asia was practically liquidated within two centuries of Muslim rule.

---

[451]Quoted in H. Narain: *Jizyah*, p.3, from Ruhollah Khomeini: *Principes Politiques, Philosophiques, Sociaux et Religieux* (Paris 1979), translated by Bat Ye'or: *The Dhimmi*, p.397.

[452]Q.9:29, Mohammed Marmaduke Pickthall's translation.

Only the Hanifite school, the one predominant in India, extends the same toleration to non-Abrahamic religions, much to the chagrin of some Indian Muslim diehards, e.g. the thirteenth-century writer Amir Khusrau, who lamented: "Had not the Zimmis enjoyed the concession of the Shari'a, all trace of the Hindus would have vanished root and branch."[453] Worse, on the established principle that Christian monks in Syria were exempt from paying the *jizya*, some of the Delhi Sultans exempted the Brahmins, the leaders of infidelism, as well.

However, Harsh Narain argues that the Quran verse is usually mistranslated, for the first part, "those who do not believe in Allah and the Last Day", cannot be referring to Jews and Christians, who *do* believe in God/Allah and the Last Day (in the Quran and the orthodox biographies of the Prophet, it is only the Pagans who are cited as ridiculing the notion of the Last Day). Instead, the verse should be understood as referring both to the Pagans, "who do not believe in Allah and the Last Day", and to non-Muslim people of the Book, who "forbid not that which Allah hath forbidden through His messenger and follow not the religion of truth".[454] So, that should be some consolation for Hindus living under Muslim rule: unless they offer armed resistance, they do not have to be given a choice of death or conversion, but may opt for the status of tolerated non-Muslims who pay the *jizya*. Against Harsh Narain's interpretation, it could be objected that this verse was "revealed" well before Mohammed had conquered the whole of Arabia and ordered the forcible conversion on pain of death of all the Arab Pagans, so that the latter policy may have abrogated the older commandment of conditional toleration; which explains why the non-Hanifite law systems refused the right of toleration to Pagans.

The regime of "toleration" included the acceptance by the unbelievers of some 20 humiliating conditions first imposed by the Caliph Umar on the Christians of Damascus.[455] These included being recognizable as a

[453]Quoted in H. Narain: *Jizyah*, p.33. Abu Hanifa (699-767?), founder of the Hanifite school, was a freed Indian (Jat) slave sent from Sindh to West Asia during Mohammed bin Qasim's conquest in 712-713, at least according to A. Wink: *Al-Hind*, vol.1, p.161.

[454]H. Narain: *Jizyah*, pp.8-9.

[455]The list is quoted in full in H. Narain: *Jizyah*, pp.21-3. Tradition ascribes this "Covenant of Umar" to the second Caliph (634-644), but some orientalists feel this is a back-projection of an arrangement formalized only after AD 750, e.g. Bat Ye'or: *The Dhimmi*, p.48.

non-Muslim by name and dress, not riding a horse, and not even a donkey where Muslims walk on foot, not excluding Muslim visitors from communal meetings, putting places of worship at the disposal of Muslim travellers as a shelter for the night, forfeiting the right to bear arms. The most important, from the viewpoint of the Islamic state, was the toleration tax or *jizya*, a tax which had to be high enough to hurt, but of which Mohammed never determined a fixed rate.

Harsh Narain analyses the nature and objectives of the *jizya*:

"1. It is meant to be an alternative to killing, plunder, enslavement, ransom, forcible conversion, as well as to be a penalty for *Kufr* [= unbelief]. ... It is a fiscal *Jihâd*, so to speak.

"2. It is a badge of humiliation for being a non-Muslim, of utter servility to Islamdom. ...

"3. The long-term policy behind it appears to be to compel or motivate the *Dhimmi*s slowly to turn to Islam and embrace it. ...

"4. It opens the door to levy of other humiliating taxes on the *Dhimmi*s such as ... *Kharâj* (land-tax)."[456]

Jizya is a kind of regulated extortion, somewhat like the "peaceful" plunder of Khaybar and other towns which submitted without a fight to the Muslim army. When there was fighting, the spoils were divided among the fighters, with one-fifth going to the Prophet or the Islamic state, but when there had been no fighting, the spoils went to the Prophet or the state in their entirety.[457]

Though *jizya* provided the unbelievers with an incentive to convert, it also provided Muslim rulers with a very tangible incentive to tolerate the non-Muslims. This effect, that it would discourage the drive to convert the whole population to Islam, had already been foreseen by the Caliph Umar, who warned the governor of Egypt not to prefer *jizya* to conversion: "I only wish that the whole bunch of them would be converted. Verily! Allah has sent Muhammad as a preacher, not as a tax-gatherer."[458] In practice, many Muslim rulers who were aware of the importance of *jizya* revenue for their treasury decided to be ruler first and Muslim next: "Thus, though Jizyah has played an enormous role in the spread of Islam, it sometimes

---

[456]H. Narain: *Jizyah*, pp.11-12.

[457]Suhas Majumdar: *Jihad*, p.6: "*Fai'*: The whole plunder accruing to the Prophet (or his representative) when the infidel army surrenders without a fight. *Jizyah* is a species of *Fai'*."

[458]H. Narain: *Jizyah*, p.16, quoting al-Wgsiti.

helped retard it as well."[459] In many cases, it is thanks to the *jizya* that non-Muslim communities have survived till today.

On the other hand, *jizya* along with land-tax has sometimes been used as an instrument of dire oppression. Particularly "Alauddin [Khilji] is notorious for having pauperized the Hindus to the utmost limit", in a deliberate policy of pushing the Hindus so deep into material hardship that they would be too busy with sheer survival to even think of rebellion.[460] While the earliest Muslim writers had described Indian prosperity, after the establishment of the Sultanate the population got impoverished, and remained so under the Moghuls: "The resultant effect of [Alauddin's] policy was that the people in the villages suffered from extreme financial hardship. The poverty of Indians was noticed in the later period by foreigners."[461]

The abolition of the *jizya* by Akbar didn't help, for the Moghul policy was to extract the highest possible land-tax: "The basic object of the Moghul administration was to obtain the revenue on an ever-ascending scale."[462] Indeed, the abolition of the *jizya* was meant precisely to promote Hindu collaboration in the administration and thereby to facilitate tax collection and increase state revenue. In some regions, half of the land revenue was taken by the state, in some two-thirds, in 1629 in Gujarat even three-fourths.[463] Moreover, the peripheral Sultans continued to levy the *jizya*.[464]

In 1679, Aurangzeb reintroduced the *jizya* at the rate of 48 dirhams for the rich (those earning more than 1000 dirhams per year), 24 for the middle-class and 12 for the poor (those earning less than 200). This was in itself much less heavy than the already existing secular tax burden. He also made Hindu traders pay a commercial tax twice as high as what Muslims paid. Like many of his predecessors, he sometimes lamented that it was

---

[459]H. Narain: *Jizyah*, p.17.

[460]H. Narain: *Jizyah*, p.29. This of course goes against the Marxist assumption that it is pauperization which leads to revolution: in reality, revolutions are typically made by self-confident upcoming classes, while the dirt-poor at best only succeed in desperate and failed revolts.

[461]K.L. Srivastava: *Position of Hindus under the Delhi Sultanate*, p.157, with reference to Francisco Pelsaert, who visited India under Jahangir: "The common people (live in) poverty so great and miserable that the life of the people can be depicted or accurately described only as the home of stark want and dwelling place of bitter woe.".

[462]K.L. Srivastava: *Position of Hindus*, p.159, quoting Irfan Habib.

[463]K.S. Lal: *Studies in Medieval Indian History*, p.191.

[464]H. Narain: *Jizyah*, pp.30-1.

very difficult to realize the *jizya*, because of the intense resistance. This had always been a problem for Muslim rulers in India: "It is also found that the Sultans had a hard nut to crack so far as goes the question of collection of Jizyah. Their Jizyah-collectors were often driven away by the local Hindu chiefs and landlords."[465]

And so, *jizya*, which combined with other taxes to create an exceedingly heavy tax burden, became a common reason for either defection of Hindus to the state religion, or rebellion, or flight from the city to the countryside and from the countryside into the forests: "With the expansion of Islam in India it appears that some migration from the cities to the villages took place, where they could get security and safety of their life and prosperity against the attacks of the Muslims."[466] The least one can say is that the unequal taxation of Hindus under Muslim rule has had a profound impact on Indian history. This was not genocide, of course, but it was a large and long-lasting fact of life in Indian society and deserves to be known for what it was.

A Muslim handful defeats the Hindu millions

The belief in Islamic egalitarianism as contrasted with Hindu caste inequality instils in modern Hindus a sense of guilt by comparison, for Hinduism may be many things but not egalitarian. It also serves as a major trump card in Islamic propaganda and polemic worldwide. Hindu thinkers have taken two distinct attitudes vis-à-vis this belief: to accept it and start a competition in egalitarianism, viz. by fighting the caste system and other forms of inequality in Hindu society; or alternatively (if not in combination with the former), to disbelieve the claim of Islamic egalitarianism and refute it.

In a debate on the 1992 Supreme Court amendments to the Mandal proposals for caste-based reservations, prominent lawyer Ram Jethmalani, who was to be BJP Justice Minister in 1998-99, said that the Hindus had been overpowered by a band of five or ten thousand invaders, simply because the Backward Castes did not care to defend their country.[467] By

---

[465]H. Narain: *Jizyah*, p.31.

[466]K.L. Srivastava, *Position of Hindus under the Delhi Sultanate*, pp.156-57.

[467]Shown in a *Newstrack* video, late 1992. A renewed polemic about the principles of caste-based reservations took place because the Supreme Court had insisted on certain modifications, especially the exclusion of the "creamy layer", i.e. the advanced upper layer of the "Backward" castes who were well-placed to corner the caste-based benefits which were of course intended to help the truly "backward".

implication, he grimly though unwittingly alleged that the Backward Caste people felt no loyalty to their country, and passively if not actively betrayed it, because it was merely the country of their hated Forward Caste rulers. Shortly after seeing this debate on video, I talked with the editor of a leading secularist daily; he declared that Hindus had been defeated by a mere two thousand Muslim invaders because of their dividedness.[468]

Against this, Hindu revivalist authors have pointed out that for five centuries, Muslim invaders in India either were swiftly repelled, or managed to get only a temporary foothold in border areas, or made short raids ending in retreat with heavy losses. Afghanistan, the Makran coast and the Maldives were the only pieces of Hindu territory permanently lost to Islam by AD 1000, and it took till 1192 before the Ghorid invaders could overrun much of North India. Were there only two thousand of them?

K.S. Lal has collected some figures. The army of Mahmud Ghaznavi (*c.* AD 1000), which sacked the Somnath temple before being thrown back with heavy losses, employed 30,000 camels only for carrying the water supplies. Mohammed Ghori, the actual conqueror of North India (AD 1192), had 120,000 cavalry. Controlling the conquered territory required even larger armies: Alauddin Khilji had 475,000 horsemen under his command, Mohammed Tughlaq had 900,000. The Bahmani sultanate in the Dekhan recruited many thousands of soldiers from the Muslim countries per year; when this inflow was reduced because the control over the Arabian Sea passed from Arab into Portuguese hands, the Bahmani sultanate collapsed.[469] This means that Islam could only conquer and occupy India by an immense military effort.

The conquest of India by Islam had taken centuries longer and required a far larger quantity of soldiers and weaponry than the conquest of West and Central Asia, North Africa and Spain. In what is probably the very first book devoted to the resistance which the Muslim invaders encountered in India, Dr. Ram Gopal Misra writes: "The political and military resistance was spread over more than five and a half centuries till its final collapse in northern India in the last decade of the twelfth century AD. For long, historians have emphasised merely the ultimate collapse of

[468]Vinod Mehta of the *Pioneer*, talking to me in Delhi, December 1992.

[469]Details of the military strength of the Muslim conquerors in K.S. Lal: "The army of the Sultanate", in *Journal of Indian History*, December 1977, pp.85-110.

the Indians, ignoring completely the resistance offered by them."[470] An excuse for this unbalanced historiography may be that most records were written by or for Muslim rulers.[471]

Even when subjugated militarily, cultural resistance continued: "The Indian resistance had another facet, which was the outcome of the resolute determination of the Indians to preserve their religious and cultural identity. While country after country, from the Straits of Gibraltar to the banks of the Indus, witnessed the rapid Islamization of their individual cultures, even Northern India managed to survive as a predominantly 'heathen' land even after five centuries of Muslim rule."[472] Moreover, unlike the Iranians and other Islamized peoples, the Hindus managed to throw the Islamic (Moghul) empire back on the defensive in the eighteenth century, when the caste system was probably at its harshest in history. If social coherence were a factor of unassailability, then clearly India's social system would have been much better and more satisfying than that of the countries to its west. It is simply not true that the caste-ridden Hindu society was less capable of putting up a defence.

The social system as a military factor

But was the social structure really a factor of much importance? Europe held out against the Islamic invasion, from Charles the Hammer at Poitiers in 732 to Jan Sobieski outside Vienna in 1683, but its feudal system could hardly be considered more egalitarian than the Indian caste system. Thus, feudalism had the same system of status-based rights and duties, including, for instance, a differentiated status-based system of punishment like the one prescribed in the *Manu-Smriti*.[473] We see the same social

---

[470]Ram Gopal Misra: *Indian Resistance to Early Muslim Invaders upto 1206 AD*, preface. Sita Ram Goel's like-minded book *History of Heroic Hindu Resistance to Muslim Invaders (636 AD to 1206 AD)* is essentially a supplement to Misra's book.

[471]Among the exceptions to this rule of Hindu disinterest in history-writing, we may mention *Padmanâbha*'s saga *Kânhadade Prabandha* (AD 1455), now available in a translation by V.S. Bhatnagar.

[472]Ram Gopal Misra: *Indian Resistance to Early Muslim Invaders upto 1206 AD*, preface.

[473]Thus, a Brahmin was punished less for murder than a Shudra, who in turn was not punished for public drunkenness while a Brahmin was. Thomas Fleming (*Politics of Human Nature*, p.3) notes, with reference to European feudalism, that "traditional societies ... rely heavily on status in assessing worth and guilt. The accidental killing of a great man can bring a greater punishment than the murder of a peasant. On the other hand, a nobleman may have to pay a more serious penalty for a crime on the grounds that he knows the law better and has greater influence."

system hold out on one and get defeated on another occasion. Between eighth-century Spain and France, there was little difference in social structure, but the former was conquered while the latter held out against the Muslim invaders. Between the Hindu society which repelled earlier Islamic invasions and the Hindu society which was overrun by Ghori in 1192, there was also very little difference. These sociological explanations for military defeats are typical constructions by armchair theorizers unacquainted with military realities.[474]

Dr. Misra quotes Mohammed Habib's classical statement that resentment against caste inequality explained the Muslim conquest and the growth of the Muslim population in India: "Face to face with the social and economic provisions of the Shariat and the Hindu Smritis as political alternatives, the Indian city-worker preferred the Shariat", so that the Ghorid conquest "was not a conquest properly so-called. This was a turn-over of public opinion—a sudden turn-over, no doubt, but still one that was long overdue."[475] This is a radically counterintuitive reading of the Ghorian conquest with its well-attested bloody battles: "The so-called Ghorian conquest of India was really a revolution of city labour led by the Ghorian Turks."[476] Likewise, K.A. Nizami: "The Rajputs and the privileged classes chafed under a sense of humiliation and defeat but the working classes joined hands with the new government and helped it in building the new cities."[477] And Aziz Ahmed claimed that "for the lower

---

[474]Here, Sita Ram Goel's thesis regarding Mao's conquest of China (developed in *Conquest of China*, 1954) applies: a victory obtained by sheer military superiority is falsely explained, in the victor's propaganda and in the writings of mediocre and uncritical foreign observers, as proof of the superiority of everything the victor stands for, including his social system or his worldview.

[475]Quoted from Habib & Nizami: *The Delhi Sultanate* (part of the *Comprehensive History of India*, graced with an approving foreword by J. Nehru), in R.G. Misra: *Indian Resistance*, p.35. Habib worked out the same thesis in vol.2 of Elliott & Dowson, *History of India*, introduction to the 1951 edition.

[476]Habib & Nizami: *Delhi Sultanate*, pp.53-4. Note also the misplaced cleverness in the marshalling of trivial facts, notably the fact that life went on, as proof of enthusiastic support to the Islamic regime. Thus, the fact that labourers dependent on wages took jobs in public works is interpreted (Habib & Nizami: *Delhi Sultanate*, p.50) as "help" to and "maintenance" of the regime: "Indian city labour, both Hindu and Muslim, *helped* to establish the new regime and it also *maintained* it, through all revolutions and revolts, for over 500 years." (emphasis added)

[477]K.A. Nizami: *Some Aspects of Religion and Politics in India during the 13th Century*, Aligarh 1961, p.85, quoted in K.L. Srivastava: *Position of Hindus under the Delhi Sultanate*, p.165.

Hindu castes acceptance of Islam meant an escape from the degraded status they had in Hindu society."[478]

A non-Muslim pioneer of this view (apart from T.W. Arnold, discussed above) was M.N. Roy, founder of the CPI. He wrote: "The phenomenal success of Islam was primarily due to its revolutionary significance and its ability to lead the masses out of the hopeless situation created by the decay of antique civilisations not only of Greece and Rome but of Persia and China—and that of India."[479] In Roy's view, "there lived in India multitudes of people who had little reason to be faithful to Hindu laws and the traditions of Brahmin orthodoxy, and were ready to forsake their heritage for the more equitable laws of Islam which offered them protection against the tyranny of triumphant Hindu reaction."[480] Today, this view that the condition of Hindu society amounted to a historical need for the imposition of Islamic rule on India, and that the masses welcomed Islam as a great liberation, is repeated as Gospel truth in numerous publications on the subject.

According to Roy, "the expansion of Islam is the most miraculous of miracles",[481] but unfortunately, "the average educated Hindu has little knowledge of, and no appreciation for, the immense revolutionary significance of Islam."[482] Therefore, he exhorts the Hindus to make a "dispassionate study" of Islam, which should have great "scientific value", "sure to be handsomely rewarded".[483] Hindu revivalist author Mayank Jain counters: "And yet, there is no scientific study on any aspect of Islamic theology or Hindu spiritualism in the entire book. ... M.N. Roy had no knowledge of Islamic theology and could only lead us to funny conclusions. His conclusions have nothing to do with scientific analysis because science is based on hard facts and not on mindlessness."[484]

M.N. Roy's enthusiasm for Islam was indeed rather starry-eyed, and

---

[478]Aziz Ahmad: *Studies in Islamic Culture in the Indian Environment* (Oxford 1964), p.82, quoted by K.S. Lal: *Indian Muslims*, p.95.

[479]M.N. Roy: *Historical Role in Islam*, p.6. In Roy's view, if India was not fully Islamized, so much the worse for India: "Unfortunately, India could not fully benefit by the heritage of Islamic culture, because she did not deserve the distinction." p.90.

[480]M.N. Roy: *Historical Role of Islam*, p.83.

[481]M.N. Roy: *Historical Role of Islam*, p.5.

[482]M.N. Roy: *Historical Role of Islam*, p.3.

[483]M.N. Roy: *Historical Role of Islam*, p.1.

[484]Mayank Jain: "Hindu-bashing through the decades", *Organiser*, 18.5.1997. Incidentally, Mayank Jain's grandfather was an associate of M.N. Roy's.

he did not give a single historical reference to support his sweeping theory. But the power equations in India are not such that Hindu revivalists can taunt their Marxist opponents for this lack of evidence and simply leave the onus of proof on them. Typically, they will go on the defensive and assume that it is up to themselves to prove M.N. Roy's innovative theory wrong, rather than wait for him to prove it right or to be seen failing in the attempt.

Ram Gopal Misra's verdict on this theory is that it is totally unsupported by data in the primary sources, the Muslim chronicles of Muslim conquest and Muslim rule, which are eloquently silent on social disaffection among the Hindu masses as a factor of Muslim victory. This may be contrasted with the situation in West Asia, where the conquest of Byzantine cities was much facilitated by disaffected minorities of Jews and Oriental Christians, who opened the city gates for besieging Muslim armies.

K.S. Lal, too, is unimpressed by the wide consensus in favour of the thesis of an egalitarian Islam entering India on an anti-caste mission: "However, contemporary writings of Persian chroniclers nowhere mention caste as a factor leading to conversions. Muslim historians of medieval India were surely aware of the existence of the caste system in Hindu society; Alberuni, Abul Fazl and emperor Jahangir, to mention a few. And yet no one mentions even once tyranny on the low caste people as cause for conversion. Their evidence shows beyond doubt that conversions in India were brought about by the same methods and processes as seen in Arabia, Persia, Central Asia, etc. ... There was no caste system in these countries and yet there were large-scale conversions there."[485]

Other Indian authors unconnected with Hindu revivalism have reached the same conclusion. None other than Mohammed Habib's son and successor (as history professor in AMU), Irfan Habib, has recently rejected "the popular conception that Islam had struck at the roots of casteism in India". He observes that the works of Muslim theologians and law scholars of the medieval period did not show "commitment to any such equality" at all. "While medieval Islamic literature referred to Hindus as 'infidels' and denounced polytheism and image worship, there was no criticism of the caste system, the theory of pollution and oppression of

[485]K.S. Lal: *Indian Muslims*, p.96.

untouchables that were rampant in medieval India", according to Irfan Habib.[486]

The Muslims did not start a crusade against caste because more generally they did not object to inequality by birth. Habib notes that inequality on the basis of birth was accepted as self-evident by leading Muslim thinkers of the period, and mentions as examples: "Minhaj Siraj, a thirteenth-century theologian, had stated that the importance of the ruling class was confined to Turks of pure lineage or Taziks of select births. Zia Barani, an orthodox and learned theologian, gave an exposition of a rigid hierarchical structure".[487]

Irfan Habib further writes: "It is true that Islam in its law recognizes differences based only upon free man and slave (and man and woman); caste, therefore, is alien to its legal system. Nevertheless, the attitude of the Muslims towards the caste system was by no means one of disapprobation. When in 711-14, the Arabs conquered Sind, their commander Muhammad Ibn Qasim readily approved of the constraints placed upon the Jatts under the previous regime, very similar to those prescribed for the Chandalas by the *Manusmriti*.[488] Muslim censures of Hinduism throughout the medieval period centre round its alleged polytheism and idol worship, and never touch the question of the inequity of caste.

"The only person who makes a mild criticism of it is the scientist (and not theologian) Alberuni (*c.*1030) who said: 'We Muslims, of course, stand entirely on the other side of the question, considering all men as equal, except in piety.'[489] But such an egalitarian statement is almost

---

[486]Summary of Irfan Habib's speech in "'Extremism should be curbed'", *Indian Express*, 27.12.1992. In spite of the scorn heaped on Irfan Habib by Hindutva authors (e.g. *Ayodhya Dispute and Prof. Irfan Habib: a Distorted Scholarship* by former ASI officer K.S. Ramachandran), and in spite of his unapologetic political inspiration (see e.g. his *Essays in Indian History: Towards a Marxist Perception*), this unconventional position of his suggests a fundamental scholarly honesty.

[487]Summary in *Indian Express*, 27.12.1992.

[488]Anonymous, *Chachnama*, Persian version of the thirteenth century, edited by U-Daudpota, Hyderabad-Dn., 1939, pp.214-16 (also see pp.47-8). A later Arab governor insisted that the Jats should, as mark of identification, be always accompanied by dogs. See Elliot and Dowson, *History of India as Told by Its Own Historians*, I, London 1867, p.129. (footnote in the original; note that secular Marxist Irfan Habib uses Elliot and Dowson's translation, which is often dismissed as biased and "colonialist" when Hindu revivalist authors use it).

[489]*Alberuni's India*, I, p.100. (footnote in the original)

unique; the fourteenth-century historian Barani in his *Tarikh-i Firuz-Shahi* fervently craved for a hierarchical order based on birth. ...

"In so far as the caste system helped, as we have seen, to generate larger revenues from the village and lower the wage costs in the cities, the Indo-Muslim regimes had every reason to protect it, however indifferent, if not hostile, they might have been to *brahmanas* as the chief idol-worshippers. (Does this not also mean that the supremacy of the *brahmanas* was by no means essential for the continuance of the caste system?)."[490]

It is routinely claimed that "Islamic egalitarianism" inspired the "egalitarian" Bhakti movements (though the genesis of the latter predated that of Islam by centuries), but Irfan Habib qualifies this belief too: "It may be that the monotheistic belief of Islam and the legal equality of the Muslim community exercised a certain influence on these movements. But their stress on equality and condemnation of caste and ritual observance was certainly much greater than is to be found in any contemporary Islamic preaching."[491]

Incidentally, the reference to "monotheism" in this context is part of a common secularist (i.c. anti-Hindu, hence anti-polytheist) argument that "the concept of one God meant the concept of social equality".[492] This is a very sweeping claim, covering many countries and several millennia, and a first glance at its non-Indian instances is not encouraging. As far as we know, pioneers of monotheism like Pharaoh Akhenaton, Moses, Saint Paul and indeed Mohammed never enjoined social equality, e.g. not one of them abolished slavery.[493] History proves that it is perfectly possible to worship one God, Creator of all mankind, and yet maintain inequality between man and woman, free man and slave, Jew and Gentile, believer and unbeliever;—just as it is possible for Hindus to believe that all human

---

[490]Irfan Habib: *Essays in Indian History*, pp.172-73.

[491]Irfan Habib: *Essays in Indian History*, p.175.

[492]Harbans Mukhia: "Medieval Indian History and the Communal Approach", in P. Lahiri, ed.: *Selected Writings on Communalism*, p.23.

[493]E.g. Paul's *Letter to Philemon* is a "covering note" sent along with a runaway slave whom he ordered to return to his master; see also his letters Eph.6:5-9 ("Servants, obey your masters"), Col.3:22, 1 Tim.6:1-2, as well as 1 Peter 2:18. Moses' laws enjoin good treatment of slaves, and sometimes their release, but by no means the abolition of slavery (though they have contributed to the principle of equality before the law for all free men). This is not to deny the involvement of later Christians in the struggle against slavery, e.g. the Quakers or Sir William Wilberforce.

(and other) beings partake of a single consciousness or *Brahman* and yet maintain inequality between the species, sexes, castes, age groups and other natural or cultural subdivisions of the biosphere and of society.

Hindu strategic failures, or was it chivalry?

Ram Gopal Misra finds the relevant difference between Hindu society and the forces of Islam not to have been a difference in social equality and justice, but a difference in military preparedness. Thus, one important military difference was that the Hindus used comparatively little cavalry. They did use elephants, but these were much less suited for warfare than horses; numerous are the occasions when elephants panicked when fire-arrows were shot, and threw the battle formation of their own side in disarray, trampling soldiers under their feet. Moreover: "The second strong point of the Turkish military machine was its mounted archery."[494] This was made possible by the Turco-Mongol invention of the stirrup. More generally, the Hindu armies came out second-best because of their slowness in adapting to improved styles of warfare: "Indians failed to keep pace with the developments of military strategy taking place in Central Asia".[495]

Why did the Rajputs not copy the stirrup, and likewise other military innovations, after having tasted its power just once? Misra suggests that it was because "the traditional Rajput chivalry looked upon the battle as a ritual or a tournament for displaying their fighting skill and swordsmanship under well-recognised rules of sport".[496] This attitude made the crucial victory of Mohammed Ghori at Tarain in 1292 possible, for a year before, at the same site and against the same army, a victorious Prithviraj Chauhan "could now have easily consummated his victory by chasing and annihilating his routed enemy. But instead, he allowed the defeated Muslim army to return unmolested."[497] One is entitled to wonder what kind of psychology clouded the minds of the Rajputs: was it an inertial clinging to some metaphysical certainty deemed stronger than common-sense reality?

According to Misra, purely military and political factors were decisive in the Hindu defeat. The Hindus did not have, and apparently never

[494]R.G. Misra: *Indian Resistance*, p.127.
[495]R.G. Misra: *Indian Resistance*, p.126.
[496]R.G. Misra: *Indian Resistance*, p.127.
[497]R.G. Misra: *Indian Resistance*, p.92.

contemplated, a forward policy of taking the battles into enemy territory, possibly due to the absence of "a strong central government for even the whole of northern India which could think and act for the whole country."[498] The Muslims, by contrast, did have the needed "spirit of aggression" and the "will to force the war in the enemy's dominions and thus destroy the base of his power."[499]

The Islamic invaders carefully prepared their invasions by means of intelligence-gathering, making use of the Muslim networks consisting of merchants and immigrants including the fabled Sufi saints: "The far-flung campaigns of Sultan Mahmud [Ghaznavi] would have been impossible without an accurate knowledge of trade routes and local resources, which was probably obtained from Muslim merchants."[500] Misra mentions the role of Hindu tolerance in furthering the cause of the enemy: "The Hindus, true to their catholicity of religious outlook and rich tradition of tolerance, never obstructed the peaceful immigrants and even zealously granted them security and full religious freedom."[501] It is with reference to such analyses that young hard-liners in Hindutva circles regularly complain: "We Hindus are too tolerant."

Even more important was the over-all military policy of the state. Unlike the Nanda and Maurya dynasties, who had a centralized state and a large standing army, the medieval Hindu empires were decentralized states where the taxes providing the centre with the means to organize national defence were very low. According to Sita Ram Goel: "The military organisation of the Rajputs was inferior as compared to that of the Muslims. The Rajputs depended mainly on feudal levies assembled on the spur of the moment."[502]

By contrast, in Misra's and Goel's view, the Islamic states were completely geared to warfare. The Abbasid Caliphate, the Sultanates, and the Ottoman Caliphate all had large standing armies which in the long run only an equally militarized state could stand up to. To the extent possible, they also made sure to be up-to-date in armament and strategy. The Moghul (actually Uzbek) invader Babar was the first in South Asia to use cannon (1525), and Abdali's victory in the third battle of Panipat (1761)

---

[498]R.G. Misra: *Indian Resistance*, p.124.
[499]R.G. Misra: *Indian Resistance*, p.123.
[500]R.G. Misra: *Indian Resistance*, pp.37-8.
[501]R.G. Misra: *Indian Resistance*, p.101.
[502]S.R. Goel: *Heroic Hindu Resistance*, p.36.

was partly due to his state-of-the-art artillery. All this requires verification on the basis of primary sources, but generally speaking, it is hardly far-fetched to propose military factors as being decisive in the outcome of military confrontations.

Low castes in revolt — against Islam

The belief that military victory is some kind of heavenly reward for having established a more just society (whether it concerns Mohammed Ghori or Mao Zedong) will be dismissed by most military historians as rank superstition. As the Belgian colonialist King Leopold II used to say: "God is always on the side of the one with the largest cannon." The sentimental determinism which promises inevitable victory to the forces of good, in particular to the egalitarian forces (as in the Latin-American slogan: *"El pueblo unido jamas sera vencido"*), has been refuted too many times by actual history.[503]

To attribute a moral superiority to the victor after his victory is usually not part of scholarly historiography which analyses the event from a distance, but typically springs up in the process of flattery and ideological self-justification which accompanies the consolidation of the victor's power. It is not because he was morally better that the victor won the war, but it is because he won the war that the history books explain his victory as the result of his (or his country's, his religion's etc.) moral superiority. In this case too, the court chroniclers of the Muslim conquerors of India did not hesitate to depict the conquest as proof of the superiority of Islam, i.e. of the Islamic religion as compared with Hindu polytheism and idolatry. But the significant point is that none of them equated this superiority with egalitarianism, nor the alleged Hindu inferiority with the baneful caste system.

Looking for the explanation of Islamic successes in the "evils of Hindu society" is historically unwarranted, but the attempt can be understood, even on the Hindu side. It is a normal phenomenon in the psychology of defeat. Many rape victims develop doubts whether they themselves are not somehow to blame for what happened to them. The

[503]The rhyming slogan, from the days of Salvador Allende and other Leftist luminaries c. 1970, means: "The people, united, will never be defeated." To drive home the point that this moralistic optimism is unwarranted, and that real military strength is decisive, the extreme Left propagated the variation: "El pueblo *armado* jamas sera vencido", poor in rhyme but rich in realism.

rationality behind this psychological mechanism is that one seeks to exorcize the defeat by situating its cause, and therefore also its future remedy, in an area which one can control, viz. in one's own behaviour. Nevertheless, the collective Hindu self-reproach would not have taken place on a substantial scale if it had not been promoted by outside forces. Because the Hindu armies were defeated, Hindu society could be dissected by guilt-mongers and declared to be the pinnacle of injustice. And because Islamic armies were victorious, Islamic doctrine and Muslim society were glorified or at least treated as enjoying immunity from criticism.

Now, let us come to specifics. Some Hindu authors have argued that low-caste Hindus not only refused to ally themselves with the Islamic invaders against their upper-caste Hindu "oppressors", but that they were also the fiercest resisters against Islamic rule. According to K.S. Lal, the best proof that the lower castes were by no means attracted to Islam nor inclined to stab their upper-caste defenders in the back in support of the invaders, is that the primary sources show us the Backward Castes as even more tenacious in their resistance to Islam than the Forward Castes. In Lal's opinion, there is plenty of testimony that these common people rose in revolt, not against their high-caste co-religionists, but against the Muslim rulers. Even when some of the high castes started collaborating, the common people gave the invaders no rest. Particularly the Delhi Sultanate was hardly a functioning empire but rather an uneasy foreign occupation, with the occupiers settled in citadels and the countryside prey to unending and uncontrollable unrest. In the Mewat region south of Delhi, the Shudras led the unrelenting resistance against the Sultans, waging a guerrilla operation from hide-outs in the forest. Sultans Nasiruddin and Balban (thirteenth century) had to clear away the forest before they could hunt down and forcibly convert a substantial part of this population.[504]

K.S. Lal quotes an inscription, dated AD 1345, in which the Reddi dynasty of Andhra describes how after the elimination of the Kshatriya defenders, the duty of defending cows and Brahmins fell on the Shudras, "born of the feet of Vishnu"; the first independent Reddi king, Vema, "restored all the agraharas of Brahmanas, which had been taken away by the wicked Mleccha kings".[505] Another inscription for the same dynasty

---

[504]K.S. Lal: *Growth of Scheduled Tribes*, pp.37-8.

[505]J. Ramayya: "Madras Museum plates of Vema", in *Epigraphica Indica*, vol.VIII (ASI 1981), p.9; v.9-12; quoted by K.S. Lal: *Growth of Scheduled Tribes*, p.98. *Agrahâra*: land grant to Brahmins, Brahmin village with land. *Mlechchha*: barbarian, non-Hindu.

proudly proclaims Vema's birth from "the victorious fourth varna", which "sprang from the feet of Vishnu", and which ruled "the remainder of the territory once ruled by the dwijas [before the Muslim conquest]", and describes how his first son Anna-Vota gave agraharas to the Brahmins and how his second son Anna-Vema freed the country of the "crowd of enemies" and used his wealth to sponsor the "men of learning".[506] It seems that the Shudras took it as a proud duty to defend the country against the Muslims and uphold the Brahminical culture.

Surprisingly, inscriptions of Shudra dynasties declare that belonging to the fourth *varna* was a matter of pride. An inscription of Singaya-Nayaka (AD 1368) says: "The three castes, viz. Brahmanas and the next [Kshatriyas and Vaishyas], were produced from the face, the arms and the thighs of the Lord; and for their support was born the fourth caste from His feet. That the latter caste is purer than the former [three] is self-evident; for this caste was born along with the river Ganga [which also springs from His feet], the purifier of the three worlds. The members of this caste are eagerly attentive to their duties, not wicked, pure-minded, and are devoid of passion and other such blemishes; they ably bear all the burden of the earth by helping those born in the kingly caste."[507] Another inscription relates how his relative Kapaya-Nayaka "rescued the Andhra country from the ravages of the Mohammedans".[508]

In taking the lead of the struggle against the Muslim invaders, the Reddi caste gained in prestige and became the dominant caste in the region. This way, the fight against the Muslim armies (if not ending in utter defeat) could lead to a rise in status for a community. Of this, another good example is the large Jat community, originally a low caste which gained prestige by fighting the Moghuls and establishing its rule in areas that passed out of the Moghul Empire's effective control in the eighteenth century.[509] Another striking example is Shivaji's Marathas.

All this is a rather different story from the conventional wisdom. K.S. Lal comments: "If it were true that the backward classes were so terribly

[506]E. Hultzsch: "Vanapalli plates of Anna-Vema", in *Epigraphica Indica*, vol.III (ASI 1979), pp.64-5, v.5, 12, 16, 20.

[507]K. Rama Sastri: "Akkalapundi grant of Singaya-Nayaka: Saka-Samvat 1290", *Epigraphica Indica*, vol.XIII (ASI reprint 1982) pp.259 ff., v.5-7.

[508]K. Rama Sastri: "Akkalapundi grant of Singaya-Nayaka: Saka-Samvat 1290", *Epigraphica Indica*, vol. XIII (ASI reprint 1982), p.261.

[509]K.S. Lal: *Growth of Scheduled Tribes*, pp.88-92.

oppressed by the Brahmanas, we would expect them to take some kind of revenge by making common cause with the Muslim persecutors of the Brahmanas. But exactly the opposite is the case. Jats and Meds helped the Brahmana and Kshatriya rulers of Sindh against Arab invaders. Jats and Khokhars joined the Hindu Shahiya Rajas of Punjab against Mahmud of Ghazni. Throughout the medieval period, the lower castes fought shoulder to shoulder with the upper castes and against the foreign invaders and tyrannical rulers."[510]

Re-evaluation of the caste system

Perhaps all the foregoing necessitates a revaluation of the caste system as it functioned in the pre-Muslim period: "The 'exploitation' by the upper castes noticeable today is because of the rigidity that caste system developed after the Hindus got bereft of political power for a long time and a moral degeneration set in. There is sufficient evidence to show that on the eve of Islamic invasions, the Hindu social system did not suffer from the defects it developed at a later stage."[511] There have been too many upper-caste attempts already to look at caste through rosy glasses, so we ought to be careful with such claims. However, Lal's point is not so much to minimize the evils usually associated with caste, to draw attention to a dimension of caste which is rarely noticed.

According to Lal, the caste system was not only innocent of the Hindu defeat, but also it should take credit for the Hindu survival and ultimate come-back: "So well coalesced was the Hindu social structure that it not only saved India from the fate of countries like Iran, Iraq, Syria and Egypt when they confronted the Islamic onslaught, but did not rest content till it had supplanted the Muslim political power in the land even though it took a thousand years to do so."[512] One hypothesis which deserves a thorough investigation here, is that because of its caste structure, Hindu society was decentralized, so that the destruction of the Hindu state did not destroy Hindu society. In proposing an alternative to the well-entrenched Marxist hypothesis, Lal may have made a start with the writing of Indian history from a native viewpoint.

The corollary of Lal's hypothesis is that much of the nastiest side of caste should have developed only during the Muslim period. He has taken

[510]K.S. Lal: *Growth of Scheduled Tribes*, p.iii.
[511]K.S. Lal: *Growth of Scheduled Tribes*, p.iii.
[512]K.S. Lal: *Growth of Scheduled Tribes*, p.iv.

it upon himself to investigate the role of Islamic rule in the genesis or aggravation of caste discrimination, in his book *Growth of Scheduled Tribes and Castes in Medieval India*. The object of the book, apart from highlighting the fierce struggle of low-caste communities against Islam, is to show that some so-called tribal communities were originally fully Hindu castes that sought refuge in the forest to escape the Islamic regime.

The best-known example is probably the Gonds, who had a large and well-organized kingdom until Akbar sent his general Asaf Khan Harvi to conquer the Gond Rani Durgavati's kingdom, and succeeded in destroying it (the queen died on the battlefield): "Thus the Gonds, a civilized people as per medieval standards, became a low tribe under Muslim rule and have remained so since then."[513] The reduction of the Gonds to colonized "natives" was completed under Aurangzeb: "The Deogarh royal family embraced Islam in order to retain their lands (1670). ... Hindu and Muhammadan cultivators were encouraged to settle in them".[514]

It is an important correction of now-common assumptions to learn that some tribes were originally peasant communities who took shelter in the forest in order to escape the revenue collectors or punitive military expeditions.[515]

Yet here, Lal promises more than he can deliver: it is not true, and in the chapters concerned he does not really pretend to prove, that "the" Scheduled Tribes are wayward Hindu castes hiding from the Sultans. Lal succeeds in showing that *some* communities considered as tribal do have such a history, first of all because medieval chroniclers themselves already "mention about people turning from civilized life in urban and rural habitats to 'savage' existence in the forests".[516] But those tribes most in focus in debates about the status and political rights of the Scheduled Tribes definitely have a different history: the Mundari-speaking tribes in Chhotanagpur and the Tibeto-Burmese-speaking tribes in the North-East show by their language that they have a separate origin. Precisely because of their relative isolation in forest or mountain areas, their experience with Islamic rule was very limited and cannot explain their socio-cultural characteristics.

It so happens, none the less, that many of these ethnically distinct

---

[513] K.S. Lal: *Growth of Scheduled Tribes*, p.82.

[514] K.S. Lal: *Growth of Scheduled Tribes*, p.83.

[515] K.S. Lal: *Growth of Scheduled Tribes*, pp.33-79.

[516] K.S. Lal: *Growth of Scheduled Tribes*, p.5.

Scheduled Tribes also have a deep-rooted hostility towards Muslims. Some of the worst communal violence has taken place between North-eastern tribals and Bangladeshi Muslim settlers on their lands, as in the case of the Nelli massacre of 1983. In Chhotanagpur in 1964, tribals organized a large-scale retaliation against local Muslims after a massacre of (mostly christianized) tribals in Bangladesh had caused a mass exodus of tribals to India.[517] A missionary observes "a remarkable abhorrence among the Santals of the Mohammedans .... According to their tradition, the sojourn of the Santal ancestors in 'the corrupt and defiled land' of the Muslims was attended with such grave harassment that contact with the Muslims must be avoided", so that even when interacting with Muslim trade partners, the Santals "do not accept food from these Muslims".[518]

It will not be surprising, therefore, that the Hindutva movement has a large following in the tribal belt of Chhotanagpur.[519] But fact remains that the Scheduled Tribe status of the population concerned has nothing to do with Muslim rule: long before the Moghul empire antagonized the tribals by imposing the Jagirdari system (absentee landlordism) and dispossessing them, the Hindus had classified the forest-dwellers among the more impure, low-ranking communities. The distance which traditional Hindus (as opposed to modern Hindu money-lenders and entrepreneurs, who joined in the Moghul and British exploitative policies) kept from the "forest-dwellers" was a better thing for the tribals than the Moghul and British encroachment, but it remains a form of inequality which is entirely native to India and for which the Muslims cannot be blamed.

Another community which is mentioned in this debate, is that of the Untouchables, people constrained to doing the ritually polluting and plainly dirtiest jobs. Mayank Jain analyses one example of a distorted perception of Hindu inequality and Muslim equality, viz. about the

---

[517]The violence subsided only after the martyrdom of the Flemish Catholic missionary Herman Rasschaert s.j., see his biography by Robert Houthaeve: *Recht, al barstte de wereld!* (Dutch: "Justice, even if the world perish for it").

[518]J. Troisi: *Tribal Religion*, p.247.

[519]L.K. Advani received an enthusiastic welcome there during his Rath Yatra in 1990. In Calcutta, November 1993, I spoke to Sujit Dhar, VHP board member who oversees the work among the tribals; though pessimistic about the situation in the North-East and in Central India, he was quite satisfied with the Hindutva presence in Chhotanagpur. When in 2000, the new state of Jharkhand was formed, the BJP formed its first government.

Bhangis, the caste of the sweepers, and tries to blame Islam for this case of untouchability: "The ancient Hindu scholar Chanakya prescribes a severe punishment on all those who would ask someone to clean or carry human faecal matter. It is quite clear from Hindu tradition that people used to defecate in the open, or behind a bush as mentioned in the *Manu Smriti*, the *Shandilya Smriti* and the *Bharadwaja Smriti*. This by itself eliminates the possibility of using the services of any community to clean or carry human waste. The so-called Bhangi community never existed before the coming of Muslims. The entire Sanskrit literature does not contain a single word which could describe Bhangi. It was the contribution of the 'progressivism' of Muslims that a toilet was put right inside the house in agreement with their *purdah* system. A large contingent of captured soldiers of defeated Hindu armies used to perform the shameful task of carrying human waste on their heads hitherto punishable in accordance with Hindu laws."[520]

So, was the untouchable Bhangi caste a gift of Muslim rule? It is quite possible that captured soldiers were forced to do the dirty work. This much of humiliation and oppression may have been the doing of Islam. But Jain probably overstates his potentially interesting argument. The story of *these* sweepers does not prove that there had never been sweepers in the pre-Muslim period, much less that there had been no untouchable castes. For one thing, is it not far-fetched to assume that before Muslim rule there was never any need for the disposal of human waste? The Hindus had cities and military forts too, where people lived close together and had no bushes where they could go and discreetly relieve themselves. And apart from waste disposal, there remain other unclean jobs to do: if pre-Muslim Hindus didn't defecate in toilets, at least they certainly died once in a while, and their decomposing bodies had to be disposed of by a specialist class of funeral workers, untouchable par excellence. Whatever the case may be with the Bhangi caste specifically, they are by no means the only untouchable caste, and a specially lowly status is attested from the pre-Muslim Smriti literature onwards (early Christian age), for example, for the caste of the funeral workers.[521] It is true that the Vedas and other ancient texts make no mention of a hereditary stigma attaching to the

[520]Mayank Jain: "Hindu-bashing", *Organiser*, 18.5.1997.

[521]The *"Antyajas"* are also mentioned by Alberuni (*India*, vol.1, pp.100-02) as "occupied with the dirty work, like the cleaning of the village and other services": fisherman, shoemaker, hunter of wild animals and birds, funeral worker etc.

specialists of such labour, and the genesis of untouchability as a definitely late development in Hinduism (clearly much younger than the caste system in general) remains to be traced in detail. But from there to reducing this whole phenomenon to a gift of Islam seems to be an unjustified leap.

Moreover, the Muslims did not make their captives "untouchable" even though they forced them to do this dirty work. Though they had their own notions of purity and impurity, in the Islamic scheme of things, doing dirty work did not make people acquire a hereditary stigma. Suppose, a rich Indian Muslim buys a Hindu slave-woman and employs her as a midwife when his harem wives give birth, with midwifery being an auspicious but highly unclean occupation (normally performed by women of the untouchable leather-working castes); and suppose further that in a fling on the side he makes the enslaved midwife pregnant as well. Then under Islamic law, the midwife's child as the son or daughter of a Muslim is entitled to freedom upon becoming adult, and hence, as a free Muslim, is allowed to intermarry with other Muslims regardless of the unclean occupation of his or her mother. Ritual uncleanliness in Islam is not hereditary. The downward change of status from captive Kshatriya warriors doing dirty work to hereditary untouchables, though caused by Muslim intervention, actually took place within the Hindu cultural framework. Moreover, the starkest forms of untouchability are found in South India (unapproachability), where Muslim rule penetrated only briefly and superficially. Indeed, we are entitled to wonder if the spread of Dravidian cultural elements (including Bhakti) in the early Christian age does not have more to do with the introduction of the notion of untouchability.

So, Mayank Jain's bid to blame Islam for untouchability can only be partly successful. Yet, for what it is worth, the role of Islam in aggravating the pre-existing institution of untouchability, or in creating new forms of caste oppression, does deserve closer investigation. A *prima facie* case could be made that when the upper castes were oppressed by Islamic rule, they themselves weighed more heavily on the lower castes, and also that oppressed societies in general become more rigid. Even M.N. Roy had quoted with approval E.B. Havell's suggestion: "The effect of the Mussalman political creed upon Hindu social life was two-fold: *it increased the rigour of the caste system* and aroused a revolt against it."[522] This certainly needs further exploration.

[522]M.N. Roy: *Historical Role of Islam*, pp.89-90, with reference to E.B. Havell: *Aryan Rule in India*; emphasis added.

Genesis of the Indian Muslim community

The first serious study of the genesis of the Indian Muslim community from a Hindu viewpoint has been undertaken by K.S. Lal in his book *Indian Muslims: Who Are They?*[523] We summarize his list of factors determining the existence and the size of the Indian Muslim community.

The first factor was immigration: the conquerors themselves, like Mohammed Ghori and Timur, did of course come from outside, but once Muslim rule had been established, there was a lot more immigration from Muslim lands into India. In particular, the devastation of Iran and Baghdad by the Mongols in the thirteenth century made the Delhi Sultanate a pole of attraction for Muslim traders, scholars and craftsmen. Muslim mercenaries were permanently welcome, and often they formed the mainstay of the armies of Muslim rulers in India. Sometimes intra-Muslim quarrels (and in the eighteenth century, the emergence of a new Hindu power) made Muslim nobles or clerics invite foreign Muslim rulers with their armies into India, for example, Babar, who stayed on to found the Moghul dynasty. In other cases the invitees, though victorious, went back, e.g. Nadir Shah and Ahmad Shah Abdali.

According to K.S. Lal, "Muslim regime of Hindustan promised and provided excellent jobs to all and sundry Muslims. ... Throughout the medieval period they came in droves, 'like ants and locusts', and were given here important and influential positions. It was naturally a one-way traffic; Muslims only came, nobody migrated from here. By the seventeenth century they formed many pressure groups—like Irani and Turani—in the Mughal empire's politics and society."[524]

Till today, a section of the Muslim elites claims foreign descent: "Many Muslims even today take pride in asserting their extra-territorial identity by adding suffixes like Iraqi and Bukhari to their names."[525] In some cases, these foreign origins are easy to trace, as in Bengal and Bihar, a community locally known as Pathans consists of the descendents of the soldiers of Sher Shah (*c.* 1540) and Bengali women. Until the Khilafat movement of *c.* 1920, when the native Muslim masses and the Muslim

[523]To be sure, partial studies of this phenomenon have been undertaken before, e.g. concerning conversion as a result of the Moghul Empire's policies, see Sri Ram Sharma: *The Religious Policy of the Mughal Emperors* (1940), pp.61-2, pp.90-2, pp.165-74. K.S. Lal takes these earlier studies into account.

[524]K.S. Lal: *Indian Muslims*, p.103.

[525]K.S. Lal: *Indian Muslims*, p.103.

aristocracy moved closer to each other, the immigrant Muslim circles looked down upon the majority of native converts.

The second factor was a high birth rate among these immigrants. This was partly due to the widespread practice of polygamy, often with the amply available enslaved Hindu women, and partly to the absence of the kind of limitations on marriage and procreation as existed in Hindu society: ban on widow remarriage, existence of a large class of celibate sadhus and sadhvis. Though mixed fairly thoroughly with native blood, a class which traced at least its paternal line of descent to foreign invaders grew into a large community and remained distinct well into the modern age.

The third factor in the genesis of the Indian Muslim community was conversion. For a general idea of the reasons for the conversion of Hindus to Islam in the Muslim period, Lal quotes the fourteenth-century author Saiyyad Muhammad bin Nasiruddin Jafar Makki al-Husaini who "held that there were five reasons which led the people to embrace Islam:

(1) fear of death;

(2) fear of their families being enslaved;

(3) propagation (of Islam) on the part of Muslims;

(4) the lust for obtaining *mawajib* (pensions or rewards) [and] *ghanaim* (booty); and

(5) *tassub* (bigotry or superstition)."[526]

Reasons 3 and 5 refer to the conversion work by Muslims (not necessarily professional clerics) and, partly overlapping, the preachings of Sufis to whom popular belief ascribed all kinds of miracles. The other three serve to confirm the classical image which Hindus have of Muslim rule and of the origin of the Indian Muslim community, viz. that brute force and materialistic allurement played a decisive role.

Apart from conversions by force, what were the motives and origins of converts? The lowest castes were certainly not the target group of Muslim proselytizers. The professional groups of Chamars, Bhangis, Chandalas etc. have remained almost exclusively Hindu, as K.S. Lal tries to show on the basis of the 1931 census figures (the last census cross-tabulating caste with other data).[527] The power-oriented sections of the upper castes were a

---

[526]K.S. Lal: *Indian Muslims*, p.95, with reference to Amir Hasan Sijzi: *Favaid-al-Fuad* (Delhi 1856), p.46.

[527]Table showing the Hindu or Muslim adherence among low-caste occupational communities in U.P., in K.S. Lal: *Indian Muslims*, p.97.

more fruitful recruiting-ground, yielding a fair number of careerist conversions. In order to gain acceptance as genuine Muslims, high-placed converts often turned into zealous persecuters, as exemplified by Malik Kafur (*c.* 1300), Alauddin Khilji's general who led expeditions to the South. What attracted these people to Islam was not its equality, but its inequality: between Muslim rulers and non-Muslim subjects, or between privileged Muslim subjects and disadvantaged non-Muslim subjects.

K.S. Lal compares the conversion rate of the upper-caste Rajputs with those of the untouchable Chamars (cobblers): "The upper castes might have sometimes submitted to force or temptation, but not the Chamars. For example, in Muzaffarnagar district there were 29,000 Hindu Rajputs and 24,000 Muslim Rajputs according to the 1901 census. Similarly, there were Hindu Rajputs and Muslim Rajputs in almost equal numbers in many western districts of U.P."[528] The religious division of the Rajputs can be explained: "The reason is that some Rajputs who loved their religion more than their land fought against Muslim invaders to the last. Many perished in the encounters. Those who survived, survived as Hindu Rajputs. Those who loved their land more than their religion converted to Islam to retain their lands and kingdoms."[529] Citing the 1931 census as recording that 99.7 per cent of the Chamars in U.P. listed themselves as Hindus, Lal argues that the said Rajput conversions "debunk the theory that low caste people converted to Islam more easily than the high castes. The Chamars did not convert, as their large numbers show."[530]

The non-untouchable Shudra castes in the cities were the numerically most important source of converts. They were numerous to start with, but unlike peasants they were dependent on patronage, so that material and social pressure related to avenues of employment could provide the incentive for conversion. Artists and artisans in the employ of courts and elite families were under strong pressure to become Muslims, a well-known example being the musicians. When Muslims play Hindu classical music, secularists will praise the "contribution of Islam to our rich

---

[528]K.S. Lal: *Growth of Scheduled Tribes*, p.17, with reference to *Imperial Gazetteer: United Provinces of Agra and Oudh*, vol.1, p.294. Remark that this was before Indian Muslims were alerted to live up to the new egalitarian image of Islam and conceal their caste background.

[529]K.S. Lal: *Growth of Scheduled Tribes*, p.17. Lal quotes the example of Raja Hara Datta, already discussed by Swami Shraddhananda.

[530]K.S. Lal: *Growth of Scheduled Tribes*, pp.16-17.

composite culture", but in fact, these are Hindu castes who had to take on Muslim names because the Hindu elite had been replaced with a new Muslim elite as the best provider of employment. The most famous example is Akbar's court musician Tansen, who had to convert to Islam in order to be allowed to marry a particular Muslim woman he loved. His musical background was entirely Hindu, and the lustre he added to the Moghul court was a Hindu and not a Muslim contribution to "composite culture".[531]

Summing up, Lal is confident that the conversion of Hindus to Islam can generally be explained without assuming either the religious attractiveness of Islam or the promise of social equality in Islam. He sees the real reasons in the use of force and milder material and social forms of pressure, and in the substantial social and professional advantages attached to being or becoming a Muslim.

We may evaluate the Hindu revivalist case against the myth of Islamic egalitarianism as by no means far-fetched. It really took the peculiar psychological conditions of twentieth-century India to make the belief in Islam's egalitarian mission possible. In particular: the Hindu, guilt-ridden over the endlessly invoked inequality of Hindu caste society, was receptive to any and every silly claim about the egalitarian qualities of all other religions as also of some "subaltern" anti-Brahminical strands within the Hindu religious commonwealth. In general, the abolition of inequality in lay society was not among the goals of any of the world's great religions. The exceptions have been a few ill-fated utopian movements which wanted to create equality overnight in the context of a theocratic state, notably the Mazdakites in sixth-century Iran and the Anabaptists in the sixteenth-century Germany: before being militarily suppressed, they made a thorough mess of the societies they had come to control, with anarchy leading to lawlessness, banditry and bloody repression. Equality as a reasonable social reform programme is typically a modern phenomenon, and religions which have their roots in tribal, slave-holding or feudal societies are taking the public for a ride when they now claim to have inherited equality as one of the goals laid down by their founders.

Even Hindu sects such as Tantrism now tend to claim caste-free

---

[531]K.S. Lal: *Legacy of Muslim Rule*, p.305; remark that even the broad-minded Akbar did not effectively abolish the Islamic prohibition on marriages between Hindu men and Muslim women.

interaction as their heritage, but in general, it appears that they ignored caste distinctions only during their spiritual practice sessions, while otherwise abiding by the dominant usage, for instance: "The Tantras did not make much discrimination between the Brahmanas and non-Brahmanas in the spiritual sphere. They admitted the right of all classes to the Tantrik Gayatri and Sandhya. All were entitled to read the Tantras and recite the Tantrik mantras. But it must be admitted that the Tantras recognized castes for all secular purposes."[532] The egalitarian claims currently made for religions may well be signs of a desirable commitment to promote social equality in the present, but as history-writing they are not to be taken seriously.

It is only because of the peculiar Indian context that Marxists there (with laudable exceptions) can inspire and later reiterate Islamic apologetic claims that Islam brought equality. Marxists elsewhere have a healthy scepticism of claims made on behalf of religions, for example, Lucas Catherine (Belgium) observes: "The Quran not only stands for economic inequality in society. Inequality at all levels is God's will. ... He who wants to nullify this inequality, is a blasphemer, especially if he belongs to the privileged himself."[533] For devout Muslims, Islam is good in itself, and it doesn't need to prove its utility in the service of secular ideologies such as egalitarianism. They consider it a sign of self-doubt to run after the latest ideological fads with slogans like: "Mohammed was the first feminist", for one who is the Prophet of God has absolutely no need of other, secular distinctions. The Quran itself is at any rate unambiguous in endorsing inequality as a God-ordained natural condition for mankind, witness Catherine's selection of verses:

"To some God has given more than He has to others. Those who are so favoured will not allow their slaves an equal share in what they have. Would they deny God's goodness?"[534]

"Your Lord gives abundantly to whom He will and sparingly to whom He pleases."[535]

---

[532]R.C. Majumdar: *History and Culture of the Indian People*, vol.7, p.638.

[533]L. Catherine: *In naam van de islam. Godsdienst als politiek argument bij Mohammed en Khomeini* (Dutch: "In the name of Islam. Religion as a political argument for Mohammed and Khomeini"), p.69.

[534]Q.16:71/73.

[535]Q.42:12/10.

"It is We who allot to them their livelihood in this world, exalting some in rank above others, so that the one may take the other into his service."[536]

Islamic history bears out the Islamic non-interest in equality, even where local custom could provide a good basis for a measure of egalitarianism. Thus, in a study on Moroccan Islam, J.M.M. van Amersfoort observes: "It is often said that the Muslim world is egalitarian. But in North Africa, this is not quite the case, and there the impulse to equality comes from the old 'heathen' tribal tradition."[537] And in India, no less an authority than Maulana Maudoodi has said that "Islam recognizes that inequality between men as a result of their different abilities and circumstances must exist to the extent that it is in conformity with nature".[538] There is nothing shameful about this, and there is no need to cover it up behind fairy-tales about Islam's egalitarian mission. All pre-modern religions accepted inequality as a fact of life, and created or sanctioned social institutions which were not informed by the modern spirit of equality.

Islamic slavery

In the medieval period, Islam was firmly associated with slavery in the Western mind. Every year, thousands of Europeans were sold as slaves in Muslim countries. A few religious orders specialized in collecting funds, tracing slaves and buying them back.[539] The Church calendar even celebrated "Our Lady of the Redemption of Slaves", on 24 September (one of the Saints abolished by Vatican II). In the early colonial period, Europeans became partners of the Muslims in the African slave-trade, while in the late colonial period, indignation about slavery was one of the "progressive" pretexts for the colonization of the remainder of Africa.[540]

---

[536]Q.43:32/31. Catherine also adds this Quran verse: "We have endowed Adam's sons ... amply above many whom We have created." (17:70/72) But it is doubtful that this concerns the inequality between human beings, rather than that between mankind on the one hand and jinns and animals on the other.

[537]J.M.M. van Amersfoort: "Islamisering, cultuurcontact en cultuurconflict", in Andreas Eppink ed.: *Cultuurcontact en Cultuurconflict*, p.115.

[538] A. Maudoodi: *The Economic Problem of Man and its Islamic Solution* (Lahore 1966), speech given in 1941.

[539]See e.g. W.H. Rudt de Collenberg: *Esclavage et Rançons des Chrétiens en Méditerranée* (French: Slavery and Ransoming of Christians in the Mediterranean").

[540]E.g. in the Belgian conquest of the Congo, the war against the Arab slave-traders in 1893 was an important element of justification. A pro-Arab account of it is L. Catherine: *Manyiema*.

Though Islam is portrayed as anti-slavery in contemporary Islamic apologetics targeting African and Afro-American audiences, Islamic countries have thrived on the slave trade for twelve centuries and have only abolished slavery under strong and persistent Western pressure. In 1855, Britain and France imposed on the Ottoman Empire the abolition of religion-based legal inequality and of the slave trade. Even then, it took decades more before this policy spread to the far corners of the Muslim world: Saudi Arabia abolished slavery in 1962, Mauretania abolished it (at least formally) in 1982, and in Sudan the practice by northern Arabic-speaking Muslims of enslavement and sale of southern Black Animists and Christians has been discovered as late as 1996.[541]

In spite of the magnitude of this subject, academic interest in the history of Islamic slavery (as compared with cases of trans-Atlantic slavery) is remarkably small. As for Islamic slavery in India, the picture is even more extreme: in contrast with the never-ending stream of publications on the Hindu caste system, critical work on Islamic slavery is exceedingly scarce. So far, a single study of Islamic slavery from the Hindu angle is in print: *Muslim Slave System in Medieval India* by K.S. Lal, who has also tried to take into account what little scholarship on this subject is available in the West.[542] A shorter survey of this history was already given in K.S. Lal: *The Legacy of Muslim Rule in India*.

K.S. Lal's work consists simply in documenting the extent of slavery in India under Muslim rule. Choosing examples "from two points of time at either extremity of Muslim rule in India", he relates: "When Mohammed bin Qasim mounted his attack on Debal in 712, all males of the age of seventeen and upwards were put to the sword and their women and children were enslaved." And after the Third Battle of Panipat (1761), the male prisoners were "beheaded ... and the women and children who survived were driven off as slaves—twenty-two thousand, many of them of the highest rank in the land".[543] And in between, the same episode was repeated over and over, or so Lal's documentation suggests.

---

[541]Michael S. Serrill: "Slaves: on sale now", *Time*, 1.7.1996.

[542]Reference is to the path-breaking study *Race and Slavery in the Middle East: An Historical Enquiry* (1990), by Bernard Lewis; and to the review of the book by David Brion Davis in his article "Slaves in Islam", *New York Review of Books*, 11.10.1990, which adds valuable information based on his own book *Slavery and Human Progress*. Valuable studies not quoted here include Daniel Pipes: *Slave Soldiers and Islam* (1981), Murray Gordon: *Slavery in the Arab World* (1989), and Claude Meillassoux: *The Anthropology of Slavery* (1991).

[543]K.S. Lal: *Muslim Slave System*, p.155.

Thus, Abu Nasr Mohammed al-Utbi, Mahmud Ghaznavi's secretary, writes that after the capture of Waihind near Peshawar in 1001-02, Mahmud took 500,000 persons of both sexes as slaves.[544] After the capture of Ninduna (1014), in Ghaznavi's homeland "slaves were so plentiful that they became very cheap; and men of respectability in their native land (India) were degraded by becoming slaves of common shopkeepers".[545] In 1015, the capture of Thanesar brought another 200,000 slaves, "so that the capital appeared like an Indian city, for every soldier of the army had several slaves and slave girls".[546] After the campaign to Mathura and Kanauj, the fifth part (*khums*) given to the Caliphate and to the descendents of the Prophet (Sayyids) included 150,000 slaves, implying a total of 750,000 Hindus enslaved.[547]

Likewise, enslavement records of the Ghorids, Sultan Iltutmish, Sultan Balban, the Khiljis, the Tughlaqs, Lodis and Moghuls are quoted. The court poet Amir Khusrau testified that "the Turks, whenever they please, can seize, buy or sell any Hindu".[548] During the Hajj season, many Hindu slaves were taken to Mecca and sold there to be taken back by pilgrims to their homelands in Turkey or Africa. A soft form of slavery was that "many women from Hindu rulers' families were forcibly married by Muslim kings throughout the Muslim period".[549]

It is to be kept in mind that "the lion's share of the state's enslavement, deportation and sale" was not taken by the emperors but by their provincial nobility, many of whom have left no surviving written records.[550] The predictable argument that court chroniclers must have exaggerated the successes of their patrons, including the numbers of their slaves, is therefore neutralized by the dark figure of unrecorded slave-takings.

---

[544]K.S. Lal: *Legacy of Muslim Rule*, p.279. This figure "is so mind-boggling that Elliot reduces it to 5000". Reference is to H.M. Elliot, whose *History of India as Told by Its Own Historians* (with J. Dowson) is decried by R.S. Sharma (*Rama's Ayodhya*), Sushil Srivastava (in S. Gopal: *Anatomy*, p.50) and Mushirul Hasan (*ibid.*, p.102) as a colonial ploy to foster an anti-Muslim prejudice among the Hindus. But in fact, Elliot *minimizes* data given in the original which could have helped in this alleged ploy.

[545]Quoted from al-Utbi's *Târîkh-i-Yaminî* by K.S. Lal: *Legacy*, p.279.

[546]Quoted from Md. Farishta's *Gulshan-i-Ibrahimi* by K.S. Lal: *Legacy*, p.279.

[547]Quoted from *Târîkh-i-Alfi* in K.S. Lal: *Legacy*, p.280.

[548]Quoted from Amir Khusrau's *Nuh Sipehr*, in Elliot & Dowson: *History of India*, vol.3, p.561, by K.S. Lal: *Legacy*, p.281. For once, a Hindu source is quoted in support of this observation, viz. Vidyapati's *Kirtilata* (pp.72-4 of the Allahabad 1923 edition).

[549]K.S. Lal: *Muslim Slave System*, p.156.

[550]K.S. Lal: *Legacy*, p.284.

Moreover, this decisive role of the relatively autonomous nobility weakened the impact of the few attested attempts to curb slave-taking, notably by the Moghul emperors Akbar and Jahangir, who prohibited the abduction of women by tax-collectors.[551] No estimate of the total number of Hindus enslaved and of Hindu slaves exported from India has been attempted so far.

K.S. Lal also tries to get an idea of the numbers of slaves and the prices they fetched, quoting price-lists from different periods. The price varied with supply and demand. Thus, Shahabuddin al-Umri wrote about the days of Sultan Mohammed bin Tughlaq (1325-51): "The Sultan never ceases to show the greatest zeal in making war upon the infidels. ... Every day thousands of slaves are sold at a very low price, so great is the number of prisoners."[552] Foreign travellers in different centuries, including the great globe-trotter Ibn Batuta, testify that Indian slaves were very cheap because they were very numerous in supply. William Finch, who lived at the Moghul court in *c.* 1610, testifies that hunting expeditions in the forest brought human as well as animal prey: "Men remain the king's slaves which he sends yearly to Kabul to barter for horses and dogs."[553] By contrast, imported slaves from the Caucasus region and Ethiopia were rarer and more expensive, the white ones being costlier than the black ones. Particularly white women were a highly prized commodity for purposes of sex slavery, a practice explicitly legitimated by the Quran.[554]

Marxist historian Irfan Habib adds: "The pressure of new circumstances led initially to large-scale slave-trading and the emergence of slave labour during the thirteenth and fourteenth centuries. The numbers of slaves in the Sultans' establishments were very high (50,000 under Alauddin Khilji, and 180,000 under Firuz Tughluq). Barani judges the level of prices by referring to slave prices, and the presence of slaves was almost all-pervasive."[555]

---

[551] K.S. Lal: *Legacy*, p.283.

[552] Quoted in K.S. Lal: *Muslim Slave System*, p.126.

[553] Quoted by K.S. Lal: *Muslim Slave System*, p.128.

[554] Q.33:50/49: "We have made lawful to you your wives to whom you pay the bride-price, and *what your right hand possesses* of what God has allotted to you as booty", i.e. enslaved women. About sex slavery, a subject which the Hindu mind closely identifies with Islam, see K.S. Lal: *Muslim Slave System*, pp.150-74, and his book *The Moghul Harem*, passim

[555] Irfan Habib: *Essays in Indian History*, p.174; with reference to Irfan Habib's own contribution to the *Cambridge Economic History of India*, vol.I, Cambridge 1982, pp.89-93.

K.S. Lal describes the emasculated slaves, thousands yearly, as the worst victims of Islamic rule: "It is not the task of the historian to pity the eunuchs or condemn those who emasculated them. But pernicious was the system in which man could exploit man to this extent. ... Many people suffered because of the medieval Muslim slave system, but undoubtedly the eunuchs suffered the most."[556] Even without mutilation, slavery was not conducive to procreation.[557] Slave women even killed or abandoned the children they did get, for fear of being separated from them or of seeing them die a miserable death. This way, large-scale enslavement of Hindus was also an indirect attack on Hindu demography.

And those slave children who did make it to adulthood, along with the children whom Muslim masters conceived on Hindu slave women, became Muslims. As Irfan Habib notes: "Slaves were, in effect, deprived of caste and, converted to Islam, could be put to almost any task or learn any trade. Manumitted in course of time, they probably created, along with artisan immigrants, the core of many artisan and labouring communities."[558] So, the victims of Islam by enslavement swelled the numbers of the very religion in the name of which they themselves had been enslaved. Similarly, the large number of Africans imported as slave soldiers on India's West Coast (large at least in absolute figures, though relatively few on the Indian scale) has left only a small remnant, the Siddi community, and they are Muslims. It is one of those ironies of history that the victims of the Muslim slave system became the defenders of Islam: the main occasion when the Siddis entered the history books was in *c.* 1660 when they fought Shivaji, the hero of Hindu liberation.[559]

With that history in mind, it is hard (and thoroughly wrong) to associate today's Indian Muslims with the Muslim invaders of yore, to scold them as *Bâbar kî aulâd* ("Babar's progeny"), as was done during the Ayodhya agitation. It should rather make the Hindus sensistive to the frailty of their own Hinduness and the sheer luck which made their own ancestors stay on the Hindu rather than fall to the Muslim side of the conflict.

---

[556]K.S. Lal: *Muslim Slave System*, p.118.

[557]Claude Meillassoux (*The Anthropology of Slavery*, part 1, chapter 3: "Sterility"), to whom K.S. Lal refers, lists childlessness as almost a defining characteristic of slavery in the Muslim world.

[558]Irfan Habib: *Essays in Indian History*, p.174; with reference to Irfan Habib's own contribution to the *Cambridge Economic History of India*, vol.I, Cambridge 1982, pp.89-93.

[559]See J. Sarkar: *Shivaji and His Times*, pp.199-211.

Some colonial observers had created a romantic picture of Islam, including a fairly positive evaluation of slavery. In 1887, the Dutch orientalist C. Snouck Hurgronje ridiculed the "fantasies" that motivated the British to work for the termination of the slave trade from Africa to the Middle East. In his report on his journey to Mecca, he claimed that "public opinion in Europe has been misled concerning Muslim slavery by a confusion between American and Oriental conditions. ... As things are now, for most of the slaves their abduction was a blessing. ... They themselves were convinced that it was slavery that first made human beings of them."[560] More recently, claiming that slavery could be a good thing has become unacceptable, so now the apologetic line is that slavery in Islam has been very much exaggerated, and that in fact Islam has contributed immensely to the abolition of slavery.[561]

In South Asia, where claims of "egalitarianism" are trump cards in the competition with "caste-ridden" Hinduism, the claim that Islam was the emancipator of the slaves is very popular. According to Syed Habib-ul Haq Nadvi, "the institution of slavery was liquidated by Islam for ever".[562] And Mohammed Iqbal, the spiritual father of Pakistan, has claimed: "We freed mankind from the chains of slavery."[563]

In the West, Bernard Lewis has thoroughly refuted this fond belief. He points out that on the contrary, when the Ottoman Government banned the slave trade in 1855, the Arab leader Shaykh Jamal issued a legal ruling "denouncing the ban on the slave trade as contrary to the holy law of Islam. Because of this anti-Islamic law, he said, together with such other anti-Islamic actions as allowing women to initiate divorce proceedings and to move around unveiled, the Turks had become apostates and heathens. It was lawful to kill them without incurring criminal penalties or bloodwit, and to enslave their children."[564] The Turks suppressed the Arab rebellion in 1856, but as a measure of reconciliation, they exempted the Hejaz area from the decree outlawing the trade in black slaves throughout the Ottoman empire. As Bernard Lewis writes: "The emergence of the holy

[560]Quoted in B. Lewis: *Race and Slavery in the Middle East*, p.82.

[561]Against the tide, a very recent whitewash of Islamic slavery is attempted by L. Catherine: *Manyiema*, p.80 ff.; on p.86 he quotes Snouck-Hurgronje with approval: "They are better off than European working-men."

[562]S.H.H. Nadvi: "The Institution of Slavery & Human Rights", in *Islamic Order* quarterly (Karachi), 1/1989, p.79.

[563]M. Iqbal: *Shikwa*, p.40.

[564]B. Lewis: *Race and Slavery*, p.80.

men and the holy places as the last-ditch defenders of slavery against reform is only an apparent paradox. They were upholding an institution sanctified by scripture, law and tradition, and one which in their eyes was necessary to the maintenance of the social structure of Muslim life."[565] Likewise, Murray Gordon asserts that "slavery ... was deeply anchored in Islamic law. ... As a result, in no part of the Muslim world was an ideological challenge ever mounted against slavery".[566]

This type of pro-slavery utterances against the rising tide of abolitionism may well be available in Indian Muslim sources too, but so far this has never been investigated as yet, at least not by the Hindu historians under consideration. It was left to Bhimrao Ambedkar, the apostate from Hinduism (to Buddhism, shortly before his death in 1956), to say more on this matter than all contemporary Hindu ideologues together, at least in general terms. Ambedkar approvingly quoted John J. Pool, who after listing some Quran statements permitting slavery, had concluded: "Thus the Koran, in this matter of slavery, is the enemy of mankind."[567] The colonial powers had abolished slavery but, wrote Ambedkar, "while it existed, much of its support was derived from Islam", because: "While the prescriptions by the Prophet regarding the just and humane treatment of slaves contained in the Koran are praiseworthy, there is nothing whatever in Islam that lends support to the abolition of this curse."[568]

The fact is that the end of Islamic slavery in India cannot be credited to any Muslim initiative. The institution declined drastically with the impoverishment of the Muslim royal and noble courts in the eighteenth century. A final stop was put to it by the formal prohibition in Act V, 1843, and by the punitive measures included in the Indian Penal Code with effect from 1 January 1862.[569] For an evaluation of Islam, the point about this is that the abolition of slavery was imposed by an outside power, the British Empire—a colonizer to some, a liberator to others.

A point which may be rich in implications is that Muslims in India and, at a later stage, in Arabia, seem to have accepted the modern

[565]B. Lewis: *Race and Slavery*, p.80.

[566]M. Gordon: *Slavery in the Arab world*, p.44.

[567]Ambedkar: *Pakistan*, p.228, with reference to J.J. Pool: *Studies in Mohammedanism*, pp.34-5.

[568]Ambedkar: *Pakistan*, p.228.

[569]K.S. Lal: *Muslim Slave System*, p.177.

prohibition of slavery. Even if the generation of Muslim jurists who had personally known the institution of slavery defended it against attempts to abolish it, among later generations of even "fundamentalist" Muslims the demand to restore slavery is simply never heard. This means that the strong attachment of orthodox Muslims to their Scriptures cannot prevent them from making revolutionary changes in their ethical sensibility. When Muslim propagandists falsely claim that Islam has abolished slavery, their distortion of history is reprehensible but at the same time, their apparent interiorization of the condemnation of slavery is commendable. The fact that Islam is trying to manufacture for itself a history of anti-slavery reform does indicate that the Muslim community has genuinely shed its belief in the righteousness of slavery. And that likewise, it might shed other Scripture-based beliefs which stand in the way of religious pluralism and co-existence.

Ambedkar's testimony

Ambedkar, a leader of the "downtrodden" (*Dalit*s), was a merciless critic of Hinduism, yet he has gained considerable popularity in Hindutva circles. His photographs are included in the portrait series above the dais at many Sangh Parivar gatherings, and he is frequently quoted in pro-Hindu papers.[570] Part of the explanation is that during his lifetime, socially conscious Hindus were too ashamed and guilt-ridden to look Ambedkar in the eye, but now that Hindu society has made some genuine headway in abolishing untouchability and easing caste discrimination, they can now acknowledge his impressive merits. For all his bitterness against Hinduism and his emphatic preference of British rule to indigenous "upper-caste rule", he is hailed as the one man who decisively stood in the way of mass conversions of the former untouchables to Christianity or Islam, guiding several million of them towards Buddhism instead.[571] Also, he was far more forthright in criticizing Islam than most Hindu leaders

[570]E.g. a series of articles in the Bombay tabloid *Blitz* reproduced all Ambedkar's arguments (in his *Thoughts on Pakistan*, 1940) against Islam. On the lorry taking L.K. Advani around on his Rath Yatra celebrating the 50th anniversary of Independence, one of the two pictures displayed was Ambedkar's, the other being Subhash Chandra Bose's. In his book *A Wounded Civilization*, V.S. Naipaul mentions seeing an Ambedkar portrait centrally displayed at a small Shiv Sena gathering.

[571]The one Hindu author who has gone out of his way to document and criticise Ambedkar's opposition to the freedom movement, is Arun Shourie: *Worshipping False Gods*.

would have dared to do. In 1947, he called on the Dalits not to side with Pakistan or with the Nizam of Hyderabad but with India: "Whatever the oppression and tyranny that the Hindus practised on them, he asserted, it should not warp their vision and swerve them from their duty. He warned the Scheduled Castes in Hyderabad not to side with the Nizam and bring disgrace upon the community by siding with one who was the enemy of India."[572] Finally, the Hindu nationalists were lucky to find in "Saint" Ambedkar's work *Thoughts on Pakistan* a wealth of anti-Islamic quotations which, if they themselves were to say them, would be denounced as "vicious Hindu chauvinist anti-Muslim hate propaganda". The reader will agree that this is sufficient explanation for his new-found popularity in Hindutva circles.

Ambedkar's starting-point was a very sound one: there are universal and objective criteria with which to evaluate religious doctrines, and rather than wallow in multicultural relativism, we should judge religions by their objective effects upon human life. We should drop the sentimental belief "that all religions are equally good and that there is no necessity of discriminating between them. Nothing can be a greater error than this. Religion is an institution or an influence and like all social influences and institutions, it may help or it may harm a society which is in its grip."[573]

Now, what evaluation of Islam can be arrived at with this criterion? Coming to specifics, he utterly rejected the notion, now spread by self-described Ambedkarites like V.T. Rajshekar in his fortnightly *Dalit Voice*, that Islamic society is more egalitarian or in other ways better than Hindu society.[574] After giving *Mother India*, Miss Katherine Mayo's book of anti-Hindu "drain inspection" (as Gandhi called it), the credit for "exposing the evils [of Hindu society]", he observed that "it created the unfortunate impression throughout the world that while the Hindus were grovelling in the mud of these social evils and were conservative, the Muslims were free from them, and as compared to the Hindus were a progressive people."[575] He proceeded to enumerate all the social evils in Hindu society, and found that they are generally also present in Muslim

---

[572]Dh. Keer: *Ambedkar*, p.399, with reference to *The Free Press Journal*, 28.11.1947.

[573]B.R. Ambedkar: *Philosophy of Hinduism*, in *Writings and Speeches*, vol.3, p.24.

[574]A Dalit criticism of *Dalit Voice*'s distortion of Ambedkar's line in a pro-Islamic sense is B.B. Biswas: *Islamisation of Dr. Ambedkar's View: a Suicidal Move* (1994).

[575]B.R. Ambedkar: *Pakistan* (*Writings and Speeches*, vol.8), pp.225 ff.

society, sometimes to a worse extent: child marriage, several forms of oppression of women, several forms of social inequality.

Ambedkar conveyed the dominant opinion that Islam imposes a uniformity of thought, and that "this uniformity is deadening and is not merely imparted to Muslims but is imposed upon them by a spirit of intolerance which is unknown anywhere outside the Muslim world for its severity and its violence and which is directed towards the suppression of all rational thinking which is in conflict with the teachings of Islam."[576] His last point about the reason for Muslim unwillingness to reform is this: "The Muslims think that the Hindus and Muslims must perpetually struggle... that in this struggle the strong will win, and that to ensure strength they must suppress or put in cold storage everything which causes dissension in their ranks."[577]

Ambedkar explained that the communal conflict which has increasingly characterized Hindu-Muslim relations, had likewise led to a stagnation in the Hindus' efforts at reform, notably in the Hindu Mahasabha. There is a parallel with the case of Congress, where it was another struggle that had taken all energy out of its efforts at reform (which had been so prominent a concern of Congress in its first two decades), viz. the struggle against the British. In all tirades by Ambedkarites against Hindu society's observed slackness at social reform, this effect of the pre-occupation with other matters should be borne in mind. Ambedkar understood that one cannot wage too many wars at the same time, and his eagerness to get society to concentrate on social reform explains his impatience with the communal conflict and his radical proposal in 1940 to solve it once and for all by means of a geographical separation of Hindus and Muslims, i.e. Partition completed by an exchange of population.

In anti-Hindu writing, you find a recurring project of a joint minorities' front including the Scheduled Castes against the upper-caste Hindus. One place where a Muslim-Dalit alliance has materialized is the city corporation of Hyderabad, where Muslims and Dalits have been taking turns as mayors in the past few decades. However, this situation is the exception, not the rule. There is a long-standing hostility between

---

[576]Ambedkar: *Pakistan*, p.234, followed by a lengthy quote from Ernest Renan (*Nationality and other Essays*) to the same effect, but harder.

[577]Ambedkar: *Pakistan*, p.237.

Muslims and Dalits, and many Hindu-Muslim riots are in effect Muslim-Dalit riots. One reason is that Muslims, like upper-caste Hindus, consider Dalits unclean: they eat pork, they have rather liberal sexual mores, and they do work which in Muslim societies was performed by slaves until recently.

Ambedkar observed that Islam also has its own caste system, quite apart from the holdovers of Hindu caste distinctions among converts. He quoted the Superintendent of the 1901 Census with approval: "The Mohammedans themselves recognize two main social divisions, 1) *Ashraf* or *Sharaf* and 2) *Ajlaf*. *Ashraf* means 'noble' and includes all undoubted descendants of foreigners and converts from high-caste Hindus. All other Mohammedans, including all occupational groups and all converts of lower ranks are known by the contemptuous terms *Ajlaf*, 'wretches' or 'mean people'. ... In some places a third class, called *Arzal* or 'lowest of all' is added. With them no other Mohammedan would associate, and they are forbidden to enter the mosque [and] to use the public burial ground. Within these groups there are castes with social precedence of exactly the same nature as one finds among the Hindus."[578]

For all his bitterness against Hindu society, Ambedkar's verdict on Muslim society was even harder: "There can thus be no manner of doubt that the Muslim society in India is afflicted by the same social evils as afflict the Hindu society. Indeed, the Muslims have all the social evils of the Hindus and something more. That something more is the compulsory system of *purdah* for Muslim women."[579] And then he sums up all the negative effects and side-effects of the *purdah* ("curtain", seclusion) system. But worse than the existence of social evils among the Muslims is, in Ambedkar's diagnosis, the lack of any attempt, even any intention, to reform their society: "The Hindus have their social evils. But there is one relieving feature about them—namely that some of them are conscious of their existence and a few of them are actively agitating for their removal. The Muslims, on the other hand, do not realize that they are evils and consequently do not agitate for their removal."[580]

Today, if not in 1940, that statement would be unfair to a considerable body of enlightened Muslims who try to make the best of it and push

---

[578] Ambedkar: *Pakistan* (republished as vol.8 of Ambedkar: *Writings and Speeches*), p.229.

[579] Ambedkar: *Pakistan*, p.230.

[580] Ambedkar: *Pakistan*, p.233.

through some social reforms within an Islamic framework. Still, the determined Muslim opposition against Civil Code reform in India suggests that there is still some truth to Ambedkar's observations. There is also a lesson implied for India's secularists: their praise for Islam as being so much more just and egalitarian than Hinduism, though addressed to the Hindus, is overheard by the Muslims as well, and has the effect of encouraging a moral smugness and discouraging the effort at social reform in the Muslim community.

Women in Islam

In the age of women's liberation, every religious marketeer adds a whiff of feminism to the projected image of his religion. Consider this Christian pamphlet: "Sita, the heroine of the 2500-year-old Ramayana epic is still held up as a model for Indian women. Silently she let her father, husband and sons decide on her life. Fortunately, other voices are heard as well. More and more, it is the women themselves who tell each other that they should not let others silence them. That is also the message which the Church and the Christians are bringing. 'Sita, speak up', they say, 'let them hear your side of the story. You who bowed your head when you were sent away, you who bowed your head for the trial, Sita speak up!'"[581] Is it pedantic to remind these trendy missionaries that Saint Paul specifically ordered Christian women to remain silent during religious meetings?[582]

For Islam, particularly South-Asian Islam, it is very hard to pose as a feminist religion, with news about the treatment of women in Pakistan and Afghanistan being hard to surpass in sheer shock value. Then again, a sufficient highlighting of the well-known atrocities on women in Hindu society still makes it possible to blame the Hindu Other as anti-woman *by comparison*.[583] In any case, one of the inequalities sanctioned by Islam is indeed the subordination of women to men.[584] It is a favourite target in modernist-Western criticism of Islam.

Until recently, Hindus had not paid much attention to this aspect of

---

[581] "India en Sri Lanka", *Oecumenisch Bulletin* of IKON (a Dutch Christian broadcasting foundation), 1.12.1996.

[582] 1 Cor. 14:33-35.

[583] As Syed Shahabuddin once said in a discussion on Muslim atrocities against women: "At least we do not burn our women."

[584] Explicitly in Q.4:34/38.

Islam's view of mankind, mostly because Hinduism itself has always allotted distinct roles to men and women, and finds itself criticized for systematic cruelty against women. Though there was slightly more equality between the sexes in the Vedic period, classical Hinduism as it has existed in the last millennium can hardly be claimed as a "pioneer of feminism", and no Hindu has tried to create such an impression. Only, the insistent culpabilization of Hinduism for its lack of equality and the glorification of Islam as a religion of equality have aroused the critical curiosity of at least one Hindu author in the status of women in Islam.

Ram Swarup notes: "The question of Muslim woman has opened up and there are voices of protest and there is demand for change. True, those voices are still feeble and not entirely unequivocal, but they can no longer be ignored and they cannot remain without influence for long."[585] In a way, his book is a gesture of sympathy for Taslima Nasreen, the Muslim-born Bangladeshi gynaecologist and writer, whose foremost concern is women's liberation, but who also drew attention to the plight of the Hindu minority in her country in her controversial novel *Lajja* ("Shame", 1993)[586]: "In this book we have praised Taslima for speaking for Muslim women who do not have many spokesmen in the Muslim world. But her real glory is that she has also spoken for the persecuted Hindus in her country—for whom no one speaks, not even the Hindus. ... Muslim orthodoxy and Muslim liberalism may be divided on the question of Muslim women, but they are one where the infidels are concerned. It is curious but true that in Muslim history there has been no protest from Muslim quarters against what Islam has done to non-Muslims.

"In this book, we have said that for sympathizing with Hindus, Taslima is not likely to be more popular with Hindu 'liberals' in India than with Muslim liberals in her own country. In some ways, Hindu 'liberals' are worse than Muslim liberals. Their first and fondest antipathy is Hinduism; and the rest of their politics is mere corollary. Taslima has described the sorry plight of the Hindus in Bangladesh. The anti-Hindu Hindu 'liberals' in India can never excuse her for that though some may

---

[585]Ram Swarup: *Woman in Islam*, p.v.

[586]Due to a collective effort of the secularist intelligentsia, *Lajja* has reached a far smaller audience than would be normal for such a headline-hitting book. It was published in English translation by the South-Asian department of Penguin publishers, not by the European and American departments; Bangladesh Government banned the book. A summarizing Hindi translation by Sita Ram Goel was published as a serial in *Panchjanya* in the summer of 1993.

make some appropriate noises to look liberal. In fact, this role of Taslima remains unrecognized and even unmentioned and every effort is made to push it under the carpet in order to suppress the very idea and need of such a role."[587]

It is a fact that Indian secularist reviewers of Taslima Nasreen's *Lajja* have not taken kindly to her interest in the plight of the minorities in Bangladesh. They have denounced her as "irresponsible" and an (unwitting?) "agent of the BJP", while reviewers in foreign papers have falsely claimed that in 1993-94, Taslima Nasreen was twice sentenced to death because of her feminism. In reality, her feminist writings, though annoying to the orthodox, had never earned her a death sentence; she was sentenced to death first for "insulting the Muslims" with her book *Lajja*, which describes Muslim atrocities on the minorities; and secondly for "insulting the Quran and the Prophet" and for "apostasy", because of her statements in several interviews that "the Quran is outdated", that "Islam is incompatible with the dignity of women", etc.[588]

The series of purportedly supportive columns by famous writers (Nadine Gordimer, Susan Sontag, Bernard-Henry Lévy *et al.*), *"Lettres ouvertes à Taslima Nasrine"*, does not contain any reference at all to her radical questioning of the Quran and to her plea in favour of the persecuted minorities in Islamic Bangladesh.[589] Instead, they try to refocus the attention on harmless liberal themes like feminism and a writer's right to dissent. None of her interviewers have inquired further about the plight of the Hindus in her country. The reader should realize the effrontery of this attitude: here is a writer who stakes her life to give a voice to the frightened Hindus of Bangladesh, and all her so-called sympathizers do everything in their power to muzzle that voice again, and to prevent the debate which their heroine had tried to open, from actually taking place.[590] So, Ram

[587]Ram Swarup: *Woman in Islam*, p.viii-ix.

[588]The interview which drew attention in both India and Bangladesh was published in *The Statesman* (Calcutta), 9.5.1994; similar strong anti-Islamic statements were made in interviews given in the following days to the Australian national TV station and to the German weekly *Der Spiegel*.

[589]The exception was Salman Rushdie, and a semi-exception was Rachid Mimouni, who drew attention to the plight of the Christians in Arab countries. The series was published in July-August 1994 in the French daily *Libération* and, in translation, in other European papers including the Flemish daily *De Morgen*.

[590]I have described and analysed this paradox in a column, "Toast the writer, burn the book", in *Observer of Business and Politics*, 27.5.1995, and in my postscript to the Indian reprint of Daniel Pipes: *The Rushdie Affair*.

Swarup is right about the treatment given to Taslima Nasreen's stand for the oppressed minorities: "every effort is made to push it under the carpet".

Now that a feminist freethinker in the Muslim world has taken the trouble of publicizing the problems which the Hindu minority faces, Ram Swarup as a Hindu revivalist author returns the gesture by paying attention to the problems of women under an Islamic dispensation. From the outset, he expresses his skepticism regarding social reform within the framework of Islam: "Islamic laws on marriage and divorce are not just social legislation which could be changed in response to new social mores and needs; they are revealed truths, Allah's commands and, therefore, unalterable. ... True, perhaps some of these laws were once current social practices among the Arabs of the time of the Prophet; but once they were adopted by Allah and acquired heavenly sanctions, they were no longer amenable to legal modifications or even normal wear and tear or silent social change. ... In this study, we have held that no worthwhile reform is possible within the present ideational framework of the Quran and the Sunnah."[591]

This, then, is obviously directed against those reformers who claim to read a message of social liberation and women's emancipation in the Quran and the model behaviour of the Prophet, and who "have already begun with their reinterpreting and in the process have given us a Quran which was not known or even suspected by Islam's best legists in the past. Similarly, though they have failed to serve the cause of Muslim women, they have certainly used the pretext for doing some fine propaganda for Islam."[592]

According to Ram Swarup, such progressive re-interpretation of the Quran "will be self-defeating. It will merely strengthen the authority of the very sources of the ideas which have kept women down."[593] He also argues that it is not convincing, e.g. the well-known attempt to read a prohibition of polygamy in the Quranic verses regulating polygamy, on the specious plea that the Quranic commandment to treat all four wives equally is humanly impossible.[594] His argument is logical enough: obviously, if Allah had wanted to abolish polygamy, which was practised only by rich

---

[591]Ram Swarup: *Woman in Islam*, p.v.

[592]Ram Swarup: *Woman in Islam*, p.vi.

[593]Ram Swarup: *Woman in Islam*, p.vi.

[594]Q.4:3, discussed in Ram Swarup: *Women in Islam*, p.18.

males, He could have said so in plain terms, just as He was not too shy to condemn idol-worship, which was practised by the entire Arab population including those rich males. And why should He give practical instructions for an institution He wanted to prohibit? Moreover, under Islamic law, men can take concubines to whom they have no duty of equal treatment, yet such an arrangement could hardly count as monogamy.

Women and the Prophet

Modern apologists for Islam, often non-Muslim secularists, have invested heavily in building a case that, on the contrary, "Mohammed was the first feminist", or at least that "compared with preceding Paganism, Islam meant a great leap forwards for women's emancipation".[595] Or in the words of the Justice Minister in Vajpayee's first effective government: "The Islam of the Prophet was a religion of equality of all and certainly of men and women."[596]

Dissidents in the Muslim world protest against this self-serving rewriting of history, for example, the Moroccan feminist Fatna Ait Sabbah says she "almost vomits when hearing yet again that story that Islam has brought freedom to women".[597] Quite apart from the doubtful historicity of Mohammed's "feminism", the argument that his policies were good by comparison with the pre-existing society is profoundly un-Islamic: "The argument which is always used against the Quranic verses contemptuous of women is at least they constituted progress vis-à-vis the pre-Islamic traditions. If you reason like this, you don't speak from an Islamic viewpoint, for to a Muslim the Quran as a whole is a divine revelation valid forever."[598]

Nevertheless, the argument that Islam is at least more feminist than Arabian Paganism and its Hindu sister religion, is frequently repeated

[595]The Arabic writers Fatima Mernissi (Morocco) and Assia Djebar (Algeria) have taken this position, applauded in a review by Hadewijch Hernalsteen: "Vrije vrouwen van de islam" (Dutch: "Free women of Islam"), *De Standaard*, 12.2.1994.

[596]Ram Jethmalani: "Muslims and Hindutva: the scope for amity", *Indian Express*, 9.12.1995.

[597]Quoted with approval and supporting evidence of women's freedom and dignity in pre-Islamic Arabia by L. Catherine: *Islam voor ongelovigen*, p.203.

[598]Hilde Keteleer: "'Met de Koran in de hand worden vrouwen onderdrukt'" (Dutch: "Quran in hand, they oppress women"), *Markant* (Antwerp), 14.7.1994, paraphrasing the German journalist Klemens Ludwig. The latter lambasts the ostracism against people who openly address the question of the status of women in Islam.

nowadays. Some Hindutva authors have in fact interiorized it, witness the opening line of an article in *Organiser*: "Some 1400 years ago Islam came as a saviour of women in the Arab world."[599] The point is made for the sake of contrast with a description of the present situation, where "Islamic fundamentalists are heaping atrocities on women in the name of Islam", but it is made none the less, as a typical example of the RSS position that Islam is all right but the Muslims are wrong.

In Ram Swarup's view, by contrast, the Prophet's injunctions regarding women were definitely a great step backwards for women's freedom and dignity. He points out that Islamic literature itself describes Pagan women as proud and entreprising individuals, most notably Mohammed's first wife Khadija and the Meccan first lady Hind. In parts of Arabia, families were matrilocal (like in Kerala and Meghalaya), and women had equal divorce rights with men.[600] Next, he discusses the institution of marriage in Islam. At first sight, it is very "progressive" and "secular" that marriage in Islam is not a sacrament but a contract. But this is vitiated by other provisions which create a stark inequality to the detriment of the woman. A woman cannot arrange her own marriage, much less her own divorce, and not even her daughter's marriage: there must always be a male guardian. A man has the right to beat his wife, not the reverse.

Then there are some special and little-known aspects to the matter. It seems obvious that a man can only marry a woman if she is not already married, given the well-known fact that Islam allows polygyny to men but not polyandry to women. Yet, the Quran itself provides for marrying a married woman in one case, viz. a woman captured in war and reduced to slavery: "And all married women are forbidden unto you save those whom your right hand possesses."[601] A famous example from Indian history, discussed by K.S. Lal, is that of Rani Kamala Devi, captured in the sack of Gujarat. Let us first hear Jawaharlal Nehru's version of the events: "Many of the [Muslim invaders] married women of the country. One of their great rulers, Alauddin Khilji, himself married a Hindu lady, and so did his son."[602] Nehru described this as "Indianization", and ever since, secularists

[599]Muzaffar Hussain: "Islamic atrocities on women", *Organiser*, 9.7.1995.

[600]Ram Swarup: *Woman in Islam*, pp.2-6.

[601]Q.4:24/28.

[602]J. Nehru: *Discovery of India*, p.238. Alauddin is called "great" because among the Indian Left he counts as a "precursor of socialism".

have been saying that the Sultan's harems have been the cradle of India's "composite culture".

Now for more detail: "Kamala Devi was captured in the sack of Gujarat (1299) and married by Alauddin Khalji. According to the Islamic law, kafir women could be married to Muslims even while their husbands were alive, for marriage is annulled by captivity. Later on her daughter Deval Devi was also captured in another campaign (1308) and ... married to Alauddin's son Khizr Khan. ... After the assassination of Khizr Khan ... she was married by Qutbuddin Mubarak Khalji (1316-20) against her will. With the murder of Qutbuddin at the hands of Khusrau Khan she was taken into the latter's harem. In short, the princess was treated as nothing more than a chattel or transferable property."[603]

These events are narrated curtly because no accompanying comment is needed to convey the desired impression of Islam as barbaric. None the less, what is described here is really a universal aspect of slavery as such: a Greek or Aztec slave-holder likewise had a right to the bodies of his slaves. In discussing the evils of Islam, one should always make the distinction between the specific input of Islam as such and the rich capacity of mankind in general for all kinds of evil. Also, the fact that Islam confers legitimacy on the induction of a captured (non-Muslim) woman into a Muslim man's harem should not make us forget that ancient Hindu law similarly recognized marriage by "capture" or by "ravishing" (*kshâtra*/warrior's and *râkshasa*/barbarian's marriage).[604] Civilization did not grow overnight.

Ram Swarup next discusses the concept of "equality" (*kifa't*) regarding marriage.[605] This does not imply an egalitarian vision; on the contrary, it means equality of the partners in social rank presupposing a hierarchy in society. A woman has a right (a claim vis-à-vis her guardian) to be married to someone of equal or of higher rank. Not that this puts a special odium on Islam: it is a worldwide phenomenon, traceable even to monkey societies, that upper-class men reserve upper-class women for themselves while also taking liberties with lower-class women, so that a

[603]K.S. Lal: *Muslim Slave System*, pp.160-61.

[604]See A.S. Altekar: *Position of Women in Hindu Civilization*, p.314. As Kedar Nath Mishra explained to me, there is a positive side to the recognition of such "marriages", viz. that an abducted woman at least had certain legal rights vis-à-vis her abductor.

[605]Ram Swarup: *Woman in Islam*, p.10, with reference to the Hanifite law codex, the *Hidayah*.

woman is normally paired off to a man who is either her equal or her superior, never to a man of lower rank. Even Hindu tradition speaks out against hypogamous (*pratiloma*) marriages but accepts hypergamous (*anuloma*) marriages.[606]

It is more surprising to learn that apart from purely social rank, there is also an ethnic hierarchy involved in these Islamic rules: highest-ranking are the Quraish, the tribe to which Mohammed belonged; next come the other Arabs, then the non-Arab Muslims or *Ajami*, and finally the first-generation converts. This means that a Quraish woman can refuse a Beduin or Persian bridegroom, just like a colonial-age white woman would generally have been considered justified in disobeying her father if he wanted to marry her off to a black man. No more surprise, then, to hear of a similar ethnic-based inequality in India, where "the principle of ranking finds a vigorous application. Those who claim foreign ancestry are the aristocracy, the *Ashraf.* They have their own ranking: Sayyids, Sheikhs, Moghuls and Pathans. They are divided into subsidiary categories, generally all endogamous. The local converts constitute the plebeian class and are frankly called *Ajlaf* and *Arzal*, Arabic words which mean the wretched, the ignoble, the mean, the triflings. ... They are further divided literally into hundreds of castes, most of them strictly endogamous."[607]

In the Western press, one of the classic icons of Islamic barbarity is the stern punishment for adultery: stoning to death of both guilty parties. As if to exonerate the Arabs and other islamized nations, Ram Swarup emphasizes that the punishment would never have been as heavy but for the personal insistence of both Mohammed and his lieutenant Omar, the second Caliph: "The Prophet himself was under some sort of psychological compulsion to stand by the Old Testament law and to do better than even the Jews, among whom the punishment of stoning in such cases had lapsed by custom. Being so unnatural, the Muslim world also wanted to forget it, but Umar insisted ... that 'stoning is a duty laid down in

---

[606]*Manu Smriti* 10:5. Incidentally, the acceptance of hypergamous marriages in the *varna* scheme shows how *varna* is not by definition an endogamous system, and must have a different origin from the tribe-originated *jâti* system, which is endogamous by definition and came about by Sanskritizing autarchic tribes into building-blocks of expanding Hindu society.

[607]Ram Swarup: *Woman in Islam*, p.11.

Allah's Book for married men and women who commit adultery'."[608] Never much of a black-and-white thinker, Ram Swarup freely acknowledges that the rules for providing the necessary proof before a judge are mercifully strict enough to ensure that the punishment is rarely implemented.

Ram Swarup does not make an attempt to blame Islam for some of the hardships of Hindu women, though people with a more polemical attitude would easily find a few indications for this. Thus, concerning the punishment of adulterous women, a negative influence from Islam might be surmised: "After about the 11th century AD lapses of women began to be treated with greater sternness."[609] There was no question of stoning (merely a stronger tendency to repudiate a woman caught in the act even once), and the general increase in Hindu prudishness was a long-term development which had started before the Muslim invasions, but the question is legitimate whether the synchronicity of this sterner treatment with the advent of Islam was more than a coincidence.

Women in Pakistan

One organization which has decided to take the polemical war into enemy territory, and to highlight Muslim misbehaviour rather than be apologetic for Hindu misbehaviour, is *Kashmir for Kashmiriat*. Founded by Hindu refugees from Kashmir, this group and its like-named periodical drew attention in the mid-1990s to human rights violations in Pakistan. Among other achievements, the group has published a booklet reproducing from Pakistani sources a number of news stories about atrocities on women.[610] Thus, it has reproduced a report by the Human Rights Commission of Pakistan summing up the legal and *de facto* discriminations against women:

1) *Hudûd* ordinances (i.e. Islamic Penal Law) "under which a woman

[608]Ram Swarup: *Woman in Islam*, p.14. On one occasion, Mohammed forced the Jews of Medina, who wanted to punish an adulterous couple by public humilation, to apply the Biblical punishment of stoning to death. Full detail in A. Guillaume: *Life of Muhammad*, pp.266/394.

[609]A.S. Altekar: *Position of Woman in Hindu Civilization*, p.313. Altekar shows an Arya Samaj-type concern that such repudiated women have no option left but to marry a non-Hindu man, leading to a "considerable swelling" of the non-Hindu population.

[610]Kashmir for Kashmiriat: *Women as Second-Class Citizens*, 1993.

reporting rape can actually be charged with and punished for adultery".[611] A woman alleging rape *ipso facto* confesses to having had illicit intercourse, and she has to produce four male witnesses to confirm that it was involuntary. If she cannot, she is considered guilty of illicit intercourse and of falsely accusing her partner. Most likely, she gets imprisoned on the spot and kept there for months; as an allegedly loose woman, she can then count on frequent rape victimization by the policemen.

2) The evidence given by two women equals the evidence given by one man, as prescribed by Islamic Law in general. (For this inequality in testimony, the Belgian convert Yahya/Jean Michot once gave the following justification: a woman is not supposed to go out alone unless she is of questionable character, so if an honourable and hence trustworthy woman is witness to some crime, her woman companion will also be a witness, so where there is one, there must be two.)[612]

3) The well-known inequality regarding multiple marriage partners and regarding unilateral divorce; a woman seeking divorce must convince a judge, while a man just has to pronounce triple *talâq* (repudiation). (Even Muslim reformers in India denounce this practice, like the *Jami'at-Ahl-e-Hadîs* has issued a fatwa declaring invalid the triple *talâq* in one session rather than in three months, once after every menstrual period as their own interpretation of Mohammed's instructions suggests.)[613]

4) Numerous cases of abduction without judicial remedy; "exchange" (*watta-satta*) marriages against the concerned women's will.

5) Literacy rate for girls half as high as for boys; infant mortality much higher for girls than for boys. Note that the ratio men/women is 51.47 per cent men in Bangladesh, 51.85 per cent in India, 52.50 per cent in Pakistan.[614] This last figure may also indicate a certain incidence of female infanticide, which was traditionally practised among some communities in Panjab and the Thar desert on both sides of the present Pakistani border. The Quranic prohibition on this practice, like the Hindu scriptural prohibition on abortion, is not capable of actually preventing it, all the less

---

[611]Kashmir for Kashmiriat: *Women as Second-Class Citizens*, p.23, from *Frontier Post*, 1.7.1993.

[612]Debate with Arif Ersoy of Refah Partisi and with myself, Leuven 1994.

[613]See: "Talaq, talaq, talaq is no talaq", *Indian Express*, 29.5.1993.

[614]*Encyclopaedia Brittannica*, Book of the Year 1992; a lower percentage of women in Pakistan as compared to India is also mentioned in: "Sixty million 'missing' women", *Observer*, 22.10.1995.

so since gender-selective abortion has made it possible to formally shun infanticide by moving it to the prenatal stage. In the West, at least, a tendency among Muslim immigrants to have foetuses gender-screened and aborted in case they are female, has been noted.[615] Though the selective pre- or post-natal elimination of baby girls is by no means confined to Muslims (its highest incidence being in China and Korea), it does undermine a classic argument in favour of Islam, viz. that it terminated infanticide.[616]

6) Numerous cases of disfigurement of women by means of acid thrown into the face, whether for refusing marriage or intercourse or for alleged un-Islamic behaviour.[617]

7) Sale of Bangladeshi girls for slave labour; kidnapping of tribal children for sale.

8) Numerous but rarely punished "kitchen fires" or "stove bursts", engineered accidents to eliminate wives, as in India's dowry murders.[618]

From some of the items cited, it is clear that Muslim and Hindu society have certain atrocities and discriminations against women in common. For the time being, Hindu polemicists are already satisfied if they can dispel the notion that Hinduism is worse than Islam, so they take comfort that even the worst of them are by no means the only sinners. Indeed, a few types of Muslim atrocities are non-existent among Hindus, for example,

---

[615]See J.A.A. van Doorn: "Aborteren op z'n buitenlands", *HP/De Tijd*, 24.1.1997. The author protests against the toleration of this practice by progressives in the name of "a woman's right to choose", when in practice, the women concerned are often coerced by their husbands. In his opinion, the Minister for Public Health had, by pleading that a Muslim woman may be justified in aborting her baby girl because she might otherwise be threatened in her marriage or her life, actually condoned a dramatic violation of the existing abortion law, which requires that the woman act *under no compulsion*.

[616]S.R. Goel possibly exaggerates when he writes (*Hindu Temples*, vol.2., pp.270-71): "It is a despicable lie that the pre-Islamic Arabs killed their children." After all, the practice has been observed among numerous nations. However, Lucas Catherine informs us (*Islam voor Ongelovigen*, p.203): "Historical research has shown that infanticide of newborn babies was by far not as widespread as we are now asked to believe. It did not only concern girls but also male babies, and it only took place in times of great drought and famine." Four Quran verses refer to infanticide: 6:137/138, 6:140/141, 6:151/152, 17:31/33; the latter two explicitly relate it to dire poverty, none specifies *female* infanticide, though the modern experience confirms that this must have been more common.

[617]"Most of the pictures accompanying this article were too gruesome to be printed": *Women as Second-Class Citizens*, p.12.

[618]See also "Dowry deaths in Pakistan", *Organiser*, 7.7.1996. The Islamabad Government hospital alone is reported to take 16 cases per month.

an item not cited in this list is that, according to a *World Development Report* brought out by the World Bank with the help of the World Health Organization, female circumcision, often thought to be confined to Africa (Pagan and Coptic as well as Muslim), does occur very marginally among South-Asian Muslims as well, even "among minorities in India".[619]

In the incorporation (or "exploitation") of women's rights in the discourse of Hindu revivalism, uneasy differences between its several segments can be noticed. Many Hindus are still not comfortable with women's equality, even if their polemic against Islam (as in the Shah Bano case) forces them to strike progressive postures.[620] Others who have assimilated modern liberalism are genuinely proud of the great strides which Hindu women have made during the twentieth century, admittedly thanks in part to Nehru's policies. Thus, in the foreword to a reprint of one of the classics of Western feminist critique, Sita Ram Goel asserts that "the one fact of which India after independence can be mighty proud is the tremendous progress which Hindu women have made in all aspects and every walk of life".[621]

In the case of the Sangh Parivar, the somewhat embarrassing position is that many of its representatives opposed the reform of Hindu Law in the 1950s, while today, pride is taken in this more liberal Hindu Law as opposed to the literally medieval Muslim Law.[622] Likewise, Sangh spokesmen like to deride Pakistan as a "feudal" country, but the Sangh's own position when Nehru and Indira Gandhi decreed land reform and abolition of feudal privileges was at best mixed. In the last few decades,

[619] "Women circumcised in India: WB report", *Indian Express*, 7.7.1993.

[620] The alleged Hindutva dilemma regarding women's emancipation is a regular feature in high-brow anti-Hindutva writing, e.g. Ratna Kapur & Brenda Cossman: "Communalising Gender/Engendering Community: Women, Legal Discourse and Saffron Agenda", *Economic and Political Weekly*, 24.4.1993.

[621] S.R. Goel, ed., in Mathilda Joslyn Gage (1826-98): *Woman, Church and State*, Voice of India reprint 1997, p.vii. The book contains estimates for the number of "witches" burned by Christians in centuries past, estimates which have recently been corrected downwards rather drastically (from 9 million to a hundred thousand) but are still being cited in anti-Christian polemic by *Wicca* neo-witches in the West.

[622] To be more precise: while Islamic Law as such does date back to the Middle Ages, its applicability to all Indian Muslims is not older than 1937, and is a gift of the British; until then, a large percentage of Indian Muslims followed their pre-conversion customary laws, partly or wholly.

an undeniable modernization of the Hindu mentality has taken place, which has brought the Sangh more or less in line with modernist positions taken by Nehru in the 1950s.

Evaluation

If Hinduism cannot claim a history of social equality, and if its home-grown anti-caste movements are not sufficient to stop the identification of Hinduism with caste, the research by authors like Bhimrao Ambedkar, Harsh Narain, Ram Swarup and K.S. Lal shows at least that Islam too has a history of radical inequality. About that, there simply cannot be the slightest doubt left: they have shown from impeccable sources that Islam teaches and practices a religiously motivated discrimination regarding non-Muslims, and that it sanctions and practices a variety of social discriminations even within the Muslim community. Mohammed Iqbal's quip that "Islam equals Communism plus Allah", assuming that in "Communism" he implied a classless society, is not true at all.[623]

A social injustice particularly closely connected with Islam, though having existed in many other societies as well, is or was slavery. The main differences between Islamic slavery and for instance, ancient Greek slavery pertain to the staggering magnitude of the Islamic slave system in both space and time, and to its religious justification. A Muslim could take a non-Muslim as a slave, not the other way around. The non-Muslim was protected from Muslim slave-raids if he was a *jizya*-paying subject of an Islamic state, but outside of the borders of the Islamic world (and inside, during rebellions etc.), non-Muslims were fair game: Europe, Africa and India each lost millions of their people to the Islamic slave-trade. So, in the blame game which nowadays tries to force people into apologizing for the sins of their forefathers, Islamic slavery is the perfect counterweight to Hindu untouchability. And that, after all, is what this polemic is all about: the Hindu party trying to get the non-Hindu critics off its back by hurling a counter-criticism devastating enough to make them shut up. To drive the nail in the coffin of Islam's moral superiority claim even deeper, it has been shown that unlike Hinduism, Islam cannot even boast of having

---

[623]Indeed, Ayatollah Khomeini was closer to the truth when he explained that Mohammed, the Meccan businessman, favoured free entreprise; which inevitably brings "inequality of outcome".

taken an initiative to abolish its most grossly unjust social institution, untouchability, i.e. slavery: Indian Islam had no Rammohun Roy, Dayananda Saraswati or Mahatma Gandhi.

Likewise, Hindu treatment of women may not meet feminist standards, but the record of Islam can be shown to be such as to prevent Muslims from attacking Hindus too loudly on that score. Regarding the position of women, Hindu society has undeniably evolved a lot more than Indian Muslim society, though this is less the doing of Hindu revivalists than of Nehruvian legal reforms and of non-ideological factors like urbanization and the greater relative and absolute size of the Hindu middle class.

At the ordinary polemical level of "My religion is better than yours", the attack on Hinduism's legitimacy with the weapon of "Islamic egalitarianism liberating the oppressed of Hindu society" has definitely been warded off, at least intellectually. However, schoolbooks and political agitators are bound to keep harping on this refuted myth for years to come, at least if the years between Ambedkar's relevant publication (1940) and the present writing are a valid indication. For now, the situation still is that Hinduism is judged far more harshly on its social record than Islam is or ever was.

As secularist commentator B.P.R. Vithal observes: "Hinduism is not unique in history in its achievements being those of a ruling elite. This has been true of every civilisation. But those civilisations managed, over time, to attract the loyalty of the large majority of their societies so that the narrow elitist origins were forgotten or forgiven, as a price to be justly paid for so magnificent a fruit. In Hinduism, however, the trend is the other way. More and more groups are getting alienated and even sins that are forgiven for others are not forgiven for Hinduism."[624] The Hindu revivalist argument surveyed in the preceding sections is bound to slowly remedy this condition.

[624]"B.P.R. Vithal on Future of Hinduism", *Muslim India*, June 1997, reproduced from *Times of India*, 19.4.1997.

Hindu nation, Hindu state

It is commonly said that the Hindutva movement wants to set up a Hindu state. This claim may be considered in the case of the HMS, RSS and VHP, who brandish the slogan *Hindû Râshtra*, though it remains to be seen whether that term is intended to be understood in its dictionary meaning of "Hindu state". The claim about working for a Hindu state is definitely misplaced in the case of most Hindu authors discussed here, and even for the BJP. They are all concerned with very specific issues (whether historical, political or religious) rather than with large schemes such as a "Hindu state". The less ambitious concept "Hindu nation" is slightly more widespread, but not uncontroversial either.

HINDU NATIONALISM: SRI AUROBINDO

Sri Aurobindo's *Uttarpara Speech*, first published in the weekly *Karmayogin*, June 1909, is a founding text of Hindu Nationalism. It was pronounced just after Aurobindo's release from prison, where he had been kept as an accomplice in a terrorist conspiracy. In this speech, he identifies the national struggle for Freedom with the struggle for the Hindu cause.

Prisoner Aurobindo sees the Light

The opening lines declare that its contents had been conceived in prison. Aurobindo first sends some thoughts to his fellow fighters for independence, some far away, some rotting in jail, some present at the meeting. He describes his impression of the atmosphere in the country which he got when coming out of jail: "When I went to jail, the whole country was alive with the cry of *Bande Mataram*, alive with the hope of a nation. ... When I came out of jail, I listened for that cry, but there was instead a silence."[1]

Yet, it had been "the Almighty Power of God which had raised that

[1]Sri Aurobindo: *Uttarpara Speech* (Pondicherry 1973 edition), p.2.

cry, that hope". If the enthusiasm for the anti-colonial struggle had faded, the reason must be that "it was the same Power which had sent down that silence ... so that the Nation might draw back for a moment and look into itself and know His will".[2]

Non-religious people would consider this God talk as a transparent rationalization of the disappointing fact that the Freedom Movement had lost its momentum. One of the tasks of a leader is to put all events including setbacks into a positive perspective, in order to give hope and courage to the rank-and-file. At any rate, Aurobindo's practical conclusion is rational enough: since the time does not seem right for action, it is just as well to use it for reflection.

Aurobindo explains that, just as Bipin Chandra Pal had testified earlier, his own reflections during his stay in prison had made him realize "God within us all, the Lord within the nation".[3] He had realized that he had to undertake the *sâdhana* (spiritual practice) prescribed in the Gita, viz. "to do work for Him without the demand for fruit, to renounce self-will" and to become "an instrument in His hands".[4] It is a typical story of a religious conversion, common in the biographies of religiously motivated persons, whether they went on to sacrifice themselves in charitable work or set out on campaigns of religious warfare, even persecution.

India in the service of Dharma

In the next breath, Aurobindo moves from his own mission to India's mission: "I realized what the Hindu religion meant. ... Other religions are preponderantly religions of faith and profession, but the Sanatan Dharma is life itself; it is a thing that has not so much to be believed as lived. This is the Dharma that for the salvation of humanity was cherished in the seclusion of this peninsula from of old. It is to give this religion that India is rising. She does not rise as other countries do, for self or when she is strong, to trample on the weak. She is rising to shed the eternal light entrusted to her over the world."[5]

---

[2]Aurobindo: *Uttarpara Speech*, p.2.

[3]Aurobindo: *Uttarpara Speech*, p.3. Similar sentiments may indeed be found in B.C. Pal's earlier as well as later speeches, e.g. in "Indian Nationalism: Hindu Standpoint" (1913).

[4]Aurobindo: *Uttarpara Speech*, p.5.

[5]Aurobindo: *Uttarpara Speech*, p.5.

So, Aurobindo attributes a universal mission to India, viz. as a beacon of Sanatana Dharma for all mankind: "When therefore it is said that India shall rise, it is the Sanatan Dharma that shall rise. ... It is for the Dharma and by the Dharma that India exists. To magnify the religion means to magnify the country."[6]

Aurobindo concludes his speech reaffirming its central message: "This Hindu nation was born with the Sanatan Dharma, with it it moves and with it it grows. When the Sanatan Dharma declines, then the nation declines, and if the Sanatan Dharma were capable of perishing, with the Sanatan Dharma it would perish. The Sanatan Dharma, that is nationalism. This is the message that I have to speak to you."[7]

What exactly is the relation between the "Hindu nation" and the *Sanâtana Dharma*? Unambiguously, it is that between a vehicle and its precious load, the vehicle being not more than the *ancilla* of the load entrusted to it: "Well, the protection of the religion, the protection and upraising before the world of the Hindu religion, that is the work before us. But what is the Hindu religion? What is this religion which we call Sanatan, eternal? It is the Hindu religion only because the Hindu nation has kept it, because it grew up in the seclusion of the sea and the Himalayas, because in this sacred and ancient land it was given as a charge to the Aryan race to preserve through the ages. But it is not circumscribed by the confines of a single country, it does not belong peculiarly and forever to a bounded part of the world."[8]

In other words: for Aurobindo, the important thing is the Sanatana Dharma, and Hindu society, or what he calls the "Hindu nation", is important only as the historical cradle and guardian of this Sanatana Dharma. The country India, in turn, is important only as the geographical setting of the civilization which gives expression to the Sanatana Dharma. In later expositions of Hindu nationalism this unequal relation between the servant (Hindu society, the country India) and his allotted task (keeping and spreading Sanatana Dharma) is blurred or even inverted. Sangh Parivar ideologues have removed Sanatana Dharma from the central position and replaced it with the country India, reducing Hindu nationalism in various degrees to a purely territorial nationalism.

---

[6]Aurobindo: *Uttarpara Speech*, p.12.
[7]Aurobindo: *Uttarpara Speech*, p.14.
[8]Aurobindo: *Uttarpara Speech*, p.13.

Universal character of Dharma

Aurobindo considers the link between India and Hinduism as a product of history: "What is this religion which we call *Sanatan*, eternal? It is the Hindu religion, only because the Hindu nation has kept it, because in this Peninsula it grew up in the seclusion of the sea and the Himalayas, because in this sacred and ancient land it was given as a charge to the Aryan race to preserve through the ages."[9] (Note that "Aryan race" here means "Hindu people", neither more nor less)

India happens to be the religion's cradle, but the religion is none the less universal, somewhat like modern science is universal in spite of its undeniably European cradle: "But it is not circumscribed by the confines of a single country, it does not belong peculiarly and forever to a bounded part of the world. That which we call Hinduism is really the eternal religion, because it is the universal religion which embraces all others. If a religion is not universal, it cannot be eternal. A narrow religion, a sectarian religion, an exclusive religion can live only for a limited time and a limited purpose."[10]

Hinduism is the religion for the modern age because it is essentially a science, an applied science: "This is the one religion that can triumph over materialism by including and anticipating the discoveries of science and the speculations of philosophy. ... It is the one religion which enables us not only to understand and believe this truth but to realize it with every part of our being."[11]

The point is extremely important in the self-perception of modern literate Hinduism. In spite of the popularization of sentimental rhetoric of the "equal truth of all religions", the more lucid tendency generated by the Hindu confrontation with modernity divides the religions in two radically different categories: irrational belief systems which are moribund before the light of science, and a vision of life and spirit which is basically scientific and therefore, after shedding some accumulated deadwood, bound to live on and flourish.

In a way, this vision of a scientific religion is thoroughly unsecular: "It is the one religion which does not separate life in any smallest detail from religion."[12] European post-Christians, convinced of the benefits of the

[9]Aurobindo: *Uttarpara Speech*, p.13.
[10]Aurobindo: *Uttarpara Speech*, p.13.
[11]Aurobindo: *Uttarpara Speech*, p.13.
[12]Aurobindo: *Uttapara Speech*, p.14.

scientific worldview, had to separate religion from public life because the religion they knew (Christianity and to a lesser degree Judaism) was a revealed religion and intrinsically unscientific. Science being universal, the very idea of exclusive prophetic revelations supposedly sent down by God was necessarily in contradiction with it. Instead of religion, the Enlightenment philosophers wanted scientific insights to penetrate every aspect of life and society in the manner of religion's omnipresence until then. It is Aurobindo's point that Hinduism basically has the scientific spirit, so that unlike the revealed religions, it is perfectly compatible with the Enlightenment, and need not be removed from public life.

THE HINDU NATION

Asserting Hindu nationhood

Hindu nationalism by definition assumes the existence of a "Hindu nation". But among India-watchers, it is the dominant opinion that the "Hindu nation" is a myth. Thus, the original subtitle of Christophe Jaffrelot's bulky book *Les Nationalistes Hindous* is *Des Nationalistes en Quête d'une Nation: les Partis Nationalistes Hindous au XXme Siècle* (French: "Nationalists in search of a nation: the nationalist Hindu parties in the twentieth century").[13] The reason usually is not so much a pedantic objection to the use of the term "nation" in favour of some other term denoting collective identity, but a radical rejection of the existence of *any* kind of collective Hindu identity, let alone one sufficient for calling it a nation.

Hindu nationalists defy the dominant opinion, with which they are familiar enough, and insist on defining the Hindus as a nation. Thus, Abhas Chatterjee affirms: "We Hindus are a nation. ... We Hindus are not just a religious community like the Mohammedans and the Christians but a nation unto ourselves. The term 'Hindu' is the name of our nationality."[14]

There are many ways of defining Hinduism, and it is an open question whether anything is gained by defining it as a "nation". An obvious advantage is that no "essentialist" definition of *Hindu* is needed, no doctrine which encapsulates the common defining beliefs of all Hindus: whatever differences and contradictions may exist within the Hindu

[13]C. Jaffrelot: *Les Nationalistes Hindous*, especially p.15.

[14]A. Chatterjee: *Hindu Nation*, pp.2-3.

nation, these are no more an obstacle to Hindu unity than the existence of different political parties to the national unity of the English or the Americans.

This definition of Hindus as a nation is also faithful to the reality that one enters Hinduism, just like one's nation, by birth; or, marginally, by marrying into it or by getting "naturalized" (converted) at one's own request and after a period of adaptation. In contrast with Christianity and Islam, nations and Hinduism do not go around to attract new members, though they may sparingly and after due evaluation admit a few who apply for membership themselves.[15]

Essence of the Hindu nation

Conceiving the Hindus as a "nation" also allows for change: in contrast with Islam, of which the teachings have been fixed forever in the Quran and Sunna, any nation may evolve over time without seeing its identity questioned. Thus, today the taboo on beef may be an element of Hindu identity, which in the Vedic age it was not; yet, the Vedic Aryans constituted the same nation (or at least a part of it) which today we call Hindu. Nations, like human beings, may change their habits, and need not remain "the same" in characteristics. At least, that would be a common-sense implication, but some Hindutva ideologues reject this purely historical view of the identity of nations.

Deendayal Upadhyaya assumes a Herderian essentialist view of the Hindu nation, which "has an innate nature, which is inborn, and is not the result of historical circumstances".[16] This genius (*chiti*) or soul of the nation remains forever the same, unaffected by historical experiences:

---

[15]The counter-example of the travelling Swamis seeking "converts" in the West (at any rate a very recent innovation), is not valid in the case of most of them, first because the initiative and finances to get them to the West mostly come from their Western followers, and secondly because they insist that their Western pupils need not convert, merely practise the yoga techniques which they have learnt. See e.g. Sri Yukteswar: *The Holy Science*, and Swami Yogananda: *Autobiography of a Yogi*, famous examples of yogic teachings embedded in an "equal truth of all religions" philosophy.

[16]Upadhyaya: *Integral Humanism*, p.41. Perhaps the expression "Herderian", practically a term of abuse in the dominant anti-nationalist discourse, does injustice to Johann Gottfried Herder (1744-1803) who was a humanist at heart, a believer in human freedom and progress. His alleged unforgivable sin is that in his *Ideas on the Philosophy of the History of Mankind*, he also emphasized the specificity of cultures as stages in the organic growth of man from the chains of nature to full humanity. This emphasis on diversity is suspect in the eyes of champions of the homogeneity of mankind, as a threat to equality. See also J. Hutchinson and A.D. Smith, eds.: *Nationalism*, pp.104-07.

"Culture does include all those things which, by the association, endeavours and the history of the society, have come to be held as good and commendable, but these are not added on to *chiti*."[17]

One might agree that certain collective traits of a nation or culture are persistent, are longer-lasting than the individual lives of its members, but it is a different matter to say that they can *never* be affected by historical experience. One can uphold the identical continuity of a culture as an ideal (in tribal and other pre-modern societies, upholding the legacy of the ancestors is often the basis of an entire code of behaviour), but it is most certainly not a natural given; unless one accepts the Herderian notion of God-given national identities having an ontological status comparable to Plato's inborn, eternal ideas.

It seems that this notion of *chiti* unnecessarily complicates matters. Instead of saying that the Hindu culture and value system (which Upadhyaya conceptualizes as "integral humanism", discussed below) are a collective heritage entrusted to the Hindu nation, which it must (as a task, not as an automatism) cherish, cultivate and pass on, Upadhyaya concretizes this effort-based cultural continuity into an emanation of some abstruse "genius". This ought to be the object of a serious debate within the Hindutva movement, but unfortunately, the movement has not yet developed much of a debating culture.

However, in practice this *chiti* concept is not that important; it is rather just a figure of speech, not of much political consequence. RSS thought is not a closely structured edifice in which every element has necessary logical implications. Upadhyaya commentator C.P. Bhishikar simply equates India's *chiti* with *dharma*, so that it merely amounts to saying that India's vocation is to uphold *Sanâtana Dharma*. And that is what we heard before from Swami Vivekananda ("Remember, the centre of our national life is not politics or economy but Dharma")[18] and from Sri Aurobindo, to whose *Uttarpara Speech* Bhishikar explicitly refers, quoting with approval:

"Our nationalism is not mere politics; it is an act of faith, it is worship. *Sanâtana Dharma* is our nationalism. Hindu Rashtra was born along with Sanatana Dharma. ... Sanatana Dharma is our nationhood."[19] Where he quotes "Hindu Rashtra", my copy of the *Uttarpara Speech* gives "Hindu

---

[17]D. Upadhyaya: *Integral Humanism*, p.41.

[18]Quoted e.g. by H.V. Seshadri: *Universal Spirit of Hindu Nationalism*, p.2.

[19]C.P. Bhishikar: *Pandit Deendayal Upadhyaya, Ideology and Perception*, vol.5, *Concept of the Rashtra*, p.98, quoting the closing para of Aurobindo's *Uttarpara Speech*.

nation". So, a nation in the service of a religion or civilization. This formula has given strength or identity to other nations before, mostly in confrontation with unbelievers.[20] But here, apparently, no confrontation is intended: the shining light of Sanatana Dharma will benefit the whole world.

And Bhishikar rewords: "Right from the time of Maharshi Vyasa till today, this *Dharma* principle has remained unbroken. ... The life-force of Bharat is in *dharma*. Brutal attacks can never annihilate Bharat. It can die only if it deviates from the path of *dharma*."[21] The idea that a nation can only come to harm if it becomes untrue to its religious vocation is familiar in the Bible, where the Prophets link Israel's past or impending defeats to its straying from the Covenant with Jahweh. It is also the rationale behind the *Tablîgh* movement and other Islamic Revivalist movements: the defeat of Islam in the eighteenth and nineteenth centuries was due to lack of zeal for Islam, so religious renewal will lead to divine favour and new victories.[22]

So here, we do not have a supernatural *chiti* as a purely inborn and inherent genius, but a contingent civilizational treasure which can expand but also diminish and even disappear: "Our nation without *dharma* will be like a mere corpse whose spirit has left the body."[23] And a corpse disintegrates: about this negative prognosis at least, all Hindu revivalists, whether "nationalist" or not, are in agreement,—that India will lose whatever unity it has if it ceases to be predominantly Hindu.

Hinduism as India's only unifier

The first argument against the notion of "Hindu nation" is always that this so-called nation is highly fragmented, and that its constituent parts have a much better claim to be called "nation". Thus, Prakash Ambedkar,

---

[20]Thus, *Gestà Dei per Francos*, "The Acts of God are performed through the Franks/French" (Middle Ages) referring to their role in the christianization of the Germanic tribes and in the Crusades; or *Alles voor Vlaanderen, Vlaanderen voor Kristus*, "Everything for Flanders, Flanders for Christ" (interbellum), related to Flanders' position as a Catholic frontline against Protestant Holland and Masonic-secular France.

[21]C.P. Bhishikar: *Concept of the Rashtra*, p.98.

[22]E.g. "The more one humbles oneself before the Lord and bears the hardship in this path, the more one is entitled to divine succour", according to Tabligh preacher Maulana Ilyas in the 1920s, quoted by Wahiduddin Khan: *Tabligh Movement*, p.15. Wahiduddin traces the doctrine to the Quran (24:55/54): "Allah has promised those of you who believe and do good works to make them masters in the land", quoted in *op.cit.*, p.20.

[23]C.P. Bhishikar: *Concept of the Rashtra*, p.98.

grandson and political successor of Bhimrao Ambedkar, says: "Every caste is a nation."[24]

It so happens that the word *jâti*, "caste", is the exact etymological counterpart of Latin *gens/gentis*, "clan", (from Proto-Indo-European *gn-ti-*) and is also related to Latin *natio* (<*gnatio*); without attaching too much importance to this etymological coincidence, is it not a strong hint that the castes are far better candidates for the status of "nation"? At the same time, the Hindus are also divided in many language communities, usually the unit of nation-building in Europe's nationalist nineteenth century. Should we not rather speak of Bengali nationalism (as the Communists sometimes do),[25] of Keralite nationalism, etc.?

Linguistic identities and caste identities are no doubt real. In fact I will grant them more reality than Benedict Anderson is willing to concede to the "nation", which he labels as an "imagined community".[26] Speaking the same language (even in non-standard but mutually intelligible form) is a very real form of community,—try getting lost in a foreign country where you have no language in common with anyone.[27] That is why mono-lingual nation-states have on average been the most successful; most separatist movements in Europe emanate from linguistic minorities. Similarly, religion constitutes real community, because the same rituals, the same broad assumptions about life, the same code of behaviour already constitute a lot of common ground between people, they create a real basis of mutual trust.

Caste identity is real, linguistic identity is real, and religious identity is also real; but the point is that one collective identity does not exclude another. Most collective identities are subdivided into smaller collective identities, some of them even more binding, starting with the family ties.

---

[24]Prakash Ambedkar: "Every caste is a nation", *Illustrated Weekly of India*, 20.4.1991.

[25]Bas Heijne, in the Rotterdam daily *NRC Handelsblad* (20.3.1993) quotes CPM office bearers Jyoti Basu and Ashok Mitra as threatening to declare Bengal independent in case the BJP comes to power; this would only be the implementation of a long-held position. However, by 1998 the CPM had lost so much of its vigour that it didn't carry out the threat.

[26]B. Anderson: *Imagined Communities*, 1983, the source of inspiration for Romila Thapar: "Imagined Religious Communities? Ancient History and the Modern Search for a Hindu Identity", *Modern Asian Studies*, Cambridge 1989, pp.209-39.

[27]B. Anderson readily concedes the role of (standardized) language in nation-building in nineteenth-century Europe and postcolonial Third World countries: *Imagined Communities*, pp.36-46, also reproduced in J. Hutchinson and A.D. Smith: *Nationalism*, in the Oxford Reader series.

Moreover, if the over-arching "national" identity were not to exist, it might still be possible to foster such an identity (as the nineteenth-century unifiers of Italy and of Germany did). Indeed, that precisely was the Nehruvian project: to "make India" out of a diverse conglomerate of separate communities.[28] Those Hindu nationalists who like to attack Nehru have to concede that some of the threats to the nation's unity which have raised their heads in recent years, particularly casteism, were unthinkable under Nehru: he and his ruling faction considered the cultivation of sub-national (except class) identities "reactionary", hence also his initial opposition to linguistic states.

But most Hindu revivalists insist that a pan-Hindu collective identity has been in existence for millennia. Thus, Shrikant Talageri affirms an ancient "clear consciousness that India was culturally one, and distinct from all other nations—a consciousness of a special Indian religio-political identity. This was manifested in the innumerable Hindu pilgrim-centres dotting the whole of India from north to south and east to west; in the consciousness of the whole of India being a 'holy land' (a *deva-nirmita bhûmi*); and in the regular pilgrimages by Hindus from one corner of India to the other (regardless of the changing borders of the various kingdoms). No Hindu on pilgrimage in another part of India ever felt conscious of being in a foreign place."[29]

This tradition of India-wide pilgrimages is very ancient: "The *Mahâbhârata* in its *Tîrthayâtra* section of the *Vanaparva*, gives details of the pilgrimage undertaken by the Pândavas to numerous sacred mountains, rivers, lakes and shrines all over India."[30] If there can be legitimate doubts about what interpolations have been made before and at the time of the *Mahabharata's* final editing, there can at least be no doubt that it took place well before the Muslim period, not to speak of Queen Victoria and Jawaharlal Nehru, who "made India".

The pilgrimage cycles (e.g. that of the twelve Shaiva *jyotirlingas*) cover every corner of India.[31] Talageri: "These Hindu pilgrim-centres range from Kailash and Mansarovar in the north to Rameshwaram in the south; and from Hinglaj in the west (in Sindh) to Parsuram Kund (in Arunachal Pradesh) in the east. The 'seven holy cities' of Hinduism include Kanchipuram in the south, Dwarka in the west and Ujjain in

[28]See M.J. Akbar: *Nehru, the Making of India.*

[29]S. Talageri: *Aryan Invasion Theory and Indian Nationalism*, pp.14-15.

[30]S. Talageri: *Indian Nationalism*, p.15.

[31]A survey of India's sacred sites is given in J.G. Sharma: *Punya-bhoomi Bharat.*

central India. ... This concept of India as a holy land has persisted ... down the ages. More than a thousand years ago, Adi Shankaracharya, who was born in Kerala, established his four *matha*s in Badrinath in the north (U.P.), Puri in the east (Orissa), Dwarka in the west (Gujarat), and Shringeri in the south (Karnataka)."[32]

Even some traditions claimed as non-Hindu pay allegiance to India as their holy land: "Jainism originated in the north-east (in Bihar), but the majority of its followers are found in western states (Rajasthan, Gujarat, Maharashtra), and the most famous statues of Gomateshawara are found in the south. Guru Nanak was born in Punjab, but throughout his writings, he speaks of Hindustan, not of Punjab. Guru Govind Singh appointed five disciples, calling them *panj pyara*s, and entrusting them with the task of ensuring that Hindu Dharma prevailed everywhere. These disciples were, respectively, from Punjab and Delhi in the north, Gujarat in the west, Orissa in the east, and Karnataka in the south. The four Takhts of Sikhism are at Nankana Sahib (Punjab now in Pakistan), Amritsar (Punjab), Patna (Bihar) and Nanded (Maharashtra)."[33]

This argument (of which we shall see more varieties) is hard to refute: there is an ancient distinction between the whole of India, which had all the Hindu places of pilgrimage, and the non-Indian outside world, which had none. It is a different matter that Hindu traders who were abroad anyway would do their devotions at foreign shrines (e.g. the pre-Islamic *Ka'ba* in Mecca); no Hindu scripture ever required Hindus to make pilgrimages abroad to earn religious merit. For Hinduism, India was big enough.

Ancient fostering of Indian unity

V.S. Agrawala, the famous art historian at Banaras Hindu University, draws attention to the *Prthivî-Sûkta* ("Earth hymn") of the Atharva-Veda, which declares the Motherland (*Mâtâbhûmi*) to be the Supreme Goddess, "bearing on her bosom peoples with many languages and religions".[34] He comments: "It is a frank and bold recognition of the diversity of languages,

---

[32]S. Talageri: *Indian Nationalism*, p.15. The exact genesis stories of these Mathas are controversial, but they are at any rate quite old.

[33]S. Talageri: *Indian Nationalism*, p.15.

[34]Atharva-Veda 12:1:45. Religion is used as the (ever inaccurate) translation of *dharma*, a term which may be used as an uncountable ("the essence of the Hindu nation is *dharma*") but also as a countable noun: Hinduism consists of many *dharma*s, i.e. the distinct traditions of each caste and sect.

of religions and of races, the three factors of *Jana*, *Bhâshâ* and *Dharma* in the making of the Indian people."[35] But even if the reading "Motherland" is conceded (could not the geographically limitless "Mother Earth" be meant?), this gives no positive indication of a conscious sense of pan-Indian national unity yet, at least not as long as the borders of this motherland have not been explicitated.

In V.S. Agrawala's opinion, the most far-sighted people then proceeded to instil a consciousness of national unity (which presupposes that they themselves already had such consciousness) by means of several deliberate techniques: "The leaders of thought were required to forge a unity out of this diversity. For this they adopted the following techniques which became the universal pattern of life in India through the ages:"[36]

"1. Worship of the Motherland. In the Atharvaveda itself this attitude is clearly stated in the words: *Mâtâ bhûmih putro aham prthivyâh* (12:1:12), 'The Earth is the Mother, I am her Son'. The concept of the Bhûmi as Devata is common to the Arya, Dravida, Kirata and Nishada cultures of India."[37] Remark that the "Mother Earth" glorified in this verse is not described as exactly coinciding with the geographical unit known as India, its confines are left unspecified. Nor is it common to exalt her as supreme deity; in that respect, the quoted verse is the exception, not the rule.

"2. Holiness of the Motherland. ... India's religious leaders preached the doctrine of apotheosis of the Motherland by distributing the holy places throughout the length and breadth of the country." Again, a deliberate strategy is imputed where a natural process sufficiently explains the pan-Indian distribution of sacred places. By the time Shankara (*c.* AD 800)[38] set up his four *mathas* in the geographical corners of India,

---

[35]V.S. Agrawala: *India—a Nation*, p.2.

[36]V.S. Agrawala: *India—a Nation*, pp.2-3.

[37]V.S. Agrawala: *India—a Nation*, p.3. At the time of his writing, *Kirâta* and *Ṇishâda* were often understood to mean "Tibeto-Burmese", "Austro-Asiatic", the two main language groups in India after Indo-Aryan and Dravidian; but this identification is flimsy. Ethnic terms were often unrelated to language, e.g. the "Turanian" enemies of the sedentary Iranians were not the Turks (until the Turkish expansion in the early Christian era) but fellow Iranians who had a more barbaric and nomadic lifestyle, broadly known *pars pro toto* as the Scythians.

[38]Among Hindus, the date of Shankara is controversial; some date him to *c.* 500 BC. In this case, I wholeheartedly support the conventional date established by indologists, among other reasons because his choice of Dwarka for his Western *matha*, and not *Hinglaj* (west of the Indus) as intended, fits neatly with the fact that the latter area had passed under Muslim control in the early eighth century.

this was of course deliberate, but the ancient flowering of places of worship into traditional "sacred places" was more likely a spontaneous behaviour of "Hindus" scattered over the Indian territory, who set up local shrines without any grand design.

"3. Geographical consciousness. ... the unity of the land was frequently emphasized and this entered the consciousness of the people, the poets, dramatists and religious teachers repeatedly declaring it."

"4. Glorification of the country. ... Several Bhârata-Prashastis, or Hymns of Glory to the Country, occur in Puranic and epic literature." Among three examples given, consider this one: "Bhârata is the most excellent continent in the whole world. Who can speak the full glory of Bhârata? What man under the sky can do is difficult even for the gods. Bhârata is verily Karma-bhûmi, a Moksha-kshetra, and the giver of both Bhakti and Mukti. In the soil of Bhârata there are seeds of all great ideals of life."[39] This definitely is an expression of a national consciousness, though it is not clear whether *"Bhârata"* refers to the whole of *Bhâratvarsha*, i.e. the subcontinent. A modern example of a hymn glorifying the country is the RSS litany *Bhârata Ekâtmatâ Stotra*.[40]

"5. Institution of Tîrtha-Yâtra. (...) Each individual was expected to travel in all the four directions to the holy centres and places of pilgrimage and to cultivate the spirit of understanding and sympathy towards all peoples. ... In this quest of a vision of the country, parochial boundaries melted away. ... The demonstration of this unity is patent even today in the Kumbha [Mela] and other big fairs drawing at one place huge masses of population."[41]

"6. Festivals and feasts." Some of these have a pan-Indian character (Diwali, Holi), but here again, it is hard to see how they could have been conceived as techniques for fostering national unity. They simply spread along with the myths to which they give expression (e.g. Vijayadashami celebrating Rama's victory over Ravana), and some are but Indian variations on truly universal festivals, e.g. Holi with its chaotic and irreverent behaviour is a typical spring festival.

---

[39]V.S. Agrawala: *India—a Nation*, p.5.

[40]Given and discussed in Harishchandra Barthwal: *The Integral Spirit of Bharat: an Eulogy. Bhârata Ekâtmatâ Stotra—An Explanation.*

[41]Reference is to the Kumbha-Mela, held in Prayag when Jupiter is in sidereal Taurus, every twelve years. The 1989 Kumbha Mela was the greatest human gathering in world history, bringing together over 40 million people, surpassed only by the 2001 Kumbha Mela, etc.

"7. Gods and goddesses. All gods and goddesses of diverse peoples and localities were accepted and given due place in the Hindu pantheon.... the overriding belief was that all the gods and goddesses are aspects of manifestations of one Deity." This sounds like a projection of modern Arya Samaj-type reinterpretations of Hindu polytheism as crypto-monotheistic on to hoary tradition, but: "This is the doctrine called *Vibhûti-yoga* in the Gita in which the Tree, River, Ocean, Animals, Sun, Moon and many others are accepted as deities. The earliest demonstration of this doctrine is to be found in the Shatarudriya Litany of the Yajurveda, which offers the god Rudra as the unifying spirit of a number of local and tribal divinities."[42]

Reference is to *Bhagavad-Gîtâ* 10, which concludes (10:41): "Whatever object is verily endowed with majesty, possessed of prosperity, or is energetic, you know for certain each of them as having a part of My power as its source." This is the basic idea of a theory of *mûrti-pûjâ*: though the Divine Person is omnipresent, one doesn't take just any object as a representation of the divine; rather, one takes what is naturally impressive (sun, lightning etc.) or artificially evocative (a well-made image). In this approach, nature-based deities can be conceived as *archanâvatâra*, "incarnation for the purpose of worship", of a more abstractly conceived God, thus incorporating more primitive types of religion into the philosophically more sophisticated and abstract Vedic-Upanishadic tradition.

"8. A common corpus of religious literature for all people to be accepted according to one's own choice." This downplays the relative exclusivism with which scriptures were guarded in secrecy, as in the case of the "esoteric" Tantras, or kept as a caste privilege, as in the case of the Vedas themselves. Then again, many philosophical and religious ideas were popularized through the medium of oral versions of the epics and other stories.

"9. The doctrine of tolerance, or as Ashoka called it, *Samvâya*, Mutual Concord." This is fine because it limits conflict, but it is not by itself a factor of *national* integration, just as secularism is not a factor of positive unity, merely a negative neutrality.

"10. One Sacred Language. From the diversity of speech one sacred language, namely Sanskrit, was accepted. Sanskrit is the Wish-fulfilling Mother of Indian culture." Sanskrit was an elite language, by no means

[42]V.S. Agrawala: *India—a Nation*, p.6.

spoken by the entire Indian population at any time. On the other hand, national unification (and politics in general) has nearly always and everywhere been an elite affair.

"11. A common pattern of domestic Samskâras for regulating the life of each individual was accepted of which three are most important: relating to birth, marriage and death."[43]

"12. *Sadâchâra*, Code of Ethical Conduct, prescribed for everyone." This needs clarification: what Indian ethical code is prescribed for "everyone"? There are lists of virtues in many Hindu scriptures, many of them expressly not applying to everyone, only to the three upper castes, or only to the members of a particular sect.[44] *Sadâchâra*, "good conduct", is listed as one of the five commandments of the Shaiva Lingayat sect, in the effective sense of: "work for one's livelihood, be righteous and help others".[45] This is commendable, but its contribution to nation-building is unclear. Perhaps more specific nation-wide common rules are meant, e.g. the taboo on cow-slaughter.

"13. Assimilative Genius and Cultural Synthesis. ... Religious anthropology has laid bare in a most surprising manner the extent of Austric borrowings in Brahmanical tradition. Even the followers of the higher philosophic way subscribed to a religion in which the primitive deities of the earth and the forest freely mingled with the gods of higher religion."

A pivotal role was played in this process by *Vyâsa*, "compiler", traditionally the compiler of the Vedas and of the *Mahâbhârata*: "*Vyâsa* stands alone as the symbol of a mighty cultural synthesis. He compiled the orthodox Vedic hymns in the *Trayî* Collection on the one hand, and admitted to an equal sanctity the Austric beliefs in the compilation of the Atharva-Veda, also reckoned as the fourth Veda. ... The *Gîtâ* was a document par excellence of this synthesis of philosophical rationalism with a proletarian belief in manifold gods and godlings."[46]

---

[43]V.S. Agrawala: *India—a Nation*, p.7.

[44]E.g. the ten Dharmic virtues in *Manu Smriti* 6:91-92, prescribed only for the Twice-Born. It is a different matter that *today*, Hindu modernists are popularizing these as a one-size-fits-all Hindu alternative to the Judeo-Christian Ten Commandments.

[45]J. Grimes: *Concise Dictionary of Indian Philosophy*, p.288.

[46]V.S. Agrawala: *India—a Nation*, p.8. That the Atharva-Veda is of Austro-Asiatic ("Austric" or Munda) provenance is a theory, not an established fact; but it is generally accepted that the AV incorporates non-Vedic practices, particularly a shamanic type of sorcery.

Through progressive synthesis, Hinduism reached its classical theistic-Puranic form: "The foreigners also who came to India from the Maurya period to the time of Harsha reached the heart of Indian culture through the doorway of Bhakti, and thus became true children of the soil. ... Puranic Hinduism represents the type of culture which was the product of a synthesis between the various social and religious groups."[47] This way, Hinduism became the truly national religion of India, the stream to which all tributaries had literally contributed.

The problem with this idyllic picture is that it seems oblivious of the role of conflict and war in human history. Was there less of it in Indian history? Or is it true that religion and war were neatly separated? The questions are not meant as purely rhetorical. The reply by V.S. Agarwala and other Hindu patriots would probably be that warfare, like the division of India into separate and sometimes hostile kingdoms, did not affect the basic cultural unity of India. If at some point certain parts of India were brought into the domain of Vedic civilization by conquest (e.g. Kerala by the mythical Parashurama), this painful beginning would still not nullify the effective cultural integration of that area into the Hindu commonwealth in subsequent centuries, so that whatever the initial scenario, the integration of every part of India into a cultural continuum is at any rate an accomplished fact twenty centuries or so.

And while such violent scenarios cannot altogether be excluded, there is ample evidence that important regions have voluntarily and by their own initiative joined the Vedic civilization, e.g. Bengali and Tamil (and Southeast-Asian) kings invited Brahmin clans to come and settle in their kingdoms to establish the Vedic tradition and add to the lustre of their dynasties. That cannot be said of, say, the Roman Empire, which expanded by purely military means.

Manu's definition of India

An ancient testimony to national consciousness is found in the *Mânava-dharma-shâstra*, which prescribes that the twice-born should make every effort to settle in the country "where the black antelope ranges by nature".[48] This is a very direct way of describing India: the black antelope

---

[47]V.S. Agrawala: *India—a Nation*, p.8.

[48]*Manu Smriti* 2:23. *Dwija* or "twice-born" is he who has received the Vedic initiation, traditionally confined to the three upper *varnas*.

is (or at least, was) found in nearly every corner of India, while the climate of neighbouring Iran, Central Asia or Tibet is less hospitable to this species. This "definition" of India is based on India's natural boundaries, which have turned India into a very specific biotope for a very specific range of animal species.

However, the reason why Manu considers this country preferable, is cultural: it is "most fit for performing sacrifices", while "beyond it is the land of the barbarians", viz. Iran, Central Asia etc., where conditions are less favourable for performing Vedic sacrifices from barbarian disrespect.[49] Hence the custom of purifying oneself after having sojourned in the *Mlechchhadesh*, the "barbarian country".

Manu's horizon did not yet reach beyond the Vindhya mountains to South India, covering only *Aryâvarta* or North India, "from the eastern sea to the western sea, between the two mountains" (Himalaya and Vindhya).[50] Of this northern India, the better part is *Madhyadesh*, from Prayag to "where the Saraswati disappears" (in the Rajasthan desert), and within that, the best parts are *Brahmâvarta*, the Vedic cradle on the Saraswati banks, and *Brahmarshidesh*, the area around the Yamuna where the *Mahabharata* events took place. Outside Madhyadesh, mores are cruder, and even before crossing the Indus to the North-West, one comes across *Mlechchha*s, "people of corrupt speech" (the same semantic development underlies Greek *barbaroi*), people who have fallen from the Aryan Way.[51] One should avoid getting polluted in these border zones and in the foreign countries, where Aryan norms are not followed.

Whatever one may think of these strictures, they prove that Manu (or the editors of the book named after him) had a definite culture-based concept of "Indian" (regardless of the changing state boundaries) and "foreign". A consciousness of belonging to one Hindu culture, of which the borders to the North, East and West were to remain fixed for millennia, already existed in the time of the final editing of the *Mânava-dharma-*

---

[49] *Manu-Smriti* 2:23.

[50] *Manu-Smriti* 2:22.

[51] In his less than accurate construction of history, Manu (10:43-45) includes the Greeks, Scythians, Persians and Chinese among those who "by failing to perform rituals" have lost caste, and now count as aliens (*dasyu*), "whether they speak Mlechchha or Arya languages". The passage shows none the less that Manu's criterion is not language, not race, not geographical provenance, but *culture*, viz. performing the Vedic sacrifices.

shâstra.[52] This was well before Queen Victoria "first united India under one sceptre", let alone before Nehru "made India".

India as Chakravarti-kshetra

Within the civilizational area recognized as home, the ancients kept alive an ideal of political unification. Shrikant Talageri sums up the typical Hindu Revivalist view: "This urge for the entire nation to be one kingdom was always there in the national consciousness since ancient times. ... The whole of India was considered to be a *chakravarti-kshetra*, and the aim of every king was to bring the whole of India into one kingdom (under himself, of course); and there was a well-established, and well-respected, code of conduct which governed this whole process. ... The concept of Bharatavarsha as one nation was the basic inspiration behind this; hence these kings never felt the need or desire to step beyond the borders of India into foreign lands to enlarge their kingdoms."[53]

The *Mahâbhârata* twice gives a list of Chakravartins, "those who turn the wheel", universal rulers (viz. of Bharatvarsha). Up to the Mahabharata age, sixteen rulers are thought to have ruled the entire Aryan country, including Rama and Nahusha, the ancestor of the "five peoples", one of them being the Puru tribe whose sages composed the Vedic hymns.[54] For the Vedic age, seven *Chakravarti*s are mentioned, starting with the Puru king Bharata after whom India/*Bhârat* is named, and the very concept of "universal rulership" itself is defined and glorified in the *Mahâbhârata.*[55]

According to Sita Ram Goel, the Chakravarti's empire was ideally not "a monolithic and militarised state", on the contrary: "Our concept of *sâmrâjya* was derived from *Sanâtana Dharma* and fostered a true federation of many *janapada*s enjoying *swarâjya*, local autonomy, on the basis of *swadharma*, local tradition and culture."[56]

---

[52]I leave the question of the date of *Manu-Smrti* undecided, though it must have been finalized by the early Gupta period (fourth century) at the latest. The point is that it carries along many older passages, some of them adapted, some of them unchanged. In this case, the recognition of the Vindhya mountains as a southern border is definitely anachronistic, for the Maurya empire in the fourth century BC already extended down to Karnataka, and Brahminical culture with it.

[53]S. Talageri: *Indian Nationalism*, p.14.

[54]*Mahâbhârata, Shântiparva* 29.

[55]Discussed in I. Armelin: *Le roi détenteur de la roue solaire en révolution (cakravartin)*, esp. pp.8-10.

[56]S.R. Goel: *Story of Islamic Imperialism*, p.129.

By the time of Kautilya, a contemporary of Chandragupta Maurya (fourth century BC), the *Chakravarti-kshetra* includes the whole subcontinent: "The area extending from the Himalayas in the north to the sea and a thousand yojanas wide from east to west is the area of operation of the King-Emperor."[57] Chandragupta Maurya, Ashoka and Samudragupta are fully historical rulers who approached the ideal of uniting the whole subcontinent, as did the Moghuls (though Queen Victoria came closest). There aren't many countries which had a sense of national unity 23 centuries ago on the basis of the same boundaries which (disregarding the Partition) are valid today.

The translator comments: "Territories beyond the subcontinent are not included, probably for the reason that the conqueror is expected to establish in the conquered territories a social order based on the Arya's *dharma*, *varna* and *âshrama* system. Kautilya perhaps considered the establishment of such a social order outside the limits of India impractical or even undesirable."[58] The chakravarti should only seek to control those territories in which the Vedic culture was established, where *yajna*s (Vedic sacrifices) were performed and the *varnâshramadharma* (system of duties differentiated for the four classes and age groups) was observed.

It is a remarkable fact of Indian history that all rulers have observed this limitation. As a recent BJP manifesto proudly proclaims: "Here, a nation, which Megasthenes noted 'never invaded others and was never invaded', existed long before the ideas of civilization evolved elsewhere."[59] While rulers from West Asia have invaded India, Hindu rulers never invaded Iran or Mesopotamia, nor Tibet or China or Myanmar.

Does India exist?

The secularist scepticism vis-à-vis the "Hindu nation" shades over into a similar scepticism vis-à-vis the "Indian nation", which the British colonizers considered as equally a figment of the imagination or a

---

[57]Kautilya: *Arthashâstra* 9:1:17, in the Penguin translation of L.N. Rangarajan, p.628. A *yojana*, according to M. Monier-Williams (*Sanskrit-English Dictionary*, p.858) has been defined as measures of distance ranging from 5/2 to 9 English miles, or about 4 to 14 km; which means that Kautilya overestimated the breadth of India, but only slightly.

[58]Kautilya's *Arthashâstra* translated by L.N. Rangarajan, p.543.

[59]BJP: *Election Manifesto 1998*, p.1; reference is to Arrian's paraphrase of Megasthenes' testimony, see R.C. Majumdar: *The Classical Accounts of India*, p.218.

misapplication of a purely geographical concept. As Winston Churchill once said: "India is a geographical term. It is no more a united nation than the Equator."[60] A recent book by C. Aloysius is titled *Nationalism without a Nation in India*, self-described as a "hard-hitting critique of the nationalist movement", i.e. not the Hindutva but the Freedom Movement. Notice its prestigious publisher (Oxford University Press, Delhi 1997): its thesis is indeed the one espoused by India's academic and the world's Indological establishment.

Most tourist guide-books start by stating, with an air of profundity, that India is not really a country, but a plurality of countries or nations, a *subcontinent*,—a term which is not so innocent from the viewpoint of Indian unity. Among secularists, India may at best be called "a nation in the making", welded out of a conglomerate of diverse nations (properly so-called) by the British and by Nehru. This view is expressed in numerous platforms, like the title of M.J. Akbar's Nehru biography: *Nehru, the Making of India*. This denial of the existence of India as a national and cultural unit is one of the many points where today's anti-Hindu-Nationalist rhetoric is an exact copy of the Muslim League's and the CPI's anti-Indian-Nationalist rhetoric before 1947.[61]

Now, the Nehruvian establishment had no personal interest in seeing India fragmented. So, it had to justify the continued unity and integrity of India, but without reference to a pre-existent Indian nation. This led to the position (at least among liberal Nehruvians as opposed to Marxists)[62] that states and state borders are sacrosanct, regardless of whether they reflect ethnic, cultural, linguistic, or simply democratic realities. Thus, after the Baltic nations had democratically decided to declare their independence

---

[60]Quoted in *The Economist*, 12.12.1992.

[61]All the anti-Hindu allegations now common in secularist literature can be found in the Muslim League's *Pirpur Report* (1939) about the "atrocities" committed by the provincial Congress Governments against Muslims (e.g. "forcing" them to sing *Vande Mâtaram*); the targets of the Muslim League's allegations were not the Hindu nationalists, but Mahatma Gandhi and even Jawaharlal Nehru. The League's "two-nation theory" is being continued in the claim that India consists of "many nations".

[62]Marxists don't hold states and borders sacred and do not uphold the principle of India's unity and integrity. Some non-Marxist Nehruvians too, such as Kuldip Nayar, have written in defence of the Khalistani and Kashmiri secessionists, but most of them have taken the position that Nehru's creation of a united India is worth preserving and that by treating the separatist militants with kid gloves, they may be cajoled into loyalty to India.

from the Soviet Union, columnist Arvind Kala condemned their decisions: "The world realises that nations cannot be fragmented even though their boundaries were redrawn arbitrarily."[63] Against such secessionism, Kala advocated a brutally imperialistic position, including the use of force: hit the secessionists really hard, it will wear them out, cause infighting and defection among them, and ultimately liquidate their rebellion. And he notes with satisfaction that all "secessionists" who have been dealt with in this manner, like the Kurds and the Tibetans, have failed.

Arvind Kala and other liberals equate this repression in defence of artificial states and empires with the struggle for India's unity, on the premise that India too is but an artificial creation. The fact that they advocate strong repression against armed secessionism will be applauded by most Hindu nationalists, whose anger is aroused mostly by Human Rights activists campaigning against the brutal treatment which captured militants receive from the Indian Army and Police, but not against the brutal treatment which the same militants have meted out to Hindu citizens and to un-cooperative Sikhs or Muslims. Yet, from a Hindu nationalist viewpoint, Arvind Kala's position is superficial and symptom-oriented. If you don't convince the Sikhs that they have a solid reason to remain in India and to feel Indian, the defeat of Sikh separatism in 1992 would only prepare the ground for a more embittered Sikh separatism tomorrow. To people like Arun Shourie, India's unity should not be based on coercion, but on a heartfelt conviction that the constitutent parts of India belong together.

Meanwhile, the winds of change have made Nehruvian secularists reconsider the matter. In a more recent column, Arvind Kala explains why India is different: "India, however, stays intact for two reasons. One is India's democracy which has been the greatest unifying force in Indian society. The second reason that cements India is an ancient Hindu civilization which has come down without a break for at least 3.000 years."[64] Likewise, Amartya Sen admits: "Obviously, we could not expect to see, historically, a pre-existing 'Indian nation' in the modern sense, lying in wait to form a nation-state, but it is difficult to miss the social and cultural linkages and identities that could serve as the basis of one. The

[63]Arvind Kala: "The battle against secessionism", *Indian Express*, 10.7.1991.

[64]Arvind Kala: "What makes India remain intact", *Hindustan Times*, 25.12.1995.

cultural transmissions across the land have been swift and comprehensive for millennia, and the economic and social connections too close to be missed in understanding Indian history."[65]

Perhaps India was not a "nation" in the modern sense, but far more than most nations which are now members of the UNO, it had enough unity on which to base, come the age of the nation-state, a nation-state. As Aurobindo said: "The 'nation idea' India never had. By that I mean the political idea of the nation. It is a modern growth. But we *had* in India the cultural and spiritual idea of the nation."[66] The fact that this is also the view of ill-reputed groupings like the RSS does not detract from the correctness of this observation.

Arun Shourie on India's national unity

Arun Shourie surveys the genesis of the modern nation-states (Germany, Italy, Indonesia etc.)[67] and concludes that many well-established nations endowed with nation-states are of very recent date: "Our intellectuals' discouraging pronouncements about India being less than entitled to continue as one country spring from their ignorance about the rest of the world."[68] By contrast, India has had a sense of civilizational unity, if not a common national feeling, for at least two thousand years: "*Yes*, India is different. A moment's reflection will show that India's case is not at par with the ones we have been considering. For those instances are of the most recent times—those nations were 'imagined', those traditions were

---

[65]A. Sen: "The vision that worked", *Times Literary Supplement*, 8.8.1997.

[66]Aurobindo: *India's Rebirth*, p.173; emphasis in the original.

[67]About Germany and Italy, it could be argued that at least as geographical terms, they have existed for more than 2,000 years, and that their dialects were more or less mutually understandable even before modern language policy tried to standardize them. Indonesia does not even have that much of a prehistory: as Shourie argues, it had nothing like a linguistic unity, and even its link language was still in the process of creation when it was chosen as *Bahasa Indonesia* ("language of Indonesia"). None the less, Hindu nationalists usually express sympathy for Indonesia, because as a Muslim-majority country it has decreed legal equality between Hindus, Buddhists, Christians and Muslims, and it honours its Hindu heritage, e.g. in contrast with Malaysia it encourages performances of the *Ramayana*. Even Indonesia's occupation of East Timor has often been justified on the analogy with India's incorporation of Goa.

[68]A. Shourie: *Secular Agenda*, p.8, with reference to E.J. Hobsbawm: *Nations and Nationalism since 1870: Programme, Myth and Reality*, showing that neither language nor religion nor common history constitutes a credible identity basis of the immense majority of modern nation-states.

'invented' just a hundred or a hundred and fifty years ago. By contrast, India has been seen as one and its people have had a common way of life for thousands of years."[69]

To be sure, other countries like Egypt, Iraq or Greece also roughly coincide geographically with ancient states and civilizational units. But: "It is not just that its history is that old, as it is in the case of the Greeks, say. *It is a continuous history.* The way of life today—the people's beliefs and practices—can be traced directly and by a chain of unsevered links to what was taught and practised thousands of years ago. Indeed, the very wail of its denouncers—that we have not shed our past—testifies to the age and continuity of the tradition. The land, its mountains and rivers are venerated in the *Rig Veda*, in the *Atharva Veda* in the very way they are in Bankim's Vande Mataram or Tagore's Jana-Gana-Mana ... because it is seen as a karma-bhumi, because it has been the place where the greatest souls revered by the people have performed great deeds—of nobility, of valour—, where they have attained the deepest insights. The *Mahabharata* and the *Ramayana* describe warring states but *they are the epics of one people*."[70]

Language played a part in this early unification, even if the link language was only used by the elite (just as all processes of political or cultural unifications have been the doings of elite classes): "Adi Shankaracharya traverses the whole country. ... He engages others in learned duels in centres thousands of miles apart—no discussant has any difficulty in following the other. The debates are held in front of large numbers. No one has any difficulty in following the interlocutors—Sanskrit is used by all. ... The debates are conducted within the framework of texts which are not just known intimately in all parts of the land, they are regarded as authoritative all over."[71] The apt comparison here would be with the role of Latin in medieval Europe, which was one civilizational space, but not one nation, though it is now trying to forge a political unity too.

Apart from the already-mentioned pilgrimage cycles, Shourie cites another aspect of Hindu ritualism which testifies to a pan-Indian consciousness: "Only Namboodiris from Kerala are to be priests at Badrinath, those in the Pashupatinath temple at Kathmandu are always

---

[69]A. Shourie: *Secular Agenda*, p.9.

[70]A. Shourie: *Secular Agenda*, p.9; emphasis added.

[71]A. Shourie: *Secular Agenda*, pp.9-10.

from South Canara in Karnataka, those at Rameshwaram in the deep South are from Maharashtra. ... Every Diwali the sari for the idol of Amba at Kolhapur comes from the Lord at Tirupati. The *Sankalpa Mantra* with which every puja commends the prayers to the deities situates the *yajyaman* with reference to the salients and sacred rivers of the entire land."[72]

From hoary antiquity, the *Sankalpa* locates the Hindu worshipper in time and space, notably in *Bhâratvarsha* (India), in a decreasing scale of geographical regions down to the city or region where the ritual is performed. Unlike the national anthem with which many events in modern nation-states begin (replacing the pre-modern prayer), the *Sankalpa* does not give an absolute value to the Motherland, to the detriment of all smaller and greater circles of identity, but gives the Motherland its due place within a framework which also acknowledges higher and lower levels of belonging. Most importantly for the present discussion, the *Sankalpa* does evince an awareness of India as a coherent and well-defined entity.

Weaken Hinduism, dismember India

Considering the above, those who trace a national consciousness to at least the *Mahabharata*, and who describe it as strongly intertwined with what we now know as Hinduism, feel assured that they have a case. As Shrikant Talageri argues, white Kashmiris speak a Dardic Indo-European language, black Tamils speak a Dravidian language, and yellow Manipuris speak a Tibeto-Burman language, so all they have in common, and the only possible reason to unite them in one Republic, is Hinduism: "The people of Manipur and China belong to the Mongoloid race, while the people of Gujarat belong to the Caucasoid race. The people of Manipur and China both speak languages belonging to the Sino-Tibetan family, while the people of Gujarat speak a language belonging to the Indo-European family. What is it, then, which can be taken to bind Manipur more closely to Gujarat than to China?"[73]

Talageri seeks one of the possible answers through the empirical finding that when subgroups of the Indian population lose their attachment

---

[72]A. Shourie: *Secular Agenda*, p.14. *Sankalpa*: "resolve", a formula recited before a ritual, in which the *yajyaman* (performer of the ritual) locates himself in space, time, genealogy and the *jâti/gotra* order.

[73]S. Talageri: *Indian Nationalism*, p.11.

to Hinduism, they tend to develop anti-Indian separatism. Indeed, the simplest way to prove Aurobindo's equation "Hinduism = Indian nationalism", is by its logical contraposition: anti-national movements in India are invariably anti-Hindu. Thus, whether or not Guru Nanak's Sikhism is part of Hinduism, Khalistani Sikhism which fought for a political separation of "Khalistan" from India is at any rate explicitly anti-Hindu: it repudiates any identification of Sikhism with Hinduism, it emphasizes non-Hindu elements (and non-Hindu reinterpretations of Hindu elements) in Sikhism, and it has often singled out Hindus in its terror campaigns. Similarly, Mizo and Naga separatism is Christian, Pakistani separatism was and Kashmiri separatism is Muslim, Dravidian separatism in the 1950s was led by the anti-religious and anti-Brahmin movement *Dravida Kazhagam*.[74]

The contraposition argument starts with the fact that "certain parts had broken away in 1947. Why did those parts break away in 1947? And why are different parts trying to break away even now? The answer is simple. Those parts of India which broke away in 1947 had cut off their links with the religion, history and culture of India, and established links with the religion, history and culture of Arabia and West Asia."[75] The fact that anti-India political movements invariably turn out to be instruments of anti-Hindu ideologies, has a paradoxical implication. The anti-Hindu forces confirm the Hindu position which the official secularist line hotly denies: that India is essentially a Hindu country. Indeed, all separatist movements identify India as "Hindu" and give that as the reason why non-Hindus should seek a place for themselves outside the Indian Republic.

Hindu revivalists argue that Hinduism is the only thing which keeps India together, the only reason why people who are geographically so distant and linguistically and racially so different as, say, white Dardic-speaking Kashmiris and black Dravidian-speaking Malayalis, should live

---

[74]Newspaper stories about the Christian hand in North-eastern separatism are fairly frequent, e.g.: "Christian missionaries, either knowingly or unknowingly, are said to be funding the purchases [of weapons for Naga separatists]. American dollars are provided to set up churches in the north-east, although it is believed that most of these funds are syphoned off to buy arms and ammunition", according to Rabin Gupta: "Law of the jungle", *Sunday*, 7.11.1993. However, the opposite also happens, viz. guerrilla fighters who see the light and embrace Christian pacifism, e.g.: "Former insurgents trade in their guns for the Bible" in Mizoram, according to Ruben Banerjee: "Look who's preaching", *India Today*, 15.1.1993.

[75]S. Talageri: *Indian Nationalism*, p.11.

together under the roof of a single state. According to Shrikant Talageri, India can only have a stable and durable existence to the extent that the vast majority of its citizens continues to feel a certain affinity with and loyalty towards Sanatana Dharma: "The main point, however, is that this Hindu religious consciousness provides the only bond which has, from very ancient times, bound every part of India to every other part in a firm bond of unity and given to this country a distinct identity of its own; and at the same time prevented any part of India from being bound to any foreign land in a similar bond."[76]

So, Talageri considers it necessary to strengthen Hinduism as the ancient and profound basis of India's unity: "Denigrating, denying or diluting this bond, and advocating, instead, the bond of a 'nation' born in 1947 with a 'composite' national identity consisting of an amalgam of the religions, cultures and histories of Arabia/West Asia, Palestine/Europe and India is nothing but a sinister conspiracy for the disintegration of India. The concept that India was not one nation in the past is, in fact, the formula for seeing to it that India ceases to be one nation in the future."[77] This, then, is the fundamental rationale of the otherwise odd-looking concept of "Hindu nationalism".

I have two remarks to Talageri's well-argued position. When people speak of "composite culture", there is no need to impute a disintegrationist design to them, a "sinister conspiracy for the disintegration of India". Nehru was the great propounder of the "composite culture" concept, giving Islam and Christianity equal rights on India along with Hinduism. Yet, Nehru stood for national unity and suppressed the separatist insurrection in Nagaland. He did not think India had a past as "nation", but saw it rather as a "nation in the making" which had to seek new grounds for unity, especially in new projects of social reform and industrial progress. None the less, this much credit must be given to him, that he believed in and worked for the future of India as a nation. In a way, the "composite culture" concept was also used (though not invented) to counter separatism, viz. to assure the Kashmiris that they, too, had a place in India even while not being Hindus themselves.

A second remark concerns Nepal, the only declared Hindu state in the world. Nepal does not need to separate from India, but it certainly insists

---

[76] S. Talageri: *Indian Nationalism*, p.16.

[77] S. Talageri: *Indian Nationalism*, p.16.

on maintaining its separateness, even by using relations with China as a counterweight against Indian interference.[78] No Hindu leader has ever spoken in favour of the annexation of Nepal, quite the opposite: Nepal at least was one Hindu state outside the control of the Nehruvians. But for theoretical purposes, if India is the natural homeland of the Hindus, why is Nepal so insistent on its separateness? Likewise, why has no Tamil separatist group in Sri Lanka sought accession to India rather than an independent Tamil Eelam? While no Hindu in India feels the need to break out, it seems that Hindus outside feel comfortable enough staying out.

On the other hand, it is also a fact that once Nepali-speaking Hindus formed a majority in the originally Tibetan-dominated kingdom of Sikkim, they voted for accession to India. Hindus in Portuguese-held Goa who agitated against colonialism did not seek independence but accession to India (in contrast with, say, the freedom fighters in East Timor and West New Guinea, who saw their countries forced into Indonesia against their will). So, the Hindus outside India's official borders also provide some testimony in favour of the thesis that India is naturally the homeland of the Hindus.

NATIONALISM AND UNIVERSALISM

Hinduism not a religion

In Hindutva thought, attempts are made to put Hinduism in a different category from the "religions" of Christianity and Islam. Scholars might agree, for instance, that unlike Christianity and Islam, Hinduism is not a belief system, at least not to the same definitional extent. It is also what Sri Aurobindo said: "Other religions are preponderatingly religions of faith and profession, but the Sanatan Dharma is life itself; it is a thing that has not so much to be believed as lived."[79]

In Hindutva circles, you hear a lot of clumsy statements with ill-defined terms, like: "Hinduism is not religion, it is faith",[80] or: "Hinduism is not religion, it is a way of life." As if every other religion were not,

[78]As Shriman Narayan, former Indian ambassador in Nepal, testifies (*India and Nepal*, p.134): after the Sino-Indian war, "I found all the Nepali newspapers, with the exception of one, were all positively anti-Indian, and several of them definitely pro-Chinese."

[79]Aurobindo: *Uttarpara Speech*, p.5.

[80]Commonly heard; also ascribed to Achyut Menon, former Chief Minister of Kerala, by H.V. Seshadri: *Universal Spirit of Hindu Nationalism*, p.3.

among other things, "a way of life". Some correctly say that "religion" is a bad translation of *dharma*, which is what Hinduism is, but then pick out a not too apt scriptural definition of *dharma*: "The ten points of duty [= *dharma*] are patience, forgiveness, self-control, not stealing, purification, mastery of the sensory powers, wisdom, learning, truth, and lack of anger."[81] But one cannot reduce a religion (or whatever we will call Hinduism) to its list of recognized virtues, just as Judaism is more than only the Ten Commandments.

Dharma means "sustaining", that which sustains the world order. Ethics can be conceived as sustaining the social order, but that is only one aspect of *dharma*. A social aspect may be the observance of *varna* differentiation; whatever modern Hindus try to make of this by reinterpretation, this has undoubtedly been considered a cornerstone of Hinduism for centuries. Another, more typically "religious" aspect is ritual, including the festival calendar: mankind participates in the cosmic cycles and upholds the cosmic order by observing religious festivals, or by doing rounds around an idol in imitation of the planetary movements.

One element of "religion" which is not included in *dharma*, is belief; *dharma* concerns behaviour, not opinion. As Frits Staal has written, a Hindu "may be a theist, pantheist, atheist, communist and believe whatever he likes, but what makes him into a Hindu are the ritual practices he performs and the rules to which he adheres, in short, what he *does*."[82] This gives Hindu nationalist ideologues a handle to press a non-religious definition of *Hindutva*.

Hinduism, universal or national?

Some Hindutva ideologues press a different and less subtle point to distinguish Hinduism from Christianity and Islam: that Hinduism is closely identified with India. RSS worker K. Suryanarayana Rao explains: "The word 'Hindu' does not mean only a religious faith just like Islam or Christianity. 'Hindu' denotes the national way of life here. ... For RSS men, the word 'Hindu' thus connotes not a particular sect, a religion or a faith, but the culture, the tradition, the way of life of the people inhabiting this part of the world from times immemorial."[83]

---

[81]*Manu-Smriti* 6:92, Wendy Doniger's translation: *The Laws of Manu*, p.123.

[82]F. Staal: *Rules without Meaning*, p.389, also quoted with approval in G. Flood: *Introduction to Hinduism*, p.12; emphasis in the original.

[83]K. Suryanarayana Rao in H.V. Seshadri *et al.*: *Why Hindu Rashtra?*, p.21.

It is undeniable that the Hindu civilization has been the "national" or at least the native civilization of the people of India for several millennia. But then what? One possibility is that the connection of this civilization is a historical fact, but that in the future, this civilization will decline and make way for a better, imported civilization: that is the view of missionaries who try to make the people of India abandon Hinduism in favour of Christianity, Islam, or Marxism. In that case, India is connected with Hinduism the way Mexico is connected with Aztec human sacrifices, or China with the tying up of women's feet: an undeniable historical link, but one which should be buried in the past never to revive.

A second possibility is that all civilizations have a right to exist, that none is better than another, and that it is best to leave everyone to his own inherited civilization, if only for the sake of maximum peace. This view, now widespread among Western intellectuals espousing cultural relativism, is also shared by most Hindus, and is implicitly but consistently present in Sangh Parivar discourse on Hindu-Muslim relations: nothing is wrong with Islam, the Arab national religion, only they should leave India alone and not try to convert Hindus.

The third possibility is that Hindu civilization should outgrow its historical confinement to India, and offer its light to the people abroad who live in darkness. As Aurobindo says: "This is the Dharma that for the salvation of humanity was cherished in the seclusion of this peninsula from of old."[84] It is like the rise of modern science in Europe: its historical location in Europe is undeniable, but its relevance is just as undeniably universal. As a euphoric A.B. Vajpayee put it: "We, the Indians, as Guru of the Nations: yes, I believe in that. We can be—or once more become—the hope of mankind. But that requires efforts and courage to be ourselves culturally. Unfortunately, we live in an age of political dwarfs, political managers without vision or courage. But their time is running out."[85] This sounds a bit like the Jewish self-perception as the Chosen People and the "Light unto the Nations", or that of the Slavophile Russians as the nation which has to save mankind.

Hindu universalism

Sri Aurobindo did not conceive of the imminent worldwide expansion of

[84]Aurobindo: *Uttarpara Speech*, p.5.

[85]Vajpayee interviewed by Erich Follath and Tiziano Terzani: "Guru der Nationen", *Der Spiegel*, 1996/19, p.163.

Hindu civilization as a conquest in the mould of the Spanish *conquista*: "It is to give this religion that India is rising. She does not rise as other countries do, for self or when she is strong, to trample on the weak. She is rising to shed the eternal light entrusted to her over the world."[86] The comparison with the spread of "European" science offers probably the best analogy of how Aurobindo conceived the spread of Hinduism. After non-European nations caught a glimpse of the achievements of modern science, their young men flocked to Western universities eager to acquire this knowledge and employ it in the service of their homelands.

It so happens that the spread of Hinduism to South-East Asia in the first centuries of the Christian era, and to the West in the twentieth century, has effectively followed this pattern. The courts in Cambodia and Java, like those in Bengal and South India before them, heard about the refined Hindu civilization from traders, and invited Brahmins to come over and "aryanize" them.[87] Western intellectuals heard about the profundities of Hindu spirituality, and started inviting Gurus over to the West. The centre of Hindu civilization did not have to spend money to finance Hindu missions, but received sponsored invitations.

In the age of science, the only tenable way to make a universal claim for Hinduism, is to incorporate science into it, even at the cost of having to shed some superstitious deadwood. The quintessential claim of the Hindu Renaissance was that Hinduism consists of scientific methods applied to areas not yet covered by Western science, viz. spirituality and the art of living.[88] So, Aurobindo claims: "That which we call Hinduism is really the eternal religion, because it is the universal religion which embraces all others. If a religion is not universal, it cannot be eternal. A narrow religion, a sectarian religion, an exclusive religion can live only for a limited time and a limited purpose. This is the one religion that can triumph over materialism by including and anticipating the discoveries of science and the speculations of philosophy. ... It is the one religion which enables us not only to understand and believe this truth but to realize it with every part of our being."[89]

---

[86]Aurobindo: *Uttarpara Speech*, p.5.

[87]Mochtar Lubis: *Het land onder de regenboog* (Dutch: "The Country under the Rainbow"): "Hinduism entered Java at the request of the royal courts" (p.41); the Javanese "brought Buddhist and Brahmin priests from India to sacralize their thrones" (p.37).

[88]The claim is found, explicitly or implicitly, in numerous books on "the Science of Yoga", e.g. Sri Yukteswar: *The Holy Science*.

[89]Aurobindo: *Uttarpara Speech*, p.13.

Given this universalist claim, Aurobindo is ready to consider the Indianness of Hinduism as a mere accident: "What is this religion which we call Sanatan, eternal? It is the Hindu religion, only because the Hindu nation has kept it, because in this Peninsula it grew up in the seclusion of the sea and the Himalayas, because in this sacred and ancient land it was given as a charge to the Aryan race to preserve through the ages. But it is not circumscribed by the confines of a single country, it does not belong peculiarly and forever to a bounded part of the world."[90] In this view, India is but the accidental birthplace of the *Sanâtana Dharma*, which has a universal vocation.

Nationalism as the ancilla of universalism

It is hard to reconcile the nationalist view of Hinduism with the said universal mission, though the Hindutva ideologues are not prepared to renounce self-flattering rhetoric about just such a universal appeal of Hinduism through the ages. They go on expressing pride that Hindu Rashtra is "the only Rashtra inspired with the vision of *Vasudhaiva Kutumbakam* (the whole world is one big family)".[91]

The expression does injustice to other countries which see themselves as the motherland of universal values such as liberty, human rights, or socialism (say, the USA, France, and the former USSR). And doesn't the European Union have an anthem declaring that *"Alle Menschen werden Brüder"* ("All human beings become brothers")? But as Ram Swarup once commented, "anybody able to rent a room and get a board painted [is] claiming to be a mini-UNO".[92] It is hardly surprising that the Hindutva movement rides with the tide and adopts its own register of do-gooder universalism.

The paradox of Hindu nationalism with a universalist self-understanding is still waiting for proper analysis by a Hindutva thinker, but a

---

[90]Aurobindo: *Uttarpara Speech*, p.13.

[91]K.S. Sudarshan: *Why Hindu Rastra*, p.17. The phrase *Vasudhaiva Kutumbakam*, "the whole world is one family", is apparently from Vishnu Sharma's *Panchatantra* 5:39, also from *Hitopadesha*, but at any rate from story-books rather than from the really authoritative Scriptures. Its frequent quotation as purportedly the quintessence of Hinduism is clearly a recent fashion.

[92]Ram Swarup: *Ramakrishna Mission in Search of a New Identity*, p.5. I am pulling the statement out of context: he used it in reference to the egalitarian claims made on behalf of every non-Hindu, anti-Hindu or reform-Hindu religion or movement in modern India; but I find it also applies to Hindu groups who claim universalism as a contribution of Hinduism.

first attempt has been made by RSS general secretary H.V. Seshadri. He writes: "If Dharma is eternal and applicable to all climes and races, why insist on calling it 'Hindu'? The answer is quite simple. It is because Hindus happened to discover these eternal laws. It is just like denoting certain scientific laws or theories after their discoverers' names. ... In fact, formerly our Dharma was called Sanâtana Dharma or Mânava Dharma. It was only when foreigners came here that a need arose for differentiating Dharma from other religious faiths and the epithet Hindu was joined to it."[93]

Seshadri seems to move away from Hindu nationalism when he writes: "So, it is clear that the word Hindu not only stands for a society, for a group of people, but for certain ideals, certain principles and life values. And the high watermark of this Hindu ethos lies in its unique holistic world perception perceiving the entire creation as one single harmonious living entity. ... Our prayers even up to this day are for universal well-being: 'Sarvepi sukhinah ...' (May all be happy, may all be free from affliction, may all see only auspicious things, and may none be struck with sorrow). In fact, in none of our prayers is there any reference to the achievement of greatness and glory of only our nation at the cost of others."[94] That is probably a commendable position when compared with the attempts of other freshly liberated nations to give themselves national pride by celebrating the memory of national heroes like Chengiz Khan, whose gift to the nation was entirely to the detriment of other nations.

To salvage nationalism, Seshadri presents it as an evolutionary stage: "Nationalism, in our view, is a stage for self-expansion of the human spirit. It is not for self-aggrandisement. It is a journey towards selflessness; towards sacrifice for the larger whole. Family is the first stage where the individual identifies himself with the joys and sorrows of the family members ... then goes on expanding his spheres of identity and reaches the stage of the nation. But the nation itself does not represent the end of the journey. ... he moves on to the entire mankind and later embraces the entire living world and finally the whole of creation. Nationalism is thus a stage of human evolution."[95]

Indian history is claimed to prove that nationalism can be a benign force, for India never attacked her neighbours: "By contrast, the very word

[93]H.V. Seshadri: *Universal Spirit of Hindu Nationalism*, pp.2-3.
[94]H.V. Seshadri: *Universal Spirit of Hindu Nationalism*, p.4.
[95]H.V. Seshadri: *Universal Spirit of Hindu Nationalism*, p.7.

'nation' has become a dirty word, a dangerous concept in the West. The reason is, whenever nationalism became powerful in these countries, its aggressive instinct was invariably roused. ... It was the same aggrandising spirit that made the colonisers carry out total liquidation of local population in continents like Australia and America."[96] Seshadri has a point. Still, a feeling remains that he has avoided the hard questions concerning the obvious divergence between universalism and nationalism.

Next year in Indraprastha

The Hindu nationalist position that Hindus are a nation can be clarified with a fairly exact parallel: the Jewish "nation". The comparison is made by Hindu nationalists themselves: "Some RSS publicists suggest that the only real analogy to this understanding of nationhood is found in Zionism."[97] The comparison is also made by their enemies: "The RSS approach in those countries where Hindus are a minority is exactly the same as that of the Jamaat-e-Islami in India. They treat Hindus the world over as one political entity even as the Jamaat treats Muslims all over the world as a single party. Both claim for their respective religious communities sole, exclusive possession of divine knowledge. The only other people who share such chauvinist megalomania are the Zionist Jews."[98] Indeed, to express his contempt for the Hindus, Jawaharlal Nehru famously wrote that "the Hindu is certainly not tolerant and is more narrow-minded than almost any person in any other country except the Jew".[99]

As usual with parallels, the differences are as instructive as the similarities. One can define Judaism as a religion, a belief system, which one can join or abandon by conversion. Effectively, conversions do occur, and in the Hellenistic and Roman periods, there was an active Jewish proselytization movement. Yet, in today's reality Jews don't inquire about beliefs when they want to decide whether someone is a Jew, except negatively: as long as a born Jew has not embraced the beliefs of another

---

[96]H.V. Seshadri: *Universal Spirit of Hindu Nationalism*, p.8.

[97]Ainslie Embree: "The function of the Rashtriya Swayamsevak Sangh: to define the Hindu nation", in M.E. Marty and R.S. Appleby, eds.: *Accounting for Fundamentalisms*, p.620.

[98]D.R. Goyal: "RSS: doctrine of disruption", *Mainstream*, 16.11.1985, p.31.

[99]J. Nehru: letter to Kailash Nath Katju, 17.11.1953, quoted in Gopal Krishna: "National integration: Nehru's failure", *Times of India*, 28.12.1988.

religion and actually joined that religion, he remains a Jew. "Is Jew, he who is born from a Jewish mother and has not joined another religion", as one well-known definition has it.

In most cases, modern believing Jews prefer an atheist Jewish-born husband for their daughter to a pious convert. Ethnic identity is stronger than religious conviction, because it is an inescapable and life-long fact of life. Since the Jewish Enlightenment (*Haskala*), millions of Jews turned to atheism, yet society continued to consider them Jews until their grandchildren had sufficiently dissolved into Gentile society by repeated intermarriage. Certain typical thought-forms were often considered as signs of a lingering Jewish identity; for example, the doctrine of Karl Marx, the atheist son of a Jewish convert to Christianity, is often described as a typical product of the Jewish spirit.[100] After Haskala and secularization, ethnic Jewish identity restructured itself around the secular nationalist movement of Zionism.

In a way, the atheist Veer Savarkar was the Hindu counterpart of a Zionist: he defined the Hindus as a Nation attached to a Motherland, rather than as a religious community. True, there is an obvious difference between the situation of the Jews, who had yet to migrate to their Motherland ("Next year in Jerusalem"), and the Hindus who merely had to remove the non-Hindu (British, then Nehruvian and, in Pakistan, Islamic) regime from their territory. The Hindus are already in Delhi, and merely have to change it into Indraprastha.[101]

The parallel between Judaism and Hinduism can be extended further, in spite of their seemingly radical religious differences, the former being the fountainhead of iconoclastic monotheism and the latter being the ultimate in idolatrous polytheism. But importantly, Judaism is not a credal but a communal religion, and this it has in common with Hinduism. As the Jewish historian Michael Arnheim remarks: "Christianity is what I have termed a *creed religion*, a religion based upon the acceptance of a

---

[100]Not only in Nazi tirades against "Judeo-Bolshevism" but also in Jewish writings, e.g.: "When we consider Marx's life and thought with hindsight, it fits so neatly in the history of the Jewish people that without any reserve, we may call him a typically Jewish thinker", writes Henri van Praag: *Karl Marx, Profeet van een Nieuwe Tijd* (Dutch: "Karl Marx, Prophet of a New Age"), p.73.

[101]Note that unlike the Shiv Sena and the Dravidianist parties which have renamed Bombay as Mumbai and Madras as Chennai, the BJP has so far not fulfilled its promises to rename Allahabad as Prayag, Ahmedabad as Karnavati, nor indeed Delhi as Indraprastha.

particular set of beliefs and standing in sharp contrast to the normal type of religion encountered in the ancient world, the *communal religion*, a category embracing religions as diverse as Judaism, Hinduism and the Roman state religion. Communal religions tend to be exclusive: they are hard to join as membership of the religion entails membership of the social community and *vice versa*, so that conversion to a communal religion is not only difficult but often practically impossible."[102]

Arnheim connects the "exclusiveness" of communal religions with their greater tolerance of religious diversity, and the proselytism of Christianity and Islam with their history of persecution and religious wars: "Yet, paradoxically, it is precisely this exclusiveness which gives communal religions their generally tolerant attitude to other religions. After all, if you are reluctant for your neighbours to embrace your religion, you can hardly blame them for persevering in their own separate faith. Indeed, the whole outlook on life of the adherents of a communal religion takes it for granted that each separate nation, state or tribe will have its own religion—a formula for tolerance."[103]

The defensive concern about proselytization is common to Hindus and Jews, precisely because they feel disinclined to counter it with proselytization of their own. The exception is the Hindu reform movements, and they specifically target only those whose ancestors left the Hindu fold, not those who never had any link with Hinduism. In the USA, there is a lot of co-operation between Hindu newcomers and the already well-organized Jews. Geopolitically, they are objective allies against Islam.

One important difference in this regard is that Hindu intellectuals increasingly believe in direct ideological confrontation with Islam, i.e. disseminating critiques of Islamic doctrine, which Jews consider contrary to their own short-term interests.[104] Israel needs to keep the Muslim world divided and any attacks on Islam as such can only strengthen Muslim unity and hostility. Hindus, by contrast, are involved in a battle for souls more than for territory, and they need to give Indian Muslims reasons for

[102]M. Arnheim: *Is Christianity True?*, p.198.

[103]M. Arnheim: *Is Christianity True?*, p.198.

[104]I was told so at the American-Israeli Political Affairs Committee in Washington DC, the fabled "Jewish lobby", April 1993. They would not, for instance, disseminate or encourage the work of the Jewish-Egyptian historian Bat Ye'or about the oppression of Christians and Jews in Muslim countries.

abandoning Islam in favour of Hinduism, and Hindus considering conversion (chiefly Scheduled Castes), reasons for not choosing Islam but rather a *Bhâratîya* religion such as Buddhism. An ideological offensive against Islam comparable to the offensive against Christianity by atheists and other modernists in eighteenth- to twentieth-century Europe is therefore unlikely to be started in Israel (though that country would greatly benefit in the long run), but may well start in India.

The most important point they have in common as far as the rest of the world is concerned, is that even the most hawkish chauvinists in the Zionist and in the Hindu Nationalist camp have a limited territorial perspective: they are satisfied with their homeland. True, there are a few disputed border zones (the West Bank, Pak-Occupied Kashmir) on which they make arguable historical claims, but this is nothing like the ambition of world conquest characterizing the Communist movement or certain historical phases of Christianity and Islam.

Nationalism as a misstatement of Hindu concerns

"The Hindu's genius is to blur issues, not to confront them."—Girilal Jain

In Sangh Parivar thinking, religious and "national" concerns are systematically identified. Thus, the RSS people often plead that on Ayodhya, the Indian state should support the Rama party against the Babar party because Rama was an "Indian" hero while Babar was a "foreign" invader. In fact, if Babar did demolish Hindu temples, it was not because of his foreign birth but because of the Islamic doctrine of iconoclasm. Many foreign invaders respected and preserved Hindu temples, lastly the British; by contrast, Indian-born Muslims destroyed temples in the name of Islam, as the convert Malik Kafur (d. 1316) did. So, formulating this conflict in terms of foreign vs. Indian is a thinly veiled and unconvincing attempt to express in terms of secular nationalism what is really a religious conflict.

The Hindu problem with Islam is not that it is *foreign*. This is amply proven by the doomsday history of another culture, as pluralist and polytheist as Hinduism, but for which Islam was not a foreign but a geographically internal enemy: the Pagan culture of Arabia which was annihilated by Mohammed and his successors Abu Bakr and Umar. One of the most original contributions of Hindu revivalists to the study and evaluation of Islam has been to draw attention to the impact of

Mohammed on Arab Pagan society *from the Pagan viewpoint*.[105] For the Arabs, Islam had the same effect on their traditions as it had on Hindu-Buddhist traditions in Turkestan, Afghanistan, the Maldives, Baluchistan and parts of South-east Asia. The Pagan Arabs fought Islam tooth and nail, until they had to acquiesce in its superior military strength. Their problem with Islam was not its geographical provenance but its intrinsic hostility to god-pluralism and idol-worship.

The fact that Islam (as Christianity, Communism) has foreign origins, is of no importance. The Parsi community has foreign origins but has harmoniously integrated itself into Hindu society. On the other hand, in Arabia itself Islam was not foreign, yet it was only imposed on the Arab Pagans by force, a fact convincingly illustrated by the pan-Arab insurrection against Islam after Mohammed's death. As the leading Islamic apologist Asghar Ali Engineer admits, "the war of *ridda* (apostasy) was a general insurrection throughout Arabia".[106]

In the opinion of thoughtful Hindus, it is a mistake to cast the Hindu revivalist programme in terms of Western secular nationalism, and to redefine a conflict between Hindu and anti-Hindu as one between "nationalist" and "anti-national". Thus, Ram Swarup said in the fifties, when "nationalism" seemed to some the only alternative to foreign-based Communism: "But foreign should not be defined in geographical terms. Then it would have no meaning except territorial or tribal patriotism. To me that alone is foreign which is foreign to truth, foreign to *Atman*."[107]

The RSS variety of Hindu nationalism puts things upside down: it starts with the Indian territory as the centre of its ideology, and then deduces that the society and the culture and religion born on this soil are worth defending. Ram Swarup, by contrast, starts from the civilization of *Sanâtana Dharma* (the "eternal value system", commonly known as Hinduism) as a value worth defending, then deduces the value of Hindu society from its upholding this *Sanâtana Dharma*, and concludes that the Indian territory and state are worth defending because and only because they house Hindu society and its civilization.

---

[105]See Ram Swarup's introductions to the Mohammed biographies by William Muir and by D.S. Margoliouth, reprinted by Voice of India; and S.R. Goel: *Hindu Temples*, vol.2, section IV and app.2.

[106]A.A. Engineer: *Origin and Development of Islam*, p.131.

[107]Quoted in S.R. Goel: *How I Became a Hindu*, 2nd ed., p.45.

Girilal Jain rejects the nationalist paradigm as a model for understanding the situation of Hindu society altogether. To him, Hinduism is first of all a *civilization*, and its status as a nation is recent and accidental: "As in the case of Europe, India could have remained a civilization and not become a nation. For it to be both, it needed the intervening agency of an effective pan-Indian modern state. The British provided us with such an agency. Regardless of whatever else they did, the importance of this contribution cannot be denied. On 15 August 1947, the Hindus finally became a *nation*, though not a *Hindu nation*."[108]

Likewise, while Aurobindo refuses to identify the Hindu-Muslim antagonism as a problem of "national" versus "foreign" (the RSS approach), he does acknowledge this antagonism and puts it in civilizational terms (like his disciple Girilal Jain): "The real problem introduced by the Mussalman conquest was not that of subjection to a foreign rule and the ability to recover freedom, but the struggle between two civilisations, one ancient and indigenous, the other mediaeval and brought in from outside."[109]

In the modern age, the state is far more important for the direction of the society it rules than in the past (organizing education and media, imposing language and cultural policies etc.). Consequently, Girilal Jain, along with all other Hindu revivalists of both nationalist and non-nationalist persuasions, applauds the existence of a state which unites most Hindus under its authority. However, he rejects the attempt to underpin this loyalty to the Indian (and potentially Hindu) state with a nationalist doctrine and the concept of an age-old "Hindu nation". According to Girilal Jain, "it is about time we recognize that we are not a *nation* in the European sense of the term, that is, we are not a fragment of a civilization claiming to be a nation on the basis of accidents of history, which is what every European nation is. ... There can, however, be no question that there had come into existence within more or less the present boundaries of South Asia a civilization pervasive enough and deep enough to give rise to a people [which] can be said to possess a collective psyche."[110]

[108]G. Jain: *The Hindu Phenomenon*, p.56.

[109]Aurobindo: *Foundations of Indian Culture*, p.379. He explains: "That which rendered the problem insoluble was the attachment of each to a powerful religion, the one militant and aggressive, the other spiritually tolerant indeed and flexible, but obstinately faithful in its discipline to its own principle and standing on the defence behind a barrier of social forms."

[110]G. Jain: *The Hindu Phenomenon*, p.21.

This could be a sterile discussion about terminology: is a community with a "collective psyche" not what nationalists would call a "nation"? But, as Girilal Jain explained to me personally, the distinction between "nation" and "civilization" has at least one important implication: the modern nationalist cult of the "nation" is a secular adaptation of the "Semitic" (meaning Christian) insistence on uniformity.[111] Just as Christian history has its share of heresy-hunting, nationalists have always sought to impose uniformity by forced assimilation of minorities who disturbed the idyllic picture of a homogeneous nation seeking rightful expression through its newly-created nation-state. Such insistence on uniformity would be unbecoming of Hindus for it is contrary to the genius of their civilization. And, said Girilal Jain, if the RSS sometimes gives the impression of aiming for a similar "national" uniformity, then that is a childhood disease of Hindu nationalism which must be remedied.

To be sure, the BJP denies that it seeks this kind of homogenization: "Diversity is an inseparable part of India's past and present national tradition. The BJP not only respects but celebrates India's regional, caste, credal, linguistic and ethnic diversity, which finds its true existence and expression only in our national unity. This rich tradition comprises not only the Vedas and Upanishads, Jainagamas and Tripitaka, Puranas and Guru Granth Sahib, the Dohas of Kabir, the various reform movements, saints and seers, warriors and writers, sculptors and artists, but also the Indian traditions of the Muslims, Christians and Parsis."[112] Perhaps, in the category of nationalist ideologies, a Hindu nationalism is a class by itself.

Savarkar and territorial nationalism

An expert on Savarkar, Dr. Shreerang Godbole, argues that even Savarkar, with his definition of "Hindu-ness" as attachment to India, never meant to confine Hinduism to its connection with the territorial entity India.[113] The identification of Hinduism with India merely happens to be the historical state of affairs, and is therefore duly registered in Savarkar's definition of *Hindutva*, but this does not imply that Hindu civilization is subordinate to its geographical location. Godbole states that to Savarkar, a true Hindu is most aware of the sacredness of the universe as a whole, rather than of Hindusthan alone. Indeed, Savarkar himself wrote: "A Hindu is most

[111]Interview in Girilal Jain's house, South Delhi, October 1990.

[112]BJP: *Election Manifesto 1998*, p.1.

[113]S. Godbole in *Organiser*, 23.2.1992.

intensely so, when he ceases to be Hindu; and with a Shankara claims the whole world for a Benares ... or with Tukaram exclaims: 'The limits of the universe—there the frontiers of my country lie.'"[114]

However, Dr. Godbole also cites a statement which in his opinion refutes the notion that Savarkar had a territorial concept of Hindutva, but which in my opinion confirms this territorial approach. To Savarkar, the fact of emigration from India need not diminish one's Hindu-ness:

"But will this simple fact of residence in lands other than Hindusthan render one a non-Hindu? Certainly not, for the first essential of Hindutva is not that a man must not reside in lands outside India, but that wherever he goes or his descendents may happen to be, he must recognize 'Sindhusthan' as the land of his forefathers. Nay more, it is not a question of recognition either. If his ancestors came from India as Hindus, he cannot help recognizing India as his 'pitrubhu' [ancestor-land]. So this definition of Hindutva is compatible with any conceivable expansion of our Hindu people. Let our colonists ... contribute all that is best in our civilization to the upbuilding of humanity. Let them enrich the people that inhabit the earth from Pole to Pole with their virtues and let them in return enrich their own country and race by imbibing all that is healthy and true wherever found. Hindutva does not clip the wings of the Himalayan eagles but only adds to their urge. ... The only geographical limits to Hindutva are the limits of our earth."[115]

What Savarkar says is that even Indians colonizing other lands remain Indians, just like the British colonizers remained British. He still considers as Hindus those who retain a link with India, even if non-resident. That, to me, is definitely a territorial definition of Hinduness. But we must admit that in a descriptive sense, Savarkar's territorial definition is acceptable because it corresponds with actual usage: few will disconnect the term Hindu from the country India. Even Western converts to certain schools of Hinduism will hesitate to call themselves "Hindu" because of this well-established geographical connotation. By contrast, second-generation Hindu immigrants born in the West will own up a religious link with India to the exact extent that they identify themselves as Hindus.

This raises a practical problem. With all the talk of alleged Muslim disloyalty to India, how should Hindus born or settled in the West define

---

[114]V.D. Savarkar: *Hindutva*, p.141.
[115]V.D. Savarkar: *Hindutva*, p.119.

their loyalties? Indian first, American second? Is this not precisely the disloyalty of which Indian Muslims are accused? In the Hindutva literature, I have not seen this matter examined yet: at most the dilemmas discussed are those of "dharma or dollar", Hindu spirituality vs. Western materialism. If Hinduism perforce has to be identified with Indian nationalism, then the question of loyalty to countries of recent Hindu settlement should be faced at some point.

After nationalism

It is undeniable that the ideological development and political growth of Hindu revivalism has been stunted by the fixation of its most numerous and best organized segment on nationalism. It has prevented any outreach to potential foreign allies, it has associated Hindu revivalism with the pettiness and narrow-mindedness so typical of nationalist movements in many countries, it has misdefined many political issues by reducing everything to questions of national vs. anti-national. Such attitudes were understandable in the colonial age and the national freedom struggle, but now they are a sign of intellectual lifelessness. Thus, while Hinduism (which prides itself on not being a belief system, hence not necessarily in conflict with reason) as such ought to have far less problems with modernity than Islam or Christian fundamentalism, Hindutva publications rarely arrive at a decent discussion of the challenges of modernity because of the interference of anti-Western sloganeering.[116] Again and again, a fundamental civilizational issue is reduced to a conflict between "us here" and "them there", often with a highly anachronistic enemy-image of the "colonialist" and "racist" West.

The fact that the colonial mind-set of the anglicized ruling class has kept the colonial/anti-colonial antagonism alive long after Independence is hardly an excuse. On the contrary, it proves precisely that even colonialism is not a matter of geography and nationality: with the proper mental conditioning, a born Hindu and native Indian can become a secularist "brown Sahib", just as in earlier centuries, he could become an Islamic idol-breaker. These foreign imprints on Hindu society are legacies of the past: they have to be dealt with, but not in a manner which disregards the fact of Independence, the fact that a Hindu majority is now master of its own destiny and responsible for any past misfortunes which it

[116]E.g. D. Upadhyaya: *Integral Humanism, passim.*

allows to linger. It is therefore high time that the nationalistic aspect of Hindu revivalism got reduced to more functional and realistic proportions.

HINDU RASHTRA

The BJP on Hindu Rashtra

The ambiguous meaning of the slogan *Hindû Râshtra*, often mentioned in texts on the BJP, has been summed up by L.K. Advani as follows. He starts by correctly pointing out that "the term *Hindû Râshtra* was never used during the Jana Sangh days, neither had it ever been mentioned in any manifesto of the BJP".[117] The BJP has mentioned *Râm Râjya*, "Rama's kingdom", a term rendered immune from criticism through its frequent use by the Mahatma.[118] But the BJP will never use the notion *Hindû Râshtra*.[119]

At the same time, Advani claimed that "those residing in the country are Hindus even if many of them believe in different religions. ... those following Islam are 'Mohammedi Hindus'. Likewise, Christians living in the country are 'Christian Hindus', while Sikhs are termed 'Sikh Hindus'. The respective identities are not undermined by such a formulation. Similarly, someone is a 'Sanatani Hindu', while the other is an 'Arya Samaji Hindu'. It would be better if such a formulation comes to be accepted. As part of the same concept, I consider this country to be a Hindu 'rashtra'. There is no need to convert it into a Hindu 'rashtra'; this needs to be understood. But I certainly do not believe in forcing people to believe in this."[120]

Likewise, RSS leader Balasaheb Deoras replied as follows to the question, "Do you consider yourself to be a Hindu first or an Indian first?"—"I don't find any difference between the two. When I use the word Hindu, I use the word in a national sense. The word Hindu does not connote any religion. For example, the sanatani Hindu believes in idol worship while the Arya Samaji does not believe in it. Both are Hindus. Our idea is that all the people, whether they are Christians, Muslims or Arya

---

[117] "Advani wants Muslims to identify with 'Hindutva'", *Times of India*, 30.1.1995.

[118] Not entirely immune, for Gandhi's Hindu revivalism and his use of the notion *Râm Râjya* have been criticized sharply by Prem Nath Bazaz: *The Shadow of Ram Rajya over India*.

[119] This was first pointed out to me, with friendly indignation at my ignorance, by BJP spokesman Kedar Nath Sahni, January 1991.

[120] "Advani wants Muslims to identify with 'Hindutva'", *Times of India*, 30.1.1995.

Samajis, are Hindus. Unfortunately, the Muslims and the Christians have not accepted this stand. When the Hindus are strong enough, the Muslims and Christians will also start saying, we are Hindus."[121]

What Advani and Deoras say here is that there is no plan to convert India into a *Hindû Râshtra*, as India already is a *Hindû Râshtra*, all Indians being Hindus.[122] In that case, there is no reason for blueprints of what a *Hindû Râshtra* should look like, as we are already in the middle of it. But in that case, there should also be no reason for the BJP to shy away from using the term *Hindû Râshtra*.

And yet, the BJP including Mr. Advani does shy away from the term, even from the term "Hindu" itself. Consider this observation by Abhas Chatterjee concerning L.K. Advani's speech at the *Virât Hindû Sammelan* (General Hindu Conference) in Ahmedabad, 1989: "In some public meetings addressed by a prominent political personage of our country, a gentleman who is regarded by most people as a champion of Hindu Rashtra, an enthusiastic audience raised the slogan: 'He alone will rule over this country who stands by the Hindu cause.' The leader lost no time in prohibiting this slogan and told the audience: 'Please say that he alone will rule over this country who stands by the nation's cause.'"[123]

In his mind, as in that of the Nehruvians, the terms "Hindu" and "the nation (of India)" are clearly not co-terminous. In many aspects of the debates to be surveyed in these chapters, it will be clear that the positions taken by Hindu Revivalist thinkers are explicitly not shared, privately or at least publicly, by what is supposed to be the biggest political vehicle of Hindu Revivalism, the BJP. On the contrary, on essential points, the BJP has moved ever closer to the Nehruvian-secularist camp.

The RSS on Hindu Rashtra

In contrast with the BJP, the RSS openly espouses the concept of *Hindû Râshtra*, but RSS statements about this central concept are not much more forthright than Advani's, in fact they are typically confused. Even the word *Râshtra* is not clearly understood:

"As Hindu Rashtra is not a religious concept, it is also not a political

[121]Balasaheb Deoras, interviewed by Nilan Singh: "Probing the Hindu Mind", *Gentleman*, September 1988, p.79.

[122]A more tenable argument for the statement that "India is a Hindu Rashtra" would be that without Hinduism, there would be no India, in the sense argued by S. Talageri: *Indian Nationalism*, p.14.

[123]Abhas Chatterjee: *Hindu Nation*, p.2.

concept. It is generally misrepresented as a theocratic state or a religious Hindu state. Nation (Rashtra) and State (Rajya) are entirely different and should never be mixed up. State is purely a political concept. ... The State changes as the political authority shifts from person to person or party to party. But the people and the Nation remain the same."[124]

The focus on the nation rather than on the state is typical for the whole RSS outlook (since Guru Golwalkar), which is wary of politics and believes in working directly on civil society. But that should not be a reason for tampering with the dictionary meaning of words: *râshtra*, from *râj*, "governance", and *-tra*, the suffix of instrumentality, is definitely synonymous with *râjya*, and does not mean "nation", but "state". Used in that sense, it could be a meaningful goal for a Hindu movement: creating a "Hindu state" might be the goal of a movement claiming to represent the "Hindu nation". Giving a nation its own state has been the stated objective of most nationalist movements.

That is also how most outsiders understand the situation: the RSS works for the creation of a Hindu state. Whether one agrees or disagrees with it, the proposition is at least not absurd. But the RSS prefers to blur the issues: if *Hindû Râshtra* means "Hindu nation", what is all the fuss about? If it merely means a Hindu nation *which is already there* (in the Hindu nationalist view at least), if it does not mean a political goal to be achieved, it promises no change in the secularist dispensation and is also no threat to the status-quo.

Admittedly, Abhas Chatterjee's book title *Hindu Nation* is a translation from Hindi, viz. *Hindû Râshtra*; the understanding of the latter term as meaning "Hindu nation" is a reality, even if it is not correct according to the dictionary. But then, precisely on this understanding, Chatterjee rejects the RSS rhetoric of "working for a *Hindû Râshtra*" as utterly confused, for Hindus already are a *Hindû Râshtra*, a Hindu nation: "We come across futuristic statements like 'we shall make a Hindu Nation (Rashtra)', or 'no one can prevent the formation of the Hindu Nation', or 'a Hindu Nation can never be created', and so on. Such statements obviously imply that no Hindu nation has been in existence so far. ... To me all this confusion appears to be quite unwarranted. As far as I have been able to understand, the concept of Hindu Nation or Hindu rashtra is extremely simple. It can

[124]K.S. Rao in H.V. Seshadri, ed.: *Why Hindu Rashtra?*, p.24.

really be spelt out in a mere five words, and these five words are: *we Hindus are a nation*."[125]

And then he goes on to argue that one of the unfulfilled rights and aspirations of that Hindu Nation is to have a state of its own, a Hindu State. Whatever his handling of the term *râshtra*, at least his political programme is clear: a Hindu state for the Hindu nation. That much clarity is not found in Sangh publications.

Perhaps this confusion is the reason why any search in RSS literature for a blueprint of this fabled *Hindû Râshtra* will be in vain. K. Suryanarayana Rao's speech from which we have been quoting gets lost in the usual complaints about the Nehruvian state's "pseudo-secularism", the anti-national designs of the mullahs with their petro-dollars, and the age-old tolerance of the Hindus. It is unclear why he had to give the speech in the first place, because it says nothing which the average RSS worker hasn't heard a hundred times before, nor does it give any perspective on any worthwhile goal to work for. Its subtitle is *"Hindu Rashtra: not a mere slogan but a vibrant reality"*, which confirms that Hindu Rashtra is not a goal to be achieved, but merely a big and sterile synonym for the already existing "Hindu nation".

Similarly, a speech on Hindu Rashtra by Vaman Das Agrawal of the Vishva Hindu Parishad goes on and on about the meaning of the word "Hindu", which is synonymous with *Bhâratîya*, which is a national and not a religious concept, etc. People with an inferiority complex are always eager for confirmation of their position by established authorities, so the professor quotes a litany of statements by secularists, for example, "Dadabhai Naoroji has said—'The word Hindu is not communal. It is indicator of nationality.' Journalist and writer Khushwant Singh has said—'In my view, the word Hindu is indicator of nationality. In countries like America, the people inhabiting this country are called Hindus even to this day.' ... *Radiance*, the English newspaper of [the Jamaat-i-Islami] has written on 1st March 1970 that 'Muslims can quite reasonably claim to be Hindus in the geographical sense'."[126]

Assuming that the quotations are correct, the question is what you gain by defining the word "Hindu" down to a mere geographical term. The

---

[125] Abhas Chatterjee: *Hindu Nation*, pp.1-2.

[126] V.D. Agrawal: *Hindu Rashtra*, pp.12-13.

result is, at any rate, that there is no longer a term to designate the religious or cultural identity now called "Hindu", while the existing secular term "Indian" gets the unsollicited company of a new synonym, "Hindu".

Hindutva stalwarts on Hindu Rashtra

It gets only a little bit better when we come to the writings of the RSS stalwarts. In an article by K.S. Sudarshan titled "Why Hindu Rashtra", in the paragraph titled "Hindu Rashtra—eternal and perennial", where we expect to be enlightened at last about this elusive concept, all we get is some more Sanskrit shlokas proving that the Vedic seers considered themselves sons of *Mâtâbhûmi*, "Motherland", and that the Puranic poets defined Bharat as the region "north of the sea and south of the Himalaya".[127]

But then, at long last, we come across a promising paragraph, "Salient features of Hindu Rashtra", one page long. The first feature is as follows: "One of the cornerstones of the cultural foundation of the ancient mansion of Hindu Rashtra is 'unity in diversity'."[128] This platitude (on condition of replacing "Hindu Rashtra" with "India") can be found in every tourist guidebook on India. It could even serve as a definition of "secularism".

K.S. Sudarshan explains "unity in diversity": "The Hindu system of thought starts by accepting the fact that every entity has a distinct role to play and a special contribution to make in the evolution of the universe. As such, it is necessary that each one should get the full scope to play his particular role in keeping with his characteristic trait. At the same time, it should be made possible for all of them to realise the intrinsic unity underlying the multitude of diversities and come together in a spirit of amity and unity."[129] This is hard to find fault with, but it says nothing new.

Unaware that the harmony model of society is quite well-known in Western thought, from the Greek philosophers and Saint Paul down to modern Christian democracy, Sudarshan seeks to prove the originality of his harmony model by contrasting it with "the West", that den of incomprehending individualism, class struggle and the conflict-prone variety of nationalism: "Unlike in the West, we did not consider family,

[127]K.S. Sudarshan in H.V. Seshadri *et al.*: *Why Hindu Rashtra?*, pp.11-12.
[128]K.S. Sudarshan in H.V. Seshadri *et al.*: *Why Hindu Rashtra?*, p.13.
[129]K.S. Sudarshan in H.V. Seshadri *et al.*: *Why Hindu Rashtra?*, p.13.

society, nation and the world as ... having conflicting interests with one another."[130]

The second feature of Hindu Rashtra (and there is no third) is but a variation on the first: "Finally, even though Truth is one whole, a human being can at best comprehend only a fraction of it at a time because of his limited powers. Thus his understanding of Truth might well be different from those of others. The celebrated saying of our scriptures is: *Ekam sat viprah bahudha vadanti*. (Truth is one, the sages call *It* variously.) As such, we have held it wrong to project only one's own view of Truth as right and that of others as false. ... And out of this basic conviction was born the principle of 'equal respect for all faiths', which forms a shining characteristic of our national tradition."[131] Again, a harmless Gandhian statement with which Nehru and most other secularists could have agreed, and which fails to explain why there should be a separate *Hindû Râshtra* movement like the RSS. Note also the sloppy logic: because the truth can be formulated from different angles, it is "deduced" that *all* doctrines must be formulations of that one truth, as if false doctrines and untruths are impossible.

C.P. Bhishikar has written a volume elucidating Deendayal Upadhyaya's thought: *Concept of the Rashtra*. But when we turn to the chapter with the promising title "The identity of Hindu Rashtra", we only find some general observations about nationalism, some bombastic neologisms (the "Science of Patriotism"),[132] and the assurance that nations with will-power are unstoppable when they work to create a state of their own.

The best publication on the "Hindu state" (no pussyfooting about the meaning of *Râshtra* here) is no doubt Balraj Madhok's: *Rationale of Hindu State*, which carries a golden swastika on the cover. Here again, we get the whole Hindutva argument about Nehruvian "pseudo-secularism", Muslim aggression, Hindu broad-mindedness and the like. The book is well-written, but on what a "Hindu state" would be like, all it offers is the assurance that it would be a pluralistic and democratic state without privileges for the minorities.

---

[130]K.S. Sudarshan in H.V. Seshadri *et al.*: *Why Hindu Rashtra?*, p.14.

[131]K.S. Sudarshan in H.V. Seshadri *et al.*: *Why Hindu Rashtra?*, p.14.

[132]C.P. Bhishikar: *Concept of the Rashtra*, p.88.

Thus, "Muslim and Christian minorities will be more safe in a Hindu state than anywhere else in the world provided they accept the Indian ideal of 'live and let live', treat others as they would like to be treated by others, and show equal respect for other religions, forms of worship and places of worship. ... In short, religious minorities in Hindu Republic of India will get much better treatment than the non-Muslim minorities in Pakistan, Bangladesh and other Islamic States of the world. But they will have to be loyal to the State and learn to respect the rights and sentiments of the nation group. They will have equal rights but no special rights."[133]

This insistence that a Hindu State will be a truly secular state is purely defensive; while there is nothing wrong with it, it fails to tell us why a Hindu state should be preferred to its alternatives, such as the Nehruvian state. At most, it could mean that the aberrations from true secularism which characterize the Nehruvian system will be replaced with real secularism. As a VHP slogan has it: "Hindu India, secular India". But then why not call your goal "secularism", a fairly clear descriptive term, instead of this murky "Hindu Rashtra"?

Rather than coming out with a blueprint of what new benefits a Hindu state will bring, all that Hindu nationalists do is to assure the world that a Hindu State is something else than what its detractors allege. This extremely defensive discourse can be understood as the result of having been vilified and pushed around for half a century, but it remains disappointing.

The BJS-BJP as a secular and modernist party

The basic closeness of the BJS/BJP to the Nehruvian mainstream of Indian politics is confirmed once more by the following statements on secularism and social reform. Under the heading "Non-communal state", the BJS declared in its 1971 Manifesto:

"Jana Sangh fully subscribes to the ancient ideal of the non-communal State. In India no one is discriminated against on grounds of his religion. The State has always looked upon all faiths as entitled to equal freedom and protection. Jana Sangh is resolved to carry forward this secular tradition.

"Jana Sangh, however, rejects the pseudo-secularism that combines

[133]Balraj Madhok: *Rationale of Hindu State*, p.167.

irreligion with appeasement. We would like followers of all religions to accept the Indian ideal of *Sarvadharma-samabhava* and cherish a feeling of not merely tolerance, but equal respect for other faiths."[134]

The manifesto continues with some more expressions of support to the modern and egalitarian consensus, under the heading "Egalitarian Society":

"Jana Sangh is pledged to the creation of an egalitarian society in which there would be no discrimination against, or in favour of, any citizen on grounds of birth, heredity, caste or creed. In this society, there would be no place for economic exploitation or social disparity.

"Jana Sangh will seek to conserve and promote all that is great, noble and sublime in Indian culture and wage a relentless battle against intolerance, superstition and obscurantism, so that our objective of building up a modern India on the basis of liberty, equality and fraternity can be achieved."[135]

That is a less well-known face of the Hindutva movement. Historically, the enthusiasm of Hindu activists for the struggle against social evils has often been in direct proportion to their Hindu radicalism. Thus, Nathuram Godse, the murderer of the Mahatma, was an active participant in and organizer of inter-caste dinners and other actions to break caste discrimination and untouchability.[136] This is only logical considering that the social evils of Hindu society are its major weakness, and that its enemies are concentrating all their efforts on exploiting these social evils.

The persistent allegation by outsiders that the BJP intends to reinstitute the caste system on the basis of the *Manu-Smriti*, is completely in conflict with every single BJS-BJP statement on the issue. Thus, to a question whether he agreed with traditionalist Swami Vamdev that the Constitution should be changed to facilitate a return to the *varna* system, A.B. Vajpayee replied: "No question of a return to the *varna* system. The *dharm sansad* (religious parliament) has clarified that it stands by the

---

[134]BJS: *Party Documents*, vol.1, p.174.

[135]BJS: *Party Documents*, vol.1, pp.174-75.

[136]I may add some examples to which I am a personal witness. Abhas Chatterjee is one of those principled Indian civil servants who refuse to attend a wedding if dowry (*dahej*) has been paid to the bridegroom's family. Sita Ram Goel refused to accept dowry at his sons' and grandson's weddings.

Constitution. There is no question of *Manusmrti* being implemented."[137] The record of the BJP Governments in the states and at the centre confirms that the party stays close to the secular and modernist trail blazed by the Nehruvian Congress.

Minorities in a Hindu State

What counts for caste also counts for religions: equality before the law for all citizens regardless of religions is an unquestioned cornerstone of the Hindutva programme. Hindu Rashtra ideologues assure us that the minorities will be safe in a Hindu state, just as they have always been safe in the Hindu states of the past, and that their members will enjoy equal rights with the Hindus. When Atal Behari Vajpayee was questioned about *Hindû Râshtra* (to which he preferred the term *Bhâratîya Râshtra*), he said: "There is no question of any section of the Indian community being disenfranchised. *Hindû Râshtra kâ matlab hai* [= its meaning is] there will be no second-class citizens on the basis of religion or caste."[138]

Hindutva spokesmen assure us that their movement could never have been anything but secular, because Hinduism is quintessentially secular: "The Hindu state has never been theocratic, there being never any institution like the Pope of Rome or the Caliph in Turkey. Therefore, to assert that the Hindu Rashtra, whose glory lies in its liberal values of life, is anti-secular, is only to betray one's gross ignorance."[139]

If the Hindu Kingdom of Nepal is taken to be a Hindu State as envisioned by the Hindu nationalists, it would tend to confirm their assurance: though backward and corrupt, Nepal is fairly peaceful and tolerant and has witnessed a mushroom growth of both the Muslim and the Christian minority in the past few decades. But the mountainous fringe state of Nepal is hardly a useful model for the glorious Hindu India of which the Hindu nationalists dream. To refute their assurance with empirical counter-evidence, we would have to wait for the effective

---

[137]A.B. Vajpayee interviewed by Nirmai Mitra: "'I have never defended the demolition'", *Sunday*, 14.2.1993. The *Dharma Sansad* is a council of *Sâdhus* convened by the VHP in order to get the generally tradition-minded *Sâdhus* on to its own reformist platform, and of course to create an embryonic pan-Hindu platform which can represent Hinduism as a whole.

[138]A.B. Vajpayee interviewed by Nirmal Mitra: "'I have never defended the demolition'", *Sunday*, 14.2.1993.

[139]K.S. Sudarshan, in H.V. Seshadri *et al.*: *Why Hindu Rashtra?*, p.19.

declaration of India as a Hindu State; unless we take a look at the pre-colonial past.

According to Hindu nationalists, history shows that a "Hindu can never be a communalist or a fundamentalist".[140] As proof, Hindu hospitality towards the Syrian Christians, the Jews and the Parsis is cited. A favourite quotation is this Israeli statement about Jewish history in India: "While most of the Jews came to Israel driven by persecution, discrimination and murder and attempts at total genocide, the Jews of India came because of their desire to participate in the building of their Jewish Commonwealth, because of their unshakable belief in the redemption of Israel. Throughout their long sojourn in India, nowhere and at no time were they subjected to intolerance, discrimination or persecution."[141]

Those minorities who expect problems are told that they have only themselves to blame: they attribute to the Hindus the very motives which have inspired their own forebears to persecution and religious wars. The minorities themselves should make a move and drop their social and political separatism. K.S. Sudarshan presents the attitude of the Parsis, India's smallest minority except for the Jews, as a model to follow:

"In 1943, the then Secretary of State, Mr. L.S. Amery, invited some Parsi representatives and suggested to them that they should ask for separate representation in various legislatures. The suggestion was emphatically spurned in a representation sent to Mr. Amery and signed by nearly 2,000 leading Parsis, and affirming that 'our interests are safe in the hands of sister communities'. Recalling this episode, R.K. Sidhwa, a prominent Parsi member of the Constituent Assembly, said that if minorities were encouraged to think in terms of permanent minority safeguards, 'there will be a kind of perpetual instinct in the mind of the minority community representatives that the safeguards are to remain forever, and it will be difficult for these small communities to come nearer to major communities.' Sidhwa added: 'The ultimate phase of political life of all Indians should be one nation, one community.'"[142]

---

[140]K.S. Rao, in H.V. Seshadri *et al.*: *Why Hindu Rashtra*, p.29. His allegation that "the British started this mischief of calling everything Hindu as communal" is a variation on the old Congress game of blaming the British for the communal problem.

[141]Quote from the booklet *Indian Jews in Israel* published by the Israel Consulate-General in India, by K.S. Rao in H.V. Seshadri: *Why Hindu Rashtra?*, p.28.

[142]K.S. Sudarshan, in H.V. Seshadri *et al.*: *Why Hindu Rashtra*, p.20.

The Hindu nationalist position is that though some minorities have attracted negative attention by being hostile to Hindu society, the Hindus are and remain willing to accommodate non-Hindus as citizens with fully equal rights, though not with special privileges. It is best summed up by Shrikant Talageri: "Muslims, whether they remain staunch Muslims or awakened (weaned-away)[143] ones, should be assured that as individuals and as general groups, they will get *full justice* in every sense of the term: the position of a Muslim individual or group will be *exactly* the same as that of a Hindu individual or group. The BJP's slogan 'justice for all, appeasement of none' says it in a nutshell. But there will be *no* religious appeasement or pampering, *no* positive discrimination in their favour, and *absolutely no* tolerance of any expansionist agenda."[144]

Remark that Talageri writes this in the context of a critique of the BJP's minority policies, which, in his view, are showing a tendency to favouritism and "appeasement" after the example of long-standing Congress policies. There is a considerable distance between the clear-cut Hindu nationalist position as outlined by Talageri, and the effective BJP policies characterized by compromise with prevalent attitudes and opinions, and with the minorities. But to understand this debate about "minority appeasement", it is necessary to study the whole list of Hindu grievances against the secular state, which they consider as unjustly favouring the non-Hindu minorities. These complaints about discrimination in favour of the minorities will be considered in the next chapter. But first we have to look into the one great attempt by an ideologue of Hindu nationalism to transcend nationalism and articulate Hindu concerns in a more universal idiom.

INTEGRAL HUMANISM

The official doctrine of the BJS/BJP is called *Integral Humanism* (Hindi: *Ekâtmatâ Mânawawâd*), a doctrine formulated in four lectures given by BJS ideologue Deendayal Upadhyaya in Pune, April 1965, vaguely on the basis of ancient Hindu social philosophy.[145] It is the alpha and omega of

---

[143]Talageri supports the reconversion of Indian Muslims in principle (though on the same page, in S.R. Goel, ed.: *Time for Stock-Taking*, p.228, he admits that a large-scale reconversion "is rather hard to imagine"), and by an "awakened Muslim", he means one who has "outgrown" Islam.

[144]S. Talageri in S.R. Goel, ed.: *Time for Stock-Taking*, pp.228-29.

[145]These four lectures were published together as a brochure titled *Integral Humanism*, which virtually every member of the BJP and of the RSS-affiliates has on his bookshelf.

ideological training sessions of RSS and BJP workers. Typically for intellectual functioning of the RSS, the term "integral humanism" had already been enshrined in the BJS's *Principles and Policies* (a programmatic statement adopted in January 1965)[146] on the basis of its intuitive meaning as explained in a single paragraph, before Upadhyaya explicitated it into a more or less full-blown philosophy in the said lectures.[147] These formed "the *Das Capital* of Jan Sangh".[148]

It is remarkable that most reputed India-watchers have never even heard of the official doctrine of the largest political party in the world's largest democracy.[149] Even when they mention it, they trivialize it and don't take it seriously. Thus, of three sentences which Salim Lakha devotes to Integral Humanism, the first is: "Upadhyaya's idea of integral humanism can be traced back to 1965 and the Jana Sangh party's attempt to define a separate ideological identity from the other major political parties." As if that separate ideological identity was an artificial creation just for the fun of having an "identity". In reality, Integral Humanism was an explication of an already well-established but insufficiently articulated identity. It is because of the BJS's underlying *Hindu* identity, that it "rejected the materialism of Western political ideologies" (Lakha's second sentence) and "argued in favour of an 'integral approach' that combined mental, physical and spiritual needs of the people" (his third).[150] Whatever the reason for their negligence, the *status quaestionis* is that, as far as the professional students of Hindutva are concerned, this topic of research is *virgo intacta*; so let us make a start.

"Integral"

Within the Indian context, the term *Integral Humanism* was used as an

---

[146]Included in BJS: *Party Documents 1951-1972*, vol.1, pp.3-43.

[147]It is therefore impossible that these lectures "were to provide the bases of the Jana Sangh's foundation of its 'principles and policies' in 1965", as claimed by Jaffrelot: *Hindu Nationalist Movement*, p.124. On the other hand, the ideas expressed in Upadhyaya's lectures had been in the air for years, and it was Upadhyaya himself who drafted the *Principles and Policies*, which at any rate are of one piece with the lectures.

[148]Chandra Mishra: "The Resurrection of the BJP", *Publik Asia*, 1.12.1989.

[149]Exceptions are the cursory mention of the term *Integral Humanism* in B. Graham: *Hindu Nationalism*, pp.86, 215; G. Heuzé: *Où va l'Inde moderne?*, pp.103, 119; and C. Jaffrelot: *The Hindu Nationalist Movement*, p.124. But none of these amounts to an actual presentation of what Integral Humanism stands for.

[150]Salim Lakha: "The Bharatiya Janata Party and Globalisation of the Indian Economy", *South Asia*, 1994, pp.213-29, specifically p.218.

answer to *Radical Humanism*, the neo-Marxist doctrine floated by M.N. Roy after he was expelled from the Communist Party of India which he himself had founded. Typifying this development, in 1948, Roy changed the name of the quarterly he published from *The Marxian Way* to *The Humanist Way*.[151] While Radical Humanism reduced man to his economic dimension, Integral Humanism wants to rehabilitate all dimensions of human life distinguished by ancient Hindu philosophy: *Kâma* (sensual enjoyment), *Artha* (worldly success), *Dharma* (integration into a larger order by doing one's duty including the participation in ritual), and a separate and typically Hindu category, *Moksha* (liberation from worldly attachments through yoga). To quote the "integral humanism" paragraph of the *Principles and Policies*:

"The individual occupies a pivotal position in our system. According to the principle of *'Yat pinde tad brahmande'* (what is in microcosm is in macrocosm) individual is the representative and chief instrument of society. Material wealth is a means to man's happiness, and not an end in itself. But a system which is based on the assumption of a mass man and fails to take into account the living man having an individuality characteristically his own is not adequate. Inadequate also is a system which looks just at one attribute of man and fails to take a comprehensive view of him as an organic being comprising of Shareer, Mana, Buddhi and Atma having a number of urges requiring to be fulfilled by the Purusharthas. Our ideal is the integral man, who has the potential to share simultaneously numerous individual and corporate entities. Integral Humanism is the corner-stone upon which our entire system needs to be built."[152]

Yat pinde tad brahmânde, "That which is in the microcosm, that is also in the macrocosm", which Deendayal himself chose as the motto of his Integral Humanism, is originally a dictum from *hatha-yoga* signifying the correspondence between the body and the universe, for example, between energy cycles in the body and planetary motions in the sky. Nowadays it is loosely used as a formula for any "holistic" or "integral" view of reality, the "holographic paradigm": just as every body cell carries the genetic

---

[151]For a comparison between Radical Humanism and Integral Humanism, see Ashok Modak: "Two Exponents of Humanism: M.N. Roy and Deendayal", in Devendra Swarup, ed.: *Deendayal Upadhyaya's Integral Humanism*, pp.141-52.

[152]BJS: *Party Documents*, vol.1, p.13. *Sharîr*: body; *mana*: mind; *budhi*: intellect; *âtma*: Self; *purushârtha*: "an individual's achievement", goal in life.

information which determines the entire body, every individual carries an imprint of the whole and is thereby conditioned to play his part in the functioning of the whole.

Secondary literature offers no data on the antecedents or sources of inspiration for Deendayal Upadhyaya's Integral Humanism.[153] Sangh Parivar spokesmen whom I questioned about this, attribute the concept *Integral Humanism* to the Bengali freedom fighter Bipin Chandra Pal (1858-1932), though none could pinpoint the exact quotation. Apparently, reference is to Pal's speech "Indian Nationalism: Hindu Standpoint" (1913), where he discusses the concept of *Nârâyana*, which he translates as "Universal Humanity".[154]

Pal's idea, developed as a superior alternative to Western self-centred individualism and ditto nationalism, is that man's "social evolution proceeds from lower and simpler to higher and more complex stages, in proportion as the range and variety of man's relations with other human units and associations expand and increase. It is by means of these larger and larger associations that man progressively realises his own personality and in the consequent development and perfection of his humanity, unveils the Divinity that is in him. For Humanity and Divinity are, indeed, one. This unity is the keynote of Hindu thought. The Hindu alone, among all the peoples of the earth, has, perhaps, one single word to denote both Humanity and Divinity. That word is Narayana. Narayana is the In-Dweller in individual humans, indeed, in all beings, severally. Narayana is also the In-Dweller in the collective life of Humanity, the Director of all social and historic movements."[155]

Reference is to the apparent relatedness of the Sanskrit word *nr-, nara*, "man" and *Nârâyana*, a deity identified with the Vedic "cosmic man" (*Purusha*) in the *Śatapatha Brâhmaṇa*, and later identified with Vishnu.[156] The "cosmic man" doctrine is an early "holographic paradigm" suggesting a homeomorphism between the part (man) and the whole (the cosmos),

---

[153]Chiefly the following Sangh publications: D.B. Thengadi, ed.: *Pandit Deendayal Upadhyaya: Ideology and Perception* (7 vols., 1988); Devendra Swarup, ed.: *Deendayal Upadhyaya's Integral Humanism* (1992); Kandarpa Ramachandra Rao: *Integral Humanism* (1995).

[154]This speech is included in B.C. Pal: *Writings and Speeches*, pp.65 ff.

[155]B.C. Pal: *Writings and Speeches*, p.78.

[156]About Nârâyana, see G. Flood: *Introduction to Hinduism*, pp.120-21; and *Śatapatha Brâhmaṇa* 12:3:4, 13:6:1.

and thereby attributing to the cosmos a functional unity similar to the functional unity in the human body.

The idea is not new nor exclusively Hindu.[157] Even the application of this paradigm to society, where the parts are said to be dependent on the whole and consequently forced to co-operate in harmony like the different organs and limbs of the body, is a metaphor found in many places and cultures. The parts are limbs of the whole, and should respect each other as such: "This Narayana or Humanity is the Whole, the different nations of the world are part of that Whole. Narayana or Humanity is the Body, the different tribalities, racialities and nationalities are limbs of that Body. The whole is implied in the parts: the organism in the organs."[158]

Deendayal Upadhyaya was aware of the limitations of the political vision which he had formulated, but he gave the broadest possible definition to his admittedly vague and still-elementary doctrine, as a guideline for future exploration: "Integral Humanism is the name we have given to the sum total of various features of Bharatiya Sanskriti, abiding, dynamic, synthesizing and sublime."[159] So, if there is any question to which you haven't found the answer in his writings, you should look into the whole treasure of Hindu civilization, for that is the real embodiment of Integral Humanism. This way, his new term implies a new understanding of what Hindu civilization stands for: just as Islam can be briefly characterized as "prophetic monotheism", Hinduism can be characterized as "integral humanism". This is arguably a modern rationalization of the "essence" of Hindu civilization, but there may be something to it.

"Humanism"

Integral Humanism is a humanism, taking the human being as its starting-point, and not any religious revelation. But the inherent risk of a humanist viewpoint is its being limited to immediate human concerns, as was allegedly visible in Western forms of humanism. Dattopant Thengadi, Upadhyaya's successor as the foremost ideologue of Integral Humanism, put it this way: "Any form of anthropocentric humanism is in its

---

[157]E.g. the Jewish-Kabbalistic doctrine of *Adam Kadmon*, "primordial man", more or less the uncreated anthropomorphic form of God, the image after which He created man; see G. Scholem: *On the Kabbalah and Its Symbolism*, pp.104 ff.

[158]B.C. Pal: *Writings and Speeches*, p.80.

[159]BJS: "Principles and Policies", *Party Documents 1951-1972*, vol.1, p.15.

final analysis an 'inhuman humanism'".[160] This notion of a non-anthropocentric humanism has recently gained ground among atheist humanists in the West (who said till the other day that "man is the measure of all things"), mostly under the impact of ecology.[161] Man is not the absolute owner and sovereign of the world, he has a responsibility towards the other creatures and the wholeness of the world as well. Or to put it in Christian-Democratic terminology, formulated independently by Mahatma Gandhi and Deendayal Upadhyaya as well: man is the *trustee* of creation.[162]

This humanism is an *integral* humanism: social and political structures must do justice to the multi-dimensionality of the human person: "Thus, even though *Dharma* regulates *Artha* and *Kâma*, all the three are interrelated and mutually complementary."[163] In its historical context, this is a reaction against the one-dimensionalization of man in a biological (racism) or economic sense (Marxism) or in terms of his religious identity. This mild talk of "the whole human person" implies, in practical politics, rejection of totalitarianism (emphasizing that "the state is not above all"[164]), a compromise between free entreprise and regulation by the state, and preservation of family values.

The contract theory of society is rejected in favour of the "organic" view of society. The RSS strongly emphasizes the distinction between society and the state, which is a mere instrument of society (whence also the disdain of RSS ideologues for politics): "Thus the state came into

---

[160]D.P. Thengadi: *Third Way*, p.195, with vague reference to an unspecified English translation, *True Humanism*, of Jacques Maritain: *Humanisme Intégral*.

[161]Examples in my home country of this ecologically reoriented humanism are Jaap Kruithof and Etienne Vermeersch, see e.g. Vermeersch: *De Ogen van de Panda* (Dutch: "The Eyes of the Panda", the panda representing the threatened species).

[162]While Gandhi cannot be left unmentioned here, it should none the less be remarked that in some instances, Gandhi's interpretation of "trusteeship" is unusual and open to criticism (and indeed much criticized at the time by the Left), viz. not that mankind is entrusted with the care of creation, but that the rich are entrusted with the care of society's collective wealth. This means that wealth equally *belongs* to the poor though it is *in the care* of the rich. This was an appeal to the rich not to indulge in their wealth but rather to see it as a responsibility entrusted to them; but Leftists read it as an appeal to the poor to forsake attempts at redistribution of wealth, since it already "belonged" to them anyway. Gandhiji's utterances on this subject have been collected in a booklet: *Trusteeship*.

[163]D. Upadhyaya: *Integral Humanism*, p.32.

[164]D. Upadhyaya: *Integral Humanism*, p.47.

existence as a contract. This contract theory can be applied to the state, but not to the nation."[165] Society precedes the individual (a view universally held until contested by individualists Jean-Jacques Rousseau and Margaret Thatcher "there is no such thing as society"): "In our view society is self-born. ... In reality, society is an entity with its own 'Self', its own life; it is a sovereign being like an individual; it is an organic entity. We have not accepted the view that society is some arbitrary association."[166] Consequently, class struggle, which is an outgrowth of the "social contract" theory, is rejected in favour of the harmony model of society.

To rephrase it in the terms of a recent BJP text: "The Bharatiya Janata Party's social agenda flows from its ideology of Integral Humanism. Our ideology rules out contradictions between society and its very components, as also between society and the individual. Our concern for the last man in the last row is as deep as that for the first man in the first row, if not more. The BJP's concept of social justice, therefore, does not seek to create rifts and schisms between various sections of society, but aims at removing social and economic disparities that have resulted in denial of a share in power, impoverishment and erosion of human dignity. An ideal society is not one that is compartmentalized in segments, but is an integral whole, harmonious and conflict-free. Hence we subscribe to *Samâjik Samarasatâ* (social harmony) and *Samâjik Nyâya* (social justice) and strive to avoid social strife."[167]

A "humanist" doctrine is hard to reconcile with the theocratic principle. Yet, Upadhyaya writes: "The ideal of the Indian State has been *Dharma Râjya*."[168] The latter term would be translated by most secularists as "religious state". However, the BJS ideologue continues: "Tolerance of and respect for all faiths and creeds is an essential feature of the Indian State. Freedom of worship and conscience is guaranteed to all and the state does not discriminate against any one on grounds of religion either in the formulation of policy or in its implementation. It is a non-sectarian state and not a Theocracy. ... The nearest English equivalent of *Dharma Râjya* is Rule of Law."[169] At that point, one is entitled to ask: if all you mean is "rule

---

[165]D. Upadhyaya: *Integral Humanism*, p.44.

[166]D. Upadhyaya: *Integral Humanism*, pp.36-7.

[167]BJP: *Election Manifesto 1998*, p.34.

[168]BJS: "Principles and Policies", *Party Documents 1951-1972*, vol.1, p.7.

[169]BJS: "Principles and Policies", *Party Documents 1951-1972*, vol.1, pp.7-8.

of law", why don't you just call it that, why create confusion by using a less straightforward or at least more complex term?

To my understanding, the term Dharma Râjya makes perfect sense as an ethical concept, but it is hard to conceive as a political concept. One of the colloquial meanings of *dharma* is "duty". And indeed, what Upadhyaya has in mind is really "the rule of duty/dutifulness", for in his ideal harmonious society, man thinks not of his own self-indulgence but of the needs of the whole: "While other concepts of state are right-oriented, the Indian concept of Dharma Râjya is duty-oriented."[170] For RSS men, activists who have chosen to dedicate themselves to an ideal, it is more natural to discharge duties than to claim rights; it is also this attitude which is inculcated in boy-scouts and in pupils of religious schools of any denomination. But it is hard to see where this takes us when we want to conceive a political structure. There is an obvious danger, viz. that rights will be denied to the individual in the name of the "rights of society" (equivalent with the duties of the individual vis-à-vis society), the old Soviet justification to muzzle dissent and reject pleas for "human rights".

But Upadhyaya is confident that this problem will not arise: "In a *Dharma Râjya*, people's rights are inviolate. It is the duty of the people to guard these rights of theirs zealously because it is through the exercise of these rights that they can fulfil their *Dharma*. In fact, according to our concept, a right is an instrument which enables the individual to carry out his duties and experience a sense of being and belonging. Duty and right are thus two sides of a triangle which has *Dharma* as its base."[171] This touches on important ethical questions regarding the relation between Freedom and the Good, but again, it remains unclear what political blueprint Upadhyaya has in mind. On the other hand, politics is not divorced from ethics, social structures cannot be separated from individual human attitudes, so perhaps Upadhyaya's reflections on rights and duties and Dharma may provide a good starting-point for a political philosophy, but as yet only a starting-point.

His thoughts on democracy are in the same mode, but quickly take us to far-reaching political conclusions: "Democracy or people's rule (*Lokatantra*) is a means for upholding *Lokâdhikâr* (people's rights) and promoting *Lokakartavya* (people's duty). Democracy has to be established

---

[170]BJS: "Principles and Policies", *Party Documents 1951-1972*, vol.1, p.8.

[171]BJS: "Principles and Policies", *Party Documents 1951-1972*, vol.1, p.8.

not only in the political field but also in the economic and social fields as well."[172] At the time (1965), it was standard Marxist parlance that "freedom" in the West was not real freedom, was a purely theoretical freedom except for the upper class, because social and economic disadvantage prevented the workers from exercising the freedoms which they legally enjoyed. For democracy to be effective, formal political democracy must be accompanied by more tangible types of democratization. Upadhyaya takes a leaf from their book: "Democracy has to be established not only in the political field but in the economic and social fields as well. ... The absence of democracy in any one sphere is bound to affect the growth of democracy in the rest."[173]

Deendayal Upadhyaya and the BJS sought to integrate modern emancipatory movements in their vision of a polity based on Hindu values. This put them in direct opposition to other tendencies and political parties, chiefly the Ram Rajya Parishad (pro-caste traditionalists), but partly also the HMS and the Swatantra Party: "There are a few political parties which voice allegiance to Bharatiya Sanskriti. They miss the dynamism of Bharatiya Sanskriti, and the eternal and enduring nature of Bharatiya values appears to them as evidence of a static and inflexible character. So they try to defend decrepit institutions and practices of the past age and plead for the *status quo*. They fail to perceive the revolutionary element in Bharatiya Sanskriti. In fact very many malpractices prevalent in society, such as untouchability, caste discrimination, dowry, ... neglect of women etc. are symptoms of ill-health and degeneration. ... Such institutions cannot be preserved in the name of Bharatiya Sanskriti."[174]

The point is often made by Hindu reformists that Hinduism itself provides the mechanisms which can free it from its social evils. Indeed, the very genesis of those evils illustrates the adaptability of Hinduism, for instance, the low status of women in the *Manu Smriti* has a prehistory which shows how Hinduism evolves: "Regarding the right of a daughter to her father's property, the opinion of Manu is quoted at length in the ancient book of Etymology and grammar, *Nirukta* of Yaska. ... He, in a discussion of the rights of girls to property, clinches the argument by giving the opinion of Manu that both sons and daughters had an equal share in the

[172]BJS: "Principles and Policies", *Party Documents 1951-1972*, vol.1, p.8.
[173]BJS: "Principles and Policies", *Party Documents 1951-1972*, vol.1, p.8.
[174]BJS: "Principles and Policies", *Party Documents 1951-1972*, vol.1, p.14.

property of their father. He claims that this decree was given in the beginning of the world. This particular shloka of Manu is not found in Manusmrti. ... The implication is that the present Manusmrti was compiled much later. And that the ancient Hindus gave equal rights to women."[175] This would mean that the so-called "Laws of Manu" were a continuously evolving document (or oral tradition), which allotted an equal share to sons and daughters at one stage and instituted inequality between them at a later stage, the stage which happens to be frozen in the *textus receptus* of the *Manu Smriti* we now know.

This also means that the traditionalists are wrong in attributing eternity to their scriptures: these are but a frozen relic of a particular stage in the continuous development of Hindu ethics and sociology. In some cases, it so turns out that a more ancient stage was more "progressive", such as here in matters of women's property rights. But even if it were found that the ancient practice was reprehensible (to modern sensibilities) at every stage, at least the principle that modifying the established practice is permitted, provides for a way forward. That is why Upadhyaya finds in *Bhâratîya Sanskrti* the principle of "dynamism" which justifies and encourages social change. The "Rule of Dharma" is therefore not to be understood as a polity based on ancient quasi-religious law-books, but rather as a dynamic polity which seeks its own solutions, guided only by very general principles of Hindu civilization, such as responsibility, social coherence, "integral humanism".

Similarities with Christian-Democracy

In its assumption that *man liveth not by bread alone* and its opting for the harmony model of society, Integral Humanism is most akin to the Christian-Democratic movement in Europe.[176] It is significant that one of the fundamental statements of the Christian-Democratic vision, by the French Neo-Thomist philosopher Jacques Maritain, is titled *Humanisme Intégral* (1936), though the homonymy is probably purely coincidental.[177] No RSS man would have been sufficiently familiar with Continental

[175]Gyan Swarup Gupta: "Hindutva and all that", *Indian Express*, 10.4.1991.

[176]According to a press survey in *BJP Today* (Jan. 1992, p.21), "Lt.-Gen. S.K. Sinha said that BJP was not a communal party, but is like the Christian-Democratic Party in Germany."

[177]An English translation is available, by Joseph W. Evans: *Integral Humanism. Temporal and Spiritual Problems of a New Christendom.*

ideological trends to be aware of this French book, and to my knowledge, until recently no Sangh Parivar publication ever mentioned it.

Indeed, Upadhyaya, with his typical Indocentric worldview, reduced Western civilization to its modern materialist manifestation and explicitly denied Western inspiration: "There have been a number of schools that have propounded humanism. But their thinking has been rooted in Western philosophies and so it is essentially materialistic. ... If you deny spiritualism, then human relations and behaviour and the relationship between man and the Universe cannot be explained."[178] As if there is no spiritualism in the West.

Nevertheless, Dattopant Thengadi, founder-president of the RSS trade-union *Bhâratîya Mazdûr Sangh* and after Deendayal the chief exponent of Integral Humanism, has at last taken note of Maritain's work, and has quoted very briefly from an unspecified English translation of Maritain's book in his own 1995 book *Third Way*,—of which the title itself is yet another point of comparison with Christian-Democracy.[179] The inspiration of both doctrines is indeed quite similar. Maritain develops a way to make a specifically Christian contribution to politics while fully accepting that secularism has come to stay; the same is true for Deendayal Upadhyaya, who insists that Hindutva fully accepts the secular framework.

Man's life, including his politics, has a transcendental dimension; yet, that does not warrant a return to medieval notions of theocracy. Indeed, one of the reasons for Jacques Maritain to write his book was the problem of the relevance of religion-based political involvement in the modern secularized world. He accepted that there could be no reversal of the secularization of public life, but at the same time he tried to articulate the inspiring role which a Christian commitment of the socially involved individual could play, as well as the universality of certain politically relevant values associated with the Christian heritage. And likewise, the Hindutva activists always emphasize that their movement is a secular movement, and that the values they promote can be accepted by Indian Muslims and Christians as well.

Another point which Integral Humanism has in common with Christian-Democracy is that both have a progressive dimension, which is

---

[178] *BJS Party Documents*, vol.1, p.13.

[179] The source is given as "Maritain's *True Humanism*", apparently not an extant translation but a simultaneous translation read out to him from the French original.

not based on an unbridled conflictual stance of one class hating another and trying to defeat it. As RSS general secretary H.V. Seshadri puts it: "Haters cannot reform".[180] Social justice can be brought about only by assuming a collective responsibility for "the evils of Hindu society", not by imputing it to one particular class and posturing as a victim with only rights to be claimed from others.[181] The Christian-Democrats have always held that "the line between good and evil runs through every man", not between classes or between nations; they reject the moral *hubris* implicit in the class struggle model (as also in the racial struggle model of Nazism), in which one class appropriates the moral high ground to itself, along with the right to disparage, oppress and even eliminate the other class.

In this respect, the Sangh merely continues and explicitates the approach taken by earlier Hindu reformers: "Probably, no declared opponent has more bitterly criticised the evil practices in Hindu society than a Vivekananda, a Dayananda, a Savarkar or a Gandhi. But still the Hindu society does not look upon them as its detractors. ... For, they loved and adored the Hindu society and stood up as its proud defenders against all its detractors. ... The Sangh too minces no words in laying bare the serious defects and distortions in the social psyche which have led to the downfall of the Hindus all these one thousand years and more. But every such criticism is invariably linked with expressions like 'we', 'ourselves' and 'our people'—expressions which reflect the spirit of identification of Sangh with the whole of society. The Sangh never stands apart on the high pedestal of a 'reformer' and [never] sermonizes to the rest of society on certain 'do's' and 'don'ts'."[182]

From this viewpoint, "negativism" (again a typical Christian-Democratic phrase used to characterize the Left) which emphasizes differences and past or existing sources of conflict is deemed "counter-productive".[183] Thus, instead of cherishing and cultivating a "Dalit" identity, as is now fashionable among certain sections of the Scheduled Castes, it is considered better to move on straight to the post-casteist age

[180]H.V. Seshadri: *The Way*, p.34, in a chapter titled: "A Study in Contrast: the Leftist and the RSS Approach".

[181]Thus, women play a key role in injustice against women, e.g. mothers-in-law extorting unreasonable dowries (or likewise in Muslim and African societies, mothers circumcising their daughters), and low-caste people have often been extra harsh in oppressing what few castes they still found below their own.

[182]H.V. Seshadri: *The Way*, pp.34-5.

[183]H.V. Seshadri: *The Way*, p.36.

and start interacting on a casteless basis right away: "All such walls of separation as untouchability, casteism, discrimination, provincialism, linguism etc. are automatically washed away by this all-powerful current of Hindu unity."[184] For this reason, the RSS solves the problem of caste discrimination not by giving special compensatory treatment to its Scheduled Caste members, but by radically ignoring caste.

I have found many times that RSS men were very reluctant to answer my questions about their caste background; if the plan is to evolve a casteless society (as most Indian political parties profess), someone has to make a start.[185] The BJP, by contrast, has a separate Scheduled Caste cell and is eager enough to publicize the low-caste background of some of its spokesmen and state ministers, whether by compromise with the caste calculus which dominates Indian party politics, or from a realization that the former Untouchables do need to go through the phase of separate identity to outgrow their depressed status in another generation or so.

At any rate, while both Christian-Democracy and Integral Humanism have a harmony model of society in mind, they also try to incorporate the existing emancipatory movements. Thus, it is Deendayal Upadhyaya himself who declared (against the liberal anti-socialists in the Swatantra Party, the traditionalists in the Ram Rajya Parishad, and their sympathizers within the BJS): "Those who are keen to preserve the status quo in the economic and social spheres are unnerved by popular movements. They are wont to create an atmosphere of despair. We are sorry we cannot cooperate with them, for many of these public agitations are natural and necessary."[186] In general terms, Deendayal Upadhyaya's Integral Humanism amounted to a social-democratic programme combined with a non-materialistic philosophy.

Integral Humanism and the world

The lack of intellectual sophistication of Integral Humanism may be deplored, but its basic intuition is rather unobjectionable, even a bit goody-goody. It could use some elaboration, which is provided in insufficient

[184]H.V. Seshadri: *The Way*, p.37.

[185]RSS general secretary H.V. Seshadri (*The Way*, p.37) gives an example: "The reflections of Bhiku Idate ... are typical. He comes from a nomadic tribe. ... He was jailed during Emergency because of his active part in Sangh. During his jail days, he once told his Socialist jail mates: 'I have been working in the Sangh for the past 12 years but none enquired my caste. For the first time, this inquiry was made in jail—and that by a Socialist!'"

[186]In *Organiser*, 21.12.1967, quoted in C. Jaffrelot: *The Hindu Nationalists*, p.235.

measure by recent RSS efforts to develop and update it through symposia and publications.

Nevertheless, the RSS believes in a great future of Integral Humanism in the modern world: "Democracy, equality, national independence and world peace are interrelated concepts. But in the West these concepts have often clashed with one another. The ideas of socialism and one-world government have stemmed from efforts at resolving this conflict. However, they have not only failed to do so but have weakened these concepts and created new problems. Bharatiya Sanskriti offers the philosophical substratum on the basis of which these concepts can be harmonised and cherished objectives realised. ... The basic truths propounded by Bharatiya Sanskriti have a validity beyond country and age. So, knowledge of these truths will provide a direction not only for our own advancement but for the world's progress as well."[187]

As Hindu nationalists, the Sangh Parivar activists have suffered of a deep inferiority complex vis-à-vis the Nehruvian elite. But as Hindus, they share in a widespread and profound confidence, deep down inside, in the ultimate superiority of Hindu civilization, a remote hold-over from the time when India was world leader in arts and sciences, thousands of years ago. This feeling that Hinduism has a tremendous liberating message for the whole world, already articulated by Swami Vivekananda, had been pushed in the background by the discovery of nationalist ideology and the remoulding of Hindu self-assertion in Savarkarite nationalist terms. Though Deendayal Upadhyaya was undeniably a nationalist too, his Integral Humanism has brought the universalist self-understanding (and ambition) of Hinduism back in focus.

Conclusion

Regarding the Hindu Nationalist position on the Indian state and nation, I may repeat here what Ainslie Embree has written about his own findings on the RSS: "The general thesis of the present chapter is that the goals of the RSS indeed place it in the mainstream of Indian nationalist aspirations, which is, of course, in accordance with the stated positions of the RSS itself."[188] In essential respects, the Sangh Parivar is continuing the vision of India enunciated by Swami Vivekananda, Sri Aurobindo and the

---

[187]BJS: "Principles and Policies", *Party Documents 1951-1972*, vol.1, p.14.

[188]Ainslie Embree: "The function of the Rashtriya Swayamsevak Sangh: to define the Hindu nation", in M.E. Marty and R.S. Appleby, eds.: *Accounting for Fundamentalisms*, p.619.

freedom movement. This is also proved *a contrario* by the continuity between the discourse of the Muslim League against the freedom movement and that of recent secularists against the Hindutva movement: "majoritarianism", "Islam/secularism in danger".

The idea of India as a Hindu state means two different things. One is that India already is a Hindu state and can only exist as a Hindu state, in the sense that Hinduism is India's natural and only unifier, that even if its Constitution does not pay any lip-service to its natural Hindu identity, India can only exist as a united state by being Hindu. The proof given for this position is that those factors which created an awareness of India as a distinct entity are intimately connected with Hinduism: the Sanskrit language nurtured by the pan-Indian Brahmin caste, the pilgrimage cycles, the Vedic rituals, the ideal of the pan-Indian ruler or *Chakravarti*, and (though the Hindu nationalists are reluctant to highlight it) the *varnâshramadharma*. Also, the literature in which the earliest awareness of cultural Indian unity is shown (*Manu-Smriti, Mahâbhârata, Arthashâstra*) is undeniably Hindu. Another proof is again *a contrario*: all separatists justify their struggle by claiming to be non-Hindu and therefore out of place in India, that obviously Hindu country.

The second meaning of "Hindu state" is simply that the Indian Republic be declared a Hindu state, just as the Kingdom of Nepal has been declared a Hindu kingdom. This goal is not pursued by the BJP, while the RSS is ambiguous about it, though many RSS stalwarts individually have embraced it. All those in and around the Sangh Parivar who care to speak out about how they envision a Hindu state, assure us that this would be a democratic and "secular" state, meaning one which knows no discrimination whatsoever on the basis of religion, and in which Muslim and Christian citizens will enjoy equal rights with Hindus, but no special privileges.

Hindu "nationalism" is in some ways a deviant branch of the broader and older Hindu revivalist movement, due to its excessive emphasis on nationalism, eclipsing larger and deeper civilizational concerns. Deendayal Upadhyaya's Integral Humanism is a corrective and a return to the mainstream, in that it attempts to formulate a recognizably Hindu political vision in universalist terms.

Specific Hindu grievances

Nothing is more revealing for the poor state of Hindutva-watching among scholars and journalists than their silence about the Hindu grievances which feed Hindutva activism, or their automatic dismissal of these grievances as being fictitious. Most observers are caught in the over-all bias of secularist writing on the phenomenon of "fundamentalism", viz. that external (non-doctrinal) factors can account for it. A very common expression of this bias is the reassuring explanation that there are no inherent religious reasons for the recent upsurge in Islamic militancy, and that it is all due to post-colonial frustrations or rising unemployment: essentially a variation on Karl Marx's dismissal of religion as "the opium of the people". In the case of "Hindu fundamentalism", the usual explanations are full of Marxist phraseology about "the urban traders seeking to assert themselves" or "an upper-caste ploy to prevent Backward-casteist mobilization", or other conspiracies of secular socio-economic interest groups *masquerading* as cultural or religious movements.

Such an approach, in my opinion, is bad scholarship. It is right to look for someone's "real" intentions *after* his ostensible intentions have been shown to be incompatible with the actual data of his situation and behaviour. But simply disregarding his explicit reasons so as to impose your own alternative explanation without giving him a fair hearing is not acceptable. We must not refuse to look at facts as they present themselves because of the a priori assumption that what you see is not what you see, that there is something else behind it. And the pertinent fact here is that Hindus as such do have a lot to complain about.

INJUSTICE IN DISCOURSE

The India-watcher in a state of denial

While any "Hindu fundamentalist" you talk to, will tell you first of all that Hindus feel like second-class citizens in India, no India-watcher has made an attempt to find out the factual basis of this complaint. Thus, BBC reporter Brian Barron was told by a Hindu interviewee, a Sadhu, that Hindus are discriminated against. Instead of jumping at this long-awaited occasion to find out the why of Hindu activism, he simply ignored the point.[1] Likewise, Susan Bayly makes it impossible for herself and her readers to comprehend Hindu activism by assuming beforehand that the said complaint is absurd considering that India guarantees "constitutional even-handedness to citizens of every religious community and ethnic group".[2] That is precisely what Hindu revivalists deny, what they have argued against at length.

If the fact of Hindu grievances (leave alone the contents of those grievances) is ever mentioned, it is invariably to laugh them off as mendacious or, in Bruno Philip's words, "fantasmatic".[3] This then is the major reason for the general misperception of the Hindu movement in the West: ignorance or denial of the objective factors of the Hindu unrest, one of them being the easily verifiable legal inequality which Hinduism suffers in India, another the distorted presentation of Hindu-Muslim relations in the dominant secularist discourse. Let us take it upon ourselves to set the record straight.

The very fact that Hindutva-watchers ignore the Hindu grievances is itself considered as an injustice towards the Hindus, an injustice of

---

[1]Brian Barron, BBC *Assignment* documentary on the Ayodhya movement, May 1991. Likewise, when L.K. Advani (whom he, unconcerned for keeping up a semblance of neutrality, introduced as a "demagogue") countered his hostile questions (e.g. about his "bloody" *Rath Yâtra* of October 1990, which was in fact entirely bloodless, though bloody riots took place in Uttar Pradesh and Hyderabad, far from Advani's itinerary) with: "You are taken in by a disinformation campaign", Barron did not pursue the point, even though a journalist ought to be on alert when the sources on which the quality of his information depends, are questioned so pointedly.

[2]Susan Bayly: "History and the Fundamentalists", *Bulletin of the American Academy of Arts and Sciences*, April 1993.

[3]Bruno Philip: "100 millions de musulmans en Inde", *Le Monde des Débats*, March 1993, reproduced in *Le Monde, Dossiers & Documents*, February 1997, p.7.

discourse. Before we come to the tangible discriminations of which Hindus complain, we should consider this alleged injustice of discourse.

Damn the Hindu victims of terrorism

The very first Hindu grievance is that *Hindus are being killed*: in Pakistan and Bangladesh, in Kashmir, during bomb attacks in Mumbai, Coimbatore and other cities. Large-scale street riots, the ones in which Muslims as well as Hindus get killed, have receded from memory in the decade following the Babri Masjid demolition, but terrorist attacks solely targeting Hindus have continued with high frequency. Moreover, Hindu activists are specifically singled out and have been assassinated in sizable numbers throughout the 1980s (including several hundreds of Sangh Parivar activists by the Khalistani terrorists) and 1990s (mostly individual murders and a few public bomb blasts, as on Advani's meeting in Coimbatore killing over 40 BJP supporters in February 1998, by Pakistan-backed Muslim groups).[4]

Among lesser-known types of anti-Hindu aggression, note the use of riots, targeted assassinations and minor forms of pestering (eve-teasing) in order to "ethnically cleanse"lucrative Hindu neighbourhoods, making the Hindus sell off their properties at dumping prices to Muslim mafia dons, as in Ahmedabad.[5] The ethnic cleansing which non-Muslims have suffered in Bangladesh has now followed the illegal Bangladeshi immigrants into the border districts of West Bengal and the north-eastern states, where Hindu and Buddhist refugees (such as the Buddhist Chakmas from the Chittagong Hill Tracts) find themselves both unwelcome from the part of the natives and chased onward by the ever-increasing Muslim settler population.[6]

None the less, such grievances can be addressed only to the trouble-makers themselves, in many cases anti-Indian (and therefore anti-Hindu) separatists. They cannot be laid at the door of the secularist intelligentsia

---

[4]See e.g. K. Jana Krishnamurthi: "Nationalist leaders being liquidated in the South", *Organiser*, 18.5.1997.

[5]See e.g. Mayank Jain: "Minority becomes majority—majority becomes minority: a first-person report from Ahmedabad", *Organiser*, 15.11.1998.

[6]Discussed in detail in Saradindu Mukherji: *Subjects, Citizens and Refugees: Tragedy in the Chittagong Hill Tracts (1947-1998)*; also in Arun Shourie: *A Secular Agenda*, pp.201-306, and in Baljit Rai: *Demographic Aggression against India*.

or the Nehruvian state except in so far as it fails to protect the citizens. Any type of regime faced with the variety of terrorists besieging India would find this an uphill battle.

The second and related grievance, however, does concern an identifiable and articulate party, a prominent section of India's establishment and of the leading international academic and media network. It is that *this killing goes on without anyone paying attention*: not the state, not the establishment media, not the scholars. Professionals paid to follow and analyse South Asia's Hindu-Muslim conflict, somehow ignore the single largest category of violence characterizing this conflict: violence against Hindus.

The total number of riot victims in India since the Partition massacres, which ended in January 1948, is variously estimated as up to almost twenty thousand, Muslims as well as Hindus, with the former outnumbering the latter three to one, and a high proportion of these Muslims having been killed in police firing.[7] However, more than that total number, and almost exclusively Hindus, were killed in 1950 in East Bengal alone.[8] Smaller massacres still rivalling the biggest Indian communal riots have been inflicted on the Hindus of East Bengal every couple of years, such as the one hitting both Hindus and Christians in 1964.[9] Recent instances took place in 1989 and 1992, both in "retaliation" for phases of the Ayodhya controversy in India, the first one being the entirely peaceful *Shilânyâs* ceremony.[10] The Hindu death toll in post-Independence riots in East Bengal already outnumbers the Muslim death toll in Hindu-Muslim clashes in the whole of South Asia by far.

What reader or writer of any book or paper on "communalism"would suspect that not Muslims but Hindus are the main victims? The impression

---

[7]Christophe Jaffrelot (*Hindu Nationalist Movement*, p.552) arrives at a total casualty figure of over 13,000 for the period 1954-93.

[8]Figures ranging from 10,000 to (unrealistically) half a million have been given in various Hindu sources, e.g.: "In 1950, nearly half a million Hindus were slaughtered in East Pakistan", according to S.K. Bhattacharyya: *Genocide in East Pakistan/Bangladesh*, p.186.

[9]A survey of the press coverage of these pogroms in 1950 and 1964 is given in A.J. Kamra: *The Prolonged Partition and Its Pogroms*.

[10]See e.g. S.G. Dastidar: "Pogroms and Riots in Bangladesh and West Bengal, 1992-93", *South Asia Forum*, fall 1993, and Taslima Nasreen: *Lajja*.

generally created is that we have to go and protect those poor hapless Muslims from the swaggering Hindu bullies.

All these riot data are, moreover, dwarfed completely by the East Bengal genocide of 1971. The first Bangladesh Government estimated the number of people killed by the Pakistanis and their local (chiefly Jamaat-i-Islami) allies at three million. This may well be an overestimate, but if we play safe and put the number at one million, it still leaves all the other communal massacres since Partition (and even the sum total of the Partition killing) far behind. Moreover, Western as well as Indian observers noticed that the prime target group were the Hindus.[11]

As for the non-Hindu victims, they too were killed by Pakistani or pro-Pakistani Muslims, not by Hindus (who were fleeing or hiding), and often also for anti-Hindu reasons: to the Pakistanis, Bengalis with their Sanskritic script, their *sari*s and their Tagore songs were still almost-Hindus, which explained their un-Islamic cultural nationalism. It should be obvious that the Bengali Muslims killed by Pakistanis do not enter the Hindu-Muslim victim tally, in case anyone was thinking of using them to obscure the steep inequality in Hindu vs. Muslim victimhood in 1971. The simple bottom-line is that since 1948, the mortal victims of Hindutva are counted at most in thousands, those of Islam in hundreds of thousands.

So, who is aware of this? In the news bulletins, names like Rwanda or Cambodia are rarely mentioned without a little background reminder of the mass killing that rocked those countries in the recent past. Even the Armenian genocide of 1915 is frequently mentioned. But Bangladesh? All South-Asian governments discourage interest in the events of 1971, particularly in the communal dimension, because each one of them wants to avert the anti-Muslim conclusions which the data might suggest to a section of the public. Foreigners, meanwhile, feel no need to know or remember the massacre. When Hindus are killed by Kashmiri terrorists, admittedly a routine occurrence, then nobody is bothered. One white Australian missionary killed by Hindu tribals is world news (Graham Staines, killed in 1998), but Hindus might as well go to the gas chambers in their millions and still nobody would care.

---

[11]Nandan Vyas ("Hindu genocide in East Pakistan", *Young India*, January 1995, pp.10-15) cites to this effect Edward Kennedy ("Hardest hit have been members of the Hindu community") and Sydney Schanberg ("Hindus, particular targets of the Muslim army").

The misperception of Hindus as bullies and minorities as their victims in turn conditions a distortion of the information flow concerning new instances of communal violence. Thus, when a series of bombs damaged churches in Goa, Karnataka and Andhra Pradesh between 21 May and 9 July 2000, Christian and secularist fingers were immediately pointed at the RSS though this organization had never been associated with the specific methods of bomb terror in the past, simply because everybody "knew" that the RSS is that big bad wolf terrorizing Christian children. In the West, even tabloids otherwise poor in international news "informed" their readers about Hindu terrorism against noble dedicated Christian missionaries, India's only cure for leprosy and caste injustice. In India, editors and Church spokesmen laughed off the RSS defence that the Pakistani ISI had to be behind it

But then on 9 July, two of the real perpetrators made a technical mistake, killing themselves and exposing their identities and the Pakistani origin of their equipment. So their gang was arrested: a branch of *Deendar Anjuman*, a Muslim sect founded in the 1920s under the Nizam's patronage to convert Lingayats (a Shaiva sect) to Islam, and now with headquarters in Pakistan. Though not an ISI intiative, the campaign did have the backing of the Pak foreign hand. If I handn't been a reader of the Indian press for professional reasons, I would not have known that the whole bomb campaign had been the handiwork of a Muslim outfit.[12] For, the Christian and secular press worldwide continued to refer to "Hindu bomb attacks on churches", obviously relaying the stories fed to them by Indian Church sources. A full two months later, Church spokesman John Dayal went before an American Congressional hearing (mandated by a law which makes US relations with foreign countries dependent on their "religious freedom", including freedom for American missionaries to proselytize) to reiterate the same old allegations of Hindu bomb attacks.

The point here is not the dishonesty of Church spokesmen, but the fact that they correctly expected to get away with repeating their calumny

---

[12]The story is told by S.V. Seshagiri Rao: "Church blasts: truth and propaganda", in David Frawley *et al.*: *Crusade in India*, pp.10-19. A similar case is the rape of four nuns in Jhabua, also in 1998 (discussed in Arun Shourie: *Harvesting Our Souls*, p.7): in spite of Christian allegations, it turned out that Hindu militancy had nothing to do with the crime and that half of the gang of perpetrators were tribal Christians themselves, yet this "rape of nuns by Hindu fanatics" keeps reappearing in press stories about "Hindu atrocities on Christians".

against the RSS even after police investigations had cleared it of any involvement and the real culprits had been arrested and had confessed. A climate has been created in which every allegation against Hindu activists enjoys a priori credibility while every complaint of Hindu victims is shrugged off or even maligned as hate propaganda.

Secular-Hindu self-hate

Leaving aside the violence department, the greatest irritant in the opinion climate for activist Hindus is the tendency to "Hindu-baiting" or "Hindu-bashing" among born Hindus who profess their adherence to "secularism". Ram Swarup explains the phenomenon as follows: "When two cultures meet on unequal military terms—as the Hindu culture met the West and earlier met Islam—it gives rise to grave problems of self-identity for the defeated party", so that in practice, many elite Hindus "disowned their nationhood and their culture and adopted the ways and attitudes of the victors whom they regarded as their superiors. They saved their self-respect through self-alienation. ... Even people who eventually came to fight the British politically surrendered to them culturally."[13]

Jawaharlal Nehru was the most typical example of this phenomenon, but most of the England-returned lawyers who led the Indian National Congress displayed this attitude to some extent. To be sure, there was also a counter-tendency of self-rediscovery and cultural self-assertion, probably best expressed by Sri Aurobindo, but the "self-alienated" tendency became the dominant one after Independence. More than the colonial dispensation, the new ruling class of free India demonstrated the most durable success of the colonizers: "A dominant ruling people or race also creates a dominant ideology. It gives birth not only to economic and political compradores but also to intellectual compradores. In India, too, we developed a local satellite ideology derived from the dominant imperialist ideology. It believed what it had been taught, namely, that India was not a nation but only a name for a geographical region occupied by successive waves of invaders, that its past was dark, its religion degraded and superstitious, and that its social system was a tyranny of castes and creeds."[14]

Much of the Hindu revivalist argument discussed in this study pertains

---

[13]Ram Swarup: *Cultural Self-Alienation and Some Problems Hinduism Faces*, p.1.

[14]Ram Swarup: *Cultural Self-Alienation*, p.5.

precisely to the "self-alienated" positions taken by Hindu members of the ruling class. For the present purpose of illustrating the anti-Hindu bias in the world view of these "alienated Hindus", we may be satisfied with a close look into one typical example, an article by Ms. J.G. Sharma published in 1993, when polarization between Hindu nationalism and the "self-alienated" secularist Hindus was at its most intense.

Ms. Sharma imagines what a BJP regime would be like, and assumes that it would first of all replace the existing legislation with the ancient code of Manu, the *Manu Smriti*. In fact, the BJP never had the intention of making the Manu Smriti into law, and it never really was a law book anyway, but let that pass.[15] So, she starts lampooning Manu: "Manusmriti is not against fashion. It is all for propagation of ethnic chic, but only in its pristine purity. That way, you spend less on cloth, and it is healthier for a warm country like ours."[16]

Western-dressed secularists describe the dress of their less advanced countrymen as "ethnic chic", a neo-colonial term,—"ethnic" meaning "tribal" or "native", and "chic" wrongly pretending that it is not the colonials but the natives who put on airs. A secularist's "ethnic chic" is simply a common man's common-sense wear, *sârîs* and *dhotîs*, praised by ecologists for their objective advantages such as being comfortable, cheap, economical with labour, and "one size fits all". Not really an important matter, but quite significant for the petty intolerance of a certain elite vis-à-vis any and every expression of native culture.

More serious is her allegation that Manu condones genocide of India's tribal populations: "As for the tribals, they would be beyond the pale, so you would not have to bother about their rights at all. You could build as many dams across their land as you wished, and drown the whole lot of them in one go."[17]

The standard reply to this is that *Shâstra*-abiding Hindus have, albeit from a distance, co-existed with the tribals for millennia, otherwise the tribals would now not be available for inclusion in anti-Hindu rhetoric. It

[15]In the eighteenth century, the East India Company based its *Code of Gentoo Law* on the Manu Smriti, though it had never been a law book comparable to modern law books or even to Shariat compendia. According to Wendy Doniger (*Laws of Manu*, p.xvii), calling it a law book "skews it towards what the British hoped to make of it: a tool with which to rule the Hindoos. A broader title like 'teaching' would better suggest what the text is".

[16]J.G. Sharma: "Manusmriti", *Sunday Mail*, 14.2.1993.

[17]J.G. Sharma: "Manusmriti", *Sunday Mail*, 14.2.1993.

was Jawaharlal Nehru, self-described as "a Hindu only by accident of birth", who applauded factories and hydro-power generators on dams as "our new temples"; and these have destroyed tribal livelihood and tribal culture far more thoroughly than Manu ever thought possible.

In fairness, it must be noted that there are different shades to the secular colour. Some vocal secularists do uphold native culture at least in some respects, see e.g. leading feminist Madhu Kishwar's attack on the English water-closet, the "imperial throne of the sahibs", in which she decries "the mindless aping of the Western drainage and sanitary systems, which are unhygienic and not suitable for Indian conditions".[18]

Some of them even criticise fellow secularists for their unsympathetic anti-Indian attitudes. Secular columnist Dipankar Gupta defends the "everyday Indian aesthetics" at which psychiatrist Sudhir Kakar has been poking fun: "Mind you, the decor of rooms that Kakar is so condescendingly describing happen to be homes of people who have been kind enough to extend hospitality to him. But locals can never do things right by Indo-Anglian standards."[19] Westerners have recently learned to be shy about inequalities, and they are shocked when they hear Hindu upper-caste traditionalists speak scornfully about low-caste people: no European aristocrat would dare to speak about the paupers in his own country like that. The same crude and unabashed condescension is in evidence when the new upper caste, the Westernized secularists, speaks about lower beings such as Hindus.

Sati, the much-highlighted ugly face of Hinduism

Secularist columnist Ms. J.G. Sharma makes the predictable allegation that Hinduism as represented by Manu is anti-woman: "O what a lovely world it would be, one governed by Manusmriti. All these women libbers would be put in their rightful places, and any talk of burning a bra would be instantly answered by a bout of bride burning. A man could marry as many times as he liked, while the women would all be suttee. And he could

[18]M. Kishwar: "Symbols of Mental Slavery", *Sunday Observer*, 24.1.1993. She also shocked India's Anglo-secularists by speaking out in favour of arranged marriage as opposed to love marriage.

[19]D. Gupta: "The Communal Psyche", a review of S. Kakar's book *The Colours of Violence*, in *India Today*, 15.12.1995. In Kakar's favour, he notes that "Kakar trains his guns at the naïveté of secular historians who believe that communal identities, like Muslim and Hindu, were non-existent in the past and are only recent colonial creations."

easily afford to marry and marry on, because every time he would get a fat dowry."[20]

The reference to the Western feminist campaign of "bra burning" (as if Manu's wife ever wore a bra) and the obsolete British spelling *suttee* say a lot about Ms. Sharma's cultural horizons. She has not bothered to actually read Manu, the arch-Hindu and proverbial bogey, and she is right in so far that one need not have read Manu to surmise that this patriarch must have "put women in their places".[21] On the other hand, actually reading his text would have taught her that neither dowry (*dahej*) nor self-immolation of widows (*satî*) figure in it.[22] Even a Manu-Smriti-abiding Hindu can do without *satî*, which always had its Hindu opponents (including some of the eighteenth-century Maratha princes who prohibited it in their domains) because momentous decisions should not be taken in the emotional condition of just having been widowed.[23] In Manu's case, we need not assume he was an opponent, he may simply have been more interested in other subjects.

Comparative study of Indo-European cultures suggests that the incidence of *satî* is *inversely* proportional to the status of women: from very common among the Celts ("massively!", says Bernard Sergent), where women were rather independent, to a mere epic memory among the Greeks, where women were men's property and not considered to have much "honour" to uphold by means of heroics.[24] The low status which Manu accords to women may then be directly related to his not acknowledging *satî*.

Satî has its defenders too, and there is at least one modern intellectual who acknowledges their *bona fides* and puts the issue in its proper

---

[20]J.G. Sharma: "Why not bring Manusmriti?", *Sunday Mail*, 14.2.1993.

[21]Famously in Manu 5:148: "In childhood a woman should be under her father's control, in youth under her husband's, and when her husband is dead, under her sons'. She should not have independence." Yet, Friedrich Nietzsche (in *Der Antichrist*, and discussed in W. Doniger: *Laws of Manu*, p.xix-xxii) praised Manu's affection for women.

[22]Manu 5:157 ff. prescribes chastity for widows; bride-price (*shulk*, i.e. the groom's family paying to the bride's) is forbidden in 3:51-54 and 9:93-100, but mentioned off-hand as an existing custom in 8:204, 8:366, 8:369.

[23]See e.g. Arvind Sharma: *Sati*, pp.15-18.

[24]Bernard Sergent: *Les Indo-Européens*, p.223. A famous case of *satî* among Indo-Europeans outside India is that of Brunhilde, widow of Sigurd/Siegfried, as described in the *Edda*: she orders her slaves (and invites her free servants) to join her in death, and before embracing death on her husband's corpse, she predicts the future of all her relatives, a testimony to the special powers attributed to a *satî* woman.

perspective: Ashis Nandy, an Indian Christian, recommends Ananda Coomaraswamy's spirited defence of *satî* "to shallow, pompous progressives and feminists who believe that one ought only to immolate oneself for secular causes like revolution and nationalism, not for old-fashioned religious or cultural causes".[25] This by itself has attracted the suspicion that Nandy is in favour of *satî*, but his critique is really more subtle than that.[26]

We are making this digression into the *satî* controversy because it illustrates the bad conscience of the "self-alienated Hindus". Indeed, Nandy informs us that the last "large-scale epidemic of sati" (in Westernizing Bengal of the early nineteenth century, where new British inheritance laws turned a surviving daughter-in-law into a pecuniary rival) was a "logical culmination of rational, secular cost-calculation against the background of a large-scale breakdown in traditional values. ... if anything, modern values, not traditional ones, were to blame".[27] Indeed, "the epidemic was a feature of exactly the part of the society—the Westernizing, culturally uprooted, urban and semi-urban Indians—that was most dismissive towards the rest of society as a bastion of superstition and atavism."[28]

This is even more true of the dowry murder plague, a typically modern, consumerist phenomenon, historically unconnected to *satî*. The Christian scholar J.N. Farquhar wrote in 1914 that "the evil seems to be largely a result of the progress of Western education".[29] He adds an example of a girl in Calcutta who committed suicide "to release her father from the impasse". The first dowry deaths in the nineteenth century were indeed *suicides* by daughters who tried to spare their fathers the huge debts, and this was in the most anglicized communities: Parsi and Sindhi businessmen. Next, consumerism and democratization spread the dowry custom to classes which could ill afford it. Though the dowry murder

---

[25]A. Nandy in J.S. Hawley: *Sati, the Blessing and the Curse*, p.136, with reference to A. Coomaraswamy: "Status of Indian Women", *The Dance of Shiva*, p.91, and to a then-recent news item of a Tamil activist who had set himself on fire in protest against the oppression of the Lankan Tamils, a small news item which caused no indignation.

[26]"When Nandy approaches tradition and modernity from a revisionist perspective, he suddenly lands himself in the conservative-reactionary camp", according to Janet Kamphorst, *India Nu*, Jan. 1996, p.5.

[27]A. Nandy in J.S. Hawley: *Sati, the Blessing and the Curse*, p.139.

[28]A. Nandy in J.S. Hawley: *Sati*, p.141.

[29]J.N. Farquhar: *Modern Religious Movements*, p.406.

plague kills thousands of women per year (as opposed to one *satî* every so many years), it is much less of an issue than *satî*, judging by the scholarly and media coverage. But, as peasant women from Deorala (where the last much-publicized sati took place in 1987) pointed out, burning to death in a Delhi suburb is no less painful than in Deorala, and "Deorala women were not accustomed to burning their daughters-in-law to death the way urban women did".[30]

However, the Indo-Anglian elite has achieved complete success in passing on its self-interested version of the facts to the outside world, as is evident in numerous anti-Hindu allegations made in passing in articles about Hindutva, such as this one by the late French commentator Jean-Edern Hallier: "The BJP [is] a party supporting the self-immolation of widows and the burning of brides for not paying sufficient dowry".[31] Or this one by David Aikman: "Widow-burning has returned to thousands of Indian villages that have no police on hand. A senior leader of the Janata party even tried to organize public rallies in support of sati. Meanwhile, there are about 500 registered cases of bride-burnings a year, the murder of young women whose financial offering to the groom is considered insufficient. As outdated as these practices may seem, they're being justified by a resurgent Hindu nationalism."[32] Aikman is a former *Time* magazine correspondent in India, and ought to know better than to:

1) grossly overstate the incidence of *satî* ("thousands");

2) confuse the Hindu-nationalist *Bhâratîya Janatâ* Party with the Left-populist *Janatâ Dal*, the party of the late Kalyan Singh Kalvi, who did indeed defend the Deorala *satî* and, less controversially, the subsequent displays of mass devotion;[33]

3) ascribe the defence of the traditional practice of *satî* to the reform-Hindu BJP;

---

[30]A. Nandy in J.S. Hawley: *Sati*, p.145.

[31]J.-E. Hallier: "La mystification. Controverse à propos de Taslima Nasreen", *Le Figaro*, 13.12.1994.

[32]David Aikman: "India's nasty currents", *American Spectator*, Oct. 1997.

[33]The two are separate issues: even opponents of *satî* and upholders of its prohibition have opposed the legal prohibition of the traditional veneration of *satî* women, see HMS ideologue Jeevan Kulkarni's unsuccessful Writ Petition (unpublished, but he gave me a copy) to the Supreme Court against the post-Deorala *Glorification of Sati (Prohibition) Act*, voted by most parties including the BJP; and feminist Madhu Kishwar's column in *Hinduism Today*, September 2000, where she calls this prohibition on *Satî* temples a threat to freedom of religion.

4) amalgamate the traditional practice of widow self-immolation with the modern secular-consumerist practice of bride-burning, falsely described as ancient ("outdated");

5) ludicrously ascribe the defence of bride-burning to the Hindu nationalists.

For one who has lived in India for years, it would be inexcusable to write such things out of sheer ignorance. Instead of inferring bad faith on David Aikman's part, I shall assume he has been misinformed by the anglicized-Indian circles in which most press correspondents hang around. At any rate, it provides an illustration of how the current demonic image of Hindu nationalism has been *created*.

Ashis Nandy finds it "remarkable how, since the Deorala event, there has been a revival of efforts by anglophone, psychologically uprooted Indians—exactly the sector that produced the last epidemic of sati in eastern India—to vend sati as primarily a stigma of Hinduism, not as one of the by-products of the entry of modern values in India."[34] The commotion about the Deorala *satî* was just one expression of the colonial mind-set of the ruling class: "At one time, most such efforts were closely associated with attempts to justify British rule in India. Now, as a cultural projection of a new form of internal colonialism, these efforts are primarily associated with the rootless, Westernized Indian *haute bourgeoisie* who control the media, either directly or through the state."[35]

The abysmally negative image which Hinduism has acquired has a lot to do with Nandy's following observation: "Colonialism has to try to discredit the cultures of the colonized to validate the colonial or quasi-colonial social relationships that it itself has created. Culture can be resistance, and those seeking hegemony in the realm of political economy cannot afford to leave that area alone. The self-declared social engineers in the Third World and their support base within the tertiary sector of that world know this fully."[36]

No Hindu revivalist could have said it better. Only, as Nandy also frequently points out, the BJP is more part of the westernized establishment than of any form of nativist opposition to it: "The BJP is designed to serve modern nationalism, the modern state, and meet the

---

[34]A. Nandy in J.S. Hawley: *Sati*, p.141.

[35]A. Nandy in J.S. Hawley: *Sati*, p.142.

[36]A. Nandy in J.S. Hawley: *Sati*, p.142.

needs of people who have lost ties with their culture."[37] On issues of women's rights, *satî*, women's protection against bride-burning, as also on the principle of secularism or the desirability of modernization, the BJP's positions differ but little from those of its main rivals. That may well be the right position on a number of counts, but at least it should make us drop any Romantic illusions about the BJP as a nativist party opposing modernity.

NO HINDU STATE

To the extent that the goal of the Hindu nationalists is the establishment of a Hindu state, their grievance consists in the absence of such a state today.

No concern for Hindu interests

For an inside view of Hindu grievances, we follow the enumeration given by Abhas Chatterjee in this and the next sections. His first grievance is that the Hindu nation does not have a Hindu state: "The significant point that merits most attention today is that though we Hindus are a nation, we are not yet an independent nation. We are still a subjugated nation. ... The plain but harsh truth is that in August 1947, the Muslim 'nation' of undivided India gained freedom, but not so the Hindus. The Muslims got recognition as a separate nation and a separate territory was carved out as their national homeland. ... But Hindus neither gained recognition as a nation, nor their own State, nor control over their national homeland."[38]

Chatterjee offers one test to verify this, viz. India's role in the international arena: "There is no state today, certainly not in India, to protect Hindu interests in the international arena, to raise voice for the Hindus. If Jews are unjustly treated in any part of the world, the State of Israel, representative of an independent Jewish nation, immediately raises its voice. ... But what is the situation of Hindus? In December 1992, no less than 600 Hindu temples were destroyed in Bangladesh, thousands of Hindu homes were burnt down, hundreds of Hindu women were paraded naked on the streets of Bhola town, a number of Hindus were killed, Hindu shops were looted, Hindu deities were desecrated, Hindu girls were dishonoured. But the Government of India remained silent. In Pakistan, 300 temples were destroyed. In Lahore a Minister of Pakistan personally

---

[37]Speaking to Anil Ramdas on Dutch television's third channel, 3.5.1993.

[38]A. Chatterjee: *Hindu Nation*, pp.30-1.

supervised the pulling down of a temple with the help of bulldozers, and several Hindus were murdered. But the Government of India remained silent. No matter how much tyranny, how much injustice is heaped on Hindus anywhere in the world, the State of India is not bothered—this is the essence of Secularism in India."[39]

This is very slightly exaggerated, e.g. the Indian Government did protest when Idi Amin threw all the Indians (but then they were not only Hindus) out of Uganda, or when Fiji overthrew a democratically elected Hindu-dominated government. But it is of course true that India is not a Hindu state the way Israel is a Jewish state. And it is true that the Nehru-Liaqat Pact of 1950, concluded with Pak Prime Minister Liaqat Ali Khan amid mass killing of Hindus in East Bengal, prevents the Government of India from any form of interference when Hindus are maltreated in Pakistan and its partial successor state Bangladesh.

As a poignant example of discrimination of Hindus abroad, Chatterjee cites the case of a Hindu worker who died in Saudi Arabia: "Some years ago, Sunil Wadhera, a Hindu, died in an accident in Saudi Arabia. In case of death like this, every Muslim gets a compensation of 6 to 7 lakh dinars in that country. But Wadhera's family was given only 17,000 dinars in compensation even when the insurance company had paid the normal amount. It was said that as Wadhera was a *Kâfir*, the value of his life was no more than a paltry sum. This is the Islamic law of that country. It is there. What is significant, however, is that even against such an inhuman, outrageous affront, there was no State which could raise its voice on behalf of the Hindu."[40] In Chatterjee's view, it is one thing to accept the fact that Saudi Arabia is a sovereign state deciding its own policies, but quite another to condone such a policy by not even lodging a formal protest. What angers Chatterjee is that India, which has always been supporting the Arab cause in Palestine, did not take up this injustice against the Wadhera family with the Saudi Government. And more generally, that the Indian state pretends there is no such thing as a specifically Hindu interest which may be hurt and which deserves protection.

No Hindu Constitution

On the Hindu nationalist assumption that there is a Hindu nation, it is

---

[39] A. Chatterjee: *Hindu Nation*, pp.41-2.

[40] A. Chatterjee: *Hindu Nation*, p.42.

undeniable that there is no state which is the political embodiment of this Hindu nation. One can verify this from the text of the Constitution: there is nothing recognizably Hindu about its conception and terminology. India's Constitution was but an adaptation of the British *Government of India Act 1935*, finalized in 1947-50 by a ruling class of anglicized Indians, mostly British-trained lawyers. Ministers of the Hindu princely states who might have made a specifically Hindu contribution (and who, unlike the Congress leaders, were experienced in the art of government), were most unwelcome in Nehru's first Cabinet.

As Abhas Chatterjee observes, "even the Preamble of the Indian Constitution does not contain any Hindu idea. It enumerates no principles based on Hindu ethos and ideals. The Preamble talks of justice, equality, fraternity and liberty as its goals. They may be good ideas in themselves, but what is the inspiration behind them? All of them are Western notions borrowed directly from the French Revolution. The national ideas of India, that is, of the Hindu nation, are—as Swami Vivekananda repeatedly reminded us—*dharma* and spirituality, renunciation and service, tolerance and harmony. ... But the present Indian Constitution has not incorporated a single idea out of these."[41]

Of course, Western Constitutions also don't mention the Ten Commandments. Moreover, it is a common boast in Sangh Parivar pamphlets that India has always been a pioneer of democracy and freedom, so these values need not be considered foreign impositions.

Chatterjee further alleges that the Constitution refuses to acknowledge the central place of Hinduism in Indian culture: "In Article 51A, Hindu culture has not been accepted as India's national culture. Instead, it has been clearly stated that India's culture is a hotch-potch 'composite' culture. This means that we have to regard Islamic culture also as our own culture and to view with reverence even such enemies of the nation as Aurangzeb and Tipu Sultan."[42]

Most Hindu revivalists reject the very notion of "composite culture", a central doctrine of Nehruvian secularism.[43] Aurobindo rejected the concept of composite culture: "a bastard culture is no sound, truth-loving

[41]A. Chatterjee: *Hindu Nation*, pp.34-5.

[42]A. Chatterjee: *Hindu Nation*, p.34.

[43]The internal contradictions of the notion of "composite culture" are discussed by Harsh Narain: *Myth of Composite Culture and Equality of Religions.*

culture. An entire return upon ourselves is our only way of salvation."[44] To this school, Indian culture is Hindu culture, other cultures present in India are either considered as honoured guests (Mazdeism, Judaism, Syrian Christianity) or as unwelcome intruders (Islam, missionary Christianity). But then, Hindu culture itself is a composite.[45] The difference is that the strands which have come to make up Hinduism have really blended, or have at least managed to co-exist in peace, unlike Christianity and Islam.

No Hindu ruling class

An obvious objection against Hindu complaints about India not being a Hindu state is that it certainly is ruled by Hindus. Considering that people with Hindu names still constitute the vast majority of India's population, it could hardly have been otherwise in a democracy. But that proves little: Stalin's first name was *Josef*, a thoroughly Christian name, yet he was a great persecutor of Christians. Among India's Prime Ministers, one could describe Lal Bahadur Shastri or Narasimha Rao as practising Hindus, but not the Nehru dynasty, V.P. Singh or I.K. Gujral; though even they never formally abandoned Hinduism.

Abhas Chatterjee rejects the inclusion of the ruling secularists in the "Hindu" category, demanding at least a minimum of loyalty to Hinduism as a criterion: "Rev. Krishna Mohan Banerjee was a Hindu, but he adopted the creed of Christianity and ceased to be a Hindu. ... Similarly, a person who starts believing in Nehruvian secularism—or Marxism for that matter—which is founded on antagonism to Hindu nationhood, cannot be logically considered to remain a Hindu, or a part of our nation. ... We mistakenly think the secularists—or Nehruvians—also to be Hindus. ... people who have been ruling this country since 1947 are totally anti-Hindu and antagonists of Hindu nationhood, although they have adopted a few superficial Hindu customs. It is wrong to consider them Hindus or to regard their regime as self-rule by the Hindu nation."[46] After going

[44]Aurobindo: *Foundations of Indian Culture*, p.386.

[45]As lovingly described in B. Sergent: *Genèse de l'Inde*. Unlike Shrikant Talageri and other nationalists, he acknowledges diverse ethnic and even geographical origins for different elements in Hindu civilization, but unlike the Dravidianists or the lunatic fringe of the Dalit movement (or their Western supporters), he does not deduce that Hindu civilization is a myth, but rather that it is an admirable synthesis.

[46]A. Chatterjee: *Hindu Nation*, pp.32-3.

through the trouble of arguing that Sikhs and Buddhists who refuse to be categorized as Hindus are none the less Hindus, Hindu spokesmen are now insisting that the mere fact of not calling oneself Hindu is sufficient to deregister the Hindu-born secularists as Hindus.

Chatterjee puts it in dramatic terms: "We are still a subjugated, enslaved nation. Nehruvian Secularists are not our own people. Their regime is not our regime. We have to liberate our motherland from their stranglehold and earn our freedom."[47] What stands between the secularist leaders (meaning the likes of Nehru, Krishna Menon, P.N. Haksar, Jyoti Basu, I.K. Gujral) and Hindu identity is not their philosophical convictions. As Hindutva pamphlets never tire of repeating, even an atheist can be a Hindu. Among the authors discussed here, Veer Savarkar and Sita Ram Goel have been declared atheists. The difference is that the latter two expressed loyalty to Hinduism, while the former category is responsible for policies which many conscious Hindus consider anti-Hindu, and that in some cases they openly rejected the label "Hindu".

Thus, while few Hindus would ever have denied the Communists the label "Hindu" in spite of their anti-Hindu policies, the Communists themselves have rejected the label. In the 1990 controversy over the access to the Kerala Devaswom boards the CPI(M)-led Kerala Government had argued that, in the name of "broad Hindu unity", Hindu-born atheists should also qualify as Hindus and hence be entitled to posts in the management of Hindu temples; but their opponents found it easy to dig up statements by the Marxists denying their Hindu identity.

Thus: "How strange that the Marxists who have been crying themselves hoarse against the very word Hindu as communal, parochial, obscurantist, reactionary and all the other abusive communist jargon, should have suddenly become the champions of 'broad-based Hindu unity'! In fact, the Marxists have always been over-eager to disclaim that they are Hindus. Some years back, in their response to a questionnaire from a leading weekly about their notions of being a Hindu, Marxist leaders like E.M.S. Namboodiripad and E.K. Nayanar had replied: 'Who told you I am a Hindu at all? The question is irrelevant to me.'[48] Now the

[47]A. Chatterjee: *Hindu Nation*, pp.44-5.

[48]Quoting from memory, I recall that to the same question of the *Illustrated Weekly of India*, the film director Satyajit Ray had replied: "I am not a Hindu, I am a Bengali." At Indological conferences, I have heard at least a dozen Hindu-born Marxists insist that they did not want to be described as Hindu. (KE)

same gentlemen have become equally eager to claim that they are Hindus!"[49] Similarly, Communist leader E.M.S. Namboodiripad, when challenged by the VHP to deny that he was a Hindu, said that he was "a man and a Communist".[50]

The lack of an established authority empowered to decide who is a Hindu makes the term "Hindu" susceptible to various manipulations of its meaning, and this has its consequences. If we try to decide this dispute by retreating to the solid ground of India's legislation, we find that Hindus who deny their Hindu origins remain legal Hindus, on par with Sikhs and Buddhists, as long as they have not embraced Christianity, Islam or Zoroastrianism. By that standard, of course all the Hindu-born secularists are still Hindus.

For the present purpose of deciding whether India's ruling class is Hindu, with the implication that it would give a Hindu character to the Indian state, it may not sound unreasonable to say that Nehru and Gujral were non-Hindus by conviction. But one cannot have it both ways: if one chooses an inclusive definition, as Hindu revivalists generally do (so as to include Buddhists and Sikhs in the Hindu category), then it is wrong to describe the "secularist ruling class" as a non-Hindu imposition, except at most for those people who explicitly and consistently reject the Hindu label (which many explicitly don't, witness the Communist attempt to cull some quotations from Vivekananda's *Complete Works* and pose as teachers of "real Hinduism"). If anything is considered wrong with the outlook of that class, the only consistent Hindu response would be to treat that as an internal problem of Hindu society.

There is, after all, a fundamental difference between the Islamic and British occupation regimes and the Nehruvian regime: the latter came and stayed in power with the consent of the governed. The anti-Hindu animus of the secularists is a hold-over from an attitude drilled into the Hindu psyche under previous colonial regimes, but it is now a free choice of the Hindus whether to tolerate or to change that mentality. The political project of the Hindu revivalists can better be construed as a matter of setting their own house in order than as a revolt against a foreign occupation force.

---

[49]H.V. Seshadri: "Marx & Muralidhar", *Indian Express*, 25.6.1990.

[50]Quoted in K. Govindan Kutty: "Politics of Temple Control", *Indian Express*, 19.7.1990.

LEGAL DISCRIMINATION

Article 30

When BJP leaders are questioned on what grievances the Hindus could possibly have in a democratic state with a Hindu majority, they often mention Article 30 of the Constitution. This lays down that the minorities can set up government-sponsored denominational schools, implying their right to a communal bias in recruitment of teachers and students and a religion-centred curriculum. When the Constitutional Assembly voted this article, many delegates probably assumed that the extension of the same rights to the Hindu majority was self-understood; but in practice, this right is denied to the Hindus.

This became hilariously clear in 1980, when the Ramakrishna Mission deemed it necessary to declare itself a non-Hindu minority (a self-definition challenged in court by its own members and finally struck down by the Supreme Court in 1995) in order to prevent the Communist West Bengal government from nationalizing its schools.[51] Hindu self-confidence and militancy were at a low ebb in 1980, hence the Ramakrishna Mission's failure to appeal to the larger Hindu society to come to its rescue. Psychologically too, the ground had been prepared for the Ramakrishna Mission's escapist solution in the sense that Hinduism was held in very low esteem, hence the permament temptation of opting out (likewise for the Sikhs, the Lingayats, even the Hare Krishnas, who have all come to profess: "We are not Hindus"). The ultimate Supreme Court ruling surprisingly did give an assurance of protection against state interference to the RK Mission schools, on grounds not of Article 30 but of the recognition of special privileges for the RK Mission under an old Bengal state law.[52] At any rate, Article 30 constitutes a very serious discrimination on grounds of religion, and is in conflict with the professed secular character of the Indian Republic.

Abhas Chatterjee alleges that "the Indian Constitution has in effect given less rights to the Hindus than to the minorities in several matters.

---

[51]About the contents of the RK Mission's plea against its own Hindu identity, see Ram Swarup: *Ramakrishna Mission in Search of a New Identity*.

[52]Deprived of legal support for its aggression, the CPI-M none the less continued to pester the RK Mission schools through other means, especially by provoking teachers' strikes, see e.g.: "Slap in the face: will the CPI-M leave RK Mission schools alone?", editorial in *The Statesman*, 3.5.1999.

Under Article 30 of the Constitution, minorities have got the most precious right of running educational institutions in accordance with their own cultures and values, but Hindus have been denied this right. This discrimination means that the Indian State is more liberal in helping propagation of alien cultures than the promotion of Hindu culture. You cannot find such a perverse provision in the constitution of any independent nation of the world."[53]

Likewise, Swaminathan Gurumurthy, convenor of the Sangh Parivar's recent Swadeshi campaigns, explains: "I don't think that the majority religion is facing oppression. But I am convinced that the Hindus are politically discriminated against. I can prove this with reference to our Constitution. Article 29 says that every minority has the right to protect its religion, language, script and culture. Article 30 says that every minority group has the right to establish and run educational institutions of its choice."[54]

The practical impact of this Article is: "If anybody wants to run in India today a school that imparts education in Islamic or Christian theology, the Central and State Governments will be giving it grants, maybe they would even meet the entire expenses of the school on many fronts. But start a school where you want to educate your children about Hindu *Dharma* and culture, teaching them the Bhagavad Gita or invocations to Goddess Saraswati, the burden of funding your school will have to be shouldered by the Kalyan Ashram, or the Friends of Tribal Society, or other voluntary organizations like them."[55] The examples given, the RSS-affiliated (Vanavasi) Kalyan Ashram and the Friends of Tribal Society, are both working among the Scheduled Tribes, the hottest area of competition between Hinduism and Christianity.

Another aspect of this discrimination is explained by BJP ideologue K.R. Malkani: "Other private schools and colleges have to reserve teaching and non-teaching jobs for SC-ST-OBCs, but minority institutions can appoint whomsoever they like. ... Private schools have to get prior permission of the Chief Educational Officer for appointing outsiders to higher posts; minority institutions don't have to follow this rule ... the Department can withdraw recognition for violation of rules. But authorities cannot withdraw recognition from a minority institution,

[53]A. Chatterjee: *Hindu Nation*, pp.33-4.

[54]Interview in *Illustrated Weekly of India*, 22.4.1990.

[55]A. Chatterjee: *Hindu Nation*, p.39.

however serious the violation of rules. ... while the Hindu institutions [have] no fundamental right to compensation in case of compulsory acquisition of their property by the state, a minority educational institution shall have the fundamental right to compensation." In Malkani's view, "a lasting solution to this problem lies only in amending Article 30 of the Constitution, giving the right to establish and administer educational institutions of their choice to all religious denominations and not only to the minorities."[56]

Speaking for a great many concerned Hindus, Jagmohan, former Governor of Jammu & Kashmir, sees a "need for having a close look at the unhealthy and unwholesome implications of Article 30", at the "disintegrative impact which Article 30 could have on the Indian state in general and Hindu society in particular".[57] Effectively, in no democratic country would a majority community tolerate such discrimination.

Unexpected support for the Hindu complaint

On the other hand, the benefits for the minorities should not be exaggerated. Their liberty to devise their own curriculum is not unlimited, for beyond certain centrally imposed standards, their diplomas are not recognized. Moreover, the Supreme Court has imposed a ceiling of 50 per cent on the number of students they can recruit on a purely communal basis.[58] To impose discriminatory measures on Hindu institutions, state governments have to take the initiative; the combative CPM Government in West Bengal did go out of its way to harass the Ramakrishna Mission schools, but most Congress Governments never did anything of the kind. And sometimes, attempts are made to take control of minority institutions as well, for example in 1992, the Tamil Nadu Assembly passed the Recognised Private Schools (Regulation) Amendments Bill and Recognised Private Colleges (Regulation) Amendments Bill, empowering the state government to exercise some control over the private schools and colleges: "The Bills are strongly supported by the unions of university, college and school teachers and other staff. But they are equally strongly opposed by Christian and Muslim school and college managements."[59]

[56] K.R. Malkani: "Privileges for all groups", *Indian Express*, 21.6.1992.

[57] Jagmohan: "Hinduism and Article 30", *Organiser*, 6.8.1995.

[58] "Minorities' educational institutions. SC allows 50 pc reservations", *Indian Express*, 7.12.1991.

[59] K.R. Malkani: "Privileges for all groups", *Indian Express*, 21.6.1992.

So, in practice, the discrimination against Hindus in education is limited. None the less, it remains unjust that it is on the statute book, even if it were not actually implemented anywhere. Indeed, the complaints about discrimination against Hindus as formulated here by Abhas Chatterjee, are considered reasonable even by some non-Hindus. Thus, a Christian author, Thomas Abraham from Madras, writes: "Let the Hindus also be given the same right as any other minority to run educational institutions, protect their language, etc. That is to say, the ambit of Article 30 in our Constitution should be changed. The state must be debarred from regulating, supervising or interfering in any way with the administration and practices followed in Hindu temples. Educational institutions run by Hindus will be free to propagate and preach Hinduism with the same constitutional protection now afforded to the minority religions."[60] What he proposes is simply the extension of the special rights enjoyed by the minorities to the Hindu majority.

On the crucial issue of Article 30, a very official form of support has come from very unexpected quarters: Syed Shahabuddin, who introduced "The Constitution (Amendment of Article 30) Bill" in the Lok Sabha, 1995. As already discussed, Article 30 discriminates against the Hindu majority by laying down the following provision: "All minorities, whether based on religion or language, shall have the right to establish and administer educational institutions of their choice." This means that minorities can establish state-subsidized schools where they have a free hand in conducting religion-based curricular, admission and recruitment policies, but the majority cannot. Shahabuddin wants to change all that. The central part of the amended version of Article 30 would read like this, as per Shahabuddin's bill: "Any section of the citizens residing in the territory of India or any part thereof, professing a distinct religion or having a distinct language, script or culture of its own or forming a distinct social group shall have the right to establish and administer educational institutions of its choice."[61] This is Shahabuddin's statement of objects and reasons:

"By judicial interpretation, the term 'minority' has been extended to include identifiable social groups which form a minority in the population of a State even if they form a majority in the Union as a whole. ... In a vast

[60]T. Abraham: "Seeds of alienation", *Indian Express*, 19.6.1990.

[61]Full text in *Muslim India*, June 1995, p.316.

and complex plural society, almost every identifiable group, whether identifiable by religion, including denomination or sect, or by language, including dialects, forms a minority at some operational or functional levels, even if it forms a majority at some other levels. In the age of ethnicity that has dawned in the world, all identifiable groups are equally anxious to maintain their identity and they too wish to have the privilege of the right to establish educational institutions of their choice. ... The aspiration for conserving and communicating religious and cultural traditions and language to succeeding generations is legitimate and applies to all groups, big or small. It is, therefore, felt that the scope of article 30 of the Constitution should be widened to include all communities and all sections of citizens who form a distinct social group at any level. Of late, Article 30 has been criticised as bestowing a privilege on the minority communities which the majority community does not enjoy. The majority community or any section thereof should also be allowed to establish and administer educational institutions of its choice, if it so desires.

"Hence this Bill.

"New Delhi, April 20, 1995.

"Syed Shahabuddin"[62]

Like so many Private Bills, Shahabuddin's Bill never made it to the voting stage, but it showed how he is aware of the mobilizing potential of the Article 30 issue. Apparently, he wanted to defuse it before the BJP would acquire the acumen to perceive and exploit this potential.

Article 370

Another *de facto* discrimination, though no religious denomination is mentioned, exists in the articles giving a special status to the Muslim-majority state of Jammu & Kashmir and the Christian-majority states of Mizoram and Nagaland. As Abhas Chatterjee says: "In whichever state of India a non-Hindu community is numerically predominant, there the state government has been granted special rights under the Indian Constitution. You are all aware, I'm sure, about the Article 370 applicable to the State of Jammu & Kashmir. Similar special provisions have been made applicable to Nagaland under Article 371A and Mizoram undere Article 371G which provide that laws made by India's Parliament would not be applicable to these states unless their own state legislatures endorse them. That is, a

[62] *Muslim India*, June 1995, p.316.

state would have greater autonomy where the legislatures have preponderance of the minorities and where the government is in the hands of the minorities. No such autonomy is available to states where Hindus predominate."[63]

As a consequence of this separate status of Kashmir under Article 370, non-Kashmiri Indians cannot acquire property and citizenship in the state: "About one lakh Hindus—Sahajdharis and Sikhs—who had fled Pakistan during the post-Partition carnage in 1947 and taken shelter in the State of Jammu & Kashmir, have not been granted state citizenship till this day. They have no right to vote in the elections to the State Legislature and the Panchayats, no right to get loans etc. from government institutions, no right to get their children admitted in the medical and engineering colleges of the State. Why? Because they are Hindus."[64]

Well, strictly speaking, they are not excluded because they are Hindus, but because they are non-Kashmiris. Formally, the law excludes non-Kashmiris on a territorial, not on a religious basis. Indeed, this law had been enacted already by the Hindu Maharaja Hari Singh before Independence, when he still hoped to win a separate independence for his state (knowing that he himself had no future in either India or Pakistan). Then again, its non-abolition upon accession to India was the choice of the new rulers, Nehru and his Kashmiri ally Sheikh Abdullah, and at that point religion did enter their calculations. At any rate, the effect of Article 370, and apparently the reason why Muslim Kashmiris are so attached to it, is to keep Hindus out and preserve the Muslim-majority character of Kashmir. The abolition of Article 370 is a long-standing promise of the BJS-BJP. As usual, the party pleads that its dependence on allies, including the Kashmiri Muslim party National Conference, precludes the promise from being carried out in the near future.

Conversion in the Constitution

The Constitution also contains several provisions which do not formally discriminate, but which are to the disadvantage of the Hindus in practice. One sore point is the right to convert, which in theory also protects the rights of Hindus to convert non-Hindus to Hinduism, but was in fact enacted (overruling Hindu opposition) to protect the rights of Christian

[63]A. Chatterjee: *Hindu Nation*, p.34.

[64]A. Chatterjee: *Hindu Nation*, p.38.

missionaries to convert Hindus to Christianity.[65] Abhas Chatterjee protests: "The right of 'propagation' of one's religion that has been bestowed by Article 25 of the Constitution on followers of different religions also means, for all practical purposes, that the adherents of alien and anti-Hindu religions will be at liberty to convert any follower of Hinduism—even if he be a minor—to their own creed."[66]

To be sure, the right of propagation applies to all religions, including Hinduism. Yet, this formal equality conceals a factual inequality: Hinduism and Zoroastrianism do not have a tradition of proselytization, while Christianity and Islam do. It is like giving wolves and sheep the "equal" liberty to eat one another.

Ram Swarup warns that giving a free hand to conversion squads can lead to the total destruction of the native culture, as exemplified by the systematic conversion of Pagan Africa to Christianity and Islam. He questions the justice of the unilateral right to convert: "Thanks to the powerful Missionary lobby in the United Nations, there is a Universal Declaration of Human Rights which states that everyone has a right to embrace the religion of his choice. But where is a similar Declaration which says that tolerant philosophies and cultures have a right to protect themselves against aggressive, systematic proselytizing?"[67]

A prohibition on missionary work in any form is in force in countries as diverse as China, Myanmar, Israel, Greece and (for non-Muslim missionaries) most Islamic states. In theory, the Hindu Kingdom of Nepal should be added to the list, for the Nepali Constitution, Article 14, says: "Right to Religion. Every person may profess his own religion as handed down from ancient times and may practise it having regard to the traditions. Provided that no person shall be entitled to convert another person from one religion to another."[68] In practice, after the replacement of the partyless *Panchâyat* system in Nepal with multi-party democracy in

[65]The Christian lobby work to get the Constituent Assembly to include the "right to propagate" in the Constitution is documented in S.R. Goel: *History of Hindu-Christian Encounters*, Ch.16: "Debate in the Constituent Assembly". As the minutes of the debate show, both proponents and opponents of the "fundamental right" to proselytize specifically had Christian conversion work in mind.

[66]A. Chatterjee: *Hindu Nation*, p.34.

[67]Ram Swarup: *Hindu View*, p.52. Reference in the first sentence is to the Missions' lobbying during the creation of the United Nations Organization, as described in S.R. Goel: *Hindu-Christian Encounters*, Ch.15: "Hoax of Human Rights", esp. pp.252-55.

[68]A. Peaslee: *Constitutions of Nations*, p.775.

1992, Christian missions are having a field day, and there are now hundreds of churches in Nepal.[69] Islamic missionaries, moving in along with the hundreds of thousands of Bangladeshi immigrants, are also active there.

The usual secular explanation given by the said countries for their prohibition on conversion work is that conversion leads to social friction, breaking up communities into hostile factions. Hindu revivalists also use this argument, and on this point, they have some allies among the anthropologists. Anthropological literature has indeed described cases of social separatism wrought within tribal communities by conversion.

Thus, this conversion-induced cleavage is evident in the socially all-important life rituals, as Christian author Joseph Troisi testifies about the Santals: "While among the non-Christians the most important part of the marriage ceremony is the Sindradan, or smearing the bride's forehead with vermillion, among the Christians the exchange of rings by bride and groom marks them as husband and wife. The applying of sindoor [= vermillion] is tabooed." The clean break is also in evidence in the funeral rites: "In the funerary ceremonies, there is little trace of non-Christian customs and modes of thought."[70]

According to Troisi, "the converts are, by and large, being alienated from their village communities. Moreover, converts also become estranged from their own kinsfolk. They are prohibited by their own religion from taking part in the ritual offerings and ceremonies [for the ancestral and other deities]. These ritual practices and ceremonies ... act as a strong unifying force among the household and family members."[71] The change in religion similarly brings about changes in food habits and many other socially important aspects of life. This way, the Christians automatically form a separate community, breaking the age-old bonds of tribal solidarity: "Cutting themselves off from many aspects of their old community life, the converts find themselves members of a new community, the Christian community."[72]

Anthropologist Christoph von Fürer-Haimendorf reports that

---

[69]The Dutch Protestant broadcasting corporation *Evangelische Omroep* regularly shows documentaries about successful conversion campaigns in Nepal, complete with Nepalese converts breaking the idols they used to worship.

[70]J. Troisi: *Tribal Religion*, p.270.

[71]J. Troisi: *Tribal Religion*, p.270.

[72]J. Troisi: *Tribal Religion*, p.271.

"missionary influence has eroded much of the tribes' cultural heritage, which was inseparably linked with the traditional mythology, beliefs and rituals, and wilted when these were abandoned. Above all, the conversion of part of a community tends to destroy the social unity of the whole tribe."[73]

Thus, the Nishi tribe in the North-East finds that in Christian mission schools "a good many Nishi youths have been converted to Christianity. This in itself need not have created any difficulty, for Nishis, like most tribals, are not greatly concerned about the beliefs of their fellow-tribesmen, and if the Christian converts had been equally tolerant, their rejection of traditional Nishi religion might have been ignored by the great mass of conservative tribesmen. However, the converts seem to have been lacking in tolerance and tact, and educated young men of villages affected by the ideological split to whom I spoke in 1980 complained bitterly that Christians deliberately disrupted the harmony of community life. They allegedly refuse to share the houses of adherents of the old faith, and this meant that old parents were abandoned by their converted children, who claimed that they could not stay in dwellings where 'devils' were worshipped. ... My informants insisted that the missions encouraged the establishment of separate settlements for Christians, and that the Christians refused to participate in village festivals, thereby demonstrating their dissociation from the tribal community. It was alleged, moreover, that converts, not satisfied with this symbolic withdrawal from village life, went a step further by abusing and physically attacking priests as they invoked the gods in the performance of traditional Nishi rituals."[74]

And this is the result: "Nishi teachers at the government high-school in Yazali, who were members of a youth organization formed to promote traditional tribal culture, told me how frustrated they were because they could not match the large sums lavished by the missions on propaganda which is undermining the old Nishi life-style."[75]

And yet, not every type of religious development or adoption of new religious practices need be the result of mission campaigns nor lead to

---

[73]C. von Fürer-Haimendorf: *Tribes of India*, p.319. Of course, it will be said that over-concern about "erosion of the tribes' cultural heritage" is an occupational hazard of the anthropological profession.

[74]C. von Fürer-Haimendorf: *Tribes of India*, p.307.

[75]C. von Fürer-Haimendorf: *Tribes of India*, p.307.

social separatism: "The conflict created by the impact of Christianity on the Nishis of the Subansiri district stands in striking contrast to the developments in the neighbouring Kameng district, where tribal groups such as the Khovas have come under the influence of Tibetan Buddhism. ... Among the Khovas there is a spontaneous trend towards Tibetan Buddhism; in two villages small *gompa* are under construction, and the villagers have invited Monpa lamas to perform Buddhist rituals. ... Unlike the Christian converts among the Nishis, those Khovas who are attracted to Buddhism do not opt out of the social life of their community and continue to participate in the traditional tribal rituals. In the same way the Sherdukpens combine their adherence to Mahayana Buddhism with the communal worship of tribal deities. ... Among the Monpas too, elements of the ancient Bon religion coexist with the dominant Buddhist faith, and the practice of both religions within the same communities has not sparked off any conflicts comparable to those which threaten to destroy the social fabric of Nishis affected by religious rivalries."[76]

This explains the assurance given by Hindu revivalists that while conversion to Christianity or Islam is socially disruptive, conversion to religions of Indian stock, in particular conversion or reconversion to Hinduism, need not have such a negative effect. However, in a modern law system, it is hardly feasible to allow one type of conversion (to any school of Hinduism in the broad sense) and to disallow another (to Christianity or Islam), though in Islamic states, this legal inequality exists. So, the choice is whether to oppose the Constitutional right to convert and suspend the Hindu reconversion programme, or to let it stand and face competition from well-organized Christian and Islamic missions in the conversion arena. This difficulty has so far prevented the BJP from taking up, even on paper, the scrapping of the "conversion" part from Article 25.

Conversion laws at the state level

In spite of the Constitutional guarantee of the right to conversion, the state of Arunachal Pradesh has a law prohibiting missionary work, though not restricting the right of an individual to choose his religion. However, a string of mission posts just across the state border has made a mockery of

[76]C. von Fürer-Haimendorf: *Tribes of India*, pp.307-08. This description gives a fair idea of how we should image the "sanskritization" process which in the past has turned numerous tribal communities into castes of Hindu society.

that law: proselytization work is going on without serious hindrance. During the 1995 state election campaign, the oppositional Janata Dal promised to repeal the law:

"The religious issue assumed a special significance with the Janata Dal promising in its election manifesto that if voted to power, it would repeal the Arunachal Pradesh Freedom of Religion [Act], 1978, which made it a cognisable offence for any one found guilty of converting the people to any religion with the lure of inducements. ... While the JD claims that the repeal of the Act has become necessary to give the State a secular character, party insiders admit that the issue was included in the manifesto under pressure from some leaders who are Christians. ... The Congress ... is said to be quiet because of the Christian leaders in the party and also because it is equally keen to woo the Christian community. But some organisations like the Tani Jagriti Foundation, which wants a revival of tribal faiths, are agitated over JD's promise and the Christian penetration in the State."[77] Note again the twist in the concept of "secularism": the right to convert, insisted on by professional clerics, may perhaps be a good thing, but there is absolutely nothing "secular" about it.

The BJP has hitherto hardly had a presence in Arunachal Pradesh, and the enactment of this law, as of similar laws in Orissa and Madhya Pradesh, was the handiwork of a Congressman: "The man who was primarily responsible for bringing in the legislation was Mr. Gegong Apang, then a Deputy Minister and now the Chief Minister for three successive terms."[78] The law has never been seriously enforced: "Besides, the State administrators never felt the need strongly enough to enforce it effectively. The result is that while the 1971 census recorded only 3,684 Christians ..., the Christian following is estimated to have swelled to over 150,000 out of the present population of 850,000."[79]

A similar but somewhat weaker law exists in Madhya Pradesh, prohibiting conversion by force or fraud and requiring the registration of conversion with a magistrate (*Madhya Pradesh Dharma Swatantratâ*

[77] Ashis Chakrabarty: "Religion casts shadow in Arunachal campaign", *Indian Express*, 10.3.1995.

[78] Ashis Chakrabarty: "Religion casts shadow in Arunachal campaign", *Indian Express*, 10.3.1995.

[79] Ashis Chakrabarty: "Religion casts shadow in Arunachal campaign", *Indian Express*, 10.3.1995.

Adhiniyam, 1968).[80] The BJP wants to enact just such a law for the whole of India: "Make fraudulent conversions, including those done by holding out the promise of economic or social benefits, a punishable offence; and introduce a system of registering all conversions".[81] At least, that is what the BJP wanted in 1996; the 1998 Election Manifesto has left that demand out, probably as part of its charm offensive toward the minorities.

The "evil" targeted for remedial action by such legislation is chiefly the use of material inducements to encourage conversions. That such inducements exist is hardly controversial, and can easily be documented from Christian sources. Consider this testimony of a Protestant missionary couple working in Pakistan in the 1960s and 70s.[82] They take it as a matter of course that hospitals and other social services are construed as instruments in the conversion drive, for example, "The evangelistic program of this hospital has been excellent".[83] Everybody who has, like the present writer, gone through the Christian school system, or belonged to a Christian parish, knows that material help is systematically used as a support to the conversion effort. The brochures which missionaries send to the homefront in a bid to garner monetary support are generally quite explicit about this. It is only in Indian secularist circles that stating this matter of common knowledge can be a cause of controversy and denounced as "Hindu chauvinist hate propaganda".

---

[80]It was because they failed to register 94 conversions of tribals to Christianity, as required by this law, that in early 1996 an 82-year-old Flemish missionary and a 50-year-old nun were sentenced to six months' imprisonment, see Neeraj Mishra: "Missionaries get six months' rigorous imprisonment for converting tribals", *Indian Express*, 30.1.1996. For pro-missionary comments, see the editorial "See no devil", *Telegraph*, 2.2.1996, and Bhavdeep Kang: "The cross and the trident", *Outlook*, 21.2.1996.

[81]BJP: *Election Manifesto 1996*, p.65. It also proposes: "Set up a Commission of Inquiry (similar to the Neogy Commission) to inquire into the activities of foreign missionaries and other organisations that have been receiving foreign funds."

[82]Frederick and Margaret Stock: *People Movements in the Punjab*. Interestingly, among Muslims their harvest was very small: "the result of twenty years' work in terms of Muslim converts was 22!" (p.294). Among non-Muslims, particularly among the Marwari-Bhil tribals in Sindh, they were luckier, and the reason was mainly non-religious, viz. fear: "Receptivity among the tribes was heightened by the 1965 and 1971 wars with India. Being Hindu in orientation, the Scheduled Castes feel insecure in a Muslim nation and fear a sudden turn of public opinion against them. This makes them more open to becoming Christians. God has used this natural instinct for safety as a means of drawing them to Himself." (p.296)

[83]Frederick and Margaret Stock: *People Movements in the Punjab*, p.294.

The most famous case of the alleged use of material inducement was the mass conversion of over a thousand Scheduled Caste people to Islam in Meenakshipuram (Tamil Nadu), 1981. It was widely alleged that they had been bought over with "Gulf money", though the alternative explanation is at least as credible: that they had sought safety from police "harassment" by joining an awe-inspiring community.[84] Either way, they sold their souls for a tangible worldly benefit. More than any other event, it was this mass conversion which alarmed Hindus that Hindu society is "under siege", and which provoked demands for curbing the right to convert people.

In other parts of India too, native communities clamour for the enactment of a similar law, for example, after summing up some discriminations imposed by the Muslim state and district authorities on the Buddhists of Kargil (in Jammu & Kashmir), representatives of the Ladakh Buddhist Association complain: "As if this is not enough, there is a deliberate and organised design to convert Kargil's Buddhists to Islam. In the last four years, about 50 girls and married women with children were allured and converted from village Wakha alone. If this continues unchecked, we fear that Buddhists will be wiped out from Kargil in the next two decades or so. Anyone objecting to such allurement and conversions is harassed. Therefore, to protect the religious and cultural identity of the Ladakhi people, an anti-conversion law must be enacted for Kargil as is presently in force in states like Arunachal Pradesh and Madhya Pradesh."[85] Similarly, the Buddhists in Sri Lanka have been campaigning for the enactment of such a law, given "the growing religious tensions in Sri Lanka due to proselytizing Christian groups. The groups are said to be dominated by Christian fundamentalists."[86]

Already in the Constituent Assembly, in the debate initiated by K.M. Munshi on whether to recognize the propagation of a religion as a "fundamental right", there had been demands for a clause specifically

---

[84]For an in-depth discussion from an Islamic angle of the Meenakshipuram case and of a surprisingly large number of similar cases, see Abdul Malik Mujahid: *Conversion to Islam, Untouchables' Strategy for Protest in India*, esp. pp.87 ff. On p.131, he claims, with reference to Government sources, that "there is no proof available to substantiate this charge" (of foreign money being used to induce cenversion).

[85]Tundup Tsering and Tsewang Nurboo, representing the Mar-yul Tsogapa, Kargil: "Ladakh visited", *Pioneer*, 4.12.1995.

[86]"Tensions between Buddhists and Christians over conversions", *Areopagus*, Easter 1994.

prohibiting conversion by material allurement and other fraudulent means. Nothing came of it, but it is worth hearing the position of Harijan member R.P. Thakur, who clarified the position of his community on conversions to Christianity thus:

"Sir, I am a member of the Depressed Classes. This clause of the Fundamental Rights is very important from the standpoint of my community. You know well, Sir, that the victims of these religious conversions are ordinarily from the Depressed Classes. The preachers of other religions approach these classes of people, take advantage of their ignorance, extend all sorts of temptations and ultimately convert them. I want to know from Mr. Munshi whether 'fraud' covers all these things. If it does not cover them, I should ask Mr. Munshi to re-draft this clause so that fraud of this nature might not be practised on these Depressed Classes. I should certainly call these 'fraud'."[87]

However, even the so-called Hindu fanatics of the BJP have never got serious about any legal curbs on proselytization. They never included a plain demand to prohibit conversion (after the erstwhile Nepali model) in their manifestoes. On the contrary, during a meeting with some Kerala Church leaders, BJP leader Murli Manohar Joshi assured them that "conversion *per se* is permissible as BJP views all religions alike. Every citizen is, therefore, at liberty to follow and practise any religion of his choice and volition."[88] Even more limited curbs on conversion through fraud and allurement have been countered rather than promoted by the BJP.

In 1997, BJP MLA Mangal Prabhat Lodha proposed a Freedom of Religion Bill (modelled on the Madhya Pradesh law) in the Maharashtra State Assembly as a private bill. However, the state party leadership refused to support him, and gave an undertaking to this effect to Catholic Church leaders. But as soon as news of the Bill came out, a Christian delegation led by Cardinal Simon Pimenta met the Chief Minister, Manohar Joshi, who assured them that this Bill was merely a Private Bill which the party as such did not support. The Bill was never heard of again in the Assembly, in spite of support by leading newspapers in

---

[87] *Constituent Assembly Debates*, vol.3, pp.490-91; reproduced in Sitaram Goel: *History of Hindu-Christian Encounters*, pp.249-50.

[88] O.M. Mathew: "Dr. Joshi's Dialogue with some Kerala Church Leaders", *BJP Today*, 16.12.1995.

Maharashtra. Finally, in a press interview in Chennai on 4 May 1997, party chairman L.K. Advani declared that his party "did not believe in use of legislation" to stop conversions.

RSS worker Shreerang Godbole protested: "I was dismayed to read the reported press statement of Shri L.K. Advani (*Indian Express*, 5.5.1997) that his party does not favour the use of legislation to ban conversions. ... In any case, this statement explains his party's dismal track record. While the secularist parties had enacted a Freedom of Religion Act in Orissa, Madhya Pradesh and Arunachal Pradesh, none of the BJP State Governments have shown similar courage. ... It is no secret that the majority of conversions in our country are through force, fraud and allurement. While the lasting solution is all-round uplift of the vulnerable sections of Hindu society, it is essential to frame, enact and implement stringent laws to prevent fraudulent proselytisation. ... If the BJP cannot muster this courage, it has no moral right to appeal to its Hindu constituency."[89]

Whether the majority of conversions are indeed "through force, fraud or allurement" is a claim open to verification by sociological research, yet the Sangh Parivar has never invested one rupee in such fact-finding. Though the conversion "frontline" is one of its main areas of activity, it does not systematically collect or process information on actual developments there. At any rate, the facts and the comments by Hindu activists gainsay the common claim that the BJP is an extremist party, or even that it is a Hindu party.

Control over temple management

The discrimination of Hindus in educational matters under Article 30 is the constitutional bedrock of similar legal or *de facto* discriminations, one of which is very consequential: the inequality implied in the inviolable right of Muslims and Christians to manage their own places of worship versus the Hindu impotence before the systematic take-over of Hindu religious institutions by the State governments. Thus, RSS sources allege: "Recently, the CPM-led government of Kerala, despite sharp criticism from Hindu organisations, has taken over the administration of the Sivagiri Mutt along with all the religious and cultural institutions governed by it. Besides, the government also proposed a Bill, Kerala

[89]Dr. Shreerang Godbole: "Ban proselytising", *Organiser*, 7.9.1997.

Hindu Religious and Charitable Institutions and Endowment Act, which intends to take over not only temples but also independent and autonomous mutts and ashrams."[90]

To get an idea of this problem, we may look into a debate which has taken place in Kerala after the Communists moved the State Assembly and the courts to eliminate the one obstacle preventing them from taking control of the temples and their funds. In 1990, the Kerala High Court ruled that only those Hindu legislators "who have faith in God and believe in temple worship" should be entitled to vote or to stand as a candidate in the election of members of temple boards (viz. the Cochin and Travancore Devaswom Boards which administer the major Hindu temples in southern and central Kerala). This means that those who have no faith in God or in the meaningfulness of worship in temples (such as the Communists), even if they are classified as Hindus, should not participate in decisions affecting the management of the temples. The Communist State government overruled the verdict by passing a law (formally an amendment to the Travancore-Cochin Religious Institutions Act, 1950, especially of its Section 4 which lays down the conditions for eligibility) defining as Hindu anyone "born as Hindu or converted to Hinduism".[91]

A newspaper reports: "The introduction of the Bill in the Assembly drew instant protests from the Hindu organisations and also unexpectedly from the Congress (I) and its allies inside the House. ... The Hindu organisations have attacked the measure as a 'black bill' and contended that it violates the fundamental right of religious denominations to establish and run religious institutions under Article 26 of the Constitution." Congress spokesman Karunakaran said that the amendment violates Article 26 of the Constitution which guarantees the rights of religious denominations to build and manage religious institutions: "Those who have no faith in temples could destroy them from within if they were given the right to run them", but the Communist Chief Minister E.K. Nayanar accused him of preferring "the misappropriation of temple property".[92]

The usual justification for imposing government control is indeed that

[90]"The Marxist design to capture Hindu religious institutions. Hand over Sivagiri Mutt to Sannyasins—RSS", *Organiser*, 29.3.1998.

[91]Discussed in K. Govindan Kutty: "Politics of Temple Control", *Indian Express*, 19.7.1990.

[92]N. Madhavan Kutty: "Row over definition of Hindu", *Indian Express*, 15.6.1990.

temple funds are misused. But anyone who has any experience with India's public sector knows that entrusting funds to government personnel is no guarantee against their misuse and disappearance. Moreover, the problem of misuse of religious funds is by no means limited to Hindu establishments. That is perhaps why in the said debate, the Muslim League legislator Mr. Seethi Haji supported the Hindus and affirmed that the administration of temples should be left to believers: the completion of the gradual government take-over of Hindu temple management could, he feared, be followed by moves to take over the mosques as well.[93] However, the position right now is that mosques and churches are immune to this government interference.

RSS General Secretary H.V. Seshadri wrote about the Kerala temple bill that "any fair and impartial lover of religious freedom would certainly conclude that the Marxist-led leftist government there has taken a drastic step to subvert the Hindu faith at its very source. Till today, a member incumbent to the Temple Management Board is required to be a Hindu who would affirm his faith in temple worship. Now, the present motion seeks to redefine the word 'Hindu' so as to allow even those not believing in temple worship, in short the Marxists themselves, to enter the management. While defending the motion, the Chief Minister and another Marxist Minister argued that they did not want to divide the Hindus in sectarian categories and would stand by the broad-based definition of Hindu which includes both the believers and the non-believers in temple worship. ... It is not the 'broad-based Hindu Unity' but the vast amounts of money, prestige and power involved in those positions that is the central point of their interest."[94]

Still, the Marxists have a point: one doesn't have to believe in the efficacity of worship in temples to be a Hindu. The Vedic rishis never worshipped in temples, and in fact even worshipping *per se* is not a requirement for being a Hindu. The RSS people themselves eagerly affirm that "even an atheist can be a Hindu".

But then, that atheist Hindu would not have (and if well-mannered, would not claim) the right to manage a temple. Seshadri: "Could anyone imagine even secular institutions appointing as their managers persons who have no faith in or are even hostile to their aims and objects? Will

[93]"Kerala Temple Bill referred to panel", *Indian Express*, 7.6.1990.

[94]H.V. Seshadri: "Marx & Muralidhar", *Indian Express*, 25.6.1990.

the Marxists themselves allow anyone who has no faith in dialectic materialism ... or who denounces communism itself to become their card holder, let alone their party manager?"[95] All the same, the Supreme Court ultimately awarded the case to the Communists: non-believing Hindus are allowed to manage temples.

The law on this matter of temple management is not uniform, but generally supports the right of the state to interfere with Hindu temples. A legal journalist summarizes the Supreme Court verdict in the case "Shri Adi Vishveshvara of the Kashi Vishvanath temple vs. Uttar Pradesh"[96] as follows: "The Hindus are not a denomination, section or sect under the Constitution. They cannot under Article 26 claim the fundamental right to maintain institutions for religious or charitable purposes, to manage their own affairs in matters of religion, to own and acquire movable and immovable property and to administer such property in accordance with law."[97] Whereas Article 26 is even-handed and recognizes rights of "every religious denomination or any section thereof" (in contrast to Article 30, which only speaks of "minorities"), this Court ruling brutally lays down that these rights are not recognized in the case of Hinduism; so that Article 26, like Article 30, must be read (and was upheld as such by the Supreme Court) as discriminating against Hinduism.

The Court's reasoning is as follows: "Public-oriented Hindu temples have a secular and a religious component. The management of such temples, their properties and endowments falls in the secular area. Hence the legislative/executive can enact laws to ensure that management is in keeping with the Constitution. Management rights are not the property of hereditary mahants, pandas or archakas. Hence a law on the lines of the UP Shri Kashi Vishvanath Temple Act, 1983, which vests the properties in the deity and entrusts the management to a Board of Trustees comprising persons qualified in Hinduism and knowledgeable about the temple, holds validity. ... Moreover, the State has not taken over the property or the management but only vested it in a Board of Trustees."[98]

---

[95]H.V. Seshadri: "Marx & Muralidhar", *Indian Express*, 25.6.1990.

[96]One of the litigants is indeed *Adi Vishveshvara*, "the original Lord of the Universe", i.e. Shiva as the deity worshipped in the Kashi Vishvanath temple; in India, a temple deity is a legal person.

[97]Krishan Mahajan: "State can take over temple management", *Indian Express*, 14.4.1997.

[98]Krishan Mahajan: "State can take over temple management", *Indian Express*, 14.4.1997.

This may sound reasonable, but how would you feel if the state left you the legal title to your house, while taking over its "management"? Hindus also object that this reasonable approach is not extended to churches and mosques. That, they argue, is and remains an inequality on the basis of religion, not permissible in a state which calls itself secular.

That the discrimination is real enough, and that the attraction of the temples' income on politicians is quite strong, was proved again when they tried to have a temple reclassified as "Hindu" in order to take it over: the Shirdi Sai Baba temple in Chanderghat Hyderabad. This saint was born in a Muslim family, though his *sâdhanâ* was purely Hindu. For the latter reason, the Government saw a chance to take it over. This time, it was not lucky: "The Supreme Court dismissed an appeal by the Commissioner for Endowments who wanted the temple declared as Hindu. The Court noted that Baba's philosophy was neither exclusively Hindu nor Muslim or Christian. The Endowment Commission controls Hindu temple administration and finances. Places of worship of other religions are free of such control."[99]

The case that Hindus are discriminated against is certainly strengthened by such incidents. As a Hindu, Shirdi Sai Baba would be susceptible to exploitation by the authorities, but being recognized as a non-Hindu, he is not. Yet all manner of experts claim that India is a secular state, except that the minorities suffer discrimination, and that it is Hindus who are threatening the secular system.

Financial discrimination

The Constitution, Article 15 (1), lays down that: "The state shall not discriminate against any citizen on grounds only of religion, race, caste, sex, place of birth or any of them."[100] On this basis, India might be called a secular state, if we keep the discriminatory articles discussed above out of our consideration. However, such discriminations by the state on grounds of religion alone do exist, and some have been formalized in laws.

According to Abhas Chatterjee, a very tangible legal discrimination is the following: "In almost all states of India, public undertakings styled as Minorities Finance Corporations have been formed. The Central

[99]*Hinduism Today*, Feb. 1996.

[100]I am using the editions of the Constitution of India (with comment) by P.M. Bakshi, by V.N. Shukla (1995 update by Mahendra P. Singh), and by B.K. Sharma (bilingual government edition, 1991).

Government is also proposing now to set up a similar undertaking by providing Rs. 500 crores as its initial capital.[101] These corporations provide loans to people below a certain level of income and help them set up their own enterprises. But there is a condition. A person would be entitled to get the loan only if he is not a Hindu! You may be a learned yet destitute Hindu, a starving Hindu today struggling to earn a penny, but you cannot be financed. Get converted tomorrow to Islam or Christianity, and you will get the loan!"[102-3]

On 16 March 1995, the Press Information Bureau of the Central government (Congress) announced that members of the religious minorities will receive assistance from the National Minorities Finance and Development Corporation (effectively established with an authorized share capital of Rs.5,000 million) if the annual family income is below double the poverty line as defined by the Planning Commission. This means that members of religious minorities need to be only half as poor as Hindus to qualify for government loans and advances on the special conditions laid down for the poor. Referring to the pre-Independence custom of water vendors to separately sell *"Hindû pânî"* and *"Muslim pânî"*, RSS commentator G.N.S. Raghavan remarks: "It has fallen to Prime Minister Narasimha Rao to extend the two-nation appellation from the drinking-water of pre-Independence days to post-Independence poverty."[104] A very tangible inequality indeed.

The Minorities' Commission

Another law enacted in defiance of the Constitutional provisions of equality regardless of religion is the 1992 Minorities Commission Act: "Article 32 of the Constitution has made a provision for protection of fundamental rights of all citizens through the judiciary. But the Central Government, and in their territories several State Governments, have passed a Minorities Commission Act to make a special arrangement for the protection of rights of those who are not Hindus. The Commissions that have been formed in pursuance of these laws grant representation to followers of alien creeds, but not to a Hindu, that is, to a follower of

---

[101] The proposal has since been put into effect. [editorial footnote in the original text]

[102] Hindus are entitled only to pay taxes for fattening the 'minority' communities. [note in the original]

[103] A. Chatterjee: *Hindu Nation*, p.35.

[104] "Rao announces Rs 500 cr minority corporation", *Indian Express*, 16.8.1994.

Sanâtana Dharma who wishes to call himself a Hindu. It appears that the Hindus neither need solution of their problems, nor the protection of their collective community rights."[105]

The Minorities Commission Act giving statutory status to the Minorities Commission was passed in 1992, but the said Minorities Commission was established in 1978, under the Janata Government in which the BJS was the senior partner. Indeed, BJS Muslim member Arif Baig was one of the godfathers of the Minorities Commission. Its first president was Swatantra Party founder Minoo Masani, representing the Parsi minority. Established to "safeguard the interests of the minorities, whether based on religion or language", it had the following 8-point programme:

1. Evaluate the workings of the various safeguards for the minorities in the Constitution and the laws passed by the Union and State Governments.
2. Recommend the most effective way to implement the laws pertaining to the minorities.
3. Look into specific complaints.
4. Conduct studies and research on the "question of avoidance of discrimination against minorities".
5. Review Union and State Government policies towards minorities.
6. Suggest appropriate legal and welfare measures to be undertaken by the Union and State Governments.
7. Serve as a national clearing house for information in respect of the conditions of the minorities.
8. Submit reports (on minorities) to the Government from time to time.[106]

The newly acquired "statutory status" means that the Minorities Commission's reports cannot formally be ignored nor withheld from Parliament by the Government (as happened in 1989-91 on the plea that these were "confidential documents"). Also, "our role as investigators can become a judicial one", according to the MC's former chairman S.M.H. Burney, who cited the right to summon witnesses in riot investigations as one of the new powers attached to the statutory status.[107]

---

[105]A. Chatterjee: *Hindu Nation*, pp.35-6.

[106]Summarized in Minu Jain: "A change of status", *Sunday*, 10.5.1992.

[107]Quoted in Minu Jain: "A change of status", *Sunday*, 10.5.1992.

Some of the demands of the Minorities Commission have struck Hindu observers as quite brazen and intrinsically anti-Hindu, e.g. "that no nationality certificates should be demanded from the Muslims seeking employment" (who are sometimes suspected of being illegal Bangladeshi immigrants), or "that 1985 should be observed as the year of the minorities and weaker sections".[108] Therefore, a standing demand of the BJP and the HMS is the replacement of the Minorities Commission with a Human Rights Commission. The BJP government of Madhya Pradesh (1989-92) has renamed the Minorities Commission as Human Rights Commission. The SS-BJP Government in Maharashtra (1995-99) has abolished the state's Minorities Commission (constituted three years before under Congress rule, with a grant of Rs. 120 million) altogether.[109]

For the national level, the BJP promises: "Disband the Minorities Commission, which has only succeeded in feeding separatist sentiments and giving rise to imagined grievances, and entrust its responsibilities to the National Human Rights Commission."[110] And again: "Entrust the responsibilities of the Minorities Commission to the Human Rights Commission, thus providing greater protection to members of minority communities".[111] Remark that the BJP feels constrained to present this change as being proposed with an eye on the minorities' welfare rather than as a matter of non-discrimination against Hindus. In the light of this BJP opposition to the Minorities Commission, it remains ironic that the earlier BJP leadership itself had co-fathered the Minorities Commission in 1978.

Lack of a Common Civil Code

In India, marriage, divorce and inheritance are regulated by religion-based law codes which are different for Hindus, Muslims, Christians and Parsis. The Hindu Personal Law applicable to Hindus consists of the Hindu Marriage Act (1955), the Hindu Succession Act (1956), the Hindu Minority and Guardianship Act (1956), and the Hindu Adoptions and Maintenance Act (1956). The legally codified Muslim Personal Law consists of the Muslim Personal Law (Shariat) Act, the Dissolution of

[108] *Indian Express*, 28.8.1990.

[109] See e.g. Muzaffar Hussain: "Great uproar over end of Minorities Commission", *Organiser*, 2.7.1995.

[110] BJP: *Election Manifesto 1996*, p.66.

[111] BJP: *Election Manifesto 1998*, p.36.

Muslim Marriages Act (1939), the Wakf Act (1913) and the Muslim Women (Protection of Rights on Divorce) Act voted during the Shah Bano controversy of 1986. Christian Personal Law consists of the Indian Christian Marriage Act (1872) and the Indian Divorce Act (1869). To Parsis, the Parsi Marriage and Divorce Act (1936) applies. The Jews follow an uncodified law known as the Jewish Law of Marriage and Divorce.

We may illustrate the situation with the stereotypical example: a Hindu who wants to marry two women knows that he will be punishable, but no longer if he converts to Islam. For this reason, there are actual cases of conversion for the sake of bigamy: "It is worth noting that the Islamic law permitting more than one marriage is actually exploited by many Hindus, who promptly convert to avoid the fuss and problems of a divorce. Film director Mahesh Bhatt converted to Islam after he faced problems divorcing his first wife to get married a second time. The Delhi press recently reported the marriage of one G.C. Ghosh, who converted to Islam to marry an office colleague. Unfortunately for Ghosh, his first wife complained to the *maulana* of the mosque where Ghosh had converted. The priest was horrified to learn the truth and promptly annulled the second marriage. Ghosh now faces charges of bigamy and fraud."[112]

This quotation deserves closer analysis. The secularist journalists quoted try to put it in such a way that Hindus are mean people who "exploit" the Islamic law permitting polygamy. This has got things backwards: Hindus can "exploit" this law only by becoming Muslims, while Muslims "exploit" this law routinely as a matter of unassailable right. And Hindus are only tempted to exploit the Islamic law in this way because this law, upheld by a so-called secular state, provides an objective advantage to Muslims. The journalists' own story ends by gleefully reporting that the said Mr. Ghosh now faces charges of bigamy; the point is that unlike this Hindu, every Muslim man is immune to such charges by sheer virtue of being a Muslim. This legal inequality is reminiscent of the legal inequality between Hindus and Muslims under Muslim rule, which then too caused many Hindus to convert to Islam.

Divorce is the most common occasion for experiencing the effects of this legal inequality. For Christian men and women, divorce laws make it

---

[112]Namita Bhandare, Louise Fernandes and Minu Jain: "A pampered minority?", *Sunday*, 7.2.1993.

very difficult to obtain a divorce; for Hindus, it is a bit easier, but divorce is the easiest for Muslims. At least for Muslim men, who only have to pronounce triple *talâq* to be legally relieved of all responsibilities to their repudiated wives; Muslim women, by contrast, have to plead their case before a judge. So, on top of inequality between the religions, the present system of religion-based personal laws perpetuates a medieval inequality between men and women.

Secularists defend the status-quo by pointing out that rather few Muslims exercise the option of polygamy, while many non-Muslims do have mistresses. Hindus argue that this is immaterial to the fact of legal inequality: the point is that Muslims can practise polygamy formally and legally, others only informally or illegally. The common "secularist" defence that real life shows more equality regarding polygamy than the letter of the unequal laws suggests, is unproven and beside the point. Justifying legal inequality on the plea that it is without object in practice is unacceptable: if equality is hard enough to realize in practice, it should at least be upheld in the ideal construction of the legal system.

Imagine someone in the USA proposing a law granting tax-exemption to billionaires "except Blacks", with the plea that "there are hardly any Black billionaires anyway"; or a tax-exemption in Germany for farmers "except Jews", justified by the factual observation that "there are no Jewish farmers anyway". Imagine the outcry such an unequal law would raise, and keep in mind that the same type of legal inequality actually exists between Hindus and Muslims in India.

Hindutva and Personal Law reform

The religion-based personal laws are not only different, they have also received different treatment from the legislative and executive powers. While no government dares to amend the Personal Law of a minority without the latter's prior consent or initiative, the secular Parliament has amended the Hindu Law in the 1950s without seeking the opinion of the Hindu community as such or of its acknowledged religious leadership. Incidentally, the BJP's earlier incarnation, the BJS, opposed the imposition of social reform on a community by the secular state. Indeed, the BJS opposed the Hindu Code Bill, not because it opposed reform (as Swami Karpatri's *Râm Râjya Parishad* did), but because it rejected interference by a secular state in internal Hindu affairs.

The 1951 BJS Manifesto was unambiguous: "Hindu Code Bill. The party holds that social reform should not come as imposition from above. It should work from within the society. Any far-reaching changes as envisaged in the Hindu Code Bill, therefore, should not be made unless there is a strong popular demand for them and a clear verdict is obtained from the electorate."[113] That is exactly what the Muslims are saying today in their pleas against the "imposition" of a Uniform Civil Code which would replace many Shariat provisions with supposedly more progressive laws.

Likewise, HMS spokesman N.C. Chatterjee argued in Parliament: "The leaders of the Congress who are Members of the Government continually harp on secularism and condemn communalism in any shape or form. It is amazing that they are introducing a 'communal' measure simply for one community. Is this Bill not wholly inconsistent with the concept of secular democracy?" But apart from this secularist argument, Chatterjee also pleaded against the contents of the reforms imposed on Hindu society, like the introduction of divorce: "We are quite sure that if any plebiscite is taken or a referendum is ordered a large majority of our citizens will turn down any proposal of introducing divorce among members of the Hindu community. ... For centuries marriage has been looked upon by the Hindus as a sacrament, and the marital bond has been held to be sacred and indissoluble." And from there back to the anti-communal line of argument: "The important provisions of the new Marriage and Divorce Bill are the enforcement of monogamy and granting the right of divorce on very easy terms. If monogamy is good for Hindus, why is it not good for Muslims?"[114]

The highly unsecular arrangement of religion-based personal laws was meant to be only temporary, for the Constitution stipulates in its directive principles (Article 44) that the State shall endeavour to enact a Common Civil Code: "The State shall endeavour to secure for the citizens a uniform civil code throughout the territory of India."[115] However, Nehru and his secularist successors never took even the slightest initiative to implement this principle, which is why the Common Civil Code had been

---

[113]BJS: *Party Documents 1951-1972*, vol.1, pp.57-8.

[114]N.C. Chatterjee's speech (1955?) was reproduced in N.C. Chatterjee: *Whither India?* (HMS, Delhi n.d.) and thence in , Donald Eugene Smith, ed.: *Religion, Politics and Social Change in the Third World*, pp.84-5.

[115]B.K. Sharma: *Bhârat kâ Samvidhân; The Constitution of India*, p.14.

parked among the non-binding Directive Principles in the first place. It is a long-standing demand of the BJS-BJP that Article 44 of the Constitution be implemented at last, for example, in its 1998 Election Manifesto, the BJP promises to: "Entrust the Law Commission to formulate a Uniform Civil Code based on the progressive practices from all traditions."[116]

The Common Civil Code demand serves as proof of the BJP's secularism, and it is of limited importance to specific Hindu interests. In a way, the present system of plural Personal Law systems is more in keeping with Hindu tradition, when every caste had its own distinctive marriage and inheritance customs.

That is perhaps why even RSS supremo Guru Golwalkar withheld his support to the Common Civil Code demand: "Questioned on this issue, Golwalkar said, 'My feeling is that nature abhors excessive uniformity.' He went on to explain that he had 'no quarrel with any class, community or sect wanting to maintain its identity so long as that identity does not detract from its patriotic feeling.' To the surprise of some RSS members, he even applied the principle to Muslims: 'A reformist's attitude is all right. But a mechanical leveller's attitude would not be correct. Let the Muslims evolve their own laws. I will be happy when they arrive at the conclusion that polygamy is not good for them, but I would not like to force my views on them.'"[117]

The Common Civil Code is not a demand of Hindu society (certainly not a priority), but is intrinsically a demand of secularism, an impeccably secular and explicitly constitutional demand. Equality before the law regardless of religion is an essential requirement of a secular state, and it is a classic example of the "perversion of India's political parlance" that BJP opponents actually defend the separate religion-based civil codes in the name of *secularism.* It is certainly strange that the entire community of Western India-watchers has failed to question the classification of the BJP as "anti-secular" and its enemies as "secular", in the light of the fact that the BJP upholds (and its enemies oppose) the very first principle of the law system in all secular democracies, viz. the uniform applicability of the laws to all citizens regardless of their religion.

But there is one serious problem with the Common Civil Code demand: with few exceptions, and with secularist support, the Muslim

[116]BJP: *Election Manifesto 1998*, p.38.

[117]Andersen & Damle: *Brotherhood in Saffron*, p.83; ref. to *Organiser*, 26.8.1972.

community opposes it tooth and nail.[118] In order to win the Muslims over, the BJP tries to invoke Muslim authority: "Separate Personal Laws on the basis of religion are neither permitted in advanced countries of the West *nor in the Islamic countries.*"[119] But this carries little conviction. In fact, it is simply not true that Islamic countries (except for those with a completely Westernized law system, like Turkey) reject a plurality of Personal Law systems: in the Ottoman *millet* system as well as in the specific arrangements for the minorities in contemporary Islamic states, separate Personal Law systems are admitted. Muslim communities may follow different schools of Islamic Law (Malikite, Shafiite, Hanbalite, Hanifite, Shiite), and non-Muslims are entitled to follow their own customary laws for all intra-community purposes including marriage and inheritance. Thus, in today's Iran or Sudan, a Muslim may unilaterally repudiate his wife but a Christian may not, unless he converts to Islam. This much may be said in favour of non-secular Islamic states, that they do not interfere with the internal affairs of the minorities.

While the BJP congratulates itself on being so clever in insisting on an impeccably secular demand like the Common Civil Code, it does not seem to be aware that, as with the Ayodhya campaign, it is making itself hated. It is a realistic prediction that an effective abolition of the religion-based Personal Law systems would provoke potentially violent agitations in *every* Muslim neighbourhood in India. After all, the Ayodhya dispute was a fairly artificial conflict, in which the common Muslim had no stake, and still it provoked a major wave of violence; but a change in the rules for marriage, divorce and inheritance affects every single Muslim personally. A secular Common Civil Code would also diminish the power of Muslim clerics within their own community greatly, so that each one of them will have a personal stake in fomenting rebellion against the implementation of Article 44.

It was no surprise that the BJP governments in May 1996 and in 1998, under pressure from numerical realities in Parliament and from the

[118]E.g. "IUML condemns Advani's demand for civil code", *Pioneer* (Varanasi), 28.12.1989 (IUML: "Indian Union Muslim League", speakers were its MPs Ebrahim Sulaiman Sait and G.M. Banatwala); or "Muslim Personal Law Board warns Sangh Parivar against demanding changes in the Shariat", *Indian Express*, 23.12.1995 (speaker was its vice-president Maulana Kalbe Sadiq).

[119]Resolution on Uniform Civil Code adopted by the BJP National Executive meeting in New Delhi on 15-16 July 1995, in BJP: *Opening Remarks by Shri L.K. Advani & Resolutions Adopted by National Executive*, p.12; emphasis added.

coalition partners, dropped the Common Civil Code project from their agendas. Yet, if given a sufficient majority, a future BJP Government would certainly try to realize this long-standing project of a Common Civil Code.

The secularists and the Common Civil Code

The campaign for a Common Civil Code got a boost when the Supreme Court, in a landmark verdict, explicitly insisted that Article 44 be implemented. On 10 May 1995, in the case of *Sarla Mudgal vs. Union of India*, the Supreme Court decided the question whether a Hindu husband, married under Hindu law and having embraced Islam for the sake of enjoying the right to marry again without having divorced his first wife (who refused both the divorce and the option of sharing her husband with a second wife), does have the right to take a second wife. In a somewhat specious reasoning, the judges ruled that "enlightened Muslims" could not possibly want conversions to Islam for such disingenuous motives, and that this avenue to polygamy should be barred. Consequently, the Court decided to declare the plaintiff's husband's second marriage invalid: "Since it is not the object of Islam nor the intention of the enlightened Muslim community that Hindu husbands should be encouraged to become Muslims merely for the purpose of evading their own personal laws by marrying again, the courts can be persuaded to adopt a construction of laws resulting in denying the husband converted to Islam the right to marry again without having his existing marriage dissolved in accordance with the law."[120]

More importantly, in an additional contemplation of the deeper reasons for the problem which had been brought before them, the judges reminded the government of Article 44 and summoned it to explain how much progress had been made in the constitutionally mandated enactment of a Common Civil Code: "One wonders how long it will take for the Government of the day to implement the mandate of the framers of the Constitution under Article 44. ... There is no justification in delaying indefinitely the introduction of a uniform personal law."[121]

---

[120]Para 25 of the verdict, quoted in Habibullah Badshah: "Uniform Civil Code—chasing a mirage", *The Hindu*, 24.12.1995.

[121]Para 30 of the verdict, quoted in Habibullah Badshah: "Uniform Civil Code—chasing a mirage", *The Hindu*, 24.12.1995.

Many secularists have responded to this authoritative plea for the secularization of Indian Personal Law with an embarrassed silence. Some, like Amartya Sen, have conceded that "there is nothing non-secular or sectarian in demanding that the provisions of Indian civil laws should apply even-handedly to all", though without ever actively supporting this demand. But then they add strange twists to somehow incriminate the Hindu (actually secular) position, like: "There are also other asymmetries, for example, between the provision for wives in the event of a divorce, where Muslim women ... have less generous guarantees. The existence of these asymmetries has been cited again and again by Hindu political activists to claim that Hindus ... are discriminated against in India. This is of course a ridiculous charge, since the discrimination is against Muslim women rather than Hindu men".[122]

Considering the fierceness with which Muslim spokesmen are defending their separate Personal Law, I don't find it "of course ridiculous" to suspect that Muslims feel privileged rather than discriminated by this arrangement. Women were a minuscule minority in the Constituent Assembly, and the privilege of a separate Personal Law (including the right to polygyny, unconditional unilateral divorce and freedom from alimony duty after divorce) was secured by Muslim men, not by Hindu women. Hindu women have merely claimed, and largely achieved, legal equality with men; Muslim men have claimed and achieved (or rather, retained) privileges denied to Hindu men and enjoyed at the expense of their own wives, who may (though rarely) be Hindu as well as Muslim.

Yet, Amartya Sen denies that this discrimination against Muslim women is at the same time a discrimination against Hindu men. As we saw, Hindus who try to avail of the same opportunity of polygamy that Muslim men can freely exercise, find themselves arrested for it. Hindu men are definitely discriminated against in that they are denied the Muslim right to legally discriminate against their wives. Not that they

---

[122]Amartya Sen: "India's secularism: the compulsions of innate pluralism", *Observer of Business and Politics*, 23.2.1993. The part about "provision for wives in the event of a divorce" is an obvious reference to the 1985 Shah Bano case, where "secular" legislation by the Congress majority corroborated the Sharia provision that a divorced woman may be supported by public foundations but (from three months after the repudiation onwards) not by her ex-husband.

should get such a right, but they do suffer an inequality compared with Muslim men: that is not "of course ridiculous" but simply obvious.

Likewise, Atul Setalvad protests that Muslims are anything but "favoured", given their underrepresentation among graduates (the result of the community's own choices, not of *any* governmental or Hindu policy). That the Muslims have a separate Civil Code is but their right, not a favour, and without it India would be a fascist state: "The only 'favour' shown to Muslims, and 'favour' is certainly not the right word, is that they ... are being allowed to exist and live the way they like to. If such 'favours' are to be stopped, we will end up with an intolerant fascist Hindu state."[123] Readers from the US, France and other countries where no Muslim Personal Law is recognized, are hereby notified that they *ipso facto* live in a fascist state.

But in India the Muslims *do* have the privilege of a separate Personal Law, yet they profess to be unhappy about it: "The failure to adopt a Uniform Civil Code" has the effect that "Muslim women suffer because they do not have an equal right of inheritance, because they cannot easily obtain a divorce, because they can be divorced by their husbands at their whim or caprice. Are Muslim women being favoured or pampered because they are treated so badly?"[124] No, they are neither favoured nor pampered by their Personal Law, but it is the Constitution and the BJP which want to change that, and their husbands, their community leaders and their secularist defenders who want to preserve it. What an effrontery to list the treatment of Muslim women among the injustices perpetrated by the overbearing Hindu majority on the Muslim minority.[125]

---

[123]Atul Setalvad: "Why we must remain secular", *Sunday Observer*, 14.1.1990.

[124]Atul Setalvad: "Why we must remain secular", *Sunday Observer*, 14.1.1990.

[125]It may be noted that, by contrast, Christian activists dissatisfied with the unequal treatment of women do take steps to reform their Personal Law or to have discriminatory clauses struck down by the Courts (e.g. the 1916 Travancore Christian Succession Act, struck down by the Supreme Court in 1986, a verdict not challenged in the streets or in Parliament the way the contemporaneous Shah Bano ruling was) rather than forever blaming Hindu communalism, see e.g. lawyer Mary Roy: "Waiting for justice", *Indian Express*, 24.3.1996, or (about one of the consequential divorce cases fought by Mary Roy) Joaquim P. Menezes: "Breaking the silence", *Illustrated Weekly of India*, 11.3.1990. Likewise concerning tribal law, see Lotika Sarkar and Malavika Karlekar: "Mizo customary law: marked bias against women", *Indian Express*, 23-5-1991, and sequel: "Growing protest against review draft", 24.5.1991.

Sen's and Setalvad's brazenly fallacious reasoning exemplifies a type of "secularist" discourse so repulsive to self-respecting Hindus that they describe it as an "Orwellian obfuscation on a massive scale", a free-for-all where "black" can mean "white".[126] At any rate, if Sen wants to do something against the discrimination of Muslim women, he should stand up and be counted among the supporters of a Common Civil Code.

As against the embarrassed silence or convoluted apologetics of many secularists, a few daredevils have plainly defended the legal inequality between the communities and argued that equality before the law (as it exists in all secular democracies) is actually *unsecular*, that "laws can never bring about social change", that "harmony between the two communities cannot be achieved by a Common Civil Code", which will "only lead to greater chaos, confusion and problems".[127] Is it any wonder that Hindu revivalists describe Indian secularism as a "mask of fundamentalism", when the top demand of all Islamist movements, viz. the enactment of Sharia-based legislation, is actively upheld as a cornerstone of secularism by some, and at least passively sustained as part of India's law system by practically *all* self-described secularists?[128]

As a son of the motherland of secularism, the French scholar Gérard Heuzé acknowledges that in central points of the communalism debate, the classical agenda of secularism is brandished not by the secularist parties but by the Hindu movement, starting with the Common Civil Code demand, "secular par excellence", which "practically all its opponents have dropped".[129] Now it becomes clear why a leading Muslim could declare: "To say that the BJP is communal is absolutely absurd and without any basis."[130] At least on this point, the BJP has genuinely appropriated the classical secular agenda.

---

[126]N.S. Rajaram: *Secularism, the New Mask of Fundamentalism*, p.2.

[127]Habibullah Badshah: "Uniform Civil Code—chasing a mirage", *The Hindu*, 24.12.1995.

[128]Secularist defenders of religions-based Personal Law systems find themselves in the company of, among other, Islamic hard-liner Syd Shahabuddin: "Trespassing on religious identity", *Observer of Business and Politics*, 25.1.1995.

[129]G. Heuzé: *Où va l'Inde moderne?*, p.81.

[130]Former Congress Minister M.C. Chagla speaking at the first BJP Plenary Session (Mumbai 1980, speech published by the BJP), also recalled in L.K. Advani: *Presidential Address*, Plenary Session, Mumbai, November 1995, p.1.

Pro-Hindu discrimination among Dalits?

While the Hindu argument about anti-Hindu discrimination goes largely unnoticed, allegations of pro-Hindu discrimination get worldwide attention. At least the world media, encouraged by the involvement of the celebrated Mother Teresa, did report the most controversial instance of alleged discrimination in favour of the Hindus on the occasion of Christian agitation demanding caste-based reservations for "Christian Dalits".[131] More than half of the Indian Christians are of Scheduled Caste origin (up to two-thirds in Tamil Nadu, even more in Andhra), nearly 20 per cent are of Scheduled Tribe origin, and the others are mostly the Mar Thoma and Jacobite "Old Christians" from Kerala, who consider themselves high-caste.[132] In the 1990s, there has been an increasing demand for extending the reservation system for Hindu-Sikh-Buddhist Scheduled Caste people to the Christian converts from Scheduled Castes. In 1996, a Bill to this effect was tabled in the Lok Sabha, and Christians including Mother Teresa demonstrated in support of it. However, it stood no chance because of the opposition of the largest party (BJP) and of influential Scheduled Caste lobbies in the other parties.

Formally, the Bill does nothing more than to add the phrase *"or the Christians"* to all the existing constitutional provisions for the Scheduled Castes. The "statement of objects and reasons" of this much-discussed Bill, proposed as Bill no.17 of 1996 by Congress leader Sitaram Kesri, is as follows: "Converts to the Christian religion who are of the Scheduled Caste origin are precluded from the statutory benefits and safeguards accruing to members of the Scheduled Castes. Demands have been made from time to time for extending these benefits and safeguards to the Christians of the Scheduled Caste origin by granting them recognition as the Scheduled Castes on the ground that change of religion has not altered their social and economic conditions. Upon due consideration of these demands, it is proposed to amend the relevant Constitution (Scheduled

---

[131]"Christians allege Govt neglect", *Indian Express*, 27.7.1990. In this first agitation, Christians who constitute less than 3 per cent of India's population "demanded that 10 per cent seats be reserved for their community in jobs and educational institutions."

[132]Figures given by M.V. Kamath: "The question of 'dalit' Christians", in Seshadri Chari: *Reservation for Christians*, p.10.

Castes) Orders to include the Christian converts from the Scheduled Castes as the Scheduled Castes therein. Hence this Bill."[133]

Why do Christians of Scheduled Caste origin not enjoy the benefit of reservations? The answer (if not necessarily the whole answer) is that the Christian leadership wanted it that way. A Christian spokesman, Father Antoni Sagayam, admits that when Ambedkar enshrined the reservations system in the Constitution, Christians of Scheduled Caste origin failed to get reservations "also at the instigation of Father Jerome D'Souza who defended the principled but all too idealistic position that Christianity does not recognizes castes".[134] That leading Christians objected to the very concept of "Dalit Christians" is only logical, for two reasons: first, Christian preachers had repeated for decades that conversion to Christianity would bring liberation from caste discrimination, i.e. from Dalit status; secondly, a clear demarcation of the Christians from the Hindu society with its notions of caste was consistent with the status of the Christians as a non-Hindu *minority*, which promised to be a highly profitable status.

In fact, the disjunction between the Scheduled Caste and Christian categories goes back even farther than the drafting of the Constitution, viz. to the drafting of the British-Indian legislation on which so much of free India's legislation is still based. As an appendix to the Government of India Act (1935), which first introduced the very notion of "Scheduled Caste", the Government of India (Scheduled Castes) Order was issued on April 30, 1936. Para 3 of that Order provided that "(a) no Indian Christian shall be deemed to be a member of a Scheduled Caste".[135]

The present Christian pleaders for the "Dalit Christian" concept with its concomitant right to reservations have a point when they argue that caste discrimination exists among Christians too. Father Antoni testifies: "Even in my new parish Dalit and non-Dalit Christians are not living as equals. Processions of non-Dalits do not pass through Dalit neighbourhoods. Non-Dalits do not go and collect subscription fees among Dalits. The corpse of a Dalit does not enter the Church but is

---

[133]Reproduced in Seshadri Chari: *Reservation for Christians*, p.6.

[134]Peter Vande Vyvere: "Over mijn lijk. Rechten voor kasteloze christenen in India" (Dutch: "Over my dead body. Rights of casteless Christians in India"), *Kerk en Leven* (official weekly of the Catholic Church in Flanders), 12.2.1997.

[135]Quoted in M.V. Kamath: "The question of 'dalit' Christians", in Seshadri Chari: *Reservation for Christians*, p.11.

brought straight to a separate graveyard. After working there for a few months, I have announced that I don't want to be part of this system and that I will treat all Christians as equals. That was not received well, caste Christians even organized a boycot."[136]

The same experience is reported by numerous observers, Christian as well as non-Christian. Thus, Dr. M. Arokiasmy, Archbishop of Madurai, reports: "The village churches in most parts of Tamil Nadu are cruciform, and Harijan Christians are in some places required to confine themselves to one wing in the House of God. ... Caste Christians never attend weddings in *cherris* (= Harijan colonies). CSCO (= Christians of Scheduled Caste Origin) marriage and funeral processions are banned from passing through the streets where upper caste Christians live."[137]

So, why should reservation be denied to Christians when it is enjoyed by Buddhists and Sikhs? RSS Sarsanghchalak Rajendra Singh states his position: "Once a Hindu becomes a Christian he is deemed to have cut himself off the Hindu mainstream. Sikhism and Buddhism have their roots deep in Hindu thought and culture. Christians themselves do not consider a convert to their faith as being part of the Hindu social order. Caste differences are no doubt a bane of the Hindu society. But unlike Sikhs and Buddhists, Christians refuse to belong to the Hindu society. How can they claim reservation for the former *dalits* who have since been 'saved by Christ'? All these years they led everyone to believe that all are equal among Christians and that Christianity does not admit of caste distinctions. ... Dalit Christian is a misnomer. If a section among Christians feels that they still suffer the ignominy of their earlier Dalit status, in spite of promises to the contrary, they should renounce Christianity. The Hindu society will welcome them back home."[138]

In the RSS supremo's view, enactment of the Bill "would deal a big blow to the Hindu society and strike at the root of the country's unity and integrity. The flood-gates of proselytisation will be opened ajar and provide a fresh impetus to the nefarious designs of foreign powers."[139] Same prediction from VHP supremo Ashok Singhal: "Once this Bill

[136]Peter Vande Vyvere: "Over mijn lijk. Rechten voor kasteloze christenen in India", *Kerk en Leven*, 12.2.1997.

[137]Recorded by Patralekha Chatterjee: "Indian Christians. Not by faith alone", *Indian Express*, 2.9.1990.

[138]Interviewed in Seshadri Chari: *Reservation for Christians*, p.8.

[139]Rajendra Singh in Seshadri Chari: *Reservation for Christians*, p.9.

becomes an Act, it will accelerate the conversion of Dalit Hindus."[140] This is quite probable, and the reason why is given by an RSS field worker in Coimbatore, one of the frontline areas of Christian proselytization: "If Dalit converts get reservations, there will be massive conversion to christianity. Today the reservations system for Hindu Dalits more or less evens out the benefits which the Christian community with all its foreign money and political astuteness can give them. But if the Christians get reservations, that balance will be broken; worse, Dalit converts will also be in a position to corner a far larger share of the reservations, so that Hindu Dalits will be at a great disadvantage."[141]

The recent debate about reservations for Christian Dalits is largely a replay of a debate in the late 1960s about the Scheduled Tribe status of tribal converts to Christianity. Just as the conceding of Scheduled Caste status to "Dalit Christians" has been blocked for years, not by the protests from the Hindutva brigade, but by the opposition of Scheduled Caste leaders (who feel directly threatened by the opening up of the reservations field to the well-organized Christians), the opposition to the existing legal inclusion of Christian converts in the Scheduled Tribes category was led by an outsider to the Hindutva movement, tribal Congress MP Kartik Oraon from Ranchi.

In 1967, the following amendment to the Constitution was proposed in Parliament by Kartik Oraon: "No person who has given up the tribal faith or faiths and has embraced either Christianity or Islam should be deemed to be a member of a Scheduled Tribe." As we have seen, it is a fact that tribal converts drop out of tribal community life, and effectively cease to be members of their tribes. The Christian practice of cornering benefits meant for tribals in spite of their social separatism and denunciation of tribal customs, is unacceptable to the genuine members of the communities concerned.

Mr. Oraon explained: "The Christian tribals have taken all the reserved positions for themselves in the colleges and government service. The Christian missions have spent crorees of rupees on the Christian tribals and built schools for them, so why should the government give them grants for their schools while the non-Christians get nothing? The

---

[140]A. Singhal: "The demand proves failure of the Church", in Seshadri Chari: *Reservation for Christians*, p.14.

[141]Interview with Krishna Kumar (manager of a network of Ayurvedic clinics) at the Hindu Conference in Frankfurt, August 1992.

government is actually supporting missionary work by giving their schools grants. In fact, why should anyone be allowed to propagate religion? When you propagate one religion, it means you must attack other religions, and that leads to hatred of one group by another. The Christians dominate everything here. ... When the government provides all these benefits, it's the Christians who get them. If the government reserved one hundred jobs, the Christians got them all."[142]

Oraon's version is confirmed by S.K. Kaul, former Deputy Commissioner for Scheduled Castes and Scheduled Tribes: "All Church-based or Church-sponsored work was a means to proselytisation, which led to the destruction of *vanavasi* culture and the way of life among the converted tribals. Even today the Church is extending its activities among isolated and defenceless tribal groups and most of the concessions and facilities go to the Christian *vanavasi*s."[143]

In March 1968, Parliament constituted the Joint Committee on Scheduled Castes and Scheduled Tribes Orders (Amendment) Bill, 1967, introduced in the Lok Sabha on August 12, 1967. Its Chairman was Anil K. Chanda, MP, who had previously worked as Commissioner for Scheduled Castes and Scheduled Tribes. The Committee recommended: "No person who has given up the tribal faith or faiths and has embraced Christianity or Islam should be deemed to be a member of the Scheduled Tribes." S.K. Kaul reports on the outcome: "Except for one Christian MP from the Garo Hills and difficulties expressed by minister-in-charge (P. Govinda Menon), the recommendation was approved by all. The credit for getting this recommendation incorporated in the report goes primarily to the late Shri Kartik Oraon of the Congress."[144]

On this basis, Kartik Oraon introduced a private bill in the Lok Sabha in November 1969, seeking to abolish the reservations granted to Christian tribals. The memorandum of the Bill was signed by 325 members of the Lok Sabha and 23 of the Rajya Sabha. When the *Scheduled Castes and Scheduled Tribes Orders (Amendment) Bill, 1967*, as amended by the above Joint Committee, finally came up for discussion, something went wrong. According to S.K. Kaul: "It is clear from the speeches delivered in

[142]M. Weiner: *Sons of the Soil*, pp.184-85.

[143]S.K. Kaul: "Sabotage of SC & ST Orders (Amendment) Bill", in Seshadri Chari: *Reservation for Christians*, pp.37-8.

[144]S.K. Kaul: "Sabotage of SC & ST Orders (Amendment) Bill", in Seshadri Chari: *Reservation for Christians*, p.38.

Parliament between November 17 and November 23, 1970, that the Bill would have been passed by both houses, but for a political eventuality. The will of the members of Parliament met with dire threats from the Nagaland chief minister. Considering the situation, the issue was discussed in the Cabinet presided over by Smt. Indira Gandhi and Shri Jagjivan Ram was deputed to persuade Shri K. Oraon to withdraw the bill. On November 24, 1970, Shri K. Oraon met Shri Jagjivan Ram at his residence and was told to withdraw the bill. He refused to do so. ... Smt. Indira Gandhi called a meeting of the MPs and the Opposition to discuss the situation and succeeded in securing postponement of voting on the bill. The bill was never put to vote as parliament was dissolved in December 1970."[145]

"An example of how Christian tribals are cornering all the benefits of reservation is the fact that most of the tribals selected by the Union Public Service Commission for entry into Indian Administrative Service and other allied Central Services are Christian tribals from the states of Meghalaya, Mizoram and Nagaland. Similarly, Christian tribals have benefited most from educational scholarships for higher studies inside and outside the country. The first generation graduates among Hindu tribals are not able to compete with Christian tribals who have had public school education for two or three generations."[146]

Meanwhile, Hindu organizations like the Vanavasi Kalyan Ashram have started to respond to social and educational needs which the missionaries had used as entries into tribal society. Still, the Christian power position in the tribal areas is very strong, and the government policy of extending Scheduled Tribes benefits to Christian tribals continues to strengthen their hand. The experience of the Scheduled Tribes definitely confirms the apprehensions of Hindutva and Scheduled Caste leaders that the entry of "Christian Dalits" into the competition for reserved jobs and college seats would be to the detriment of non-Christian Dalits.

At any rate, the non-allotment of reservations to Christians of Scheduled Caste origin was never imposed by the Hindus. It was decided on by the British administrators in collaboration with Christian missionary spokesmen. It can, therefore, not be construed as a discrimination which the Hindus have inflicted on the minorities. And given the special benefits

---

[145] S.K. Kaul: "Sabotage of SC & ST Orders (Amendment) Bill", in Seshadri Chari: *Reservation for Christians*, p.39.

[146] S.K. Kaul: "Sabotage of SC & ST Orders (Amendment) Bill", in Seshadri Chari: *Reservation for Christians*, p.39.

for Christians as a minority and the foreign funding for Christian institutions, it is in practice not much of a discrimination anyway.

DISCRIMINATORY POLICIES

The creation of Malappuram

An old grievance of Hindu nationalists concerns the privileges conceded to the Moplah Muslims in Kerala: "You are aware of a Muslim group in Kerala called the Moplahs. The only contribution of these people in the Freedom Movement was that, during the Khilafat agitation of 1921, they carried out a brutal massacre of Hindus in Malabar. They plundered thousands of Hindu homes and burnt Hindu villages, they raped Hindu women and destroyed Hindu temples. But you know what? Such of those Moplahs as are still alive are honoured by the Government of India as 'freedom fighters' and given monthly pension on that basis!"[147] As Hindus like to point out again and again: the Moplahs were recognized as "freedom fighters" not because they took up arms against the British, but because the British took up arms against them, viz. in a determined suppression of Moplah terror against the Hindus.

While the generation of Moplahs involved in the said riots has almost died out, a new Moplah-related grievance was generated in the 1960s: the Muslims in Malabar could get the Communist state government of Kerala to redraw (what Americans call "gerrymander") district boundaries so as to create a Muslim-majority district, Malappuram. The very existence of Malappuram serves as a standing example of the policy of "Muslim appeasement", a term which dates back to the HMS critique of the Congress policy of concessions to the Muslim League, starting with the Lucknow Pact of 1916 (accepting the principle of separate electorates and weightage in favour of the Muslims) and culminating in the acceptance of Partition in 1947. The homonymy with Neville Chamberlain's "appeasement" policy vis-à-vis Hitler is intentional: just like the British appeasement policy over Czechoslovakia merely whetted Hitler's appetite for more conquests, the secularist appeasement policy vis-à-vis Muslim communalism is held responsible for the steady rise in Muslim demands

[147] A. Chatterjee: *Hindu Nation*, p.36. *Moplah* (or strictly, *Mapilla*) is said to mean "son-in-law", referring to Arab traders to whom Keralite women were given in marriage; they are thus certified to be one Muslim community whose presence in India is not due to armed invasion but to Hindu hospitality.

culminating in the Partition. The RSS alleges that this pre-Independence policy of "appeasement" is being repeated, and is bound to have similarly disastrous consequences.[148]

It is the considered opinion of thoughtful Hindu revivalists that India's problems mostly result from a psychology of "spoilt children" among certain communities.[149] Thus, no matter how justified the grievances of the Tamils in Sri Lanka, their resorting to armed separatism is at least partly explained as being due to their history of privilege under British rule. The Sikhs were the privileged group par excellence, neatly carved out of the native society to serve the British interests in special Army units; and when they lost their privileges in 1947, the ground was prepared for Sikh separatism ultimately culminating in Khalistani terrorism in the 1980s. The largest privileged group were the Muslims, and their history of receiving one concession after another, not just from the British but also from the Congress movement, strengthened their resolve never to accept a status of ordinary equality with Hindu citizens, so that Partition became nearly inevitable.

According to Hindu revivalist thinkers of every denomination, the cure for this problem, as for the problem of making a spoilt child reasonable again, is firmness. Special treatment should be replaced with simple equality, and firmness should be applied in maintaining that equality. But so far, the BJP has never announced any plans of redrawing the boundaries of Malappuram again. While this may certainly be explained as a rational attitude of avoiding trouble over such minor matters, it may also be a sign of the typical Hindu nationalist habit of endless complaining without much resolve to do something.

Pilgrimage taxes

So far, the Hindu nationalist parties have concentrated less on doing anything than on adding ever more complaints to their "Muslim appeasement" litany. One sore symbolic issue is pilgrimage taxes. Thus, while pilgrims to Hindu sacred sites like Amarnath have to *pay* a special tax of Rs.50 to finance the security and material facilities provided by the government (which the VHP described as "*jizya* which used to be

---

[148]"Appeasement that led to partition being repeated in Independent Bharat—RSS", text of RSS resolutions in *Organiser*, 20.7.1997.

[149]This view was expressed to me on separate occasions by Girilal Jain, Ram Swarup, Sita Ram Goel and others.

imposed during the rule of Aurangzeb"),[150] Muslims *receive a subsidy* for going on pilgrimage to Mecca:

"It has recently been reported by newspapers that Haj pilgrims are financed by the Government of India to the tune of Rs. 16,000 per head, and that 18,000 such pilgrims are involved annually. This reveals how crores of rupees are spent from the public exchequer every year to render an altogether uncalled-for service to those who go on Haj pilgrimage. Salvation is strictly for the personal benefit of individuals. Under which law the Government of a secular country is rendering this financial help for the personal benefit of a particular community is difficult to comprehend."[151]

One might, of course, argue that at least the tax on Hindu pilgrimages can be justified by the fact that the Indian State does have to employ a lot of people to create smooth arrangements for pilgrimages inside India, expenses which it does not incur for the arrangements made in distant Mecca. The Hajj allowance is the result of the Hajj Bill which Nehru himself introduced in Parliament in 1959. According to N.S. Rajaram, it now costs the State Rs. 930 million annually.[152]

However, the complaints about "Muslim appeasement" have come to sound hollow when uttered by BJP men, for the BJP's record in State governments is not very different from that of other parties. Thus, the BJP protested when in 1990 Prime Minister V.P. Singh earmarked 5 million Rupees for the upkeep of the Jama Masjid of Delhi, the mosque of his political friend Imam Abdullah Bukhari. But soon after, the BJP state government of Rajasthan, in a bid to prove its secularist sensitivity to Muslim interests, awarded 67 million Rupees to the Ajmer Dargah of Muinuddin Chishti (*c.* 1200), a fanatical anti-Hindu preacher who co-operated closely with the Ghorid conquerors, and whose mausoleum was built with the debris of demolished Hindu temples. As Chief Minister of Uttar Pradesh, Kalyan Singh doubled the Hajj allowance. And Prime Minister Vajpayee's additional generosity to Muslim pilgrims earned him, in Varsha Bhosle's unsparing satirical columns, the alias *Hajjpayee*. Much to the dismay of some non-BJP Hindu revivalists, the record shows that the BJP is entirely serious when it announces that it stands for "secularism".

---

[150]"Registration 'fee' for Amarnath Yatra", *Organiser*, 18.8.1996.

[151]S.P. Khanna: "Subsidising Haj", *Indian Express*, 3.6.1993.

[152]N.S. Rajaram: "Secular perversion: from Somnath to Hajj", *Organiser*, 20.7.1997.

Encouraging illegal immigration

"Infiltration" from Bangladesh is one of the top concerns of Hindu nationalists. Immigration from Bangladesh is of two types. First, there are members of the minority communities fleeing occasional waves of persecution or the more general sense of being second-class citizens under the Islamic dispensation.[153] Since 1974, Hindus have been crossing the border to India at the rate of 475 per day, or nearly 3 million in 1974-91.[154] Few Hindus would dispute the right of these non-Muslim refugees to settle down in India and to receive Indian citizenship.[155]

Secondly, there are Muslims seeking economic opportunities or sheer living space, which Bangladesh cannot offer to the ever-larger numbers of newcomers on the housing and labour market. Bangladeshi intellectuals openly claim the right to *Lebensraum* ("living space") for their tightly concentrated nation, proposing the timely argument that "along with the new international order there should also be a world demographic order and a globalised manpower market to facilitate movement and settlement of population to avoid critical demographic pressure in pockets of high concentration".[156]

In other countries, Bangladeshis find they are not too welcome, or only temporarily: "At the end of last year [1996], there were still more than 100,000 illegal immigrant workers from Bangladesh in Malaysia. As of early February 1997 they are massively expelled by the Malay Government. ... Bangladesh has some experience with such disasters: last year already, Saudi Arabia, the United Arab Emirates and Qatar expelled some 50,000 illegal Bangladeshis. ... Three years ago, the Malaysian

---

[153]Published information about the oppression of and the violence against the minorities in Bangladesh is extremely scarce. The most accessible general information can be found in Taslima Nasreen's controversial fact-novel *Lajja*; an actual report is *Communal Discrimination in Bangladesh: Facts and Documents*, compiled and published by the Bangladesh Hindu-Buddhist-Christian Unity Council, 1993.

[154]Mohiuddin Ahmed: "The missing population", *Holiday* (Dhaka), 7.1.1994, quoted by South Asia Research Society (Calcutta): "Population explosion in West Bengal: a survey", included in S.R. Goel, ed.: *Time for Stock-Taking*, p.446.

[155]On 10 January 1996, the Supreme Court upheld the right of Buddhist Chakma refugees from the Chittagong Hill Tracts in Bangladesh to apply for Indian citizenship, see T.K. Rajalakshmi: "Cheer for Chakmas. Supreme Court upholds their right to citizenship", *Frontline*, 9.2.1996.

[156]Sadiq Khan: "The question of Lebensraum", *Holiday* (Dhaka), October 1990, paraphrased by T.V. Rajeshwar: "Migration or invasion?", included in S.R. Goel: *Time for Stock-Taking*, p.460.

government signed an agreement with the government in Dhaka agreeing to take in 50,000 new guest workers from Bangladesh. But when more and more Bangladeshis entered the country secretly and started to work without work permit, Malaysia cancelled the agreement unilaterally."[157] Therefore, contiguous India is the safest destination for Bangladeshis seeking new pastures.

What angers many Hindus, is that secularist governments at the central and state levels have been passively tolerating illegal immigration by Bangladeshi Muslims on a massive scale: "Every free nation or state, no matter how small or weak it may be, protects—or at least attempts to protect—its own international borders against entry of aliens. But in India, the Central Government as well as the State Governments of Assam, West Bengal, Bihar, Delhi etc. have been willingly permitting millions of Bangladeshi Muslims to infiltrate into our country. In fact, they are conniving with these infiltrators, giving them indirect encouragement and protection, showing a keenness to give them full benefits of citizenship by issuing ration cards to them, entering their names in voters' lists, and so on."[158]

According to BJP spokeswoman Sushma Swaraj, there is a remarkable contrast with the policy vis-à-vis genuine refugees: "Religious persecution, abduction, rape and forcible occupation of their lands by the Muslims left the Chakmas with no choice but to leave Bangladesh", yet "while the Congress Government had welcomed Bangladeshi infiltrators for vote-bank politics, Chakmas were being pushed out even though they were victims of religious persecution."[159] It is exaggerated to say that Chakmas are pushed back across the Bangladeshi border, but in the areas of India's North-East, they are indeed being pushed out (to adjoining areas) or seriously harassed by the local population, partly because they are already overburdened with the constant influx of Muslim Bangladeshis.

The BJP has always demanded that the authorities flush out the illegal Bangladeshi immigrants. However, none of the BJP state governments has made any effort to fulfil this long-standing election promise. In 1995, Delhi Chief Minister Madan Lal Khurana proposed to issue permits of residence to Bangladeshis (perhaps justifiable as a "lesser evil" certifying

---

[157]*De Wereld Morgen*, April 1997, p.17.

[158]A. Chatterjee: *Hindu Nation*, p.36.

[159]Quoted in: "SC comes to the aid of Chakmas", *Organiser*, 11.2.1996.

their foreigner status to pre-empt their silent acquisition of Indian citizenship), and MP Uma Bharati proposed some financial support for them. Even on paper, the intention to send them back is now not honoured any longer. The BJP's 1998 Election Manifesto only promises this: "The total number of illegal infiltrators from Bangladesh is officially ascertained at over 1.7 crore. ... Our government will:

"1) Take more stringent measures to intercept illegal infiltrators and turn them back. Fencing of the border wherever possible will be urgently taken up. Border patrolling will be intensified;

"2) Initiate steps to detect illegal infiltrators and delete their names from electoral rolls; and,

"3) Maintain a national register of citizens."[160]

But no promise is made to send the 17 million "illegal infiltrators" back. Among non-BJP nationalists, this abdication by the BJP goes to strengthen the old doomsday scenarios of a Muslim demographic take-over.[161] Former police officer Baljit Rai believes that India is bound by demography to become a Muslim-dominated state and ultimately an Islamic state,—unless India is declared a Hindu state in the near future: "Hindus, Sikhs, Christians, Parsis, Buddhists and others (Muslims excluded) living in India have no option but to live either in a Hindu Rashtra or Muslim India, i.e. India as Dar-ul-Islam. That is the stark reality."[162] He fails to explain how the declaration of India as a Hindu state would stop the Muslim increase leading to a Muslim majority, but presumably it would include a policy of sending illegal Muslim immigrants back to their country of origin.

Arrest warrants for Hindus, not for Muslims

The alleged pro-Muslim policy goes as far as condoning infiltration by Pakistani agents: "The ISI, the intelligence agency of Pakistan, has virtually covered the whole of India with an elaborate network of its own. Here are the intelligence activities of an enemy country penetrating our territory deeply, our own intelligence departments have reported this with concern from every affected state, but the Indian State sits practically idle to let this threat to our security thrive. The reason? The reason is that the network concerned consists of Muslims. When our Intelligence Bureau

---

[160]BJP: *Election Manifesto 1998*, p.33.

[161]Developed in Baljit Rai: *Demographic Aggression against India.*

[162]Baljit Rai: *Is India Going Islamic?*, p.107.

sent an officer from Bombay to Patna earlier this year to arrest a maulvi who was an active agent of the ISI, the Chief Minister of Bihar, Laloo Prasad Yadav, himself intervened to thwart the arrest. The situation in UP and West Bengal is no different."[163]

Shortly after Abhas Chatterjee finished his manuscript, a similar incident sensationally illustrated the tendency described by him: "The subsequent events at the Nadwa College at Lucknow in November 1994 prove that the Government of India actually encourages ISI activists in India. When Abu Bakr, a hard-core agent of the ISI, was nabbed in a raid on the College hostel which he had been using as a hideout for the last eight years to carry out terrorist and subversive activities all over India, the Government intervened swiftly to let him escape, apologized to the Rector of the College for the arrest, promised to him not to make such arrests in his institution in future, set up a high-level enquiry and took to task the officials of the Indian Intelligence Bureau and UP State Police who had conducted the raid."[164] The said Rector of the Nadwat-ul-Ulema College in Lucknow was Maulana Syed Abul Hassan Ali Nadwi, also known as Ali Mian, chairman of the Muslim Personal Law Board and prominent member of the *Rabita*, the Hejaz-based World Islamic Council, and therefore (i.e. because of his say in the allotment of huge Arab finances to selected Islamic initiatives) probably the most powerful man within India's Muslim community.[165]

What is alleged here is that the Indian state protects agents who are working to undermine that same Indian state. This does not mean that the security forces are neglecting their constitutional duty of protecting the state, on the contrary: the point is precisely that security personnel are often thwarted in the performance of their duty and sometimes even punished by the political authorities.

Abhas Chatterjee alleges that Muslim leaders are allowed to get away with law-breaking activities without having to fear arrest: "For people who openly indulge in anti-India activities, incite the minorities to mischief, and boldly proclaim themselves to be representatives of a marauding culture, arrest warrants from Indian courts are not applicable. Warrants for the arrest of Abdullah Bukhari, Imam of Jama Masjid at Delhi, have been

---

[163]A. Chatterjee: *Hindu Nation*, pp.36-7. ISI = "Inter Services Intelligence".

[164]Editorial note in A. Chatterjee: *Hindu Nation*, p.37.

[165]Details in S. Sahay: "Nadwa raid was right", *Organiser*, 18.12.1994, courtesy the *Hindustan Times*.

issued long ago by courts in Kerala, UP and Bihar, but the armed police force of India have not the courage to take him into custody."[166] If the police sometimes "have not the courage" for making such arrests, part of the reason is precisely that the officers making the arrest can look forward to being punished themselves (as were those who pursued Abu Bakr in the incident in Lucknow) or at least being punitively transferred to another town, upsetting their housing and social arrangements and the school careers of their children.

The same leniency is not extended to Hindu religious leaders, some of whom have been imprisoned during the anti-cow-slaughter movements of *c.* 1950 and *c.* 1966 and the Ayodhya movement of *c.* 1991: "In contrast, any Hindu holy man, let him be Shankaracharya Swaroopanandaji or any one else, can be arrested at any time under any pretext."[167] The trend was set by Jawaharlal Nehru himself: during the first post-Independence agitation against cow slaughter, when Swami Karpatri sat in front of Nehru's office in protest, Nehru and his sister Vijayalakshmi Pandit came out, grabbed him by his hair, kicked him and literally threw him on to the street.[168] Of course, this and Chatterjee's evidence is only anecdotal, and a more detailed count should be made to verify the impression that Muslims, from ISI agents to religious dignitaries, are given a more lenient treatment than Hindus.

Hindu refugees

A discrimination for which the Indian State cannot be held responsible, but which deserves to be better known none the less, is the selective killing of Hindus by separatist militants (i.e. fighters *against* the Indian State): "Over the last few years, there have been several incidents in Punjab and Jammu, in which some passengers were segregated and dragged out of buses to be lined up on the roadside and shot to death. You should remember that in each one of these incidents, the victims of the butchery, persons killed like dogs, were Hindus and Hindus alone, and they were so killed because they were Hindus."[169]

---

[166]A. Chatterjee: *Hindu Nation*, p.38.

[167]A. Chatterjee: *Hindu Nation*, p.39. The Shankaracharya and other leading Hindu clerics had been imprisoned for their role in the Ayodhya agitation.

[168]Related to me by James Michaels, then India correspondent for several American papers (more recently editor of *Forbes* magazine). There is a hint of this episode in S.R. Goel: *How I Became a Hindu*, p.65.

[169]A. Chatterjee: *Hindu Nation*, p.37.

But according to Hindu activists, the Indian State *can* be held responsible for the follow-up of such terrorist attacks on Hindus: "The entire Hindu population of the Valley of Kashmir, a province of our own country, has been languishing for the last five years in makeshift tents. In the face of inhuman cruelty and terror inflicted by Muslims, these people had to leave their hearths and homes. ... During these five years [1989-94], there have been three Prime Ministers in the country, but not one of them had a day's time or the decency to even visit any of these camps. Why? Because the sufferers are Hindus. The Government of India has not even stated categorically till this day that it is committed to the safe return of these people to their own homes and properties."[170]

Incidentally, while the Hindu refugees are being housed in temporary camps, the government of Jammu and Kashmir has planned colonies (i.e. permanent settlement) for Kashmiri Muslims in Jammu, allegedly in a bid to "change the demographic complexion of Hindu-majority Jammu, the city of temples".[171]

Similarly, Chatterjee complains that the secularists pay absolutely no attention when Hindus are killed in terrorist attacks: "Muslims exploded a powerful bomb in the Madras office of the RSS. The explosion destroyed the building and left seven persons dead, but Rajesh Pilot, the Minister of State in the Home Ministry, Government of India, stated that the occurrence was not serious enough to warrant a CBI investigation. Why? Because the RSS is a Hindu organization."[172]

Ultimately, a part of the blame should be passed on to Hindu public opinion. If a Minister were to sense that Hindu public opinion cared about receiving due attention from politicians, he would not risk failing to take action on such occasions.

Symbolic discriminations

Symbolic issues are not immediately consequential, but tend to speak to the imagination more strongly than many bread-and-butter issues. Hence the ill-feeling among Hindus about the communal suppression of *Vande Mâtaram*, the battle-song of the 1905 Swadeshi movement, on the ground that Muslims consider it a hymn to goddess Durga, hence a form of idolatry.

---

[170]A. Chatterjee: *Hindu Nation*, pp.37-8.

[171]Khajuria S. Kant: "Islamisation of Jammu begins", *Organiser*, 18.5.1997.

[172]A. Chatterjee: *Hindu Nation*, p.38.

On 17 October 1937, the Muslim League passed a resolution condemning the Congress for "foisting *Bande Mâtaram* as the national anthem upon the country in callous disregard of the feelings of Muslims".[173] Nehru was Congress president, and the Congress Working Committee which met in Calcutta a few weeks later "recognizing the validity of the objections raised by the Muslims to certain parts of the *Bande Mâtaram* song, recommended that at the national gatherings the first two stanzas only of the song should be sung".[174] Nehru's subsequent lobbying against *Vande Mâtaram* in 1937-50 provides an interesting case study in his thought and working-style.[175] At any rate, against an overwhelming majority of ordinary Congressmen in favour of *Vande Mâtaram*, he proved stronger: on 24 January 1950, two days before the first Republic Day, Rabindranath Tagore's *Jana Gana Mana* was accepted as India's national anthem. According to Sita Ram Goel, "the national movement stood humiliated."[176]

Abhas Chatterjee protests: "Is there a single independent nation in the world which does not have the right to sing its national song in its own Parliament? But in India, *Vande Mâtaram* which we have recognized as our national song was not allowed to be sung in the Parliament because some Muslims members objected to it!"[177] Meanwhile, a BJP initiative has remedied this condition: *Vande Mâtaram* can be sung in Parliament, though not on an equal footing with the official anthem *Jana Gana Mana*. Also, the BJP State governments of Delhi and Gujarat have introduced the daily singing of *Vande Mâtaram* in the public schools. But restoring *Vande Mâtaram* as national anthem is a different matter yet.

The national flag provides a similar story. The first flag of the Freedom Movement was the one unfurled by the Parsi nationalist Madam Bhikaji Cama at the International Socialist Congress in Stuttgart in 1907: horizontal stripes of green, yellow and red, the top green one carrying eight white lotuses (for the then eight provinces), the middle yellow one

---

[173]Sarvepalli Gopal, ed.: *Selected Works of Jawaharlal Nehru*, first series, vol.8, p.185n.

[174]Sarvepalli Gopal, ed.: *Selected Works of Jawaharlal Nehru*, first series, vol.8, p.236n.

[175]Sarvepalli Gopal, ed.: *Selected Works of Jawaharlal Nehru*, second series, vol.3, pp.85-6, pp.189-92; vol.5, p.455; vol.6, pp.277-84.

[176]S.R. Goel: "Nehru promoted Jana Gana Mana", *Observer of Business and Politics*, 10.9.1995.

[177]A. Chatterjee: *Hindu Nation*, p.36.

the white Devanagari caption *Vande Mâtaram*, and the bottom red one carried a sun towards the fly and a crescent towards the hoist.[178] With modifications, this became the Congress flag, but when the Congress seriously considered designing a national flag for the future Republic, the Congress Flag Committee (1931) proposed the plain saffron flag (with blue charkha) as a historically rooted, truly national flag for independent India.[179] However, Muslims inside the Congress insisted on including green, conventionally the emblematic colour of Islam. Disregarding the Committee's advice, the Congress leadership opted for the tricolour scheme which served as party flag, and which was commonly read as a communal compromise, with the top saffron stripe symbolizing Hinduism and the bottom green stripe symbolizing Islam.

It really troubled Aurobindo in the Congress policy of Hindu-Muslim unity that this unity was sought in the erasing of all distinctly Hindu elements from its conception of India, as exemplified by symbolic issues in the 1930s, such as the choice of a flag (saffron flag rejected in favour of a communal tricolour including green as representing Islam) and an anthem (*Vande Mâtaram* rejected in spite of its long association with the freedom movement): "As for the Hindu-Muslim affair, I saw no reason why the greatness of India's past or her spirituality should be thrown into the waste paper basket in order to conciliate the Moslems who would not at all be conciliated by such policy."[180]

Another symbolic grievance concerns the names of public buildings, towns and streets, for instance: "In the capital city of our country, there are still roads commemorating persons like Aurangzeb, Sikander Lodi, Firoz Tughlaq etc. There is no conceivable tyranny that these barbarians did not practise on our national society and culture; there is no effort they spared to destroy us. Even their names should evoke revulsion in us. But the State in India has been glorifying them."[181]

The Delhi units of Sangh Parivar organizations call themselves *Indraprastha* units, after the ancient city of the Pandavas near which Delhi was built. Their intention is to rename the capital as *Indraprastha* as an

---

[178]See M.M. Lal: "Madame Cama—an ardent nationalist", *Organiser*, 29.1.1995. The original flag was smuggled back into India and is now on display in the library of the *Mahratta* and *Kesri* newspapers in Pune.

[179]The story is told by K.R. Malkani: *The Politics of Ayodhya and Hindu-Muslim Relations*, pp.175-79.

[180]Aurobindo (1934): *India's Rebirth*, p.189.

[181]A. Chatterjee: *Hindu Nation*, p.38.

internationally audible statement of Hindu revival, but the BJP resolve in this direction seems weak; as Delhi's state government in 1993-98, and as national government since 1998, the BJP had not made any move in this direction. The SS-BJP government of Maharashtra officially renamed *Bombay* as *Mumbaî*, but the BJP state governments in Gujarat and Uttar Pradesh never got around to fulfilling the long-standing promise of renaming *Ahmedâbâd* as *Karnâvatî* and *Allahâbâd* as *Prayâg*. As always, the BJP proved to be less radical and more subject to inertia than both its supporters and its enemies believe.

Cultural discrimination

Another complaint concerns the neglect and depreciation of Hindu culture, starting with the demotion of Sanskrit in the school curriculum: "Sanskrit, the sacred language of the Hindus, is being slowly but systematically edged out. State Governments in the country are now working to even throw it out of the school curriculum. By contrast, Urdu which is primarily the language of the Muslims, which is written in a foreign script, which is the official language of Pakistan, and which had played a prominent part in fanning Muslim separatism leading to the Partition, is being blatantly encouraged. Today it is made the official language of some states, tomorrow it is recognized as a medium of examination, the day after it becomes a language of Doordarshan, and so on."[182]

Regarding Sanskrit, the situation is not as bad as Chatterjee seems to fear. The language received a setback under the V.P. Singh Government (1990), when the time allotted to it in the school curriculum was substantially decreased.[183] However, private organizations are very active in promoting Sanskrit, both as a study subject and as a living spoken language.[184] Moreover, on 6 October 1994, the Supreme Court rejected the plea that teaching Sanskrit is in conflict with secularism, and directed the Central Board of Secondary Education to include Sanskrit as an elective subject in its Secondary School syllabus. As the CBSE had pleaded that

---

[182]A. Chatterjee: *Hindu Nation*, p.39.

[183]Sukumar Bhattacharji: "New education policy and Sanskrit", *Economic and Political Weekly*, 1.12.1990, pp.2641-42, on VHP's Acharya Ramnath Suman: *Naî Shikshâ Nîti kâ Sanskṛt par Prahâr* (New education policy's blow to Sanskrit).

[184]On Krishna Sastry's work to propagate spoken Sanskrit, see: "Sanskrit revival", *Hinduism Today*, Feb. 1986.

the inclusion of Sanskrit would force it to provide similar facilities for the teaching of Persian and Arabic, the apex Court even added that it was perfectly justified to give Sanskrit a status which is withheld from Persian and Arabic.[185]

Abhas Chatterjee also complains of the hostile contents of many programmes on India's state television: "Look at our national media of communication, the Doordarshan—DD. It presents as a national hero no less a villain than Tipu Sultan who demolished 8,000 Hindu temples, slaughtered Hindus in large numbers, forcibly converted thousands of them by circumcision and feeding of beef. The DD shows for months a serial styled 'The Sword of Tipu Sultan' even when that sword bears on it a carved message expressing the man's eagerness to extinguish Hinduism and eradicate the Hindu populace. That sword is still preserved in the Mysore Museum for anyone to see. Amir Khusro, a man who abused Hindus and Bhagwan Shiva in such filthy language that I cannot even repeat it before an audience which includes women, is projected by the DD as a Sufi saint, a great national hero. In the 'Firdaus' programme of the DD, the terrorist Muslims of Kashmir are depicted as liberal, tolerant and gentle people while the Hindus, the victims of their atrocities, are painted as mean and mischievous rogues."[186]

I don't know whether Tipu Sultan ever managed to destroy as many as 8,000 temples in the fairly small territory which he controlled, but it is certain that the Doordarshan serial *The Sword of Tipu Sultan* has painted him in unhistorical rosy colours.[187] But a Muslim could easily reply that in the epic serials, the Hindu heroes Rama and Krishna are also shown in the best colours, though they too committed some acts of injustice. Doordarshan may have been politically anti-BJP in its news-reporting as long as anti-BJP parties were in power, but it may be exaggerated to impute to Doordarshan an anti-Hindu bias in its cultural programmes.

Some politicians take their care to uphold "secularism" quite far. In a Lok Sabha debate with Union Railway Minister Ram Vilas Paswan, Uma Bharati complained that "when she boarded the Rajdhani Express bound for Ahmedabad in the morning recently, she could not hear the soothing

---

[185]Reported in *Vedic Light* (Arya Samaj monthly), February 1995, pp.4 ff., courtesy *Hindustan Times*.

[186]A. Chatterjee: *Hindu Nation*, pp.40-1.

[187]To set the record on Tipu Sultan straight, the Bombay Malayali Samajam has collected articles on his alleged wrongdoings in a booklet, *Tipu Sultan, Hero or Villain?*

bhajans which used to be played over the public address system. In its place was instrumental music which made no sense. When she called up a Railway official and inquired about the change in the musical menu, she was told that the new Railway Minister did not want religious songs which would compromise the 'secular' image of the Railways. Bharati asked the Minister not to go to ridiculous lengths to prove secularism."[188]

This small incident raises fundamental questions about the very feasibility and desirability of a "secular" cultural policy. Should government-sponsored concerts exclude religiously inspired music? Can a government-sponsored exhibition of national art history, in any country, display paintings on religious themes? In that case, European authorities would have to cover up the best paintings of Michelangelo Buonarotti or Pieter-Pauwel Rubens, and silence the best music of Johann Sebastian Bach or Georg Friedrich Händel. The exclusion of religious themes would mean the exclusion of the best works of art.

Private-sector cultural discrimination

The private-sector (partly underworld-controlled) Mumbai film industry toes the same anti-Hindu line, according to Shrikant Talageri: "When two persons meet, in a Hindi film, and one is a Hindu and the other a Muslim, they do not greet one another with *namaste* or *Râm Râm*; nor does one say *namaste* and the other *as-salâm âleykum* ...; both greet each other with *âdâb arz hai* or *as-salâm âleykum*. When a Hindu, in a Hindi film, is faced with some great affliction, he starts doing the rounds, turn by turn, of a temple, a mosque and a church, but a Muslim or Christian is never shown finding it necessary to approach other shrines. These are just two of many examples—each subtle by itself, perhaps not even consciously noticed in spite of their repeated occurrence—which, in the cumulative effect, serve to create the intended psychological environment. The entertainment media have played no mean role in carrying on this brand of propaganda. The calculated glorification of Urdu, of Lucknow *tehzîb*, of the Mughals, of *ghazals* and *qawâllîs*, etc., and the subtle ridicule of Sanskritised Hindi, has been a basic feature of the Hindi film industy."[189]

---

[188]"Uma Bharati praises rail budget", *Indian Express*, 11.3.1997.

[189]S. Talageri: *Aryan Invasion Theory and Indian Nationalism*, p.33. The part about Hindus adopting the Muslim greeting when meeting a Muslim is quite realistic; I have seen it happen a number of times at the BJP office when a member of the BJP Minority Cell came in.

Talageri also notes the asymmetry between Hindu and Muslim culture in the treatment given to them by public figures in an effort to make the right secular noises: "every aspect of India's mainstream culture, which existed in India prior to the arrival of Islamic culture from West Asia, represents 'communalism'. Thus, it is perfectly secular for Indian politicians to don *fez* caps, visit mosques, perform *namâz* to clicking cameras, etc. But it is 'communal' for them to visit temples, or bow down before Hindu holy men, or to wave *ârti*, or break coconuts while inaugurating a function, since the customs of visiting temples, bowing before holy men, waving *ârti* and breaking coconuts, all existed in India before the arrival of Islam".[190]

The only comparison which comes to mind for this ill-treatment of the majority culture is the disparaging of Christianity in the media by the dominant secularists in France, Belgium or the USA. In 1995, the authorities in some British cities prohibited the display of Christian symbols in public decorations for Christmas, on the plea that these would be offensive to the minorities. This kind of "multiculturism" amounting to the self-effacing of the "dominant" culture is perhaps the best handle Westerners have to get a feel of what secularism means to Hindus.

The news media are also part of this climate, according to Abhas Chatterjee: "In the major newspapers and periodicals of India, the situation today is: write whatever trash you like castigating Hindu Dharma, Hindu culture and Hindu society, let it even be utterly baseless and outright abusive, your piece will be published like a shot. But write a piece on Mohammed or Islam, let it be a factual, logical, truthful article written in decent language and based on impeccable sources, you would not be able to find space for it in any newspaper or periodical. It is as if a policy of strict Islamic censorship is operating in the country."[191]

This, I am afraid, was indeed the situation in the leading English-language media at the time when Chatterjee wrote his *Concept of Hindu Nation* (1993), though even then, there were still sizable loopholes, like the opinion page of *Indian Express*, where Chatterjee himself could present historical evidence for the existence of a Rama temple at the site where later the Babri Masjid was built.[192] At any rate, the climate has changed considerably. Thus, Arun Shourie's hard-hitting book about the

---

[190] S. Talageri: *Aryan Invasion Theory and Indian Nationalism*, p.33.

[191] A. Chatterjee: *Hindu Nation*, p.41.

[192] Articles included in the second edition of S.R. Goel, ed.: *Hindu Temples*, vol.1.

real-life role of Islamic Law in Indian Muslim communities, *The World of Fatwas* (1995), was reviewed in most papers, often lengthy excerpts were included, and in 1997, the prestigious publishing-house HarperCollins decided to republish it in a paper back edition. But Chatterjee remains in the right when he insists on an inequality in the editors' policies: while the attention paid to the Fatwa book remained an exceptional event and outright praise for it confined to a few dailies, the disparaging of Hinduism remains an entirely routine affair in all media.

Banning Hindu political parties

There is also discrimination against Hindu politicians by the courts: "Secularism, which is a synonym for anti-Hinduism, has not been defined in our Constitution, but the highest court of the land passes a judgment that as such-and-such party does not support Secularism, therefore it has no right to function through State Governments. The Chief Election Commissioner issues an order for intensive revision of electoral rolls in Assam so that the rolls may be purged of names of Bangladeshi infiltrators, but the courts rule that it would be illegal to do so."[193-94]

Specifically, courts have challenged the right of Hindu election candidates to stand on an explicitly Hindu platform, all the while condoning the explicitly Islamist programmes of the Ittehad-ul-Muslimeen (Hyderabad) or the Indian Union Muslim League (Kerala): "The Bombay High Court on Tuesday set aside the election of Shiv Sena candidate Suryakant Mahadik from Nehru Nagar constituency in the state Assembly elections of February 1990 for having garnered votes on the basis of Hindutva and a religious appeal. ... The judge held Mr. Mahadik guilty of using corrupt practices mentioned in section 123, sub-sections (3) and (3A) of the Representation of the People Act and set aside his election from Nehru Nagar constituency". The plaintiff, the defeated Congress candidate Mrs. Saroj Bhosale-Naik, had alleged that at Mr. Mahadik's election meetings, SS and BJP leaders had "appealed to voters to cast their votes on the basis of Hindutva".[195]

Though the BJP avoids explicit references to themes like *Hindû*

---

[193]Recently there have been some more judgments which display the same disposition, notably the Supreme Court judgments on Ayodhya Reference and the photo-identity cards. (editorial note in the original)

[194]A. Chatterjee: *Hindu Nation*, p.40.

[195]"High Court sets aside election of Shiv Sena MLA", *Indian Express*, 24.4.1991.

Râshtra, it feels threatened by these judicial moves: "The Bharatiya Janata Party is worried about the legal and political impact of the unseating of its Member of Parliament from Thane in Maharashtra, Mr. Ram Kapse, through a verdict of the Bombay High Court. ... Although a few Shiv Sena MLAs have earlier lost their seats in the Maharashtra Assembly as a result of court verdicts, this is the first time an MP has been found guilty of corrupt practice of using religion to raise his vote count, for violation of section 123 of the Representation of the People Act."[196]

The BJP itself has indeed been targeted by censoring decrees, e.g.: "The election commission today censored the election speech of BJP leader Kalyan Singh to be broadcast over All-India Radio on the ground that it has misused religion for electoral purposes. In a directive to the chief electoral officer of Uttar Pradesh, the three-member commission asked him to ensure that the references to the BJP leader's promise on the construction of a Ram temple at Ayodhya are deleted."[197] More seriously, on 11 March 1994, a nine-judge bench of the Supreme Court upheld the dismissal of the erstwhile BJP governments which had been dismissed following the Babri Masjid demolition. The Supreme Court had stated that "religion and politics cannot be mixed" and that "any State Government which pursues unsecular policies or unsecular course of action, acts contrary to the constitutional mandate and renders itself amenable to action under Article 356"[198] (i.e. dismissal by the Central government and imposition of President's Rule on the state).

However, the courts are by no means uniformly hostile to the pleas of the Hindu candidates concerned. On 19 February 1992, the Election Commission under T.N. Seshan rejected petitions by Congress leader Arjun Singh and four others demanding the deregistration of the BJP as a political party. The petitioners pleaded that the BJP had mixed religion and politics by organizing a religious procession, viz. L.K. Advani's 1990 Rath Yatra to Ayodhya (stopped in Bihar with Advani's arrest), and that the use during the procession of the party symbol, the lotus flower, confirmed the suspicion that this was a purely religious symbol which should henceforth be barred from use in electoral propaganda. Seshan explained: "Objections cannot be entertained on the ground that the

[196]"Court verdict puts BJP in a fix", *The Hindu* (international edition), 23.4.1994.
[197]"EC censors Kalyan's campaign speech", *Indian Express*, 17.4.1996.
[198]"Court verdict puts BJP in a fix", *The Hindu* (international edition), 23.4.1994.

ideologies, policies and programmes of a certain political party are opposed to those of another political party".[199]

In 1995 the Supreme Court upheld the right of several Shiv Sena and BJP candidates to appeal to the voters in the name of "Hindutva".[200] The Supreme Court held that the mere mention of the words Hindu and Hindutva in a speech does not bring it within the prohibitions listed in the Representation of the People Act: "It may well be that these words are used in a speech to promote secularism or emphasise the way of life of the Indian people and Indian culture or ethos, or criticise the policy of any political party as discriminatory or intolerant."[201] And in 1996, the Delhi High Court struck down the 1992 decision of the Election Commission to deregister the Hindu Mahasabha for being an explicitly "Hindu" and therefore "communal" party.[202]

In 1993, the Congress government tried to push through Parliament two Bills of which the effect would be to impose deregistration on a party which brings religion into politics: the Constitution (Eightieth Amendment) Bill and the Representation of the People (Amendment) Bill. The operative part of the latter read: "Where (a) any party bears a religious name; or (b) the memorandum or rules and regulations [or the activities] of the political party no longer conform to the provisions of subsection (5) of section 29-A ..., its registration as a political party under section 29-A shall be liable to be cancelled by an order of the High Court within whose jurisdiction the main office of that political party is situated."[203]

The said section 29-A subsection (5) of the Representation of the People Act prohibits parties from fomenting ill-will between different classes of the population on grounds of religion, race, language, caste or

---

[199]Quoted by J.C. Jetli: "BJP wins symbol case against Arjun Singh, JD, SJP, Leftists", *BJP Today*, 16.3.1992. T.N. Seshan has become an icon of incorruptibility in the administration; he presents his views in two books, authored with the help of Sanjoy Hazarika: *The Degeneration of India* and *The Regeneration of India* (both 1995).

[200]See Rama Jois: *Supreme Court Judgment on 'Hindutva'*. This and related judgments are sharply criticized by Brenda Cossman and Ratna Kapur: *Secularism's Last Sigh?* Ch.2.

[201]Sarita Rani, Namita Bhandare, Lyla Bavadam: "The day of judgement. Mixing religion with politics: the Supreme Court clears Manohar Joshi but censures Bal Thackeray", *Sunday*, 24.12.1995.

[202]See D.C. Tyagi: "At long last, it was Savarkar's epic definition of Hindu", in Tyagi, ed.: *Sâvarkar Saurabh Smriti Granth*, pp.169-73.

[203]Quoted in: "A Bill that poses more questions than it answers", *Indian Express*, 30.7.1993.

regional provenance. The Constitutional amendment which the Congress government proposed in 1993 aimed at enshrining that very provision in the Constitution: "Parliament may, by law, provide that any association or body of individuals be banned, if it, by words, either spoken or written, or by signs or by visible representations or otherwise, promotes or attempts to promote disharmony or feelings of enmity, hatred or ill-will between different classes of citizens of India (i) on grounds of religion; or (ii) on grounds of race, place of birth, residence, language, caste or community."[204]

In its note of dissent, the BJP pointed out that while the *Statement of Objects and Reasons* appended to the Bills, on the pattern of earlier legislation of this type, mentions the aim of curbing disharmony "on grounds of religion, race, caste, community, language, place of birth or residence", the actual text of the Bills only deal with the factor "religion", and thereby implicitly "virtually confer legitimacy on the abuse" of divisions based on caste or language.[205] The BJP further alleged that the Bills constituted a serious infringement on the freedom of association, because it would "arm the Executive with wide-ranging powers to outlaw not only political parties and trade-unions ... but even social and religious organizations like the Arya Samaj!"[206]

The BJP claimed that democracy itself was at stake: "Democracy is a system wherein all political parties and ideologies must be allowed to grow. Ideologies can be countered ideologically and never by legislative oppression. The proposed Eightieth Amendment to the Constitution strikes at the roots of this concept. This Bill has focussed on one ideology and seeks to block its growth by these amendments. If the country acquiesces in this, tomorrow yet another ideology would be targetted. This is the path to one-party rule. A controlled democracy with a Tribunal acting as ideological ombudsman spells disaster for the very system."[207]

The Bills were defeated because other parties joined the BJP in

---

[204]Quoted in: "A Bill that poses more questions than it answers", *Indian Express*, 30.7.1993. It may be noted in passing that *economic class* is conspicuous by its absence in this list, so the doctrine of class struggle can be freely propagated.

[205]BJP: *Note of Dissent by BJP regarding Constitution (80th Amendment) Bill, 1993, and the Representation of People (Amendment) Bill, 1993*, p.2.

[206]BJP: *Note of Dissent by BJP regarding Constitution (80th Amendment) Bill, 1993, and the Representation of People (Amendment) Bill, 1993*, p.6.

[207]BJP: *Note of Dissent by BJP regarding Constitution (80th Amendment) Bill, 1993, and the Representation of People (Amendment) Bill, 1993*, p.7.

opposing it. The main reason cited was that politicians who remembered the Emergency dictatorship heard an alarm bell ring when faced with a Bill which would give an occasional majority in Parliament or even an unelected High Court judge the power to outlaw and dissolve a political party. When you consider moreover that the Bill was aimed specifically at creating an instrument to outlaw the largest opposition party, the BJP, representative of more than 20 per cent of the voters, it was clear that this Bill would open the floodgates for a high-handed muzzling of opposition voices by the establishment.

Janata Dal spokesman George Fernandes referred to the Emergency and the legal covers which Indira Gandhi had used to impose dictatorship, and said: "This is even more unlawful. Though it is meant to fight communalism, it will give absolute powers to the Government to deny democratic rights of the people. It strikes at the very roots of fundamental rights and the structure of the Constitution. In the name of fighting communalism, the Government cannot be allowed to snatch away the religious rights enshrined in the Constitution."[208]

Moreover, while banning a party would still involve a truly public procedure, barring an individual candidate from contesting could be done at a fairly low administrative level without any democratic control: "Legal experts fear that every returning officer will get the power to decide whether a person is disqualified. He can reject the nomination of a candidate at the very stage of scrutiny on these grounds. If a returning officer feels that a candidate, after taking oath, has made use of religion or promoted ill-will between classes of citizens on the grounds mentioned in the amendment, he can reject the nomination outright. The effect of the proposed amendment would thus be to take India towards a 'controlled democracy'."[209]

Commentators wondered aloud whether the government had properly considered the implications of its own proposals. Thus, the small print of the amendment to the Representation of the People's Act held that a person will be disqualified for being elected to the Central or State Parliaments if he "makes use of religion, including religious symbols, for the purposes of the said election". To this, the *Indian Express* editors remark: "Indian semiology is essentially religious. There is perhaps no

[208]Quoted in "Oppn eyes Religion Bill with suspicion", *Indian Express*, 30.7.1993.

[209]Editorial comment in: "A Bill that poses more questions than it answers", *Indian Express*, 30.7.1993.

sign or symbol which is clinically secular. Whether it is hand or cow or wheel or lotus or crescent, [it has] an acute religious association in the Indian context. Will the use of these symbols attract the newly proposed constitutional provision? The apostles of secularism, particularly communists, will not have to worry. Sickle or hammer are not seen as religious symbols."[210]

A BJP leader commented: "By what leap of logic does a compulsory rote of the *Red Book* remain 'democratic and secular', when Marxism-Leninism is in practice a state religion, and yet, any other expression of faith becomes a near sacrilegious act against secularism."[211] Indeed, even though this doctrine is responsible for the largest mass killings in world history, for thousands of killings during Communist uprisings in India, and for hundreds of murders of Hindu activists even in recent years, its operative category of discrimination and hatred, viz. *economic class*, is conspicuous by its absence in the list of unmentionable social divisions: religion, language, caste etc. The strictures against "mixing religion with politics" are not based on objective human rights concerns, because religion, for all its frequent inhumanity, has not done worse than purely secular ideologies like National-Socialism and Communism.

Coming back to actually religious symbols, there is reason to wonder whether the Bill would prohibit candidates from wearing things which are identified with a religion: can a Hindu candidate have a tilak on his forehead, or a Sikh candidate a turban?[212] The ground reality is that a Sikh candidate in rural Panjab who shows up at election meetings bare-headed and clean-shaven is bound to lose votes. Wearing the Khalsa uniform sends the message to the Sikh voter that whatever else the candidate promises, he is "one of us", he will not betray Sikh interests. This is also true at the level of language, whether because of language chauvinism or, again, for the religious connotations which a language carries: try speaking Urdu before a Hindu audience, or proper Hindi in Aligarh Muslim University or before a Dravidian audience. All these details of

[210]Quoted in: "A Bill that poses more questions than it answers", *Indian Express*, 30.7.1993.

[211]Jaswant Singh: "The politics of secularism", *Indian Express*, 4.6.1990.

[212]Speaking of which: CPI(M) president Harkishen Singh Surjeet, a Sikh-born atheist still sporting a Sikh turban and beard, has said that he had wanted to drop this religion-based attire, but that the party had advised him to keep it, for whereas Hindu symbols count as "communal", sporting minority symbols is deemed "secular".

language, dress and other symbols carry communal weight with a number of voters, and may decide whether a candidate gets elected or not.

And what about names? To take this logic to its extreme: "The Representation of the People's Act is being amended to provide for a ban on political parties with religious names, after all, on the assumption that names transmit a religious message. If that is the philosophy behind this legislation, when a party can send a religious message, will not an individual's?"[213] The Prime Minister at the time was called Narasimha, the name of one of Vishnu's incarnations. Surely many Hindu voters would feel more comfortable voting for a Narasimha than for an Ahmed or Ali.

The more fundamental question of democracy which these Bills raise, is: why should religion be a less legitimate consideration on which to base voting choices than any other? Democracy has no business with the considerations which lead the voters to vote for this candidate, party and party programme rather than for another. If the voters in one country vote against abortion rights while those in another country vote in favour, then one can say from an ideological angle (whether it is feminism or the moral doctrines of the Church or any other) that the voters in one of these two countries were morally or politically *wrong* in voting the way they did. Yet, from the viewpoint of democracy, there is no ground for interfering with their sovereign choice.

Moreover, voters are free to be guided by their conscience, by calculations of their individual or class interests, by their religious beliefs, or by any other consideration they may fancy. Religious leaders, along with the spokesmen of secular ideologies and interest groups, are perfectly allowed to issue electoral advice to their flock, and in many democracies they have always done so and they still do. For the same reason, candidates have a right to identify with a religion-based cause: if that is what the voters want to see represented in Parliament, they are entitled to have it. Any interference with this right leads to what the *Indian Express* editors have aptly called a "controlled democracy".

CONCLUSION

Many of the Hindu complaints about discrimination sound shrill and some are indeed found to be exaggerated. But the general tendency to take Hindus for granted while showing special consideration to the minorities

[213]"A Bill that poses more questions than it answers", *Indian Express*, 30.7.1993.

has been sufficiently demonstrated by BJP spokesmen and by Abhas Chatterjee, selected here as a forthright independent spokesman of a widespread Hindu unrest.

To an extent, special provisions for minorities are in conformity with international practice, as for instance Tony Blair's policy of "devolution" in Great Britain means that the minority nations of Wales and Scotland get their own parliaments, while the majority English will have to make do with the joint British parliament, in which the semi-autonomous Welsh and Scotsmen also have a say. But even that arrangement has attracted criticism and will probably prove to be only temporary. At any rate, the inequalities which have been created in Indian law and political practice seriously harm the professed secular and democratic character of the Indian Republic. Thus, a statutory Minorities Commission with specific official powers, no matter how limited, and with the minorities involved being defined as *religious* minorities, is unthinkable in normal secular states.

Demanding equality before the law is hardly a revolutionary position in a republic committed to equality and democracy. Thus, there is no secular excuse for not supporting the Hindu demand of equality under Article 30: under the laws of any genuinely secular state, the Hindus would be enjoying the same rights in setting up denominational subsidized schools or in managing their own places of worship as the minorities. It is in fact a serious indictment of the spokesmen of secularism and of their foreign sympathizers that they have left this concern to denominational Hindu interest groups. There is nothing "communal" about demanding equality before the law regardless of religion.

In some cases, however, it is possible that the gains do not outweigh the price which would have to be paid for reform. In particular, the imposition of a Common Civil Code on the minorities would meet with such opposition that it could lead to serious disturbances and a genuine Muslim estrangement from the Indian state, and probably the BJP would be wise to keep this project in cold storage for the time being. At the same time, it should be kept in focus at least as a long-term project, a matter of principle whose implementation may be postponed but not abjured.

General conclusion

SUMMARY

Hindu revivalism is a broad trend in the nineteenth- and twentieth-century India which seeks to revitalize Hinduism after a millennium of political, ideological and psychological subjection to Islamic and Western hegemony. Unlike Hindu traditionalism, it seeks to co-opt modernity in its project of Hindu revival or Hindu reconstruction.

Hindu nationalism, or *"Hindutva"*, as given expression by the *Hindû Mahâsabhâ* (HMS, 1915-) and the family of organizations around the *Râshtrîya Swayamsevak Sangh* (RSS, 1925-), including the *Bhâratîya Jana Sangh* (BJS, 1951-77) and the *Bhâratîya Janatâ* Party (BJP, 1980-), is the numerically most important tendency within this broad movement. So far, most scholarly publications on these organizations have paid little attention to their ideological development as given in the primary sources. To an extent, this neglect was justified: there simply is not much ideology in Hindu nationalism. Beyond some elementary love of the Motherland, it is all quite straightforward and not very developed intellectually. All the same, a closer study of what is available would have led to a more correct picture of the movement's ideological position than is extant in the scholarly literature so far.

From the ideological viewpoint, the most interesting formulations of Hindu revivalist thought have been provided by individuals outside the said organizations, from Bankimchandra Chatterjee (1838-1894) and Sri Aurobindo (1872-1950) to Ram Swarup (1920-1998), Sita Ram Goel (1921-) and their younger friends. While the said organizations focused precisely on "organization", *sangathan*, on the assumption that this was what Hindus had lacked and what could make them invincible again, these authors focus on consciousness-raising about the exact nature of the different forces in the field. About their work, at least that of the post-Independence generation of Hindu revivalist authors, no scholarly research has been undertaken until now. Yet it is they more than the Hindutva organizations who are the true heirs of the colonial-age trail-blazers of Hindu revival.

As a preparation to a proper investigation of this fairly controversial subject, the present study has opened with a survey of the numerous terminological problems in this field. Most notable among them is the controversial term "secularism", appropriated both by the BJP and by its opponents. The latter denounce the BJP as religious fundamentalists, while the BJP itself claims to represent a religion which is inherently tolerant and pluralistic and argues that its proposals of legislative reform would change India in a direction which is called "secular" elsewhere, most importantly its long-standing demand that a Common Civil Code replace the present system of separate Hindu, Muslim, Christian and Parsi personal law systems.

Closely connected with this terminological confusion is the politicized climate of Hindutva studies, mostly in the sense of an unabashed hostility. A brief look into some remarkable cases of partisan reporting on the Hindutva movement shows us how great the impact of the Indian Marxist school has been on bonafide Western scholarship, which tends to dismiss as ridiculous and mischievous many of the positions taken by the Hindutva movement, even when these positions studied in isolation turn out to stand up to critical verification, like the claim that the controversial Babri Masjid stood on a destroyed Hindu temple, or that Muslim demography is eroding Hinduism's majority position in parts of India, or that the BJP demand for a Common Civil Code is in conformity with secularism as understood in the rest of the world. It is noted, however, that the recent rise of the BJP, its accession to power and the conspicuous failure of all the dramatic predictions about BJP rule ("the BJP will build gas chambers for the Muslims") have already caused a softening of this hostility in wider circles of observers though not among the hard core of ideological opponents.

Next, we have provided a historical survey of Hindu revivalism, brief when describing the already much-discussed Hindutva organizations, more detailed when presenting for the first time the work of individual thinkers like Ram Swarup. Though we have primarily focused on the 1980s and 90s, a proper understanding of our subject required us to extend its horizon back to the contributions of authors of the late nineteenth century like Dayananda Saraswati (1824-1883) and Swami Vivekananda

(1863-1902), and of the early twentieth century like Swami Shraddhananda (1857-1926) and Sri Aurobindo. A brief overview has been given of the pioneers of Hindu revivalism, from the *Brahmo Samâj* (1828-) to the early HMS. In greater detail, we have traced the history of the mature HMS, the genesis and growth of the RSS and its affiliate organizations including the BJP, some smaller but related movements including the traditionalist *Râm Râjya Parishad* (1948-) and the national-populist *Shiv Senâ* (1966-), and the careers of some individual authors.

The literature of the organized Hindutva movement shows a strange poverty of thought actually cultivated by an anti-intellectual RSS leadership. Its political analysis rarely rises above the most elementary pamphlet level, its power to convince outsiders is correspondingly limited, and its argumentation against hostile ideologies is likewise poor. Only recently has there been a slight change for the better, partly thanks to the successful outreach of Hindutva to the upcoming professionals whose influence is reorienting the movement to more modern goals and standards of excellence. The polemical exchanges with Christianity and Marxism, briefly surveyed here, and those with Islam, related in some detail, all show a sharp difference between the organized Hindutva movement and a number of individual authors. While many among the latter have formulated principled critiques of the doctrinal basis and the historical record of Christianity, Islam and Marxism, often also drawing on Western scholarship, the former has systematically limited its critique to a question of "loyalty to the nation": these foreign doctrines are accused of fostering extra-territorial loyalties and of being instrumentalized by foreign countries. The RSS has one-dimensionalized its worldview to a conflict between "nationalism" and the "anti-national forces", disregarding all subtler ideological differences between Hinduism and its challengers.

Even the Hindu-Muslim conflict is distortingly conceived as a struggle between "national" and "foreign". On closer analysis, this reductionist worldview owes much to the RSS's charm offensive towards the Indian Muslims ("it's not your *religion* we object to") and to their eagerness for recognition as a "secular" movement. Indeed, the RSS now propagates the belief that the Hindu-Muslim conflict is a British creation, a belief ridiculed by Hindu revivalist authors from Pandit Lekh Ram (1858-97) to Sita Ram Goel, but identical to the Gandhian and Nehruvian-secularist explanation of this conflict. One of the reasons of reviving the somewhat quaint term "revivalism" is precisely that we can see a continuity between the old revivalists of the Bengal Hindu Renaissance and the recent independent authors discussed here, while the large and much-discussed Hindutva movement is only a somewhat aberrant branch of this revivalist mainstream. Its main aberration consists in its refusal to speak plainly about the religious conflict, which it fudges by construing it in secular terms.

Hindu revivalism, with the temporary exception of the *Arya Samâj* (1875-), is by no means a "fundamentalist" movement. The notion "fundamentalism" refers to the effort by purists within a religion to impose their scripturalist views on a more lax or more modernist majority *within their own religion*. That is not at all the issue for the movement under consideration. To the extent that it is an "anti" movement, it may be anti-Islamic and anti-Western, but it is not particularly worried about impure or modernist forms of Hinduism. To the extent that it criticizes born Hindus, these will not be Hindus who smuggle Western ideas into Hinduism, but Hindu-born secularists who attack Hinduism, more as outsiders than as insider harbingers of impurity. This way, the Hindutva movement is by no means a danger to non-mainstream groups within Hinduism, the way Islamic fundamentalism has proven to be a headache for minorities within Islam such as the Shiites and Ahmadiyas in Pakistan.

Until now, most scholarly literature on Hindutva has had a very slender basis in primary sources. It has therefore been necessary to invite the reader to simply go over the explicit programmatic statements of the Hindu nationalist organizations. So far, all Western observers of Hindutva have somehow managed to ignore the official ideology of the RSS and BJP, Deendayal Upadhyaya's "Integral Humanism". An inspection of the texts formulating this doctrine suggests that Integral Humanism is in many respects an exact Indian counterpart of the European doctrine of Christian-Democracy. One thing which comes out very clearly from the election manifestoes of the BJS-BJP, and from similar texts by related organizations such as the Vishva Hindu Parishad (1964-), is that nationalism is a higher priority for them than any specifically religious issue, for in every case, the toughest language is used in denouncing real or perceived threats to the unity and integrity of India.

Another discovery is that the Hindu nationalists speak a progressive and egalitarian language in their designs for political reform, from socialist land redistribution plans in the 1960s to women's emancipation and "empowerment" in the 1990s. Skeptics may deride this as mendacious or as hollow election promises, but the fact is that at least in its official expressions, Hindu nationalism does not live up to the "fundamentalist" and reactionary image which its critics have propagated.

THE COLONIZED MIND

Hindu revivalism perceives itself as the cultural chapter of India's decolonization, which tries to free the Indians from the colonial condition at the mental and cultural level, to complete the process of political and economic decolonization. The emerging analysis among Hindus of their own society's condition is as follows.

During the past millennium, India has gone through two colonizations, one by Islam and one by semi-Christian, semi-secular Europe. At the political level, the native society proved relatively victorious against both, though not without retaining a considerable residue of what they brought. The problem with that, for Hindus attached to their culture, is not that in the wake of the Islamic conquests, a considerable amount of West- and Central-Asian human material enriched the Indian gene pool, nor that British rule brought an immense transformation in material culture. What they see as the problem for Hindu society is that the Islamic and Western regimes brought world-views which instil a profound contempt for and hostility to Hinduism.

The challenge facing Hindu activists is that for half a century after India's formal Independence, Hindu society has remained under the spell of a colonial psychology, in three different ways. First, power came in the hands of a westernized elite which had been estranged from the native culture, and which had established the same relationship with native culture which the British overlords used to have. If anything, its members displayed more animosity in their assertion of a non-Hindu identity for themselves and for India, apparently because they had to exorcize the remnants of Hinduness out of themselves. At the same time, they had the self-confidence, not to say arrogance, which comes with being securely in power.

The meaning of the term "secularism" which this elite had appropriated to itself, is alleged to be, for all practical purposes: an aversion to the native culture, not only in its strictly religious but in all its distinctive aspects. If the damage this ideology-cum-attitude could inflict remained limited, it was because the Indian "colonial" elite had penetrated Indian society and culture much less deeply than its counterpart in countries like China had managed to do. While the conflict between this class and the Hindu activists has produced a lot of verbal sound and fury, its hostility is ultimately based on opportunism, on collaboration with the colonizer or with the global dominance of the West, which is a relatively superficial motive liable to give way once the power equation changes. To an extent, the 1990s have indeed produced the beginnings of such a change in opinion climate.

The second face of the lingering colonial condition as defined by Hindu revivalists is that a sizable section of the native society has passed under the spell of the religions brought by past imperialisms. They have been (or are being) artificially estranged from their mother society, at least in their core religious convictions (in the case of the Christians) and often in their entire culture and way of life (in the case of the Muslims). For Hindu revivalists, decolonization in the case of the estranged minorities would mean: freeing them from the beliefs and concomitant loyalties instilled in them by past imperialisms. The main Hindu revivalist position on this, since the late nineteenth century, is that Muslims and Christians should be persuaded to return to their ancestral culture. By contrast, the Sangh Parivar has settled for the less ambitious and somewhat unclear position that the minorities should "Indianize" themselves, develop love and loyalty for India, though it is never explained how that would square with their dictinctive religious beliefs.

The idea that the Muslim minority is seen as a "residue of a past imperialism" may come as a shock to many. If this were to mean that present-day Muslims are held responsible for the wrongdoings of the past Islamic invaders and rulers, that would indeed be worrying. Most authors assure us that that is not their intention at all. On the other hand, as a matter of history, a fair case can be made that except in marginal instances, the genesis of the Indian Muslim community is inseparable from the conditions of Muslim hegemony which prevailed from the late twelfth till the eighteenth century. But ultimately, such facts of history may not be a sufficient reason to argue against the legitimacy of Islam being in India: many national histories have their blood-soaked episodes without thereby delegitimizing the existence of the nations concerned. However, some

Hindu scholars have endeavoured to supply this reason by means of a fundamental critique of Islam: regardless of whether Islam is foreign, regardless of whether it was imposed by force, if it can be shown that Islam is not good, or not true, that should suffice to make Indian Muslims reconsider their religious beliefs.

Meanwhile, the Hindu mind has remained a colonized mind, and this is the third residue of the colonial condition. In spite of occasional bouts of bluster about past greatness, or of genuine admiration for the ancestral heritage, the Hindu as Hindu still had little self-respect or self-confidence, often showing the effects of a deep inferiority feeling. Some sections of Hindu society, most strikingly the Sikhs, have even reformulated their own religion in the mould of the prophetic-monotheist religions and turned against the mother society, though probably not in a definitive way. Here again, the historic factor of opportunistic collaboration with the powerful or the prestigious ideology suggests that the aversion to Hinduism is fairly superficial and may be reversed easily once Hinduism acquires more prestige again. A related phenomenon is that contemporary educated Hindus have been getting increasingly ignorant about Hindu tradition, and this affects not only the secularists but also the emerging Hindu middle class which votes for the BJP.

However, certain objective trends encourage the restoration of self-consciousness and pride in Hindu society: internationally, the decline of Europe and the implosion of the Soviet Union as available models in favour of fellow Asian countries have brought India out of the psychological shadow; internally, the economic breakthrough and the communications revolution have been creating a new middle class that can provide leadership and is in a position to embellish its new status with a dimension of cultural revival. At the same time, decades of organizational and (to a lesser extent) ideological work by Hindu activists are having their effect. This way, Hindu revivalism, though existing as an ideological and cultural trend for well over a century, now finally seems like an idea whose time has come. In 1991, its main (though highly imperfect) political embodiment, the BJP, became the largest opposition party; in 1996, it became the largest party, before Congress; and in 1998, it managed to win a vote of confidence for a BJP-led government, confirmed again after elections in 1999. Though not very consequential in itself, this willingness of the electorate to give the BJP a chance is symptomatic of a deeper change in the opinion climate.

A final thing to note here is that the situation just outlined pertains only to four-fifths of the territory and population for whose freedom the Indian national movement has fought. In Pakistan and Bangladesh, there is no decolonization of Hindu society whatsoever. There, the stranglehold of the Islamic occupation force is stronger than ever in history. In the Hindu revivalist vision, these parts of Indic civilization will one day also have to be liberated, though this mission of honour is not on anyone's agenda for the near future. But the implosion of Soviet Communism has alerted people to the possibility that giants on clay feet can crumble surprisingly fast, and in particular, that Pakistan and indeed the rest of the Islamic world may soon see the collapse of their dominant ideology from within.

HINDU SOCIETY UNDER SIEGE

It has been a standard perception of Hindu revivalists in the twentieth century, from at least Swami Shraddhananda to Sita Ram Goel, that Hinduism is "under siege". This view could be summarized as follows:

1. Hindu civilization has been badly wounded by foreign invasions and occupations, it is the tired and exhausted survivor of two determined attacks which were intended to be deadly: the Islamic invasion which sought to replace Hinduism with Islam and managed to destroy numerous Hindu people and institutions, and the European invasion, which sought to replace Hinduism with either Christianity or secularism, and which had a less brutally destructive but far more penetrating impact.

2. In spite of its breakthrough to freedom in 1947, Hindu society has not definitively shaken off its old enemies; it has enemies inside India, each with its allies abroad, chiefly Christianity, Islam and Marxism.

3. In India, these forces have suspended their mutual differences for a joint fight against their main enemy, Hinduism.

4. This fight sometimes takes the form of physical attacks on Hindus (as in West Panjab 1947, East Bengal 1971, Kashmir 1989-90), but mostly tries to destroy Hinduism in the minds of Hindus, by converting them or at least by making them lose all respect for and attachment to Hinduism.

5. The main strengths of these enemies are their organization, their (mostly foreign) money-power, their devotion to their project of conquest, in the case of Islam also sheer demography, but most of all the weaknesses of the Hindus: disunity, lack of organization, unconcern based on lack of knowledge and understanding of the forces in the field, lack of energy or self-esteem.

So, the basic inspiration of the Hindu revivalist movement is a sense of being threatened and of losing ground, combined with the conviction that Hindu civilization deserves to survive. The movement is a fight for survival. At the same time, there is a sense that Hindu society could only be put this badly on the defensive because of its own flaws, which various authors diagnose differently, from lack of social justice to the loss of a martial spirit. The solutions offered are chiefly the following:

1. Social reform, first because social justice is good in itself, but secondly also to pre-empt the use of inter-Hindu social conflict as a handle to weaken Hindu society further.

2. *Shuddhi*, reconversion, which is, in a sense, the final solution, for if all Indians can be brought "back" (in the case of converts or their progeny) into Hinduism, the main threat becomes geographically external and in that respect already easier to handle.

3. *Sangathan*, "organization", creating a trans-caste, transregional structure which unites the Hindus and defends their interests; the main Hindu political parties and associations are the fruit of the Sangathanist drive.

4. Intellectual mobilization, the creation of a polemical discourse, not so much in dialogue with the alleged enemies of Hinduism (their "conversion" is a different project) but first of all in order to inform the Hindus themselves about the nature of the conflict, about the virtues of Hinduism and the vices of its challengers.

It should be understood that this sense of being besieged is not a thing of the past. The threat emanating from Communism may have receded, but the cultural threat of globalization has taken its place. India may prove a winner in a globalized economy, but will this come at the price of cultural Americanization and self-forgetfulness, now not just at the elite but also at the mass level? It is all very fine to point to the decline of Christianity in its heartlands, but the conversion bulletins of the missionaries still show gains to Christianity, while Hindus count their losses. Islam may feel challenged by modernization and the information revolution penetrating its societies, but demographically it continues to make inroads in ever more parts of India. Even a Hindu nationalist government proves unable to stop the penetration of India by millions of Bangladeshi illegal immigrants and the continuous slaughter of Hindu and Sikh citizens by Pakistan-backed terror squads. In spite of the new self-confidence which Hindu society is drawing from its recent technological and economic successes, the sense of foreboding and encirclement by hostile forces refuses to subside.

THE INCOMPLETE DECOLONIZATION

In his famous Independence speech, Jawaharlal Nehru said: "A moment comes, which comes but rarely in history, when we step out from the old to the new, when an age ends and when the soul of a nation, long suppressed, finds utterance." But was this really the case? To many conscious Hindus, it seemed that *the soul of the nation remained suppressed.* The colonial views of Indian religion and history, far from being shaken off, was further interiorized and propagated among the masses. Linguistically, India became less self-reliant than ever.

The colonial psychology has also affected the very movement which seeks to reassert Hindu sovereignty, in particular its organized, Hindu nationalist wing. The first assertions of Hinduism's right to survive expressed an interiorized subservience to the colonial power by trying to mould Hinduism after the colonizer's expectations of what religion should be. In the nineteenth century, the Brahmo Samaj and the Arya Samaj tried to make Hinduism monotheistic and aniconic, even iconoclastic: they transplanted a controversy from Judeo-Christian history into Hinduism where it had no relevance. They even assumed that Hindu India had suffered a deserved defeat against the colonizers because of its wrong religious orientation.

In the case of Swami Vivekananda, the Western influence was of the reverse type: trying to present Hinduism as contrasting with the "materialist West", trying to live up to the Western orientalist image of the "spiritual East" as the West's Other. This reduction of Hindu civilization to its spiritual component was unjust to the variegated Hindu traditions in art, architecture, statecraft, mathematics etc., not to speak of India's historical status as a country of fabulous wealth. At the same time, Vivekananda also imitated Western models, for instance, by involving his Ramakrishna Mission in social service work after the Christian model (not that Hindu society had no notion of social relief work, but it was not the business of monks), and by advertising *Vedânta* as a "scientific" religion.

In the early twentieth century, with the prospect of political self-rule on the horizon, some Hindu revivalists tried to cast Hinduism into another borrowed mould: that of nationalism. This notion was not entirely new to

Hinduism, ancient elements of a national consciousness could genuinely be identified, but the Western-inspired desire for a monolithic uniformity as the guarantee of national unity crept into it. Thus, V.D. Savarkar's plea for a biological unification of all Hindu castes through intermarriage, though perhaps commendable from the viewpoint of social equality, showed a Jacobin desire to even out all other types of community in favour of a homogeneous nation (the idea also never caught on; if castes are now starting to mingle, it is not out of nationalistic enthusiasm but merely because their differences in occupational opportunities as well as in their everyday lifestyles are disappearing).

In some cases, from Sri Aurobindo to Arun Shourie (1941-), the intellectual leadership roles in Hindu revivalism have been taken by people who were quite at home in Western civilization, and who were consequently less exalted about it and more discerning in choosing what to adopt from among its contributions. The option to simply go back to the pre-colonial period as if nothing had happened is of course not really open, and a purely traditionalist leadership is inevitably marginal and not in a position to change the existing power equations. Moreover, in the more universalist segment of the Hindu movement, from a Rammohun Roy to a Ram Swarup, there is no objection to things Western, not because these authors are any the less Hindu, but because they see Hinduism as part of a continuum of human civilization.

In the case of the Hindu nationalists, the colonized mentality goes even deeper than the mindless aping of once-hegemonic foreign models. Many of them are morbidly stuck with the desire for the approval of others, of those with prestige, ergo of those who belong to the hostile but hegemonic camp. Even after acceding to political power at the centre, they have been displaying the tendency to see themselves through the eyes of their opponents, to live up to the standards set by their (nominally disempowered) enemies and to beg certificates of good conduct from them.

FROM SECULARISM AS ANTI-HINDUISM TO THE HINDU STATE

A very large part of Hindu nationalist discourse consists of complaints about the injustices which Hindu society suffers at the hands of the secular state: discrimination in favour of the minorities in education, in the management and financing of places of worship, in government-aided loans, in the extraordinary autonomy for non-Hindu-majority provinces, in the treatment of religion-based Personal Law systems, in cultural and media policies; discriminations against Hindus by the Constitution, the laws, the political practice and the cultural institutions of the Indian Republic. They go as far as alleging that secularism so far has only meant anti-Hinduism.

Some of these complaints are contrived and ungenerous, others are undeniably valid. The most important legal grievance concerns Article 30 of the Constitution, which allows the minorities but not the Hindus to set up state-subsidized denominational schools. That the discrimination sanctioned by this article is real enough, has been demonstrated by the attempt of the Ramakrishna Mission to get registered as a non-Hindu sect entitled to this educational privilege, after hostile attempts by provincial governments to nationalize its schools. Likewise, discrimination in matters of temple management has been illustrated by the authorities' attempt to get the Shirdi Sai Baba temple reclassified as a Hindu temple so as to create legal grounds for taking it over.

Many complaints are directed against the private sector, especially against the media, the academic world and the Indian film industry, all of whom are accused of having an anti-Hindu bias. Of course, the truth of this wide-ranging allegation has to be established case by case. One important case where it can effectively be verified is the processing of the East Bengali massacre by the Pakistani Army (1971) in all types of information channels; we find that this massacre is given little attention, its predominantly anti-Hindu thrust even less, and that attempts to give it more attention are either muzzled or maligned as "anti-Muslim propaganda". More generally, the impression which the public has acquired of Hindu-Muslim relations is seriously skewed in the sense of not conceding to the Hindus their martyrs, i.e. of denying or obscuring the fact that the victim toll has so far been far higher on the Hindu than on the Muslim side, both in premodern and in recent history. However, a general observation concerning such wrong but widespread impressions which imposes itself is that Hindus largely have themselves to blame: being the majority, they could easily influence the opinion climate and the decision-making bodies to their own advantage if only they applied themselves to such action rather than to sterile complaining.

These complaints are often factual, but the litany raises a few questions. First of all, how come a majority accepts this discriminatory treatment? Probably this too is a symptom of the colonial condition: Hindus sit sulking in a corner, saying to themselves that it is not fair, but they are not sufficiently sure of their rights to rise in revolt and abolish these discriminations. And secondly, why is the BJP not doing anything about this? So far, the BJP's enthusiasm to tackle these discriminations has not been proven by much action, except for the assurance that "once we come to power", everything will change. And once they came to power, the assurance was that "once we have a clear majority", everything will change. But so far, the BJP has always failed to explore the avenues of bringing pressure on other parties to push through the desired changes jointly, simply because taking up issues of religious discrimination would confirm it in its image of a pro-Hindu and "communal" party.

In their public statements, Hindu nationalist leaders emphasize that there is no conflict between Hinduism and secularism, assuming that secularism means *nirapekshatâ* ("neutrality") between sects or religions, as the Hindi text of the Constitution has it. With only slight exaggeration, they assert that Hindu states have always practised equal treatment to all sects. They claim the support of history when they insist that non-Hindu minorities have always been safe and free to practise their religions in Hindu states. A projected *Hindû Râshtra* will, on the unanimous assurance of all Hindu leaders who care to speak out, resume this tradition of respecting and honouring all religions.

In the Hindu revivalist perception, the ideology which has dominated independent India in its first half century, Nehruvian secularism, consists in a permanent vigilance against religion, suspended only in the case of non-Hindu religions deemed useful as allies against Hinduism. This "secularism" is not neutral vis-à-vis religion in general, it is negatively predisposed towards religion as such (though more so towards Hinduism than towards its rivals). This anti-religious variety of secularism is yet another lingering manifestation of the colonial condition, for in its distrust of religion and its vigilance to keep the slightest taint of religion out of public life, it builds on the European experience of Church-State relations. This would make it a pure transplant which ignores the radically different experience of Hindu history.

The perception of European secularists was that man had to be emancipated from the mind control exerted by authoritarian religious establishments in the name of dogmatic and irrational belief systems. In the Hindu view, such a situation never obtained in India at all: while religion in the sense of belief in supernatural interventions was certainly widespread, Hindu tradition always had a rational core as well, which may now be promoted at the mass level through the modern education system. Most importantly, Hinduism has always had a pluralistic attitude: it never tried to stifle debate and free enquiry and constituted no threat to civic freedoms, in this respect at least. Therefore, declaring India a Hindu state is an altogether less dramatic event than the declaration of Pakistan as an Islamic state was. The Hindu assurance is that declaring India a Hindu state will have no effect on freedom of opinion or religious pluralism or non-discrimination on religious grounds: "Hindu India, secular India!"

To rename or reclassify India as a "Hindu state" would therefore not make much difference, certainly not of a threatening nature. And in a way, it would only formalize a state of affairs already imposed by reality in spite of the hot denials by the secularists. Attacks on Hindu nationalism or simply on Hinduism are more often than not also attacks on India. Conversely, verbal as well as armed attacks on India are invariably committed by anti-Hindu forces, whether "Khalistani" neo-Sikhs, Muslims, Christians or Communists, and their targets are also mostly Hindus as such. This means that India is perceived by its enemies as a naturally Hindu state in which non-Hindus or non-Hindu provinces have no place and no reason to remain. The declared enemies of Hinduism thereby testify that "India is a Hindu state", not because its political and legal system has a pro-Hindu bias (which it doesn't), but simply because it encompasses a mostly Hindu-majority territory which Hindus consider their homeland, and of which the very landscape has acquired a Hindu character by virtue of its millennial integration in Hindu religious practice.

Most Hindu revivalists agree with this perception of the intrinsically Hindu character of India, pointing to the fact that the common Hindu cultural background is the only conceivable reason for bringing so many racially and linguistically diverse communities together in one state. In their view, declaring India a Hindu state is merely a confirmation of a well-established historical fact on which Hindus and anti-Hindu separatists agree. History and religious customs are brought in to deepen this insight: the Hindu pilgrimage cycles and other pan-Indian institutions have contributed mightily to a sense of Indianness, of Indian "nationhood" in modern terms, firmly rooted in Hindu civilization. When we consider the evidence, we must admit at least this much, that India has had a sense of cultural distinctness and of its geographical boundaries for much longer than most existing nation-states.

The unity and integrity of India is one point on which all tendencies of Hindu revivalism agree, regardless of whether they profess a nationalist political philosophy. While in the past, cultural unity of the subcontinent could subsist without political unity, in the modern age the state has acquired such importance that a unitary state is the best expression and guarantee of India's cultural unity. Moreover, the sorry fate of Hindus in non-Hindu states serves as a constant reminder of the need for a state which Hindus can call their own.

The notion of "Hindu state" is assumed by outside observers to represent a Hindu counterpart to the better-known concept of an "Islamic state", a theocratic state with a state religion and with legislation based on divine revelation. Such a notion may exist among politically powerless Hindu traditionalists, and even there only very vaguely, but it is completely absent in Hindu revivalist discourse, which belongs to the reformist tendency in Hinduism. Indeed, all Hindutva authors who have cared to speak out on the notion of a "Hindu state" assure us that they mean a state which has the basic features of what we would call a secular state, including full freedom of religion and total equality of all citizens before the law. Their position is that Hindu states in the past have always been pluralistic, and that the benefits which secularism has brought to most Christian and a few Muslim countries have always been cultivated by Hindu civilization.

A strictly modern component of the concept of "Hindu state" is the underlying assumption that there is a "Hindu nation", as boldly asserted for example by Abhas Chatterjee (1941-). Hindu nationalists like Savarkar borrowed the concept of "nationhood" from European nationalists like Giuseppe Mazzini and tried to rethink the problems before Hindu society in terms of "national unity" and "national sovereignty". However, Girilal Jain (1922-1993), Ram Swarup and other Hindu authors have objected that this recasting of Hinduism in the nationalist mould was not a felicitous idea. At the same time, however, all Hindu revivalists are united around the practical need to defend India's unity and integrity as a material precondition for making a renewed flowering of Hindu civilization possible.

HINDU REVIVALIST VIEW OF ISLAM

The first thing which colonial underlings are taught, is to look up to their colonial masters. They are to depreciate their own culture and glorify the colonizer's beneficial contributions. They are to be grateful to the colonizer for his breaking open their closed and stagnant little world and making them receptive to the benefits of his civilizing mission. In the relation between the Hindus and the British, this pattern is obvious. Though the secularists accused the British of creating the Hindu-Muslim problem and of exporting India's wealth to England, they praised them for bringing modernity to India, with all its material, moral and intellectual benefits. And quite a few Hindu revivalists go along with this view, though they question some of the ideological conditioning which the British brought, including the distorted perception of Hinduism and Indian history which was propagated among Hindus on the strength of modern (but fallible and partisan) scholarship.

In the relation between Hindus and Muslims, this Hindu debt of gratitude was obvious to the Muslim rulers of yore, in this sense that the Muslims brought the Hindus the only true religion, not in any other sense. The Muslim invaders acknowledged Hindu superiority in many other respects, from the sciences to the beauty of Hindu women; but that could not match the unique virtue of the true religion, key to eternal beatitude. However, Hindu revivalists along with the Hindu masses are generally not impressed with the Muslim claim on Hindu gratitude. The replacement of the native languages with Persian and Urdu, of temples with mosques, of Hindu architecture with Indo-Saracen architecture, of vegetarianism with meat dishes, of saris with so-called Panjabi dress or *hijâb*, none of these Muslim innovations could be considered "progress" in the sense that the British-Indian railway system has undeniably constituted progress. On the contrary, the Muslim contribution is often only noticed for having been made at the expense of its Hindu counterpart, most materially in the case of architecture, where thousands of Hindu buildings have been forcibly replaced with the rather simpler beauties of the Indo-Saracen building style.

The one genuine contribution of the Muslim invaders which the Hindu gracefully accept is that they have brought the word "Hindu" to India. By their application of this term to all Indians not subscribing to the West-Asian monotheisms, they have given an outsider's testimony *in tempore non suspecto* that there is such a thing as a Hindu identity, even if it had to be defined negatively.

In two respects, however, the Hindu including even the Hindu-revivalist attitude to Islam is or has been that of colonial underlings. First, the *Arya Samâj* and a large part of the urban Hindu middle-class have interiorized the Islamic objection against idolatry and polytheism, which is why they assert that all Hindu gods are but different faces of the One God. Secondly, many Hindus including Hindu nationalists have interiorized the unhistorical notion that Islam brought equality. Against these tendencies, a fundamental critique of Islam has recently been developed. On the first point, it is argued that the Islamic focus on iconcoclasm, for all its large-scale destructiveness, is at bottom simply a sign of an immature religious consciousness: God is an uncountable, and quarrels over his oneness or manifoldness constitute a projection of all-too-human categories onto God,—an understandable mistake but certainly not one worth killing for. On the second point, it is concluded from the documentary record that the anti-caste egalitarianism of Islam is a figment of the apologists' imagination, its current popularity being inversely proportional to its historical plausibility.

The most original and compelling (and to unprepared readers, downright frightening) contribution of the Hindu revivalist school of history is its critique of the very basis of Islam. Partly drawing on international scholarship, partly on the categories of yogic psychology, they have argued that the Quranic revelation was nothing but an unhealthy psychopathological phenomenon, perhaps due to improperly practised mystical exercises. Moreover, they have marshalled evidence to show that all the undesirable traits of Islam, its notion of *jihâd*, its extortion and expulsion of non-Muslim communities, its elimination of apostates and critics of the Prophet, are directly due to the example set by the Prophet himself. Their conclusion is what to Muslims may sound as the ultimate blasphemy: the problem with Islam is Mohammed. Rather than trying to pull Muslims back into Hinduism through conversion campaigns, they suggest that Muslims properly inform themselves about Mohammed's career, not in a theologically streamlined but in an objective way, and then decide for themselves if they want to remain in the Muslim fold.

In actual politics, the main Hindu revivalist party, the BJP, has been cultivating good relations with the Muslim community ever since its foundation in 1980. Internationally, it has continued the friendly relations with the Muslim world, even going quite far in its peace overtures to Pakistan. Indeed, it is criticized for replicating Mahatma Gandhi's policy of "Muslim appeasement". Its record in state governments suggests that it means the Muslims no harm. However, sceptics can easily point to more anti-Muslim tendencies in other segments of the Sangh Parivar, and in other Hindu parties like the Shiv Sena.

Between the political attitude of flattering the Muslims all the while attacking Pakistan and alleged Pakistani agents sabotaging India (the BJP story) and the occasionally violent fits and starts of radical Hindu groups (Shiv Sena, the VHP youth wing Bajrang Dal) during moments of Hindu-Muslim crisis, there is a large practical difference, one which suggests an easy moral choice between the two, viz. appeasement rather than violence. But equally important is the common intellectual and psychological basis between the flatterers and the streetfighters, viz. an unwillingness to seriously study Islam. The two attitudes may jointly be contrasted with the ideological attitude of criticizing Islam down to the bone while refraining from any act of hostility towards the actual Muslims and trying to talk with them on a non-communal, purely humanistic basis (the position of a Sita Ram Goel or an Arun Shourie).

In this more fundamental contrast, the preference of rational people should definitely go to the latter option. The former position is too unstable and has led to fairly large-scale bloodshed in recent years, though the fault is of course not that of the Hindu parties alone. Indeed, at every step in communal escalations within living memory, Hindus have essentially only reacted to Islamic aggression; but there are cruder and more intelligent ways of reacting to provocation, and the difference is consequential.

Hindu revivalists have an acute apprehension that, short of an implosion of Islam in the footsteps of Communism, the demographic evolution leads straight to a Muslim majority and the Islamization of the Indian polity. Considering the sorry fate of Hindus in the Muslim-majority states of Afghanistan, Pakistan, Bangladesh and Malaysia, they all agree that this would be a very ominous development for Hinduism. Those who look beyond their individual deaths into the next few centuries feel burdened with a responsibility to prevent this development for the sake of their great-grandchildren. Some of them propose fantastic, unworkable or inhumane schemes to face this challenge, such as outright demographic competition or an exchange of population with the Muslim-dominated neighbouring states. Others offer a purely verbal solution: rebaptizing the Muslims as "Mohammedi Hindus" as a shortcut to the Muslims' complete integration into a Hindu India, thus illustrating once more that Hindus are good at theoretical solutions for practical problems.

However, from a more enlightened and sober Hindu viewpoint, there is enough time to reverse the onward march of Islam in a very real and durable sense before its demographic presence can overwhelm Hindu society, viz. to destroy the fence with which Islam keeps its sheep together, the Muslims' attachment to the beliefs instilled in them from childhood. In spite of martial terminology ("destroy"), this merely amounts to engineering a shift in public opinion, a process of education comparable to the secularization and scientific enlightenment of the Christian countries in the last couple of centuries. For the time being, this solution is equally theoretical, because it requires a mobilization of Hindu activists for this rather sophisticated goal, many of whom are now dissipating their energies in fantastic schemes of converting mosques into temples, rather than Muslims into Hindus.

HAS HINDU REVIVALISM SUCCEEDED?

It is undeniable that Hindu revivalism has been the biggest mobilizing force in modern Indian history, at least in terms of the crowds it got walking or cheering. This was first demonstrated during the freedom movement: mass mobilization for the anti-colonial struggle was in direct proportion to the dose of Hindu religion which B.G. Tilak, Sri Aurobindo and Mahatma Gandhi mixed with their political agitation. More recently, the Ayodhya campaign became the largest-ever mass movement in India.

Though impressive, this show of numerical strength has yielded very little result, for example the Ayodhya agitation has not won Hindus the acknowledged right to build their temple at the contentious site. It has achieved nothing at all in terms of relieving the legal anti-Hindu discriminations. The common front of most other parties against the Hindu parties has created a situation where not a single Hindu demand has any chance of being met as long as the Hindu parties have no solid majority in Parliament. Indeed, even the parties *politically* allying themselves with the BJP in Governments generally remain ideological opponents when it comes to communally sensitive issues, at least to the extent that they would exercise a veto if the BJP were to get serious about election promises like the enactment of a Common Civil Code or the full constitutional integration of Kashmir into India.

This way, whether in opposition or in power, the Hindutva movement has been unable to set the agenda and implement its own programme. It is also to be noted that the BJP has shown very little creativity in exploring indirect ways of furthering Hindu interests. Thus, one way of bettering the problematic financial situation of many Hindu temples and their priests would be through tax reforms encouraging private donations to temples. One indirect way of neutralizing the discrimination inherent in Article 30 could be through reinterpretation (in the sense of deeming the rights given to the minorities as implicitly also applying to the Hindu majority), esp. requesting the Supreme Court for a formal interpretation of the article along these lines, rather than through the laborious route of amending the Constitution. We can only note that the organized Hindu nationalist movement has not given proof of much imagination and initiative in this regard.

In terms of actual realizations, Hindu revivalism owes more to the conservative fraction of Congress than to the BJP, like the choice of sanskritized Hindi over "Hindustani" as India's link language, or the enactment of laws restraining missionary activities in several tribal-concentration states. If points of the BJP wish-list were ever realized, it was by Congress: Pakistan was broken in two by Congress socialist Indira Gandhi, while Congress conservative Narasimha Rao eliminated the Khalistan movement, normalized relations with Israel, liberalized the economy, and effectively condoned the demolition of the Babri Masjid,—which RSS and BJP leaders on the spot were trying to halt.

The main Hindutva party's desire for secularist respectability is such that it never seriously contemplates putting any of its communally sensitive points on the agenda. Since mid-1991, and very decisively since the demolition of the Babri Masjid in Ayodhya on 6 December 1992, the BJP has opted for a strategy of non-polarization, which in the minds of many BJP cadres and supporters is more than merely a strategy: to tread softly, to abandon provocative postures, to avoid expressions of hostility towards the minorities, bridge-building, inviting them in. This has greatly helped the BJP in winning allies and coming to power, it has also helped in defusing Hindu-Muslim tension on the streets, but it has not brought the

Hindu state visibly closer. Now that the potential scale of a Hindu-Muslim conflict has multiplied by the availability of modern weapons including the nuclear option, it may well be reassuring to note the consistent evolution in BJP parlance and actual BJP policy towards communal reconciliation.

This evolution was necessary for allowing the BJP to replace Congress as the central force in Indian politics. It may help the BJP to steer a responsible course at the helm of the emerging superpower, India. It may at last win the BJP some sympathy among India-watchers, the day they agree to base their opinions on facts rather than on the opinions of their privileged Indian contacts. But in the face of a determined enemy like Pakistan's Inter Services Intelligence, not everyone is convinced that this niceness is always the best policy. It is also proving difficult to please both the general public (not to mention the secularists) and the movement's activist basis, which has repeatedly uttered its dissatisfaction with the BJP's soft line. One thing to watch therefore is whether an alternative centre of Hindu political activism may come up, especially in moments of renewed communal crisis. Also, the increasingly quaint-looking RSS style of mass mobilization may give way to newer forms of activism.

At the ideological level, the attempt of Hindu thinkers to free themselves from the impact of the hegemonic thought systems has not gone smoothly, with even the best minds often interiorizing assumptions from the very thought systems which they opposed. It was probably inevitable that Hindus, including Hindu anti-colonialists, would look at their own situation and at the other factors in the field through the conceptual categories which the Islamic and European colonizers themselves had introduced. By the 1990s, however, it was clear that Hinduism's intellectual vanguard had climbed out of this self-estranged perception and was coming into its own. Yet, this has so far only meant a breakthrough on paper. In general, it is axiomatic that ideas have consequences, and that this new Hindu revivalist thinking will have its effect, but it remains to be seen *to what extent* it will actually influence the Hindu nationalist decision-makers and the indian polity. Naturally, this is something which only time will tell.

Bibliography

Names of cities are given as in the book itself, so that both *Bombay* and *Mumbai* may appear, and similarly Madras/Chennai, Benares/Varanasi, Poona/Pune. Names of Indian authors are generally not analysed the way Western authors and international publishers and bibliographers tend to understand them, but as Indians do. Thus, "Ram Swarup" is really a first name ("nature of Ram"), to which a Hindu may or may not add his *gotra*/clan title (GARG, Ram Swarup), his *jâti*/caste title (AGRAWAL, Ram Swarup), or his general *varna*/caste title (GUPTA, Ram Swarup). If he chooses not to add such a title habitually, his first name ends up functioning as his full name, e.g. AUROBINDO functioning as the reference name of the author who grew up as Aurobindo GHOSE. In such cases, non-Hindus will tend to split this first name into a first and a last name: "SWARUP, Ram", so that he would be referred to as "Mr. Swarup". However, that would be a mistake. So, disregarding conformity with other international bibliographies, I follow the Indian pattern in the few cases where it applies, e.g. RAM SWARUP under R, JAGMOHAN under J, RAGHU VIR under R, HARSH NARAIN under H.

Primary publications: Arya Samaj

AYODHYA PRASAD: *Vedic Thoughts*. Sarvadeshik Arya Pratinidhi Sabha, Delhi, n.d. (*c.*1978).

DAYANANDA Saraswati, Swami: *Satyârtha Prakâsh*. Arsha Sahitya Prachar Trust, Delhi VS 2045.

—: *Light of Truth*. Sarvadeshik Arya Pratinidhi Sabha, Delhi 1989 (1882, 1895).

—: *Selected Letters*. Bahadur Ch. Narain Singh Pratap Singh Dharamarth Nyas, Karnal (Haryana), n.d.

DEVI CHAND: *The Yajurveda in English*. Sarvadeshik Arya Pratinidhi Sabha, Delhi 1992 (1964).

FEROZ CHAND: *Lajpat Rai, Life and Work*. Ministry of Information, Delhi 1989.

KAPUR, Karam Narain: *Sublimity of the Vedas*. Sarvadeshik Arya Pratinidhi Sabha, Delhi 1994.

KORATKAR, Kranti Kumar: *A Glorious Chapter from the Annals of the Arya Samaj*. Delhi 1995.

KSHITISH Vedalankar: *Storm in Punjab*. Word Publ., Delhi 1985 (1984).

PANDIT, Kumari Saraswati: *A Critical Study of the Contribution of the Arya Samaj to Indian Education*. Maharaja Sayajirao University, Baroda 1974.

PATHAK, Raghunath Prasad: *Achievements of Arya Samaj*. Sarvadeshik Arya Pratinidhi Sabha, Delhi 1975.

RAI, Lala Lajpat: *The Arya Samaj. An Account of Its Origins, Doctrines and Activities* (edited by S.K. Bhatia). Reliance Publ., Delhi 1991.

RAO, Vandematharam Ramachandra: *Swamy Dayananda's Satyartha Prakash. Spot-light on Truth*. Udgeetha Prakashan Samstha, Hyderabad 1988.

—: *Maharana Pratap*. Sarvadeshik Arya Pratinidhi Sabha, Delhi 1993.

RAO, Vandematharam Veerabhadra: *Life Sketch of Swami Dayananda*. Sarvadeshik Arya Pratinidhi Sabha, Delhi, 1987.

SHASTRI, Acharya Vaidyanath: *The Arya Samaj, Its Cult and Creed*. Sarvadeshik Arya Pratinidhi Sabha, 1988 (1965).

—: *Science in the Vedas*. Sarvadeshik Arya Pratinidhi Sabha, 1970.

SHRADDHANANDA, Swami: *Inside the Congress*.

—: *Hindu Sangathan, Saviour of the Dying Race*. Delhi 1926.

NARAYAN SWAMY, Mahatma: *What is Arya Samaj* (2nd ed.). Sarvadeshik Arya Pratinidhi Sabha, Delhi, n.d.

TYAGI, O.P., ed.: *Achievements of the Arya Samaj*. Sarvadeshik Arya Pratinidhi Sabha, Delhi 1975.

VABLE, D.: *The Arya Samaj. Hindu without Hinduism*. Vikas Publ., Delhi 1983.

—: *The Arya Samaj. The Most Revolutionary Reform Movement in India*. Sarvadeshik Arya Pratinidhi Sabha, Delhi, 1987.

VEDALANKAR, Pandit Nardev: *Basic Teachings of Hinduism*. Veda Niketan, Durban 1978 (1973).

—, and MANOHAR, Somera: *Arya Samaj and Indians Abroad*. Sarvadeshik Arya Pratinidhi Sabha, Delhi 1975.

Periodical

Vedic Light, Delhi

Primary Publications: Hindu Mahasabha

BANERJEE, Nitya Narayan: *Hindu Polity, Positive and Perverted*. Hindutva Publ., Delhi 1985.

—: *Hindu Outlook*. Hindutva Publ., Calcutta 1990.

BAKHLE, Pandit: *Heroes of the Freedom Struggle*. Swatantryaveer Savarkar Rahstriya Smarak, Mumbai, n.d.

CHATTERJEE, Nirmal Chandra: *Hindu Politics. The Message of the Mahasabha. Collected Speeches of Sj. N.C. Chatterjee*. Ramesh Bannerjee, Calcutta 1945.

"CHITRAGUPTA": *Life of Barrister Savarkar*. Veer Savarkar Prakashan, Bombay 1987 (1926).

GODBOLE, Arvind: *Sâvarkar Vichâradarshan*. Popular Prakashan, Mumbai 1983.

GODSE, Gopal: *Gandhiji's Murder and After*. Surya Prakashan, Delhi 1989 (Marathi 1967).

—: *An Introduction to the Family of the Trinity of Revolutionary Savarkar Brothers*. Akhil Bharatiya Hindu Mahasabha, Delhi, no date given (ca. 1985).

GODSE, Nathuram: *May It Please Your Honour*. Surya Prakashan, Delhi 1989 (1948).

—: *Why I Assassinated Mahatma Gandhi*. Surya Bharati Prakashan, Delhi 1993 (1948).

GROVER, Verinder, ed.: *V.D. Savarkar*. Deep & Deep Publ., Delhi 1993.

INDRA PRAKASH: *Hindu Mahasabha, Its Contribution to Indian Politics*. Akhil Bharatiya Hindu Mahasabha, Delhi 1966.

—: *A Prophet of Modern Times*. Akhil Bharatiya Hindu Mahasabha, Delhi 1975.

—: *They Count Their Gains, We Calculate Our Losses*. HMS, Delhi 1979.

KULKARNI, Jeevan: *Historical Truths & Untruths Exposed*. Itihas Patrika Prakashan, Thane 1991.
MISHRA, Anil Kumar: *Hindû Mahâsabhâ: Ek Adhyayan*. Madanlal Goel, Delhi 1988.
OAK, Vikram Ganesh: *Hindu Maha Sabha, Its Aims and Ideals*. HMS, Delhi 1983.
OAK, Purushottam Nagesh: *Taj Mahal, the True Story*. A. Ghosh, Houston n.d.
—: *Islamic Havoc in Indian History*. A. Ghosh, Houston 1996.
SAVARKAR, Balarao: *Vîr Sâvarkar aur Gândhîjî*. HMS, Delhi, n.d.
SAVARKAR, Vinayak Damodar: *The Indian War of Independence 1857*. Rajdhani Granthagar, Delhi 1988 (1909).
—: *Hindutva*. Bharati Sahitya Sadan, Delhi 1989 (1923).
—: *Hindu Pad Padashahi. Story of the Maratha Struggle to Re-establish Sovereign Hindu Power*. Bharati Sahitya Sadan, Delhi 1971 (1925).
—: *Hindu Rashtra Darshan*. Veer Savarkar Prakashan, Bombay 1984 (1937-42).
—: *My Transportation for Life*. Veer Savarkar Prakashan, Bombay 1984 (1949).
—: *Six Glorious Epochs of Indian History*. Veer Savarkar Prakashan, Bombay 1985 (1963).
—: *Historic Statements*. Veer Savarkar Prakashan, Bombay 1992 (1941-65).
SHIV SARAN: *Life Sketch of Devtaswarup Bhai Parmanand*. HMS, Delhi 1994.
SINGH, Jagjit: *Savarkar*. Savarkar Darshan Pratishthan, Bombay 1989.
SRIVASTAVA, Harindra: *Five Stormy Years: Savarkar in London*. Allied Publ., Delhi 1983.

Periodical

Hindu Vartta

Primary Publications: RSS Parivar

ADVANI, Lal Krishna: *A Prisoner's Scrap-book*. Arnold-Heinemann, Delhi 1978.
—: *The People Betrayed*. Vision Books, Delhi 1979.
—: *Presidential Address*, Vijayawada 1987.
—: *The Gravest-Ever Challenge to Our Nationhood*. Jagrita Bharata Prakashana, Bangalore 1991.
—: *Presidential Address*. Mumbai/Delhi 1995
—: *Supreme Court on 'Hindutva' and 'Hinduism'*. Delhi 1995.
AGRAWAL, Vaman Das: *Hindu Rashtra*. Vishva Hindu Parishad, Delhi, n.d. (1990).
—: *The People Betrayed*. Vision Books, Delhi 1979.
—: *Why Rathyatra?* Jagarana Prakashan, Bangalore 1990.
AHUJA, Gurdas M.: *BJP and Indian Politics*. Ram Company, Delhi 1994.
BAJAJ, Jitendra, ed.: *Ayodhya and the Future India*. Centre for Policy Studies, Madras 1993.
BAKHT, Sikander: *"Angry Hindu"/Why Hindus in the Dock?* Suruchi Prakashan, Delhi 1988.
BAKSHI, Chandrakant: *Hindus Are Disturbed Because...* Bombay 1993.
BARTHWAL, Harishchandra: *The Integral Spirit of Bharat: an Eulogy. Bhârata Ekâtmatâ Stotra: an Explanation*. Suruchi Prakashan, Delhi 1995.
BHANDARI, C.S., & RAMASWAMY, S.R.: *Dr. Bhimrao Ambedkar, an Outstanding Patriot*. Suruchi Prakashan, Delhi 1991.

BHARATIYA JANA SANGH: *Party Documents 1951-1972* (5 vols.). BJS, Delhi 1973.
BHARATIYA JANATA PARTY: *Jamshedpur Riots: The Truth Unmasked.* Delhi 1981.
—: *The Meenakshipuram Report.* Delhi 1981.
—: *Hindu-Sikh Unity at all Cost.* Delhi 1984.
—: *Resolution on Shah Bano Case.* (Chandigarh) 1986.
—: *Constitution and Rules (as amended by the National Council at Gandhinagar, Gujarat, on 2nd May 1992).* Delhi 1992.
—: *White Paper on Ayodhya & the Rama Temple Movement.* Delhi 1993.
—: *The GATT Treaty, a Total Surrender.* Delhi 1993.
—: *Note of Dissent regarding Constitution (80th Amendment) Bill, 1993, and the Representation of the People (Amendment) Bill, 1993.* Delhi 1993.
—: *Foreign Policy and Resolutions.* Delhi 1995.
—: *BJP on Kashmir.* Delhi, 1995.
—: *Resolutions Adopted at National Executive Meeting, Jaipur, November 15-17, 1996.* Delhi 1996.
BHATNAGAR, Brij Bhushan: *A 100-Year Fraud of the Pseudo-Secularists on Hindus.* Indraprastha VHP, Delhi 1991.
BOKARE, M.G.: *Hindu Economics.* Janaki Prakashan, Delhi 1993.
CHITKARA, M.G.: *Hindutva.* APH Publ., Delhi 1997.
CHOWGULE, Ashok: *A Frustrating Dialogue.* Hindu Vivek Kendra, Mumbai 1997.
DEORAS, Madhukar Dattatreya (Balasaheb): *Social Equality and Hindu Consolidation,* Jagaran Prakashan, Bangalore 1974.
—: *With Delhi Newsmen.* Suruchi Sahitya, Delhi 1979.
—: *RSS and the Present Controversy.* Suruchi Sahitya, Delhi 1979.
—: *Speech in Jamshedpur.* Suruchi Sahitya, Delhi 1981 (1979).
—: *The Malady and the Remedy.* RSS Madras, 1980.
—: *Country's Unity a Must.* Suruchi Prakashan, Delhi 1985.
DEVENDRA SWARUP, ed.: *Politics of Conversion.* Deendayal Research Institute, Delhi 1986.
—, ed.: *Integral Humanism. Documents, Interpretation, Comparisons.* Deendayal Research Institute, Delhi 1992.
DHAR, Sujit: *Scourge of Infiltration. Gravest Threat to Our National Security.* Seemanta Shanto o Suraksha Samiti, Calcutta 1986.
—: *Bangladesh Islamised—What Next?* Seemanta Shanto o Suraksha Samiti, Calcutta 1988.
GOLWALKAR, Madhav Sadashiv: *We. Our Nationhood Defined.* Bharat Prakashan, Nagpur 1947 (1939).
—: *Bunch of Thoughts.* Jagaran Prakashan, Bangalore 1984 (1966).
—: *The Answer to All Questions.* RSS, Delhi 1968.
—: *Homage to the Mahatma,* RSS Prakashan Vibhag, Bangalore 1969.
—, *et al.*: *Integral Approach.* Suruchi Prakashan, Delhi 1991 (1965-74).
—: *Shri Guruji Meets Delhi Newsmen.* Suruchi Sahitya, Delhi 1970.
— (with Saiffuddin JEELANY): *Shri Guruji on the Muslim Problem.* Suruchi Sahitya, Delhi 1971.
—: *Spotlights.* Sahitya Sindhu Prakashan, Bangalore 1975 (1974).
GURUMURTHY, S.: *Hindu Heritage, Assimilative, Not Divisive.* Vigil, Madras 1993.

JAGARANA PRAKASHANA: *The Shah Bano Case: Nation Speaks Out*. Bangalore 1986.

JAMMU KASHMIR SAHAYATA SAMITI: *Genocide of Hindus in Kashmir*. Suruchi Prakashan, Delhi 1991.

JOG, B.N.: *Threat of Islam: Indian Dimensions*. Unnati Prakashan, Mumbai 1994.

JOIS, Justice M. Rama: *Legal and Constitutional History of India*, vol.1, *Ancient Legal, Judicial and Constitutional System*. N.M. Tripathi, Bombay 1990 (1984).

—: *Our Fraternity*. Suruchi Prakashan, Delhi 1996.

—: *Supreme Court Judgment on "Hindutva". An Important Landmark*. Suruchi Prakashan, Delhi 1996.

KAUL, Utpal, et al.: *Agony of Kashmir*. Suruchi Prakashan, Delhi 1992.

MADHOK, Balraj: *India's Foreign Policy and National Affairs*. Bharati Sahitya Sadan, Delhi 1969.

—: *Indianisation*. Orient Paperbacks, Delhi 1970.

—: *Rationale of Hindu State*. Indian Book Gallery, Delhi 1982.

—: *RSS and Politics*. Hindu World Publ., Delhi 1986.

—: *Case for Hindu State*. Hindu World Publ., Delhi 1989.

--: *Kashmir. The Storm Center of the World*. A. Ghosh, Houston 1992.

MALHOTRA, Vijay Kumar: *Why Image of Bharat is So Bad Abroad*. VHP, Delhi (no date given; *c*. 1990).

—: *Is It a Sin to Be Hindu in India?* VHP, Delhi (no date given; *c*. 1990).

MALKANI, K.R.: *India Tomorrow*. Rashtra Dharma Pustak Prakashan, Lucknow 1972.

—: *The Midnight Knock*. Vikas Publ., Delhi 1978.

—: *The RSS Story*. Impex India, Delhi 1980.

—: *The Sindh Story*. Allied Publ., Delhi 1984.

—: *The Politics of Ayodhya*. Har-Anand Publ., Delhi 1993.

MUKTANANDA Saraswati, Swami: *Vartamân Indian Samvidhân*. Akhil Bharatiya Sant Samiti, Vrindavan 1991.

NADAR, Thanulinga, ed.: *Unrest at Kanyakumari*. Hindu Munnani, Madras 1983.

NAIK, J.A.: *Death or Resurrection. A Story of the Hindus*. Ajanta, Delhi 1994.

NARAYANA, C.K. Saji: *Multi-Nationals, Anti-Nationals*. Bharat Prakasan, Vijayawada 1992.

PANDYA, Anand Shankar: *Hindu Thought and World Harmony*. Bharatiya Vidya Bhavan, Bombay 1989.

—: *Hypocrisy of Secularism (Injustice to Hindus)*. VHP, Karnavati 1990.

—: *Relevance of Hinduism in the Modern Age*. Vishva Hindu Parishad, Delhi, no date given (1990).

—: *Role of Hinduism in 21st Century*. Bombay 1995.

PARAMESWARAN, P.: *Narayan Guru. The Prophet of Renaissance*. Suruchi Sahitya, Delhi 1979.

RAJENDRA SINGH (Rajju Bhaiya), ed.: *Our Kashmir*. Suruchi Prakashan, Delhi 1991.

—: *Ever-Vigilant We Have to Be*. Suruchi Prakashan, Delhi 1994.

—: *Sarsanghchalak Speaks Abroad*. Suruchi Prakashan, Delhi 1996.

RAM PRAKASH: *Guru Tegh Bahadur, the Patriot by Excellence*. Suruchi Prakashan, Delhi 1987.

RAO, Kandarpa Ramachandra: *Integral Humanism*. Academy of Integral Humanism, Hyderabad 1995.

RAO, K. Suryanarayana: *Hindu Rashtra: Not a Mere Slogan but the Vibrant Reality*. Vigil, Madras 1990.

RAO, S.V. Seshagiri: *Collapse of Communist Oligarchy. The Great 1989 Revolution*. Suruchi Prakashan, Delhi 1991.

RASHTRIYA SWAYAMSEVAK SANGH: *Shri Guruji*. RSS, Delhi, no date given, *c*. 1965.

—: *High Courts on RSS*. RSS Prakashan Vibhag, Bangalore 1983 (1972).

—: *Facts about RSS*. Suruchi Sahitya, Delhi, no date given (1978).

—: *RSS Marches on the Path of National Truth*, Jagaran Prakashan, Bangalore 1979.

—: *RSS, Ready for Selfless Service*, Jagarana Prakashan, Bangalore 1979.

—: *RSS Resolves... Full Text of Resolutions 1950-83*. RSS Prakashan Vibhag, Bangalore 1983.

—: *RSS Spearheading National Renaissance*. RSS Prakashan Vibhag, Bangalore 1985.

—: *Heralding a New Era. A Bird's-Eye View of Dr. Hedgewar Birth Centenary Celebrations*. Jagaran Prakashan, Bangalore 1989.

SAHASRABUDDHE, P.G., and VAJPAYEE, M.C.: *The People vs. the Emergency: a Saga of Struggle*. Suruchi Prakashan, Delhi 1991.

SAPRE, Prasanna Damodar: *Hamâre Vanavâsî aur Kalyân Ashram*. Lokahit Prakashan, Lucknow 1994.

SASTRY, Shripaty: *Christianity in India. A Retrospect*. Bharatiya Vichar Sadhana, Pune 1984.

SESHADRI, H.V., ed.: *Dr. Hedgewar, the Epoch-Maker*. Sahitya Sindhu, Bangalore 1981.

—: *Warning of Meenakshipuram*. Jagaran Prakashan, Bangalore 1981.

—: *The Tragic Story of Partition*. Jagaran Prakashan, Bangalore 1984 (1982).

—: *Hindu Renaissance under Way*. Jagaran Prakashan, Bangalore 1984.

—: *RSS: A Vision in Action*. Jagaran Prakashan, Bangalore 1988.

—: *Hindus Abroad—The Dilemma: Dollar or Dharma?* Suruchi Prakashan, Delhi 1990.

—: *Universal Spirit of Hindu Nationalism*. Vigil, Madras 1991.

—: *The Way*. Suruchi Prakashan, Delhi 1991.

— et al.: *Why Hindu Rashtra?* Suruchi Prakashan, Delhi 1990.

SHARMA, Jugal Kishore: *Punya-Bhoomi Bharat*. Suruchi Prakashan, Delhi 1993.

SHARMA, K.L.: *The Great Betrayers*. Delhi (n.d.; *c*. 1988).

THENGADI, Dattopant, et al.: *Pandit Deendayal Upadhyaya, Ideology and Perception* (7 vols.). Suruchi Prakashan, Delhi 1988-89.

—: *Nationalist Pursuit*. Sahitya Sindhu Prakashana, Bangalore 1992.

—: *Third Way*. Janaki Prakashan, Delhi 1995.

UPADHYAYA, Deendayal: *Integral Humanism*. BJP, Delhi, *c*.1990 (1965).

—: *Political Diary*. Suruchi Prakashan, Delhi 1992.

VAJPAYEE, Atal Behari: *Back to Square One*. BJP, Delhi 1988.

—: *Secularism: the Indian Concept*. BJP, Delhi 1992.

VARSHNEY, Manga Ram: *Jana Sangh/RSS and Balraj Madhok*, privately published by the author, Aligarh, no date given (*c*. 1980).

VIGIL: *The 5 Hours and After. The English Press on Ayodhya after Dec. 6, 1992*. Madras 1993.

—: *Kashmir Temple Controversy: Secular Liars*. Madras 1993.

VISHVA HINDU PARISHAD, ed.: *5th European Hindu Conference, Frankfurt 28-30 August 1992*. VHP e.V. of Germany, Frankfurt 1992.

Periodicals

BJP Today, BJP national office, Delhi.
Manthan, Deendayal Research Institute, Delhi.
Organiser, RSS headquarters, Delhi.
Panchjanya, RSS headquarters, Delhi.

Primary Publications: Independent Authors

AGRAWALA, Vasudeva S.: *India — a Nation*. Prithivi Prakashan, Varanasi 1983 (1943-64).
AUROBINDO (Ghose), Sri: *Bande Mataram. Early Political Writings*. Sri Aurobindo Ashram, Pondicherry 1973 (1890-1908).
—: *Uttarpara Speech*. Sri Aurobindo Ashram, Pondicherry 1973 (1909).
—: *The Spirit and Form of Indian Polity*. Sri Aurobindo Ashram, Pondicherry 1966 (1918-21).
—: *The Foundations of Indian Culture*. Sri Aurobindo Ashram, Pondicherry 1984 (1918-21).
—: *Essays on the Gita*. Sri Aurobindo Ashram, Pondicherry 1983 (1916-20).
—: *Bankim, Tilak, Dayananda*. Sri Aurobindo Ashram, Pondicherry 1970 (1940).
—: *Secret of the Veda*. Sri Aurobindo Ashram Trust, Pondicherry 1972.
—: *Dayananda and the Veda*. Sarvadeshik Arya Pratinidhi Sabha, Delhi 1982.
—: *Evening Talks with Sri Aurobindo, Recorded by A.B. Purani*. Sri Aurobindo Ashram Trust, Pondicherry 1982.
—: *India's Rebirth*. Institut de Recherches Evolutives, Paris 1994.
BESANT, Annie: *The Ancient Wisdom*. Theosophical Publ., Adyar 1998 (1897).
—: *In Defence of Hinduism*. Madras 1919.
BHARTI, Brahma Datt: *Christian Conversions and Abuse of Religious Freedom in India*. Era Books, Vellore 1979.
—: *A Short History of Subversion and Sabotage of Indian Education by Christianism*. Era Books, Vellore 1990.
—: *Gandhi and Gandhism Unmasked: Was Gandhi a Traitor?* Era Books, Vellore 1992.
BOMBAY MALAYALEE SAMAJAM, ed.: *Tipu Sultan, Villain or Hero? An Anthology*. Voice of India, Delhi 1993.
CHAMAN LAL, Bhikshu: *India, Mother of Us All*. Published by the author, Delhi 1968.
CHATTERJEE, Abhas Kumar: *The Concept of Hindu Nation*. Voice of India, Delhi 1995.
CHATTERJEE, Bankimchandra: *Essentials of Dharma*. Sanskrit Book Depot, Calcutta 1979 (Bengali 1885).
—: *Ananda Math*. Orient Paperbacks, Delhi 1992 (1881).
CHON, Kuttikhat Purushothama: *Remedy the Frauds in Hinduism*. Bombay 1991.
COOMARASWAMY, Ananda Kentish: *Buddha and the Gospel of Buddhism*, Citadel Press, Secaucus NJ, 1988 (1916).
—: *Metaphysics* (edited by Roger Lipsey). Princeton University Press 1977.
—: *Spiritual Authority and Temporal Power in the Indian Theory of Government*. Munshiram Manoharlal, Delhi 1978 (1942).

"DADOO MIYAN": *100 Years of Muslim Appeasement*. Dar-ul-Hind, Baroda 1995.
DATE, S.R.: *Hindu Nationalism. A Viewpoint*. Kal Prakashan, Pune, no date given (1984).
FRAWLEY, David: *Arise Arjuna. Hinduism and the Modern World*. Voice of India, Delhi 1995.
—: *Hinduism, the Eternal Tradition (Sanatana Dharma)*. Voice of India, Delhi, 1995.
—, and RAJARAM, N.S.: *Crusade in India. Christianity's Struggle for Survival in the Post-Colonial World*. Naimisha Research Foundation, Bangalore 2000.
GHOSH, Arvind: *Hindus! Where Will You Go Now?* Houston 1997.
—: *Impostors Galore, Take Your Pick*. Houston 1999.
HARSH NARAIN: *Myths of Composite Culture and Equality of Religions*. Voice of India, Delhi 1991.
—: *Jizya and the Spread of Islam*. Voice of India, Delhi 1992.
—: *The Ayodhya Temple-Mosque Dispute. Focus on Muslim Sources*. Penman, Delhi 1993.
JAGMOHAN: *My Frozen Turbulence in Kashmir*. Allied Publ., Delhi 1991.
JAGTIANI, G.M.: *Burning Questions on Hindutva*. Privately published, Bombay, no date given (ca. 1990).
—: *Swami Vivekananda on Islam*. Society of Hindu Missionaries, Bombay, n.d. (ca. 1992).
GOEL, Sita Ram: *Samyak Sambuddha*. Bhârat-Bhâratî, Delhi 1997 (1957).
—: *Hindu Society under Siege*. Voice of India, Delhi 1992 (1981).
—: *The Story of Islamic Imperialism*. Voice of India, Delhi 1994 (1982).
—: *How I Became a Hindu*. Voice of India, Delhi 1993 (1982).
—: *The Emerging National Vision*. Voice of India, Delhi 1983.
—: *Defence of Hindu Society*. Voice of India, Delhi 1994 (1983).
—: *Heroic Hindu Resistance to Muslim Invaders*. Voice of India, Delhi 1994 (1984).
—: *Perversion of India's Political Parlance*. Voice of India, Delhi 1984.
—: *Saikyularizm, Râshtradroha kâ Dûsrâ Nâm*. Bhârat-Bhâratî, Delhi 1985.
—: *Muslim Separatism, Causes and Consequences*. Voice of India, Delhi 1987.
—, ed.: *Catholic Ashrams, Adapting and Adopting Hindu Dharma*. Voice of India, Delhi 1994 (1988).
—: *History of Hindu-Christian Encounters*. Voice of India, Delhi, 1996 (1989).
—: *Hindu Temples, What Happened to Them* (2 vols.). Voice of India, Delhi 1990-93.
—: *Islam vis-à-vis Hindu Temples*. Voice of India, Delhi 1993.
—: *Hindu and Hinduism, Manipulation of Meanings*. Voice of India, Delhi 1993.
—: *Genesis and Growth of Nehruism*. Voice of India, Delhi 1993 (1960).
—: *Jesus Christ, an Artifice for Aggression*. Voice of India, Delhi 1994.
—, ed.: *Time for Stock-Taking. Whither Sangh Parivar?* Voice of India, Delhi 1997.
—, ed.: *Vindicated by Time. The Niyogi Committee Report on Christian Missionary Activities*. Voice of India, Delhi 1998.
—: *Pseudo-Secularism, Christian Missions and Hindu Resistance*. Voice of India, Delhi 1998.
JAIN, Girilal: *The Hindu Phenomenon*. UBSPD, Delhi 1994.
LAL, K.S.: *Growth of Muslim Population in India*. Research Publ., Delhi 1973.
—: *Early Muslims in India*. Delhi 1984.
—: *Indian Muslims, Who Are They?* Voice of India, Delhi 1990.
—: *Legacy of Muslim Rule in India*. Aditya Prakashan, Delhi 1992.

—: *Muslim Slave System in Medieval India*. Id., 1994.

—: *Growth of Scheduled Tribes and Castes in Medieval India*. Id., 1995.

LOHIA, Hari Prasad, ed.: *Political Vandalism*. Delhi 1990.

MADHAVDAS, Baba, ed.: *Report of the Christian Missionary Activities Enquiry Committee, Madhya Pradesh* (abridged edition). Brindavan, n.d.

MAHESWARI, Anil: *Crescent over Kashmir. Politics of Mullaism*. Rupa, Delhi 1993.

MAJUMDAR, Suhas: *Jihâd. The Islamic Doctrine of Permanent War*. Voice of India, Delhi 1994.

MISRA, Ram Gopal: *Indian Resistance to Early Muslim Invaders upto 1206 AD*. Anu Books, Meerut 1992 (1983).

NIVEDITA, Sister (= NOBLE, Margaret E.): *Footfalls of Indian History*. Advaita Ashrama, Calcutta 1980.

PADMANABHA: *Kanhadade Prabandha. India's Greatest Patriotic Saga of Medieval Times* (tra. V.S. Bhatnagar). Voice of India, Delhi 1991.

PAL, Bipin Chandra: *Swadeshi and Swaraj. Speeches and Writings of B.C. Pal*. Calcutta Yugayatri Prakashak, 1954 (1923).

—: *Introduction to the Study of Hinduism*. Calcutta 1908.

PALIWAL, Krishna Vallabh, and BHARTI, Brahm Datt: *The Hindu?* Era Books, Delhi 1994.

RAI, Baljit: *Muslim Fundamentalism in the Indian Subcontinent*. B.S. Publ., Chandigarh 1991.

—: *Demographic Aggression against India: Muslim Avalanche from Bangladesh*. B.S. Publ., Chandigarh 1993.

—: *Is India Going Islamic?* B.S. Publ., Chandigarh 1994.

RAMACHANDRAN, K.S.: *Ayodhya Dispute and Prof. Irfan Habib: a Distorted Scholarship*. Historians' Forum, Delhi 1992.

RAM GOPAL: *Hindu Culture during and After Muslim Rule. Survival and Subsequent Challenges*. M.D. Publ., Delhi 1994.

RAM SWARUP: *Buddhism vis-à-vis Hinduism*, Voice of India, Delhi, 1983 (1958).

—: *Manna, the Heavenly Food*. Delhi, n.d.

—: *The Hindu View of Education*. Delhi 1971.

—: *The Word as Revelation. Names of Gods*. Impex India, Delhi 1980.

—: *Hinduism vis-à-vis Christianity and Islam*. Voice of India, Delhi 1992 (revised, 1982).

—: *Understanding Islam through Hadis. Religious Faith or Fanaticism*. Voice of India, Delhi 1989 (1983).

—: *Hindu-Sikh Relationship*, Voice of India, Delhi 1985.

—: *Ramakrishna Mission in Search of a New Identity*. Voice of India, Delhi 1986.

—: *Cultural Alienation and Some Problems Hinduism Faces*. Voice of India, Delhi 1987.

—: *Whither Sikhism?* Voice of India, Delhi 1991.

—: *Hindu View of Christianity and Islam*. Voice of India, Delhi 1992.

—: *Woman in Islam*. Voice of India, Delhi 1994.

—: *Pope John-Paul II on Eastern Religions and Yoga, a Hindu-Buddhist Rejoinder*. Voice of India, Delhi 1995.

—: *On Hinduism. Reviews and Reflections*. Voice of India, Delhi 1999.

—: *Meditations. Yoga, Gods, Religions*. Voice of India, Delhi 2000.

RAY, Siva Prasad: *Turning of the Wheel*. A. Ghosh, Calcutta 1985.

SANYAL, B.S.: *Hindu Ideology Made Simple*. Vichar-o-Prachar, Varanasi 1986.
"SAVITRI DEVI (Mukherji)", née PORTAS, Maximiani: *Souvenirs et Réflexions d'une Aryenne*, privately published, Delhi 1976.
SHAIKH, Anwar: *Eternity*. Principality Publ., Cardiff 1990.
—: *Islam, the Arab National Movement*. Principality Publ., 1994.
—: *The Tale of Two Gujarati Saints*. A. Ghosh, Houston 1997.
SHOURIE, Arun: *Hinduism, Essence and Consequence*. Vikas Publ., Delhi 1979.
—: *Symptoms of Fascism*. Vikas Publ., Delhi 1978.
—: *Religion in Politics*. Roli Books, Delhi 1989 (1987).
—: *The Only Fatherland*. ASA, Delhi 1991.
—: *Indian Controversies*. ASA, Delhi 1993.
—: *A Secular Agenda. For Saving Our Country, for Welding It*. ASA, Delhi 1993.
—: *Missionaries in India*. ASA, Delhi 1994.
—: *Arun Shourie and His Christian Critic*. Voice of India, Delhi 1995.
—: *The World of Fatwas*. ASA, Delhi 1995.
—: *Worshipping False Gods. Ambedkar, and the Facts which Have Been Erased*. ASA, Delhi 1997.
—: *Eminent Historians. Their Technology, Their Line, Their Fraud*. ASA, Delhi 1998.
—: *Harvesting Our Souls*. ASA, Delhi 1999.
TALAGERI, Shrikant: *Aryan Invasion Theory and Indian Nationalism*. Voice of India, Delhi 1993.
—: *The Rigveda, a Historical Analysis*. Aditya Prakashan, Delhi 2000.
TALREJA, Kanayalal M.: *Philosophy of Vedas*. Talreja Publ., Mumbai 1982.
—: *200 Himalayan Blunders*. Rashtriya Chetana Prakashan, Delhi 1997.
TAPASYANANDA, Swami, ed.: *The Nationalistic and Religious Lectures of Swami Vivekananda*, Ramakrishna Math, Madras 1985.
VEDANTHAM, Major T.R.: *Christianity—a Political Problem*. Madras 1984.
VIVEKANANDA, Swami: *Caste, Culture and Socialism*. Advaita Ashram, Calcutta 1983.
—: *Proletariat! Win Equal Rights*. Advaita Ashram, Calcutta, 1984.
—: *Our Women*. Advaita Ashram, Calcutta, 1987.
—: *Complete Works*. Advaita Ashram, Calcutta, 1992.

Periodicals

Tattva Darshana, Madras
Young India, Wellingborough, England
Sword of Truth (electronic), Houston

Secondary Publications on Hindu Revivalism

AKBAR, M.J.: *India, the Siege Within*. Penguin 1985.
—: *Nehru, the Making of India*. Penguin 1991.
ALI, S. Mahmud: *The Fearful State*. Zed Books, London 1993.
ALLEN, Douglas: *Religion and Political Conflict in South Asia*. Greenwood Press, Westport (Connecticut) 1992.
ALOYSIUS, C.: *Nationalism without a Nation in India*. OUP, Delhi 1997.
ANDERSEN, Walter K., and Shridhar D., DAMLE: *The Brotherhood in Saffron. The Rashtriya Swayamsevak Sangha and Hindu Revivalism*. Vistaar Publ., Delhi 1987.

ARSLAN, Mehdi, and Janaki RAJAN: *Communalism in India: Challenge and Response*. Manohar, Delhi 1994.
BAIRD, Robert D.: *Religion in Modern India*. Manohar, Delhi 1991.
—: *Religion and Law in Independent India*. Manohar, Delhi 1993.
BANERJEE, Subrata: *Secularism and Indian Polity*. Joshi-Adhikari Institute of Social Studies, Delhi 1987.
BASU, Tapan et al.: *Khaki Shorts and Saffron Flags*. Orient Longman, Delhi 1993.
BAXTER, Craig: *The Jana Sangh. A Biography of an Indian Political Party*. Oxford University Press, Delhi 1971.
BAZAZ, Prem Nath: *The Shadow of Ram Rajya over India*. Shark Publ., Delhi 1980.
BHATT, Chetan: *Liberation and Purity. Race, New Religious Movements and the Ethics of Postmodernity*. UCL Press, London 1997.
BHALLA, G.S. et al.: *India, Nation-State and Communalism*. Patriot Publ., Delhi 1989.
BIDWAI, Praful, Harbans MUKHIA and Achin VANAIK: *Religion, Religiosity and Communalism*. Manohar, Delhi 1996.
BIPAN CHANDRA: *Communalism in Modern India*. Vikas, Delhi 1987 (1984).
BJRKMAN, J.W.: *Fundamentalism, Revivalists and Violence in South Asia*. Manohar, Delhi 1988.
BONNER, Arthur: *Democracy in India, a Hollow Shell*. American University Press, Washington DC, 1994.
BRASS, Paul R.: *The Politics of India since Independence*, 2nd ed. (*New Cambridge History of India* IV.1). Cambridge University Press, Cambridge 1994 (1990).
CHAKRABARTY, Bidyut, ed.: *Secularism and Indian Polity*. Segment, Delhi 1990.
CHAKRAVARTTY, Gargi: *Gandhi, a Challenge to Communalism*. Eastern Books, Delhi 1991 (1987).
CHAKRAVARTY, Papia: *Hindu Response to Nationalist Ferment*. Subarnarekha, Calcutta 1992.
CHATTERJI, P.C., ed.: *Self-Images, Identity and Nationality*. Indian Institute of Advanced Study, Shimla 1989.
—: *Secular Values for Secular India*. Manohar, Delhi 1995.
CHATTERJI, Rakhahari, ed.: *Religion, Politics and Communalism. The South Asian Experience*. South Asian Publ., Delhi 1994.
COSSMAN, Brenda, and KAPUR, Ratna: *Secularism's Last Sigh? Hindutva and the (Mis)Rule of Law*. OUP, Delhi 1999.
D'CRUZ, Emil: *Indian Secularism, a Fragile Myth*. Indian Social Institute, Delhi 1988.
DEVAHUTI, ed.: *Bias in Indian Historiography*. D.K. publ., Delhi 1980.
ELENJIMITTAN, Anthony: *Philosophy and Action of the RSS for the Hind Swaraj*. Laxmi Publ., Bombay 1951.
ELST, Koenraad: *Ram Janmabhoomi vs. Babri Masjid*. Voice of India, Delhi 1990.
—: *The Saffron Swastika. The Notion of "Hindu Fascism"*. Voice of India, Delhi 2001.
—: *De Moord op de Mahatma*. Davidsfonds, Leuven 1998.
ENGINEER, Asghar Ali, ed.: *Babri Masjid Ram Janmabhoomi Controversy*. Ajanta, Bombay 1990.
—, ed.: *Politics of Confrontration*. Ajanta, Bombay 1992.
—: *Communalism in India. A Historical and Empirical Study*. Vikas Publ., Delhi 1995.
FARQUHAR, J.N.: *Modern Religious Movements in India*. Munshiram Manoharlal, Delhi

1977 (1914).

FREITAG, Sandria: *Public Arenas and the Emergence of Communalism in North India.* OUP, Delhi 1990.

GAUTIER, François: *Rewriting Indian History.* Vikas Publ., 1996.

GHOSH, Muktishree: *Concept of Secular Education in India.* B.R. Publ., Delhi 1991.

GHOSH, Tapan: *The Gandhi Murder Trial.* Asia Publ., Delhi 1973 (1961).

GOPAL, Sarvepalli: *Anatomy of a Confrontation. The Babri Masjid Ram Janmabhumi Issue,* 2nd ed. Penguin, 1991 (1990).

GORIS, Gie: *God met ons. Wereldwijde verhalen over godsdienst en geweld.* Icarus, Antwerp 1997.

GRAHAM, Bruce: *Hindu Nationalism and Indian Politics. The Origins and Development of the Bharatiya Jana Sangh.* Cambridge University Press, Cambridge 1990.

GUPTA, Dipankar: *Nativism in a Metropolis. Shiv Sena in Bombay.* Manohar, Delhi 1982.

GUPTA, N.L.: *Nehru on Communalism.* Sampradayikta Virodhi Committee, Delhi 1965.

HAQ, Jalalul: *Nation and Nation-Worship in India.* Genuine Publ., Delhi 1992.

HASAN, Zoya, ed.: *Forging Identities. Gender, Communities and the State in India.* Westview Press, Boulder 1994.

HEUZE, Gèrard: *Oî Va l'Inde Moderne?* L'Harmattan, Paris 1993.

INAMDAR, P.L.: *The Story of the Red Fort Trial 1948-49.* Popular Prakashan, Bombay 1979.

IQBAL NARAIN: *Secularism in India.* Classic Publ., Jaipur 1995.

JAFFRELOT, Christophe: *Les Nationalistes Hindous.* Presse de la Fondation Nationale des Sciences Politiques, Paris 1993.

—: *The Hindu Nationalist Movement in India.* Viking/Penguin, London/Delhi 1996.

—: *L'Inde Contemporaine: de 1950 à nos jours.* Fayard, Paris 1996.

JAYAPRASAD, K.: *RSS and Hindu Nationalism. Inroads in a Leftist Stronghold.* Deep & Deep Publ., Delhi 1991.

JEFFREY, Robin: *What's Happening to India? Punjab, Ethnic Conflict and the Test for Federalism* (2nd ed.). Macmillan, London 1994 (1986).

JORDENS, J.T.F.: *Swami Shraddhananda, His Life and Causes.* OUP, Delhi 1981.

JUERGENSMEYER, Mark: *The New Cold War? Religious Nationalism Confronts the Secular State.* University of California Press, Berkeley 1994 (1993).

KEER, Dhananjay: *Veer Savarkar* (3rd ed.). Popular Prakashan, Bombay 1988 (1950).

—: *Lokamanya Tilak. Father of the Indian Freedom Struggle* (2nd ed.). Popular Prakashan, Bombay 1969 (1959).

KHOSLA, G.D.: *Murder of the Mahatma.* Jaico Press, Bombay 1977 (1963).

—: *Stern Reckoning. A Survey of the Events Leading Up To and Following the Partition of India.* OUP, Delhi 1989.

KING, Christopher R., ed.: *One Language, Two Scripts. The Hindi Movement in Nineteenth Century North India.* OUP, Delhi 1994.

KISHORE, Mohammed Ali: *Jana Sangh and Indian Foreign Policy.* Associated Publ., Delhi 1969.

KOTNALA, M.C.: *Raja Rammohun Roy and Indian Awakening.* Gitanjali Prakashan, Delhi 1975.

KOPF, David: *The Brahmo Samaj and the Shaping of the Modern Indian Mind.* Princeton University Press, 1979.

KULKARNI, Atmaram: *The Advent of Advani*. Aditya Prakashan, Bombay 1995.

LAHIRI, Pratul, ed.: *Selected Writings on Communalism*. People's Publishing House, Delhi 1994.

LLEWELLYN, J.E.: *The Arya Samaj as a Fundamentalist Movement. A Study in Comparative Fundamentalism*. Manohar, Delhi 1993.

LUDDEN, David: *Making India Hindu. Religion, Community and the Politics of Democracy in India*. OUP, Delhi 1996.

LÜTT, Jlrgen: *Hindu Nationalismus in Uttar Pradesh 1867-1900*. Ernst Klett Verlag, Stuttgart 1970.

MALGONKAR, Manohar: *The Men Who Killed Gandhi*. Orient, Delhi 1981.

MALIK, Yogendra K., and SINGH, V.B.: *Hindu Nationalists in India. The Rise of the Bharatiya Janata Party*. Vistaar Publ., Delhi 1994.

McGUIRE, John; Peter REEVES; and Howard BRASTED: *Politics of Violence. From Ayodhya to Behrampura*. Sage Publ., Thousand Oaks (Colorado)/Delhi 1996.

McKEAN, Lise: *Divine Enterprise. Gurus and the Hindu Nationalist Movement*. Chicago University Press, 1996.

MEHTA, V.R.: *Foundations of Indian Political Thought*. Manohar, Delhi 1996.

NAIPAUL, V.S.: *An Area of Darkness*. Penguin, London 1968.

—: *India, a Wounded Civilization*. Penguin 1985 (1977).

—: *India. A Million Mutinies Now*. Minerva, London 1990.

—: *Beyond Belief*. London 1997.

NANDY, Ashis: *The Intimate Enemy. Loss and Recovery of Self under Colonialism*. OUP, Delhi 1995 (1983).

--: *At the Edge of Psychology. Essays in Politics and Culture*. OUP, Delhi 1990

—: *The Illegitimacy of Nationalism. Rabindranath Tagore and the Politics of Self*. OUP, Delhi 1994.

— et al.: *Creating a Nationality. The Ramjanmabhumi Movement and Fear of the Self*. OUP, Delhi 1995.

NAYAK, Pradeep: *The Politics of the Ayodhya Dispute*. Commonwealth Publ., Delhi 1993.

NIELSEN jr., Niels C.: *Fundamentalism, Mythos and World Religions*. SUNY, Albany 1993.

PANDEY, Gyanendra: *The Construction of Communalism in Colonial North India*. OUP, Delhi 1990.

—, ed.: *Hindus and Others. The Question of Identity in India Today*. Viking/Penguin, Delhi 1993.

PANIKKAR, K.N.: *Communalism in India. A Perspective for Intervention*. People's Publishing House, Delhi 1991.

—: *Communalism in India. History, Politics and Culture*. Manohar, Delhi 1991.

PATEL, Sujata, and Alice THORNER: *Bombay. Metaphor for Modern India*. OUP, Delhi 1997.

PEREIRA, Myron J.: *Partly True, Wholly False. A Study Guide on Communal Stereotypes*. Xavier Institute of Communications. Bombay, *c*. 1991.

PUROHIT, B.R.: *Hindu Revivalism and Indian Nationalism*. Sathi Prakashan, Sagar (MP) 1965.

RADHEY MOHAN, ed.: *Secularism in India*. Zakir Hussain Educational & Cultural Foundation, Delhi 1990.

ROBB, Peter, ed.: *The Concept of Race in South Asia*. OUP, Delhi 1995.

ROY, Binoy K.: *Socio-Political Views of Vivekananda*. People's Publishing House, Delhi 1986 (1970).

SAMPRADAYIKTA VIRODHI COMMITTEE: *Shiv Sena Menace*. Sampradayikta Virodhi Committee, Delhi n.d., *c.* 1970.

SANKHDER, M.M.: *Secularism in India*. Deep & Deep Publ., Delhi 1992.

SARDESAI, S.G.: *Fascist Menace and Democratic Unity*. People's Publishing House, Bombay 1970.

SARKAR, Tanika, and Urvashi BUTALIA: *Women and the Hindu Right*. Kali for Women, Delhi 1995.

SCRASE, Timothy J.: *Image, Ideology and Inequality. Cultural Domination, Hegemony and Schooling in India*. Sage Publ., Delhi 1993.

SEN, Amiya P.: *Hindu Revivalism in Bengal 1872-1905*. OUP, Delhi 1993.

SHASHI BHUSHAN: *Fundamentalism, a Weapon against Human Aspirations*. National Convention on Secularism, Delhi 1986.

SINGH, Khushwant, and BIPAN CHANDRA: *Many Faces of Communalism*. CRRID, Chandigarh 1985.

THAKUR, Janardan: *All the Janata Men*. Vikas Publ., Delhi 1978.

VAJPEYI, Dhirendra, & Yogendra K., MALIK: *Religious and Ethnic Minority Politics in South Asia*. Manohar, Delhi 1989.

VAN DER VEER, Peter: *Gods on Earth. The Management of Religious Experience and Identity in a North-Indian Pilgrimage Centre*. Athlone Press, London 1988.

—: *Religious Nationalism. Hindus and Muslims in India*. University of California Press, Berkeley 1994.

VAZIRANI, Gulab: *Lal Advani. The Man and his Mission*. Arnold Publ., Delhi 1991.

WAIDYA, Prabhakar: *Shiv Sena: the Fascist Menace behind the Pseudo-Maharashtrian Mask*. Communist Party of India, Maharashtra; Bombay n.d., *c.* 1969.

YOUNG, Richard F.: *Resistant Hinduism. Sanskrit Surces on Anti-Christian Apologetics in Early Nineteenth-Century India*. De Nobili Research Library, Wien 1981.

Periodicals and newspapers

Asian Profile, Richmond (British Columbia)
Frontline, Chennai
Indian Express, Delhi
India, Brussels (1992-97)
India Nu, Utrecht
India Post, USA
Indo-Iranian Journal, Leiden
Hinduism Today, Honolulu
Hindustan Times, Delhi
Journal of South Asian and Middle Eastern Studies, Villanova PA
Journal of Hindu Studies, Quèbec
Mainstream, Delhi
New India Digest, Pune
Political and Economic Weekly, Delhi
Observer of Business and Politics, Delhi
Relations Internationales et Stratègiques, Paris

Seminar, Delhi
South Asia, New England (Australia)
South Asia Bulletin, USA
Times of India, Delhi/Mumbai et al.

Other publications: Indian Politics

ACHARYA, SriKumar: *The Changing Pattern of Education in Early Nineteenth-Century Bengal*. Punthi-Pustak, Calcutta 1992.
ALI, Tariq: *The Nehrus and the Gandhis, an Indian Dynasty*. Pan (Picador), London 1985.
BAKKER, Hans: *Gandhi and the Gita*. Canadian Scholars' Press, Toronto 1993.
BAKSHI, P.M.: *The Constitution of India*. Universal Books, Delhi 1995.
BAKSHI, S.R.: *Revolutionaries and the British Raj*. Atlantic Publ., Delhi 1988.
BANATWALA, G.M.: *Religion and Politics in India*. Bombay 1992.
BARAL, Lok Raj: *Nepal's Politics of Referendum. A Study of Groups, Personalities & Trends*. Vikas Publ., Delhi 1983.
BHAT, Sudhakar: *India and China*. Popular Book Service, Delhi 1967.
BHATTACHERJE, S.B.: *Encyclopaedia of Indian Events & Dates*. Sterling Publ., Delhi 1995 (1986).
BIPAN CHANDRA: *India's Struggle for Independence*. Penguin, Harmondsworth 1988.
CHAKRAVARTI, P.C.: *India-China Relations*. K.L. Mukhopadhyay, Calcutta 1961.
DALTON, Dennis: *Mahatma Gandhi. Non-Violent Power in Action*. Columbia University Press, New York 1993.
DESAI, M.P.: *The Problem of English*. Navajivan Publ., Ahmedabad 1964.
DUTT, V.P.: *India's Foreign Policy*. Vani Educational Books, Delhi 1984.
DWIVEDI, S.: *Hindi on Trial*. Vikas Publ., Delhi 1981.
EASWARAN, Eknath: *Gandhi the Man*. Jaico, Delhi 1997.
GALBRAITH, John Kenneth: *Ambassador's Journal: an American View of India*. Jaico, Bombay 1972.
GANDHI, Mohandas Karamchand: *Truth Is God*. Navjivan Publ., Ahmedabad 1955.
—: *Trusteeship*. Navjivan Publ., Ahmedabad 1960.
—: *The Hindu-Muslim Unity*, selected by Anand T. Hingorani. Bharatiya Vidya Bhavan, Bombay 1965.
GANDHI, Rajmohan: *Patel, a Life*. Navajivan Publ., Ahmedabad 1991.
—: *Revenge and Reconciliation. Understanding South-Asian History*. Penguin, 1999.
GHOSH, Manomohan: *China's Conflict with India and the Soviet Union*. World Press, Calcutta 1969.
GOPAL, Sarvepalli: *Jawaharlal Nehru: a Biography*, vol.1-2-3. OUP, Delhi 1976-79-84.
—, ed.: *Selected Works of Jawaharlal Nehru* (first series), 15 vols. Orient Longman, Delhi 1970-82.
—, ed.: *Selected Works of Jawaharlal Nehru* (second series), 16 vols. OUP, Delhi 1982-93.
GHURYE, G.S.: *India Recreates Democracy*. Popular Prakashan, Bombay 1978.
GUPTA, Pranay: *India, the Challenge of Change*. Methuen/Mandarin, London 1989.
HABIB, Irfan: *Essays in Indian History. Towards a Marxist Perspective*. Tulika, Delhi 1995.
HAKSAR, P.N.: *One More Life*, vol 1: *1913-1929*. OUP, Delhi 1990.
HEEHS, Peter: *The Bomb in Bengal. The Rise of Revolutionary Terrorism in India*. OUP, Delhi 1993.

HUSAIN, S. Abid: *The National Culture of India*. National Book Trust, Delhi 1987 (1956).

JHA, D.C.: *Indo-Pakistan Relations*. Bharati Bhawan, Patna 1972.

JOHRI, Major Sita Ram: *Chinese Invasion of NEFA*. Himalaya Publ., Lucknow 1968.

KADIAN, Rajesh: *India's Sri Lanka Fiasco. Peacekeepers at War*. Vision Books, Delhi 1990.

KARANJIA, R.K.: *The Mind of Mr. Nehru*. Allen & Unwin, London 1960.

KEER, Dhananjay: *Lokamanya Tilak*. Popular Prakashan, Bombay 1969 (1959).

KHAN, Rasheeduddin: *Composite Culture of India and National Integration*. Indian Institute of Advanced Study, Simla 1987.

KING, Robert D.: *Nehru and the Language Politics of India*. OUP, Delhi 1997.

KOOIMAN, Dick: *India: Mensen, Politiek, Economie, Cultuur*. Koninklijk Instituut voor de Tropen, Amsterdam, 1994.

KOTHARI, Rajni: *Politics in India*. Orient Longman, Delhi 1970.

KULKE, H., and D. ROTHERMUND: *A History of India*. Rupa, Delhi 1991.

LOHIA, Ram Manohar: *India, China and Northern Frontiers*. Navahind, Hyderabad 1963.

MAJUMDAR, R.C., ed.: *History and Culture of the Indian People*, vol.1, *The Vedic Age*. Bharatiya Vidya Bhavan, Mumbai 1988 (1951).

—: vol.6, *The Delhi Sultanate*, 1990 (1960).

—: vol.7, *The Mughal Empire*, 1994 (1974);

—: vol.9-10, *British Paramountcy and Indian Renaissance*, 1988 (1963).

—: vol.11, *Struggle for Freedom*, 1988 (1969).

—: *History of the Freedom Movement in India*. Firma KLM, Calcutta, 1963.

MARX, Karl: *Notes on Indian History*. Progress Publ., Moscow 1986 (1858).

MASANI, Minoo: *Against the Tide*. Vikas Publ., Delhi 1981.

MATHEW, K.M., ed.: *Manorama Yearbook 1996*. Kottayam 1996.

MEHTA, V.R.: *Foundations of Indian Political Thought*. Manohar, Delhi 1996.

MENDE, Tibor: *Conversations with Mr. Nehru*. Secker & Warburg, London 1956.

MENEZES, S.L.: *The Indian Army*. Viking, Delhi 1993.

METCALF, Thomas: *The Aftermath of the Revolt: India 1857-1870*. Princeton University Press, Princeton 1964.

MISHRA, D.P.: *The Post-Nehru Era*. Delhi 1993.

MUKHERJEE, Haridas & Uma: *B.C. Pal and India's Struggle for Swaraj*. K.L. Mukhopadhyaya, Calcutta 1958.

NANDA, B.R.: *Gandhi and His Critics*. Oxford University Press, Delhi 1993 (1985).

NARAYAN, Jayaprakash: *Nation-Building in India*. Navachetna Prakashan, Varanasi *c*. 1965.

NARAYAN, Shriman: *India and Nepal*. Orient/ Hind Pocket Books, Delhi 1971.

NAYAR, Kuldip: *India after Nehru*. Vikas Publ., Delhi 1975.

NEHRU, Jawaharlal: *Glimpses of World History*. Asia Publ., Delhi 1934.

—: *The Discovery of India*. OUP, Delhi 1982 (1946).

PANDEY, B.N.: *The Indian Nationalist Movement 1885-1947. Select Documents*. Macmillan Press, London/Delhi 1979.

PARK, Richard L., and Irene TINKER, eds.: *Leadership and Political Institutions in India*. Princeton 1959.

PHILIPS, C.H.: *Select Documents on the History of India and Pakistan*. OUP, London 1962.

POCHHAMMER, Wilhelm von: *India's Road to Nationhood: a Political History of the Sub-Continent*. Allied Publ., Bombay 1961.

RIENCOURT, Amaury de: *The Soul of India*, Jonathan Cape, London 1961.

ROWLAND, John: *A History of Sino-Indian Relations*. Allied Publ., Bombay 1971 (1967).

SARASWATHI, S.: *Minorities in Madras State. Group Interests in Modern Politics*. Impex India, Delhi 1974.

SESHAN, T.N., with HAZARIKA, Sanjoy: *The Degeneration of India*. Viking/Penguin, Delhi 1995.

—: *The Regeneration of India*. Viking/Penguin, Delhi 1995.

SHARMA, B.K.: *Bhârat kâ Samvidhân; Constitution of India*. Government of India, Delhi 1991.

SHARMA, B.L.: *The Pakistan-China Axis*. Asia Publ., Delhi 1968.

SMITH, Donald Eugene, ed.: *Religion, Politics and Social Change in the Third World. A Sourcebook*. Free Press, New York 1971.

SPEAR, Percival: *A History of India*, vol.2. Penguin, London 1979 (1965).

THAPAR, Romila: *A History of India*, vol.1. Penguin, London.

TRIVEDI, Ram Naresh: *Sino-Indian Border Dispute and its Impact on Indo-Pakistan Relations*. Associated Publ., Delhi 1977.

TULLY, Mark: *No Full Stops in India*. Viking/Penguin, Delhi 1992 (1991).

VARMA, V.P.: *Modern Indian Political Thought*. Laxmi Narain Agarwal, Agra 1987 (1961).

WOLPERT, Stanley A.: *Tilak and Gokhale: Revolution and Reform in the Making of Modern India*. OUP, Delhi 1989 (1961).

Other publications: Hinduism

AGEHANANDA Bharati, Swami: *The Light at the Center. Context and Pretext of Modern Mysticism*. Ross-Erikson, Santa Barbara 1976.

ALTEKAR, A.S.: *State and Government in Ancient India*. Motilal Banarsidass, Delhi 1984 (1949).

—: *The Position of Women in Hindu Civilization*. Motilal Banarsidass, Delhi 1987 (1959).

AMBEDKAR, Dr. Babasaheb: *Writings and Speeches*, vol.1-9, Education Department, Government of Maharashtra, 1986-1990.

—: *Annihilation of Caste*. Arnold Publ., Bangalore 1990.

BASHAM, A.L., ed.: *A Cultural History of India*. OUP, Delhi 1997 (1975).

BHARATI KRISHNA Tirtha, Shri: *Secret of India's Greatness: Sanatana Vaidika Dharma*. Jagriti Prakashan, Noida 1998 (1934).

BHATTACHARJEE, A.M.: *Hindu Law and the Constitution*. Eastern Law House, Calcutta 1994.

BROCKINGTON, J.L.: *The Sacred Thread. A Short History of Hinduism*. OUP, Delhi 1992 (1981).

—: *Righteous Rama. The Evolution of an Epic*. OUP, Delhi 1985.

CALLEWAERT, Winand M.: *India, Betoverende Verscheidenheid*. Davidsfonds, Leuven 1996.

CHATTERJI, Suniti Kumar: *Indo-Aryan and Hindi*. K.L. Mukhopadhyaya, Calcutta 1969 (1940).

—: *Balts and Aryans*. Indian Institute of Advanced Study, Simla 1968.

CHATTOPADHYAYA, Sudhakar: *Ethnic Elements in Ancient Hinduism*, Sanskrit College, Calcutta 1979.

COWARD, H.G.; J.J. LIPNER; and K.K. YOUNG: *Hindu Ethics: Purity, Abortion and Euthanasia*. State University of New York Press, Albany 1989.

DANIELOU, Alain: *Histoire de l'Inde*, Fayard, Paris 1983 (1971).

—: *Les Quatre Sens de la Vie, La Structure Sociale de l'Inde Traditionnelle*, Buchet-Chastel, Paris 1984 (1975).

—: *Le Chemin du Labyrinthe. Souvenirs d'Orient et d'Occident*. Ed. du Rocher, Paris 1993.

DAYANANDA Saraswati, Swami: *The Teaching Tradition of Advaita Vedanta*. Arsha Vidya Gurukulam, Saylorsburg PA 1993

DEVAHUTI: *Harsha, a Political Study*. Oxford University Press, Delhi 1983.

DE VRIES, Sjoerd: *Hindoeïsme voor Beginners. Een Heldere Inleiding tot de Oudste nog Levende Wereldgodsdienst*. Forum, Amsterdam 1996.

DIWAN, Paras: *Modern Hindu Law*. Allahabad Law Agency, Allahabad 1985 (1972).

DONIGER, Wendy, and Brian K., SMITH, eds.: *The Laws of Manu*, Penguin 1991.

EDAKKANDIYAL, V.: *Daddy, Am I a Hindu?* Bharatiya Vidya Bhavan, Bombay 1988.

ELIADE, Mircea: *Journal des Indes*, L'Herne, Paris 1992.

—: *Yoga. Immortality and Freedom* (Bollingen Series 56). Princeton University Press 1969 (1954).

FEUERSTEIN, Georg; Subhash KAK; and David FRAWLEY: *In Search of the Cradle of Civilization*. Quest Books, Wheaton, Ill., 1995.

FLOOD, Gavin: *An Introduction to Hinduism*. Cambridge University Press, 1996.

GANDHI, Maneka: *Heads and Tails*. The Other India Press, Mapusa (Goa) 1994.

GANGULI, Kisori Mohan, tra.: *The Mahabharata*. Munshiram Manoharlal, Delhi 1997.

GHURYE, G.S.: *The Aborigines—So-Called—and Their Future*. Gokhale Institute of Politics and Economics, Pune 1943.

—: *Indian Sadhus*. Popular Prakashan, Bombay 1995 (1953).

—: *Indian Acculturation. Agastya and Skanda*. Popular Prakashan, Bombay 1997.

GRIMES, John: *A Concise Dictionary of Indian Philosophy*. Radhakrishnan Institute, University of Madras, 1988.

GUPTA, Mahendranath, and (tra.) Swami NIKHILANANDA: *The Gospel of Sri Ramakrishna*. Sri Ramakrishna Math, Madras 1942.

HARIHARANANDA Giri, Swami: *Secrets and Significance of Idol Worship among the Hindus*. Karar Ashram, Puri 1984.

HAWLEY, John Stratton, ed.: *Sati, the Blessing and the Curse. The Burning of Wives in India*. Oxford University Press, Oxford 1994.

HINNELLS, John, and SHARPE, Eric, eds.: *Hinduism*. Oriel Press, Newcastle upon Tyne, 1972.

GOPALAKRISHNAN, M.D.: *Periyar, Father of the Tamil Race*. Emerald Publ., Madras 1991.

ILAIAH, Kancha: *Why I Am Not a Hindu: A Sudra Critique of Hindutva Philosophy, Culture and Political Economy*. Samya (Bhatkal and Sen), Calcutta 1996.

IYENGAR, B.K.S.: *Light on the Yoga Sutras of Patanjali*. Aquarian Press, London 1993.

JETTMAR, Karl: *The Religions of the Hindukush*, vol.1: *The Religion of the Kafirs, the Pre-Islamic Heritage of Afghan Nuristan*. Oxford & IBH, Delhi 1986.

KANE, P.V.: *History of Dharma-Shâstra*. Bhandarkar Oriental Research Institute, Pune 1990 (1930-62).

KEER, Dhananjay: *Dr. Ambedkar, Life and Mission*. Popular Prakashan, Bombay 1987 (1962).

—: *Mahatma Jotirao Phooley, Father of Indian Social Revolution*. Popular Prakashan, Mumbai 1964.

KETKAR, S.V.: *History of Caste in India*, Low Price Publ., Delhi 1990 (1909).

KLOSTERMAIER, Klaus K.: *A Survey of Hinduism*, State University of New York Press, Albany 1989.

KOSAMBI, D.D.: *The Culture and Civilisation of Ancient India in Historical Outline*, Vikas Publ., Delhi 1988 (1964).

KRISHNAMACHARYA, Kulapati Ekkirala: *Our Heritage*. World Teacher Trust, Visakhapatnam 1983.

LOKESH CHANDRA, *et al.*, eds.: *India's Contribution to World Thought and Culture*. Vivekananda Trust, Kanyakumari/Delhi, n.d.

MAJUPURIA, Trilok Chandra and Rohit Kumar: *Sadhus and Saints of India and Nepal*. Tecpress, Bangkok 1996.

MARRIOTT, McKim: *India through Hindu Categories*. Sage Publ., Delhi 1989.

NAQVI, Saeed: *The Last Brahmin Prime Minister in India*. Har-Anand Publ., Delhi, 1996.

NARASIMHAN, C.V.: *The Mahabharata. An English Version Based on Selected Verses*. OUP, Delhi 1996.

NARLA, V.R.: *The Truth about the Gita*. Narla Institute, Hyderabad 1988.

NUGTEREN, Albertina: *Hindoeïsme, Heden en Verleden*. Garant, Leuven/Apeldoorn 1992.

PANDIT, M.D.: *Mathematics as Known to the Vedic Samhitas*. Sri Satguru Publ., Delhi 1993.

POLLET, Gilbert, ed.: *Indian Epic Values*. Peeters, Leuven 1995.

PRIME, Ranchor: *Hinduism and Ecology*. Motilal Banarsidass, Delhi 1994.

PHULE, Mahatma Jotirao: *Collected Works*, vol.1-2. Education Department, Government of Maharashtra, 1991-92.

RANGARAJAN, L.N., tra./ed.: *Kautilya: The Arthashastra*. Penguin, Delhi 1987.

RAY, Purnima, tra.: *Vasistha's Dhanurveda Samhitâ*. JP Publ., Delhi 1991.

SARKAR, Jadunath: *Shivaji and His Times*. Orient Longman, Delhi 1992 (1952).

SASTRI, Nilakantha: *A History of South India*. OUP, Delhi 1988 (4th ed.; 1955).

SASTRI, P.S.: *Ananda K. Coomaraswamy*. Arnold-Heinemann Publ., Delhi 1974.

SCHLEICHER, Irene, ed.: *Vedic Heritage Teaching Program*. Arsha Vidya Gurukulam, Coimbatore, *c.* 1994.

SERGENT, Bernard: *Les Indo-Européens. Histoire, Langues, Mythes*. Payot, Paris 1995.

—: *Genèse de l'Inde*. Payot, Paris 1997.

SETHNA, K.D.: *The Problem of Aryan Origins*, Aditya Prakashan, Delhi 1992 (1980).

—: *Karpâsa. A cultural and chronological Clue*. Aditya Prakashan, Delhi 1989.

SHARMA, Chandradhar: *A Critical Survey of Indian Philosophy*. Motilal Banarsidass, Delhi 1987 (1960).

SONTHEIMER, Gunther, and KULKE, Herman, eds.: *Hinduism Reconsidered*. Manohar, Delhi 1989.

STAAL, Frits: *Een Wijsgeer in het Oosten. Op Reis door Java en Kalimantan*. Meulenhoof, Amsterdam 1988.

—: *Zin en Onzin in Filosofie, Religie en Wetenschap*. Meulenhoff, Amsterdam 1989 (1986).
—: *Ritual and Mantras: Rules without Meaning*. Motilal Banarsidass, Delhi 1996 (1989).
SUBBIAH, Ganapathy: *Roots of Tamil Religious Thought*. Pondicherry Institute of Linguistics and Culture, 1991.
TATACHARIAR, Agnihotram Ramanuja: *Eternal Relevance of Vedas*. Tirumala Tirupati Devasthanams, Tirupati 1985.
TRIPATHI, L.K., ed.: *Position and Status of Hindu Women in Ancient India*. BHU, Varanasi 1988.
TULL, Herman W.: *The Vedic Origins of Karma. Cosmos as Man in Ancient Indian Myth and Ritual*. SUNY, Albany 1989.
VAN DER BURG, C.J.G., and KRANENBORG, R.: *Hindoeïsme en Boeddhisme*, in the series *Religieuze bewegingen in Nederland*, part 23, VU uitgeverij, Amsterdam 1991.
VAN LYSEBETH, André: *Tantra, le Culte de la Féminité*. Flammarion, Fribourg 1988.
WEBER, Max: *The Religion of India. The Sociology of Hinduism and Buddhism*. Munshiram Manoharlal, Delhi 1992 (*c.* 1910).
WINTERNITZ, Maurice: *A History of Indian Literature*. Motilal Banarsidass, Delhi 1987 (1907).
YOGANANDA, Swami: *Autobiography of a Yogi*. Self-Realization Fellowship, Los Angeles 1979 (1946).
YOGI, Maharishi Mahesh: *Invincibility to Every Nation*. Seelisburg (Switzerland) 1977.
YUKTESWAR, Sri: *The Holy Science*. Self-Realization Fellowship, Los Angeles 1977.
VANNUCCI, M.: *Ecological Readings in the Veda*. DK Printworld, Delhi 1994 (1993).
WATERSTONE, Richard: *De Wijsheid van India*. Kosmos, Utrecht 1995.
ZELLIOT, Eleanor, and BERNTSEN, Maxime, eds.: *The Experience of Hinduism*. SUNY, Albany 1988.

Other publications: Islam

AHMAD, Barakat: *Muhammad and the Jews. A Re-Examination*. Vikas Publ., Delhi 1979.
AHMAD, Imtiaz, ed.: *Caste and Social Stratification among Muslims in India*. Manohar, Delhi 1978.
AHMAD, Hazrat Haji Mirza Bashir-ud-din Mahmud: *Invitation to Ahmadiyyat*. Routledge & Kegan Paul, London 1980 (1926).
AHMED, Akbar S.: *Discovering Islam. Making Sense of Muslim History and Society*. Vistaar Publ., Delhi 1990 (1988).
—: *Postmodernism and Islam: Predicament and Promise*. Routledge, London 1992.
—: *Living Islam. From Samarkand to Stornoway*. BBC Books/Penguin, London 1993.
AJNAT, Surendra: *Ambedkar on Islam*. Buddhist Publ., Jalandhar 1986.
AKHTAR, Shabbir: *Be Careful with Muhammad! The Salman Rushdie Affair*. Bellew Publ., London 1989.
ALI, B. Sheik: *Tipu Sultan*. National Book Trust, Delhi 1991 (1972).
ANDRAE, Tor: *Mohammad, the Man and his Faith*. London 1956.
ARMSTRONG, Karen: *Mohammed. Een Westerse Poging tot Begrip van de Islam*. Anthos, Amsterdam 1996 (1991).
ARNOLD, T.W.: *The Preaching of Islam*. Low Price Publ., Delhi 1990 (1913).
AZIZ, K.K.: *Muslims under Congress Rule 1937-39. A Documentary Record*. Renaissance Publ., Delhi 1986 (1978).

BALJON, J.M.S.: *A Mystical Interpretation of Prophetic Tales by an Indian Muslim. Shâh Walî Allâh's Ta'wîl al-Ahâdîth*. Brill, Leiden 1973.

BARREAU, Jean-Claude: *De l'Islam en Général et du Monde Moderne en Particulier*. Le Pré aux Clercs, Paris 1991.

BAT YE'OR: *Les Chrétiens d'Orient entre Jihad et Dhimmitude*. Le Cerf, Paris 1991.

—: *The Dhimmi*. Fairleigh Dickinson University Press, London 1984 (1980).

BISWAS, B.B.: *Islamisation of Dr. Ambedkar's View: a Suicidal Move*. Vivekananda Sahitya Kendra, Calcutta 1994.

BURGGRAEVE, Roger and Johan DE TAVERNIER: *Strijden op de Weg van Jahwe, God, Allah? De 'heilige oorlog' in het Oude Testament, Westers Christendom en Islam*. Acco, Leuven 1989.

CATHERINE, Lucas: *In Naam van de Islam. Godsdienst als Politiek Argument bij Mohammed en Khomeini*. EPO, Antwerp 1985.

—: *Manyiema. De Enige Oorlog die België Won*. Hadewijch, Antwerp 1994.

—: *De Gelaagde Religie*. EPO, Antwerp 1996.

—: *Islam voor Ongelovigen*. EPO, Antwerp 1997.

CLEARY, Thomas: *The Essential Koran*. Harper-Collins-Indus, Delhi 1994.

CRONE, Patricia, and Michael COOK: *Hagarism: The Making of the Islamic World*. Cambridge University Press, 1977.

CRONE, Patricia: *Meccan Trade and the Rise of Islam*. Princeton University Press, Princeton 1987.

DALWAI, Hamid: *Muslim Politics in Secular India*. Hind Pockets 1968.

DEWEESE, Devin: *Islamization and Native Religion in the Golden Horde. Baba Tükles and Conversion to Islam in Historical and Epic Tradition*. Pennsylvania University Press, 1994.

DOUGLAS, Ian Henderson: *Abul Kalam Azad. An Intellectual and Religious Biography*. OUP, Oxford 1993 (1988).

EATON, Richard Maxwell: *Sufis of Bijapur (1300-1700)*. Princeton University Press, Princeton 1978.

—: *The Rise of Islam and the Bengal Frontier 1204-1760*. OUP, Delhi 1997.

—: *Essays on Islam and Indian History*. OUP, Delhi 2000.

ELLIOT, Henry M., and John DOWSON: *History of India as Told by Its Own Historians*, 8 vols. Low price Publ., Delhi 1990 (London 1867-77).

ELST, Koenraad: *De Islamitische Zuil. Verslag van de 6de Konferentie van Moslims in Europa*. Leuven 1992.

ENGINEER, Asghar Ali: *Origin and Development of Islam*. Orient Longman, Delhi 1987.

—, ed.: *The Shah Bano Controversy*. Orient Longman, Delhi 1987.

EPPINK, Andreas, ed.: *Cultuurcontact en Cultuurconflict*. Dick Coutinho, Muiderberg (Netherlands) 1988.

FREDERIC, Louis: *L'Inde de l'Islam*. Arthaud, Paris 1989.

FRIEDMANN, Yohanan: *Shaykh Ahmad Sirhindi. An Outline of His Thought and a Study of His Image in the Eyes of Posterity*. McGill Queen's University Press, Montreal 1971.

GABORIEAU, Marc: *Islam et Société en Asie du Sud*. Editions de l'Ecole des Hautes Etudes en Sciences Sociales, Paris 1986.

GANDHI, Rajmohan: *Understanding the Muslim Mind*. Penguin, Delhi 1987 (1986).

GESE, Hartmut, HOEFNER, Maria, and RUDOLPH, Kurt: *Die Religionen Altsyriens, Altarabiens und der Mandäer*. W. Kohlhammer-Verlag, Stuttgart 1970.
GHANI, Abdul: *I Am for India, India for Me*. Damal Varati, Calcutta 1993.
GIBB, H.A.R., and J.H. KRAMERS: *Shorter Encyclopaedia of Islam*. E.J. Brill, Leiden 1953.
GORDON, Murray: *Slavery in the Arab World*. New Amsterdam, New York 1989 (1987).
GUILLAUME, Alfred: *Islam*. Penguin 1990 (1954).
—, tra.: *Life of Muhammad. The Sirat Rasul Allah of Ibn Ishaq*. OUP, Karachi 1990 (1955).
HABIB, Mohammed: *Introduction* to reprint of Elliot & Dowson's *History of India*, vol.2. Aligarh 1951.
—, and NIZAMI, K.A.: *A Comprehensive History of India*, vol.5, *The Delhi Sultanate*. Delhi 1970.
HARDY, Peter: *Partners in Freedom—and True Muslims. The Political Thought of Some Muslim Scholars in British India 1912-47*. Scandinavian Institute of Asian Studies, Lund 1971.
HIRO, Dilip: *Islamic Fundamentalism*. Paladin, London 1989 (1988).
HISKETT, Mervyn: *Some to Mecca Turn to Pray*. Claridge Press, Saint Albans (GB) 1993.
HUGHES, Thomas Patrick: *Dictionary of Islam*. Rupa, Calcutta 1988 (1885).
IMRAN, Mohammed: *Ideal Woman in Islam*. Markazi Maktab Islami, Delhi 1994 (1981).
IQBAL, Sir Mohammed: *Shikwa & Jawab-i-Shikwa. Complaint and Answer. Iqbal's Dialogue with Allah*. Translated from the Urdu with an introduction by Khushwant Singh. OUP, Delhi 1981.
IQBAL, Sheikh Mohammed: *The Mission of Islam*. Vikas Publ., Delhi 1977.
ISRAELI, Raphael: *Muslims in China*. Scandinavian Institute of Asian Studies Monograph Series, no. 29, MalmĨ 1980).
JANSEN, J.J.G.: *Inleiding tot de Islam*. Coutinho, Muiderberg 1987.
KABIR, Mohammed Ghulam: *Minority Politics in Bangladesh*. Nawroze Kitabistan, Dhaka 1980.
KHAN, Ansar Hussain: *The Rediscovery of India. A New Subcontinent*. Orient Longman, Delhi 1995.
KHAN, Majid Ali: *Muqaddas Ayat*. Islamic Research Foundation, Delhi 1989.
KHAN, Maulana Wahiduddin: *Tabligh Movement*. Islamic Centre, Delhi 1986.
—: *Mohammed, the Prophet of Revolution*. Islamic Centre, Delhi 1994 (1986).
—: *Indian Muslims. The Need for a Positive Outlook*. Al-Risala Books, Delhi 1994.
—: *Uniform Civil Code. A Critical Study*. Islamic Centre, Delhi 1996.
KHOURY, A.-Th.: *Polémiquę Byzantine contre l'Islam*. Brill, Leiden 1972.
KORBEL, Josef: *Danger in Kashmir*. Princeton University Press, Princeton 1954.
KRAMER, J.H.: *De Koran*. First edition, Amsterdam 1956; and second, revised edition, Agon, Amsterdam 1992.
LAFFIN, John: *Holy War*. Grafton, London 1988.
LEWIS, Bernard, ed.: *Islam from the Prophet Muhammad to the Capture of Constantinople*, vol.1.: *Politics and War*.
—: *Race and Slavery in the Middle East. An Historical Enquiry*. OUP, New York 1990.
LUBIS, Mochtar: *Het Land onder de Regenboog. De Geschiedenis van IndonesiÎ*. A.W. Sijthoff, Utrecht 1992 (1989).
MALCOLM, Noel: *Bosnia. A Short History*. Papermac, London 1994.
MALIK, S.K.: *The Quranic Concept of War*. Himalayan Books, Delhi 1986.

MARGOLIOUTH, D.S.: *Mohammed and the Rise of Islam.* Voice of India, Delhi 1985 (1905).

MAUDOODI, Abul-Ala: *Towards Understanding Islam.* Lahore 1960 (1932).

—: *Jihad in Islam.* Delhi 1993 (1939).

—: *The Economic Problem of Man and its Islamic Solution.* Lahore 1966 (1941).

MEILLASSOUX, Claude: *The Anthropology of Slavery.* University of Chicago Press, Chicago 1991 (1986).

MOREY, Robert: *The Islamic Invasion. Confronting the World's Fastest Growing Religion.* Harvest House Publ., Eugene (Oregon) 1992.

MUIR, William: *The Life of Mahomet from Original Sources.* Voice of India, Delhi 1992 (1894).

MUJAHID, Abdul Malik: *Conversion to Islam. Untouchables' Strategy for Protest in India.* Anima Books, Chambersburg (Pennsylvania) 1989.

NADVI, Mohsin Usmani: *Ahânat-i Rasûl kî Sazâ.* Islamic Research Foundation, Delhi 1989.

NAQVI, Saeed: *Reflections of an Indian Muslim.* Har-Anand, Delhi 1993.

NATH, R.: *The Tajmahal and Its Incarnation. Original Persian Data on Its Builders, Materials, Costs, Measurements etc.* Historical Research Documentation Programme, Jaipur 1985.

—: *The Baburi Masjid of Ayodhya.* Historical Research Documentation Programme, Jaipur 1991.

PADMASHA: *Indian National Congress and the Muslims.* Delhi,

PENRICE, John: *A Dictionary and Glossary of the Koran.* Curzon Press, London 1979 (1873).

PETERS, Rudolph: *Jihad in Classical and Modern Islam.* Markus Wiener, Princeton 1997.

PIPES, Daniel: *Slave Soldiers in Islam: the Genesis of a Military System.* Yale University Press, New Haven 1981.

—: *In the Path of God: Islam and Political Power.* Basic Books, New York 1983.

—: *The Rushdie Affair. The Novel, the Ayatollah and the West.* Carol Publ., New York 1990; Indian reprint, Voice of India, Delhi 1998.

PLATTS, John T.: *A Grammar of the Hindustani or Urdu Language.* Munshiram Manoharlal, Delhi 1990 (1878).

RAM NATH: *Dalit-Muslim Unity. Why? And How?* Dalit Sahitya Akademy, Bangalore 1995.

"RASOEL, Mohamed": *De ondergang van Nederland, land der naïeve dwazen.* Timmer Publ., Amsterdam 1991.

RIZVI, Saiyyad Athar Abbas: *A History of Sufism in India*, 2 vols. Delhi 1978-83.

ROBERTSON, George S.: *The Kafirs of the Hindu-Kush.* OUP, Karachi 1987 (1896)

RODINSON, Maxime: *Mohammed.* Penguin, 1973 (1968).

ROY, M.N.: *Role of Islam in History.* Ajanta, Delhi 1990 (1939).

ROY, Olivier: *The Failure of Political Islam.* HUP, 1994.

RUDT DE COLLENBERG, Wipertus H.: *Esclavage et Rançons des Chretiens en Mediterranée (1570-1600)*, Le Leopard d'Or, Paris 1987.

SARDAR, Ziauddin, and Merryl Wyn DAVIES: *Distorted Imagination. Lessons from the Rushdie Affair.* Grey Seal, London 1990.

SARKAR, Jadunath: *Anecdotes of Aurangzib*. Orient Longman, Delhi 1988 (1912).
—: *Fall of the Mughal Empire* (4 vols.). Orient Longman, Delhi 1991 (1934).
SHAYEGAN, Daryush: *Hindouïsme et Soufisme. Une lecture du 'Confluent des Deux Océans'*. Albin Michel, Paris 1997.
SIDDIQUI, M.K.A.: *Hindu-Muslim Relations*. Abadi Publ., Calcutta 1993.
SOMERS, Herman: *Een Andere Mohammed*. Hadewijch, Antwerp 1992.
SRIVASTAVA: Kanhaiya Lall: *The Position of Hindus under the Delhi Sultanate 1206-1526*. Munshiram Manoharlal, Delhi 1980.
STEENBRINK, Karel: *Dutch Colonialism and Indonesian Islam. Contacts and Conflicts 1596-1950*. Rodopi, Amsterdam/Atlanta 1993.
TITUS, Murray: *Islam in India and Pakistan*. Calcutta 1959.
WAARDENBURG, Jacques: *Islam. Norm, Ideaal en Werkelijkheid*. Standaard, Antwerp 1984.
WARRAQ, Ibn: *Why I Am Not a Muslim*. Prometheus Books, New York 1995.
WATT, Montgomery: *Muhammad's Mecca. History in the Qur'ân*. Edinburgh University Press, 1988.
WEISSMAN, Steve, and Herbert KROSNEY: *The Islamic Bomb*. Orient, Delhi 1983 (1981).
WINK, André: *Al-Hind, the Making of the Indo-Islamic World*, vol.1, *Early Medieval India*. OUP, Delhi 1990.
ZAKARIA, Rafiq: *Muhammad and the Quran*. Penguin 1991.

Periodicals

Islam and Christian-Muslim Relations, Birmingham UK and Washington DC.
Middle East Quarterly, Philadelphia
Muslim India, Delhi
Radiance, Delhi

Other publications: communal violence

AKBAR, M.J.: *Riot after Riot*. Penguin 1988.
BARRIER, N.G.: *Roots of Communal Politics. The Congres Report That Was Banned in 1933*. South Asia Books, Columbia (Missouri), n.d.
BANGLADESH HINDU-BUDDHIST-CHRISTIAN UNITY COUNCIL: *Communal Discrimination in Bangladesh*. Dhaka 1993.
BHATTACHARYYA, S.K.: *Genocide in East Pakistan/Bangladesh*. A. Ghosh, Houston 1987.
BRASS, Paul: *Theft of an Idol*. Delhi 1998.
DAS, Suranjan: *Communal Riots in Bengal 1905-1947*. OUP, Delhi 1991.
DAS, Veena: *Communities, Riots and Survivors in South Asia*. OUP 1990.
ENGINEER, Asghar Ali: *Communalism and Communal Violence in India. An Analytical Approach to Hindu-Muslim Conflict*. Ajanta Publ., Delhi 1989.
—: *Lifting the Veil. Communal Violence and Communal Harmony in Contemporary India*. Sangam, Hyderabad 1995.
GHOSH, S.K.: *Communal Riots in India. Meet the Challenge Unitedly*. Ashish Publ., Delhi 1987.
KAKAR, Sudhir: *The Colours of Violence*. Viking, Delhi 1995.

KAMRA, A.J.: *Bangladesh, a Vast Concentration Camp for Hindus*. Delhi 1996.
—: *The Prolonged Partition and Its Pogroms. Violence against Hindus in East Bengal 1946-64*. Voice of India, Delhi 2000.
KUMAR, Pramod: *Polluting Sacred Faith. A Study on Communalism and Violence*. Privately published, Delhi 1992.
MUKHERJI, Saradindu: *Subjects, Citizens and Refugees: Tragedy in the Chittagong Hill Tracts (1947-1998)*. Voice of India, Delhi 2000.
NARAYAN, Jitendra: *Communal Riots in India*. Ashish Publ., Delhi 1992.
NASREEN, Taslima: *Lajja (Shame)*. Penguin India, Delhi 1994 (1993).
RAJAGOPAL, P.R.: *Communal Violence in India*. Uppal Publ., Delhi 1987.
SAKSENA, N.S. *Communal Riots in India*. Trishul Publ., Noida 1990.
SHETH, Pravin, and Ramesh MENON: *Caste and Communal Time-Bomb*. Het Varsha Prakashan, Ahmedabad 1989 (1986).
SUNIL, ed.: *Bhârat men Sâmpradâyik Hinsâ: Ye Barbartâ kahân Chhupî Thî?* Amrit Publ., Delhi 1985.

Other publications: Christianity and Judaism

AHMAD of QADIAN, Hazrat Mirza Ghulam: *Jesus in India*. Islam Internation Publ., Tilford UK 1989 (1899).
ANANDA: *Hindu View of Judaism*. APC Publ., Delhi 1996.
ARNHEIM, Michael: *Is Christianity True?* Duckworth, London 1984.
COOLEN, Mario: *Tussen God en Goud. Vijfhonderd Jaar Evangelisatie van Indianen in Latijns-Amerika*. Bisschoppelijke Adviescommissie voor Latijns-Amerika, The Hague 1992.
CORNILLE, Catherine: *The Guru in Indian Catholicism*. Peeters, Leuven 1991.
DE MOOR, J.C.: *The Rise of Yahwism. The Roots of Israelite Monotheism*. Peeters, Leuven 1997 (1990).
DENA, Lal: *Christian Missionaries and Colonialism*. Vendrame Institute, Shillong 1988.
GAGE, Mathilda Joslyn: *Woman, Church and State*, Voice of India reprint 1997 (*c.* 1880).
GRIFFITHS: *The Marriage of East and West*. Fount Paperbacks, London 1983 (1982).
HALBERTAL, Moshe, and Avishai MARGALIT: *Idolatry*, Harvard University Press, 1994 (1992).
HOUTHAEVE, Robert: *"Recht, al barstte de wereld!"* Privately published, Moorslede (Belgium) 1995.
JESUDASAN, Ignatius s.j.: *A Gandhian Theology of Liberation*. Maryknoll NY, 1984.
KULANDAY, Victor: *The Paganization of the Church in India*. Galilee, Madras 1988.
MANGALWADI, Vishal: *Missionary Conspiracy. Letters to a Postmodern Hindu*. Good Books, Mussoorie 1996.
NECKEBROUCK, Valeer: *De stomme duivelen. Het anti-missionair syndroom in de Westerse Kerk*. Tabor, Bruges 1990.
O'BRIEN, Justin: *Yoga and Christianity*. Himalayan International Institute, Pennsylvania 1978.
PANIKKAR, K.M.: *Malabar and the Portuguese*. Voice of India, Delhi 1997 (1929).
PANIKKAR, Raimundo: *The Unknown Christ of Hinduism*. Darton, Longman & Todd, London 1964.
PRAET, Dany: *God der Goden*. Pelckmans/Kok/Agora 1996.

PUTHANANGADY, Paul, ed.: *Towards an Indian Theology of Liberation*, Indian Theological Association, Bangalore 1986.

RADIN, P.: *Monotheism among Primitive Peoples*. London 1954.

RAJ, Sunder: *The Confusion Called Conversion*. TRACI, Delhi 1986.

RAJSHEKAR (SHETTY), V.T.: *Dialogue of the Bhoodevatas. Sacred Brahmins versus Socialist Brahmins*. Dalit Sahitya Akademy, Bangalore 1993.

SCOTT-WARING, Major J. (originally signing "A Bengal Officer"): *Vindication of the Hindoos from the Aspersions of the Rev. Claudius Buchanan, MA, with a Refutation of the Arguments Exhibited in His Memoir on the Expediency of an Ecclesiastical Establishment for British India*. London 1808.

SMITH, Morton: *Jesus the Magician*. Victor Gollancz Ltd., London 1978.

SCHOLEM, Gershom: *On the Kabbalah and Its Symbolism*. Schocken Books, New York 1965 (1960).

—: *Sabbatai Zwi, der mystische Messias*. Juedischer Verlag, Frankfurt 1992.

SOARES, A., ed.: *Truth Shall Prevail*. Catholic Association of Bombay, 1957.

SOARES-PRABHU, M.: *Tribal Values in the Bible*. *Jeevadhara* vol.24, no.140, Delhi 1994.

STARK, Rodney: *The Rise of Christianity. A Sociologist Reconsiders History*. Princeton University Press, Princeton 1996.

STOCK, Frederick & Margaret: *People Movements in the Punjab*. Gospel Literature Service, Bombay 1978 (1975).

SUMITHRA, Sunand: *Christian Theologies from an Indian Perspective*. Theological Book Trust, Bangalore 1995.

TAYLOR, Joan: *Christians and the Holy Places*. Oxford University Press, 1993.

THOMAS, M.M.: *The Acknowledged Christ of the Indian Renaissance*. Madras 1976.

TROISI, J.: *Tribal Religion*. South Asia Books/Manohar, Delhi 1978.

VAN PRAAG, Henri: *Karl Marx, Profeet van een Nieuwe Tijd*. Ankh-Hermes, Deventer 1976.

VERKUYL, J.: *De New Age Beweging*. J.H. Kok, Kampen 1989.

VON FÜRER-HAIMENDORF, Christoph: *Tribes of India. The Struggle for Survival*. Oxford University Press, Delhi 1989.

WILSON, A.N.: *Paul, the Mind of the Apostle*. Sinclair 1997.

Periodicals

Areopagus, Hong Kong
Asian Journal of Theology, Bangalore
Dalit Voice, Bangalore
Indian Missionary Journal, Shillong
Journal of Dharma, Pondicherry
Sevârtham, Ranchi
Studia Missionalia, Rome
Wereldwijd, Antwerp

Other publications: general/miscellaneous

ALVARES, Claude: *Decolonizing History. Technology and Culture in India, China and the West, 1492 to the Present Day*. The Other India Press, Mapusa (Goa) 1991 (1979).

ANDERSON, Benedict: *Imagined Communities*. Verso, London 1991 (1983).

BOTTOMORE, Tom: *A Dictionary of Marxist Thought*. Blackwell, Oxford 1988 (1983).

CHALK, Frank, and Kurt JONASSOHN: *The History and Sociology of Genocide*. Yale University Press, New Haven 1990.

CORNILLE, Catherine: *De Wereldgodsdiensten over Schepping, Verlossing en Leven na de Dood*. Davidsfonds, Leuven 1997.

DURANT, Will: *The Story of Civilization*, vol.1, *Our Oriental Heritage*. New York 1972.

FLEMING, Thomas: *The Politics of Human Nature*. Transaction Publ., New Brunswick NJ 1993 (1988).

HOBSBAWM, E.J.: *Nations and Nationalism since 1870: Programme, Myth and Reality*. Cambridge 1990.

HUTCHINSON, John, and SMITH, Anthony D.: *Nationalism*. OUP, Oxford 1994.

JOHNSON, Paul: *Modern Times. A History of the World from the 1920s to the 1990s*. Orion, London 1992.

KOHN, Hans: *Nationalism, Its Meaning and History*. Krieger Publ., Malabar (Florida) 1982 (1965).

KORZEC, Michel: *Het Voelen van de Draak*. Bert Bakker, Amsterdam 1986.

LEVINAS, Emmanuel: *Totalité et Infini: Essais sur l'Extériorité*. Kluwer, Dordrecht 1993 (1971).

LEVY, Bernard-Henri: *Le Testament de Dieu*. Paris 1979.

—: *La Pureté Dangereuse*. Grasset, Paris 1994.

LLEWELYN, John: *Emmanuel Lévinas. The Genealogy of Ethics*. Routledge, London 1995.

MARITAIN, Jacques: *Integral Humanism. Temporal and Spiritual Problems of a New Christendom*. University of Notre Dame Press, Indiana 1986 (1936).

MOOREHEAD, Caroline: *Bertrand Russell*. Sinclair Stevenson, London 1992.

MOSHER, Steven: *China Misperceived. American Illusions and Chinese Reality*. BasicBooks, New York 1990.

MÜNSTER, Arno, ed.: *La Différence comme Non-Indifférence. Ethique et Altérité chez Emmanuel Lévinas*. Kimé, Paris 1995.

PEASLEE, Amos J.: *Constitutions of Nations*. Martinus Nijhoff, The Hague 1956.

POLIAKOV, Léon: *Le Mythe Aryen*. Editions Complexe, Paris 1987 (1971).

—: *Histoire de l'Antisémitisme 1945-93*. Paris 1994.

ROTTHIER, Rudi: *Kinderen van de Krokodil*. Antwerp 1996.

SHARMA, Arvind, ed.: *Our Religions. The 7 World Religions Introduced by Preeminent Scholars from Each Tradition*. Harper, San Francisco 1995 (1993).

SCRUTON, Roger: *Modern Philosophy*. Mandarin, London 1996 (1994).

SAID, Edward: *Orientalism*. New York 1978.

SAUNDERS, Frances Stonor: *The CIA and the Cultural Cold War*. Granta, London 1999.

SOLZHENITSYN, Aleksandr: *Rebuilding Russia*. Harvill (HarperCollins), London 1991 (1990).

SPENCE, Jonathan: *The Gate of Heavenly Peace*. Viking, New York 1981.

STORMER, John A.: *None Dare Call It Treason*. Liberty Bell Press, Florissant (Missouri) 1964.

TINDEMANS, Leo: *De Toekomst van een Idee*. Pelckmans, Kapellen 1993.

TUCHMAN, Barbara W.: *Notes from China*. Collier, New York 1972.

VAN DER VEER, Peter: *Modern Oriëntalisme*. Meulenhoff, Amsterdam 1995.

Papers and periodicals

Le Figaro, Paris
De Groene Amsterdammer, Amsterdam
HP/De Tijd, The Hague
London Review of Books, London
Markant, Antwerp (d. 1995)
Le Monde, Paris
New York Review of Books, New York
Le Nouvel Observateur, Paris
NRC-Handelsblad, Rotterdam
Der Spiegel, Hamburg
De Standaard, Brussels
The Times Literary Supplement, London
etc.

Interviews

In brackets, their positions at the time of our meeting.

Arya Samaj: Vandematharam Ramachandra Rao (president Arya Sarvadeshik Pratinidhi Sabha).

HMS: Shiv Saran (president), Vikram Savarkar (former president), Gopal Godse (accomplice in Mahatma murder), Madanlal Pahwa (idem), Indra Sen, Jeevan Kulkarni, Harindra Srivastava (Savarkar biographer).

RSS: Balasaheb Madhukar Dattatreya Deoras (Sarsanghchalak), Rajendra Singh (Sarsanghchalak), Bhaurao Deoras, H.V. Seshadri, K.S. Sudarshan (Sarsanghchalak), Dattopant Thengadi (founder-president BMS), Chaman Lal, K.K. Mittal, Seshadri Chari (editor *Organiser*), Tarun Vijay (editor *Panchjanya*), Nana Deshmukh (founder DRI), Devendra Swarup (DRI), L.S. Bhide (DRI), Amarnath Dogra (BMS), Manohar Shinde (convenor FISI Los Angeles).

VHP: Ashok Singhal (secretary-general), Anand Shankar Pandya (treasurer), Vishnu Hari Dalmia, Sujit Dhar, Giriraj Kishore, Hari Babu Kansal, Ram Shankar Agnihotri, Surya Krishna, Ashok Chowgule (Mumbai president), S.P. Gupta (director Devahuti Institute), Raj Dave (Chicago president), Krishna Kumar (Shree Chakra Foundation), Prema Pandurang, Vinay Katiyar (Bajrang Dal president), Krishna Kumar Sharaf (spokesman Purvanchal Kalyan Ashram).

BJP: L.K. Advani (president), M.M. Joshi (president), Kalyan Singh (UP Chief Minister), K.R. Malkani (editor-in-chief *BJP Today*), Vijayaraje Scindia, Jagmohan (former Governor of Jammu & Kashmir), K.L. Sharma, J.P. Mathur, K.N. Sahni (MP), K.N. Govindacharya, B.L. Sharma Prem (MP), Brijesh Mishra (MP), M.L. Sondhi, Jagdish Jetli (editor *BJP Today*), Daya Prakash Sinha (BJP office administrator), Bangaru Lakshman (secretary BJP Scheduled Castes Front), Bansilal Sonee (secretary North-East States Co-ordination Council).

Reconstituted BJS: Balraj Madhok (president).

SS: Bal Thackeray (president).

Institutional Hinduism: the 144th and 145th Jagatguru Shankaracharya of Puri; the retired Kanchipuram Shankaracharya Jayendra Saraswati; Veer Bhadra Mishra (mahant of Sankat Mochan Mandir, Varanasi, and convenor of Swacha Ganga Campaign).

Independent Hindu authors: Girilal Jain, Harsh Narain, Suhas Majumdar, Ram Swarup, Sita Ram Goel, Arun Shourie, N.S. Rajaram, Shrikant Talageri, Abhas Chatterjee, Damodar Nene, Rajendra Singh, Kanayalal Talreja, Arvind Ghosh, Mayank Jain, *et al.*

Others: authors Nirad C. Chaudhary, Khushwant Singh, R.K. Karanjia, Kashinath Singh; Kanshi Ram (BSP president); Rammohan Rao (information adviser to the J&K Government); Prof. K.N. Pandita (secretary Friends of Kashmir); Mohan P. Upadhyaya (Nepal's Consul-General in Calcutta).

Index